born *in blood*

Collection Volume I

bound *by honor*

bound *by duty*

bound *by hatred*

bound *by temptation*

Cora Reilly

Subscribe to Cora's newsletter to find out about her next books, bonus content and giveaways! (corareillyauthor.blogspot.de/p/newsletter.html)

Cover design by Romantic Book Affairs Design

bound *by honor*

(Born in Blood Mafia Chronicles, #1)

prologue

My fingers shook like leaves in the breeze as I raised them, my heartbeat hummingbird quick. Luca's strong hand was firm and steady as he took mine and slipped the ring onto my finger.

White gold with twenty small diamonds.

What was meant as a sign of love and devotion for other couples was nothing but a testament of his ownership of me. A daily reminder of the golden cage I'd be trapped in for the rest of my life. Until death do us part wasn't an empty promise, as with so many other couples that entered the holy bond of marriage. There was no way out of this union for me. I was Luca's until the bitter end. The last few words of the oath men swore when they were inducted into the mafia could just as well have been the closing of my wedding vow:

"I enter alive and I will have to get out dead."

I should have run when I still had the chance. Now, as hundreds of faces from the Chicago and New York Famiglias stared back at us, flight was no longer an option. Nor was divorce. Death was the only acceptable end to a marriage in our world. Even if I still managed to escape Luca's watchful eyes and those of his henchmen, my breach of our agreement would mean war. Nothing my father could say would prevent Luca's Famiglia from exercising vengeance for making them lose face.

My feelings didn't matter, never had. I'd grown up in a world where no choices were given, especially to women.

This wedding wasn't about love or trust or choice. It was about duty and honor, about doing what was expected.

A bond to ensure peace.

I wasn't an idiot. I knew what else this was about: money and power. Both were dwindling since the Russian mob—"the Bratva"—, and other crime organizations had been trying to expand their influence into our territories. The Italian Famiglias across the US needed to lay their feuds to rest and work together to beat down their enemies. I should be honored to marry the oldest son of the New York Famiglia. That's what my father and every other male relative had tried to tell me since my betrothal to Luca. I knew that, and it wasn't as if I hadn't had time to prepare for this exact moment, yet fear still corseted my body in a relentless grip.

"You may kiss the bride," the priest said.

I raised my head. Every pair of eyes in the pavilion scrutinized me, waiting for a flicker of weakness. Father would be furious if I let my terror show, and Luca's Famiglia would use it against us. But I had grown up in a world where a perfect mask was the only protection afforded to women and had no trouble forcing my face into a placid expression. Nobody would know how much I wanted to escape. Nobody but Luca. I couldn't hide from him, no matter how much I tried. My body wouldn't stop shaking. As my gaze met Luca's cold gray eyes, I could tell that he knew. How often had he instilled fear in others? Recognizing it was probably second nature to him.

He bent down to bridge the ten inches he towered over me. There was no sign of hesitation, fear or doubt on his face. My lips trembled against his mouth as his eyes bored into me. Their message was clear: *You are mine.*

chapter
one

Three years earlier

I WAS CURLED UP ON THE CHAISE LOUNGE IN OUR LIBRARY, READING, when a knock sounded. Liliana's head rested in my lap, and she didn't even stir when the dark wooden door opened and our mother stepped in, her dark blonde hair pulled back in a tight bun at the back of her head. Mother was pale, her face drawn with worry.

"Did something happen?" I asked.

She smiled, but it was her fake smile. "Your father wants to talk to you in his office."

I carefully moved out from under Lily's head and put it down on the chaise. She drew her legs up against her body. She was small for an eleven-year-old, but I wasn't exactly tall either at five foot four. None of the women in our family were. Mother avoided my eyes as I walked toward her.

"Am I in trouble?" I didn't know what I could have done wrong. Usually Lily and I were the obedient ones; Gianna was the one who always broke the rules and got punished.

"Hurry. Don't let your father wait," Mother said simply.

My stomach was in knots when I arrived in front of Father's office. After a moment to stifle my nerves, I knocked.

"Come in."

I entered, forcing my face to remain carefully guarded. Father sat behind his mahogany desk in a wide black leather armchair; behind him rose the mahogany shelves filled with books that Father had never read, but they hid a secret entrance to the basement and a corridor leading off the premises.

He looked up from a pile of sheets, gray hair slicked back. "Sit."

I sank down on one of the chairs across from his desk and folded my hands in my lap, trying not to gnaw on my lower lip. Father hated that. I waited for him to start talking. He had a strange expression on his face as he scrutinized me. "The Bratva and the Triad are trying to claim our territories. They are getting bolder by the day. We're luckier than the Las Vegas

Famiglia who also has to deal with the Mexicans, but we can't ignore the threat the Russians and the Taiwanese pose any longer."

Confusion filled me. Father never talked about practicalities to us. Girls didn't need to know about the finer details of the mob business. I knew better than to interrupt him.

"We have to lay our feud with the New York Famiglia to rest and combine forces if we want to fight the Bratva." Peace with the Famiglia? Father and every other member of the Chicago Outfit hated the Famiglia. They had been killing each other for decades and only recently decided to ignore each other in favor of killing off the members of other crime organizations, like the Bratva and the Triad. "There is no stronger bond than blood. At least the Famiglia got that right."

I frowned.

"Born in blood. Sworn in blood. That's their motto."

I nodded, but my confusion only grew.

"I met with Salvatore Vitiello yesterday." Father met with the Capo dei Capi, the head of the New York mob? A meeting between New York and Chicago hadn't taken place in a decade, and the last time hadn't ended well. It was still referred to as Bloody Thursday. And Father wasn't even the Boss. He was only the Consigliere, the adviser to Fiore Cavallaro, who ruled over the Outfit and with it, organized crime in the Midwest.

"We agreed that for peace to be an option, we had to become family." Father's eyes bored into me, and suddenly I didn't want to hear what else he had to say. "Cavallaro and I determined that you would marry his oldest son Luca, the future Capo dei Capi of the Famiglia."

I felt like I was falling. "Why me?"

"Vitiello and Fiore have talked on the phone several times in the last few weeks, and Vitiello wanted the most beautiful girl for his son. Of course, we couldn't give him the daughter of one of our soldiers. Fiore doesn't have unmarried daughters, so he said you were the most beautiful girl available." Gianna was just as beautiful, but she was younger. That probably saved her.

"There are so many beautiful girls," I choked out. I couldn't breathe. Father looked at me as if I were his most prized possession.

"There aren't many Italian girls with hair like yours. Fiore described it as golden." Father guffawed. "You are our door into the New York Famiglia."

"But, Father, I'm fifteen. I can't marry."

Father made a dismissive gesture. "If I were to agree, you could. What do we care for laws?"

I gripped the armrests so tightly, my knuckles were turning white, but I didn't feel pain. Instead, numbness was working its way through my body.

"But I told Salvatore that the wedding would have to wait until you turn eighteen. Your mother was adamant you be of age and finish school. Fiore let her begging get to him."

So the Boss had told my father the wedding had to wait. My own father would have thrown me into the arms of my future husband at this very moment. My *husband*. A wave of sickness crashed over me. I knew only two things about Luca Vitiello: he would become the head of the New York mob once his father retired or died, and he got his nickname "The Vice" for crushing a man's throat with his bare hands. I didn't know how old he was. My cousin Bibiana had to marry a man thirty years her senior. Luca couldn't be that old, if his father hadn't retired yet. At least, that's what I hoped. Was he cruel?

He'd crushed a man's throat. He'll be the head of the New York mob.

"Father," I whispered. "Please don't force me to marry that man."

Father's expression tightened. "You will marry Luca Vitiello. I shook hands on it with his father Salvatore. You will be a good wife to Luca, and when you meet him for the engagement celebrations, you'll act like an obedient lady."

"Engagement?" I echoed. My voice sounded distant, as if a veil of fog covered my ears.

"Of course. It's a good way to establish bonds between our families, and it'll give Luca the chance to see what he's getting out of the deal. We don't want to disappoint him."

"When?" I cleared my throat but the lump remained. "When is the engagement party?"

"August. We haven't set a date yet."

That was in two months. I nodded numbly. I loved reading romance novels and whenever the couples in them married, I'd pictured how my wedding would be. I'd always imagined it would be filled with excitement and love. Empty dreams of a stupid girl.

"So I'm allowed to keep attending school?" What did it even matter if I graduated? I would never go to college, never work. All I'd be allowed to do was to warm my husband's bed. My throat tightened further and tears prickled in my eyes, but I willed them not to fall. Father hated it when we lost control.

"Yes. I told Vitiello that you attend an all-girls Catholic school, which seemed to please him." Of course, it did. Couldn't risk my getting anywhere near boys.

"Is that all?"

"For now."

I walked out of the office as if in a trance. I'd turned fifteen four months ago. My birthday had felt like a huge step toward my future, and I'd been excited. Silly me. My life was already over before it even began. Everything was decided for me.

I couldn't stop crying. Gianna stroked my hair as my head lay in her lap. She was thirteen, only eighteen months younger than me, but today those eighteen months meant the difference between freedom and a life in a loveless prison. I tried very hard not to resent her for it. It wasn't her fault.

"You could try to talk to Father again. Maybe he'll change his mind," Gianna said in a soft voice.

"He won't."

"Maybe Mama will be able to convince him."

As if Father would ever let a woman make a decision for him. "Nothing anyone could say or do will make a difference," I said miserably. I hadn't seen Mother since she'd sent me into Father's office. She probably couldn't face me, knowing what she'd condemned me to.

"But Aria—"

I lifted my head and wiped the tears from my face. Gianna stared at me with pitiful blue eyes, the same cloudless summer-sky blue as my own. But where my hair was blonde, hers was red. Father sometimes called her "witch;" it wasn't an endearment. "He shook hands on it with Luca's father."

"They met?"

That's what I'd wondered as well. Why had he found time to meet with the head of the New York Famiglia, but not to tell me about his plans to sell me off like a high-class whore? I shook off the frustration and despair trying to claw their way out of my body.

"That's what Father told me."

"There has to be something we can do," Gianna said.

"There isn't."

"But you haven't even met the guy. You don't even know how he looks! He could be ugly, fat and old."

Ugly, fat and old. I wished those were the only features of Luca I had to worry about. "Let's google him. There have to be photos of him on the Internet."

Gianna jumped up and took my laptop from my desk, then she sat down beside me, our sides pressed against each other.

We found several photos and articles about Luca. He had the coldest gray eyes I'd ever seen. I could imagine only too well how those eyes looked down at his victims before he put a bullet in their heads.

"He's taller than everyone," Gianna said in amazement. He was; in all the photos he was several inches taller than whoever stood beside him, and he was muscled. That probably explained why some people called him the Bull behind his back. That was the nickname the articles used, and they identified him as the heir of businessman and club owner Salvatore Vitiello. *Businessman*. Maybe on the outside. Everybody knew what Salvatore Vitiello really was, but of course nobody was stupid enough to write about it.

"He's with a new girl in every photo."

I stared down at the emotionless face of my future husband. The newspaper called him the most sought-after bachelor in New York, heir to hundreds of millions of dollars. *Heir to an imperium of death and blood,* that was what it should say.

Gianna huffed. "God, girls are throwing themselves at him. I suppose he's good-looking."

"They can have him," I said bitterly. In our world a handsome exterior often hid the monster within. The society girls saw his good looks and wealth. They thought the bad-boy aura was a game. They fawned over his predator-like charisma because it radiated power. But what they didn't know was that blood and death lurked beneath the arrogant smile.

I stood abruptly. "I need to talk to Umberto."

Umberto was almost fifty and my father's loyal soldier. He was also Gianna's and my bodyguard. He knew everything about everyone. Mother called him a scandalmonger. But if anyone knew more about Luca, it was Umberto.

"He became a Made Man at eleven," Umberto said, sharpening his knife on a grinder as he did every day. The smell of tomato and oregano filled the kitchen, but it didn't give me a sense of comfort as it usually did.

"At eleven?" I asked, trying to keep my voice even. Most people didn't become fully initiated members of the mafia until they were sixteen. "Because of his father?"

Umberto grinned, revealing a gold incisor, and paused in his movements. "You think he got it easy because he's the Boss's son? He *killed* his first man at eleven, that's why it was decided to initiate him early."

Gianna gasped. "He's a monster."

Umberto shrugged. "He's what he needs to be. Ruling over New York, you can't be a pussy." He gave an apologetic smile. "A wuss."

"What happened?" I wasn't sure I really wanted to know. If Luca had killed his first man at eleven, then how many more had he killed in the nine years since?

Umberto shook his shaved head, and scratched the long scar that ran from his temple down to his chin. He was thin, and didn't look like much, but Mother told me few were faster with a knife than him. I'd never seen him fight. "Can't say. I'm not that familiar with New York."

I watched our cook as she prepared dinner, trying to focus on something that wasn't my churning stomach and my overwhelming fear. Umberto scanned my face. "He's a good catch. He'll be the most powerful man on the East Coast soon enough. He'll protect you."

"And who will protect me from him?" I hissed.

Umberto didn't say anything because the answer was clear: nobody could protect me from Luca after our wedding. Not Umberto, and not my father if he felt so inclined. Women in our world belonged to their husband. They were his property to deal with however he pleased. I glanced at the now gleaming blade in Umberto's hand and shivered.

chapter *two*

THE LAST COUPLE OF MONTHS HAD GONE BY TOO FAST NO MATTER how much I wanted them to slow, to give me more time to prepare. Only two days until my engagement party. Mother was busy ordering the servants around, making sure the house was spotless and nothing went wrong. It wasn't even a big celebration. Only our family, Luca's family and the families of the respective heads of New York and Chicago were invited. Umberto said it was for safety reasons. The truce was still too fresh to risk a gathering of hundreds of guests.

I wished they'd cancel it altogether. For all I cared, I didn't have to meet Luca until the day of our wedding. Now, as I hid from the party preparations in my room, Fabiano jumped up and down on my bed, a pout on his face. He was only five and had entirely too much energy. "I want to play!"

"Mother doesn't want you to race through the house. Everything needs to be perfect for the guests."

"But they aren't even here!" Thank God. Luca and the rest of the New York guests wouldn't arrive till tomorrow. Only one more night until I'd be meeting my future husband, a man who killed with his bare hands. I closed my eyes.

"Are you crying again?" Fabiano hopped off the bed and walked up to me, slipping his hand into mine. His dark blond hair was a mess. I tried to smooth it down but Fabiano jerked his head away.

"What do you mean?" I'd tried to hide my tears from him. Mostly I cried at night when I was protected by darkness.

"Lily says you cry all the time because Luca has bought you."

I froze. I'd have to tell Liliana to stop saying such things. It would only get me in trouble. "He didn't buy me." *Liar. Liar.*

"Same difference," Gianna said from the doorway, startling me.

"Shhh. What if Father hears us?"

Gianna shrugged. "He knows that I hate how he sold you like a cow."

"Gianna," I warned, nodding toward Fabiano. He peered up at me.

"I don't want you to leave," he whispered.

"I'm not leaving for a long time, Fabi."

He seemed satisfied with my answer, and the worry disappeared from his face and was replaced by his up-to-no good expression. "Catch me!" he screamed and stormed off, pushing Gianna aside as he darted past her.

Gianna tore after him. "I'll kick your ass, you little monster!"

I rushed into the corridor. Liliana poked her head out of her door, and then she too ran after my brother and sister. Mother would have my head if they smashed another family heirloom. I flew down the stairs. Fabiano was still in the lead. He was fast, but Liliana had almost caught him, while Gianna and I were too slow in the high heels my mother forced us to wear for practice. Fabiano dashed into the corridor leading into the west wing of the house, and the rest of us followed. I wanted to shout at him to stop. Father's office was in this part of the house. We'd be in so much trouble if he caught us playing around. Fabiano was supposed to act like a man. What five-year-old acted like a man?

We passed Father's door and relief washed over me, but then three men rounded the corner at the end of the corridor. I parted my lips to shout a warning, but it was too late. Though Fabiano skidded to a halt, Liliana ran into the man in the middle with full force. Most people would have lost their balance. Most people weren't six foot five and built like a bull.

I jerked to a halt as time seemed to grind to a stop around me. Gianna gasped beside me, but my gaze was frozen on my future husband. He was looking down at the blonde head of my little sister, steadying her with his strong hands. Hands he'd used to crush a man's throat.

"Liliana," I said, my voice shrill with fear. I never called my sister by her full name unless she was in trouble or something was seriously wrong. I wished I was better at hiding my terror. Now everyone was staring at me, including Luca. His cold gray eyes scanned me from head to toe, lingering on my hair.

God, he was tall. The men beside him were both over six feet, yet he dwarfed them. His hands were still on Lily's shoulders. "Liliana, come here," I said firmly, holding out a hand. I wanted her far away from Luca. She stumbled backward, then flew into my arms, burying her face against my shoulder. Luca raised one black eyebrow.

"That's Luca Vitiello!" Gianna said helpfully, not even bothering to hide her disgust. Fabiano made a sound like an enraged wildcat, stormed toward Luca, and started pummeling his legs and stomach with his small fists. "Leave Aria alone! You don't get her!"

My heart stopped right then. The man to Luca's side took a step forward. The outline of a gun was visible under his vest. He had to be Luca's bodyguard, though I really couldn't see why he needed one.

"No, Cesare," Luca said simply, and the man stilled. Luca caught my brother's hands in one of his, stopping the assault. I doubted he'd even felt the blows. I pushed Lily toward Gianna, who wrapped a protective arm around her, then I approached Luca. I was scared out of my mind, but I needed to get Fabiano away from him. Maybe New York and Chicago were trying to lay their feud to rest, but alliances could break in a blink. It wouldn't be the first time. Luca and his men were still the enemy.

"What a warm welcome we get. That's the infamous hospitality of the Outfit," said the other man with Luca; he had the same black hair but his eyes were darker. He was a couple of inches shorter than Luca and not as broad, but they were unmistakably brothers.

"Matteo," Luca said in a low voice that made me shiver. Fabiano was still snarling and struggling like a wild animal, but Luca held him at arm's length.

"Fabiano," I said firmly, gripping his upper arm. "It's enough. That's not how we treat guests."

Fabiano froze, then gazed up at me over his shoulder. "He's not a guest. He wants to steal you away, Aria."

Matteo chuckled. "This is too good. I'm glad Father convinced me to come."

"Ordered you," Luca corrected, but he didn't take his eyes off of me. I couldn't return his gaze. My cheeks blazed with heat at his scrutiny. My father and his bodyguards made sure that Gianna, Lily and I weren't around men very often, and the ones he let near us were either relatives or ancient. Luca was neither family, nor old. He was only five years older than me, but he looked like a man and made me feel like a small girl in comparison.

Luca let go of Fabiano and I pulled him toward me, his back against my legs. I folded my hands over his small heaving chest. He didn't stop glaring at Luca. I wished I had his courage, but he was a boy, an heir to my father's title. He wouldn't be forced to obey anyone, except for the Boss. He could *afford* courage.

"I'm sorry," I said, even if the words tasted foul. "My brother didn't mean to be disrespectful."

"I did!" Fabiano shouted. I covered his mouth with my palm and he squirmed in my hold, but I didn't let him go.

"Don't apologize," Gianna said sharply, ignoring the warning look I shot her. "It's not our fault that he and his bodyguards take up so much room in the corridor. At least Fabiano speaks the truth. Everyone else thinks they need to blow sugar up his ass because he's going to be Capo—"

"Gianna!" My voice was like a whip. She snapped her lips shut, staring at me with wide eyes. "Take Lily and Fabiano to their rooms. Now."

"But—" She glanced behind me. I was glad I couldn't see Luca's expression.

"Now!"

She grabbed Fabiano's hand and dragged him and Lily away. I didn't think my first encounter with my future husband could possibly have gone any worse. Bracing myself, I faced him and his men. I expected to be greeted by fury, but I found a smirk on Luca's face instead. My cheeks were burning with embarrassment, and now that I was alone with the three men, nerves twisted my stomach. Mother would freak out if she found out I wasn't dressed up for my first meeting with Luca. I was wearing one of my favorite maxi dresses with sleeves that reached my elbows, and I was silently glad for the protection all the fabric offered me. I folded my arms in front of my body, unsure of what to do. "I apologize for my sister and brother. They are—" I struggled for a word other than rude.

"Protective of you," Luca said simply. His voice was even, deep, emotionless. "This is my brother Matteo."

Matteo's lips were pulled into a wide grin. I was glad he didn't try to take my hand. I didn't think I could have kept my composure if either of them had moved any closer. "And this is my right hand, Cesare." Cesare gave me the briefest nod before he returned to his task of scanning the corridor. What was he waiting for? We didn't have assassins stashed in secret trap doors.

I focused on Luca's chin and hoped it appeared as if I was actually looking at his eyes. I took a step back. "I should go to my siblings."

Luca had a knowing expression on his face, but I didn't care if he saw how uncomfortable, how *scared* he made me. Not waiting for him to excuse me—he wasn't my husband nor my fiancé yet—I turned and quickly walked off, proud that I hadn't given in to the urge to run.

Mother tugged at the dress Father had chosen for the occasion. For the meat show, as Gianna called it. No matter how much Mother tugged, though, the dress didn't get any longer. I stared at myself in the mirror uncertainly. I'd never worn anything this revealing. The black dress clung to my butt and waist and ended at my upper thighs; the top was a glittery golden bustier with black tulle straps. "I can't wear this, Mother."

Mother met my gaze in the mirror. Her blonde hair was pinned up; it was a few shades darker than mine. She was wearing a floor-length elegant dress. I wished I was allowed something that modest. "You look like a woman," she whispered.

I cringed. "I look like a hooker."

"Hookers can't afford a dress like that."

Father's mistress had clothes that cost more than some people spent on a car. Mother put her hands on my waist. "You have a wasp waist, and the dress makes your legs look very long. I'm sure Luca will appreciate it."

I stared down at my cleavage. I had small breasts; even the push-up effect of the bustier couldn't change that. I was a fifteen-year-old dressed up to look like a woman.

"Here." Mother handed me five-inch black heels. Maybe I'd reach Luca's chin when I wore them. I slipped into them. Mother forced her fake smile onto her face and smoothed down my long hair. "Hold your head high. Fiore Cavallaro called you the most beautiful woman of Chicago. Show Luca and his entourage that you are more beautiful than any women in New York too. After all, Luca *knows* almost all of them." The way she said it, I was sure she'd read the articles about Luca's conquests as well, or maybe Father had told her something.

"Mother," I said hesitantly, but she stepped back.

"Now go. I'll come after you, but this is your day. You should enter the room alone. The men will be waiting. Your father will present you to Luca, and then we'll all come together in the dining room for dinner." She'd told me this dozens of times already.

For a moment, I wanted to take her hand and beg her to accompany me; instead I turned and walked out of my room. I was glad that my mother had forced me to wear heels in the last few weeks. When I arrived in front of the door to the fireplace lounge on the first floor of the west wing, my heart was beating in my throat. I wished Gianna was at my side, but Mother was probably warning her to behave right now. I had to go through this alone. Nobody was supposed to steal the show from the bride-to-be.

I stared at the dark wood of the door and considered running away. Male laughter rang out behind it—my father and the Boss. A room filled with the most powerful and dangerous men in the country, and I was supposed to go in. A lamb alone with wolves. I shook my head. I needed to stop thinking like that. I'd made them wait too long already.

I gripped the handle and pressed down. I slipped in, not yet looking at anyone as I closed the door. Gathering my courage, I faced the room. Conversation died. Was I supposed to say something? I shivered and hoped they couldn't see it. My father looked like the cat that got the cream. My eyes sought Luca and his piercing stare rendered me motionless. I held my breath. He put down a glass with a dark liquid with an audible clank.

If nobody said something soon, I'd flee the room. I quickly scanned the faces of the gathered men. From New York there were Matteo, Luca and Salvatore Vitiello, and two bodyguards: Cesare and a young man I didn't know. From the Chicago Outfit there were my father, Fiore Cavallaro, and his son, the future head Dante Cavallaro, as well as Umberto and my cousin Raffaele, whom I hated with the fiery passion of a thousand suns. And off to the side stood poor Fabiano, who had to wear a black suit like everyone else. I could see that he wanted to run toward me to seek solace, but he knew what Father would say to that.

Father finally moved toward me, put a hand on my back and led me toward the gathered men like a lamb toward slaughter. The only man who looked positively bored out of his mind was Dante Cavallaro; he had eyes only for his Scotch. Our family had attended the funeral of his wife two months ago. A widower in his thirties. I would have felt pity for him if he didn't scare me senseless, almost as much as Luca scared me.

Of course Father steered me straight toward my future husband with a challenging expression, as if he expected Luca to fall on his knees from awe. Going from his expression, Luca might as well have been staring at a rock. His gray eyes were hard and cold as they focused on my father.

"This is my daughter, Aria."

Apparently, Luca hadn't mentioned our embarrassing encounter. Fiore Cavallaro spoke up. "I didn't promise too much, did I?"

I wished the ground would open and swallow me whole. I had never been submitted to so much...attention. The way Raffaele looked at me made my skin crawl. He'd been initiated only recently and had turned eighteen two weeks ago. Since then he'd been even more obnoxious than before.

"You didn't," Luca said simply.

Father looked obviously put off. Without anyone noticing, Fabiano had snuck up behind me and slipped his hand into mine. Well, Luca had noticed and was staring at my brother, which brought his gaze entirely too close to my naked thighs. I shifted nervously and Luca looked away.

"Maybe the future bride and husband want to be alone for a few minutes?" Salvatore Vitiello suggested. My eyes jerked in his direction and I didn't manage to hide my shock fast enough. I was sure Luca had noticed, but he didn't seem to care.

My father smiled and turned to leave. I couldn't believe it.

"Should I stay?" Umberto asked. I gave him a quick smile, which disappeared when my father shook his head. "Give them a few minutes alone," he said. Salvatore Vitiello actually *winked* at Luca. They all filed out until only Luca, Fabiano and I were left.

"Fabiano," came my father's sharp voice. "Get out of there *now*."

Fabiano reluctantly let go of my hand and left, but not before sending Luca the deadliest look a five-year-old could manage. Luca's lips quirked. Then the door closed and we were alone. What had Luca's father's wink meant?

I peeked up at Luca. I had been right: with my high heels, the top of my head grazed his chin. He looked out the window, not sparing me a single glance. Dressing me up like a hooker didn't make Luca any more interested in me. Why would he be? I'd seen the women he dated in New York. They would have filled out the bustier better.

"Did you choose the dress?"

I jumped, startled that he'd spoken. His voice was deep and calm. Was he ever anything but? "No," I admitted. "My father did."

Luca's jaw twitched. I couldn't read him and it was making me increasingly nervous. He reached into the inside of his jacket, and for a ridiculous second I actually thought he was pulling a gun on me. Instead he held a black box in his hand. He turned toward me and I stared intently at his black shirt. Black shirt, black tie, black jacket. Black like his soul.

This was a moment millions of women dreamed of, but I felt cold when Luca opened the box. Inside sat a white gold ring with a big diamond in the center, sandwiched between two marginally smaller diamonds. I didn't move.

Luca held out his hand when the awkwardness between us reached its peak. I flushed and extended my hand. I flinched when his skin brushed mine. He slipped the engagement ring on my finger, then released me.

"Thank you." I felt obligated to say the words and even look up into his face, which was impassive, though the same couldn't be said for his eyes. They looked angry. Had I done something wrong? He held out his arm and I linked mine through it, letting him lead me out of the lounge and toward the dining room. We didn't speak. Maybe Luca was disappointed enough with me that he'd cancel the arrangement? But he wouldn't have put the ring on my finger if that were the case.

When we stepped into the dining room, the women of my family had joined the men. The Vitiellos hadn't brought female company. Maybe because they didn't trust my father and the Cavallaros enough to risk bringing women into our house.

I couldn't blame them. I wouldn't trust my father or the Boss either. Luca dropped his arm and I quickly joined my mother and sisters, who pretended to admire my ring. Gianna gave me a look. What had our mother threatened her with to keep her silent? I could tell that Gianna had a scathing comment on the tip of her tongue. I shook my head at her and she rolled her eyes. Dinner was a blur. The men discussed business while we women remained quiet. My eyes kept drifting toward the ring on my finger. It felt too heavy, too tight, *entirely too much*. Luca had marked me as his possession.

After dinner the men moved on to the lounge to drink and smoke and discuss whatever else needed to be discussed. I returned to my room, but couldn't fall asleep. Eventually, I put a bathrobe over my pajamas, slipped out of my room and crept downstairs. In a fit of craziness, I took the passage that led to the secret door behind the wall in the lounge. My grandfather thought it was necessary to have secret escapes in the office and the fireplace lounge because that's where the men of the family usually held their meetings. I wondered what he thought would happen to the women after the men had all fled through the secret passage?

I found Gianna with her eyes pressed against the peephole of the disguised door. Of course, she was already there. She whirled around, eyes wide, but relaxed when she spotted me.

"What's going on in there?" I said in a bare whisper, worried the men in the lounge would overhear us.

Gianna moved to the side, so I could peer through the second peephole. "Almost everyone's already gone. Father and Cavallaro have details to discuss with Salvatore Vitiello. It's only Luca and his entourage now."

I squinted through the hole, which gave me a perfect view of the chairs crowded around the fireplace. Luca leaned against the marble ledge of the fireplace, legs casually crossed, a glass of Scotch in his hand. His brother Matteo lounged in an armchair beside him, legs wide apart and that wolfish grin on his face. Cesare and the second bodyguard they'd called Romero during dinner sat in the other armchairs. Romero looked to be the same age of Matteo, so around eighteen. Barely men by society's standard, but not in our world.

"It could have been worse," Matteo said, grinning. He might not have looked quite as deadly as Luca, but something in his eyes told me he was only able to hide it better. "She could have been ugly. But, holy fuck, your little fiancée is a vision. That dress. That body. That hair and face." Matteo whistled. It seemed as if he was provoking his brother on purpose.

"She's a child," Luca said dismissively. Indignation rose in me, but I knew I should be glad that he didn't look at me like a man looked at a woman.

"She didn't look like a child to me," Matteo said, then clucked his tongue. He nudged the older man, Cesare. "What do you say? Is Luca blind?"

Cesare shrugged with a careful glance at Luca. "I didn't look at her closely."

"What about you, Romero? You got functioning eyes in your head?"

Romero glanced up, then quickly looked back down to his drink.

Matteo threw his head back and laughed. "Fuck, Luca, did you tell your men you'd cut their dicks off if they looked at that girl? You aren't even married to her."

"She's mine," Luca said quietly, sending a chill down my back with his voice, not to mention his eyes.

He looked at Matteo, who shook his head. "For the next three years, you'll be in New York and she will be here. You can't always keep an eye on her, or do you intend to threaten every man in the Outfit? You can't cut off all of their dicks. Maybe Scuderi knows of a few eunuchs who can keep watch over her."

"I'll do what I have to," Luca said, swirling the drink in his glass. "Cesare, find the two idiots who are supposed to guard Aria." The way my name rolled off his tongue made me shiver. I didn't even know I had two guards now. Umberto had always protected me and my sisters.

Cesare left immediately and returned ten minutes later with Umberto and Raffaele, both looking butt-hurt that they'd been summoned like dogs by someone from New York. Father was a step behind them.

"What's the meaning of this?" Father asked.

"I want to have a word with the men you chose to protect what's *mine*."

Gianna huffed beside me, but I pinched her. Nobody could know we were listening in on this conversation. Father would throw a fit if we revealed the position of his secret door.

"They are good soldiers, both of them. Raffaele is Aria's cousin, and Umberto has worked for me for almost two decades."

"I'd like to decide for myself if I trust them," Luca said. I held my breath. That was as close to an insult as he could get without actually speaking against my father openly. Father's lips thinned, but he gave a curt nod. He remained in the room. Luca stepped up to Umberto. "I hear you are good with the knife."

"The best," Father interjected. A muscle in Luca's jaw twitched.

"Not as good as your brother, as rumor has it," Umberto said with a nod toward Matteo, who flashed him a shark grin. "But better than any other man in our territory," Umberto admitted eventually.

"Are you married?"

Umberto nodded. "For twenty-one years."

"That's a long time," Matteo said. "Aria must look awfully delicious in comparison to your *old* wife." I stifled a gasp.

Umberto's hand twitched an inch toward the holster around his waist. Everyone saw it. Father watched like a hawk but didn't interfere. Umberto cleared his throat. "I've known Aria since her birth. She is a *child*."

"She won't be a child for much longer," Luca said.

"She will always be a child in my eyes. And I'm faithful to my wife." Umberto glared at Matteo. "If you insult my wife again, I'll ask your father for permission to challenge you in a knife fight to defend her honor, and I'll kill you."

This would end badly.

Matteo inclined his head. "You could try." He bared his white teeth. "But you would not succeed."

Luca crossed his arms, then gave a nod. "I think you are a good choice, Umberto." Umberto stepped back, but kept his gaze fixed on Matteo, who ignored him.

Luca's eyes settled on Raffaele, and he dropped whatever civility had cloaked the monster within until that point. He moved so close to Raffaele that my cousin had to tilt his head back to return the stare. Raffaele tried to keep his expression arrogant and self-confident, but he looked like a Chihuahua pup attempting to impress a Bengal tiger. He and Luca might as well have been two different species.

"He's family. Are you honestly going to accuse him of having an interest in my daughter?"

"I saw how you looked at Aria," Luca said, never taking his eyes off of Raffaele.

"Like a juicy peach you wanted to pluck," Matteo threw in, enjoying this entirely too much.

Raffaele's eyes darted toward my father, looking for help.

"Don't deny it. I know want when I see it. And you want Aria," Luca growled. Raffaele didn't deny it. "If I find out you are looking at her like that again. If I find out you are in a room alone with her. If I find out you touch as much as her hand, I will kill you."

Raffaele flushed red. "You aren't a member of the Outfit. Nobody would tell you anything even if I *raped* her. I could break her in for you." *God, Raffaele, shut your mouth.* Couldn't he see murder in Luca's eyes? "Maybe I'll even film it for you."

Before I could even blink, Luca had thrown Raffaele to the ground, dug a knee into his spine, and twisted one of my cousin's arms behind him. Raffaele struggled and cursed, but Luca held him fast. One of his hands gripped Raffaele's wrist while he reached under his vest with the other, pulling out a knife.

My legs turned weak. "Leave now," I told Gianna in a whisper. She didn't listen.

Look away, Aria.

But I couldn't. Father would surely stop Luca. But Father's expression was disgusted as he stared down at Raffaele. Luca's eyes sought Father's gaze—Raffaele wasn't his soldier. This wasn't even his territory. Honor demanded he got permission from the Consigliere—and when my father gave a nod, Luca brought the knife down and cut Raffaele's pinky off. The screams rang in my ears as my vision turned black. I bit down on my fist to stifle a sound. Gianna didn't. She let out a screech that could have woken the dead before she threw up. At least she'd turned and aimed away from me. Her vomit spilled down the steps.

Behind the doors, silence reigned. They had heard us. I gripped Gianna's upper arms when the secret door was ripped open, revealing Father's furious face. Behind him stood Cesare and Romero, both with their weapons drawn. When they saw Gianna and me, they returned them to the holsters under their jackets.

Gianna didn't cry. She seldom did, but her face was pale and she leaned heavily against me. If I didn't have to hold her up, my own legs would have crumpled. But I had to be strong for her.

"Of course," Father hissed, scowling at Gianna. "I should have known it was you causing trouble again." He wrenched her away from me and into the lounge, raised his hand and slapped her hard across the face.

I took a step in his direction to protect her, and Father lifted his arm again. I braced myself for the slap, but Luca caught my father's wrist with his left hand. His right hand was still grasping the knife he'd used to cut off Raffaele's finger. Both the knife and Luca's hand were coated with blood. My eyes widened. Father was the master of the house, the master over us. Luca's intervention was an insult against my father's honor.

Umberto drew his knife and Father had his hand on his gun. Matteo, Romero and Cesare had drawn their own guns. Raffaele was huddled on the floor, bent over his hand, his whimpers the only sound in the room. Had there ever been a red engagement?

"I didn't mean disrespect," Luca said calmly, as if war between New York and Chicago wasn't on the verge of breaking out. "But Aria is no longer your responsibility. You lost your right to punish her when you made her my fiancée. She's mine to deal with now."

Father glanced down at the ring on my finger, then inclined his head. Luca let go of his wrist, and the other men in the room relaxed slightly, but didn't put their weapons back. "That's true." He stepped back and gestured at me. "Then would you like the honor of beating some sense into her?"

Luca's hard gaze settled on me, and I stopped breathing. "She didn't disobey me."

Father's lips thinned. "You are right. But as I see it, Aria will be living under my roof until the wedding, and since honor forbids me to raise my hand against her, I'll have to find another way to make her obey *me*." He glowered at Gianna and hit her a second time. "For every one of your wrongdoings, Aria, your sister will accept the punishment in your stead."

I pressed my lips together, tears prickling in my eyes. I wouldn't look at either man again, until I could find a way to hide my hatred from them.

"Umberto, take Gianna and Aria to their rooms and make sure they stay there." Umberto sheathed his knife and gestured at us to follow him. I stepped past my father, dragging Gianna with me, her head bowed. She stiffened as we stepped over the blood on the hardwood floor and the cut-off finger lying abandoned in it. My eyes darted to Raffaele, who was clutching his wound to still the bleeding. His hands, shirt and pants were covered with blood. Gianna retched as if she was going to throw up again.

"No," I said firmly. "Look at me."

She drew her eyes away from the blood and met my gaze. There were tears in her eyes, and a cut on her lower lip was dripping blood on her chin and her nightgown. My hand on hers tightened. *I'm here for you*. Our locked eyes seemed her only anchor as Umberto led us out of the room.

"Women," my father said in a scoffing tone. "They can't even bear the sight of a bit of blood." I could practically feel Luca's eyes boring into my back before the door closed. Gianna wiped her bleeding lip as we hurried after Umberto through the corridor and up the stairs. "I hate him," she muttered. "I hate them all."

"Shh." I didn't want her to talk like that in front of Umberto. He cared for us, but he was my father's soldier through and through.

He stopped me when I wanted to follow Gianna into her room. I didn't want her to be alone tonight. And I didn't want to be alone either. "You heard what your father said."

I glared at Umberto. "I need to help Gianna with her lip."

Umberto shook his head. "It's nothing. You two in a room together always bodes trouble. Do you think it's wise to irk your father any more tonight?" Umberto closed Gianna's door and gently pushed me in the direction of my room next to hers.

I stepped in, then turned to him. "A room full of grown men watches a man beat a helpless girl—that's the famous courage of *Made Men*?"

"Your future husband stopped your father."

"From hitting *me*, not Gianna."

Umberto smiled like I was a stupid child. "Luca might rule over New York, but this is Chicago and your father is Consigliere."

"You admire Luca," I said incredulously. "You watched him cut off Raffaele's finger and you admire him."

"Your cousin is lucky The Vice didn't cut off something else. Luca did what every man would have done."

Maybe every man in our world.

Umberto patted my head like I was an adorable kitten. "Go to sleep."

"Will you be guarding my door all night to make sure I don't sneak out again?" I challenged him.

"Better get used to it. Now that Luca's put a ring on your finger, he'll make sure you're always guarded."

I slammed the door shut. Guarded. Even from afar Luca would be controlling me. I'd thought my life would go on as it used to until the wedding, but how could it when everyone knew what the ring on my finger meant? Raffaele's pinky was a signal, a warning. Luca had made his claim on me and would enforce it in cold blood.

I didn't extinguish the lights that night, worried the darkness would bring back images of blood and cut-off limbs. They came anyway.

chapter *three*

My breath clouded as it left my lips. Even my thick coat couldn't protect me from Chicago's winter. Snow crunched under my boots as I followed Mother along the pavement toward the brick building, which harbored the most luxurious wedding store in the Midwest. Umberto trailed closely behind, my constant shadow. Another of my father's soldiers made up the rear, behind my sisters.

Revolving brass doors let us into the brightly lit store and the owner and her two assistants immediately greeted us. "Happy birthday, Ms. Scuderi," she said in her lilting voice.

I forced a smile. My eighteenth birthday was supposed to be a day for celebration. Instead it only meant I was another step closer to marrying Luca. I hadn't seen him since that night he'd cut off Raffaele's finger. He'd sent me expensive jewelry for my birthdays, Christmas holidays, Valentine's days and the anniversary of our engagement, but that was the extent of our contact in the last thirty months. I'd seen photos of him with other women on the Internet, but even that would stop today when our engagement would be leaked to the press. At least in public he wouldn't flaunt his whores anymore.

I didn't kid myself into thinking he wasn't still sleeping with them. And I didn't care. As long as he had other women to screw, he'd hopefully not think about me in that way.

"Only six months until your wedding, if I'm correctly informed?" the shop owner piped. She was the only person who looked excited. No surprise really—she would make a lot of money today. The wedding that marked the final union of the Chicago and the New York mafia was supposed to be a splendid affair. Money was irrelevant.

I inclined my head. One hundred sixty-six days until I had to exchange one golden cage for another. Gianna gave me a look that made it clear what she thought of the matter, but she kept her mouth shut. At sixteen and a half, Gianna had finally learned to rein in her outbursts, *mostly*.

The shop owner led us into the fitting room. Umberto and the other man stayed outside the drawn curtains. Lily and Gianna plopped down on the plush white couch while Mother began browsing the wedding gowns on display. I stood in the middle of the room. The sight of all the white tulle, silk, gossamer, and brocade, and my knowledge of what it stood for, corded up my throat. I'd be a married woman soon. Quotes about love decorated the walls of the fitting room; they felt like a taunt considering the harsh reality that was my life. What was love but a silly dream?

I could feel the eyes of the shop owner and her assistants on me, and squared my shoulders before I joined my mother. Nobody could know that I wasn't the happy bride-to-be, but a pawn in a game of power. Eventually, the shop owner approached us and showed us her most expensive gowns.

"What kind of gown would your future husband prefer?" she asked pleasantly.

"The naked kind," Gianna said, and my mother shot her a glare. I flushed, but the shop owner laughed as if it was all too delightful.

"There's time for that on the wedding night, don't you think?" She winked.

I reached for the most expensive dress in the collection, a dream of brocade; the bustier was embroidered with pearls and silvery threads forming a delicate flower pattern. "Those are platinum threads," the shop owner said. That explained the price. "I think your groom will be pleased with your choice."

Then she knew him better than I did. Luca was as much a stranger to me today as he had been almost three years ago.

The wedding would be held in the vast gardens of the Vitiello mansion in the Hamptons. Everyone was already abuzz with the preparations. I hadn't set foot into the house or even the premises yet, but my mother kept me up-to-date, not that I'd asked her to.

The moment my family had arrived in New York a few hours ago, my sisters and I had huddled together in our suite in the Mandarin Oriental Hotel in Manhattan. Salvatore Vitiello had suggested we live in one of the many rooms in the mansion until the wedding in five days, but my father had declined. Three years of tentative cooperation and they still didn't trust each other. I was glad. I didn't want to set foot into the mansion until I had to.

Father had agreed to let me share a suite with Lily and Gianna, so he and Mother had a suite for themselves. Of course, a bodyguard was stationed in front all three doors to our suite.

"Do we really have to attend the bridal shower tomorrow?" Lily asked, her bare legs swung over the backrest of the sofa. Mother always said Nabokov must have had Liliana in mind when he wrote *Lolita*. While Gianna provoked with her words, Lily used her body for that. She'd turned fourteen in April, a child who flaunted her tentative curves to get a rise out of everyone around us. She looked like the teen model Thylane Blondeau, only her hair was a bit lighter and she didn't have a gap between her front teeth.

It worried me. I knew it was her way of rebelling against the gilded cage that was our life, but while Father's soldiers regarded her flirting with amusement, there were others out there who would love to misunderstand it.

"Of course, we have to," Gianna muttered. "Aria is the happy bride, remember?"

Lily snorted. "Sure." She sat up abruptly. "I'm bored. Let's go shopping."

Umberto wasn't enthused about the suggestion; even with another of my father's bodyguards at his side, he claimed it was almost impossible to keep us under control. Eventually he relented, as he always did.

We were shopping in a store that sold sexy rocker-chick-like outfits that Lily desperately wanted to try on when I got a message from Luca. It was the first time he'd contacted me directly, and for a long time I could only stare at my screen. Gianna peered over my shoulder in the dressing room. "'Meet me at your hotel at six. Luca.' How nice of him to *ask*."

"What does he want?" I whispered. I'd hoped I wouldn't have to see him until August 10th, the day of our wedding.

"Only one way to find out," Gianna said, checking her reflection.

I was nervous. I hadn't seen Luca in a long time. I smoothed my hair down, then straightened my shirt. Gianna had convinced me to wear the tight black skinny jeans I'd bought today. Now I wondered if something that drew less attention to my body might have been better. I still had fifteen minutes before Luca wanted to meet me. I didn't even know where yet. I assumed he'd call me once he arrived and ask me to come down into the lobby.

"Stop fiddling," Gianna said from her spot on the sofa, reading a magazine.

"I really don't think this outfit is a good idea."

"It is. It's easy to manipulate men. Lily is fourteen and has already figured it out. Father always says we're the weak sex because we don't carry around guns. We have our own weapons, Aria, and you'll have to start using them. If you want to survive a marriage with that man, you'll have to use your body to manipulate him. Men, even cold-hearted bastards like them, have a weakness, and it hangs between their legs."

I didn't think Luca could be manipulated that easily. He didn't seem like someone who ever lost control, unless he wanted to, and I wasn't sure I wanted him to notice my body like that.

A knock made me jump and my eyes flew to the clock. It was still too early for Luca, and he wouldn't really come up to our suite, would he?

Lily dashed out of her bedroom before Gianna or I could even move. She was wearing her rocker-chic outfit: tight leather pants and a tight black tee. She thought she looked so adult with it. Gianna and I thought she looked like a fourteen-year-old trying too hard.

She opened the door, jutting her hip out, trying to look sexy. Gianna groaned but I wasn't paying attention to her.

"Hi, Luca," Lily piped. I walked closer so I could see Luca. He was staring down at Lily, obviously trying to figure out who she was. Matteo, Romero and Cesare stood behind him. Wow, he'd brought his entourage. Where was Umberto?

"You are Liliana, the youngest sister," Luca said, ignoring Lily's flirty expression.

Lily frowned. "I'm not that young."

"Yes, you are," I said firmly, walking up to her and putting my hands on her shoulders. She was only a couple of inches shorter than me. "Go to Gianna."

Lily gave me an incredulous look, but then she slinked away.

My pulse was racing as I turned to Luca. His gaze lingered on my legs, then slowly moved up until it arrived at my face. That look hadn't been in his eyes the last time I'd seen him. And I realized with a start it was desire. "I didn't know we'd meet in my suite," I said, then realized I should have greeted him, or at least tried to sound less rude.

"Are you going to let me in?"

I hesitated, then I stepped back and let the men walk past me. Only Cesare stayed outside. He closed the door even though I would have preferred to keep it ajar.

Matteo sauntered over to Gianna, who quickly sat up and gave him her nastiest look. Lily, of course, smiled at him. "Can I see your gun?"

Matteo grinned at her but before he could reply, I said. "No, you can't."

I could feel Luca's eyes on me, lingering on my legs and butt again. Gianna gave me an I-told-you-so-look. She wanted me to use my body; the problem was I preferred Luca ignoring my body because the alternative terrified me.

"You shouldn't be here alone with us," Gianna muttered. "It's not appropriate." I almost snorted. As if Gianna gave a damn about appropriateness.

Luca narrowed his eyes. "Where is Umberto? Shouldn't he be guarding this door?"

"He's probably on a toilet or cigarette break," I said, shrugging.

"Does it happen often that he leaves you without protection?"

"Oh, all the time," Gianna said mockingly. "You see, Lily, Aria and I sneak out every weekend because we have a bet going who can pick up more guys." Lily let out her bell-like laugh.

"I want to have a word with you, Aria," Luca said, fixing me with his cold stare.

Gianna rose from the sofa and came toward us. "I was joking, for god's sake!" she said, trying to step between Luca and me, but Matteo gripped her wrist and pulled her back. Lily watched everything with wide eyes and Romero stood against the door, pretending this didn't concern him.

"Let go of me, or I'll break your fingers," Gianna growled. Matteo raised his hands with a wide grin.

"Come on," Luca said, his hand touching my lower back. I swallowed a gasp. If he noticed, he didn't comment. "Where's your bedroom?"

My heartbeat stuttered as I nodded toward the door to the left. Luca led me in that direction, ignoring Gianna's protests. "I'll call our father! You can't do that."

We stepped into my bedroom and Luca closed the door. I couldn't help but be afraid. Gianna shouldn't have said those things. The moment Luca faced me, I said, "Gianna was joking. I haven't even kissed anyone yet, I swear." Heat crept into my face at the admission, but I didn't want Luca to get angry for something I hadn't even done.

Luca's gray eyes held me with their intensity. "I know."

My lips parted. "Oh. Then why are you angry?"

"Do I look angry to you?"

I decided not to reply.

He smirked. "You don't know me very well."

"That's not my fault," I muttered.

He touched my chin and I turned into a pillar of salt. "You are like a skittish doe in the clutches of a wolf." He didn't know how close that came to what I thought of him. "I'm not going to maul you."

I must have looked doubtful because he released a small laugh, lowering his head toward mine.

"What are you doing?" I whispered nervously.

"I'm not going to take you, if that's what you're worried about. I can wait a few more days. I've waited three years, after all."

I couldn't believe he'd said that. Of course, I knew what was expected on a wedding night, but I'd almost convinced myself that Luca wasn't interested in me that way. "You called me a child last time."

"But you aren't a child anymore," Luca said with a predatory smirk. His lips were less than an inch from mine. "You're making this really hard. I can't kiss you if you look at me like that."

"Then maybe I should give you that look on our wedding night," I challenged.

"Then maybe I'll have to take you from behind so I don't have to see it."

My face fell and I stumbled away, my back colliding with the wall.

Luca shook his head. "Relax. I was joking," he said quietly. "I'm not a monster."

"Aren't you?"

His expression hardened and he straightened, drawing up to his full height again. I regretted my words, even though they were the truth. "I wanted to discuss the matter of your protection with you," he said in an emotionless, formal voice. "Once you move into my penthouse after the wedding, Cesare and Romero will be responsible for your safety. But I want Romero at your side until then."

"I have Umberto," I protested, but he shook his head. "Apparently, he's taking too many toilet breaks. Romero won't leave your side from now on."

"Will he watch me when I shower too?"

"If I want him to."

I raised my chin, trying to quench my anger. "You would let another man see me naked? You must really trust Romero not to take advantage of the situation."

Luca's eyes blazed. "Romero is loyal." He leaned close. "Don't worry—I'll be the only man to ever see you naked. I can't wait." His eyes traveled over my body.

I crossed my arms over my chest and averted my eyes. "What about Lily? She and Gianna share this suite with me. You saw how Lily can be. She will flirt with Romero. She will do anything to get a rise out of him. She doesn't realize what she could get herself into. I need to know that she's safe."

"Romero won't touch your sister. Liliana is playing around. She's a little girl. Romero likes his women of age and willing."

And you don't? I almost asked, but swallowed the words and nodded instead.

My eyes darted toward my bed. This was a horrible reminder of what would happen soon.

"There's something else. Are you taking the pill?"

The blood drained from my face as I stared at him. "Of course not."

Luca scrutinized me with unsettling calm. "Your mother could have made you start it in preparation for the wedding."

I was pretty sure I was going to have a nervous breakdown any moment. "My mother would never do that. She won't even talk to me about these things."

Luca raised one eyebrow. "But you do know what happens between a man and a woman on their wedding night?"

He was mocking me, the bastard. "I do know what happens between normal couples. In our case, I think the word you're looking for is rape."

Luca's eyes flashed with emotion. "I want you to start taking the pill." He handed me a small packet. It was birth control.

"Don't I need to see a doctor before I start taking birth control?"

"We have a doctor who's been working for the Famiglia for decades. This is from him. You need to start taking the pill immediately. It takes forty-eight hours for them to start working."

I couldn't believe him. He seemed really eager to sleep with me. My stomach tightened. "And what if I don't?"

Luca shrugged. "Then I'll use a condom. Either way, on our wedding night you are mine."

He opened the door and gestured for me to move. As if in a trance, I walked into the living area of the suite. I hadn't meant to make him angry, but now it was too late. It probably wasn't the last time anyway.

Umberto stood beside Gianna and Lily, looking annoyed. He frowned at Luca. "What are you doing here?"

"You should pay better attention in the future and keep your breaks to a minimum," Luca told him.

"I was gone for only a few minutes and there were guards in front of the other doors."

Gianna smirked. Matteo's eyes were locked on her. "What are you looking at?" she snapped.

Matteo leaned forward. "At your hot body."

"Then keep looking." She gave a one-shoulder shrug. "Because that's all you ever get to do with my *hot body*."

"Stop it," Umberto warned.

I wasn't looking at him, but at Matteo, who had a calculating expression on his face.

"Romero will take over the watch duty until the wedding," Luca said. Umberto opened his mouth, but Luca raised a hand. "It's done." He turned to Romero, who straightened at once. They walked a few steps away from us. Gianna pressed up to me. "What does he mean?"

"Romero is my new bodyguard."

"He just wants to control you."

"Shh." I was watching Luca and Romero. After a moment, Romero glanced at Lily, then nodded and said something. They finally returned to us. "Romero will stay with you," Luca said simply. He was so cold since I'd as good as called him a monster.

"And what am I supposed to do?" Umberto asked.

"You can guard their door."

"Or you can join our stag party," Matteo suggested.

"I'm not interested," Umberto said.

Luca shrugged. "Suit yourself. Scuderi is coming with us."

My father would go with them? I didn't even want to know what they were up to.

Luca turned to me. "Remember what I told you."

I didn't say anything, only clutched the pill packet in my hand. Without another word, Luca and Matteo left. Romero held the door open. "You can leave too," he told Umberto, who glared but walked out after a moment. Romero shut the door and locked it.

Gianna gaped. "You can't be *serious*."

Romero leaned against the door, arms clasped in front of him. He didn't react.

"Come, Gianna." I pulled her with me toward the couch and plopped down. Lily was already kneeling on the armchair, watching Romero with rapt attention. Gianna's eyes flitted down to my hand. "What's this?"

"Birth control."

"Don't tell me that asshole gave it to you just now so he can screw you on your wedding night."

I pressed my lips together.

"You aren't going to take them, right?"

"I have to. It won't stop Luca if I don't. He'll only be angry."

Gianna shook her head, but I gave her a pleading look. "I don't want to argue with you. Let's watch a movie, okay? I really need the distraction." After a moment, Gianna nodded. We picked out a random movie, but it was difficult to focus with Romero guarding us.

"Are you going to stand there all night?" I asked eventually. "You're making me nervous. Can't you sit down at least?"

He moved toward the vacant armchair and sank down. He shrugged off his jacket, revealing a white shirt and a holster holding two guns and a long knife.

"Wow," Lily breathed. She stood and walked over to him. He kept his attention on the door. She stepped in his way and he had no choice but to look up at her. She smiled, then quickly slipped into his lap, and he tensed. I leaped off the sofa and wrenched her off him. "Lily, what's the matter with you? You can't act like that. One day a man is going to take advantage of you." Many men had trouble understanding that provocative clothes and actions didn't mean a woman was *asking for it*.

Romero straightened in the chair.

"He won't hurt me. Luca forbade him, right?"

"He could steal your virtue and cut your throat afterward, so you can't tell anyone," Gianna said offhandedly. I shot her a glare.

Lily's eyes grew wide.

"I wouldn't," Romero said, startling us with his voice.

"You shouldn't have said that," Gianna muttered. "Now she's going to fawn over you."

"Lily, go to bed," I ordered, and she did under loud protest.

"I'm sorry," I said. "She doesn't know what she's doing."

Romero nodded. "Don't worry. I have a sister her age."

"How old are you?"

"Twenty."

"And how long have you been working for Luca?" Gianna turned off the TV to focus on her interrogation. I settled against the backrest.

"Four years, but I've been a Made Man for six years."

"You must be good if Luca chose you to protect Aria."

Romero shrugged. "Knowing how to handle myself in a fight isn't the main reason. Luca knows I'm loyal."

"Meaning you won't paw at Aria."

I rolled my eyes at Gianna. Romero probably regretted ever leaving his spot at the door. "Luca knows he can trust me with what's his."

Gianna's lips thinned. Wrong thing to say. "So if Aria came out of her room naked tonight and you got a hard-on because you can't really help it, Luca wouldn't cut off your dick?"

Romero was obviously taken aback. He stared at me, as if he actually worried I would do that. "Ignore her. I won't."

"Where are Luca and the other men going for stag night?"

Romero didn't reply.

"Probably a strip club and afterward one of the whorehouses the Famiglia has going," Gianna muttered. "Why is it that men can whore around while we have to save our virginity for the wedding night? And why can Luca fuck whoever he wants while Aria can't even kiss a guy?"

"I didn't make the rules," Romero said simply.

"But you make sure that we don't break them. You aren't our protector—you are our warden."

"Have you ever considered that I'm protecting guys who don't know who Aria is?" he asked.

I frowned.

"Luca would kill anyone who dared to touch you. Of course, you could go out, flirt with a guy and move on, because you wouldn't be the one Luca would gut."

"Luca isn't my fiancé," Gianna said.

"Your father would kill any man that got near you, because he wouldn't want anyone to spoil his most prized possessions."

For the first time, I realized the fact that I'd been given to Luca didn't mean Gianna wouldn't be forced to marry someone else. I felt suddenly very tired. "I'm going to bed."

I lay awake most of the night, thinking of ways to get out of the wedding, but the only option would be to run, and while Gianna would definitely come with me, what about Liliana? I couldn't keep them both safe. And what about Fabiano? What about my mother? I couldn't leave everything behind. This was my life. I didn't know anything else. Maybe I was a coward, though marrying a man like Luca probably required more courage than running away.

chapter *four*

THE LIVING ROOM OF THE SUITE WAS DECORATED FOR THE BRIDAL shower. I'd hoped to be spared that tradition, but my mother had insisted it would be an affront to the women of Luca's family if they couldn't meet me before the wedding.

I smoothed out the green cocktail dress. It was a color that was supposed to bring good luck. I knew my interpretation of what would be good luck at this point differed widely from Luca's and my father's opinions.

Lily wasn't allowed to attend the bridal shower since she was deemed too young, but Gianna had argued her way into staying. Though I worried that there might be another reason behind Mother's agreement. Gianna had turned seventeen a few days ago. That meant she was almost old enough to be married off as well. I pushed the thought aside. I could hear Mother and Gianna arguing in the bedroom about what Gianna was supposed to wear when a knock sounded at the suite door. It was a bit early; the guests weren't supposed to arrive for another ten minutes.

I opened the door. Valentina stood in front of me, Umberto behind her. She was my cousin but five years older than me. Her mother and my mother were sisters. She smiled apologetically. "I know I'm early."

"It's okay," I said, stepping back so she could walk in. Umberto sat back on the chair outside my door. I really liked Valentina, so I didn't mind spending some time alone with her. She was tall and graceful, with dark brown, almost black hair and eyes that were the darkest green imaginable. She wore a black dress with a pencil skirt that reached her knees. Her husband Antonio had died six months ago, and my wedding would be the first time that she'd wear something other than black. Sometimes widows, especially older women, were expected to wear mourning attire for a year after their husband's death, but Valentina was only twenty-three. Luca's age. I caught myself wishing her husband had died sooner so she could have married Luca, and then I felt horrible. I shouldn't be thinking like that. Romero hovered beside the window.

"Could you please wait outside? A bridal shower is no place for a man."

He tilted his head, then walked out without another word.

"Your husband sent you his own bodyguard?" Valentina asked.

"He isn't my husband yet."

"No, you're right. You look sad," she said with a knowing expression as she sank down on the sofa. Champagne, soft drinks and an array of finger food were set up on a table behind it.

I swallowed. "So do you." And I felt immediately stupid for saying something like that.

"My father wants me to remarry," she said, twisting her wedding band.

My eyes widened. "So soon?"

"Not right away. Apparently he's already talking to someone."

I couldn't believe it. "Can't you say no? You were already married."

"But it was a childless marriage, and I'm too young to stay alone. I had to move back in with my family. My father insisted on it to protect me."

We both knew that code. Women always needed protection from the outside world, especially if they were of a marriageable age. "I'm sorry," I said.

"It is what it is. You know that as well as I do."

I laughed bitterly. "Yeah."

"I saw your future husband when I visited the Vitiello mansion with my parents yesterday. He's…imposing."

"Terrifying," I added quietly. Valentina's expression softened, but our conversation was cut short when Mother and Gianna came out of the bedroom. And soon after that more guests arrived.

The gifts were everything from lingerie and jewelry to certificates for a day at a luxury spa in New York. The lingerie was the worst though, and when I opened the gift from Luca's stepmother Nina I had trouble keeping a straight face. I lifted the barely there white nightgown and smiled tightly. The entire middle was see-through, and it was so short it wouldn't even cover much of my legs. Beneath it in the gift box was an even smaller piece of clothing: white lace panties that would reveal most of my butt and were held together by a bow in the back. A chorus of appreciative murmurs came from the women around me.

I gaped at the lingerie. Gianna tipped her finger inconspicuously against her temple.

"This is for your wedding night," Nina said with a calculating glint in her eyes. "I bet Luca will love unwrapping you. We need to please our husbands. Luca will certainly expect something this daring."

I nodded. "Thank you."

Had Luca set his stepmother up to give this to me? I wouldn't put it past him. Not after he'd gotten birth control for me. My stomach twisted with worry, and it only got worse when the women started talking about their wedding nights.

"I was so embarrassed when it was time for the presentation of the sheets!" Luca's cousin Cosima stage-whispered.

"The presentation of the sheets?" I asked.

Nina's smile was patronizing when she said, "Didn't your mother explain it to you?"

I glanced at my mother who pressed her lips together, two red blotches appearing on her cheeks.

"It's a Sicilian tradition that the Famiglia has proudly upheld for generations," Nina explained, eyes fixed on my face. "After the wedding night, the women of the groom's family come to the bridal pair to collect the sheets they spent the night on. Then those sheets are presented to the fathers of the bride and the groom and whoever else wants to see proof that the marriage has been consummated and that the bride was pure."

Cosima giggled. "It's also called the tradition of the bloody sheets for that reason."

My face was frozen.

"That's a barbaric tradition!" Gianna hissed. "Mother, you can't allow it."

"It's not up to me," Mother said.

"That's right. We won't abandon our traditions." Nina turned to me. "And from what I know you've been well-protected from male attention, so there's nothing for you to fear. The sheets will prove your honor."

Gianna's lips curled, but all I could think about was that this tradition meant I definitely had to sleep with Luca.

chapter *five*

THE AFTERNOON BEFORE THE WEDDING DAY, MY FAMILY MOVED out of the Mandarin Oriental and headed for the Vitiello mansion in the Hamptons. It was a huge building inspired by Italian palazzos, surrounded by almost three acres of park-like grounds. The driveway was long and winding, and led past four double garages and two guesthouses until it ended in front of the mansion with its white front and red shingled roof. White marble statues stood at the base of the double staircase leading up to the front door.

Inside, coffered ceilings, white marble columns and floors, and a view of the bay and the long pool through the panoramic windows took my breath away. Luca's father and stepmother led us toward the second floor of the left wing, where our bedrooms were situated.

Gianna and I insisted on sharing a room. I didn't care if it made us look immature. I needed her at my side. From the window we could watch how the workers began setting up the huge pavilion that would serve as church tomorrow. Beyond it the ocean churned. Luca wouldn't arrive until the next day so we couldn't cross paths by accident before the wedding, which would mean bad luck. I honestly didn't know how I could experience any more bad luck than I already had.

"Today's the day!" Mother said with fake cheer.

I dragged myself out of bed. Gianna pulled the blankets over her head, grumbling something about it being too early.

Mother sighed. "I can't believe you shared a room like five-year-olds."

"Someone had to make sure Luca didn't sneak in," Gianna said from beneath the blanket.

"Umberto patrolled the corridor."

"As if he would protect Aria from Luca," Gianna muttered, finally sitting up. Her red hair was a mess.

Mother pursed her lips. "Your sister doesn't need protection from her husband."

Gianna snorted, but Mother ignored her and ushered me into the bathroom. "We have to get you ready. The beautician will be here any second. Grab a quick shower."

As the hot water poured down on me, realization set in. This was it, the day I'd been dreading for so long. Tonight I'd be Aria Vitiello, wife to the future Capo dei Capi, and former virgin. I leaned against the shower cabin. I wished I were like other brides. I wished I could enjoy this day. I wished I didn't have to dread my wedding night, but I'd learned a long time ago that wishing didn't change a thing.

When I stepped out of the shower, I felt cold. Even my fluffy bathrobe couldn't stop my shivering. Someone knocked and Gianna entered with a cup and a bowl in her hand. "Coffee and fruit salad. Apparently you aren't allowed to have pancakes because it could cause bloating. What bullshit."

I took the coffee but shook my head at the food. "I'm not hungry."

"You can't go all day without eating or you'll faint when you walk down the aisle." She paused. "Though, on second thought, I'd love to see Luca's face when you do."

I sipped at the coffee, then took the bowl from Gianna and ate a few pieces of banana. I really didn't want to faint. Father would be furious, and Luca probably wouldn't be too happy about it either.

"The beautician has arrived with her entourage. You would think they need to prettify an army of fishwives," Gianna muttered.

I smiled weakly. "Let's not make them wait."

Gianna's worried gaze followed me as I walked into the bedroom, where Lily and my mother were already waiting with the three beauticians. They began their work at once, waxing our legs and armpits. When I thought the torture was over, the beautician asked, "Bikini zone? Do you know what your husband prefers?"

My cheeks exploded with heat. Mother actually looked at me for an answer. As if I knew the first thing about Luca and his preferences, especially concerning body hair.

"Maybe we could call one of his whores," Gianna suggested.

Mother gasped. "Gianna!"

Lily looked clueless about the whole situation. She might have been the queen of flirting, but that was all.

"I'll remove everything except for a small triangle, okay?" the beautician said in a gentle voice and I nodded, giving her a grateful smile.

It took hours to get us ready. When our makeup was in place and my hair was pinned up in an elaborate updo that would later hold the veil and diamond headpiece, my aunts Livia and Ornatella came in carrying my wedding dress as well as the bridesmaid dresses for Lily and Gianna. There was only one hour left until the wedding ceremony.

I stared at my reflection. The dress was gorgeous; the chapel train fanned out behind me, the platinum embroidery glittering wherever the sunlight hit it, and the empire waist was accentuated by a white satin ribbon.

"I love the sweetheart neckline. It gives you breathtaking cleavage," Aunt Livia gushed. She was Valentina's mother.

"Luca will surely appreciate it," Aunt Ornatella said.

Something on my face must have made my mother realize I was close to having a nervous breakdown, so she ushered my aunts out. "Let the three girls have a moment."

Gianna stepped into view beside me. Her red hair contrasted beautifully with the mint dress. She opened the box with the necklace. Diamonds and pearls surrounded by intricate white gold threads. "Luca doesn't spare any costs, does he? That necklace and your headpiece probably cost more than most people pay for their house."

The conversation and laughter of the gathered guests carried up from the gardens through the open window into the room. Every now and then a clunk could be heard.

"What's that noise?" I asked, trying to distract myself. Gianna walked over to the window and peered out. "The men are taking off their guns and putting them into plastic boxes."

"How many?"

Gianna cocked an eyebrow.

"How many guns does each man put away?"

"One." She frowned, then it dawned on her, and I nodded grimly.

"Only a fool would leave the house with less than two guns."

"Then why the show?"

"It's symbolic," I said. *Like this horrid wedding.*

"But if they all want peace, why not attend unarmed? It's a wedding, after all."

"There have been red weddings before. I saw pictures from a wedding where you couldn't tell the color of the bride's dress anymore. It was soaked in blood."

Lily shuddered. "That won't happen today, right?"

Anything was possible. "No, Chicago and New York need each other too much. They can't risk spilling blood among each other as long as the Bratva and the Taiwanese pose a threat."

Gianna snorted. "Oh great, that's comforting."

"It is," I said firmly. "At least we know nobody will come to harm today." My stomach twisted into a knot. Except for me, maybe. Probably.

Gianna wrapped her arms around me from behind and rested her chin on my bare shoulder. "We could still run. We could get you out of your dress and sneak out. They're all busy. Nobody would notice."

Lily nodded her head vigorously and got up from where she'd perched on the bed.

Luca would notice. I forced a brave smile. "No. It's too late."

"It's not," Gianna hissed. "Don't give up."

"There would be blood on my hands if I broke the agreement. They would kill each other in retribution."

"They all have blood on their hands. Every single fucking person in the garden."

"Don't curse."

"Really? A lady doesn't curse," Gianna mimicked our father's voice. "Where did behaving like an obedient little lady get you?"

I looked away. She was right. It had brought me straight into the arms of one of the deadliest men in the country.

"I'm sorry," Gianna whispered. "I didn't mean it."

I linked our fingers. "I know. And you are right. Most of the people in the garden have blood on their hands and would deserve to die, but they are our family, the only one we've got. And there are innocents like Fabiano."

"Fabiano will have blood on his hands soon enough," Gianna said bitterly. "He'll become a killer."

I didn't deny it. Fabiano would start his initiation process at twelve. If what Umberto had said was true, Luca had killed his first man at eleven. "But he's innocent now, and there are other children out there as well, and women."

Gianna fixed me with a hard look in the mirror. "Do you really believe that any one of us is innocent?"

Being born into our world meant being born with blood on your hands.

With every breath we took, sin was engraved deeper into our skin. Born in blood. Sworn in blood, like the motto of the New York Famiglia. "No."

Gianna smiled grimly. Lily walked over to the bed and picked up my veil attached to the headpiece. I bent my knees so she could fix it atop my head. She gently smoothed it out.

"I wish you were marrying for love. I wish we could giggle about your wedding night. I wish you didn't look so fucking sad," Gianna said fiercely.

The silence between us stretched. Lily eventually nodded toward the bed. "Is this where you'll sleep tonight?"

My throat tightened. "No, Luca and I will spend the night in the master bedroom." I didn't think I'd get much, if any, sleep.

A knock sounded and I squared my shoulders, putting on my outside face. Bibiana and Valentina stepped in, followed by Mother.

"Wow, Aria, you are gorgeous. Your hair looks like spun gold," Valentina said. She was already wearing her bridesmaid dress, and the mint color looked gorgeous with her dark hair. Technically, only unmarried women were allowed to be bridesmaids, but my uncle had insisted we make an exemption for Valentina. He was really keen to find a new husband for her. Bibiana wore a floor-length maroon dress with long sleeves, despite the summer heat. It was probably meant to hide how thin she'd gotten.

I forced a smile. Mother took Lily's arm. "Come on, Liliana, your cousins need to talk to your sister." She led Lily out of the room, then looked back at Gianna, who sat cross-legged on the sofa. "Gianna?"

Gianna ignored her. "I'm staying. I won't leave Aria alone."

Mother knew better than to argue with my sister when she was in a mood, and so she closed the door.

"What are you supposed to talk to me about?"

"Your wedding night," Valentina said with an apologetic smile. Bibiana made a face, which reminded me how young she was. Only twenty-two. I couldn't believe they'd chosen to send those two to talk to me about my wedding night. Bibiana's face spoke of her unhappiness. Since her wedding to a man almost thirty years her senior, she'd been fading away. Was that meant to soothe my fears? And Valentina had lost her husband six months ago in an altercation with the Russians. How could they expect her to talk about wedded bliss?

I smoothed my dress nervously.

Gianna shook her head. "Who sent you anyway? Luca?"

"Your mother," Bibiana said. "She wants to make sure you know what's expected of you."

"Expected of her?" Gianna hissed. "What about what Aria wants?"

"It is what it is," Bibiana said bitterly. "Tonight Luca will expect to claim his rights. At least he's good-looking and young."

Pity for her kindled in me, but at the same time my own anxiety made it hard to console her. She was right. Luca was good-looking. I couldn't deny it, but that didn't change the fact that I was terrified of being intimate with him. He didn't strike me as a man who was gentle in bed. My stomach lurched again.

Valentina cleared her throat. "Luca will know what to do."

"You just lie on your back and give him what he wants," Bibiana added. "Don't try to fight him; that will only make it worse."

We all stared at her, and she looked away.

Valentina touched my shoulder. "We're not doing a good job of consoling you. Sorry. I'm sure it'll be all right."

Gianna snorted. "Maybe Mother should have invited one of the women Luca's fucked to the wedding. They could have told you what to expect."

"Grace is here," Bibiana said, then she turned red and stammered, "I mean, that's only a rumor. I—" She looked toward Valentina for help.

"One of Luca's old girlfriends is here?" I whispered.

Bibiana cringed. "I thought you knew. And she wasn't really his girlfriend, more like a plaything. Luca's been with many women." She snapped her mouth shut. I was fighting for control. I couldn't let people see how weak I was. Why did I even care if Luca's whore was at the wedding?

"Okay," Gianna said, getting up. "Who the fuck is Grace, and why the fuck is she invited to this wedding?"

"Grace Parker. She's the daughter of a New York senator who's on the payroll of the mafia," Valentina explained. "They had to invite his family."

Tears blurred my vision and Gianna rushed toward me. "Oh don't cry, Aria. It's not worth it. Luca's an asshole. You knew that. You can't let his actions get to you."

Valentina handed me a Kleenex. "You'll ruin your makeup."

I blinked a few times until I had a grip on my emotions. "I'm sorry. I'm just being emotional."

"I think it's best if you leave now," Gianna said sharply, not even looking at Bibiana and Valentina. There was rustling and then the door opened and closed. Gianna wrapped her arms around me. "If he hurts you, I'll kill him. I swear it. I'll take one of those fucking guns and put a hole into his head."

I leaned against her. "He survived the Bratva and the Triad, and he's the most feared fighter in the New York Famiglia, Gianna. He'd kill you first."

Gianna shrugged. "I'd do it for you."

I pulled back. "You're still my little sister. I should protect you."

"We will protect each other," she whispered. "Our bond is stronger than their stupid oaths and the Omerta and their blood vows."

"I don't want to leave you. I hate that I have to move to New York."

Gianna swallowed. "I'll visit often. Father will be glad to be rid of me."

There was a knock and Mother walked in. "It's time." She scanned our faces but didn't comment. Gianna took a step back, eyes burning into me. Then she turned and walked out. Mother's eyes zoomed in on the white lace garter on my vanity. "Do you need help putting it on?"

I shook my head and slid it up until it came to rest on my upper thigh. Later tonight, Luca would remove it with his mouth and throw it into the group of gathered bachelors. I smoothed down my wedding dress.

"Come," Mother said. "Everyone's waiting." She handed me my bouquet, a beautiful arrangement of white roses, mother-of-pearl roses, and pink ranunculus.

We walked in silence through the empty house, my heels clacking on the marble floors. My heart pounded in my chest as we stepped through the glass sliding door onto the veranda overlooking the backyard and the beach. The front of the garden was occupied by the huge white pavilion where the wedding ceremony would be held, but behind the pavilion dozens of tables had been set up for the following feast. Voices carried over to me from inside the pavilion, where the guests were waiting for my arrival. A path of red rose petals led from the veranda toward the entrance. I followed Mother into the small room between the outside and the main part of the pavilion. Father was waiting and straightened when we entered. Mother gave him the briefest nod before slipping into the makeshift chapel. His smile was earnest when he offered me his arm. "You look beautiful," he said quietly. "Luca won't know what hit him."

I ducked my head. "Thanks, Father."

"Be a good wife, Aria. Luca is powerful and once he takes his father's place, his word will be law. Make me proud, make the Outfit proud."

I nodded, my throat too tight for words. The music started to play: a string quartet and a piano. Father lowered my veil. I was glad for the extra layer of protection, no matter how thin. Maybe it would hide my expression from afar.

Father led me toward the entrance and gave a low command. The fabric was pulled apart, revealing the long aisle and the many hundred guests to either side of it. My eyes were drawn to the end of the aisle where Luca stood. Tall and imposing in his charcoal suit and vest with the silver tie and the white shirt. His groomsmen were dressed in vests and dress pants of a lighter gray, and wore no jackets and bowties instead of ties. Fabiano was one of them, only eight and much shorter than the men.

My father tugged me along, and my legs seemed to carry me of their own accord as my body shook with nerves. I tried not to look at Luca and instead watched Gianna and Liliana from the corner of my eye. They were the first two bridesmaids, and seeing them gave me the strength to hold my head high and not bolt outside.

White rose petals covered my path and were squashed under my shoes. Kind of symbolic in itself, though I was sure it wasn't meant to be.

The walk down the aisle took forever, and yet it was over too soon. Luca extended his hand, palm upwards. My father gripped the corners of my veil and lifted it, then he handed my hand over to Luca, whose gray eyes seemed to burn up with an emotion I couldn't place. Could he feel me shaking? I didn't meet his gaze.

The priest in his white frock greeted us, then the guests, before he began his opening prayer. I tried not to pass out. Luca's grip was the one thing keeping me focused. I had to be strong. When the priest finally came to the closing lines of the Gospel, my legs could barely hold me up. He announced the rite of marriage and the guests all rose from their chairs.

"Luca and Aria," the priest addressed us. "Have you come here freely and without reservation to give yourselves to each other in marriage? Will you love and honor each other as man and wife for the rest of your lives?"

Lying was a sin, but so was killing. This room *breathed* sin. "Yes," Luca said in his deep voice, and a moment later my own "yes" followed. It came out strong and firm.

"Since it is your intention to enter into marriage, join your right hands, and declare your consent before God and his Church." Luca clasped my hands. His were hot against my cold skin. We faced each other, and I had no choice but to look up into his eyes. Luca spoke first: "I, Luca Vitiello, take you, Aria Scuderi, to be my wife. I promise to be true to you in good times and in bad, in sickness and in health. I will love you and honor you all the days of my life." How sweet the lies sounded coming from his mouth.

I recited the words expected of me, and the priest blessed our rings.

Luca picked up my ring off the red cushion. My fingers shook like leaves in the breeze as I raised them, my heartbeat hummingbird quick. Luca's strong hand was firm and steady as he took mine. "Aria, take this ring as a sign of my love and fidelity. In the name of the Father, and of the Son, and of the Holy Spirit."

He slipped the ring onto my finger. White gold with twenty small diamonds. What was meant as a sign of love and devotion for other couples was nothing but a testament of his ownership of me. A daily reminder of the golden cage I'd be trapped in for the rest of my life. Until death do us part wasn't an empty promise, as with so many other couples that entered the holy bond of marriage. There was no way out of this union for me. I was Luca's until the bitter end. The last few words of the oath men swore when they were inducted into the mafia could just as well have been the closing of my wedding vow:

"I enter alive and I will leave dead."

It was my turn to say the words and slip the ring onto Luca's finger. For a moment, I wasn't sure if I could manage it. The tremor rocking my body was so strong that Luca had to steady my hand and help me. I hoped nobody had noticed, but as usual Matteo's keen eyes rested on my fingers. He and Luca were close; they'd probably laugh about my fear for a long time.

I should have run when I still had the chance. Now, as hundreds of faces from the Chicago and New York Famiglias stared back at us, flight was no longer an option. Nor was divorce. Death was the only acceptable end to a marriage in our world. Even if I still managed to escape Luca's watchful eyes and those of his henchmen, my breach of our agreement would mean war. Nothing my father could say would prevent Luca's Famiglia from exercising vengeance for making them lose face.

My feelings didn't matter, never had. I'd grown up in a world where no choices were given, especially to women.

This wedding wasn't about love or trust or choice. It was about duty and honor, about doing what was expected. A bond to ensure peace.

I wasn't an idiot. I knew what else this was about: money and power. Both were dwindling since the Bratva had been trying to expand their influence into our territories. The Italian Famiglias across the US needed to lay their feuds to rest and work together to beat down their enemies. I should be honored to marry the oldest son of the New York Famiglia. That's what my father and every other male relative had tried to tell me since my betrothal to Luca. I knew that, and it wasn't as if I hadn't had time to prepare for this exact moment, and yet fear corseted my body in a relentless grip.

"You may kiss the bride," the priest said.

I raised my head. Every pair of eyes in the pavilion scrutinized me, waiting for a flicker of weakness. Father would be furious if I let my terror show, and Luca's Famiglia would use it against us. But I had grown up in a world where a perfect mask was the only protection afforded to women and had no trouble forcing my face into a placid expression. Nobody would know how much I wanted to escape. Nobody but Luca. I couldn't hide from him, no matter how much I tried. My body wouldn't stop shaking and his grip on my hands tightened. As my gaze met Luca's cold gray eyes, I could tell that he knew. How often had he instilled fear in others? Recognizing it was probably second nature to him.

He bent down to bridge the ten inches he towered over me. There was no sign of hesitation, fear or doubt on his face. My lips trembled against his mouth. My first kiss, if it could even be called that. His eyes bored into me, even as he pulled back. Their message was clear: *You are mine.*

Not quite. But I would be tonight. A shudder passed through me, and Luca's eyes narrowed briefly before his face broke into a tight smile as we faced the applauding guests. He could change his expression in a heartbeat. I had to learn to do so as well, if I wanted to stand any chance in this marriage.

Luca and I walked down the aisle past the standing and clapping guests, and left the pavilion. Outside, dozens of waiters offered glasses of champagne and small plates with canapés. It was now our turn to accept the blessings and congratulations of every guest before we could move on to the tables and sit down for dinner. Luca took two glasses of champagne and handed one to me. Then he grabbed my hand again, and it didn't appear as if he had any intention of letting go anytime soon. He bent down, lips brushing my ear, and whispered, "Smile. You are the happy bride, remember?"

I stiffened, but I forced my brightest smile onto my face as the first guests piled out of the pavilion and lined up to talk to us.

My legs began to hurt as we'd made it through half of our guests. The words directed at us were always the same. Praise for me on my beauty and congrats to Luca for having such a beautiful wife—as if that was an achievement—always followed by not-so-hidden hints about the wedding night. I wasn't sure if my face remained as bright through all of them. Luca kept glancing at me as if to make sure I kept up the charade.

Bibiana and her husband were next. He was small, fat and bald. When he kissed my hand I had to stop myself from shuddering. After a few mandatory words of congratulations, Bibiana gripped my arms and pulled me toward her body to whisper into my ear. "Make him be good to you. Make him love you if you can. It's the only way to get through this."

She let go of me and her husband wrapped his arm around her waist, meaty hand on her hip, and then they were gone.

"What did she say?" Luca asked.

"Nothing," I said quickly, glad for the next well-wishers who prevented Luca from asking more questions. I nodded and smiled, but my mind whirred around what Bibiana had said. I wasn't sure if anyone could make Luca do anything he didn't want to do. Could I make him *want* to be good to me? Could I make him *want* to love me? Was he even capable of such an emotion?

I risked a glance up at him as he talked to a soldier of the New York mob. He was smiling. Feeling my eyes on him, he turned, and for a moment our gazes locked. There was darkness and a burning possessiveness in his eyes that sent a shiver of fear down my back. I doubted there was a flicker of gentleness or love in his black heart.

"Congrats, Luca," a high female voice said. Luca and I turned toward it, and something in his demeanor shifted ever so slightly.

"Grace," Luca said with a nod.

My eyes froze on the woman, even though her father, Senator Parker, had started talking to me. She was beautiful in an artificial way with a too narrow nose, full lips and cleavage that made my moderate chest look like child's play. I didn't think any of it was natural. Or maybe my jealousy was talking. I dismissed the thought as quickly as it had come.

With a look in my direction, she leaned up and said something to Luca. His face remained a passive mask. Finally, she turned to me and actually pulled me into a hug. I had to force myself not to stiffen. "I should warn you. Luca's a beast in the bedroom and hung like one too. It'll hurt when he takes you and he won't care. He doesn't care about you or your silly emotions. He will fuck you like an animal. He will fuck you bloody," she murmured, then she stepped back and followed after her parents.

I could feel the color drain from my face. Luca reached for my hand and I flinched, but he clasped it anyway. I steeled myself and ignored him. I couldn't face him now, not after what that woman had just said. I didn't care that it was required to invite her and her parents. Luca should have kept them away.

I could tell Luca grew frustrated with my continued refusal to meet his gaze as we spoke to the last few guests. When we walked toward the tables that had been set up under a roof of garlands attached to wooden beams, he said, "You can't ignore me forever, Aria. We are married now."

I ignored that as well. I was hanging on to my composure with desperate abandon, and still I could feel it slipping through my fingers like sand. I could not, I *would not* break into tears at my own wedding, especially since nobody would mistake them for tears of happiness.

Before we could take our seats, a chorus of "*Bacio, Bacio*" broke out among our guests. I'd forgotten about that tradition. Whenever the guests shouted the words, we'd have to kiss until they were satisfied. Luca pulled me against his rock-hard chest and pressed another kiss to my lips. I tried in vain not to be as stiff as a porcelain doll, to no avail. Luca released me, and finally we were allowed to sit down.

Gianna took a seat beside me, then leaned over to whisper in my ear. "I'm glad he didn't shove his tongue down your throat. I don't think I could get any food down if I had to witness that." I was glad too. I was already tense enough. If Luca actually tried to deepen a kiss in front of hundreds of guests, I might lose it altogether.

Matteo sat beside Luca and said something to him that made both of them laugh. I didn't even want to know what kind of lewd joke that might have been. The rest of the seats at our table belonged to my parents, Fabiano and Lily, and Luca's father and stepmother, as well as Fiore Cavallaro, his wife and their son Dante. I knew I should be starving. The only thing I'd eaten all day was the few pieces of banana in the morning, but my stomach seemed content to live on fear alone.

Matteo rose from his chair after everyone had settled down and clinked his knife against the champagne glass to silence the crowd. With a nod toward Luca and me, he began his toast. "Ladies and gentlemen, old and new friends, we've come here today to celebrate the wedding of my brother Luca and his stunningly beautiful wife Aria..."

Gianna reached for my hand under the table. I hated having the attention of everyone on me, but I mustered up a bright smile. Matteo soon made several inappropriate jokes that had almost everyone roaring and even Luca leaned back in his chair with a smirk, which seemed to be the only form of smile he allowed himself most of the time. After Matteo, it was my father's turn; he praised the great collaboration of the New York mob and the Chicago Outfit, making it sound as if this was a business merger and not a wedding feast. Of course he also dropped a few hints that it was a wife's duty to obey and please her husband.

Gianna clutched my hand so tightly by then that I was worried it would fall off. At last, it was Luca's father's turn to toast us. Salvatore Vitiello wasn't quite as impressive but whenever his eyes settled on me, I had to stifle a shiver. The only good thing about listening to the toast was that nobody could call "*Bacio, Bacio,*" and that Luca's attention was focused elsewhere. That reprieve was short-lived, however.

The servers began piling the tables with antipasti: everything from Veal Carpaccio, Vitello Tonnato, and Mozzarella di Bufala, to an entire leg of Parma ham, over a selection of Italian cheeses, octopus salad, and marinated calamari as well as green salads and ciabatta. Gianna grabbed a piece of bread and tore into it, then said, "I wanted to make a toast as your bridesmaid, but Father forbade it. He seemed worried I would say something to embarrass our family."

Luca and Matteo glanced our way. Gianna hadn't bothered lowering her voice and pointedly ignored Father's death glare. I tugged at her arm. I didn't want her to get in trouble. With a huff, she filled her plate with antipasti and dug in. My plate was still empty. A server filled my glass with white wine and I took a sip. I'd already drunk a glass of champagne; that combined with the fact that I hadn't eaten much all day made me feel slightly foggy.

Luca put a hand on mine, preventing me from taking another gulp. "You should eat." If I hadn't felt the eyes of everyone at the table on me, I'd have ignored his warning and downed the wine. I grabbed a slice of bread, took a bite, then put the rest onto my plate. Luca's lips tightened but he didn't try to coax me into eating more, not even when soup was served and I let it go back untouched. They served lamb roast for the main course. The sight of the whole lambs made my stomach turn, but it was traditional. The cook rolled a rotisserie table toward us, since we had to be served first. Luca, as the husband, got the first slice, and before I could decline he told the cook to give me a slice as well. The center of the table was loaded with roasted rosemary potatoes, truffled mashed potatoes, grilled asparagus and much more.

I forced a bite of lamb and potato into my mouth before I set down my cutlery. My throat was too tight for food. I washed it down with another gulp of wine. Luckily Luca was busy talking to the men at the table about a club the Russians had attacked in New York. Even Dante Cavallaro, the future Boss of the Outfit, looked almost animated when he talked about business.

A band started playing when dinner was over, the signal that it was time for the obligatory dance. Luca stood, holding out his hand. I let him pull me to my feet, and at once "*Bacio, Bacio*" rang out again. Gianna narrowed her eyes and searched the guests, as if she was thinking of attacking the culprit who'd started the chanting.

When Luca tugged me toward him, I stumbled against his chest as dizziness caught up with me. Luckily, nobody noticed because Luca's arms around me held me firm. His eyes pierced mine as he lowered his lips and brushed them against mine. The band played faster and faster, urging us to finally enter the dance floor; the tables had been set up in circles around it. Luca kept his arm around my waist as he led me toward the center. To everyone around us it looked like a loving embrace, but it was the only thing keeping me upright.

Luca pulled me against his chest for the waltz, and I had no choice but to rest my cheek against it. I could feel a gun under his vest. Even the groom couldn't come to his wedding unarmed. For the first time I was glad for Luca's strength. He had no trouble keeping me on my feet during the dance. When it ended, he leaned down. "Once we're back at the table, you'll eat. I don't want you to pass out during our celebration, and much less during our wedding night."

I did as he asked and forced down a few more bites of now cold potato and meat. Luca's alert gaze kept checking on me while he talked to Matteo. The dance floor was filled with other people now. Lily rose from her chair and asked Romero to dance. No surprise there. He couldn't refuse her, of course. Neither could I refuse when Luca's father asked me for a dance. After that I was handed from one man to the next until I lost count of their names and faces. All through it Luca's eyes followed my every move, even when he danced with the women of our families. Gianna, too, couldn't escape the dance floor. I caught her dancing with Matteo at least three times, and her face grew more sullen by the minute.

"May I?"

I startled at the distantly familiar voice that sent a thrill of fear through my body. Dante Cavallaro took the place of whomever I'd danced with before. He was tall, albeit not as tall as Luca, and not as muscled. "You don't look impressed with the festivities."

"Everything's perfect," I said mechanically.

"But you didn't choose this marriage."

I gaped at him. His dark blond hair and blue eyes gave him a look of cold efficiency, while Luca radiated fierce brutality. Different sides of the same coin. In a few years the East Coast and Midwest would tremble under the judgement of these two men. I snapped my mouth shut. "It's an honor."

"And your duty. We all have to do things we don't want to. Sometimes it might seem as if we don't have any choice at all."

"You are a man. What do you know about not having a choice?" I said harshly, then stiffened and ducked my head. "I'm sorry. That was out of turn." I couldn't talk to someone who was practically my Boss like that. Then I remembered he no longer was. I didn't fall under the rule of the Chicago Outfit anymore. With my marriage, I'd become part of the New York mob and thus Luca's and his father's rule.

"I think your husband is eager to have you back in his arms," Dante said with a tilt of his head, then handed me over to Luca, who gave him a hard look. Two predators facing off.

Once we were out of earshot of Dante Cavallaro, Luca looked down at me. "What did Cavallaro want?"

"To congratulate me on the festivities."

Luca gave me a look that made it clear he didn't believe me. There was a hint of mistrust in his expression.

The music stopped and Matteo clapped his hands, silencing the guests. "Time to throw the garter!"

Luca and I stopped as well as the guests gathered around the dance floor to watch the show. A few even stood on chairs or held up their kids so everyone could get a good look. Luca knelt before me under the cheers of our guests and raised his eyebrows. I gripped my gown and lifted it up to my knees. Luca slid his hands up my calves, over my knees and up my thighs. I stilled completely at the feel of his fingers on my naked skin. Goose bumps erupted all over my body. The touch was light and not uncomfortable, and yet it terrified me.

Luca's eyes were intent as they watched my face. His fingers brushed the garter on my right thigh and he pushed my gown up for everyone to see, revealing the entire length of my leg. I gripped the hem and he put his arms behind his back, then he bent over my thigh, his lips brushing the skin under the garter. I sucked in a deep breath but tried to keep my face in happy-bride mode. Luca closed his teeth around the edge of the garter and pulled it down my leg until it landed in a heap at my white high heels. I raised my foot so Luca could pick the piece of lace up. He straightened and presented the garter to the applauding crowd. I forced a smile and clapped as well. The only person who wasn't smiling was Gianna.

"Bachelors," Luca called in his deep voice. "Gather around. Maybe you'll be the lucky one to marry next!"

Even the youngest boys stepped forward, Fabiano among them. He was scowling. Mother had probably forced him to participate. I winked at him and he poked out his tongue. I couldn't help but laugh, the first genuine gesture I'd managed during the wedding feast.

Luca's eyes darted toward me, a strange expression on his face. I quickly looked away. Luca raised his arm, the garter in his fist, before he thrust it into the cluster of waiting men.

Matteo snatched it out of the air with an impressive lunge. "Any willing Outfit ladies out there that want to further the bond between our families?" he boomed, wiggling his eyebrows.

Cheering and laughter sounded from many married and unmarried women. Of course, Lily was among them, jumping up and down with a bright smile. Everything was a game for her. I didn't want Matteo's eyes on her, I didn't even want her name in his mind when he thought of marriage. As was tradition, he had to pick an unmarried woman to dance with.

Luca stepped close to me, his arm sneaking around my waist in casual possessiveness. I flinched at the unexpected contact and Luca's body became rigid.

Matteo extended his hand toward Lily, who looked close to exploding from excitement over being chosen. My chest tightened. I knew it was a joke right now. Nobody took a fourteen-year-old girl seriously.

As Luca and I waltzed over the dance floor, I kept an eye on Lily and Matteo. His hand was high on her back, his expression teasing. He didn't look like a man who'd set his eyes on his future wife.

"If my brother married your sister, you'd have family in New York," Luca said.

"I won't let him have Lily." The words were fierce. How could I be tough when it came to protecting my sister, but not when it was about me?

"It's not Lily he wants."

My eyes flew to Gianna, who stood with her arms wrapped around her chest, eyes like a hawk as they followed us. Father wouldn't give away another of his daughters to New York. If he wanted to strengthen the position of our family in the Chicago Outfit, he needed to make sure he had enough family around him.

After the waltz was over, a faster beat began and the dance floor was once again flooded with guests. Luca started dancing with my mother, and I used the moment to slip away. I needed a few moments to myself or I'd lose it. I lifted my gown off the ground and hurried to the edge of the garden where the grass met the bay before I walked down the few steps to the dock, where a yacht was lying in wait. To my right a long beach stretched out. The ocean was black under the night sky, and the breeze tugged at my dress and ripped strands from my updo. I stepped out of my high heels and jumped off the dock, my feet landing in the cool sand. Closing my eyes, I listened to the sound of the waves. The wooden boards creaked, and I tensed before glancing over my shoulder and spotting Gianna. She shook off her own shoes and joined me on the beach, wrapping an arm around me.

"Tomorrow you'll leave for New York and I'll head back to Chicago," she whispered.

I swallowed hard. "I'm scared."

"Of tonight?"

"Yes," I admitted. "Of tonight and every night that follows. Of being alone with Luca in a city I don't know, surrounded by people I know even less, people who might still be the enemy. Of getting to know Luca and finding out he's the monster I think he is. Of being without you and Lily and Fabiano."

"We will come to visit as often as Father allows it. And about tonight." Gianna's voice turned hard. "He can't force you."

I let out a choked laugh. Sometimes I forgot that Gianna was younger than me. These were the moments that reminded me. "He can. He *will*."

"Then you'll fight him with all you've got."

"Gianna," I said in a whisper. "Luca is going to be Capo dei Capi. He's a born fighter. He'll laugh at me if I try to resist. Or my refusal will make him angry, and then he'll really want to hurt me." I paused. "Bibiana told me I should give him what he wants, that I should try to make him be good to me, try to make him love me."

"Stupid Bibiana, what does she know?" Gianna glared at me. "Look at her, the way she cowers in front of that fat fool. How she lets him touch her with his sausage fingers. I'd rather die than lie under a man like that."

"Do you think I can make Luca love me?"

Gianna shook her head. "Maybe you can make him respect you. I don't think men like him have a heart to be capable of love."

"Even the most cold-hearted bastards have a heart."

"Well, then it's as black as tar. Don't waste your time on love, Aria. You won't find it in our world."

She was right, of course, but I couldn't help hoping.

"Promise me you'll be strong. Promise me you won't let him treat you like a whore. You are his wife."

"Is there a difference?"

"Yeah—whores at least get to sleep with other men and don't have to live in a golden cage. They are better off."

I snorted. "You are impossible."

Gianna shrugged. "It made you smile." She turned and her expression darkened. "Luca sent his lapdog. Maybe he was worried you'd run."

I followed her gaze to find Romero standing at the crest of the small hill overlooking the bay and the dock.

"We should have taken that yacht and run away," Gianna said.

"Where could I run? He'd follow me to the end of the world." I glanced at the elegant golden watch around my wrist. I didn't know Luca, but I knew men of his kind. They were possessive. Once you belonged to them, there was no escaping. "We should go back. The wedding cake will be presented soon."

We put our shoes back on and walked back toward the noise. I ignored Romero but Gianna scowled at him. "Does Luca need you for everything? Or can he at least take a piss on his own?"

"Luca is the groom and needs to attend to the guests," Romero said simply, but of course it was a reprimand in my direction.

Luca's eyes settled on me the moment I returned to the festivities. Many guests were already drunk, and some had moved up to where the pool was and were taking a swim fully clothed. Luca held his hand out, and I bridged the distance between us and took it. "Where were you?"

"I just needed a moment to myself."

There was no time for further discussions as the cook rolled a table with our wedding cake toward the center. It was white, had six tiers and was decorated with peach flowers. Luca and I cut it under another round of applause, followed by *"Bacio, Bacio,"* and put the first piece onto our plate. Luca picked up a fork and fed me a bite as a sign that he'd provide for me, and I then fed him a piece as a sign that I'd take care of him as a good wife was supposed to.

It was close to midnight when the first shouts rang out that suggested Luca and I retire to the bedroom. "You wed her, now bed her!" Matteo shouted, throwing his arms up and bumping into a chair. He'd drunk his fair share of wine, whiskey, Grappa and whatever else he could get his hands on. Luca, on the other hand, was sober. The small inkling of hope I'd harbored that he'd be too drunk to consummate our marriage evaporated. Luca's answering grin, all predator, all hunger, all want, made my heart pound in my chest. Soon most of the men and even many women joined in the chorus.

Luca rose from his chair and I did the same, even though I wanted to cling to it with desperate abandon, but I had no choice. A few looks of understanding and compassion from other women were directed my way, but they were almost as bad as the jeering.

Gianna rose from her chair but Mother gripped her upper arm, holding her back. Salvatore Vitiello shouted something about a bedsheet, but the sounds and colors seemed dimmed to me, as if I was trapped in fog. Luca's grip around my hand as he led me toward the house was the only thing keeping me in motion. My body seemed on autopilot. A large crowd, mainly consisting of men, followed after us, their chant of "Bed her, Bed her!" growing louder as we entered the house and ascended the staircase toward the master bedroom on the second floor. Fear was an insistent throbbing in my chest.

I tasted copper and realized I'd bitten the inside of my cheek hard. We finally arrived in front of the dark wooden double doors of the master bedroom. The men kept clapping Luca's back and shoulders. Nobody touched me. I would have wilted if they had. Luca opened the door and I walked in, glad to bring some distance between the leering crowd and myself. The shouting rang in my head, and it was all I could do not to clamp my hands over my ears. "Bed her! Bed her!"

Luca slammed the door shut. Now we were alone for our wedding night.

chapter *six*

THE COMMOTION IN FRONT OF THE DOOR STOPPED EXCEPT FOR Matteo, who was still shouting lewd suggestions of what Luca could do to me, or I to him.

"Shut up, Matteo, and go find a whore to fuck," Luca growled.

Silence reigned outside. My eyes wandered toward the king-sized bed in the center of the room and terror gripped me. Luca had his own whore to fuck tonight and until the end of days. The price for my body hadn't been paid in money, but it might as well have been. I wrapped my arms around my middle, trying to quench my panic.

Luca turned around to face me with a predatory glint in his eyes. My legs turned weak. Maybe if I fainted, I'd be spared, and even if he didn't care if I was conscious and took me anyway, at least I wouldn't remember anything. He thrust his jacket over the armchair next to the window, the muscles in his forearms flexing. He was muscle and strength and power, and I might as well have been made from glass. One wrong touch and I would shatter.

Luca took his time admiring me. Wherever his eyes touched my body, they branded me as his possession, the word *mine* edged into my skin over and over again.

"When my father told me I was to marry you, he said you were the most beautiful woman the Chicago Outfit had to offer, even more beautiful than the women in New York."

To offer? As if I was a piece of meat. I dug my teeth into my tongue.

"I didn't believe him." He stalked up to me and grabbed my waist. I swallowed the gasp and forced myself to be still as I stared at his chest. Why did he have to be so tall? He leaned down until his mouth was less than an inch from my throat. "But he told the truth. You are the most beautiful woman I've ever seen, and tonight you are mine." His hot lips touched my skin. Could he feel the terror pounding in my veins? His hands on my waist tightened. Tears pressed against my eyeballs, but I forced them back. I wouldn't cry, but Grace's words slammed into my brain. *He'll fuck you bloody.*

Be strong. I was a Scuderi. Gianna's words flashed in my mind. *Don't let him treat you like a whore.*

"No!" The word ripped from my throat like a battle cry. I wrenched myself away from him, stumbling a few steps back. Everything seemed to still then. What had I just done?

Luca's expression was stunned, then it hardened. "No?"

"What?" I snapped. "Have you never heard the word 'no' before?" *Shut up, Aria. For God's sake shut up.*

"Oh, I hear it often. The guy whose throat I crushed, he said it over and over and over again until he couldn't say it anymore."

I took a step back, bristling. "So you're going to crush my throat too?" I was like a cornered dog, biting and snapping, but my opponent was a wolf. A very big and dangerous wolf.

A cold smile twisted his lips. "No, that would defy the purpose of our marriage, don't you think?"

I shuddered. Of course it would. He couldn't kill me. At least not if he wanted to maintain peace between Chicago and New York. That didn't mean he couldn't beat or force himself on me. "I don't think my father would be happy if you hurt me."

The look in his eyes made me take another step back. "Is that a threat?"

I averted my eyes from his. My father might risk war over my death—not because he loved me, but to keep face—but definitely not over a few bruises or rape. For my father it wouldn't even be rape; Luca was my husband and my body was his to take whenever he wanted. "No," I said softly. I hated myself for being submissive, like a bitch bowing to her alpha, almost as much as I hated him for making me do it.

"But you deny me what's mine?"

I glared. Damn being submissive. Damn my father for selling me off like cattle, and damn Luca for accepting the offer. "I can't deny you something that you don't have the right to take in the first place. My body doesn't belong to you. It's mine."

He will kill me. The thought shot through my mind a second before Luca drew himself up before me. Six foot five was scarily tall. I saw his hand move in my peripheral vision and flinched in anticipation of the blow, my eyes slamming shut. Nothing happened. The only sound was Luca's harsh breathing and the pounding of my pulse in my ears. I risked a peek up at him. Luca was staring at me, his eyes like a stormy summer sky. "I could take what I want," he said, but the viciousness was gone from his voice.

There was no use denying it. He was much stronger than me. And even if I screamed nobody would come to my aid. Many men in my and Luca's family would probably even hold me down to make it easier for him, not that Luca would have any trouble restraining me. "You could," I admitted. "And I would hate you for it until the end of my days."

He smirked. "Do you think I care about that? This isn't a marriage of love. And you already hate me. I can see it in your eyes."

He was right on both counts. This wasn't about love and I hated him already, but hearing him say it crushed the last bit of foolish hope I had. I didn't say anything.

He gestured at the squeaky clean sheets of the bed. "You heard what my father said about our tradition?"

My blood turned ice cold. I had, but until now I'd put it out of my mind. My courage had been for nothing. I stepped up to the bed and stared down at the sheets, my eyes boring into the spot where the proof of my lost virginity would have to be. Tomorrow morning the women of Luca's family would knock at our door and take the sheets to present to Luca's and my father, so they could inspect the proof of our consummated marriage. It was a sick tradition, but it wasn't one I could evade. The fight drained out of me.

I could hear Luca coming up behind me. He grasped my shoulders and I closed my eyes. I wouldn't make a sound. But my fight not to cry was a losing battle. The first tears already clung to my lashes, then dripped onto my skin and burned a trail down my cheeks and chin. Luca slid his hands over my collarbones, then down to the edge of my dress. My lips quivered and I could feel a tear dropping from my chin. Luca's hands tensed against my body.

For a moment, neither of us moved. He turned me to face him and pushed my chin up. His cold gray eyes scanned my face. My cheeks were wet with silent tears but I made no sound, only returned his gaze. He dropped his hands, jerked back with a string of Italian curses, and then he drove his fist into the wall. I gasped and jumped back, pressing my lips together as I watched Luca's back. He was facing the wall, shoulders heaving. I quickly wiped the tears off my face.

You've done it. You've made him really angry.

My eyes darted toward the door. Maybe I could reach it before Luca. Maybe I could even get outside before he caught up with me, but I'd never make it off the premises. He turned around and removed his vest, revealing a black knife and gun holster. His fingers closed around the handle of the knife, his knuckles already turning red from the impact with the wall, and he pulled it out. The blade was curved like a claw: short, sharp and deadly. It was black like the handle, so it couldn't easily be seen in the dark. A karambit knife for close combat. Who knew Fabiano's obsession with knives would ever be of use to me? Now I could at least identify the knife that would cut me open. Hysteric laughter wanted to fight its way out of my throat, but I swallowed it.

Luca stared intently at the blade. Was he trying to decide which part of me to slice open first?

Beg him. But I knew it wouldn't save me. People probably begged him all the time, and from what I heard it never saved them. Luca didn't show mercy. He would become the next Capo dei Capi in New York, and he would rule with cold brutality.

Luca came toward me and I flinched. A dark smile curled his lips. He pressed the sharp tip of the knife into the soft skin below the crook of his arm, drawing blood. My lips parted in surprise. He put the knife down on the small table between the two armchairs, grabbed a glass and held his wound over it, then watched his blood drip down without a flicker of emotion before finally disappearing in the adjoining bathroom.

I heard water running and then he returned into the bedroom. The mix of water and blood in the glass had a light red color. He approached the bed, dipped his fingers into the liquid and then smeared it onto the center of the sheet. My cheeks flushed with realization. I approached him slowly and stopped when I was still out of arm's reach, not that it would do me much good. I stared down at the stained sheets. "What are you doing?" I whispered.

"They want blood. They get blood."

"Why the water?"

"Blood doesn't always look the same." *He would know.*

"Is it enough blood?"

"Did you expect a bloodbath?" He gave me a sardonic smile. "It's sex, not a knife fight."

He will fuck you bloody. The words were burnt into my brain, but I didn't repeat them.

Just how many virgins have you taken to know about this? And how many of them came willingly into your bed? The words lay on the tip of my tongue, but I wasn't suicidal.

"Won't they know that it's your blood?"

"No." He walked back over to the table and poured Scotch into the glass with the remaining water and blood. His eyes held mine as he downed it in one gulp. I couldn't help but wrinkle my nose in disgust. Was he trying to intimidate me? Drinking blood really wasn't necessary for that. I'd been terrified of him before I'd ever met him. I'd probably still be terrified of him when I bowed my head over his open casket.

"What about a DNA test?"

He laughed. It wasn't exactly a joyful sound. "They will take me by my word. Nobody will doubt that I've taken your virginity the moment we were alone. They won't because I am who I am."

Yes, you are. Then why did you spare me? Another thought to never leave my lips. But Luca must have been thinking the same because his dark brows drew together as his eyes roamed the length of my body.

I stiffened and took a step back.

"No," he said in a low voice. I froze. "That is the fifth time you shied back from me tonight." He set down the glass and took the knife in his hand. Then he advanced on me. "Did your father never teach you to hide your fear from monsters? They give chase if you run."

Maybe he expected me to contradict his claim to be a monster, but I wasn't that good a liar. If there were monsters, the men in my world were among them. When he arrived in front of me, I had to tilt my head back to look him in the face.

"That blood on the sheets needs a story," he said simply as he brought the knife up. I flinched and he murmured, "That's six times."

He hooked the blade under the edge of the bodice of my wedding dress and slowly moved the knife down. The fabric gave way until it finally pooled at my feet. The blade never once touched my skin. "It's tradition in our family to undress the bride like this."

His family had many disgusting traditions.

Finally I stood before him in my tight white corset with its laces in the back and my panties with the bow over my butt. Goose bumps covered every inch of my body. Luca's gaze was like fire on my skin. I drew back.

"Seven," he said quietly.

Anger surged through me. If he was tired of me flinching away from him, then maybe he should stop being so intimidating.

"Turn around."

I did as he ordered, and the sharp intake of his breath made me regret it instantly. He moved closer, and I felt a gentle tug on the bow that was holding my panties up. *A present to unwrap. How could any man possibly resist?* The words of Luca's stepmother popped unwantedly into my head. I knew that below the bow, the top of my butt would be exposed. *Say something to distract him from that stupid bow over your butt.*

"You already bled for me," I said in a shaky voice, and then almost inaudibly, "Please don't." My father would be ashamed of my open display of weakness. But he was a man. The world was his for the taking. Women were his for the taking. And we women were always supposed to give without protest.

Luca didn't say anything, but his knuckles brushed the skin between my shoulder blades as he raised the knife to my corset. With a hiss the fabric came apart under the blade. I brought my hands up before that barrier of protection could fall as well and pressed the corset against my chest.

Luca wrapped his arm across my chest possessively, trapping my arm under his and gripped my shoulder, pressing me against him. I gasped when something hard poked me in the lower back. That wasn't his gun. Heat flooded my cheeks and fear gripped my body.

His lips brushed my ear. "Tonight you beg me to spare you, but one day you're going to beg me to fuck you." No. *Never,* I swore to myself. His breath was hot against my skin, and I closed my eyes. "Don't think because I don't claim my rights tonight that you aren't mine, Aria. No other man will ever have what belongs to me. You are mine." I nodded, but he wasn't done yet. "If I catch a man kissing you, I'll cut out his tongue. If I catch a man touching you, I'll cut off his fingers, one at a time. If I catch a guy fucking you, I'll cut off his dick and his balls, and I'll feed them to him. And I'll make you watch."

He dropped his arm and stepped back. From the corner of my eye, I watched him stride over to the armchair and sink down in it. He reached for the bottle of Scotch and poured himself a generous amount. Before he could change his mind, I quickly walked into the bathroom, closed the door and turned the lock, then cringed at how stupid that was. A lock wasn't any protection from him; neither was a door. Nothing in this world could protect me.

I scrutinized my face in the mirror. My eyes were red and my cheeks wet. I let the remains of my corset drop to the floor and picked up the nightgown that one of the servants had folded on the chair for me. A choked laugh escaped my mouth after I'd put it on over my bow panties. The part over my breasts was made from lace, but at least it wasn't see-through, unlike the entire middle of the nightgown. It was the finest gossamer I'd ever seen, and it didn't leave anything to the imagination. My bare stomach and the panties were on display. It ended above my knees with a hem of more lace. I could just as well walk out of this room naked and be done with it, but I wasn't that brave.

I washed my makeup off, brushed my teeth, let down my hair, and when I couldn't prolong the inevitable any longer, I grabbed the door handle. Would it be so bad if I slept in the bathroom?

Taking a deep breath, I opened the door and stepped back into the bedroom. Luca was still sitting in the armchair. The Scotch bottle was almost half-empty. Drunk men were never a good thing. His eyes found me and he laughed without humor. "That's what you choose to wear when you don't want me to fuck you?"

I flushed at his crude language. It was the Scotch talking, but I couldn't tell him to stop drinking. I was toeing the line as it was. "I didn't choose it." I crossed my arms, torn between staying on my feet and slipping under the covers of the bed. But lying down felt like a bad idea. I didn't want to make myself any more vulnerable than I already was. Yet standing in front of Luca half-naked wasn't the best choice either.

"My stepmother?" he asked.

I nodded simply. He put down his glass and rose. Of course, I flinched. His expression darkened. He didn't say anything as he walked past me into the bathroom, not even when I gasped as his arm brushed mine. The moment the door closed, I released a harsh breath. Slowly I approached the bed, my eyes finding the light red stain. I perched on the edge of the mattress. Water was running in the bathroom, but eventually Luca would come back out.

I lay down on the edge of the mattress, turned on my side and pulled the covers up to my chin, then squeezed my eyes shut, willing myself to fall asleep. I wanted this day to end, even if it was only the beginning of many hellish days and nights to come.

The water stopped and a few minutes later Luca emerged from the bathroom. I tried to make my breathing even to appear as if I was already sleeping. I risked a quick peek through half-closed eyes, my face mostly covered by the blanket, and turned to stone. Luca was only wearing black briefs. And if Luca was impressive when dressed, he was a whole new level of intimidating when half-naked. He was pure muscle and his skin was littered with scars, some thin and long as if a knife had sliced cleanly through, and some round and rigid as if a bullet had torn into his flesh. Letters were inked into the skin over his heart. I couldn't read them from afar, but I had a feeling it was their motto. "Born in blood. Sworn in blood. I enter alive and I leave dead."

He walked over to the main light switch and turned it off, bathing us in darkness. Suddenly I felt like I was alone in a forest at night, knowing that somewhere something was stalking me. The bed dipped under Luca's weight, and I clutched the edge of the bedframe. I pressed my lips together, allowing myself only shallow breaths.

The mattress shifted when Luca lay down. I held my breath, waiting for him to reach out for me and take what was *his*. Would it always be like this? Would I be miserable for the rest of my life? My nights filled with fear?

The pressure of the last few weeks, or maybe even years, crashed down on me. Helplessness, fear and anger washed over me. Hatred for my father filled me up, but even worse was the hot knife of disappointment and sadness. He'd given me to a man he didn't know anything about, except for his reputation as a skilled killer; he'd offered me to the enemy to do with as he pleased. The man who should have protected me from harm had shoved me into the arms of a monster for the sole purpose of securing power.

Hot tears spilled out of my eyes, but the weight on my chest didn't lift. It grew heavier and heavier until I couldn't hold it in anymore and a gasped sob burst out of me. *Get yourself under control, Aria.* I tried to fight it, but another choked sob slipped past my lips.

"Will you cry all night?" came Luca's cold voice out of the blackness. Of course, he wasn't asleep yet. For a man in his position, it was best to always keep an eye open.

I buried my face into the pillow but now that the floodgates had opened, I couldn't close them again.

"I can't see how you could possibly have cried any worse, if I'd taken you. Maybe I should fuck you to give you a real reason to cry."

I pulled my legs up against my chest, making myself as small as possible. I knew I needed to stop. I hadn't been beaten or worse, but I couldn't get a grip on my emotions.

Luca moved and a soft light flooded the room. He'd turned on the lamp on his nightstand. I waited. I knew he was watching me, but I kept my face pressed against the pillow. Maybe he'd leave the room if he got fed up with the noise. He touched my arm, and I jerked so violently that I would have fallen off the bed if Luca hadn't pulled me toward him.

"That's enough," he said in a low voice.

That voice. I stilled immediately and let him roll me onto my back. Slowly I uncurled my legs and arms, and lay as unmoving as a corpse.

"Look at me," he ordered, and I did. Was that the voice that had made him notorious? "I want you to stop crying. I want you to stop flinching from my touch."

I nodded numbly.

He shook his head. "That nod means nothing. Don't you think I recognize fear when it stares back at me? The moment I turn out the light, you'll be back to crying as if I'd fucking raped you."

I didn't know what he wanted me to do. It wasn't as if I enjoyed being scared out of my mind. Not that fear was the only reason for my breakdown, but he wouldn't understand. How could he possibly understand that I felt like my life was ripped away from me? My sisters, Fabiano, my family, Chicago; they were all I had ever known, and now I had to give them up.

"So to give you peace of mind and shut you up, I'm going to swear an oath."

I licked my lips, tasting the saltiness of tears on them. Luca's fingers tensed on my arm. "An oath?" I whispered.

He took my hand and pressed my palm against the tattoo over his heart. I exhaled as his muscles flexed under my touch. He was warm, the skin much softer than I'd anticipated.

"Born in blood, sworn in blood, I swear that I won't try to steal your virginity or harm you in any way tonight." His lips quirked and he nodded toward the cut on his arm. "I already bled for you, so that seals it. Born in blood. Sworn in blood." He covered my hand with his over the tattoo, looking at me expectantly.

"Born in blood, sworn in blood," I said softly. He released my hand and I lowered it to my stomach, stunned and confused. An oath was a big deal. Without another word, he extinguished the light and returned to his side of the bed.

I listened to his rhythmic breathing, knowing that he wasn't asleep. I closed my eyes. He wouldn't break his oath.

chapter *seven*

Sunlight hit my face. I tried to stretch, but an arm was thrown over my waist and a firm chest pressed against my back. It took me a moment to remember where I was and what had happened yesterday, and then I stiffened.

"Good, you're awake," Luca said in a voice that was gruff with sleep.

Realization hit me. Luca. My husband. I was a married woman, but Luca had kept his promise. He hadn't consummated the marriage. I opened my eyes. Luca's hand gripped my hip and he turned me on my back. He was propped up on one elbow as his eyes took in my face. I wished I knew what he was thinking. It was strange to be in bed with a man. I could feel Luca's heat, even though our bodies weren't touching. In the sunlight the scars on his skin were somehow less prominent than last night, but his muscles were just as impressive. I wondered how they'd feel to the touch.

He reached up and took a strand of my hair between two fingers. I held my breath, but he released it after a moment, his face becoming calculating. "It won't be long until my stepmother, my aunts and the other married women of my family knock at our door to gather up the sheets and carry them into the dining room, where undoubtedly everyone else is already waiting for the fucking spectacle to begin."

A blush spread over my cheeks and something in Luca's eyes changed, some of the coldness replaced by another emotion. My eyes found the small cut on Luca's arm. It hadn't been deep and was already scabbing.

Luca nodded. "My blood will give them what they want. It'll be the foundation of our story, but we'll be expected to fill in the details. I know I'm a convincing liar. But will you be able to lie to everyone's face, even your mother's, when you tell them about our wedding night? Nobody can know what happened. It would make me look weak." His lips tightened with regret. Regret for having spared me and gotten himself in the position of depending on my lying skills.

"Weak because you didn't want to rape your wife?" I whispered.

Luca's fingers on my hip tightened. I hadn't even realized they were still there. *Make him want to be good to you.* Bibiana's words flitted through my mind. Luca was a monster, there was no doubt about it. He couldn't be anything else in order to survive as a leader in our world, but maybe I could make him keep the monster in chains when he was with me. It was more than I'd hoped for when he'd led me toward the bedroom last night.

Luca smiled coldly. "Weak for not taking what was mine for the taking. The tradition of bloody sheets in the Sicilian mafia is as much a proof of the bride's purity as of the husband's relentlessness. So what do you think it will say about me that I had you lying half-naked in my bed, vulnerable and *mine*, and yet here you are untouched as you were before our wedding?"

"Nobody will know. I won't tell anyone."

"Why should I trust you? I don't make a habit of trusting people, especially people who hate me."

I rested my palm against the cut on his arm, feeling his muscles flex beneath my touch. It felt as if I were touching stone. How was it possible that muscles could be unyielding like bone? *Make him be good to you, make him love you.* "I don't hate you." He narrowed his eyes, but it was mostly the truth. I would have hated him if he had forced himself on me. I certainly hated what marriage to him meant for me, but I didn't know him well enough for real hate. Maybe it would come with time. "And you can trust me because I am your wife. I didn't choose this marriage, but I can at least choose to make the best out of our bond. I have nothing to gain from betraying your trust, but everything to gain by showing you that I'm loyal."

There was a flicker of something, maybe respect, in his expression. "The men waiting in that dining room are predators. They prey on the weak, and they've been waiting more than a decade for a sign of weakness from me. The moment they see one, they'll pounce."

"But your father—"

"If my father thinks I'm too weak to control the Famiglia, he'll gladly let them tear me apart."

What kind of life was it to have to be strong all the time, even around your closest family? At least I had my sisters and my brother, and even to some extent my mother and people like Valentina. Women were forgiven weakness in our world.

Luca's eyes were hard. Maybe this would be the moment he'd decide it really wasn't worth the risk and take me, but when his gaze finally settled back on my face, the darkness was at bay.

"What about Matteo?"

"I trust Matteo. But Matteo is hotheaded. He'd get himself killed trying to defend me."

It was strange talking to Luca—to my husband—like this, almost like we knew each other. "Nobody will doubt me," I said. "I'll give them what they want to see."

Luca sat up and my eyes were drawn to the tattoo over his heart, then took in the muscles of his chest and stomach. My cheeks heated when I met his gaze.

"You should be wearing more than this pitiful excuse for a nightgown when the harpies arrive. I don't want them to see your body, especially your hips and upper thighs. It's better when they wonder if I left marks on you," he said. Then he smirked. "But we can't hide your face from them."

He bent over me and his hand came toward my face. I squeezed my eyes shut, flinching.

"This is the second time you thought I was going to hit you," he said in a low voice.

My eyes flew open. "I thought you said..." I trailed off.

"What? That everyone expects you to have bruises on your face after a night with me? I don't hit women."

I remembered when he'd stopped my father from slapping me. He'd never raised his hand against me. I knew many men in the Chicago Outfit had a strange code of rules they followed. You couldn't stab a man in the back, but you could cut his throat that way, for example. I wasn't sure what made one better than the other. Luca seemed to have his own rules as well. Crushing someone's throat with your bare hands was acceptable; hitting your wife was not.

"How am I supposed to believe you can convince everyone we've consummated our marriage when you keep flinching away from my touch?"

"Believe me, the flinching will make everyone believe the lie even more, because I definitely wouldn't have stopped flinching away from your touch if you'd *taken what's yours*. The more I flinch, the more they will take you for the monster you want them to think you are."

Luca chuckled. "I think you might know more about playing the game of power than I expected."

I shrugged. "My father is Consigliere."

He tilted his head in acknowledgement, then he brought his hand up and cupped my face. "What I meant earlier was that your face doesn't look like you've been kissed."

My eyes widened. "I've never…" But of course he knew that already.

His lips collided with mine and my palms came up against his chest, but I didn't push him away. His tongue teased my lips, demanding entrance. I gave in and hesitantly touched my tongue to his. I wasn't sure what to do and looked at Luca wide-eyed, but he took the lead as his tongue and lips ravished my mouth. It was strange allowing that sort of intimacy, but it wasn't unpleasant. I lost track of time as he kissed me, demanding and possessive, his hand warm against my cheek. His stubble rubbed against my lips and skin, but the friction made me tingle instead of bothering me. I could feel the restrained strength as his body pressed against me. Eventually he pulled back, eyes dark with desire. I shivered, not only from fear.

Insistent knocking sounded, and Luca swung his legs out of bed and stood. I sucked in a breath at the sight of the bulge in his briefs.

He smirked. "A man is supposed to have a boner when he wakes up beside his bride, don't you think? They want a show, they'll get a show." He nodded toward the bathroom. "Now go and grab a bathrobe."

I quickly leaped out of the bed with its stained bedsheet and hurried into the bathroom, where I grabbed the long white satin bathrobe and put it over my nightgown before I picked up the remnants of my corset that I'd dropped last night.

When I stepped back into the bedroom, I watched Luca putting his gun and knife holster on over his naked chest, donning another knife strap with a longer hunting knife onto his forearm, covering the small cut, and repositioning his stiffness so it was even more obvious.

My cheeks hot, I moved further into the room and threw the corset down beside my ruined wedding dress. Luca was a magnificent sight with his tall frame, muscles and holster, not to mention the bulge in his pants. A hint of curiosity filled me. How did he look without the underwear?

I leaned against the wall beside the window and wrapped an arm around myself, suddenly worried that someone would realize Luca hadn't slept with me. These were all married women. Would they see something wasn't right?

I braced myself when he opened the door wide, standing before the gathered women in all his half-naked glory. There were gasps, giggles and even a few muttered Italian words, which might have been prayers or curses—they were spoken too fast and quiet for me to hear. I had to stifle a snort.

"We've come to collect the sheets," Luca's stepmother said in what was barely hidden glee.

Luca stepped back, opening the door wider. At once several women stepped in, their eyes darting to the bed and the stain, then to me. I knew my face was red, even though it wasn't my blood on the sheets. How could these women jump at the chance to see proof of my taken virginity? Didn't they have any compassion? Maybe they thought it was only fair I went through the same ordeal they had. I looked away, unable to bear their scrutiny. Let them make from that what they wanted. Most guests had left, especially politicians and other non-mafia folk; only the closest family was supposed to bear witness to the presentation of the sheets, but from the number of women gathered in the corridor and bedroom, you wouldn't have known.

Only women of marriage age were allowed to be present when the sheets were taken down—so as not to frighten the pure virgin eyes of younger girls. I could see my aunts among the spectators, as well as my mother, Valentina and Bibiana, but the women from Luca's family were in the front since it was their tradition, not ours. *Now it is yours as well,* I reminded myself with a twinge. Luca met my eyes briefly from across the room. We shared a secret now. I couldn't help but feel grateful toward my husband, even though I didn't want to be grateful for something like that. But in our world you had to be thankful for the smallest kindness, especially from a man like Luca, especially when he didn't have to be kind.

Luca's stepmother Nina and his cousin Cosima began stripping the bed. "Luca," Nina said with feigned indignation. "Did nobody tell you to be gentle to your virgin bride?"

That actually got her a few embarrassed giggles and I lowered my eyes, even though I wanted to scowl at her. Luca did a fine job of that, then he flashed her a wolfish smile that raised the hairs on my neck. "You are married to my father. Does he strike you as a man who teaches his sons to be gentle to *anyone?*"

Her lips thinned but she didn't stop smiling. I could feel everyone's eyes on me and squirmed under the attention. When I risked a peek toward my family, I saw shock and pity on many of their faces.

"Let me through!" came Gianna's panicked voice. My head shot up. She was fighting her way through the gathered women and avoided Mother, who tried to stop her. Gianna wasn't even supposed to be here. But when did Gianna ever do what she was supposed to do? She shoved a very thin woman out of her way and staggered into the bedroom. Her face flashed with disgust when she spotted the sheets Luca's stepmother was holding up and spreading over Cosima's outstretched arms.

Her eyes found my face, lingering on my swollen lips, disheveled hair and my arms, which were still wrapped around my middle. I wished there was a way to let her know I was fine, that it wasn't as it looked, but I couldn't with all those women around us. She turned to Luca, who at least didn't have a boner anymore. The look in her eyes would have sent most people running. Luca raised his eyebrows with a smirk.

She took a step in his direction. "Gianna," I said quietly. "Will you help me get dressed?" I let my arms fall to my sides and walked toward the bathroom, trying to wince now and then as if I was sore and hoping I wasn't overdoing it. I'd never seen a bride, or anyone else, after they'd supposedly lost their virginity.

The moment the door closed behind Gianna and me, she threw her arms around me. "I hate him. I hate them all. I want to kill him."

"He didn't do anything," I murmured.

Gianna pulled back, and I put my finger to my lips. Confusion filled her face. "What do you mean?"

"He didn't force me."

"Just because you didn't fight him doesn't mean it wasn't rape."

I covered her mouth with my hand. "I'm still a virgin."

Gianna stepped back so my hand dropped from her lips. "But the blood," she whispered.

"He cut himself."

She stared at me in disbelief. "Do you have Stockholm syndrome?"

I rolled my eyes. "Shh. I'm telling the truth."

"Then why the show?"

"Because nobody can know. Nobody. Not even Mother or Lily. You can't tell anyone, Gianna."

Gianna frowned. "Why would he do that?"

"I don't know. Maybe he doesn't like to hurt me."

"That man would kill a baby fawn if it looked at him the wrong way."

"You don't know him."

"Neither do you." She shook her head. "Don't tell me you trust him now. Just because he didn't fuck you last night doesn't mean he won't do it soon. Maybe he prefers to do it in his penthouse with a view over New York. You are his wife, and any man with a working dick would want to get in your pants."

"Father really wasted all of his lady comments on you," I said with a smile. Gianna kept glaring. "Gianna, I knew when I married Luca that I would have to sleep with him eventually, and I accepted that. But I'm glad that I get the chance to at least get to know him a bit better first." Though I wasn't sure I'd like the parts of him I'd get to know. But his kisses hadn't been unpleasant at all. My skin still warmed when I thought of it. And Luca definitely was nice to look at. Not that good looks could cancel out cruelty, but so far he hadn't been cruel to me, and somehow I thought he wouldn't be, at least not intentionally.

Gianna sighed. "Yeah, you're probably right." She sank down on the toilet lid. "I didn't sleep all night from worrying about you. Couldn't you have sent me a text saying Luca didn't pop your cherry?"

I began undressing. "Sure. And then Father or Umberto would check your mobile and see it, and I'd be doomed."

Gianna's eyes scanned me from head to toe as I stepped into the shower, probably still looking for a sign that Luca had manhandled me.

"You still have to act as if you hate Luca when you see him later, or people will get suspicious," I told her.

"Don't worry. That won't be a problem because I still hate him for taking you away from me, and for *being him*. I don't believe for one second that he's capable of kindness."

"Luca can't know I told you either." I turned the shower on and let the hot water wash away the last hints of tiredness. I needed to be fully alert for the show in the dining room later. My tense muscles began relaxing as the stream of water massaged them.

"You can't come in," Gianna said angrily, startling me. "I don't care that you are her husband." I opened my eyes to see Luca pushing his way into the bathroom. Gianna stepped in his way. I quickly turned my back to them.

"I need to get ready," Luca growled. "And there's nothing here that I haven't already seen." Liar. "Now leave, or you'll see your first cock, girl, because I'm going to undress now." He took off his chest holster and wrist strap.

"You arrogant asshole, I—"

"Leave!" I shouted.

Gianna left, but not without calling Luca by a few choice words. The door banged shut and we were alone. I wasn't sure what Luca was doing and I wouldn't turn around to check. I couldn't hear him from the splashing of the water. I knew I couldn't stay in the shower forever, so I shut off the water and faced the room.

Luca was spreading shaving cream on his chin with a brush, but his eyes were watching me in the mirror. I resisted the urge to cover myself, even though I felt a blush spreading over my body. He set the brush down and reached for one of the plush bath towels hanging over the heated towel rack, then walked over to me, still in his briefs. I opened the shower and took the towel from him with a quick thanks. He didn't move, eyes unfathomable as they roamed my body. I wrapped the towel around myself, then stepped out. Without high heels, the top of my head only reached Luca's chest.

"I bet you're already regretting your decision," I said quietly. I didn't need to explain; he knew what I meant.

Without a word, he returned to the wash table, picked up the brush and resumed what he'd been doing before. I was on my way into the bedroom, when his voice startled me. "No." I glanced back and met his eyes. "When I claim your body, I want you writhing beneath me in pleasure and not fear."

chapter *eight*

I was already dressed in an orange summer maxi dress and a golden belt to accentuate my waist when Luca stepped out of the bathroom in nothing but a towel. I sat on the chair in front of my vanity, putting on makeup, but froze with the mascara brush inches from my eye when I saw Luca. He walked toward the wardrobe and picked out black pants and a white shirt before he dropped his towel without shame. I didn't look away fast enough and was rewarded with his firm backside. I lowered my eyes and busied myself with checking my nails until I dared to face the mirror again and put on mascara.

Luca buttoned his shirt, except for the upper two. He strapped a knife to his forearm and rolled the sleeve over it, then put a gun holster around his calf. I turned around. "Do you ever go anywhere without guns?" No chest holster this time because it couldn't be hidden well with only a white shirt and it would have been bad taste to display weapons openly at a family gathering.

"Not if I can avoid it." He considered me. "Do you know how to shoot a gun or use a knife?"

"No. My father doesn't think women should get involved in fights."

"Sometimes fights come to you. The Bratva and the Triad don't distinguish between men and women."

"So you've never killed a woman?"

His expression tightened. "I didn't say that." I waited for him to elaborate but he didn't. Maybe it was for the best.

I stood, smoothing out my dress, nervous about meeting my father and Salvatore Vitiello after the wedding night. "Good choice," Luca said. "The dress covers your legs."

"Someone could lift the skirt and inspect my thighs."

It was meant as a joke, but Luca's lips pulled into a snarl. "Someone tries to touch you, they lose their hand."

I didn't say anything. His protectiveness thrilled and scared me in equal parts. He waited for me at the door and I approached him uncertainly. His words from the bathroom still rang in my ears. *Writhe in pleasure.* I wasn't sure I was even close to being relaxed enough around him for anything coming close to pleasure. Gianna was right. I couldn't allow myself to trust him that easily. He could be manipulating me.

He rested his hand on my lower back as we walked out. When we reached the top of the stairs, I could already hear conversation, and a few scattered guests were talking in small groups in the huge entrance hall.

I froze. "Are they all waiting to see a bloody sheet?" I whispered, appalled.

Luca peered down at me, smirking. "Many of them, especially the women. The men might hope for dirty details, others might hope to talk about business, ask a favor, get on my good side." He gently pressed me forward and we walked down the steps.

Romero was waiting at the foot of the stairs, his brown hair in disarray. He tilted his head toward Luca, then gave me a brief smile. "How are you?" he asked me, then grimaced, the tips of his ears actually turning red.

Luca chuckled. I didn't know any of the other men in the hall, but they all gave Luca winks or broad grins. Embarrassment crept up my neck. I knew what they were all thinking, could practically feel them undressing me with their eyes. I shifted closer to Luca and he curled his fingers around my waist.

"Matteo and the rest of your family are in the dining room."

"Poring over the sheets?"

"As if they could read them like tea leaves," Romero confirmed, then gave me an apologetic look. He didn't seem to suspect anything.

"Come," Luca said, nudging me toward the double doors. The moment we stepped into the dining room, every pair of eyes was on us. The women of the family were gathered on one side of the room, divided into small clusters, while the men sat around the long dining table, which was piled with ciabatta, grapes, ham, mortadella, cheese, fruit platters, and biscotti. I realized I was actually quite hungry. It was already almost lunchtime. Matteo snuck up beside Luca and me, an espresso in his hand.

"You look like shit," Luca said.

Matteo nodded. "My tenth espresso and I'm still not awake. Drank too much last night."

"You were trashed," Luca said. "I'd have had your tongue cut out for some of the things you said to Aria if you weren't my brother."

Matteo grinned at me. "I hope Luca didn't do half of the things I suggested."

I wasn't sure what to say to that. Matteo still made me nervous. He exchanged a look with Luca, who ran a thumb over my side, making me jump.

"Quite a work of art you presented us," Matteo said with a nod toward the back of the room, where the sheets were draped over a coat rack for better display.

I tensed. What did he mean?

But Luca didn't look worried; instead he shook his head. Salvatore Vitiello and my father were waving at us to join them, and it would have been impolite to make them wait any longer. Father rose when we arrived at the table and wrapped me in his arms. I was surprised by this open display of affection. He touched the back of my head and whispered, "I'm proud of you."

I gave him a forced smile when we pulled apart. Proud for what? For losing my virginity? For spreading my legs?

Salvatore put a hand on my and Luca's shoulders, and gave us a smile. "I hope we can expect small Vitiellos soon."

I managed not to let my shock show. Hadn't Luca mentioned that I was on birth control?

"I want to enjoy Aria alone for a long while. And with the Bratva closing in, I wouldn't want to have children to worry over," Luca said tightly. There was no word to describe how relieved I was about Luca's words. I really wasn't ready for children. I'd already had enough changes thrown my way without the added bonus of a baby.

His father nodded. "Yes, yes, of course. Understandable."

After that they launched into a conversation about the Bratva, and it became pretty clear I was dismissed. I slipped out of Luca's grasp and walked toward the women. Gianna met me halfway. "Disgusting," she muttered with a scowl toward the sheets.

"I know."

I looked around, but couldn't see Fabiano or Lily. "Where are—"

"Upstairs in their room with Umberto. Mother didn't want them to be there for the reveal of the sheets." She leaned in conspiratorially. "I'm so glad you're finally here. Those women have been sharing their bloody sheet stories for hours. What the fuck is wrong with the New York Famiglia? If I hear one more word about it, I'm going to give them a real bloodbath."

"Now that I'm here, I doubt they'll be talking about anything but the bloody sheets over there," I muttered. It turned out I was right. Almost every woman felt the need to hug me and offer me words of advice that only made me nervous. *It'll get better. Sometimes it takes a bit for a woman to be comfortable.* And the best: *Believe me, it took me years to enjoy it.*

Valentina didn't say anything as she wrapped her arms around me, just touched her palm to my cheek and smiled, before stepping back to make room for another woman. Mother kept her distance. I wasn't sure why. She stood with her hands clasped in front of her, disapproval written across her face. I was glad she wasn't sharing stories of her wedding night with Father. I stepped toward her and she pulled me into a tight hug. Like my father, she wasn't an overly affectionate person, but I was glad for her closeness. ""I wish I could have protected you from all this," she whispered before pulling back. There was a flicker of guilt on her face. I nodded. I didn't blame her. What could she have done? Father wouldn't have let her talk him out of the agreement.

"Luca can't stop watching you. You must have left quite an impression on him," Luca's stepmother said teasingly.

I turned to her and smiled politely. Luca probably just wanted to make sure I didn't give away our secret by accident. From the corner of my eye, I saw the door at the back open and Lily slink in, followed by Fabiano. They'd probably used Umberto's toilet break to get away. Gianna made a face when our brother stopped in front of the sheets.

I excused myself and walked over to them with Gianna at my heels. Mother was wrapped up in overly polite conversation with Luca's stepmother.

"What are you doing here, you little monster?" Gianna asked, grasping Fabiano's shoulders.

"Why's there blood on the sheets?" he half shouted. "Has someone been killed?"

Gianna burst into laughter while Lily looked honestly distressed by the sight of the sheets. I supposed it burst her bubble of fairy-tale princes and lovemaking under the stars. The men at the table behind us also started laughing, and Fabiano's face scrunched up in anger. Although he was only eight, he had a temper. I hoped he'd calm down soon, or he'd get in trouble once he was initiated. Gianna ruffled his hair.

"Are you going to New York with Luca?" Fabiano asked suddenly.

I bit my lip. "Yeah."

"But I want you to come home with us."

I blinked, trying to hide my anguish over hearing him say that. "I know."

Lily tore her eyes away from the sheets for a moment. "Won't you go on a honeymoon?"

"Not right now. The Russians and the Taiwanese are giving Luca trouble."

Fabiano nodded as if he understood, and maybe he did. With every year that passed he'd learn more of the dark world we lived in.

"Stop staring at the sheets," Gianna said in a low voice, but Lily seemed too caught up in the sight.

Her face scrunched up. "I think I'm going to be sick." I wrapped an arm around her shoulder and steered her outside. She shook in my grip.

"Hold it back," I ordered as we half ran out of the room, everyone's eyes following us. We stumbled into the hall. "Where's the bathroom?" This mansion had too many rooms.

Romero motioned us to the end of the hall and opened a door, then closed it when we were inside. I held Lily's hair as she threw up in the toilet bowl, then made her sit down on the ground. I wiped her face with a wet towel and a bit of soap. "I still feel strange."

"Put your head between your knees." I crouched before her. "What's the matter?"

She gave a small shrug.

"I'll get you some tea." I straightened.

"Don't let Romero see me like this."

"Romero isn't..." I trailed off. Lily obviously had a crush on him. It was futile, but I could at least allow her that small fantasy, when the sight of the sheets had already distressed her so much. "I'll keep him out," I promised instead and slipped out of the bathroom.

Romero and Luca waited in front of it.

"Is your sister okay?" Luca asked. Was he actually concerned or only polite?

"The sheets made her queasy."

Romero's expression darkened. "They shouldn't allow young girls to witness something like that. It'll only scare them."

He glanced at Luca as if catching himself. But Luca waved dismissively. "You are right."

"Lily needs some tea."

"I can get it for her, and stay with her so you can return to your guests," Romero suggested.

I smiled. "That's nice, but Lily doesn't want you to see her."

Romero frowned. "Is she scared of me?"

"You sound like that isn't a possibility," I said with a laugh. "You are a soldier of the mafia. What's not to be scared of?" I decided not to play with him anymore and lowered my voice. "But that's not it. Lily has a major crush on you and doesn't want you to see her like that." That, and I didn't want any of Luca's men alone with Lily until I knew them better.

Luca grinned. "Romero, you still got it. Capturing the hearts of fourteen-year-old girls left and right." Then he turned his attention to me. "But we have to return. The women will be mortally offended if you don't give them all your attention."

"I'll take care of Lily," Gianna said, appearing in the hall with Fabiano.

I smiled. "Thanks," I said as I brushed her hand in passing. The moment I was back in the dining room, the women flocked around me again, trying to extract more details from me. I pretended to be too embarrassed to speak about it—which I would have been, if it had taken place—and only gave them vague answers. Guests eventually started to leave, and I knew it would soon be time to say goodbye to my family and embark on my new life.

Fabiano pressed his face against my ribs almost painfully and I stroked his hair, feeling him tremble. Father was watching with a disapproving frown. He thought Fabiano was too old to show emotions like that, as if a boy couldn't be sad. They would have to leave for the airport soon. Father needed to return to Chicago to conduct business as usual. I wished they could have stayed longer, but Luca and I would leave for New York today as well.

Fabiano sniffed, then pulled back, looking up at me. Tears pressed against my eyes but I held them back. If I started crying now, things would only get harder for everyone, especially Gianna and Lily. They both hovered a couple of steps behind Fabiano, waiting for their turn to say goodbye. Father stood already beside the black rental Mercedes, impatient to leave.

"I will see you again soon," I promised, but I wasn't sure when soon would be. Christmas? That was still four months away. The thought settled like a heavy stone in the pit of my stomach.

"When?" Fabiano jutted out his lower lip.

"Soon."

"We don't have forever. The plane will leave without us," Father said sharply. "Come here, Fabiano."

With a last longing look at me, Fabiano shuffled over to Father, who immediately began scolding him. My heart felt so heavy, I wasn't sure how it could remain in my chest without crushing my ribs. Luca pulled up behind the Mercedes in his steel-gray Aston Martin Vanquish and got out, but my attention shifted to Lily, who threw her arms around me, and after a moment Gianna joined in the hug. My sisters, my best friends, my confidantes, my *world*.

I couldn't hold back the tears anymore. I never wanted to let them go. I wanted to take them with me to New York. They could live in our apartment, or even get their own. At least then I'd have someone whom I loved and who loved me back.

"I'm going to miss you so much," Lily whispered between hiccupped sobs. Gianna didn't say anything. She only pressed her face into the crook of my neck and cried. Gianna, who almost never cried. My strong, impulsive Gianna. I wasn't sure how long we held on to each other, and I didn't care who saw this open display of weakness. Let them all see what true love meant. Most of them would never experience it.

"We have to leave," Father called. Gravel crunched.

I lifted my face. Mother walked up to us, briefly touched my cheek, then took Lily's arm and led her away from me. Another piece of myself gone. Gianna didn't loosen her iron grip on me.

"Gianna!" Father's voice was like a whip.

She raised her head, eyes red, her freckles standing out even more. We locked gazes and for a moment neither of us said anything. "Call me every day. Every single day," Gianna said fiercely. "Swear it."

"I swear," I choked out.

"Gianna, for Christ's sake! Do I have to come get you?"

She backed away from me slowly, then she whirled around and practically fled into the car. I walked a few steps after them as their car drove down the long driveway. Neither of my sisters turned around. When they finally turned a corner and were gone, I was strangely relieved. I cried for myself for a while, and nobody interrupted me. Yet I knew I wasn't alone. At least, not in the physical sense.

When I finally turned around, Luca and Matteo stood on the steps behind me. Luca stared at me with a look I didn't have the energy to read. He probably thought me pathetic and weak. That was the second time I'd cried in front of him. But today hurt worse. He came down the steps while Matteo stayed behind.

"Chicago isn't the end of the world," Luca said calmly.

He couldn't understand. "It might as well be. I've never been separated from my sisters and brother. They were my whole world."

Luca didn't say anything. He gestured to his car. "We should leave. I have a meeting tonight."

I nodded. Nothing kept me here. Everyone I cared about was gone.

"I'll be behind you," Matteo said, then headed for a motorcycle.

I sank into the taupe-colored leather seats of the Aston Martin. Luca closed the door, walked around the hood and settled behind the steering wheel.

"No bodyguard?" I asked tonelessly.

"I don't need bodyguards. Romero is for you. And this car doesn't exactly have room for additional passengers." He started the engine, the deep rumbling filling the inside. I faced the window as we drew away from the Vitiello mansion. It felt surreal that my life could change so drastically because of a wedding. But it had, and would only change even more.

chapter *nine*

The drive to New York passed in silence. I was glad Luca hadn't tried to make conversation. I wanted to be alone with my thoughts and sadness. Soon skyscrapers rose up around the car as we crept through New York at a glacial pace. I didn't care. The longer the drive took, the longer I could pretend I didn't have a new home, but eventually we pulled into an underground garage. We got out of the car without a word and Luca took our bags from the trunk. Most of my belongings had already been brought to Luca's apartment a few days ago, but this would be the first time I saw where he lived.

I lingered next to the car as Luca headed for the elevator doors. He glanced over his shoulder and stopped as well. "Thinking about running?"

Every single day.

I walked up to him. "You would find me," I said simply.

"I would." There was steel in his voice. He jabbed a card into a slot and the elevator doors glided open, revealing marble, mirrors and a small chandelier. The opulence made it clear that this wasn't a normal apartment building. We stepped inside, and nerves twisted my stomach.

I'd been alone with Luca last night and during the ride here, but the thought of being alone in his penthouse was somehow worse. This was his kingdom. Who was I kidding? Pretty much all of New York was his empire. He leaned against the mirrored wall and watched me as the elevator began its ascent. I wished he'd say something, *anything, really*. It would distract me from the panic rising up my throat. My eyes flitted to the screen showing which floor we were on. We were already on floor twenty and hadn't stopped yet.

"The elevator is private. It leads only to the last two floors of the building. My penthouse is at the top, and Matteo has his apartment on the floor below."

"Can he come into our penthouse whenever he wants?"

Luca scanned my face. "Are you scared of Matteo?"

"I'm scared of the both of you. But Matteo seems more volatile, while I doubt you'd ever do anything you haven't thought through. You seem like someone who's always firmly in control."

"Sometimes I lose control."

I twisted my wedding ring around my finger, avoiding his eyes. That was information I didn't need to know.

"You have nothing to worry about when it comes to Matteo. He's used to coming over to my place whenever he wants, but things will change now that I'm married. Most of our business takes place somewhere else anyway."

The elevator beeped and came to a stop, then the doors slid apart. Luca gestured for me to step out first. I did and immediately found myself in a huge living space with sleek white sofas, dark hardwood floors, a modern glass and metal fireplace, black sideboards and tables, as well as avant-garde chandeliers. There was hardly any color at all, except for a few pieces of modern art on the walls and art pieces made from glass. But the entire wall facing the elevator was glass. The windows offered a view toward a terrace and roof garden, and beyond that skyscrapers and Central Park. The ceiling opened up above the main part of the living area, and a staircase led up to the second floor of the penthouse.

I walked farther into the apartment and tilted my head up. Glass banisters allowed a clear view of the upper floor: a bright gallery with several doors branching off of it.

An open kitchen took up the left side of the living area, and a massive black dining table marked the border between dining and living area. I could feel Luca's eyes on me as I took everything in, approaching the windows and peering out. I'd never lived in an apartment; even a roof garden didn't change the fact that it was a prison that rose high above the city streets.

"Your things are in the bedroom upstairs. Marianna wasn't sure if you wanted to put them away yourself, so she left them in your suitcases."

"Who's Marianna?"

Luca came up behind me. Our gazes met in the reflection in the window. "She's my housekeeper. She's here a couple of days per week."

I wondered if she was also his mistress. Some men in our world actually dared to insult their wives by bringing their whores into their own home. "How old is she?"

Luca's lips twitched. "Are you jealous?" He rested his hands on my hips and I tensed. He didn't pull away, but I could see anger crossing his face. But I also noted that he didn't answer my question.

I stepped out of his hold and headed for a glass door leading out onto the roof garden. I turned to Luca. "Can I go outside?"

His jaw was tight. He wasn't stupid. He had noticed how quickly I'd shaken off his touch. "This is your home now too."

It didn't feel that way. I wasn't sure it ever would. I opened the door and stepped outside. It was windy, and distant honking carried up from the streets below. White lounge furniture took up the terrace, but beyond it a small well-kept garden stretched out toward a glass barrier. There was even a square in-ground Jacuzzi big enough for six people. Two sunchairs were set up beside it. I strode toward the edge of the garden and let my gaze wander over Central Park. It was a beautiful view.

"You're not thinking about jumping, are you?" Luca asked, gripping the banister beside me.

I tilted my face up to him, trying to gauge if this was his attempt at humor. He looked serious. "Why would I kill myself?"

"Some women in our world see it as their only way to gain freedom. This marriage is your prison."

I appraised the distance between the roof and the ground. Death was certain. But I'd never considered killing myself. Before doing that, I'd run. "I wouldn't do that to my family. Lily, Fabi and Gianna would be heartbroken."

Luca nodded. I couldn't read his expression and it was driving me crazy. "Let's go back inside," he said, putting a hand on my lower back and steering me into the apartment. He closed the door, then turned back to me. "I have a meeting in thirty minutes, but I'll be back in a few hours. I want to take you to my favorite restaurant for dinner."

"Oh," I said, surprised. "Like a date?"

The corners of Luca's mouth twitched, but he didn't smile. "You could call it that. We haven't been on a real date yet." He wrapped an arm around my middle and pulled me against him. I froze, and the lightness disappeared from his eyes.

"When will you stop being afraid of me?"

"You don't want me to be afraid of you?" I'd always thought it would make his life easier if I was terrified of him. Would make it easier to keep me in check.

Luca's dark brows drew together. "You are my wife. We'll spend our lives together. I don't want a cowering woman at my side."

That really surprised me. Mother loved Father, but she also feared him. "Are there people out there who don't fear you?"

"A few," he said before lowering his head and pressing his lips against mine. He kissed me without hurry until I relaxed under his touch and parted my lips for him. I raised my arm and hesitantly touched the back of his neck, my fingers brushing his hair. My other hand pressed against his chest, enjoying the feel of his muscles. He pulled away.

"I have half a mind to cancel this fucking meeting." He rubbed his thumb over my lips. "But there's still more than enough time for this later." He glanced at his watch. "I really need to go now. Romero will be here when I'm gone. Take your time to look around and make yourself comfortable." With that, he headed for the door and left.

For a moment, I stared at the door, wondering if anyone would stop me if I walked out of this building. Instead I moved toward the staircase and walked up to the second floor. Only one of the white doors was ajar, and I pushed it open. The master bedroom opened up before me. As with the living area, an entire wall was made up of windows overlooking New York. The king-sized bed was facing them. I wondered how it would be to watch the sunrise from bed. The wall behind the bed was upholstered with black fabric. At the end of the room a doorway led into a walk-in closet, and to its right I could see a freestanding bathtub through the glass wall separating the bedroom from the bathroom.

I walked toward it. Even from the bathtub you could watch the city. Despite the glass wall, the washbasins and the shower weren't visible from the bedroom, and the toilet was in its own small room.

"Aria?"

I gasped. My heart pounded in my chest as I slowly followed the voice and found Romero on the gallery, carrying my bags. "I didn't mean to startle you," he said when he saw my face. I nodded. "Where do you want me to put your bags?"

I'd forgotten Luca had dropped them on the sofa. "I don't know. Maybe the walk-in closet?"

He strode past me and set the bags down on a bench in the closet. My three suitcases as well as two moving boxes were beside it. "Do you know if I need to dress up for tonight? Luca said he wants to take me to his favorite restaurant, but he didn't tell me if it has a dress code."

Romero smiled. "No. Definitely no dress code."

"Why? Is it a KFC?" I'd actually never eaten at a KFC. Father and Mother would have never taken us to a place like that. Gianna, Lily and I had once convinced Umberto to take us to a McDonalds, but that was the extent of my experience with fast-food joints.

"Not really. I think Luca wants to surprise you."

I doubted that. "Maybe I should unpack then." I gestured at my suitcases.

Romero kept a careful distance from me. He was nice but professional. "Do you need help?"

I really didn't want Romero to touch my underwear. "No. I'd prefer to be alone."

Compassion filled Romero's face before he turned and left. I waited until I was certain that he was back downstairs before I opened the first box. On top was a photo of me with Gianna, Lily and Fabi. I cried for the third time in less than twenty-four hours. I'd seen them only this morning, so how could I already feel so alone?

When Luca came home almost five hours later, I'd changed into a skirt and a flimsy, sleeveless blouse. Despite my best efforts, my eyes were still slightly red from crying. There was a limit to what makeup could do. Luca noticed immediately, his gaze lingering on my eyes, then darting to the photo of my family on the nightstand.

"I wasn't sure which was your side. I can move it to the other nightstand if you want," I said.

"No, it's okay." Exhaustion was written plainly on his face.

"Was the meeting okay?"

Luca looked away. "Let's not talk about it. I'm starving." He held out his hand and I took it and followed him to the elevator. He was tense and barely said a word as we rode in his car. I wasn't sure if he expected me to make conversation, and I was too emotionally drained to put up an effort.

When we stopped at a red light, he glanced over. "You look great."

"Thanks."

He parked the car in a gated parking area where they stashed the cars on top of each other, then we headed down a street with small restaurants offering everything from Indian cuisine, to Lebanese and Sushi. He stopped at a Korean restaurant and held the door open for me. Stunned, I walked into the crowded, narrow dining room.

Small tables were set closely together, and a bar at the front offered alcoholic beverages with labels I couldn't even read. A waiter came up to us and upon spotting Luca, he led us toward the back of the restaurant and gave us the last available table. The people at the table beside ours stared at Luca with wide eyes, probably wondering how he'd fit. I took the seat on the bench running the entire length of the room, and Luca folded himself into the chair across from me. The man beside him shifted his chair to the side, so Luca would have more room. Did they know who he was or were they being polite?

"You look surprised," Luca said after the waiter had taken our drink orders and left us with the menu.

"I didn't think you'd go for Asian food, considering *everything*." That was all I could say in a crowded restaurant, but Luca knew I was talking about the Taiwanese Triad.

"This is the best Asian restaurant in town, and it doesn't belong to an Asian *chain*."

I frowned. Was it under the protection of the Famiglia?

"It's independent."

"There are independent restaurants in New York?"

The couple at the table beside us gave me a strange look. For them our conversation probably seemed more than a little weird.

"A few, but we're in negotiations right now."

I snorted.

Luca pointed at my menu. "Do you need help?"

"Yeah, I've never tried Korean."

"The marinated silk tofu and the bulgogi beef are delicious."

"You eat *tofu*?"

Luca shrugged. "If it's prepared like this, then yes."

I shook my head. This was surreal. "Just order what you think is best. I eat everything except for liver."

"I like women that eat more than salad."

The waiter returned and took our orders. I fumbled with the chopsticks, trying to figure out the best way to use them.

"Have you never used sticks before?" Luca asked with a smirk. Was he mocking me?

"My parents only took us to their favorite Italian restaurant, and I wasn't really allowed to go anywhere alone." Bitterness rang in my voice.

"You can go anywhere you want now."

"Really? Alone?"

Luca lowered his voice. "With Romero or me, or Cesare when Romero isn't available."

Of course.

"Here, let me show you." He took his own chopsticks and held them up. I tried to imitate his grip and after a few tries, I managed to move the sticks without dropping them. When our food arrived, I realized that it was much harder to grab on to something with sticks.

Luca watched with obvious amusement as I took three tries to bring a piece of tofu to my lips.

"No wonder New York girls are so thin if they eat like this all the time."

"You are more beautiful than all of them," he said. I scanned his face, trying to figure out if he was being truthful, but as usual his face was unreadable. I allowed myself to admire his eyes. They were unusual, with their darker ring around the gray. They weren't exactly cold right now, but I remembered them being that way.

Luca snatched a piece of marinated beef and held it out in front of me. My eyebrows shot up in surprise. Luca mirrored my expression, but his was more challenging. I leaned forward and closed my lips around the sticks, then pulled back, savoring the taste of the bulgogi beef. Luca's eyes seemed to darken as he watched me.

"Delicious," I said. Luca picked up a piece of tofu next, and I took it eagerly. This was better than trying to wrangle the chopsticks into submission.

I was grateful that Luca showed me this normal side of him. It gave me hope. Maybe that was his intention, but I didn't care.

The relaxation I'd felt during dinner evaporated when Luca and I returned to our penthouse and stepped into the bedroom. I went into the bathroom and took my time getting ready before I returned.

Luca's eyes took in my long, dark satin nightgown. It reached my calves but had a slit that went up to my thighs. It was still much more modest than the horrible thing I'd worn on our wedding night. And yet I was sure there was desire in his eyes.

Once he'd disappeared into the bathroom, I walked toward the window and busied myself watching the nighttime skyline. I was almost as nervous as last night. I knew I wasn't ready for more than kissing. When I heard Luca come up beside me, I didn't turn. His impressive stature was reflected in the windows. Like yesterday, he was only wearing briefs. I watched him reach out for me, and every muscle in my body tensed. If he noticed my reaction, he didn't let it show. He trailed a knuckle down the length of my spine, sending a tingling sensation through my body. When I didn't react he extended his hand, palm upward—an invitation, not a command, and yet I knew there was only one right answer.

I faced him, but my eyes were drawn to the long scar on his palm. I ran my fingertips over it. "Is that from the blood oath?" I peered up into his unreadable face. I knew during the initiation ceremony, men had to let blood while reciting the words of the oath.

"No. This is." He turned his other hand, where a small scar marred his palm. "That," he said with a nod toward the scar I was still touching. "...happened in a fight. I had to stave off a knife attack with my hand."

I wanted to ask him about the first time he killed a man, but he curled his fingers around my wrist and led me toward the bed. My throat became too tight for words when he sat on the mattress and pulled me between his legs. I tried to relax into his kiss, and when he made no move to take things further, I actually felt the tension slip away and began to enjoy his experienced mouth, but then he lay back and pulled me onto the bed with him.

His kisses became more forceful, and I could feel his erection pressed up against my thigh. Still I didn't pull back. I could do this. I knew it was coming. His hand cupped my breast and I stiffened despite my best intentions not to. He didn't remove it, but didn't move it either. His kisses made thinking difficult. Would it really be so bad to sleep with Luca? He drew back a couple of inches and trailed kisses toward my ear. "I've never wanted to fuck a woman as much as I want to fuck you right now."

I froze. His words made me feel cheap. He was my husband and he had a right to my body—if you asked anyone in our family, anyway—but I deserved better than that. I didn't want to be fucked like he was used to doing with other women. I was his wife. I wanted more.

I turned my head and pushed my palms against his chest. After a moment, he relented.

"I don't want this," I said, not bothering to hide my aversion from him.

I didn't look at him, but I could practically feel his frustration. What did he think? That I would suddenly feel comfortable enough to sleep with him because he'd taken me out for dinner once? Was that how it worked with his other girls? For a long time he did nothing but stare at me, then he untangled himself from me.

He shut off the light without a word and lay on his side of the bed. I wished he'd at least hold me. This was my first night so far away from my family. It would have been nice if he'd comforted me, but I didn't ask him to. Instead I pulled the covers up and closed my eyes.

When I woke the next morning, Luca was gone. There was no note, not even a text on my phone. He was really pissed. I shoved my blankets off. *Bastard.* He knew I didn't know anyone in New York, and yet he didn't care.

I grabbed my laptop and opened my email account. Gianna had already sent me three new emails. The last one was almost threatening. I picked up the phone. Only hearing her voice was enough to make me feel better. I didn't need Luca or anyone else, as long as I had Gianna.

The scent of coffee and something sweeter eventually drew me out of the bedroom and downstairs. Pans were clanking in the kitchen and as I turned the corner, I found a small, plump woman who looked old enough to be my grandma at the stove, making pancakes. Her dark gray hair was secured with a hairnet. Romero was perched on a stool at the bar attached to the kitchen island, a cup of coffee in front of him. He turned when I approached, his eyes taking in my nightgown before jerking his head away. Really?

The woman turned and smiled kindly. "You must be Aria. I'm Marianna."

I walked up to her to shake her hand but she pulled me into a hug, pressing me against her ample chest. "You are a beauty, *bambina*. No wonder Luca is smitten with you."

I swallowed a snide comment. "That smells delicious."

"Sit. Breakfast is ready in a couple of minutes. It's enough for Romero and you."

I sat beside Romero on a stool. He was still pointedly looking the other direction. "What's your problem? I'm not naked," I said when I couldn't take it anymore.

Marianna laughed. "The boy is worried Luca finds out he ogled his girl."

I shook my head, annoyed. If Romero insisted on being a coward, he'd have to eat with closed eyes. I wasn't putting a bathrobe on because I needed a bodyguard in my own home.

I was already dozing off when Luca came home that night. While he'd spent his day outside doing God knows what, I was a prisoner in this stupid penthouse. The only people who kept me company were Marianna and Romero, but she'd left after preparing dinner, and Romero wasn't exactly the most communicative companion. I watched as Luca emerged from the bathroom, freshly showered. He barely acknowledged me. Did he think I cared? When he lay down beside me and extinguished the lights, I said into the darkness, "Can I walk through the city tomorrow?"

"As long as you take Romero with you," was his short reply.

I swallowed my hurt and frustration. When he'd taken me to his favorite restaurant, I'd thought he'd try to make this marriage work, but it had only been a ploy to get me into bed. And now he punished me with the silent treatment.

But I didn't need him, never would. I listened to his rhythmic breathing, pretending to be asleep. Shortly before I drifted off to sleep, the mattress shifted as he left the bed. Part of me wanted to stop him, but I remained silent.

I awoke in the middle of the night from a nightmare. Luca's arm was wrapped around me, my body spooned by his. I could have pulled away, but his closeness felt too good. A part of me still wanted this marriage to work.

I missed Gianna and Lily so much, it was almost a physical thing.

Romero tried to be invisible, but he was always there. "Do you want to go shopping?"

I almost laughed. Did he think shopping made everything better? Maybe that worked for some people, but definitely not for me. "No, but I'd like to grab something to eat. Gianna sent me an email with a few restaurants she wants to try when she visits. I'd like to go to one of them today."

Romero looked uncertain for an instant, and I exploded. "I asked Luca for permission a couple of nights ago, so you don't have to worry. I'm allowed to leave this prison."

He frowned. "I know. He told me."

This was ridiculous. I left him standing in the middle of the living area and hurried up the stairs to the bedroom. I quickly changed into a nice summer dress and sandals, then grabbed my bag and sunglasses before heading back down. Romero hadn't moved from his spot. Why couldn't he pretend he was something other than my bodyguard?

"Let's go," I ordered. If he wanted to act like my bodyguard, I'd treat him that way. Romero pulled a jacket over his shirt to hide his holster, then pushed the elevator button. We didn't talk during the ride down. This was actually the first time I saw the lobby of the apartment building. It was sleek, black marble, modern art, white high-gloss counter behind which a middle-aged receptionist in a black suit sat. He inclined his head toward Romero before his eyes zoomed in on me with obvious curiosity. "Good day,

Mrs. Vitiello," he said in an overly polite voice. I almost stumbled at hearing him call me that. It was easy to forget I wasn't a Scuderi anymore. After all, my husband never seemed to be present.

I nodded in acknowledgement, then quickly rushed outside. Heat blasted against my body as I left the air-conditioned building. Summer in the city, nothing to be excited about. The smell of exhaust and garbage seemed to carry through the streets like fog. Romero was a step behind me, and I wondered how he could bear the heat in his outfit.

"I think we need to take a taxi," I said, as I stepped toward the curb. Romero shook his head, but I'd already raised my arm, and a taxi swerved to the side and stopped beside me.

Romero hung a few steps back, his alert gaze on my back. It was driving me crazy. People were giving us strange looks. "Can you please walk beside me?" I asked as we walked down Greenwich Street where the restaurant was. "I don't want people to think you're guarding me." He was probably still pissed that I'd made him take a taxi, instead of the black BMW that screamed mafia from afar.

"I'm guarding you."

I stopped until he fell into step beside me. The outside of the restaurant was surrounded by wildflowers growing in terra-cotta pots, and the inside reminded me of British pubs I'd read about. It seemed as if every single waiter was tattooed, and the tables were set so closely together you could have eaten from your neighbor's plate. I could see why Gianna would love it.

Romero's lips twisted in obvious disapproval. It was probably a bodyguard's nightmare. "Do you have a reservation?" a tall woman with a septum piercing asked.

"No." Romero narrowed his eyes as if he couldn't believe someone was actually asking something like that. I loved it. Here I was only Aria. "But it's just the two of us. And we won't take long," I said politely.

The woman looked between Romero and me, then smiled. "You have one hour. You are a cute couple."

She turned to lead us toward our table, which was why she didn't see Romero's expression. "Why didn't you correct her?" he asked quietly.

"Why should I?"

"Because we aren't a couple. You are Luca's."

"I am. And I'm not."

Romero didn't argue again, but I could tell it made him uncomfortable to act like we were anything but bodyguard and his boss's wife. I ate a salad with the most delicious dressing and enjoyed watching the people around us, while Romero ate a burger and monitored our surroundings. I couldn't wait to take Gianna here. Sadness filled me at the thought. I had never been so lonely in my life. Only two days into my new life, and I really didn't know how to survive the many thousands of days that would follow. "So Luca will be home late again tonight?"

"I suppose," Romero said evasively.

After we'd eaten, I forced Romero to stroll through the neighborhood of the restaurant for a bit longer, but eventually I got frustrated with his stiff posture and obvious discomfort, and agreed to return to the apartment.

When the taxi pulled up in front of the apartment building, Romero paid the driver and I slipped out of the car. As I approached the glass front, I noticed one of Luca's cousins sitting inside the lobby. What was she doing here? We hadn't spoken more than a few sentences to each other at the wedding, and I hadn't gotten the impression that she was interested in friendship. Confused, I stepped into the lobby. Cosima's eyes snapped to me, and she walked up to me without hesitation. To my surprise, she hugged me, then she pressed something into my hand. "Here. Don't let Romero or anyone else see it. Now smile."

I did, stunned. I could feel a folded piece of paper and what felt like a key in my palm. I quickly stashed them in my purse when Romero appeared beside me. "What are you doing here, Cosima?" There was a hint of suspicion in his voice.

She flashed her teeth at him. "I wanted to see how Aria was doing and asked her if we could meet for lunch soon. But now I need to go. I have a hair appointment." She gave me a warning look, then she walked out, high heels clacking on the marble floor.

Romero was watching me. "What did she say?"

"What she told you," I said, raising my chin. "I want to go up now." He wanted me to act like his boss, so he couldn't expect me to open up to him. He nodded and led me toward the elevator with a curt nod toward the two receptionists.

The moment we entered the penthouse, I excused myself and headed into the guest bathroom. I pulled out what Cosima had given me and unfolded the piece of paper.

Aria,

The key is for one of the apartments the Vitiellos own. Come over tonight at ten p.m. to see what your husband is really up to while you warm his bed. Be careful and quiet, and don't tell anyone. Romero will try to stop you. Shake him off.

The address was at the bottom of the page. The note wasn't signed and it was written with a computer. Was it from Cosima? It would make sense. I read it over and over again. It could be a trick, or worse, a trap, but curiosity burned through me. Luca hadn't exactly been the most present husband so far. The only problem was how to get to the apartment and how to get rid of Romero. He never left my side.

I convinced Romero to take me out to dinner at a restaurant that, according to Google maps, was only a five-minute walk from the address Cosima had given me. When Romero used the guest bathroom in our apartment, I used the moment to take a small gun Luca kept in one of the top drawers in the walk-in closet. I'd noticed it when I'd unpacked my suitcases and folded my clothes into drawers. I hid it in the side pocket of my bag. Even though I didn't have much experience with guns, I knew how to handle them in theory. Better safe than sorry.

It was a quarter past nine. Romero and I had just finished our starter, when I stood to head for the bathroom. Romero pushed back his chair and was about to stand as well.

I glared. "You won't follow me to the bathroom. Do you think I'll get lost on the way? People will be staring. Nobody knows who I am here. I'm safe."

Romero sank back down. The bathroom was past a corner, closer to the door than our table. I slipped out of the restaurant, took flats from my purse and put them on. Then I hurried toward the address. It would take at least five minutes before Romero would venture toward the bathroom, and hopefully even longer before he'd barge in to check on me.

When I arrived in front of the brownstone building, I hesitated. It didn't have a reception, only a narrow corridor and a steep staircase. Then I took a deep breath and entered. The key said the apartment was on the third floor. I took the elevator hidden in a dark corner behind the stairs. During the ride up, doubt overcame me. Maybe I shouldn't have listened to the letter. The elevator came to a halt and the door rattled open. My eyes darted to the button that would take me back to the ground floor, but instead I stepped out and found the apartment door. It wasn't completely shut.

My heart fluttered with fear. This seemed like a really bad idea, but curiosity was stronger than worry. I pushed the door open and peered in. The living room was dark and empty, but light was coming from somewhere else. I rested my hand on the gun in my purse, then crept further in, but froze when I heard a woman cry out. "Yes! Harder!"

Dread settled in me as I followed the voice. I had heard it before. The light was spilling out of an open door. I stopped in front of it, hesitating. I could still turn around and pretend I'd never received the letter. Another moan drifted out of the room, and I peeked inside. Heat rushed up my face, then seemed to drain out of my body completely. Grace Parker was on her knees and forearms on the bed while Luca fucked her from behind. The slaps of his body hitting her ass filled the silence, only occasionally disrupted by her encouraging cries and moans. Luca's eyes were closed as his fingers dug into her hips and he rammed into her over and over again. Grace turned her head to meet my eyes, and smiled triumphantly. Bile traveled up my throat. So this was what Luca had been up to the last two nights.

For a crazy moment, I considered taking the gun out and throwing it at her head. I wouldn't shoot her, even if I wanted to. I wasn't a mobster. I wasn't Luca. My shoulders slumped and I took a step back. I needed to get away. Luca's eyes shot open, hand reaching for a gun on the bed beside him, but then he found me. He jerked, then froze.

"What's the matter, Luca?" Grace asked, wiggling her ass against him. He was still buried inside her. Luca and I stared at each other, and I could feel tears gathering in my eyes.

I whirled around and ran. I needed to get away. Just away. The moment I stepped out of the elevator on the first floor, I began shaking, but I didn't stop. I rushed outside, almost bumping into Romero, who must have followed my phone's GPS. He stumbled back, looked at my face, then at the building, and his eyes widened. He knew. Everyone seemed to know, except for stupid me.

I stormed away, running faster than I'd ever run in my life. When I crossed the street toward the underground station, I caught a glimpse of Luca in an unbuttoned shirt and pants staggering out of the door. Romero was already chasing me.

But I was fast. Years of working out on the treadmill finally paid off. I practically flew down the steps, fumbling for the Metro card my sisters and I had purchased before the wedding, after we'd forced Umberto to show us the subway. I managed to squeeze into the already closing doors of a subway wagon. I wasn't even sure where it was going. But as I saw Luca and Romero heading for the tracks, all that mattered was that it was taking me away. Away from the triumphant smile Grace had given me, from the sound of Luca's body pounding her ass, from his betrayal.

On our wedding night I'd told Luca I didn't hate him. I wished he'd ask me again tonight. I sank down on a free seat, but I was still shaking. Where was I going?

I couldn't run away. Luca was probably already sending every soldier at his disposal after me. I let out a choked laugh and got a few strange looks from other passengers. What did they know? They were free.

I grabbed my mobile and called Gianna. She answered at the second ring. "Aria?"

"I caught Luca in bed with Grace." More people looked my way. What did it even matter? They didn't know who I was. The wedding announcements in the newspaper had never included a photo of me. I really didn't need any more attention.

"Holy fuck."

"Yeah." I got out at the next station as I began telling the whole story to Gianna. I quickly moved away from the subway, because that would be the place they'd look first. Eventually I landed in a loud and dark place where burgers and beer were sold. I ordered a Coke and a burger, though I had no intention of drinking or eating.

"Where are you now?" Gianna asked.

"Somewhere. I don't even know. In a restaurant, sort of."

"Be careful." I didn't say anything. "Are you crying?"

I was. Again I stayed silent.

"Don't. Not when I'm not around to console you and kick Luca's fucking ass. I knew he was an asshole. Fucking bastard. You haven't slept with him yet, right?"

"No, I haven't. That's probably why he's off cheating on me."

"Don't you dare blame yourself, Aria. Any decent man would have kept his dick in his pants or used his hand."

The burger and Coke arrived, and I thanked the waitress who lingered beside my table for a couple of seconds, her gaze focusing on my tears. I gave her a smile and she finally took the hint and left.

"What will you do now? Are you thinking of coming back home?"

"Do you really think Father will let me leave Luca because he cheated on me? Father has had a mistress for *years*." Nor would Luca allow it. I was his, as Romero never ceased to remind me.

"Men are all pigs."

"I can't forget the look Grace gave me. She looked like she'd won."

"She wanted you to see it—she wanted to humiliate you." Gianna fell silent. "You are the wife of the future Capo dei Capi. If someone humiliates you, they are practically insulting Luca."

"Well, he was busy helping her insult me."

Gianna snorted. "I hope his dick falls off."

"I'm not holding my breath."

"I bet Romero's getting his ass kicked for letting you slip away. Serves him right."

I almost felt sorry for Romero, but then I reminded myself that he'd known about Grace all along. It had been written all over his face. God, how many people knew? Were they all laughing about me behind my back?

"Are you talking to Aria?" I could hear Lily's excited voice in the background.

"That's none of your business. Get out of my room, you little snoop."

"I want to talk to her! She's my sister too!"

"Not now. This is private." There was shouting, then the bang of a door, followed by fists hammering against wood. My heart swelled with warmth and I smiled. This had been my life not too long ago. Now I only had a cheating husband to return to.

"So what now?" Gianna asked eventually.

"I honestly don't know." I paid and left the restaurant, returning to roaming the streets. It was dark, but they were still crowded with people on their way home from dinner or heading to a club or bar.

"You can't let him treat you like that. You must fight back."

"I don't know if fighting Luca is something I want to do."

"What can he do to you? You aren't his enemy or his soldier, and he said he didn't beat women, nor would he force himself on you. What's left? Lock you in your room without dinner?"

I sighed.

"Maybe you should cheat on him. Go to a club, find a hot guy and sleep with him."

That would go over well with Luca. "He'd kill him. I don't want blood on my hands."

"Then do something else. I don't care as long as you pay Luca back for what he's doing to you. He'll probably just keep cheating on you. Fight back."

But Gianna was the fighter. I preferred subtle tactics. "I should get rid of this phone now. I need more time to think and don't want Luca to track me down."

"Call me as soon as you can. No matter the time. If I don't hear from you tomorrow morning, I don't care who I have to take down to fly to New York."

"Okay. Love you." Before Gianna could say any more, I turned my phone off, disabled it and threw it into a dustbin before walking the streets aimlessly. It was past midnight and I was getting tired. The only thing that kept me going was the image of Luca going crazy because he couldn't find me. He hated not being in control. And now I'd slipped away from him. I wished I could see it.

I bought a coffee and wrapped my fingers around the warm paper cup as I leaned against the facade of the diner and let my eyes wander over the thinning number of passersby. Every time a couple walked past me, holding hands, kissing and laughing and being in love, my chest tightened. My eyes burnt from exhaustion and my earlier crying. I was so tired.

I hailed a taxi and let it take me to our apartment building. As I stepped into the lobby, the receptionist immediately picked up the phone. *Good dog*, I wanted to say. Instead I twisted my mouth into a smile and stepped into the elevator, then slipped in the card so it would take me to the right floor. I was almost calm now, at least on the outside. Was Luca in the penthouse? Or was he out hunting me? Or maybe he'd returned to his whore and let his men do the work for him. When I'd woken with Luca's arms around me, or when he'd kissed me, I'd let myself believe that maybe I could make him love me. When we'd had dinner together, I'd thought I could fall for him.

I entered the penthouse. Romero was there and practically sagged with relief. "She's here," he said into his phone, then nodded before ending the call.

"Where's Luca? Back with his whore?"

Romero frowned. "Searching for you."

"I'm surprised he bothers. He could have sent you or one of his other lapdogs. After all, you do everything he says. Even cover for him while he's out cheating on me." Romero didn't say anything. I wasn't sure why I was lashing out at him.

I walked away.

"Where are you going?"

"I'm going to undress and shower. If you want to watch, be my guest." Romero stopped, but his eyes followed me up the stairs. I slammed the bedroom door shut after me, then locked it before walking into the bathroom to take a shower. I turned the temperature as high as I could bear, but the water couldn't wash away the images that had taken refuge in my brain. Luca buried in Grace. Her smile. The sound of his hips slamming against her ass. I wasn't exactly sure what I was feeling. Disappointment. Jealousy? I hadn't chosen Luca, but he was my husband. I wanted him to be faithful to me. I wanted him to want only me. I wanted to be enough.

There was banging at the bedroom door when I got out of the shower. I wrapped a towel around myself and slowly walked out of the bathroom into the bedroom.

"Aria, let me in!" There was anger in his voice. He was *angry?*

I dropped the towel and slipped a silk nightgown over my body.

"I'm going to kick in the door, if you don't let me in."

I'd like to see you do it. Maybe you'll dislocate a shoulder.

"Aria, open the fucking door!"

I was too tired to keep playing with him. I wanted this day to be over. I wanted sleep to magically take away my memory. I unlocked the door, then turned and walked back to the bed. The door flew open, banging against the wall, and Luca stormed in. He grasped my arm and fury burned through me. How dare he lay hands on me after gripping that whore's ass with them?

"Don't touch me!" I shrieked, wrenching out of his grip. He was panting, eyes wild with emotion. His hair was a mess and his shirt wasn't buttoned properly. Matteo stood in the doorway, Romero and Cesare a few steps behind.

"Where have you been?" he said in a low voice. He reached for me again and I stumbled back. "No! Don't ever touch me again. Not when you use those same hands to touch your *whore*."

His face became very still. "Out, everyone. Now."

Matteo turned, and he and the other two men disappeared from view.

"Where have you been?"

"I wasn't cheating on you if that's what you're worried about. I would never do that. I think faithfulness is the most important thing in a marriage.

So you can calm yourself now—my body is still only yours." I practically spat the last few words. "I only walked around the city."

"You walked around New York at night *alone?*"

I stared into his eyes, hoping he could see how much I hated him for what I'd seen, how much it hurt to know he respected me so little. "You have no right to be angry with me, Luca. Not after what I saw today. You cheated on me."

Luca snarled. "How can I be cheating when we don't have a real marriage? I can't even fuck my own wife. Do you think I'll live like a monk until you decide you can stand my closeness?"

That arrogant pig. He and my father had made sure I didn't even talk to other men until my wedding to Luca. "God forbid. How dare I expect my husband to be faithful to me? How dare I hope for this small decency in a monster?"

"I'm not a monster. I've treated you with respect."

"Respect?" My voice rose higher. "I caught you with another woman! Maybe I should go out, bring a random guy back with me and let him fuck me in front of your eyes. How would that make you feel?"

Suddenly he flung me on the bed and was on top of me, my arms pinned above my head. Pushing through the choking fear, I said, "Do it. Take me, so I can really hate you." His eyes were the most terrifying thing I'd ever seen.

His nostrils flared. I turned my face away and closed my eyes. He was breathing harshly, his grip on my wrists too tight. My heart pounded against my ribcage as I lay unmoving beneath him. He shifted and pressed his face into my shoulder, releasing a harsh breath. "God, Aria."

I opened my eyes. He released my wrists but I kept my arms above my head. Slowly he raised his eyes. The anger was gone from his face. He reached for my cheek, but I turned away. "Don't touch me with *her* on you."

He sat up. "I'm going to take a shower now, and we will both calm down, and then I want us to talk."

"What's there left to talk about?"

"Us. This marriage."

I lowered my arms. "You fucked a woman in front of my eyes today. Do you think there's still a chance for this marriage?"

"I didn't want you to see that."

"Why? So you could cheat in peace and quiet behind my back?"

He sighed, and began unbuttoning his shirt. "Let me take a shower. You were right. I shouldn't disrespect you further by touching you like this."

I shrugged. Right now I didn't think I'd ever want him to touch me again, no matter how many showers he took. He disappeared in the bathroom. The shower ran for a long time. I sat against the headboard, sheets pulled up to my hips, when Luca finally emerged. I averted my eyes when he dropped his towel and put on boxer shorts, then he slipped into bed beside me with his back against the headboard. He didn't try to touch me. "Did you cry?" he asked in a puzzled voice.

"Did you think I wouldn't care?"

"Many women in our world are glad when their husbands use whores or take on a mistress. As you said, there are few marriages based on love. If a woman can't stand her husband's touch, she won't mind him having affairs to satisfy his needs."

I scoffed. "His needs."

"I'm not a good man, Aria. I never pretended otherwise. There are no good men in the mafia."

My eyes rested on the tattoo over his heart. "I know." I swallowed. "But you made me think that I could trust you and that you wouldn't hurt me."

"I never hurt you."

Did he really not get it? "It hurt seeing you with *her*."

His expression softened. "Aria, I didn't get the feeling that you wanted to sleep with me. I thought you'd be glad if I didn't touch you."

"When did I say that?"

"When I told you I wanted you, you pulled back. You looked disgusted."

"We were kissing, and you said you wanted to fuck me more than any other women. Of course, I pulled back. I'm not some whore you can use when you feel like it. You are never home. How am I supposed to get to know you?" He looked frustrated. Mafia men seemed even more clueless than normal ones. "What did you think? I've never done anything. You are the only man I've kissed. You knew that when we married. You and my father made sure it was the case, and despite that you expect me to go from never having kissed a guy to spreading my legs for you. I wanted to take it slow. I wanted to get to know you so I could relax; I wanted to kiss you and *do other things* first before we slept together."

Realization finally settled on his features, then he smirked. "Other things? What kinds of other things?"

I glared. I wasn't in the mood for jokes. "This is useless."

"No, don't." He turned my face back to him, then dropped his hand. He'd learned his lesson. "I get it. For men the first time isn't a big deal, or at least it wasn't for the men I know."

"When was your first time?"

"I was thirteen and my father thought it was time for me to become a real man, since I'd already been initiated. 'You can't be a virgin and a killer.' That's what he said." Luca smiled coldly. "He paid two noble prostitutes to spend a weekend with me and teach me everything they knew."

"That's horrible."

"Yeah, I suppose it is," Luca said quietly. "But I was a thirteen-year-old teenage boy who wanted to prove himself. I was the youngest member in the New York Famiglia. I didn't want the older men to think of me as a boy. And I felt like a big deal when the weekend was over. I doubt the prostitutes were overly impressed with my performance, but they pretended that I was the best lover they'd ever had. My father probably paid them extra for it. It took me a bit to figure out that not all women like it if you come all over their face when they give you a blow job."

I wrinkled my nose and Luca let out a laugh. "Yeah," he murmured, then reached for a strand of my hair and let it glide over his finger. I wasn't sure why he always did that. "I was really worried tonight."

"Worried that I'd let someone have what's yours."

"No," he said firmly. "I knew, I *know* you are loyal. Things with the Bratva are escalating. If they got their hands on you..." He shook his head.

"They didn't."

"They *won't*."

I shifted away from his hand that had moved on from my hair to my throat. I didn't want his touch. He sighed. "You're going to make this really difficult, aren't you?"

I stared.

"I'm sorry for what you saw today."

"But not sorry for what you did."

He looked exasperated. "I rarely say I'm sorry. When I say it, I mean it."

"Maybe you should say it more often."

He took a deep breath. "There's no way out of this marriage for you, nor for me. Do you really want to be miserable?"

He was right. There was no way out. And even if there was, what would be the point? My father would marry me off to the next man. Maybe a man like Bibiana's husband. And no matter how much I wanted to deny it, I could imagine developing feelings for the Luca I saw in the restaurant. It wouldn't have hurt so much seeing him with that woman, if I didn't. When he'd touched my hair or kissed me or wrapped his arms around me during the night, I'd felt myself wanting to fall in love with him. I wished I could hate him with all my heart. If Gianna had been in my stead, she would rather have gone through life hating her husband and being miserable than ever giving him and our father the satisfaction of coming to care for him. "No," I said. "But I can't pretend I never saw you with her."

"I don't expect you to, but let's just pretend our marriage begins today. A clean start."

"It's not that easy. What about her? Tonight wasn't the first time you were with her. Do you love her?" My voice trembled as I said it.

Luca noticed, of course. He looked at me as if I was a puzzle he couldn't figure out. "Love? No. I don't have feelings for Grace."

"Then why do you keep seeing her? The truth."

"Because she knows how to suck a cock and because she's a good fuck. Truthful enough?"

I flushed. Luca brushed a finger over my cheek. "I love how you blush whenever I say something dirty. I can't wait to see your blush when I *do* something dirty to you."

Why couldn't he stop touching me? "If you really want to make this marriage work, if you *ever* want the chance to do something dirty to me, then you'll have to stop seeing other women. Maybe other wives don't care, but I won't have you touching me as long as there is anyone else."

Luca nodded. "I promise. I'll touch only you from now on."

I considered him. "Grace won't like it."

"Who gives a fuck what she thinks?"

"Won't her father give you trouble?"

"We pay for his campaigns, and he has a son following in his footsteps who needs our money soon as well. What does he care about a daughter who isn't good for anything but shopping and eventually marrying a rich man?"

The same could be said for me and every other woman in our world. Sons could follow in their father's footsteps—they could become members of the mafia. I still remembered how much Father had celebrated when he'd found out his fourth child was finally a son.

"She probably hoped you'd be that man."

"We don't marry outsiders. Never. She knew that, and it wasn't like she was the only woman I fucked."

I gave him a look. "You said it yourself. You have your needs. So how can you tell me you won't cheat on me again soon if you get tired of waiting for me to sleep with you?"

Luca tilted his head, eyes narrowed in thought. "Do you intend to make me wait long?"

"I think we have very different concepts of the words 'long wait.'"

"I'm not a patient man. If long means a year..." He trailed off. I couldn't believe him. I sent him a reproachful look.

"What do you want me to say, Aria? I kill and blackmail and torture people. I'm the Boss of men who do the same when I order them to, and soon I'll be the Capo dei Capi, the leader of the most powerful crime organization on the East Coast, and probably the US. You thought I'd take you against your will on our wedding night, and now you're angry because I don't want to wait months to sleep with you?"

I closed my eyes. "I'm tired. It's late." It was so late it was actually early.

"No," Luca said, touching my waist. "I want to understand. I'm your husband. You aren't like other girls who can choose the man they're going to lose it to. Are you scared I'm going to be rough with you because of what you saw today? I won't be. I told you I want you to writhe beneath me in pleasure, and while that probably won't happen the first time I take you, I'll make you come as often as you want with my tongue and my fingers until you can come when I'm inside you. I don't mind going slow, but what do you want to wait for?"

I watched him through half-lidded eyes. *For something that will never happen: that you'll want to* make love *to me and not* take *me like I'm your possession.* Part of me didn't want to settle for less; the other part knew I had to. *Love is something girls hope for when they don't know better, something women long for when they lie awake at night, and something they'll only ever get from their children. Men don't have time for such notions.* That's what my father always said. "I won't make you wait for months," I said instead of what I really wanted to say, and then I finally fell asleep.

chapter *ten*

LUCA CANCELLED HIS PLANS FOR THE NEXT DAY AND SENT MATTEO out to do whatever needed to be done. As a woman in our world, you quickly learned not to ask too many questions because the answers were rarely good.

Luca got ready first and when I walked into the kitchen dressed and showered, he was staring into the fridge with a frown on his face. "Can you cook?"

I snorted. "Don't tell me you've never made breakfast for yourself?"

"I usually grab something on my way to work, except on the days when Marianna is here and prepares something for me." His eyes scanned my body. I'd chosen shorts, a tank top and sandals since it was supposed to get really hot today. "I love your legs."

I shook my head, then walked toward him to peek into the fridge. He didn't step back and our arms brushed. This time I managed not to flinch. His touch wasn't uncomfortable and when he didn't startle me, I could actually imagine enjoying it.

The fridge was well stocked. The problem was I'd never cooked either, but I wouldn't mention that to Luca. I grabbed the egg carton and red peppers, and set them down on the kitchen counter. It couldn't be that hard to prepare an omelet. I'd watched our cook a few times in the past.

Luca leaned against the kitchen island and crossed his arms as I grabbed a pan from the cupboard and turned on the stove. I glanced over my shoulder at him. "Won't you help me? You can chop the peppers. You know how to handle a knife from what I hear."

That made the corners of his lips twitch, but he pulled a knife out of the block and stepped up to my side. The top of my head came only up to his chest with my flat sandals. I had to admit I kind of liked it. I handed him the pepper and pointed toward a wooden cutting board, because I got the feeling Luca would have started chopping right on the expensive black granite countertops. We worked in silence but Luca kept sneaking glances at me. I put a bit of butter into the pan, then seasoned the beaten eggs. I wasn't sure if

I needed to add milk or cream, but decided against it. I poured the eggs into the sizzling pan.

Luca pointed his knife at the chopped peppers. "What happens to these?"

"Shit," I whispered. The peppers should have gone in first.

"Have you ever cooked?"

I ignored him and chucked the peppers into the pan with the eggs. I'd turned the stove to maximum heat, and soon the hint of a burning smell reached my nose. I quickly grabbed a spatula and tried to flip the omelet over, but it stuck to the pan. Luca was watching me with a smirk.

"Why don't you make coffee for us?" I snapped as I scraped the half-burnt eggs from the bottom of the pan.

When I thought the eggs were safe to eat, I spooned them onto two plates. They didn't really look all that tasty. Luca's brows rose when I put a plate down in front of him. He sank down on the barstool and I hopped onto the one beside him. I watched him as he picked up the fork and speared a piece of egg, then brought it to his lips. He swallowed, but it was obvious he wasn't too impressed. I took a bite as well and almost spat it back out. The eggs were too dry and too salty. I dropped my fork and gulped down half of my coffee, not even caring that it was hot and black. "Oh my God, that's disgusting."

There was a hint of amusement in Luca's face. The more relaxed expression made him look so much more approachable. "Maybe we should go out for breakfast."

I glowered at my coffee. "How hard can it be to make an omelet?"

Luca let out what might have been a laugh. Then his eyes flitted back down to my bare legs, which were almost touching his. He put his hand down on my knee, and I froze with my cup against my lips. He didn't do anything, just lightly traced his thumb back and forth over my skin. "What would you like to do today?"

I pondered that, even if his hand was very distracting. I was alternating between wanting to shove it off my knee and ask him to keep caressing me. "The morning after our wedding night, you asked me if I knew how to fight, so maybe you can teach me how to use a knife or a gun, and maybe some self-defense."

Surprise crossed Luca's face. "Thinking about using them against me?"

I huffed. "As if I could ever beat you in a fair fight."

"I don't fight fair."

Of course he didn't. "So will you teach me?"

"I want to teach you a lot of things." His fingers tightened on my knee.

"Luca," I said quietly. "I'm serious. I know I have Romero and you, but I want to be able to defend myself if something happens. You said it yourself, the Bratva won't care that I'm a woman."

That got him. He nodded. "Okay. We have a gym where we work out and do fight training. We could go there."

I smiled, excited about getting out of the penthouse and doing something useful. "I'll grab my workout clothes." I hopped off the stool and ran upstairs. I snatched up my mobile from my nightstand and sent Gianna a short text to let her know I was okay. Knowing her and dreading the flood of questions she'd be firing at me, I didn't take my phone with me as I headed back downstairs.

Thirty minutes later we parked in front of a shabby building after having grabbed muffins for breakfast. I was bursting with excitement, and I was glad to have something to distract myself from what had happened yesterday. Luca and I got out of the car, and he carried our bags as we headed through a rusty steel door. Security cameras were everywhere, and a middle-aged man sat in a nook that held a table and chair as well as a TV. Two guns were in his holster. He straightened when he saw Luca, then he spotted me and his eyes grew wide.

"My wife," Luca said with a hint of warning, and the man's gaze jerked away from me. Luca put a hand on the small of my back and guided me through another door that led into a huge hall. There was a boxing ring, all kinds of exercise machines, dummies for fight and knife training, and a corner with mats where a few men were sparring. I was the only woman.

Luca grimaced. "Our changing rooms are men only. We don't usually have female visitors."

"I know you'll make sure nobody sees me naked."

"You bet I will."

I laughed, and a few faces turned our way, then more until everyone was staring. They quickly returned to what they'd been doing when Luca led me toward a door on the side, but they kept throwing badly disguised glances my way. A few of the older men called out a greeting to Luca. He opened the door, then stopped. "Let me check if someone's in there." I nodded, then leaned against the wall as Luca disappeared inside the changing room. The moment he was gone, I could feel the full force of the men's attention shifting my way. I tried not to let them see how nervous their scrutiny made me and almost breathed a sigh of relief when Luca came back out, followed by a few men who pretended they didn't notice me. I wondered what Luca had told them.

"Come." He held the door open for me, and we walked into a low-ceilinged room filled with humidity and the smell of too many hard-working male bodies. I scrunched my nose up. Luca laughed. "We're not catering to sensitive female noses."

I grabbed my bag from him and walked toward a locker. Luca followed and set his own bag down on the scratched wooden bench.

"Aren't you going to give me some privacy?" I asked, hands on the hem of my shirt.

Luca raised one eyebrow at me before removing his holster and then pulling his own shirt over his head, revealing his muscled and tanned torso. He dropped his shirt on the bench, then reached for his belt, that challenging look still in his eyes.

Gritting my teeth, I turned my back to him and slid my tank top over my head. I reached behind me to open the clasp of my bra, but Luca's hand was there and did it for me expertly. Bastard. Of course, he could open a bra with one finger. I grabbed my jogging bra and put it on, trying not to think about Luca, who was undoubtedly watching every move. I stripped off my shorts and could have kicked myself for choosing a thong this morning. I pulled it down as well, and heard Luca sucking in his breath when I bent forward slightly. My cheeks blasted with heat, realizing what kind of view I'd just given him. I snatched a pair of the plain black panties I always wore when I worked out on the treadmill, then I put my jogging shorts on over them and turned back around to Luca. He'd put on black sweatpants and an ultra-tight white shirt that showcased his spectacular body. There was a bulge in his pants. All because of my butt?

"That's what you're wearing for self-defense lessons?"

I looked down at myself. "I don't have anything else. This is what I wear when I go jogging." The shorts were tight and ended high up on my thighs, but I didn't like too much fabric when I ran.

"You realize I'll have to kick every guy's ass who looks at you the wrong way, right? And looking like that, my men will have a hard time not looking at you the wrong way."

I shrugged. "It's not my job to make them control themselves. Just because I'm wearing revealing clothes doesn't mean I'm inviting them to look. If they can't behave themselves, that's their problem."

Luca led me out of the changing room and toward the sparring mats. The men there immediately backed away, pointedly not looking at me. I followed Luca toward a display of knives. His eyes scanned them, then he chose one with a long smooth blade and handed it to me. He didn't take one for himself.

He positioned himself across from me, looking utterly relaxed. He must have known everyone was watching us, but he acted as if he couldn't care less. This wasn't private. He had to put up a show for his men. "Attack me, but try not to cut yourself."

"Won't you get a knife too?"

Luca shook his head. "I don't need one. I'll have yours in a minute."

I narrowed my eyes at his self-assured tone. He was probably right, but I didn't like him saying it. "So what am I supposed to do?"

"Try to land a hit. If you manage to cut me, you win. I want to see how you move."

I took a breath and tried to forget the men watching me. I tightened my grip on the knife, then I dashed forward. Luca moved fast. He dodged my jab, grabbed my wrist and whirled me around until my back collided with his chest.

"You don't have my knife yet," I gasped out. His fingers around my wrist tightened a fraction, uncomfortably but not painfully. His lips brushed my ear. "I would have to hurt you to get it. I could break your wrist, for example, or just bruise it." He released me and I stumbled forward.

"Again," Luca said. I tried a few times, but didn't get anywhere close to cutting him. For my next try, I decided to stop playing fair. I advanced on him, then as he made a grab for me, I aimed a kick between his legs. The men cheered, but Luca's hand caught my foot before it could make impact and before I knew what was happening I landed on my back with a heavy thud. My breath rushed out of me and the knife slipped out of my hand. I squeezed my eyes shut. Luca touched my stomach, and my muscles constricted under his warm palm. "Are you okay?" he asked quietly.

I opened my eyes. "Yeah. Just trying to catch my breath." Then I scanned the crowd. "Don't you have a soldier who's only five foot something and terrified of his own shadow who would be willing to fight me?"

"My men aren't terrified of anything," Luca said loudly. He held out his hand and pulled me to my feet. He addressed his soldiers. "Anyone willing to fight my wife?"

Of course nobody stepped forward. They were probably worried Luca would skin them alive. Some of them shook their heads, chuckling.

The shadow of a grin crossed Luca's face. "You'll have to fight me."

A few more attack attempts later, I was out of breath and annoyed by my inability to hurt Luca the tiniest bit, but then a chance offered itself. He held me against his body and his upper arm was close to my face, so I turned and bit him. He was so startled he actually released me and I tried to jab him with the knife, but he gripped my wrist. "Did you bite me?" he asked as he stared at my teeth marks on his bicep.

"Not hard enough. There isn't even blood," I said.

Luca's shoulders twitched once, then again. He was fighting laughter. Not the effect I'd intended when I bit him, but I had to admit I loved the sound of his deep chuckle. "I think you've done enough damage for one day," he said.

We grabbed something to eat on our way home, then settled on the rattan sofa on the roof terrace with a glass of wine.

"I'm surprised," I said eventually. Luca and I sat close together, almost touching, and his arm was thrown over the backrest behind me but so far he had held back. "I didn't think you'd really try."

"I told you I would. I keep my word."

"I bet this is hard for you." I gestured at the space between us.

"You have no idea. I want to kiss you really fucking bad."

I hesitated. Kissing him had felt good. Luca set the glass down, then he moved a bit closer and touched my waist. "Tell me you don't want me to kiss you."

I parted my lips but nothing came out. Luca's eyes darkened and he leaned toward me, capturing my mouth in a kiss, and I lost myself in the sensation of his tongue and lips. Luca didn't push it, never moved his hand from my waist, but he'd begun rubbing my skin there lightly and his other hand massaged my scalp. How could I feel that all the way between my legs?

Eventually I lay back on the sofa, Luca propped up above me. I could feel myself getting wet but I didn't have the time or necessary focus to feel embarrassed. Luca's kisses kept me busy. The tingling in my center became difficult to ignore, and I tried to alleviate the tension by pressing my legs together.

Luca drew back with a knowing expression. Heat rose into my cheeks.

"I could make you feel good, Aria," he murmured, his hand on my waist tightening. "You want to come, don't you?"

Oh my God, yes. I'd overheard girls in school go into detail about how amazing it could be, but I'd never managed to make myself feel anything close to what they'd described. My body was screaming for it. "I'm fine. Thank you."

Luca choked on a laugh. "You are so stubborn." He didn't say it in a mean way. His lips came down on mine again and I could tell he gave it his all, determined to break my resolve, and a few times I got close. I was throbbing between my legs but I wouldn't give in, not so soon. I had more control than that.

That night I fell asleep with Luca's arms around me and his erection an insistent presence against my upper thigh. Maybe we really could make this marriage work.

chapter *eleven*

When I woke the next morning, I was alone in bed. I sat up, disappointed that Luca hadn't woken me. I slipped out of bed when he came into the bedroom from the hallway, already dressed in black, with a chest holster that held two knives and two guns, and who knew how many more holsters on the rest of his body with more weapons. "Are you leaving already?"

He grimaced. "The Bratva got one of ours. They left him in tiny pieces around one of our clubs."

"Somebody I know?" I asked with dread. Luca shook his head. "Will the police get involved?"

"Not if I can help it." Luca cupped my face. "I'll try to be home early, okay?"

I nodded. He lowered his head, watching me the entire time to see if I would pull back. His lips brushed over mine. I opened my mouth for him and sank into the kiss, but it was over too quick. I watched his back as he left. Then I picked up the phone and called Gianna.

"I thought you'd never call," was the first thing out of her mouth.

I smiled. "I haven't even showered yet, and it's only eight in Chicago. You can't have been awake for long."

"You didn't call yesterday and all I got was a short text. I was sick with worry. I couldn't sleep because of *you*. I hate that we are so far apart and I can't see for myself if you're okay. Are you okay?"

"Yes, I am." I told her about my conversation with Luca and how we'd spent yesterday together.

"How noble of him to agree to not cheat on you again and actually try to make the marriage work. Give that man flowers."

"He isn't a good man, Gianna. There are no good men in our world. But I think he really wants to try. And I want it too."

"Why don't you ask him if I can come visit for a few days? I don't have school for another two weeks and I'm bored out of my mind without you. We could spend a couple of days at the beach in the Hamptons and go shopping in Manhattan."

"What about Father? Did you ask him?"

"He told me to ask you and Luca."

"I will ask him. I don't think he'll mind. It's not like he's home very often at the moment. Most days I'm alone with Romero."

"Why don't you ask Luca if you can go to college? You've got perfect grades. You would have no trouble getting into Columbia."

"What for? I won't ever be allowed to work. It's too dangerous."

"You could help Luca with his clubs. You could be his secretary or whatever. You'll go crazy if you stay in that penthouse all the time."

"Don't worry, I'll be fine," I said, even though I really wasn't sure. Gianna had a point. "I will talk to Luca about your visit. Now I really need to take a shower and grab something to eat."

"Call me as soon as possible. I need to book a flight."

I smiled. "I will. Stay out of trouble."

"You too."

I hung up. Then I got ready and dressed in a breezy summer dress. It was sunny outside and I wanted to walk through Central Park. When I stepped into the living room, Romero was sitting at the dining room table with a cup of coffee in front of him.

"Was Luca very angry with you?" I asked as I walked past him toward the huge open kitchen. Homemade carrot cake set on the counter and I could hear Marianna humming somewhere. She was probably cleaning. Romero got up, took his cup and leaned against the kitchen island. "He wasn't happy. You could have been killed. I'm supposed to protect you."

"What's Luca doing today?"

Romero shook his head.

"What is he doing? I want to know details. Why is he taking so many guns with him?"

"He, Matteo and a few others are going to find the guys who killed our man, and then they're going to get revenge."

"That sounds dangerous." A hint of worry filled me. Revenge was never the end of things. The Bratva would take revenge in turn for Luca's revenge. It was a never-ending cycle

"Luca and Matteo have been doing this for a long time. They are the best, and so are the men with them."

"And instead of being in on the fun, you have to babysit me."

Romero gave a shrug, then he smiled. "It's an honor."

I rolled my eyes. "I'd like to go jogging in Central Park."

"Will you try to run away again?"

"Why would I? There's nowhere I can run. And I doubt you'll let me escape again. You look fit enough."

Romero straightened. "Okay." I could tell that he was still suspicious of my motives.

I put on my shorts, a tank top and my running shoes, then went back out. Romero had changed into sweatpants and a T-shirt. He kept a stash of clothes in one of our guest bedrooms, but he lived in an apartment about ten minutes from here. "Where have you hidden your guns?"

"That's my secret," he said with a rare grin, then he caught himself and put on his professional face.

Romero was fit and could easily keep up with me as we jogged through the many pathways in Central Park for the next hour. It felt wonderful to actually run outside for once instead of always being limited to the treadmill. I felt free and almost as if I belonged among all the people doing ordinary things, like walking their dogs or playing baseball. Maybe Luca would run with me one day, when the Russians weren't giving him so much trouble anymore. But when would that ever be?

Later that day I sat on the roof terrace, watching the sunset, my legs pulled up against my body. Romero was checking his phone. "Luca will have more time for you soon."

I looked at him. Had I appeared lonely to him? "Did he tell you when he'd be home today?"

"He hasn't written yet," he said slowly.

"That's a bad sign, right?"

Romero didn't say anything, only frowned down at his phone.

I went inside when it became too cold, put on my nightgown and curled up on the couch, turning on the TV. I couldn't help but get more worried as the clock edged closer to midnight, but eventually I drifted off.

I woke when I was lifted off the couch. My eyes fluttered open and I peered up into Luca's face. It was too dark to make out much. Romero must have extinguished the lights at some point. "Luca?" I murmured.

He didn't say anything. I put a hand against his chest. His shirt was slick with something—water? Blood?

His breathing was even, steps measured. His heartbeat was calm under my palm. But I couldn't read his mood. It was strange. He carried me up the stairs as if I weighed nothing. We reached our bedroom and he put me down on the bed. I could only see his tall shape looming above me. Why wasn't he saying anything?

I stretched and fumbled for the main switch beside the bed. I brushed it with my fingertips and the lights came on, and I gasped. Luca's shirt was covered in blood. Soaked in it. There was a small cut at Luca's throat and if the rips in his shirt were any indication, he probably had more wounds. Then my eyes found his face and I became very still, like a fawn trying to blend in so as not to attract the attention of the wolf. I'd thought I'd seen Luca's darkness on a few occasions, had thought I'd glimpsed the monster beneath the civil mask before. Now I realized I hadn't. His expression was void of emotion, but his eyes made the hairs on my neck rise.

I licked my lips. "Luca?"

He started unbuttoning his shirt, revealing small cuts and a longer wound below his ribs. His skin was covered with blood. But it couldn't all have come from him, especially not all the blood on the shirt. It worried me that he still hadn't spoken. He shed his shirt and dropped it on the ground. Then he unbuckled his belt.

"Luca," I said. "You're scaring me. What happened?"

He pushed his pants down and stepped out of them. He was barefoot and now only in his briefs as he knelt on the bed and brought one knee between my legs. I began to regret wearing only a nightgown. He slowly moved up until his head hovered over me. Terror gripped my throat, turned my heartbeat into a flutter.

His eyes made me want to bolt, to cry and scream, to escape. Instead I lifted my hand and cupped his cheek. His expression shifted, a chink in the monstrous mask. He leaned into the touch, then he lowered his face and pressed it into the crook of my neck. He breathed in deeply and didn't move for a long time. I tried not to panic. My hand was shaking against his cheek.

"Luca?" I said softly.

He raised his head again. I could see a flicker of the Luca I knew. He slid off the bed and headed for the bathroom. When he was out of sight, I let out a deep breath. Whatever had gone down today must have been horrible. I sat up as I listened to the running shower. In what kind of mood would Luca return into the bedroom? The monster in check, or almost unleashed like a moment ago?

The water stopped and I quickly lay down on my side of the bed and pulled the covers up. A few minutes later, the door opened and Luca walked in with a towel around his waist. It was white, but a few droplets of blood had dripped from his wound and stained the fabric. He didn't walk toward the cupboard to grab boxer shorts as he usually did; instead he came directly toward the bed. When he reached for the towel, I averted my eyes and turned on my other side, my back toward him. He lifted the blanket and the mattress shifted under his weight. He pressed up against me, his hand curled over my hip in an almost bruising grip before he turned me toward him.

My mind screamed at me to stop him. He was completely naked and in a terrifying mood. He'd spent the day picking up the pieces of one of his men and the remainder of it killing his enemies. He grabbed the hem of my nightgown and began pulling it up. I put my hand over his.

"Luca," I whispered.

His eyes met mine. I relaxed slightly. There was still darkness in them, but it was more contained. "I want to feel your body against mine tonight. I want to hold you."

I could almost hear the unspoken words: *I need you*. I swallowed. "Only hold me?"

"I swear." His voice was gruff, as if he'd spent hours screaming orders.

I lowered my hand and let him pull my nightgown off. He released a low breath as he gazed at my naked breasts. I had to fight the urge to cover myself. His fingertips brushed the hem of my panties, but when I tensed they retreated, and he rolled onto his back and lifted me on top of him. I straddled his stomach, my knees on either side of him, my breasts pressed against his chest. I tried to keep my weight off him because I didn't want to hurt his wounds, but he wrapped one arm around my back and pressed me tightly against him. His other hand touched my butt, making me jump. He began moving his thumb across my lower back and ass, and I relaxed slowly. The entire time his eyes were boring into mine, and with every passing moment, another tiny piece of the darkness dissipated.

"Doesn't your cut need stitches?"

He bent forward and kissed me sweetly. "Tomorrow." He kept stroking my backside and kissing me slowly, as if he wanted to savor every moment. I was completely overwhelmed but it felt good. I loved that he was suddenly so gentle. If he was like that when he took my virginity, then maybe it wouldn't be so bad. My eyelids felt heavy, but I couldn't look away from Luca. I touched his throat, an inch below the cut. I wasn't sure why, but I leaned forward and pressed a featherlight kiss against the wound. It was small and wouldn't need stitches, not like the one below his ribs. When I drew back, Luca looked almost surprised. His hand moved lower, cupping my ass cheek. His little finger was almost touching me *there*. He squeezed my cheek, and for a moment his finger brushed my opening through the fabric.

I sucked in a breath, shocked by the jolt the small touch had sent through me. Heat gathered between my legs and I could feel myself getting wet. I squirmed in embarrassment, not wanting Luca to realize that a bare brush and his stroking of my butt had caused such a reaction. Maybe I wasn't experienced, but I'd been imagining certain things, had caressed myself on many nights. It wasn't that I was frigid. Luca's body turned me on. Maybe I wanted love, but my body wanted something else. The feeling of Luca's strong chest and muscled stomach under me, his gentle kisses, his soft touch…they made me want something more, even if my mind told me it was a bad idea.

Luca's eyes narrowed a fraction as he studied me, like I was a difficult equation he wanted to figure out. Then he lightly grazed the crotch of my panties with his fingertips, and I knew he could feel it. *I* could feel that the thin fabric was soaked. My cheeks flamed in mortification and I lowered my eyes, but I couldn't bring myself to slide off him or even close my legs. His fingertips against my core felt good, even if they'd stopped moving.

"Look at me, Aria," Luca said in a rough voice.

I peered into his eyes even as my face felt close to exploding from shame. "Are you embarrassed because of this?" He traced a finger over my wet panties. My pelvis arched and I exhaled harshly.

I couldn't say anything. My lips parted as small sounds that weren't quite moans slid out. Luca moved his finger up and down, gently, teasingly, and small shivers of pleasure slithered through my body. I'd always thought that passion and orgasms came as a forceful wave leaving nothing in their wake, something almost intimidating, but this was like a slow trickling; a deliciously sweet tension mounting to something bigger.

I quivered on top of Luca, my fingers clinging to his shoulders. He never sped up his stroking, but the pleasure rose with every brush. His eyes bored into mine as he slid two fingers over my opening, then between my folds, and pressed down on my clit. How could this feel so intense? He wasn't even touching my skin. I gasped and trembled as sparks of pleasure shot through my body. I buried my face against Luca's neck as I clung to him. His finger rubbed my clit through my panties, slower and slower until he simply rested his hand possessively over my folds.

Luca pressed his face into my hair. "God, you're so wet, Aria. If you knew how much I want you right now, you'd run away." He laughed darkly. "I can almost feel your wetness on my cock."

I didn't say anything, only tried to calm my breathing. Luca's heartbeat was strong and fast beneath my cheek. He shifted and his length briefly brushed my inner thigh. He felt hot and hard.

"Do you want me to touch you?" I said in the quietest whisper. I was half-scared and half-excited about seeing him naked and actually touching him. I wanted to lay my claim on him, wanted to make him forget about the women of his past. Luca's hand on my back tightened and he drew in a deep breath, his chest expanding under me.

"No," he growled, and I lifted my head in confusion and a little hurt. Some of it must have showed, because Luca smiled grimly. "I'm not quite myself yet, Aria. There's too much darkness on the surface, too much blood and anger. Today was bad." He shook his head. "When I came home today and found you lying on the sofa, so innocent and vulnerable and mine..." Something flickered in his eyes, some of the darkness he'd mentioned. "I'm glad you don't know the thoughts that ran through my head then. You are my wife and I swore to protect you, if necessary even from myself."

"You think you'd lose control?" I whispered.

"I know it."

"Maybe you underestimate yourself." I trailed my fingers over his shoulders. I wasn't sure if I was trying to convince him or myself. He had scared me, there was no denying it. But he had snapped out of it.

"Maybe you trust me too much." He ran a finger over my spine, sending a new wave of tingling toward my core. "When I lay you down on the bed like a sacrificial lamb, you should have run."

"Someone once told me not to run from monsters because they give chase."

The ghost of a smile crossed his face. "Next time, you run. Or if you can't, you ram your knee into my balls."

He wasn't joking. "If I'd done that today, you would have lost control. The only reason you didn't was because I treated you like my husband, not a monster."

He traced my lips with his thumb, then brushed my cheek. "You are far too beautiful and innocent to be married to someone like me, but I'm too much of a selfish bastard to ever let you go. You are mine. Forever."

"I know," I said, then lowered my cheek back to his chest. Luca extinguished the lights, and I fell asleep listening to his heartbeat. I knew a normal person would have run from Luca, but I'd grown up among predators. Decent, normal guys with jobs that didn't involve breaking laws were a foreign species to me. And deep down, a primal part of me couldn't imagine being with someone who wasn't an alpha like Luca. It thrilled me to know that a man like him could be gentle with me. It thrilled me that he was mine and I was his.

The sky was only just turning gray over New York's skyline when I woke the next morning. I was still lying on Luca's chest, my naked breasts pressed against his hot skin, but I'd slid down his body overnight and his stiff length was pressed against my leg. I shifted carefully and peered up into Luca's face. His eyes were closed and he looked so peaceful in sleep, it was hard to belief that the same face had harbored so much violence and darkness last night.

Curiosity gripped me. I'd never seen a naked erection, but I was worried about waking Luca. After what he'd said, I really didn't want to risk him losing control. I tried to peek over my shoulder at Luca's boner, but with the way we were positioned I'd have to break my neck to see it.

Suddenly a buzzing came from the nightstand, and Luca sat up so fast I squeaked. He took me with him, one arm steadying me around the waist, the other reaching for his mobile. But the new position had made me slide down his body and now his erection was between my legs, its length pressed up against my core. I was practically riding it like a broom. I'd never been more grateful for my underwear.

I stiffened and so did Luca, the mobile already pressed against his ear. I tried to maneuver into a less problematic position, but that only made his cock rub against me. He groaned and I froze. Luca's eyes dilated as his fingers on my waist tightened.

"I'm fine, Matteo," he rasped. "I'm *fucking* fine. No. I can handle this. I don't need to see the Doc. Now let me sleep." Luca hung up, put the phone back on the nightstand and stared at me. I was so stiff he could have used me as an ironing board.

He sank back slowly, with all the control only lots of sit-ups could give you. I remained in a sitting position, straddling his hips, but quickly draped one arm in front of my breasts. Now that he was lying down, his erection was no longer touching me. Gathering my courage, I swung my leg over his hips, accidentally brushing Luca's boner.

"Fuck," Luca growled, jerking beneath me. I had to stifle a smile. I knelt beside him, my arm still covering my breasts, and then I allowed myself to look. Wow. I had nothing to compare him to, but I couldn't imagine he could be any bigger. He was long and thick, and circumcised. Gianna had won her stupid bet.

"You're going to be the death of me, Aria," Luca said in a low voice.

I turned, embarrassed. I'd been *staring*. There was hunger on Luca's face when I met his eyes. One of his hands rested on his stomach, while the other was thrown over his head. His abs were taut with tension; actually, every inch of his body seemed that way. Suddenly I was overcome with shyness. Why had I thought it was a good idea to take a look at him? I risked another peek.

"If you keep looking at my cock with that stunned expression, I'm going to combust."

"I'm sorry if my expression bothers you, but this is new for me. I've never seen a naked man. Every first I'll experience will be with you, *so*..."

Luca sat up. His voice dropped an octave. "It doesn't bother me. It's fucking hot, and I'll enjoy every first you'll share with me." He stroked my cheek. "You don't even realize how much you turn me on."

With him sitting, our faces were close and Luca pulled me in for a kiss. I pressed my palm against his shoulder, then slowly ran it down his chest to his stomach. Luca paused the kiss. "Last night you asked me if I wanted you to touch me."

"Yeah," I said, my breath catching. "Do you want me to touch you now?"

The fire in his eyes darkened. "Fuck yes. More than anything." He reached out for my arm pressed against my breasts. "Let me see you." He curled his fingers around my wrist but didn't pull. I hesitated. He'd seen them yesterday, but now I felt more exposed. Slowly I eased my arm down. I sat very still as Luca's eyes roamed over me. "I know they're not big."

"You're fucking beautiful, Aria."

I didn't know what to say.

"Do you want to touch me now?" he said in a low voice.

I nodded and licked my lips. I glanced down, then tentatively reached out and ran my finger over his length. He felt soft, hot and firm. Luca let out a harsh breath, the muscles in his arms straining from holding himself up. I brushed the tip, marveling at how soft he was. Luca gritted his teeth.

I felt a strange sense of power over him as I ran my fingertips up and down slowly, fascinated by his silkiness.

Luca quivered under my touch. "Take me in your hand," he said in a low voice.

I wrapped my fingers around his shaft lightly, worried about hurting him. I moved my hand down, then up, surprised at how heavy he felt in my palm. Luca lay back. I knew he was watching me but I couldn't meet his gaze, too mortified by my own courage.

"You can grip harder," he said after a few more of my tentative strokes.

I tightened my fingers.

"Harder. It won't fall off."

I flushed and turned away, dropping my hand. "I didn't want to hurt you." God, this was embarrassing. I couldn't even do this. Maybe Luca should go back to his whore Grace. She knew what to do.

"Hey," Luca said calmly, pulling me against him. "I was teasing you. It's okay." He kissed me. His mouth moved against mine, unyielding but gentle, and his hand snaked down my arm, my hip and over the curve of my butt until his finger slipped between my legs and grazed over my folds. He slid back and forth lightly before moving the tip of his finger under my panties. I held my breath at the feel of him against my bare skin. He dipped between my folds, then slid up to my clit, coating it with my wetness. I moaned against his lips before slipping my tongue into his mouth to dance with his. Pleasure swept through me as he twirled his finger over my sensitive nub.

He tore his mouth away from mine, his eyes boring into me. "Want to try again?" he rasped with a nod toward his hard length.

His finger flicked over me again and I gasped, barely able to think straight, much less form a coherent sentence. My body ached with a need I'd never felt before. I slid my hand down his muscled torso, following the fine trail of dark hair to his erection. I curled my hand around it and it jumped under my touch.

Luca's fingers slid faster against my wet flesh. His steady caresses made me pant, but I was too far gone to care. Luca covered my hand around his length with his, showing me how hard to grip him. Then he moved our hands up and down his shaft. I watched in fascination. We moved faster and harder than I would have dared. Luca's fingers between my folds rubbed me faster too, until I could barely breathe and my pulse pounded in my veins. I was about to topple over the edge.

"Luca," I gasped and he flicked my clit, sending me spiraling out of control. Spasms shot through my body as I moaned. My hand pumped Luca's length even faster, and with a guttural growl Luca's release washed over him. I shivered against him as I watched him come over our hands and his stomach. My nipples were hard and rubbed against his chest, sending ripples of pleasure through me. His erection, still throbbing in my palm, softened slowly. Luca pulled his fingers out from beneath my panties and rested them on my butt.

I closed my eyes, listening to the thundering of his heart. Luca kissed the top of my head, startling me with the loving gesture. My heart burst with new hope. Gradually our breathing slowed. Luca reached out for a tissue box on the nightstand and handed me a tissue, before wiping himself clean. I felt self-conscious as I cleaned his sperm from my hand. I couldn't believe I'd touched him like that. I was still sensitive between my legs, and yet I wanted to feel his fingers again. Was it wrong that I enjoyed Luca's touch so much?

He was my husband, but still. My mother had always treated sex like something only men desired. Women simply did their duty. Luca rubbed my arm and I decided not to think about it too much. I'd do what felt right. I released a small breath, but then my eyes focused on the cut below Luca's ribs. Blood was trickling from it.

I sat up. "You're bleeding." I'd forgotten all about it. "Does it hurt?"

Luca looked utterly relaxed. He cast his gaze down to his wound. "Not much. It's nothing. I'm used to it."

I touched the skin below the cut. "It needs stitches. What if it gets infected?"

"Maybe you'll get lucky and become a young widow."

I glared. "That's not funny." Not after what we'd just done. I felt closer to him than ever, and my father would only find me a new husband anyway.

"If it bothers you so much, why don't you grab the first-aid kit from the bathroom and bring it to me."

I jumped out of bed and rushed into the bathroom. "Where is it?"

"In the drawer below the sink."

There wasn't only one first-aid kit. There were about two dozen of them. I picked one and returned to the bedroom but before I joined Luca in bed, I grabbed my nightgown from the ground and put it on. Luca sat against the headboard, still gloriously naked. I concentrated on his torso, embarrassed by his unabashed nudity.

Luca stroked my cheek when I settled next to him. "Still too shy to look at me after what happened." He tugged at the hem of my nightgown. "I liked you better without it."

I pursed my lips. "What do you want me to do?" I set the first-aid kit between us and opened it.

"Many things," Luca murmured.

I rolled my eyes. "With your cut."

"There are disinfectant wipes. Clean my wound and I'll prepare the needle."

I ripped open one of the packets. The overpowering smell of disinfectant clogged my nose. I pulled the wipe out, unfolded it and dabbed it against the cut. Luca twitched but didn't make a sound. "Does it burn?"

"I'm fine," he said simply. "Wipe harder."

I did, and though he jerked a few times, he never told me to stop. Eventually I threw the wipe into the trash and leaned back. Luca pierced his skin with the needle and began stitching himself up, his hands steady and sure. Watching him made me queasy. I couldn't imagine doing that to myself, but as my eyes wandered over Luca's body and the many scars, I realized it probably wasn't the first time he did this. When Luca was satisfied with his job, he chucked away the needle.

"We need to cover it," I said. I rummaged in the kit for bandages, but Luca shook his head. "It'll heal faster if it's allowed to breathe."

"Really? Are you sure? What if dirt gets in?"

Luca chuckled. "You don't need to worry. This won't be the last time I'll come home injured." Was I worried? Yes. And I didn't like the thought of him taking his health so lightly.

Luca opened his arms. "Come."

"Don't you have to leave?" I glanced at the clock. It was only eight, but on most days Luca had been gone by then.

"Not today. The Bratva is dealt with for the moment. I'll have to be in one of the Famiglia's clubs in the afternoon."

I smiled slightly. I couldn't help it. Glad I didn't have to be alone all day again, I snuggled against Luca's side and he wrapped his arm around me.

"I didn't expect you to look so happy," he said quietly.

"I'm lonely." I hated how weak that made me sound, but it was the truth. Luca's fingers on my arm tightened.

"I have a few cousins you could hang out with. I'm sure they'd enjoy going shopping with you."

"Why does everyone think I want to go shopping?"

"Then do something else. Have a coffee, or go to a spa, or I don't know."

"I still have a spa certificate that I got at my bridal shower."

"See? If you want I can ask a few of my cousins."

I shook my head. "I'm not too keen on meeting with another one of your cousins after what Cosima did."

"What did she do?" He grew rigid beneath me.

I drew back, looking at Luca. Then I realized I'd never told him how I'd found him in bed with Grace, and after all the confusion of the last few days he'd never asked. He'd probably had more than enough on his plate with the Bratva.

"She gave me the letter that led me to you and Grace." Saying her name made my stomach turn again, and unwanted memories resurfaced. I sat up, away from Luca's warmth. I drew my legs up against my chest, overwhelmed by all that had happened.

Luca pushed himself into a sitting position and pressed a kiss against my shoulder. "Cosima gave you a letter that told you to go the apartment?" His voice was tight with barely controlled anger.

I nodded, then swallowed before I dared to speak. "And a key. It's still in my bag."

"That fucking bitch," he growled.

"Who?"

"Both of them. Grace and Cosima. They're friends. Grace must have put Cosima up to this. That cunt."

I flinched away from the fury in his voice. He let out a harsh breath and sneaked an arm around my waist, pulling me against his chest and burying his face in my hair.

"Grace wanted to humiliate me. She looked really happy when I found you."

"I bet," he said. "She's a fucking rat trying to humiliate a queen. She's nothing." Wow, he was furious. And I couldn't help but feel schadenfreude toward Grace.

"How did she react when you told her that you couldn't see her anymore?"

He was silent. I tensed. "You promised you wouldn't see her or other women again." My voice shook and I tried to pull away from him, but he held me fast. Had he lied to me? I couldn't believe I'd believed him, couldn't believe I'd let him touch me there, and actually touched him in turn.

"I did, and I won't. But I didn't talk to Grace. Why should I? I don't owe her an explanation, just like I don't owe a fucking explanation to the other sluts I fucked." His body might have been made from stone, he was so tense. I wanted to believe him. He grabbed my chin between his thumb and index finger and tilted my face around until I was looking at him. "You are the only one I want. I'll keep my promise, Aria."

"So you won't see her again."

"Oh, I will see her again to tell her what I think about her little stunt."

"Don't."

He frowned.

"I don't want you to talk to her again. Let's just forget her." I could see that he didn't want to forget. "Please."

He exhaled, then nodded. "I don't like it, but if that's what you want..."

"It is," I said decidedly. "Let's not even talk about her anymore. Pretend she doesn't exist."

Luca lifted his hand and rubbed his thumb over my lower lip. "Your lips are too fucking kissable." I ducked my head to hide my pleased smile.

"There's something I wanted to talk to you about," I said.

"More bad news?"

"Well, I guess that depends on your viewpoint. I want Gianna to visit me. Her school doesn't begin for another two weeks, and I miss her."

"It's been only a few days since you saw her."

"I know."

"Where would she stay?"

"I don't know. Maybe in our guest room?" We had three of them on the lower floor of the penthouse.

"Your sister is a major pain in the ass."

I gave him a pleading look.

"How about a deal?" he said in a husky voice.

Nerves fluttered in my stomach. "A deal?"

"Don't look so nervous." Luca smiled sardonically. "I'm not going to ask you to sleep with me so you can see your sister. I'm not that big of an asshole."

"No?" I teased, and he slammed his lips against me in a kiss that sent lightning sensations all the way down to my toes.

"No," he said against my lips. "But I'd like to explore your body."

I raised my eyebrows. "What do you mean?"

"Tonight, I'll try to be home early from the meeting at the club, and I want us to soak in the Jacuzzi for a bit, and then I want you to lie back and let me touch you and kiss you wherever I want." He licked my ear. "You'll love it."

I parted my lips in surprise. This was moving way faster than I'd thought it would, than I thought it should.

Luca must have seen the uncertainty in my expression, because he slipped his hand between my legs and pressed the heel of his palm against my clit over the fabric of my panties. I bucked and let a moan slip out before I could stop myself. God, this was ridiculous. This was what happened when you were forced to live abstinent for so long.

"You like this, Aria. I know you do. Admit it."

He pressed harder and I jerked against him. "Yes," I gasped out. He moved his palm slowly over me, sending spikes of pleasure through my body. "Don't stop."

"I won't," he said, nibbling my throat. "So will you let me have my way with you tonight? I won't do anything you don't want."

I wasn't even sure what I wanted right now. Except for Luca not to stop what he was doing with his hand. I would have promised him anything in that moment. "Yes."

He increased the pressure on my clit and suckled at my throat, then flicked his tongue over my collarbone, and I exploded.

Luca kissed me below my chin before pulling back with a smirk. Once I came down from my high, I needed to figure out a way to balance the power between us. He wanted me more than I wanted him. I was sure about it. I needed to take advantage of it.

I rested my forehead against his shoulder. "So can I call Gianna and tell her to buy plane tickets?"

Luca chuckled. "Sure, but remember our deal." His phone buzzed on the nightstand. He picked it up. "For fuck's sake, Matteo, what now?"

I pulled back. Luca got up and began pacing the bedroom, completely naked. "We've got his back. I won't let another fucking restaurant go to the Russians. Yeah. Yeah. I'll be ready in thirty minutes." He flung his phone on the nightstand.

"I'll have to talk to the owner of a restaurant chain."

"Okay," I said, trying to hide my disappointment.

"Call your sister and tell her she can come. And I'll be back in time for dinner, okay? I have a few take-out menus in the kitchen. Order whatever you want." He leaned down and kissed me. "Let Romero take you to a museum or something like that."

Fifteen minutes later, he was gone, and I was left with my doubts. How could I have agreed to his deal? Because I loved the pleasure he gave me. Why not enjoy it? Maybe I would have to live without love, but that didn't mean I would have to be miserable.

Gianna was ecstatic when I called to tell her she could visit. I didn't tell her about the deal. I couldn't talk about something like that on the phone, or ever. I knew she wouldn't approve of me giving in to Luca so quickly.

As promised, Luca was home early. I was incredibly nervous. I'd chosen a beautiful yellow dress and set the table on the roof terrace. Surprise flashed across Luca's face when he found me outside.

"I thought we could eat here?"

He wrapped his arms around me and pulled me in for lingering kiss. Butterflies fluttered in my stomach. "I ordered Indian food."

"I'm hungry for only one thing."

I shivered. "Let's eat." What would Luca do if I told him the deal was off? I took a seat. Luca watched me with intensity. Eventually he sank down on the chair across from me. The gentle breeze on the rooftop caressed my skin and tugged at my hair.

"You look fucking sexy."

I started eating. "Romero took me to the Metropolitan today. It was amazing."

"Good," Luca said with a hint of amusement. Could he see how nervous I was?

"What about the restaurant owner? Did you convince him that the Famiglia will protect him from the Russians?"

"Of course. He's been under our protection for more than a decade. There's no reason to change that now."

"Sure," I said distractedly, taking a gulp of the white wine.

Luca put down his fork. "Aria?"

"Hm?" I nudged a piece of cauliflower on my plate, not meeting Luca's gaze.

"Aria." His voice sent a chill down my back and I peered up at him. He leaned back in his chair, arms crossed over his strong chest. "You are scared."

"I'm not." He narrowed his eyes. "Maybe a bit, but mostly I'm nervous."

He got up from the chair and came around the table. "Come on." He held out his hand. After a brief moment of hesitation, I took it and let me pull him to my feet. "Let's get into the Jacuzzi, okay? That'll relax you."

I doubted being in a hot tub with him in only swimwear would make me less nervous. I didn't know what to expect and that terrified me.

"Why don't you grab your bikini and I'll set up the Jacuzzi?"

I nodded and went back inside. I picked my favorite white bikini with pink dots. I pulled my hair into a ponytail, then stared at myself in the bathroom mirror. I wasn't sure why this made me so nervous. This morning Luca's touch had set my skin aflame. He'd promised not to do anything I didn't want.

I took a deep breath and walked into the bedroom. Luca was waiting for me in black shorts; they did nothing to hide his strong body. All muscles and power. His eyes traveled over me, then he slipped a hand over my hip. "You are perfect," he said in a low voice. With a gentle nudge, he led me out of the bedroom, down the stairs and onto the roof terrace.

I shivered in my bikini. The breeze had picked up, and it was definitely too cold to stand outside in nothing but a bikini. Luca lifted me into his arms. I gasped in surprise, my hand coming up against the tattoo over his heart.

My own heart was galloping in my chest. I buried my face in the crook of Luca's neck, trying to relax. Luca's grip on me tightened as he stepped into the Jacuzzi and slowly lowered us into the hot bubbling water. I sat on his lap, my face still hidden against his skin. Luca rubbed his hand up and down my spine. "There's no reason for you to be scared."

"Says the man who crushed a man's throat with his bare hands," I meant to say it teasingly, but my voice came out shaky.

"That's got nothing to do with us, Aria. That's business."

"I know. I shouldn't have brought it up."

"What's really the problem?"

"I'm nervous because I feel vulnerable, like I'm at your mercy because of the deal."

"Aria, forget about the deal. Why don't you try to relax and enjoy this?" He nudged my chin up until our lips were almost touching and our eyes were locked.

"Promise you won't force me to do something I don't want to do." I lowered my gaze to his chest. "Promise me that you won't hurt me."

"Why would I hurt you?" Luca asked. "I told you I won't sleep with you unless you want me to."

"So you will hurt me when we sleep together?"

Luca's lips twisted into a wry smile. "Not on purpose, no, but I don't think there's a way around it." He kissed the spot below my ear. "But tonight I want to make you writhe in pleasure. Trust me."

I wanted to, but trust was a dangerous thing in our world. Part of me wanted to hold on to the flicker of hate I'd felt when I'd caught him with Grace. But another, bigger part wanted to pretend we hadn't been forced into this union, wanted to pretend that we could love each other.

Luca's tongue trailed over my throat. He stopped over my pounding pulse and sucked my skin into his mouth. I shivered from the sensation. His body was hot and hard against mine and I loved sitting in his lap, though it wasn't exactly comfortable. There wasn't much softness about Luca's body, only firm muscle. He shifted, pressing his erection against my butt as his lips claimed my mouth. The kiss sent small lightning bolts through my body, but I needed this to be more than physical. I wanted to know more about the man I'd spend the rest of my life with.

I pulled back, getting a growl from Luca in response. His fingers on my waist tightened, his gray eyes questioning as they settled on my face. I kissed his cheek and slung my arms around his neck. "Can we talk for a bit?"

It was obvious from Luca's expression that talking was the last thing on his mind, but he leaned against the wall of the Jacuzzi. "What do you want to talk about?"

One of his hands slid lower and began caressing my butt. I didn't allow it to distract me from my goal, even if it was *very* distracting. The hungry look in Luca's eyes didn't help either.

"What happened to your mother?" I knew she'd died when Luca had been a young boy, but Umberto hadn't said much more, either because he didn't know or because he thought I shouldn't know.

Luca's body turned rigid, eyes hard. "She died." He turned his face away, jaw flexing. "That's not the kind of thing I want to talk about tonight."

His rebuke stung. I wanted to get closer to him, wanted to get to know more sides of him, but it was clear he wouldn't let me. I nodded.

Luca removed his hand from my backside and slowly trailed it over my hip, then lower until he reached my inner thigh. He slipped under my bikini bottoms, rubbing his finger along my folds. I should have pushed him away, but instead I opened my legs a bit wider. Luca nuzzled my neck, then drew back. He hooked the fingers of his other hand under my bikini top and pulled it down so it bunched around my ribcage. My breasts sprang free, gooseflesh covering my skin and my nipples erect from the contact with the cold breeze.

Luca made a sound low in his throat as he stared at my chest. Then he bowed low and sucked my nipple into his mouth, and at the same time rubbed his thumb over my clit. I cried out from the sensation. He growled against my skin and released my nipple with an audible pop. His gaze snapped up to me as his tongue lavished my nub. I tried to look away, but he snarled, "No. Look at me."

And I did. I watched my nipple disappear in his mouth once more, watched him as he teased it with his tongue, his hungry gray eyes on me. He bit down gently, and my hips bucked against his hand still teasing my folds. Release shuddered through my body. Luca pulled back lightning fast, gripped my hips and lifted me onto the edge of the Jacuzzi.

"Luca, what—" Luca tore my bikini bottoms off me, pretty much ripping them in half. I gasped and tried to close my legs, but Luca positioned himself between them, shoved my legs as far apart as possible and lowered his head.

I gasped again, horrified and stunned and…oh God. Luca ran his tongue all the way from my opening up to my clit.

"Fuck, yes," he growled.

My eyes darted around. What if people saw? Only part of the Jacuzzi was encompassed by a screen, but Luca sucked my outer lips into his mouth and I didn't care anymore.

"Look at me," he ordered against my folds, the feel of his breath against my heated flesh making me shudder. I peered down, my skin burning with embarrassment and arousal as I met his gaze. His eyes locked on mine, he slowly slid his tongue between my folds. I moaned.

"You are mine," he said harshly. He licked me again, more firmly but even slower. "Say it."

"I'm yours," I said breathlessly. His thumbs parted me even further, revealing my small pink nub. He released a low breath, a smirk curling his lips. I wanted him to touch me there, wanted nothing more. He leaned forward, eyes on me, and circled his tongue around my nub. I whimpered, my hand shooting out and grabbing Luca's hair. I came violently, shuddering and crying out, writhing against Luca's lips.

He didn't stop. He was relentless. I threw my head back, staring up at the night sky. Luca didn't tell me to look at him this time. But I could hear everything he was doing. How he sucked and licked, how he hummed with approval, how he blew against my heated flesh, then licked again. My entire body was aflame, shaking. I couldn't take much more, but Luca pushed his tongue into me and I came, my muscles clenching around him. I squeezed my eyes shut, my back arching off the cold marble. I was so wet. How could anyone be so wet? The sounds of Luca lapping at me were so wrong, but they aroused me like nothing ever had.

Luca pulled his tongue out as the last spikes of my orgasm wrecked me. Before I knew what was happening, I felt his finger against my opening and he slid it almost all the way in. The intrusion was foreign and unexpected. I jerked and gasped from the pain. My body became rigid as I tried to catch my breath. I'd never even used tampons because they were too uncomfortable and because my mother worried I might accidentally rupture my hymen.

"Fuck, you're so fucking tight, Aria."

I flattened my palms against the Jacuzzi rim, trying to relax. Water sloshed as Luca moved out of the water to lean over me, his finger still in me. I bit my lip but didn't look at him.

"Hey," he said in a rough voice. I met his gaze. "I should have entered more slowly, but you were so wet."

I nodded but didn't say anything. I couldn't get over the feeling of his finger inside me. It didn't move, but it was there, filling me. Luca kissed my lips. His eyes were darker than I'd ever seen them, and filled with so much want and hunger that it scared and aroused me at the same time.

"Does it still hurt?" he rasped.

I shifted my hip slightly, trying to find words for the sensation. "It's uncomfortable and it burns a bit." I flushed.

Luca licked my lips, then sucked the lower lip into his mouth. "I know I'm an asshole for saying it, but the thought of my cock inside your tight pussy makes me so hard."

My eyes widened but he shook his head. "Don't look so terrified. I told you I wouldn't try it tonight."

"You also told me you wouldn't hurt me." The words were meant more to provoke him than because I was really mad at him. I was slowly getting used to his finger in me, and what he'd done before that had been paradise. I already wanted his lips and tongue back on me.

Something in Luca's expression shifted, but I couldn't read the emotion. "I didn't think it would, Aria," he said softly. "You were so wet and willing. I thought my finger would go in without trouble. I wanted to finger you for your fourth orgasm."

I shivered, and a small spike of pleasure built in my core again. I almost wanted Luca to move his finger now. "Did it hurt because you took my, you know…" Heat rushed into my cheeks and something flashed in Luca's eyes.

"Your virginity? No, *principessa*. I'm not that deep in, and I want to claim that part of you with my cock, not my finger."

Principessa? Warmth settled in my chest. Slowly he pulled his finger out, my muscles clenching around him and sending a strange prickling through my core. He traced the same finger over my lip and dipped it into my mouth. I circled it with my tongue without even knowing why.

Luca groaned. He jerked his finger out and shoved his tongue between my lips. I pressed myself against his chest, my tongue battling with his. "Let's go inside. I want to lick you again."

I exhaled.

"Will you let me put my finger into you again? This time I'll go really slow."

"Yes," I said. He leaped out of the Jacuzzi and helped me to my feet. Then he lifted me into his arms, my legs wrapping around his waist as he carried me inside.

He lowered me to my feet in front of our bed and disappeared in the bathroom only to return with a towel. He helped me out of my bikini top, wrapped the towel around me and started to gently rub me dry. I closed my eyes, enjoying the feel of it. I couldn't believe I'd let Luca do what he'd done. I couldn't believe I wanted him to do it again. Everything was overwhelming. I knew it was too fast, but as Luca had said, what was I waiting for? He was my husband.

"Are you cold?"

My eyes peeled open. Luca dropped the towel, leaving me naked. His hands slid up and down my arms. My entire body was covered in goose bumps. "A bit."

Luca made me lie down on the bed before he straightened and slid down his shorts. His erection sprang free, hard and long, and suddenly anxiety gripped me. He'd put his finger into me, maybe now he wanted to take the next step. Maybe I was confused about a few things at the moment, but I knew one thing: I wasn't ready for that.

I still barely knew the man in front of me, and sleeping with him, letting him into me like that was too much, too intimate. Maybe this evening had been his way of manipulating me. Nobody got that far in the mafia without being a master in manipulation. I pressed my legs together and scrambled back. Luca paused, one knee already on the bed.

"Aria?" His fingers curled around my calf, and I jerked back and pulled my legs against my chest. He sighed. "What now?"

He sat beside me, his length almost brushing my leg. "Say something."

"This is too fast," I said quietly.

"Because I got naked? You've seen my cock before. You even jerked me off."

My face burned. "I think you're trying to manipulate me. If I gave you the chance, you'd go all the way today."

"You bet I would, but I can't see what manipulation has to do with it," he said with a hint of anger in his voice. "I want you. I never lied to you about that. I'm going to take whatever you are willing to give, and you were willing in the Jacuzzi."

"Not about the finger," I snapped, suddenly getting angry too. "Maybe you'll try the same with sex." I knew it sounded ridiculous.

Luca actually laughed. He leaned very close. "That won't work. My cock won't slide in that easily, believe me, and it will hurt a lot more."

I flinched, remembering what Grace had said at our wedding. *He'll fuck you bloody*. Luca released a harsh breath. "I shouldn't have said that. I didn't mean to scare you."

I watched him over my legs. He ran his knuckles lightly down my side. The hard set of his lips loosened. "Tell me that you enjoyed what I did to you on the roof," Luca murmured. There was a hint of need in his voice, maybe even vulnerability.

"Yes," I said breathlessly. He leaned closer, his lips on my ear. "What did you enjoy the most? My tongue fucking you? Or when I ran my tongue all the way over your pussy? Or when I sucked your clit?"

Oh god. I was getting wet again. Luca's deep voice vibrated through my body. "I don't know."

"Maybe I need to show you again?" Luca pushed against my ankles, pressing them against me until there was enough room for his hand to slip between them and my upper thighs. He cupped me with his palm. I was about to lie down to make it easier for him, but he shook his head. "No," he rasped. "Stay like that." His fingers began to move against my folds, teasing, circling, rubbing.

I rested my chin on my knees, breathing heavily. Luca kissed my ear and wrapped an arm around my shoulder, pulling me against his side. It was strange, sitting up with my legs pressed against my chest as he touched me, but it felt incredibly good. Luca's erection rubbed against my outer thigh, his breathing hot against my ear.

"Relax," he said in a low voice. There was a gentle pressure against my opening. I peered down between my legs. Luca teased me with his little finger. He dipped the tip in, then circled my opening before entering me again, sliding a bit deeper every time he did.

"Look at me."

I did, caught up in the intensity of his gray eyes. "You are so wet and soft and tight. You can't imagine how fucking good this feels." His length slid along my outer thigh again. His lips pressed against mine, his tongue demanding entrance. His finger slipped into me, this time all the way. It was only his little finger, but I was thrilled. He began moving it inside me and I gasped into his mouth, jerking my hips, needing more. He pumped in and out slowly, his thumb rubbing my clit. I could feel pleasure building again and I moved my pelvis in sync with his finger. He pulled his hand away, eliciting a sound of protest from me.

Luca laughed, a deep rumbling in his chest. He knelt in front of me and pushed my legs apart, then he looked up at me. He traced his index finger over my folds, then rubbed my opening with it. Never looking away from my face, he pushed the tip in. My muscles clenched, and I released a low breath. It didn't hurt and I relaxed. Slowly he started sliding in and out, moving a bit deeper every time, like he'd done with his little finger. His mouth closed over my clit.

I whimpered, my legs falling wider apart. My pleasure was mounting scarily fast as Luca worked me with his finger and lips. With a cry, I tumbled over, my legs shaking, hips bucking. My fingers clutched the blanket as I shattered into pieces. Luca removed his finger, kissed my belly button, then lay down beside me, his erection red and glistening. I reached out, spreading the droplet of liquid that had trickled out all over his tip.

Luca growled, his abs flexing. "I want your mouth on me," he said in a low voice. I froze, my hand on him stilling. It seemed only fair after what he'd just done, but I had no clue how to actually go down on him. "Blow job" was a pretty confusing name, because I knew I wasn't supposed to blow on his erection, but sadly I wasn't exactly sure what to do. And what if I didn't like it?

I remembered his words about Grace, that she knew how to suck a cock. Not that I wanted to be anything like Grace. I had no intention of becoming Luca's whore, but I didn't want to fail completely either. I was overthinking this.

"Is this because you don't want to, or because you don't know how?" Luca asked calmly, but I could tell he had trouble keeping the tension out of his voice. He'd given me several orgasms. He was probably bursting. "You can jerk me off like last time," he said when I stayed silent. His hand brushed a strand of blonde hair away from my face, his gray eyes questioning.

"No, I mean, I think I want to do it."

"You think?" Amusement tinged Luca's voice. "But?"

"What if I don't like it?"

Luca shrugged, but it was obvious from his expression that he didn't like the idea. "Then you don't. I won't force you."

I nodded and brought my face a bit closer to his erection, which hadn't softened at all during our conversation. Luca tensed in anticipation, his fingertips against my scalp twitching. Embarrassed, I admitted, "I don't know what to do."

His erection jerked in response. I couldn't help but laugh, and Luca grinned his predator grin. "You like to torture me with your innocence, don't you?"

I blew against his tip, making him groan. "I don't think that's why it's called blow job, right?"

He actually laughed a real laugh, and the sound filled my stomach with butterflies. "You're going to be the death of me, *principessa*."

"Don't laugh," I said with a smile. "I don't want to do something wrong."

"Do you want me to tell you what to do?" Excitement blazed in his eyes.

I nodded.

"Okay," he said hoarsely. "Close your lips around the tip and be careful with your teeth. I don't mind it a bit rougher, but don't chew on it."

I snorted, then nerves made me go quiet. Luca's fingers slipped through my hair until they came to rest on the back of my head. He didn't push me, but from the way he tensed I could tell he wanted to. I took the tip into my mouth. He was thick, and I had to be careful not to graze him with my teeth. His tip was slightly salty, but not in a bad way.

"Now swirl your tongue around it. Yes, just like that." He watched me, his jaw clenched. "Take a bit more of me into your mouth and move your head up and down. Now suck as you move. Yes, fuck." His hips bucked when I was as far as I could take him, driving his erection even further inside. I gagged and pulled back, coughing.

He stroked my hair. "Fuck, sorry." He rubbed his thumb over my lips. "I'll try to stay still."

Instead of taking him back into my mouth, I licked him from his base to the tip. He groaned. "Is that okay?" I whispered before doing it again.

"Fuck yes."

I took my time licking every inch of him, but especially his tip. I loved the feel of it against my tongue.

"This feels really fucking good, but I really want to come."

I glanced up uncertainly. I could come when he stroked and licked me gently. Did he need it rougher? Would he need it rough during sex too? Grace's stupid words jumped into my head again, but I pushed them aside. I wouldn't let that whore ruin this for me. "What do you need me to do?" I whispered.

"Suck me harder and keep looking at me with your fucking beautiful eyes."

I fixed my gaze on him and took him into my mouth until he hit the back of my throat, then bobbed my head up and down fast and hard, my lips tight around him. Luca moaned, his hips rocking lightly. His eyes burnt into me, his teeth gritted. "If you don't want to swallow, you need to get away…"

I jerked away, releasing him with a pop, and a moment later he spilled his seed on his stomach and legs. Luca closed his eyes as his erection twitched. His hand was still in my hair, gently stroking my neck and scalp. Slowly he eased it down, but I gripped his hand and pressed my cheek into it, needing his closeness after what we'd done. His eyes flew open with an unreadable look in them. His thumb brushed my cheekbone gently. We stayed like that for a couple of heartbeats, then Luca sat up, taking in the mess on his upper thighs and abs. "I need a fucking shower." Luca reached for a tissue and cleaned off the sperm before swinging his legs out and standing.

I nodded, strangely disappointed that he'd slip out of bed so quickly. I felt suddenly self-conscious about what I'd done.

Luca held out his hand. "Come on. I don't want to shower alone."

I scrambled off the bed, put my hand in his and followed him into the bathroom.

As the hot water poured down on us, Luca began lathering my body with soap and I closed my eyes, enjoying the feel of his hands on me. He pressed up to my back, one arm circling my stomach. "So was it okay for you?" he asked quietly.

He was probably worried I wouldn't go down on him again, if it wasn't. "Yeah."

He kissed my throat. He did that a lot. It felt so gentle, loving and intimate, but I knew it wasn't meant like that. "I'm glad, because I really enjoy being in your mouth."

I flushed with embarrassment and a strange sense of accomplishment.

Ridiculous. "Are you angry that I didn't, you know, swallow? I bet the women you've been with so far always did."

"No, I'm not angry. I won't lie, I'd love to come in your mouth but if you don't want that, it's okay."

We stepped out of the shower and dried off before we crawled back into bed. I rested my head on Luca's chest. He turned off the lights, bathing us in darkness. He lightly stroked my hip, and the touch and his warmth made feel safe enough to ask a question that had been bothering me for years. "When your father told you to marry me, what was your reaction?" I murmured.

Luca's fingers on my hips paused. "I'd expected it. I knew I'd have to marry for tactical reasons. As future Capo, you can't let emotions or desires rule any part of your life."

I was glad for the darkness so Luca couldn't see my face. He sounded so detached and emotionless. His touches and kisses made me want to believe that maybe he was starting to care for me, but now I wasn't so sure anymore.

"And what about you?" he asked.

"I was terrified."

"You were only fifteen. Of course, you were terrified."

"I was still terrified on the day of our marriage. I'm still not entirely sure you don't terrify me."

Luca was silent a moment, as if he didn't know how to react to my admission. "I told you, you have no reason to fear me. I'll protect and take care of you. I'll give you anything you want and need."

Except for one thing: love.

"But the Famiglia always comes first," I said lightly. "If you had to kill me to protect the business, you would."

Luca became rigid, but he didn't deny it. My father always said there's only room for one true love in the life of a Made Man, and that's the mafia.

chapter *twelve*

GIANNA MANAGED TO GET A TICKET FOR A FLIGHT TWO DAYS later. I was brimming with excitement that day. It hadn't been long since I'd last seen her, but it felt like an eternity. It was already getting dark outside when Luca and I pulled up at JFK. I wished Gianna could have gotten a morning or afternoon flight instead.

Since my comment that Luca would kill me in order to protect the Famiglia, he'd been emotionally withdrawn, not that he'd been an open book before that. The only way we interacted was at night when Luca pleasured me with his hands and mouth, and I him in turn. Maybe without Gianna's impending visit, I'd have tried to talk to him or even pleaded with him to show me where he worked; instead I'd given him the space he obviously wanted.

Luca parked the car close to the terminal where Gianna would arrive and we got out. He didn't try to take my hand. I didn't think he was the type of man who held hands, but he touched my lower back as we entered the arrival area of the airport.

"Are you sure you'll be okay with Gianna staying with us for the next few days?"

"Yes. And I promised your father to protect her. It's easier when she's living in our apartment."

"She will provoke you," I said.

"I can handle a little girl."

"She's not that little. She's barely younger than me."

"I can handle her."

"Luca," I said firmly. "Gianna knows how to push people's buttons. If you aren't absolutely sure that you can control yourself, I won't let her near you."

Luca's eyes blazed. He'd been on edge all day. "Don't worry. I won't kill her *or you* in the next few days."

I took a step back. Where did that come from? Was he angry because of what I'd said? It was the truth; we both knew it.

"Aria!"

I whirled around. Gianna rushed toward me, dropping her trolley on the way. We collided almost painfully, but I clutched her to my chest tightly. "I'm so glad you're here," I whispered.

She nodded, then pulled back, searching my face. "No visible bruises," she said loudly, her gaze darting behind me toward Luca. "You only hit places that are covered by clothes?"

I gripped her hand and gave her a warning look.

"Get your luggage," Luca ordered. "I don't want to stand here all night."

Gianna glared at him but retrieved her trolley and returned to us. "A gentleman would have got it for me."

"A gentleman, yes," Luca said with a tight smile.

We walked back to our car, my arm linked with Gianna's. Luca walked a few steps ahead and got behind the steering wheel without a word.

"What's the matter with him? He's even more of an asshole than I remember."

"I think the Russians are giving him trouble."

"Aren't they always?" Gianna put her trolley into the trunk of the car before we both sat in the backseat.

Luca raised his eyebrows at me. "I'm not your driver. Get in the front with me."

I was taken aback by his harshness, but I did as he said and sat shotgun. Gianna's face was scrunched up with anger. "You shouldn't talk to her like that."

"She's my wife. I can do and say to her what I want."

I frowned. Luca turned to me, meeting my gaze. I couldn't place the look in his eyes. He turned back to the street.

"How are Lily and Fabi?"

"Annoying as hell. Especially Lily. She doesn't stop talking about Romero. She's in love with him."

I laughed, and even Luca's lips twitched. I wasn't sure why but I reached out and put my hand on his leg. His eyes snapped toward me briefly, then he covered my hand with his until he needed it to shift gears again. Gianna's eyes were attentive as they watched. She'd bombard me with questions the moment we were alone, no doubt.

When we stepped into the apartment, the smell of roasted lamb and rosemary wafted over to us.

"I told Marianna to prepare a nice dinner," Luca said. Gianna's red eyebrows shot up in surprise.

"Thank you," I said.

Luca nodded. "Show your sister to her room and then we can eat." He was still withdrawn and stiff. I watched him head around the corner toward the kitchen area.

I showed Gianna her guest room, but she quickly pulled me inside and closed the door. "Are you okay?"

"Yes. I told you on the phone. I'm fine."

"I prefer to hear you say it when I can see your face."

"I'm not lying to you, Gianna."

She gripped my hand. "Did he force you to sleep with him?"

"No, he didn't. And I haven't."

Her eyes widened. "But something happened between the two of you. I want details."

I pulled away. "We need to have dinner now. Marianna will be mad if the food gets cold. We can talk tomorrow when Luca's busy with business."

"Tomorrow," Gianna said firmly.

I opened the door and led her toward the dining area. Her eyes took everything in, then became slits when she saw who else would be having dinner with us: Matteo. He and Luca stood beside the table, discussing something, but stepped apart when they noticed us.

"What's he doing here?" Gianna said, her nose wrinkled.

Flashing his shark grin, Matteo walked toward her and gripped her hand to kiss it. "Nice to see you again, Gianna."

Gianna snatched her hand away. "Don't touch me."

She needed to stop provoking him; he liked it way too much. Luca and I sat beside each other and Matteo beside Gianna. I wasn't sure that was the best decision. I glanced at Luca, but his cautious gaze rested on his brother and my sister.

Marianna bustled in, serving roast lamb, rosemary potatoes and green beans. We ate in silence for a while until Gianna couldn't hold her tongue anymore. "Why did you crush that guy's throat?"

I put my fork down, expecting Luca to explode, but he only leaned back in his chair and crossed his arms over his chest.

Gianna huffed. "Come on. It can't be that big of a secret. You got your nickname for it."

Matteo grinned. "The Vice is a nice name."

Luca shook his head. "I hate it."

"You earned it," Matteo said. "Now tell them the story or I will."

I'd been curious about it for a while. Nobody from the Chicago mob wanted to give me details, and I hadn't dared to ask Romero yet.

"I was seventeen," Luca began. "Our father has many brothers and sisters, and one of my cousins climbed the ranks in the mafia alongside me. He was several years older and wanted to become Capo. He knew my father would choose me, so he invited me to his house and tried to stab me in the back. The knife only grazed my arm and when I got the chance, I wrapped my hands around his throat and choked him."

"Why didn't you shoot him?" Gianna asked.

"He was family, and it used to be tradition that we put down our weapons when we entered the home of a family member," Luca said coldly. "Not anymore, of course."

"The betrayal made Luca so angry, he completely crushed our cousin's throat. He choked on his blood because the bones in his neck cut through his artery. It was a mess. I'd never seen anything like it." Matteo looked like a kid on Christmas morning. It was more than a little disturbing.

Luca glared down at his plate, hands clutching his thighs. No wonder he was reluctant to trust people. To be betrayed by family must have been horrible.

"That's why Luca always sleeps with an eye open. He never even spends the night with a woman without a gun under the pillow or somewhere at his body."

Luca shot his brother a glower.

Matteo raised his hands. "It's not like Aria doesn't know you screwed around with other women."

I didn't think that was the reason for Luca's reaction.

"So are you wearing a gun now?" Gianna asked. "We're all family, after all."

"Luca always wears a gun." Matteo leaned toward Gianna. "Don't take it personally. I don't think even I have seen him without a gun since that day. It's Luca's tic."

Luca didn't wear a gun when we were alone. He wore one when Romero or Marianna was there, even when Matteo was there, but when Luca and I shared a bed, there wasn't a gun under his pillow or anywhere else. *That's probably because he could overpower you with his hands bound behind his back.* Still it seemed like an unnecessary risk.

Luca spent the rest of dinner tense and silent, but Gianna's and Matteo's arguments filled the silence. I wasn't sure who got off more on their fights.

When we were done eating, I got up to clean the table. Marianna had already left and I didn't want to leave the dirty dishes waiting for her when she came back tomorrow. Luca surprised me when he rose as well and carried the serving platters and plates over to the dishwasher. I yawned, exhausted.

"Let's go to bed," Luca said quietly.

I glanced at Gianna. There was so much I wanted to talk to her about, but it was late and tomorrow was another day. "Not before Matteo leaves. I won't leave him and my sister alone."

Luca nodded grimly. "You are right. She shouldn't be alone with him." He went over to Matteo and put a hand on his shoulder before leaning down and saying something into his ear. Matteo's face darkened with anger but he rose smoothly, gave Gianna his shark grin and then walked out of the apartment without another word.

Gianna came toward me. "He's obsessed with me."

Worry clawed at my insides. "Then stop teasing him. He likes it."

"I don't care what he likes."

Luca leaned beside me against the counter, his arm sneaking around my waist to Gianna's obvious displeasure. "Matteo is a hunter. He loves the chase. You'd better not make him want to chase you."

I worried it might already be too late for that warning. Gianna rolled her eyes. "He can hunt me all he wants. He won't get me." She looked at me. "You don't intend to go to bed now, right?"

"I'm really tired," I said guiltily.

Gianna's shoulders slumped. "Yeah, me too. But tomorrow I want you all to myself." She gave Luca a pointed look before heading off toward her room. She paused in her doorway. "If I hear screams, no gun under a pillow will save you, Luca." With that, she closed her door.

Luca brushed my ear with his lips. "Will you scream for me tonight?" He licked my skin and I shivered.

"Not with my sister under the same roof," I said, even as a tingling between my legs betrayed me.

"We'll see about that," Luca growled, then gently bit my throat. I moaned, but quickly bit my lip to stifle the sound. Luca took my hand and pulled me upstairs. With every step that we got closer to the bedroom, the pressure between my legs increased. I couldn't believe how eager my body was for his touch, for the release he brought me. In just a few days, Luca's touch had gone from something that terrified me to the only time I forgot everything about my life, the only time I was free of the shackles in our world.

Luca slammed the door shut behind us, and I hoped it wouldn't draw Gianna's attention. But I didn't have much time for worry because Luca pulled my dress off, then he lifted me into his arms, only to lay me down in the middle of the bed. Luca pressed a kiss against my lace panties, inhaling, before he kissed my stomach and my ribs, then my breasts through the lace of my bra.

"Mine," he growled against my skin, making me tremble with arousal. He slid his hands under my back and unclasped my bra and slowly pulled it off. My nipples were hard. "I fucking love your nipples. They're pink and small and perfect."

I pressed my legs together, but Luca gripped my panties and slipped them down. He ran a finger over my folds, smirking. His hungry gaze returned to my breasts, and he bent his head and trailed his tongue from one nipple to the other. I moaned softly. He took his time with my breasts and when he slowly moved lower, I was already panting. His lips found my folds, teasing and gentle, then suddenly his tongue slid out hard and fast, and I covered my mouth with my palm, stifling my gasps and cries.

"No," Luca snarled. He gripped both of my wrists in his hand and pressed them against my stomach, trapping them there.

My eyes widened. "Gianna will hear."

He smirked and sucked my clit hard and fast, then gentle and soft. I whimpered and moaned, my body trembling from the effort to keep quiet. "Oh god," I gasped as Luca slipped his finger achingly slow into me, then eased in and out in rhythm with his sucks on my clit. I buried my face in the pillow. Luca's grip on my wrists tightened and pleasure ripped through me. I cried out into the pillow, my back arching, legs quavering.

Luca moved up my body until he bent over me, knees between my spread legs. "When will you let me take you?" he whispered harshly against my throat.

I turned to stone. Luca raised his head, eyes meeting mine. "Fuck. Why do you have to look so fucking scared when I ask you that question?"

"I'm sorry," I said quietly. "I just need more time."

Luca nodded, but there was a deep need in his eyes that seemed to grow every day.

I ran my hands over his chest, feeling his gun holster beneath the shirt. He sat back and I leaned forward, beginning to unbutton his shirt, revealing his toned torso and the black holster with his gun and knife. Luca took off his shirt and I opened the holster, helping him out of it. He thrust it to the ground. Matteo's words came back to me and I ran my hands over Luca's naked chest.

I pressed a kiss against Luca's tattoo, then against the healing wound over his ribs. I brushed Luca's nipples with my fingertips and he groaned in response. He quickly slipped out of his pants. I lowered my lips to his erection but paused an inch from his tip. "If you're not quiet, I'll stop."

Luca's eyes flashed. He put his hand on my head. "Maybe I won't allow you to stop."

"Maybe I'll bite."

Luca chuckled. "Have your way with me, I won't make a sound. Don't want to offend your sister's virgin ears."

"What about my virgin ears?" I kissed his tip.

"You shouldn't still be one," Luca said in a low voice. I took his erection into my mouth to distract him. He made a sound deep in his throat, then quieted as I took care of him.

I pulled back again before he came.

After he'd cleaned himself, Luca spooned me.

"I'm sorry for what your cousin did," I said into the darkness.

"I should have known better than to trust anyone. Trust is a luxury people in my position can't afford."

You can trust me, I wanted to say, because he could. No matter how much I tried to fight it, I had fallen for him. "Life without trust is lonely."

"Yes, it is." He kissed the back of my neck, then we fell silent.

Luca was asleep when I woke, his body wrapped around mine, his hardness pressing against my lower back. I untangled myself and slipped into the bathroom. It wasn't late yet, but Gianna was an early riser and I couldn't wait to spend the day with her. I took a long shower, feeling more awake already. I got out of the shower and wrapped a towel around myself, then went back into the bedroom. Luca sat on the edge of the bed but got up when I entered. His erection jutted out. I gave him a teasing smile as he curled his fingers over my hipbones. "Hard again?"

He growled. "I'm always hard for you. One day my balls are going to explode."

I could hear movement somewhere in the apartment, then a curse. Gianna was awake. "I should go to her."

"Oh no, you won't," Luca rasped. He kissed me possessively and I stood on my tiptoes to make it easier for him. One kiss couldn't hurt, but the way Luca was grinding himself against me, I knew he wanted more than a kiss. He turned me around and pulled me flush against his chest so his erection pressed into my back.

I gasped. We were facing the floor-length mirror across from the bed. Luca gripped the towel and pulled it down, leaving me naked. He kissed my throat, eyes on me through the mirror. His strong hands traveled up my sides and cupped my breasts. He captured my nipples between his forefinger and thumb, and twirled them. My lips parted and a soft moan escaped.

I could hear Gianna coming up the stairs toward our floor. Oh god.

Luca pinched my nipples, then tugged. I closed my eyes at the delicious sensation that swept through me. He peppered my throat and collarbone with kisses and licks while his hand slid down the valley between my breasts, over my stomach and between my thighs. Gianna stopped outside of our bedroom. Luca flicked his thumb over my clit, and I bit down on my lip to stop myself from moaning.

"Aria? Are you awake?"

"Your sister is a fucking nuisance," Luca muttered in my ear, then licked the skin below before sucking it. His index finger slid between my folds, then entered me. I exhaled. "But you're so fucking wet, *principessa*." A new wave of wetness pooled between my legs. "Yes," Luca growled into my ear. His eyes bored into me in the mirror and I couldn't look away. His finger slipped in and out of me, spreading my wetness all over my folds.

I couldn't believe he was making me watch him fingering me. I couldn't believe how much it turned me on. His fingers pinched my nipple again, harder this time, and I could feel it all the way in my clit. I whimpered.

"Aria?" Gianna hammered against the door. God, she wouldn't stop. I tried to pull away. This was wrong. I couldn't do this with my sister outside of the door. Luca smirked, his grip on me tightening. His second hand moved down and rubbed my clit while his other kept slipping in and out of me. I was spiraling out of control. His lips crashed down on mine, swallowing my moans as pleasure washed over me. My legs spasmed and I rocked myself against Luca's hands as I came hard. Luca didn't stop moving his hands, even as I tried to step away. Instead he pushed against my shoulders until I leaned forward, my hands coming up to support me against the mirror. My eyes grew wide when he knelt behind me, palming my butt and then spreading me. And then his tongue was there, sliding over my folds. He licked the entire length of me. I tensed when his tip slid along my back entrance and he quickly returned his mouth to my clit. I lost all sense of myself, even as I heard Gianna's insistent knocking and her occasional calls. All that mattered was Luca's tongue as it drove me higher and higher. This had to be wrong, but it felt too good. I bit the inside of my cheek and as pain and pleasure mingled, my second orgasm crashed over me. My legs gave way and I fell to my knees beside Luca, panting and gasping, and hoping Gianna couldn't hear it.

I glared at Luca, but he smirked, hunger on his face. He stood, and his erection twitched. I watched as he began stroking himself in front of my face. I knew what he wanted. I parted my lips and he slid his tip in. The saltiness of his pre-cum spread on my tongue. I couldn't believe I was blowing Luca with Gianna close by, but the wrongness of it turned me on even more. What was wrong with me? Luca caressed my cheek as his other hand cupped the back of my head. His eyes never left me as he slowly slid in and out of my mouth. I wasn't sure why I liked it, but I did.

"You're so beautiful, Aria," he murmured, pushing a bit deeper into my mouth. I swirled my tongue around his tip and he exhaled sharply, so I did it again.

Gianna's step receded down the stairs but I kept sucking Luca, slow and sensually. Luca's hand guided me, a light pressure against my head. I sucked him faster, increasing the pressure of my lips. "Cup my balls."

I did. I loved how soft they felt in my palm. Luca rocked his hips faster. "I want to come in your mouth, *principessa*," he said harshly. I wasn't sure if that was something I'd like, but Luca didn't mind tasting me down there, so I thought I should at least give it a try. I nodded and sucked him deeper into my mouth. Luca growled, his hips bucking faster. After a few more thrusts, he came in my mouth. I swallowed. It tasted strange and was more than I'd thought it would be, but it wasn't exactly bad.

Luca still stroked my cheek as he softened in my mouth. He pulled back, his penis sliding out from between my lips. I swallowed again. Luca grabbed my arm and lifted me to my feet, his mouth crashing down on mine in a fierce kiss. He didn't mind tasting himself on me. "I hope you remember this all day."

Luca left shortly after breakfast and Gianna immediately pulled me out onto the roof terrace, away from Romero's attentive ears.

"What's going on? You've been acting strange all morning. Why didn't you answer when I called you this morning?"

I looked away, a blush spreading on my cheeks. Gianna's eyes shot open. "What did he do?"

"He went down on me," I admitted.

"You let him?"

I laughed. "Yes." More heat rose into my cheeks at the sound of eagerness in my voice.

Gianna leaned forward. "You like it?"

"I love it."

Gianna bit her lip. "I hate thinking about you with him, but you really seem to enjoy it. I guess it has its advantages that Luca fucked every society girl in New York."

I didn't want to think about it.

"So how does it feel?"

"As if I'm shattering. It's overwhelming and amazing, and I don't know how to describe it."

"But you didn't sleep with him?"

I shook my head. "Not yet, but I don't think Luca wants to wait much longer."

"Fuck him. He can screw himself." She narrowed her eyes. "Did he make you blow him?"

"He didn't make me. I wanted to do it."

Gianna looked doubtful. "And? Tell me more. You know I have to vicariously live through you. I'm so fucking tired of being under surveillance all day. I want a boyfriend. I want to have sex and have orgasms."

I snorted. "I doubt Father will allow it."

"I don't intend to ask him," Gianna said with a shrug. "I'm here now. Nobody's stopping me from having fun, right?"

My eyes widened. "Father would kill me if I let you hook up with guys while you were here."

"He doesn't have to know, does he?" She shrugged again. "It's not like I would tell him."

I gaped, then laughed. "Well, unless you want to seduce Romero or Matteo, your options are kind of limited."

"Ugh, no. I don't want either of them. I want a normal guy. A guy who doesn't know who I am."

"Well, I don't know how we could find a guy for you."

Gianna grinned. "How about we hit a club?"

"Romero won't let me out of his sight after I ran away from him once. There's no way we can escape him and go off to a club."

Gianna contemplated this. I worried about the crazy plan she might come up with, though I actually liked the idea of going out for a night of dancing. I'd always imagined how it would be to spend a night on the dance floor and let loose.

"Romero can come with us. He's guarding you, not me. Maybe I can slip away."

"And then what? A quickie in a restroom stall? Do you really want to experience all your firsts like that?"

Gianna glared. "At least, I'd experience them on my own terms. It would be my choice. You don't have a choice at all. Luca and Father took them all away. I don't get how you can be so calm about it. How can you not hate Luca?"

Sometimes I wondered that myself. "I should hate him."

Gianna's face crumbled. "But you don't. Fuck, Aria, do you actually care about him? Love him?"

"Would you really prefer I hate him and be miserable?"

"He treats you like a prisoner. You don't really believe Romero is just for your protection, right? He keeps an eye on you, so no other guy gets a piece of you."

I knew that. "Let's go shopping."

"Really? That's so trophy wife of you."

"Shut up," I said teasingly, wanting to lighten the mood. "Shopping for hot outfits for tonight. We can hit one of Luca's clubs."

Gianna grinned. "I want to wear something that gives guys a fucking boner from looking at me."

Romero had waited outside the store while we went shopping. He'd probably checked beforehand if there was a back entrance we could use to escape. I hadn't told him about our plan to head out to a club yet. It was better if I sprang it on him at the last moment.

Gianna whistled as I turned around so she could admire my outfit. "Holy shit. You are sex on legs. Or maybe death on legs, because Luca will probably kill every guy that looks at you the wrong way."

I rolled my eyes. "Luca won't kill anyone for looking."

"Wanna bet on that?"

No, I wouldn't. I'd never worn anything that sexy in public. The black leather pants hugged my body so tightly, they looked like a second skin. The sheer black sleeveless blouse I'd tucked into my waistband, revealed my sparkly push-up bra below.

"You don't look too shabby either," I said.

Gianna jumped up from my bed. "You think?" She flashed me a seductive smile. She really looked smoking hot in her black shirt and black leather hot pants.

"You're jailbait." Good thing we didn't have to worry about getting carded. I linked our arms and led her out of the bedroom and down the staircase. Romero was sitting on the sofa, cleaning his knife. His eyes darted up and he stilled completely. His gaze wandered over our bodies. He'd never openly stared at me.

"Are you checking us out?" I couldn't help but tease him. He was always so controlled. This small flicker of humanness was a relief.

He stood abruptly, sheathing the knife into its holder. His eyes were again firmly focused on my face. "What's going on?" There was a hint of strain in his voice.

I walked up to him, and he actually tensed as if he thought I would jump him. That almost made me laugh. "Gianna and I want to go to Marquee." That was one of the hottest clubs in town.

Romero shook his head. "That belongs to the Bratva."

"Oh, what's the hottest club that belongs to the Famiglia then?"

Romero didn't say anything at first. He reached into his pocket and pulled out his phone, probably to call Luca. Something snapped in me then. I couldn't believe he needed to ask Luca permission. I gave Gianna a look and nodded toward Romero, who had started typing. She sidled up to him and actually squeezed his butt. He jumped and I used the moment to snatch his phone from him. He took a threatening step toward me, eyes blazing with anger, then he froze. "Aria," he said. "Give it back."

I slipped the phone into my waistband. The pants were tight enough that there wasn't a risk of it slipping down.

Gianna stepped away from Romero, grinning. "Why don't you shove your hand down Aria's pants and get it. I'll take a pic and send it to Luca."

Romero's eyes lingered on the shape of his phone in my pants, but I knew he wouldn't try to get it. "This isn't funny."

"No it isn't, you're right," I said sharply. "I'm an adult. If I tell you to take me to a club, I don't want you to ask my husband for permission. I'm not a child, nor am I his property."

"You are Luca's," Romero said calmly.

I stepped up to him, so close that I had to tilt my head back. "Gianna and I are going to a club. So unless you want to keep me at gunpoint, you'll drive us there or let us leave alone."

Romero's jaw tightened. The look in his eyes made me realize why he was my bodyguard. For the first time I was reminded that Romero was a killer. "I'll drive you. But you will go to Sphere. It's Luca's."

"Is it any good?" Gianna asked.

"It's hotter than the fucking Marquee." Romero was really pissed.

"Take us there, then."

He put on his jacket and led us to the elevator. "Luca won't like it," he said.

Gianna and I sat in the back as Romero steered the car through traffic. I pulled the phone out and checked what Romero had been writing.

A wants to hit a club. Permission?

He had managed to send it off before I'd snatched it, but Luca's reply had come afterward.

No

My blood boiled. Gianna huffed. "I can't fucking believe his nerve."

Romero glanced at us through the rearview mirror. "Did Luca reply?"

"Yeah," I said. "He said you should stay close at all times."

Romero bought my lie and actually relaxed. Gianna winked. Luca would go through the roof, but I really couldn't bring myself to care. Romero parked the car in a side alley and led us around the building. A long line of partygoers waited in front of the entrance, but Romero ushered us past them.

"Hey you stupid fucker, there's a line," a guy shouted. Romero stopped, a cold anger replacing his usual calm.

"Go ahead," Romero said to us before he turned around to the guy. Gianna gripped my hand and dragged me toward the two bouncers at the front. They were as tall and muscled as Luca.

"You don't look old enough to hit a club," the dark-skinned man said.

"Is that a problem?" Gianna asked with a flirty smile.

The man's eyes moved to something behind me. "Romero," he said with a hint of confusion.

"She belongs to the Boss, Jorge. This is Aria Vitiello and her sister Gianna Scuderi of the Chicago Outfit."

Both men stared at me, then stepped back respectfully. "We didn't know she was coming tonight. The Boss didn't say anything," Jorge said.

Romero grimaced, but didn't respond. Instead he led Gianna and me inside, past the cloakroom tinged in bluish light and a bar area. Behind it the doors opened to a dark dance floor. Blue and white light flashed and hip-hop beats blasted toward us. Gianna tugged at my hand, wanting to go in that direction.

"We should go to Luca first," Romero said.

"He's here?" I asked, surprised.

Romero nodded. "The club has several back rooms and a basement where we handle some business."

"Why don't you go tell him I'm here while Gianna and I hit the dance floor."

Romero gave me a look. "No chance in hell."

"That's your problem then. Gianna and I are going dancing." Romero grasped my wrist. I tensed. "Let me go right this second," I hissed and he did, his chest heaving. Gianna and I walked into the club. The beat vibrated under our feet as if the floor had come to life. The club was crowded with writhing bodies. Romero shadowed my sister and me as we squeezed through the throng of dancers toward another bar area.

"Two gin and tonics," I said. The barman frowned briefly before noticing Romero, then he prepared our drinks and handed them to us. Romero leaned over the bar and said something to the man, who nodded and walked around the bar. I knew what it meant. I took a deep gulp of my drink, then set it down and moved onto the dance floor.

I let the music claim my body and started writhing to the beat. Gianna grinned widely, throwing her head back. She looked happier than I'd seen her in a long time. She moved her hips and butt, shaking and rotating her hips. I stepped closer and mimicked her motions. Our eyes locked as we lost all sense of everything around us, as we let the beat carry away who we were. I wasn't sure where Romero was and I didn't care. This felt like freedom.

Men were watching us. I didn't return their hungry gazes. It wouldn't be fair to lead them on. Gianna didn't share my restraint. She smiled and flirted, batted her eyelashes and ran her hands through her hair. A few men started dancing around us. Gianna pressed up to one of them, hands on his chest. Another man raised his eyebrows at me, but I shook my head. He opened his mouth then closed it and backed away.

I didn't need to look back. I kept dancing because it was obvious who was behind me from the looks of respect from the men around me, from the looks of admiration from the women. Rotating my hips, I thrust my butt out, raised my arms. Firm hands came down on my hips. For a second I worried they belonged to some suicidal idiot, but they were the big, strong hands I knew. I arched, pressing my butt against a crotch, and smiled. I was wrenched against a muscled body and Luca's hot breath brushed my ear. "Who are you dancing for?"

I tilted my head to stare into his blazing gray eyes. "You. Only you."

Luca's expression was hungry, but there was still a hint of anger too. "What are you doing here?"

"Dancing."

He narrowed his eyes. "I told Romero 'no'"

"I'm not your possession, Luca. Don't treat me like one."

His fingers on my waist tightened. "You are mine, Aria, and I protect what's mine."

"I don't mind being protected, but I do mind being imprisoned." I turned in Luca's arms, catching a glimpse of Gianna in a heated argument with Matteo. "Dance with me," I shouted.

And Luca did. I knew from photos on the Internet that he'd often been to clubs in the past, and it became obvious when he moved his body. A man as tall and muscled as him shouldn't be able to move so smoothly. His eyes never left mine, his hands possessive on my waist. Luca bent his head toward me to whisper in my ear. "You look fucking hot, Aria. Every man in the club wants you and I want to kill them all."

"I'm only yours," I said fiercely, and God help me it was the truth, not just because of the ring on my finger that marked me as his. Luca's lips crashed down on mine, fierce and demanding and possessive, and I opened up for him, letting him claim me in front of everyone.

"I'm so fucking hard," Luca growled against my lips and I could feel his erection against my stomach. "Fuck. I have a call set up with one of our distributors in five minutes." I didn't ask what they were distributing. I didn't want to know.

"It's okay," I said. "Come back when you have time. I'm going to grab a drink."

"Go to the VIP area."

I shook my head. "I want to pretend I'm an ordinary girl tonight."

"Nobody who looks at you will think you are ordinary." His eyes travelled the length of my body and I shivered. Then he took a step back, regret obvious on his face. "Cesare and Romero will keep an eye on you." I was about to nod when I noticed a familiar face in the VIP area, watching me. Grace.

My breath caught. She sat on another man's lap so she wasn't here for Luca, but the look in her eyes said it all. She wasn't over him. Luca followed my gaze and cursed. "She's not here because of me."

"Yes, she is."

"I can't throw her out. She comes here all the time to party. I haven't seen her since that night. I usually stay in the back."

I nodded, a lump forming in my throat. Luca took my chin between his thumb and index finger, forcing me to meet his eyes. "There's only you, Aria." He glanced at his watch, then pulled back. "I really need to go now. I'll be back as soon as I can." He turned and strode through the crowd that parted for him. Matteo followed after him and Gianna stepped up beside me. "That asshole."

"Who?" I said distractedly. Grace had disappeared from the VIP area.

"Matteo. The guy has the nerve to tell me not to dance with other men. What is he, my owner? Fuck him." She paused. "Are you okay?"

"Yeah," I whispered. "Let's go to the bar." Romero and Cesare fell into step behind us but I turned around to them, feeling on edge. "Can you watch us from afar? You're driving me crazy." Without a word they separated and took positions in corners of the club. I released a breath and settled on a barstool.

I ordered two new gin and tonics and took a deep gulp from the cool liquid, trying to relax. Gianna jiggled her leg. "You can go dancing," I told her, but she shook her head and bobbed her head to the music.

"In a few minutes. You look pale."

"I'm okay," I said, my eyes searching the club for a sign of Grace, but she seemed to have vanished into thin air. There were too many people on the dance floor to find her anyway.

"I really need to go to the restroom," Gianna said after a while. Her gin and tonic was almost gone.

"I need to sit for a few more minutes."

Gianna gave me a worried look, but then she slipped away and Cesare followed at a safe distance.

I put my head in my palm, taking a deep breath. An arm bumped against mine, startling me. I drew back as a man with long blond hair leaned against the counter beside me. He reached past me for a straw. His jacket brushed my breast and I leaned even further back, glancing away, uncomfortable with the look he was giving me.

"What's your name?" he shouted.

I tried to ignore him. Something about him was seriously giving me the creeps. I took a sip from my drink and tried to pretend I was busy searching for someone. The man kept leering at me with an ugly smile on his unshaven face. "Are you waiting for someone?"

I turned away, really trying to ignore him and not make a big deal out of this. If I started freaking out, Romero would come over and make a scene. Maybe he was already on his way. My vision started to blur and my stomach gave a lurch. I took another sip from my drink but it didn't help. I slid off the stool, but my legs were shaky and I felt dizzy. I grabbed the counter behind me. Suddenly, the man's mouth was at my ear, his stale-cigarette breath on my face. "I'm going to fuck your tight ass. I'll make you scream, bitch." His grip on my arm was crushing as he tried to drag me away from the bar. My eyes found Romero, who was steering toward me, hand under his jacket where his gun and knife were. Impatient with our slow progress, my attacker wrapped an arm around me like a loving boyfriend ready to help his drunk girlfriend out of the club. "I'll fuck you like an animal. I'll fuck you bloody, cunt," he rasped into my ear. I stared at him, my limbs heavy, my mouth filled with cotton. I'd heard those exact words not too long ago.

I forced my lips into a smile. "You are a dead man."

Confusion flickered across the man's face a second before it contorted in agony. He released me and my legs gave way, but Cesare caught me, his arm replacing that of the man. My eyes darted around for Gianna. She hovered beside Cesare, face drawn in worry. Romero was close behind my attacker, his knife buried in the man's upper thigh. "You will follow us. If you try to run, you'll die."

"Take her drink," Cesare said to Gianna. "But don't drink."

Cesare half carried me toward the back of the club and down a flight of stairs. He shouldered open a door and we walked into a sort of office. Matteo rose from his chair. "What's going on?"

"Probably roofies," Romero said, giving the man he was holding a good shake.

"I'll get Luca," Matteo said with a twisted smile. He walked through another door and a moment later Luca stalked into the room, as tall and impressive as ever. I hung in Cesare's grasp, my face half-pressed against his chest. Luca's eyes narrowed, then flitted between me and my attacker.

"What happened?" he snarled.

Suddenly he was in front of me, lifting me into his arms. My head lolled against his chest as I gazed up at him. He put me down on the couch. Gianna knelt beside me, gripping my hand. "What's happening to her?" she cried.

"Roofies," Romero said again. "This sick fuck was trying to drag her outside."

Luca drew himself up before my attacker. "You put roofies in my wife's drink, Rick?"

Luca knew that man? Confusion flickered in my hazy mind.

"Wife! I didn't know she was yours. I didn't. I swear!" The man's lower lip was trembling.

Luca pushed away Romero's hand and curled his fingers around the handle of the knife still buried in Rick's leg. He twisted and the man screamed. Romero held him upright by the arms. "What did you plan to do to her once you had her outside?"

"Nothing!" the man cried.

"Nothing? So if my men hadn't stopped you, you would have just dropped her off at a hospital?" Luca's voice was pleasant, calm, his face devoid of emotion.

Gianna's grip on my hand was painful. I swallowed and cleared my throat. "I'll fuck your tight ass," I whispered.

Luca's head whirled around, then he was at my side, his face so close to mine, I could have kissed him. Maybe it was the roofies, but I really wanted to kiss him senseless in that moment, wanted to rip his shirt off, wanted to…

"What did you say, Aria?"

"'I'll fuck your tight ass. I'll make you scream, bitch. I'll fuck you bloody, cunt.' That's what he said to me." Luca stared into my eyes, a muscle in his jaw working. Before he could move, Gianna had leaped to her feet and flew at Rick. She hit his face and kicked his groin, and struggled ferociously against Matteo's grip as he dragged her away from Rick.

"You will die!" she screamed.

Luca straightened and she stopped moving.

"Let me go," she hissed.

"You promise to behave?" Matteo asked with an amused smile.

She nodded, her stare fixed on Rick. Matteo dropped his arms and she straightened her clothes. "They will make you bleed," she said coldly. "And I hope they will rape your ugly ass with that broomstick over there."

"Gianna," I rasped. She came over to me and sank down on the edge of the couch, taking my hand again.

Matteo didn't take his eyes off her. "I'll make him pay, Gianna."

"No," Luca said firmly. Rick looked ready to burst from relief. "He's my responsibility." Matteo and Luca exchanged a long look, then Matteo nodded.

Luca brought his face close to Rick's. "You wanted to fuck my wife? Wanted to make her scream?" His voice tore through my growing dizziness and sent a shiver down my back. I was glad it wasn't directed at me. I'd been scared of Luca before, but never had he sounded anything like this.

Rick shook his head frantically. "No, please."

Luca wrapped his hand around Rick's throat and lifted him until he stood on his tiptoes and his face was turning red. Then he tossed him away, and Rick collided with the wall and crumpled to the floor.

"I hope you're hungry," Luca snarled. "Because I'm going to feed you your cock."

"Take the girls to the car, Romero," Matteo ordered as Luca unsheathed his knife. Romero lifted me into his arms and walked out the back door, Gianna close behind. Dizziness cloaked my brain and I pressed my face into Romero's jacket. He stiffened.

Gianna snorted. "Do you think Luca will cut off your dick too because she leaned against you while she was sick?"

"Luca is my boss and Aria is his."

Gianna muttered something under her breath, but I couldn't make out the words.

"Open the door for me," Romero said, and then I was lying on cool leather. Gianna lifted my head and put it in her lap. Her fingers untangled my hair and she rested her forehead against mine. "That guy gets what he deserves."

I closed my eyes. I had condemned a man to his death with my words. My first murder. But what about the girls he would have attacked in the future? They were safe now.

"Your bodyguard doesn't even dare to wait in a car with us. Luca is a beast."

"Romero keeps watch," I whispered.

"Sure." I must have dozed off because suddenly the door was ripped open and Luca spoke. "How is she?"

"Holy fuck," Gianna said, voice shrill. "You're covered in blood."

I opened my eyes, but had trouble focusing.

"Only my shirt," Luca said, annoyance clear in his voice. There was rustling.

"You have no shame," Gianna said.

"I'm taking off my shirt, not my fucking pants. Do you ever shut your mouth?"

"Here, Boss."

Blurrily I saw Luca putting on a new shirt. "Burn that one and take care of everything, Romero. I'll drive."

A hand brushed my cheek and Luca's face hovered over me. Then he was gone, the door closed and he slipped behind the driver's seat. The car started moving and my stomach churned.

Gianna leaned forward, her head between the seats. "You are quite a hunk, you know that? If you weren't married to my sister and not such an asshole, I might consider giving you a go."

"Gianna," I groaned. When she was scared or nervous or angry, she never stopped talking, and the longer she talked the more offensive she got. And around Luca she was constantly angry.

"What, cat got your tongue? I hear you usually jump everything that doesn't have a dick," Gianna said.

Luca still didn't say anything. I wished I could see his face to find out how close to exploding he was. He'd killed a man not long ago; Gianna should really shut up.

Gianna sat back, but I knew she wasn't done yet. She wouldn't give up until she got a rise out of him. He pulled into the underground garage of our apartment building. "We're here," Gianna whispered into my ear. I wished she would talk as reasonably to Luca as she did to me.

The car door swung open and Luca hoisted me into his arms. He carried me toward the private elevator and stepped in. The bright halogen lights hurt my eyes, but I kept them open to watch Gianna and Luca in the mirror. She leaned beside him and her expression didn't bode well. "Have you ever had a threesome?"

Luca didn't move a muscle. He was looking down at me but I kept my attention on the mirror, trying to send Gianna a silent message to close her mouth. "How many women have you raped before my sister?"

Luca's head shot up, eyes burning as he stared at Gianna. I pressed my palm gently against his chest, and he glanced down at me. The tension remained. "Can't you do something else with your mouth than yap?"

Gianna straightened. "Like what? Give you a blow job?"

Luca laughed. "Girl, you've never even seen a dick. Just keep your lips shut."

"Gianna," I croaked in warning.

At last, we arrived on the top floor and Luca stepped out into our penthouse. He headed for the stairs to our bedroom when Gianna blocked his way. "Where are you taking her?"

"To bed," Luca said, trying to sidestep my sister, but she followed his movements.

"She's high on roofies. That's probably the chance you've been waiting for. I won't let her alone with you."

Luca became very still, like a wolf on the verge of attacking. "I'm going to say it only once, and you'd better obey: get out of my way and go to bed."

"Or what?"

"Gianna, please," I pleaded. She searched my face, then she nodded once and quickly kissed my cheek. "Get better."

Luca walked past her, carried me up the stairs and then into the master bedroom. The sickness that had been a distant pressure in my stomach turned into an insistent throbbing. "I'm going to be sick."

Luca carried me into the bathroom and held me over the toilet as I retched. When I was done, I said, "I'm sorry."

"What for?" He helped me stand, though the only thing keeping me upright was his steely grip on my waist.

"For throwing up."

Luca shook his head and handed me a wet towel. My hands shook as I wiped my face with it. "It's good that you got some of that shit out of your system. Fucking roofies. It's the only way for ugly fucks like Rick to get their dicks into a pussy."

He led me back into the bedroom and toward the bed. "Can you undress?"

"Yeah." The moment he let go, I fell backward and landed on the mattress. Laughter bubbled out of me, then a new wave of dizziness hit me and I groaned. He leaned over me, his face slightly blurry.

"I'm going to get you out of your clothes. They stink of smoke and vomit." I wasn't sure why he was telling me. It wasn't as if he hadn't seen me naked before. He grabbed the hem of my shirt and pulled it over my head. I watched him as he unzipped my leather pants and slid them down my legs, his knuckles brushing my skin, leaving goose bumps in their wake. He unhooked my glittery bra and threw it to the ground before he straightened and stared down at me. He turned abruptly and disappeared from my view. Dots danced in and out of my vision and I was on the brink of another laughing fit when Luca returned and helped me into one of his shirts. He was only in his briefs. He slid his arms under my knees and shoulder blades and moved me up until my head rested on the pillow, then he got into bed beside me.

"You're impressive, you know?" I babbled.

Luca scanned my face, then pressed a palm against my forehead. I giggled and reached out, wanting to touch his tattoo but misjudging the distance and brushing my fingertips across his abdomen and then lower. He hissed, snatched my hand away and pressed it against my stomach. "Aria, you're drugged. Try to sleep."

"Maybe I don't want to sleep." I wriggled in his grip.

"Yes, you do."

I yawned. "Will you hold me?"

Luca didn't say anything, but he extinguished the lights and wrapped his arms around me from behind. "You'd better lie on your side in case you feel sick again."

"Did you kill him?"

There was a pause. "Yes."

"Now there's blood on my hands."

"You didn't kill him."

"But you killed him because of me."

"I'm a killer, Aria. It had nothing to do with you." It had everything to do with me, but I was too tired to argue.

I listened to his breathing for a few heartbeats. "You know, sometimes I wish I could hate you, but I can't. I think I love you. I never thought I could. And sometimes I wonder how it would be if you made love to me."

Luca pressed his lips against my neck. "Sleep."

"But you don't love me," I mumbled. "You don't want to make love to me. You want to fuck me because you own me." His arm tightened around me. "Sometimes I wish you had taken me in our wedding night; then at least I wouldn't still wish for something that will never be. You want to fuck me like you fucked Grace, like an animal. That's why she told me you would fuck me bloody, right?"

My tongue felt heavy and my eyelids stuck together. I was talking nonsense, a garble of words I shouldn't say.

"When did she say that? Aria, when?"

Luca's sharp voice couldn't rip through the fog blanketing my thoughts, and blackness claimed me.

chapter *thirteen*

A WAVE OF SICKNESS WRENCHED ME FROM SLEEP. I STUMBLED toward the bathroom and threw up again, kneeling on the cold marble floor, too exhausted to get up. I shuddered. Luca reached over me and flushed the toilet before stroking my hair back from my forehead. "Not that hot anymore, am I?" I laughed hoarsely.

"That shouldn't have happened. I should have kept you safe."

"You did." I gripped the toilet seat and staggered to my feet. Luca's hands grasped my waist.

"Maybe a bath will help."

"I think I'll drown if I lie in the bathtub now."

Luca turned the water on in the tub while still holding me with one hand. The sky was turning gray over New York. "We can take a bath together."

I tried a teasing smile. "You just want to grab a feel."

"I won't touch you while you're still vulnerable."

"A Capo with morals?"

Luca's face was serious. "I'm not Capo yet. And I have morals. Not many, but a couple."

"I'm only teasing," I whispered as I leaned my forehead against his naked chest. He rubbed my back and the motion sent a sweet tingling down into my core. I drew back and carefully walked over to the washbasin to brush my teeth and wash my face.

Luca shut the water off when the tub was almost full. Then he helped me out of my panties and got out of his boxers before he lifted me into the tub. I ducked my face under the water for a moment, hoping it would clear the remaining fog from my head. Luca slid in behind me and pulled me back against his chest. His erection pressed against my thigh. I turned so I was facing Luca, and his length slid between my legs and brushed my entrance. I stiffened. Luca would only have to push his hips upward to enter me. He groaned, gritted his teeth, then he reached between us and pushed his erection back so it rested against my thigh again and pulled me flat on his torso.

"Some men would have taken advantage of the situation," I murmured.

Luca's jaw clenched. "I'm that kind of man, Aria. Don't kid yourself into believing I'm a good man. I'm neither noble nor a gentleman. I'm a cruel bastard."

"Not to me." I pressed my nose against the crook of his neck, breathing in his familiar, musky scent.

Luca kissed the top of my head. "It's better if you hate me. There's less chance of you getting hurt that way."

What had I told him last night when I was out of it? Had I told him I'd fallen in love with him? I couldn't remember. "But I don't hate you."

Luca kissed my head again. I wished he'd say something. I wished he'd say that he…

"You mentioned something Grace said to you." His voice was casual but tension gripped his body. "Something about fucking you bloody."

"Oh, yeah. She said you'd hurt me, fuck me like an animal, fuck me bloody when she talked to me during our wedding reception. Scared me out of my mind." Then I frowned. "I think that guy last night almost said the same thing."

"Before I killed him, he said one of the women who bought dope from him told him you were a skank who needed to be taught a lesson. She gave him cash."

I lifted my head. "Do you think it was Grace?"

Luca's eyes were like a stormy sky. "I'm sure it was her. The description fits, and who else would have an interest in attacking you."

"What are you going to do?"

"I can't kill her, even if I want to cut her fucking throat—that would cause too much trouble with her father and brother. I'll have to talk to them, though. Tell them they need to put her on a fucking leash or there won't be any more money from us."

"What if they refuse?"

"They won't. Grace has been fucking things up for a long time. They'll probably ship her off to Europe or Asia for rehab or some shit like that."

I kissed him, but the tension didn't leave Luca's body. "I can't stop thinking about what would have happened if Romero and Cesare hadn't been there, if that fucker had gotten you out of the club. The thought of his dirty hands on you makes me want to kill him again. The thought that he might have…" He shook his head.

I knew his turmoil wasn't because Luca had emotions for me. He was possessive. He couldn't bear the thought that someone might have gotten his hands on me, that someone might have taken what Luca considered his. Resignation filled me. "When Gianna leaves in a few days, you can have me," I whispered against his throat. Luca's hands stilled on my back. He didn't ask me if I was sure. I hadn't expected him to. Luca had said it himself; he wasn't a good man.

Gianna and I had spent the last few days trying different cafés and restaurants, talking and laughing and shopping, but today Gianna had to go back to Chicago. My arms around her were tight as we stood in the departure hall of JFK. Gianna needed to go through security soon, but I didn't want to let her go. Not only because I'd miss her terribly but also because I was anxious about my promise to Luca.

I braced myself and took a step back from Gianna. "Visit again soon, okay?"

She nodded, her lips pressed together. "You call me every day, don't forget."

"I won't," I promised. She backed away slowly, then turned and headed for the line at security. I waited until she walked through and disappeared from view.

Luca stood a few steps behind me. I rushed over to him and pressed my face against him. He stroked my back. "I thought we could grab dinner and then have a relaxing evening." He sounded hungry and excited, but not for food.

"Sounds good," I said with a small smile. Something shifted in Luca's face, but then it was gone.

I hadn't eaten much; my stomach was already churning. I didn't want to take any risks. Luca pretended not to notice. He ate what I didn't. When we stepped back into our penthouse, I headed for the liquor cabinet, looking for some liquid courage, but Luca gripped my wrist and pulled me against him. "Don't."

He lifted me into his arms and carried me upstairs into our bedroom. When he set me down on the edge of the bed, my eyes found his crotch. He was already hard. Nerves twisted my insides. He wanted me. I wouldn't deny him, not tonight.

Luca climbed on the bed and I lay back, my palms flat against the blanket. His lips found mine, his tongue dipping in, and I relaxed under his skillful mouth. This was good, familiar, comforting. My leg muscles loosened. Luca ripped his mouth away from me and sucked my nipple into his mouth through the fabric of my dress. I cupped his head, letting his experienced ministrations carry away my fear. There was an urgency to his kisses and touches that I'd never felt before.

He tugged at my dress and slid it down my body, leaving me in only my panties. He took a moment to admire my body before he moved down and buried his face between my legs, his tongue sliding between my folds over my panties. With a growl, he gripped them and ripped them off, then tossed them away. His mouth was hot and demanding, but too quickly he stopped and thrust a finger into me. Then he stood abruptly and slipped out of his shirt before he removed his holder and pants. His body was taut with tension and his erection harder than I'd ever seen it. The raw hunger on his face sent a spike of fear through me. "You're mine."

And then Luca loomed over me, his knees parting my legs and his tip nudged against my entrance. My muscles seized up, and I dug my nails into his shoulders and squeezed my eyes shut. This was too fast. He seemed barely in control. I pressed my face into the crook of his neck, trying to let his smell calm me.

Luca didn't move, his erection still only lightly touching my entrance.

"Aria," he said in low voice. "Look at me." I did. His gaze was hunger mixed with something gentler. I tried to focus on the gentle. For a long time we gazed at each other. He closed his eyes and lowered himself so his body was flush with mine. "I'm an asshole," he rasped. He kissed my cheek and my temple.

Confusion filled me. "Why?" God, was that small voice mine? Luca was my husband and I sounded as if I was terrified.

I *was* terrified, but I should have hidden it better.

"You are scared, and I almost lose control. I should know better. I should prepare you properly, and instead I almost shove my cock into you."

I didn't know what to say. I shifted and Luca's erection rubbed over my entrance, making me gasp. Luca released a harsh breath, squeezing his eyes shut. When he opened them again, the hunger was contained. He slid down until his head hovered over my breasts and his abs pressed against my folds. I exhaled at the friction and Luca's muscles flexed. I could tell he was still on edge.

"You are my wife," he said fiercely as if to remind himself. Then his fingers closed around my nipples and he tugged at them. I moaned, bucking my pelvis, making my core rub against Luca's abs again.

"Stop squirming," Luca ordered, almost pleadingly. He tugged again, and this time I forced myself to stay still, but a moan escaped my lips. Luca's expression was one of concentration and restraint as he tugged and twisted, twirled and rubbed. I arched my back, practically pushing my breasts into his face, and he gladly took me up on my invitation and sucked my nipple into his mouth. I closed my eyes as he suckled one breast while his fingers pinched my other. He shifted and ghosted his fingers over my ribs, my hips, my sides before his tongue followed the same trail. He bit the skin over my hipbones, then soothed the spot with his tongue. My entire body was on fire, desperate for release.

His fingers began massaging my thighs, parting me further as he moved lower. He kissed my mound, then my inner thigh before biting gently. I gasped and rocked my hips. He slid his hand under my butt and lifted me a few inches, then he kissed my folds. I whimpered at the soft touch. He kissed me again, his lips moving against my folds, then he pulled back. My eyes peeled open. He watched me, then he kissed my opening and I could feel wetness pool out of me. Luca's thumbs spread my lips for him and he licked his tongue over my wetness.

I shuddered and felt another trickle. Luca gently lapped at me, not once touching my clit. He sucked my folds, licked them, circled his tongue around my entrance but never touched me where I needed him.

"Luca, please." I bucked my hips again.

"You want this?" Luca nudged my clit with his tongue, and I cried out.

"Yes."

"Soon," he growled and eased a finger into me, fucking me with it slowly as his tongue slid around my opening, coating me with his saliva. His tongue moved up, finally circling my clit. I relaxed with a moan. Luca took my clit into his mouth and suckled, bringing me closer and closer to the edge.

"Tell me when you come," Luca said against my wet flesh.

He fingered me faster and pressed his tongue against my clit.

"I'm com—"

Luca pulled his finger out, then entered me again with two fingers. I gasped in discomfort but my orgasm ripped through me, pain mingling with pleasure as my body tried to adapt to the fullness. Luca kissed my inner thigh, then groaned. "You're so fucking tight, Aria. Your muscles are squeezing the life out of my fingers."

My pulse was slowing and I glanced at Luca. He was watching me, two fingers buried in me. He slid them out a couple of inches and I winced, but he slowly found a rhythm as he slid in and out.

"Relax," Luca murmured, and I tried. "I need to widen you, *principessa*." Luca traced his tongue over my folds and clit again. I hummed in pleasure. The discomfort in my core lessened with every stroke from Luca's tongue, and I could feel myself approaching another release. Luca must have felt it too. He pulled his fingers out and moved up until he was propped up over me. He lined himself up and shifted my legs and hips until he found the angle he wanted, then his tip brushed my entrance. And just like that I froze up again. I wanted to cry in frustration. Why couldn't my body work with me?

Luca kissed my chin, then my lips. "Aria." My eyes finally met his. His expression reflected some kind of inner struggle. I wrapped my arms around him, my palms coming to rest on his flexing back. Resolve claimed his expression.

He shifted his hips and the pressure increased. I tensed even further and Luca let out a harsh breath. "Relax," he said as he cupped my cheek and kissed my lips. "I'm not even in yet." His hand caressed my side down to my thigh. He cupped it and opened me a bit wider. Then he pushed in slowly. I tightened my hold on him, pressing my lips together. It hurt. God, it hurt like hell. He would never fit. I whimpered when the tearing sensation got to be too much and tensed even further. Luca halted in his movement, jaw clenched. He brought one of his hands up and cupped my breast, rubbing and twisting my nipple.

"You are so beautiful," he murmured into my ear. "So perfect, *principessa*." His words and his teasing of my breast made me relax slightly, and he pushed in a bit further. I tensed again. Luca kissed my mouth. "Almost there." He slid his hand down my body, fingers ghosting over my belly until he brushed my folds. He rubbed my clit slowly and I exhaled. Through the pain and discomfort I could feel small bolts of pleasure. Luca took his time teasing my clit and kissing me. His lips were hot and gentle, and his finger sent tingling sensations through my body. Slowly, my muscles loosened around his cock.

Rocking his hips forward, he pushed all the way in and I gasped, my back arching off the bed. I squeezed my eyes shut, breathing through my nose to get through the pain. I felt too full, as if I was going to rip apart. I buried my face against Luca's throat and started to count, trying to distract myself. *It gets better*, that's what the women said at my bridal shower, but when?

Luca moved, slowly and just an inch, but it hurt too much. "Please don't move," I gasped, then I pressed my lips together in shame. Other women had gone through this, and they had lain back and suffered through it. Why couldn't I? Luca's body became taut like a bowstring. He touched my cheek as he pulled back, forcing me to look at him.

"Does it hurt that much?" His voice was pure restraint, eyes dark with an emotion I couldn't place.

Get a grip, Aria. "No, not that much." My voice caught on the last word because Luca had twitched. "It's okay, Luca. Just move. I won't be mad at you. You don't have to hold back for me. Just get it over with."

"Do you think I want to use you like that? I can see how fucking painful this is. I've done many horrible things in my life, but I won't add this to my list."

"Why? You hurt people all the time. You don't have to pretend to care for my feelings only because we're married."

His eyes flashed. "What makes you think I have to pretend?"

My lips parted. I didn't dare to hope, didn't dare to read too much into his words, but God, did I want to.

"Tell me what to do," he said harshly.

"Can you hold me close for a while? But don't move."

"I won't," he promised, then kissed my lips. He gritted his teeth as he lowered himself completely. We were incredibly close—not even a sheet of paper would have fit between us. Luca curled one arm under my shoulders and pressed me against his chest, and then we kissed, our lips gliding over each other, our tongues tangling, soft and teasing. Luca caressed my side and my ribs before sneaking a hand between us and drawing small circles on my nipple. Slowly my body became slack under his soft caress and the taste of his mouth on mine. The pain between my legs turned to a dull ache and my core loosened around Luca, my body growing accustomed to his size. Luca didn't seem to notice, or he chose to ignore it; instead he kept kissing me. His fingernail scraped my nipple and a flicker of pleasure spiked between my legs. I drew back, my lips raw and hot from our kiss. Luca's eyes were hooded.

"Can you still...?" I asked.

He shifted and I could feel how hard he was. He hadn't softened at all. My eyes widened in surprise.

"I told you I'm not a good man. Even though I know you're hurting, I still have a boner because I'm inside you."

"Because you want me."

"I've never wanted anything more in my life," Luca admitted.

"Can we go slow?"

"Of course, *principessa*." Still holding me close, he withdrew a few inches, watching my face. The look of concern on his face released a knot in my chest.

I exhaled. It still hurt but not nearly as much as before, and behind the pain was the hint of something better. Luca eased back into me and found a slow and gentle rhythm. I soaked in the feel of Luca's strong body pressed against me, the sharp lines of his face. His eyes never left my face. He didn't seem to mind the slow pace; the tension in his shoulders and neck was the only sign of how difficult this was for him. He changed the angle and a spark of pleasure shot through me. I gasped. Luca halted. "Did that hurt?"

"No, it felt good," I said with a shaky smile. Luca smiled and repeated the motion, sending another tingle through me. He lowered his lips to mine. I wasn't sure how long he kept up the slow rhythm, but I was getting sore and I knew I wouldn't come. I wasn't even close, despite the occasional flickers of pleasure. Dull pain still covered too much of it. I didn't know how to say what I needed to say. He must have seen something on my face because he said. "Are you okay?"

I bit my lip. "How long until you…?"

"Not long, if I go a bit faster." He scanned my face and I nodded. He propped himself up on his elbows and thrust faster and a bit harder, and I pressed my lips together and buried my face against his shoulder, clutching his back. The pain was back, but I wanted Luca to come. "Aria?" Luca rasped.

"Keep going. Please. I want you to come."

He growled and kept thrusting. His pants came faster. He thrust deeper than before and I bit down on his shoulder to keep from whimpering in pain. Luca tensed with a groan, then he shuddered and I could feel him expand even further in me, filling me up until I was sure I'd come apart. He stopped moving, his lips against my throat. I could feel him softening in me and I almost breathed a sigh of relief. I held on to Luca, relishing the feel of his quick heartbeat and the sound of his harsh breathing.

Luca pulled out and lay down beside me, pulling me into his arms. He brushed back my hair from my sweaty face. I felt something trickling out of me and shifted uncomfortably.

"I'll get a washcloth." Luca got out of bed to head for the bathroom. Feeling cold without him, I stretched my legs but winced. I sat up and my eyes widened. There was blood smeared on my thighs and the bed, mingled with Luca's semen. Luca knelt on the bed beside me. He must have cleaned himself because there wasn't any blood on him. "There's much more blood than the fake scene you created during our wedding night." My voice was shaky.

Luca nudged my legs apart and pressed the warm wet washcloth against me. I sucked in a breath. Luca kissed my knee. "You were a lot tighter than I thought," he said quietly. He pulled the washcloth away and I flushed, but he discarded it on the floor without another glance before he pressed his hand against my abdomen. "How bad is it?"

I put my head back on the pillow. "Not that bad. How can I complain when you're covered in scars from knife and bullet wounds?"

"We're not talking about me. I want to know how you feel, Aria. On a scale of one to ten, how much does it hurt?"

"Now? Five?"

Luca tensed. He lowered himself beside me, curled an arm around me and scanned my face. "And during?"

I avoided his eyes. "If ten is for the worst pain I've ever felt, then eight."

"The truth."

"Ten," I whispered.

Luca clenched his jaw. "Next time will be better."

"I don't think I can again so soon."

"I didn't mean now," he said firmly, kissing my temple. "You'll be sore for a while."

"On a scale of one to ten, how fast and hard did you go? The truth," I mimicked his words.

"Two."

"Two?"

I must have looked pretty horrified, because Luca rubbed my stomach lightly. "We have time. I will go as gentle as you need me to."

"I can't believe Luca—The Vice—Vitiello said 'gentle,'" I said teasingly to lighten the mood.

Luca smirked. He cupped my face and leaned close. "It'll be our secret."

Emotions crowded in my chest. "Thanks for being gentle. I never thought you would be."

Luca laughed, a raw sound. "Believe me, nobody's more surprised about this than me."

I rolled onto my side, wincing, and snuggled against Luca's shoulder. "You've never been gentle to someone?"

"No," he said bitterly. "Our father taught Matteo and me that any kind of gentleness was a weakness. And there was never any room in my life for it."

Even if the words wanted to get stuck in my throat, I said, "What about the girls you were with?"

"They were a means to an end. I wanted to fuck, so I looked for a girl and fucked her. It was hard and fast, definitely not gentle. I mostly fucked them from behind so I didn't have to look them in the eyes and pretend I gave a shit about them."

He sounded cold and cruel.

I kissed his tattoo, wanting to banish that part of him again. His arms around me tightened. "The only person who could have taught me how to be gentle was my mother." I held my breath. Would he tell me about her now? "But she killed herself when I was nine."

"I'm sorry." I wanted to ask what happened, but I didn't want to push him and make him retreat behind his cold mask. Instead I cupped his cheek. He looked startled by the gesture but didn't pull away. I licked my lip, trying to suppress my curiosity.

"Does it still hurt?" he asked suddenly. For a moment, I didn't know what he was talking about. He brushed a hand across my abdomen. "Yeah, but talking helps."

"How does it help?"

"It distracts me." I gathered my courage. "Can you tell me more about your mother?"

"My father hit her. He raped her. I was young but I understood what was going on. She couldn't bear my father anymore, so she decided to slice her wrists and overdose on dope."

"She shouldn't have left you and Matteo alone."

"I found her."

I jerked up and stared. "You found your mother after she'd cut her wrists?"

"That was actually the first body I saw. Of course it wasn't the last." He shrugged as if it didn't matter. "The floor was covered with her blood and I slipped on it and fell. My clothes were soaked with her blood." His voice was calm, detached. "I ran out of the bathroom screaming and crying. My father found me and slapped me. Told me to be a man and clean myself up. I did. I never cried again."

"This is horrible. You must have been terrified. You were only a boy."

He was silent. "It made me tough. At one point every boy has to lose his innocence. The mafia isn't a place for the weak."

I knew that. I'd seen how Father had tried to shape Fabiano in the last few years, and it always broke my heart when my little brother had to act like a man instead of the young boy that he was. "Emotions aren't a weakness."

"Yes, they are. Enemies always aim where they can hurt you most."

"And where would the Bratva aim if they wanted to hurt you?"

Luca extinguished the lights. "They won't ever find out."

That wasn't the answer I'd hoped for, but I was too tired to ponder it. Instead I closed my eyes and let sleep claim me.

chapter *fourteen*

Going to the toilet burnt like hell, and walking wasn't exactly comfortable either. I winced as I stepped back into the bedroom where Luca lay with his head propped up on his arm. He watched me. "Sore?"

I nodded, blushing. "Yeah. I'm sorry."

"Why are you sorry?"

I lay down beside him. "I thought you might want to do it again, but I don't think I can."

Luca traced his fingertips over my ribs. "I know. I didn't expect you to be ready so soon." He rubbed my stomach, then inched a bit lower. "I could lick you if you're up for it."

My core tightened and I really wanted to say yes. "I don't think that's a good idea."

Luca nodded and settled back against the pillows. The blanket crowded around his hips, revealing his muscled torso and the scars there.

I moved closer and propped myself up above him. I traced Luca's scars, wondering what kind of stories hid behind each of them. I wanted to know all of them, wanted to figure Luca out scar by scar like a puzzle. Where did he get the long scar on his shoulder and the bullet wound below his ribs? Luca was doing his own exploring with his eyes, wandering over my breasts and face. He ran his thumb over my nipples. "Your breasts are fucking perfect." His touch was more possessive than sexual, but I could feel it all the way between my legs anyway.

Trying to distract myself, I paused with my fingertips against a mostly faded scar on his abs. "Where did you get this scar?"

"I was eleven." My eyes grew wide. I was pretty sure where the story was going. "The Famiglia wasn't as united as it is now. A few men thought they could grab power by killing my father and his sons. It was the middle of the night when I heard screaming and shooting. Before I could get out of bed, a man stepped into the room and pointed his gun at me. I knew I'd die as I stared into the barrel. I wasn't as scared as I thought I'd be. He would have killed me, if Matteo hadn't jumped him from behind when he pulled the trigger. The bullet went a lot lower than it was supposed to and hit my middle. It hurt like a motherfucker. I was screaming and probably would have passed out if the man hadn't turned on Matteo to kill him. I had a gun stashed in the drawer of my nightstand, took it out and put a bullet in the man's head before he could kill Matteo."

"That was your first murder, right?" I whispered.

Luca's eyes, which had been lost in another time, focused on me. "Yeah. The first of many."

"When did you kill again?"

"That same night." He smiled humorlessly. "After that first man, I told Matteo to hide in my closet. He protested, but I was bigger and locked him in. By then I'd lost quite a bit of blood, but I was high on adrenaline and could still hear shooting downstairs, so I headed for the noise with my gun. My father was in a shooting match with two attackers. I came down the stairs but nobody paid me any attention, and then I shot one of them from behind. My father took the other down with a shot in the shoulder."

"Why didn't he kill him?"

"He wanted to question him to find out if there were other traitors in the Famiglia."

"So what did he do with the guy while he took you to the hospital?"

Luca gave me a wry look. I gasped. "Don't tell me he didn't take you."

"He called the Doc of the Famiglia, told me to put pressure on the wound and went ahead and started torturing the guy for information."

I couldn't believe a father would let his child suffer through pain and risk his life, so he could gather information.

"You could have died. Some things need to be treated in a hospital. How could he do that?"

"The Famiglia comes first. We never take our injured to a hospital. They ask too many questions and the police get involved, and it's an admittance of weakness. And my father had to make sure the traitor spoke before he got a chance to kill himself."

"So you agree with what he did? You would have watched someone you love bleed to death so you could protect the Famiglia and your power."

"My father doesn't love me. Matteo and I are his guarantee for power and a way to keep the family name alive. Love has nothing to do with it."

"I hate this life. I hate the mafia. Sometimes I wish there was a way to escape."

Luca's face became still. "From me?"

"No," I said, surprising myself. "From this world. Have you never wanted to live a normal life?"

"No. This is who I am, who I was born to be, Aria. It's the only life I know, the only life I want. For me to commit to a normal life would be like an eagle living in a small cage in a zoo." He paused. "Your marriage to me shackles you to the mafia. Blood and death will be your life as long as I live."

"Then so be it. I'll go where you go no matter how dark the path."

For a moment, Luca held his breath, then he gripped the back of my head and kissed me fiercely.

I'd thought Luca would want to sleep with me again soon after our first time, but he didn't push me. Even though I tried to hide it, he could tell that I was sore for a few days after. He pleasured me with his tongue a few times, never even entering me with his finger, and I made him come with my mouth in turn.

I wasn't sure if he was waiting for an okay from me but when he came home one night a week after he'd taken my virginity, looking exhausted and angry, I wanted to make him feel better. After he'd showered, he stumbled toward the bed in only his boxers, his eyes filled with darkness.

"Bad day?" I whispered as he flung himself on the bed beside me. He lay on his back and stared up at the ceiling with empty eyes.

"Luca?"

"I lost three of my men today."

"What happened?"

"The Bratva attacked one of our warehouses." His lips thinned, chest heaving. "We'll make them pay. Our retribution will make them bleed."

"What can I do?" I said softly, my hand stroking his chest.

"I need you."

"Okay." I slid my nightgown over my head and pushed down my panties. I knelt beside Luca. He got rid of his boxers and his erection sprang free. Gripping my hips, he made me straddle his stomach. Nerves twisted my insides. I'd hoped that for my second time Luca would still be on top. The thought of lowering myself on his length after how much it had hurt last time terrified me, but if Luca needed me, then I could do it. I cried out in surprise when Luca gripped my butt and hoisted me toward his face, so I was hovering over his mouth. He pressed me down and I screamed out in pleasure, my hands coming up to press against the headboard. This was more intense than anything Luca had ever done to me.

His tongue slipped into me deeply and he massaged my butt with firm fingertips. I peered down into Luca's eyes as he closed his mouth over my clit. I rocked my hips, pressing myself against his mouth. He growled. The vibration sent pleasure through me and I started rotating my hips, riding Luca's face. I closed my eyes, let my head fall back as Luca fucked me with his tongue again, humming all the while. And then I shattered, rocking against Luca's mouth and screaming his name. Somewhere deep inside, a part of me wanted to be embarrassed, but I was too aroused.

When my orgasm subsided, I tried to pull away from Luca's lips but he held me fast, his eyes burning into me as he licked me with slow strokes. It was too much, but he was relentless. With soft caresses and nudges from his tongue he slowly built my pleasure up again. My pants came quicker and I didn't try to escape anymore; instead I let Luca move my hips back and forth as he licked me. I was seconds away from my second orgasm. Without warning he pulled back, and in one fluid motion he flicked me on my back and knelt between my legs, his erection pressed against my entrance.

I tensed up but Luca didn't enter. He bowed his head so he could suck my nipple into his mouth and rubbed the tip of his erection back and forth over my clit. I mewed helplessly at the sensation. I'd been so close to coming before and could feel myself getting there again. Then he dipped only the tip into my opening. I gasped at the brief pain, but he retreated quickly and slid his slick tip over my clit again. He did this over and over until I was panting and so wet I could hear it, then he released my nipple and brought his face up to mine. His tip slipped into my opening, but this time he didn't retreat.

Slowly he slid into me all the way, never taking his eyes off me. I bit my lip to stifle a gasp. It wasn't as painful as last time but still uncomfortable. I felt too stretched, too full. Luca cupped the back of my head and began moving. My breath hitched despite the slow pace, but Luca didn't falter. He slid in and out at an excruciatingly slow and gentle rhythm until my breath stopped catching in my throat. He sped up, but I clawed his arms and he slowed again. He lowered his mouth to my ear, his voice low and husky as he spoke. "I loved the taste of you, *principessa*. I loved how you rode my fucking mouth. I loved my tongue in you. I love your pussy and your tits, and I love that you're all mine." Luca kept up his steady thrusting as he whispered into my ear. And I forgot about the dull pain, and moaned. Nothing was sexier than Luca talking dirty to me in his deep baritone.

Through the discomfort I could feel an orgasm building as Luca's low voice washed over me. He sneaked his hand between us and found my clit, rubbing frantically as he thrust into me. His movements sped up a bit, and I whimpered from both pain and pleasure. Luca didn't slow. He was panting, his skin slick with sweat as he fought for control. I could see on his face how his grip on it was fading, but he didn't lose it. I moaned as he slid deeper into me than before. Pleasure radiated through my body.

"Come for me, Aria," he rasped, increasing the pressure on my clit. Another spike of pleasure mixed with pain slammed through me and I fell apart, gasping and moaning as my orgasm rocked my body. Luca growled and thrust harder. I clung to him, fingers digging into his shoulders as he approached his own peak. With a guttural groan, Luca tensed above me, and I could feel him release into me. I moaned at how full and stretched I felt. Luca kept thrusting until I could feel him soften. He pulled out but stayed on top of me, his weight supported on his forearms. "Was I too rough?" he asked thickly.

"No, it was okay." I didn't dare ask how much harder he could go.

He kissed the corner of my mouth, then my lower lip until he dipped his tongue into me for a delicious kiss. We kissed for a long time, our slick bodies pressed against each other. I wasn't sure how long we lay like that, kissing, but eventually I could feel Luca getting hard again.

My eyes grew wide in surprise. "So soon? I thought men needed time to rest."

Luca laughed, a deep sexy sound. "Not with your naked body beneath me." He kneaded my butt. "How sore are you?"

Too sore, but the way he rubbed his erection lightly against my folds, I couldn't say it. "Not too sore."

Luca gave me a look that made it clear he recognized the lie but he rolled on his back, taking me with him. I straddled his abs. He must have seen how nervous I was because he stroked my sides gently. "Take your time. You are in control."

He rocked his hips, rubbing his length over my butt cheeks.

"I want you in control," I admitted.

Luca's eyes darkened. "Don't say something like that to a man like me." But he gripped my hips and positioned me above his erection. From this vantage point he looked even bigger. He rubbed his tip in small circles over my clit as his other hand trailed up toward my breast and cupped it. He lined himself up with my opening before grabbing my hips and slowly guiding me down. When he was almost all the way in, I paused, catching my breath. I lay my palms flat against his chest as I tried to get used to the new position. He felt bigger, and my muscles clenched tightly around his erection. Luca gritted his teeth. He ran his hands up my torso and cupped my breasts again, twirling my nipples between his fingers. I moaned and made small rocking motions with my hips. Luca pressed his thumb against my clit and flicked, then as I moaned he pushed me all the way down to the base of his erection.

I cried out in surprise more than pain and froze, exhaling slowly to adjust to the feeling of utter fullness.

"Aria," Luca rasped. I met his gaze. A hint of uncertainty flickered in his eyes.

I forced my lips into a smile. "Give me a moment."

He nodded, his hands resting lightly on my waist as he watched me. I released another breath, then shifted my hips experimentally. There was a twinge but there was also pleasure. "Help me?" I whispered, gazing at him through my lashes.

He clasped my waist, his fingers splaying across my butt, and guided me into a slow rhythm of rocking and rotating. It was exhilarating to feel the strength of his body beneath my hands, to feel his pectoral muscles flex under my fingertips, but even better was the look in his eyes as he watched me on top of him. The hunger and admiration mixed with another emotion I didn't dare to guess. Luca's chest heaved under my palms, his breath coming faster as he started thrusting upwards, driving himself into me harder and faster. His thumb flicked back and forth over my clit as he drove into me. I cried out. Luca gripped my hips in a bruising grip and thrust faster. I threw my head back, riding through my orgasm as I felt Luca tense and release into me with a low moan.

I shivered helplessly on top of him as I came down from my high. I slumped forward on Luca's chest and pressed my lips to his. His heart pounded against my breasts. He slung his arms around my back and pressed me against him tightly.

"I won't lose you," he growled, startling me.

"You won't."

"The Bratva is closing in. How can I protect you?"

Why would the Bratva have any interest in me? "You will find a way."

chapter *fifteen*

A COUPLE OF WEEKS HAD PASSED AND SEX GOT BETTER EVERY TIME we did it. I had a feeling Luca was still holding back quite a bit, but I didn't mind. Sometimes I wondered if maybe he needed the gentle lovemaking as much as I did after all the stress he went through with the Bratva.

Lovemaking? No matter how much I tried to ignore my feelings, I knew I loved Luca. Maybe it was natural to fall in love with the person you were married to, the person you shared intimacy with. I wasn't sure why I had fallen for Luca despite my best intentions not to let him into my heart; I only knew that I had. I knew what men like Luca thought of love. I hadn't told him about my feelings, though a few times the words had been on the tip of my tongue after we'd laid in each other's arms, sweaty and sated after sex. I knew Luca wouldn't say it back, and I didn't want to make myself vulnerable like that.

I watched the sun set over New York from my position in the lounge chair on the roof terrace. Romero was inside, reading a sports magazine on the sofa. A few times I'd considered asking Luca to stop Romero's constant presence—nothing could happen to me in our penthouse—but then I couldn't go through with it. I would have felt more alone without Romero in the apartment, even if we didn't talk all that much. Marianna only came in around lunchtime to clean and prepare lunch and dinner, and Luca was gone most days. I still hadn't met any of the women from the Famiglia for coffee. After Cosima's betrayal, I really wasn't keen on meeting more of Luca's family anyway.

My phone vibrated on the small table. I snatched it up, seeing Gianna's name flash on the screen. Happiness burst in my chest. We had talked this morning, but it wasn't unusual for my sister to call more than once per day and I didn't mind.

The moment I heard her voice, I sat up, my heart pounding in my chest like crazy.

"Aria," she whispered, her voice thick with tears.

"Gianna, what happened? What's going on? Are you hurt?"

"Father's giving me to Matteo."

I didn't understand, couldn't. "What do you mean he's giving you to Matteo?" My voice shook and tears already burnt in my eyes as I listened to Gianna's heart-wrenching sobs.

"Salvatore Vitiello spoke to Father and told him that Matteo wanted to marry me. And Father agreed!"

I couldn't breathe. I'd worried that Matteo wouldn't let Gianna get away with her rudeness toward him. He was a man who didn't like to be refused, but how could Father have agreed? "Did Father say why? I don't understand. I'm already in New York. He didn't need to marry you off to the Famiglia too."

I stood, couldn't sit still anymore. I started pacing the roof, trying to calm my racing pulse with low breaths.

"I don't know why. Maybe Father wants to punish me for saying what I think. He knows how much I despise our men, and how much I hate Matteo. He wants to see me suffer."

I wanted to disagree, but I wasn't sure Gianna was wrong. Father thought women needed to be put in their place, and what better way to do that with Gianna than bind her to a man like Matteo? Behind his grins lurked something dark and angry, and I had a feeling Gianna wouldn't have the sense not to provoke him until he lost it.

"Oh, Gianna. I'm so sorry. Maybe I can tell Luca and he can change Matteo's mind."

"Aria, don't be naïve. Luca knew all along. He's Matteo's brother and the future Capo. Something like that isn't decided without him being involved."

I knew she was right, but I didn't want to accept it. Why hadn't Luca told me about this? "When did they make the decision?"

"A few weeks ago, even before I came to visit."

My heart clenched. Luca had slept with me, had made me trust him and love him, and hadn't bothered to tell me that my sister was being sold to his brother.

"I can't believe him!" I whispered harshly. Romero was watching me through the windows, already getting up from the sofa. "I'm going to kill him. He knows how much I love you. He knows I wouldn't have allowed it. I would have done anything to prevent the agreement."

Gianna was silent on the other end. "Don't get in trouble because of me. It's too late anyway. New York and Chicago shook hands on it. It's a made deal, and Matteo won't let me out of his clutches."

"I want to help you, but I don't know how."

"I love you, Aria. The only thing that stops me from cutting my wrists right now is the knowledge that my marriage to Matteo means I'll live in New York with you."

Fear crushed my heart. "Gianna, you are the strongest person I know. Promise me you won't do anything stupid. If you hurt yourself, I couldn't live with myself."

"You are much stronger than me, Aria. I have a big mouth and flashy bravado, but you are resilient. You married Luca, you live with a man like him. I don't think I could have done it. I don't think I can."

"We'll figure it out, Gianna."

The elevator doors opened and Luca stepped into our apartment. His eyes darted from Romero to me, his brows drawing together.

"He's here. I'll call you tomorrow." I hung up as fury burnt through me. I hadn't thought I could ever hate Luca again, not even for a moment, but in this second I wanted to hurt him. I stormed inside, my hands balled into fists as I headed toward Luca. He didn't move a muscle, only watched me with calm scrutiny. That calm fueled my rage more than anything else. I wasn't sure what he thought I was going to do, but it wasn't attack—that was obvious from his reaction. My fists hammered his chest as hard as I could. Shock flashed across Luca's face, his entire body exploding with tension. From the corner of my eye I saw Romero take a step in our direction, obviously unsure if he was supposed to do something. He was my bodyguard, but Luca was his boss. Of course, Luca didn't have trouble handling me. After a moment, he gripped both of my wrists in his hand. I hated that he could overpower me so easily. "Aria, what—"

He didn't get to finish because I rammed my knee upward, and only his quick reflexes prevented me from hitting my goal. The sound of Gianna's sobs rang in my mind, made me lose whatever rationality I had.

"Get out," Luca ordered sharply. Romero did so without protest. Luca's blazing eyes met mine, but I was past being scared. I would die for Gianna. I tried another kick and grazed Luca's groin this time. He snarled and pushed me down on the sofa, my legs pinned down by his knees and my arms pushed above my head. "For god's sake, Aria. What's gotten into you?"

I glared. "I know about Gianna and Matteo," I spat, and then I lost it completely and I started crying, big, gasping sobs raking my body. Luca released my wrists and sat back so I could move my legs. He regarded me like I was a creature he would never understand.

"That's what this is about?" He sounded incredulous.

"Of course you don't understand, because you never loved anyone more than your own life. You can't possibly understand how it is to feel your own heart breaking at the thought of the person you love getting hurt. I would die for the people I love."

His eyes were hard and cold as he stood. "You are right. I don't understand." The cold mask was back. I hadn't seen it directed at me in weeks.

I wiped my eyes and stood as well. "Why didn't you tell me? You've known for weeks."

"Because I knew you wouldn't like it."

I shook my head. "You knew I'd be mad at you, and you didn't want to ruin your chances of fucking me." I didn't blush, even though I never used the word.

Luca became rigid. "Of course I wanted to fuck you. But I got the impression you enjoyed our *fucking sessions*."

I wanted to hurt him. He was so cold. Of course it had always been about taking what was his, about claiming my body. He didn't give a shit about me, or anyone. "And you worried I wasn't a good enough actress to fool everyone after our little trick on our wedding night. But it turns out, I even fooled you." I let out an ugly laugh. "I made you believe I actually enjoyed it."

Something flickered in Luca's eyes, something that made me want to take back my words for a moment, but then his mouth pulled into a cruel smile. "Don't lie to me. I've fucked enough whores to know an orgasm when I see one."

I flinched as if he'd hit me. Had he just compared me to his whores? I said the ugliest thing I could think of. "Some women even experience an orgasm when they're being raped. It's not because they're enjoying it. It's their body's way of coping."

For a long time Luca didn't say anything. His nostrils flared and his chest heaved and his hands were clenched to fists. He looked like he wanted to kill me on the spot. Then the scariest thing happened: the anger slipped off his face. His expression became emotionless, his eyes as smooth and impenetrable as steel. "Your sister should be happy that Matteo wants her. Few men can stand her gab."

"God, that's the reason, isn't it?" I said in disgust. "It's because she told him that he'd never get her hot body that day in the hotel. He didn't like it. He couldn't bear that she was immune to his creepy charm."

"She shouldn't have challenged him. Matteo is a determined hunter. He gets what he wants." Still not a flicker of emotion, not even in Luca's voice. It was like he was made from ice.

"He gets what he wants? It's not hunting if he forces her into marriage by asking my father for her hand. That is cowardice."

"It doesn't matter. They're getting married." He turned his back to me, as if he was dismissing me.

Luca didn't get it. He couldn't. He didn't know Gianna as well as I did. She wouldn't go into this union quietly like I had. I stormed toward the elevator. "Aria, what the fuck are you doing?"

I was in the elevator before Luca could reach it and was on my way one floor down. I stepped out into Matteo's apartment. It was basically a mirror image of our own, except that it wasn't a duplex. Matteo was sitting in an armchair, listening to some kind of crappy rap music when he saw me. He rose, eying me cautiously as he came toward me. "What are you doing here?"

I pushed my palms against his chest when he stopped in front of me. "Take your proposal back. Tell my father you don't want Gianna."

Matteo laughed. "Why would I? I want her. I always get what I want. Gianna shouldn't have played games with the big boys."

I lost it and slapped him across the face. My stupid Italian temperament. I usually reined it in, better than my other siblings at least, but not today. He gripped my arm, shoved me back so my spine collided painfully with the wall, and trapped me between it and his body. I gasped. "You are lucky that you are my brother's wife."

The elevator dinged as it stopped and opened. "Let her go," Luca growled, stepping out. Matteo backed away at once and gave me a cold smile.

Luca walked up to me, eyes scanning my body before facing his brother. "You won't do that again."

"Then teach her manners. I won't let her hit me again." Teach her manners? His marriage to Gianna would end in an utter catastrophe.

Luca's voice dropped an octave. "You won't touch my wife again, Matteo. You are my brother and I'd take a bullet for you, but if you do that again, you'll have to live with the consequences." They faced each other, and for a moment I worried they'd pull knives and fight each other. That wasn't what I'd intended. I knew how much Luca cared about his brother—more than he cared about me, anyway. Matteo was the only person Luca trusted. For a while I'd thought I might be that person, but if that were the case, today would have gone very differently. I knew his protecting me was a power game and not about emotions. By touching me, Matteo had shown disrespect toward Luca, and of course Luca couldn't let that slide.

"I won't hit you again, Matteo," I ground out, though the words tasted foul in my mouth. "I shouldn't have done it."

Both men turned to me in surprise. Matteo relaxed his stance. Luca didn't.

"I'm sorry if I hurt or scared you," Matteo said. I couldn't tell if he meant it or not. He had the emotionless mask down just like his brother.

"You didn't."

Luca smirked, then he stepped up to me and pulled me against him possessively. Our eyes met and as if he remembered our earlier words, his smirk disappeared and his lips tightened. He didn't release me, but his hold on me loosened.

I turned away from him, not able to bear his expression any longer, and faced Matteo. "Don't marry Gianna," I tried again, and Luca's grip on my waist tightened in warning. I ignored him. "She doesn't want to marry you."

"You didn't want to marry Luca either, yet here you are," Matteo said with his shark grin.

"Gianna isn't like me. She won't come to terms with an arranged marriage."

Luca dropped his hand from my waist.

"She will become my wife the moment she turns eighteen. No power in this universe will stop me from making her mine."

"You disgust me. You all do," I said. With that I stepped back into the elevator. Luca didn't follow. He didn't even watch me to see if I was returning to our apartment. He knew I wouldn't go anywhere. Even if I still wanted to run, I couldn't. My heart belonged to him even if he didn't have a heart that he could give me in turn.

chapter *sixteen*

I twisted and turned, not able to fall asleep. I wasn't used to being alone in bed anymore. Even though Luca and I had barely spoken in the last three days since our fight and hadn't had sex, we'd always ended up in each other's arms during the night. Of course, the moment we woke we moved apart. I missed Luca's closeness. I missed talking to him, missed his kisses, his touch, his hot tongue between my legs. I sighed as I became wet. I wouldn't give in. How much longer could Luca go without sex anyway?

What if he wasn't? What if he'd fucked Grace again? She was supposedly in England, but who knew if that was the truth. Or maybe he'd found a new woman to fuck. My eyes found the clock. It was almost two in the morning. A heavy weight settled on my chest. Was Luca giving up on our marriage that easily?

Why not? He'd gotten what he wanted. He'd claimed my body. It wasn't like I was the only person who could give him what he wanted.

A bang sounded downstairs, followed by deep voices. Romero was one of them, the other was Luca. I slipped out of bed and quickly rushed out of the bedroom in my nightgown. I froze on the staircase. The lights were out, but the moon and the surrounding skyscrapers provided enough light for me to see what was going on. Luca had Romero in a chokehold. I took another step down and Luca's eyes shot toward me, furious and wild. The monster was back. His arms were covered in blood. Romero stopped struggling when he realized Luca was too strong.

"I would never betray the Famiglia," Romero choked out, then coughed. "I'm loyal. I'd die for you. If I were a traitor, Aria wouldn't be here, safe and unscathed. She'd be in the hands of the Bratva."

Luca loosened his hold and Romero fell to his knees, gasping for breath. I walked down the remaining steps, ignoring Romero shaking his head at me. What was going on? Luca had never been this unhinged.

"Out, now," he snarled at Romero. When Romero didn't move, Luca grabbed him by the collar and dragged him into the elevator. Before the doors slid shut, Romero's worried gaze settled on me. Luca jabbed a code into the panel beside the elevator that deactivated it and stopped people from coming into our apartment, then he turned to me. Not only his arms, but his shirt too was covered in blood. I didn't see any bullet holes in his shirt or pants.

"Are you okay?" I said, but even my whisper felt too loud in the silence.

I approached Luca slowly as his eyes followed my movement like a tiger would watch the antelope. A strange flicker of excitement filled me. Despite what I'd witnessed, I knew Luca wouldn't really hurt me. When I'd almost reached him, Luca stalked toward me and crashed his lips against mine. I gasped and he thrust his tongue into my mouth. His hands ripped at my nightgown, tearing it from my body. When it fluttered to the ground, he tore my thin lace panties off. His hungry gaze traveled over me, then he wrenched me toward him and bit into my throat, then my nipple. I gasped in pain and arousal. I should have run as Luca had told me a long time ago, but this side of him actually excited me, and my arousal spoke louder than my fear, even when Luca pushed me toward the sofa and bent me over the backrest. His hand held my neck as his other hand slid between my folds. He pushed two fingers into me and found me wet and aching. I released a harsh breath as my walls clamped tightly around his fingers. He pulled them out. I heard him open his belt and unzip his pants, and I shivered with fear and excitement. Luca bit into my butt cheek, then my lower back and shoulder blade, before he shoved his entire length into me without warning.

I cried out, but Luca didn't hesitate. He pressed his chest against my back while he held me captive with one arm around my chest, and then he started pounding into me hard and fast. I bit down on my lip. It hurt but it felt also good. Every time he pushed into me, he hit a spot deep inside me that sent sparks of pleasure through me. Luca reached down, his hot breath against my neck, and rubbed his fingers over my clit. I cried and gasped and whimpered. I could feel the tension building. The sound of Luca's pants and growls turned me on even more. His fingers twisted my nipple almost painfully and he bit down on the crook of my neck, and stars erupted before my vision as I exploded. I screamed Luca's name over and over again as I trembled in the wake of my orgasm, but he didn't slow. He drove into me hard and fast, his fingers on my clit relentless as his breathing grew labored, and then I came again, shattering into a thousand tiny pieces of pleasure. My legs crumbled, but Luca pinned me against the backrest with his body. With a growl, he gripped my hips and fucked me even harder. I'd be bruised and sore tomorrow, but I couldn't bring myself to care. When he shuddered against me and bit the other side of my throat, I hung limply over the sofa. I was too sated and exhausted to do anything as he came inside me.

I thought it was over, but Luca lifted me off the backrest and lowered me to the ground. He shoved my legs as wide apart as they would go. I was oversensitive and couldn't possibly come again, but Luca's eyes pinned me with their intensity. He grasped my wrists and pushed my arms up above my head, then he rubbed two fingers along my folds, back and forth, before circling my opening and sliding them in inch by inch. My eyes rolled back in my head as he fingered me in a torturously slow way. My walls clamped around his fingers and I heard sounds coming from the back of my throat I didn't recognize. He didn't touch my clit, just fucked me with his fingers with an intense look on his face.

"Is this a fucking lie?" he asked roughly as he curled his fingers in me and made me gasp in pleasure. "Tell me, Aria. Tell me you enjoy this as much as I do." The despair in his voice startled me.

He curled his fingers again and I whimpered. "Yes, Luca. I enjoy this."

He flicked my clit with his thumb and I arched off the ground, but he pulled his thumb away despite my mew of protest and kept fingering me. "So you lied? Why?"

He was driving me insane with need. I wanted him to touch my clit, wanted him to finger me faster, wanted him to fuck me. "Yes, I lied!" I squirmed in his hold, wanting to free my hands to reach for his cock. He was already growing hard and I wanted to convince him to stop my torture, but he was too strong and too relentless.

"Why?" he growled. He paused his fingers and I wanted to scream in frustration.

"I lied because I hate that I love you, because I hate that you can hurt me without ever laying a finger on me, because I hate myself for loving you even though you won't ever love me back." Luca released my wrists, eyes dark and questioning.

I didn't want to talk. I reached for his erection and gave it a hard squeeze. "Now fuck me."

He grabbed my legs and pulled me toward him, my feet pressed up against his shoulders, and then he slid into me in one hard stroke and I came around him, my muscles clenching around his cock so tightly that he grunted. He fucked me even harder, and I scratched my fingers over the wooden floor as my eyes shut tightly. I was coming apart from pleasure and emotions. My back rubbed against the hard floor, I was sore and my legs were stiff, but I came again when Luca hit his release, and then I passed out.

My entire body hurt. I groaned when I shifted and realized I was lying in our bed. Luca must have carried me upstairs last night. My eyes fluttered open and found Luca watching me with a strange look on his face.

"What did I do?" he asked in a harsh whisper.

I frowned, then looked down at myself. The blankets were pulled back, revealing the entire length of my body and the proof of last night's actions. There were finger-shaped bruises on my hips and wrists. My throat and shoulders were tender where Luca had marked me, and my inner thighs were red from the friction. I looked like a mess. I sat up and winced from the sharp soreness between my legs. Yet I couldn't find it in me to regret anything. I didn't always want it this rough, but once in a while it was a nice change of pace.

"Aria, please tell me. Did I…?"

I searched his eyes, trying to figure out what he was talking about. Self-hatred flashed on his face, and then I realized what he thought. "You don't remember?"

"I remember bits and pieces. I remember holding you down." His voice caught. He wasn't touching me. In fact he perched on the edge of the bed, as far from me as possible. He looked exhausted and broken.

"You didn't hurt me."

His eyes flickered to the bruises. "Don't lie to me."

I knelt and moved toward him even when he stiffened. "You were a bit rougher than usual, but I wanted it. I enjoyed it."

Luca didn't say anything, but I could tell he didn't believe me.

"No, really, Luca." I kissed his cheek and lowered my voice. "I came at least four times. I don't exactly remember everything. I passed out from sensory overload." Relief washed away some of the darkness in Luca's eyes, but I was surprised that he didn't tease me for my comment.

"I don't understand what got into you. You even attacked Romero."

"My father is dead."

I jerked. "What? How?"

"Last night. He was having dinner at a small restaurant in Brooklyn when a sniper put a bullet into his head."

"What about your stepmother?"

"She wasn't there. He was with his mistress. She was shot too, probably because the Bratva thought she was his wife. Someone must have told them where to find him. Very few people knew he went there. He was in disguise. Nobody could have recognized him. There has to be a traitor among us."

chapter
seventeen

The sky over New York was hung with heavy clouds, but it didn't rain. It fit the occasion. For the funeral of Salvatore Vitiello, the elite of New York and the Famiglia, as well as the most important members of the Chicago Outfit, had gathered at the cemetery. The perimeter around it had been closed off, and most of the soldiers of the New York mafia were keeping guard to make sure the Bratva didn't disturb the funeral. A gathering of the most important members from both New York and Chicago at this time was a risk, but paying respect to the Capo dei Capi was more important.

Luca stood tall and stoic beside his father's grave. He was now the new Capo and he couldn't show a flicker of weakness, not even after the death of his father. Luca and his father hadn't been close in the traditional sense, but losing your parent, no matter how cruel and cold he'd been, always ripped a hole into you.

I could tell that many of the older men in the Famiglia watched Luca with a calculating look in their eyes. Luca didn't give any indication that he noticed, but that was definitely an act. This was the most dangerous time, so soon after he'd come into power. I hadn't known Salvatore Vitiello very well, and I wasn't sorry about that. For me the funeral meant only one thing: I got the chance to see my family again.

Gianna, Fabi and Lily stood with Father and Mother among the guests from the Chicago Outfit. They'd arrived this morning and I couldn't wait to spend some time with them. Every guest shook Luca's hand, clapped his shoulder and said a few words of comfort, most of them lies. How many of these men were waiting for a chance to rip the power from Luca's hands?

When it was my father's turn, I had to stop myself from attacking him for agreeing to marry Gianna off to Matteo. Instead I gritted my teeth and gave him a cold smile. Gianna pointedly avoided Matteo's eyes. She'd lost weight, and it broke my heart to see her so hopeless.

I was glad when the funeral was over. The men had a meeting scheduled for the evening to discuss the rising threat of the Russians. In our world there wasn't time to mourn the dead for long. Chicago and New York needed to figure out a way to stop the Bratva before another Capo lost his life. And that would be either Luca, or Dante Cavallaro.

Luca wanted me out of New York, so he sent me to the Vitiello mansion in the Hamptons. Gianna, Lily and Fabi were allowed to accompany me for the night before they'd have to leave for Chicago tomorrow evening. I had a feeling Father hoped I would talk some sense into Gianna about her arranged marriage with Matteo. The engagement party was planned for the beginning of November, so Gianna didn't have all that long to come to terms with it. Mother stayed with Father in Manhattan, but they sent Umberto with us. He, Cesare and Romero were supposed to keep us safe.

We arrived at the mansion around dinnertime, and the staff had already prepared a meal for us. My heart swelled with happiness as Lily, Fabi, Gianna and I settled around the long dining table, but it was dimmed by the fact that our three bodyguards discussed the Russian threat in hushed voices and by Gianna's refusal to eat more than two bites. I didn't want to discuss her betrothal to Matteo with everyone there. Later, when they'd gone to bed, Gianna and I would have enough time for that.

Fabi was the only one who kept the conversation on our side of the table going as he told me excitedly about the collection of knives Father had given him. Lily was busy sneaking admiring glances at Romero, who was completely oblivious to her pining.

After dinner, we moved on to the loggia overlooking the ocean. The night sky out here twinkled with stars. In New York you rarely got a glimpse at them. Cesare had gone off to do God knows what, probably check the security system, and Umberto and Romero had settled in the living room; from there they could watch us without overhearing our conversation. Fabi lay curled up beside Lily, fast asleep, as she typed something on her phone while checking out Romero occasionally.

"Do you want to talk?" I whispered to Gianna who sat beside me, legs pressed up against her chest. She shook her head. It felt as if a rift had grown between us since she'd gotten the news about her betrothal, and I didn't know why. "Gianna, please."

"There's nothing to talk about."

"Maybe it's not as bad as you think." She gave me an incredulous look but

I kept talking. "When I found out I had to marry Luca, I was terrified, but I've come to terms with it. Luca and I are getting along better than I thought possible."

Gianna glared. "I'm not like you, Aria. You're eager to please him, to do anything he says. I'm not like that. I won't submit to anyone."

I flinched. Gianna had never lashed out at me like that.

She jumped up. I tried to catch her arm but she shook me off. "Leave me alone. I can't talk to you right now." She whirled around and stormed off toward the beach. I stood, unsure if I should follow her, but I knew she wouldn't listen to me when she was like that. Umberto stepped outside. I raised a hand. "No, give her a few minutes to herself. She's upset."

Umberto nodded, then his eyes darted to Fabi. "I should take him to bed."

I was about to nod when an ear-splitting alarm broke the silence, but it stopped a few seconds later. Fabi's eyes were wide as he clung to Lily, both of them looking at me as if I knew what was going on. Romero stormed toward us, two guns drawn, when a red dot appeared on Umberto's forehead. I cried out but it was too late. There was a shot and Umberto's head flung back, blood splattering everywhere. Lily started screaming, and I still couldn't move. I stared at the dead eyes of Umberto. A man I'd known all my life.

Romero flung himself at me, and we landed on the ground as a second bullet blasted the glass door, sending shards flying.

"What's going on?" I screamed, hysteria rocking my body.

"The Bratva," was all Romero said as he dragged me toward the living room. I struggled against him. Lily and Fabi cowered beside a lounge chair, still in shooting range of the sniper. "Get them!"

But Romero ignored my command, and he was too strong for me. He shoved me against a wall inside the living room, his grip biting into my skin, his eyes hard and wild. "Stay here. Don't move."

"Lily and Fabi," I gasped.

He nodded, then ducked and rushed back outside. I was shaking all over. Romero returned with my sister and brother, who clung to him desperately. I wrapped my arms around them tightly the moment they were at my side. And then my world tilted.

"Gianna," I whispered.

Romero didn't hear me. He was shouting into his phone. "Where? How many?" His face paled. "Fuck." He turned to me, and his expression made my stomach drop. "The Russians are on the property. Too many for us. I'll take you to the panic room in the basement where we'll wait until backup arrives."

He gripped my arm but I pulled away. "Take Fabi and Lily there. I need to warn Gianna."

"You are my responsibility," Romero hissed. Somewhere in the house glass shattered. Shots rang out.

"I don't care. I won't come with you. You will do as I say. Take them to the panic room. If something happens to Lily or Fabi, I will kill myself, and nothing you or Luca or any other power in this world can do will change that. I want you to protect them. Keep them safe. That's all that matters to me."

"You should come with us."

I shook my head. "I have to find Gianna."

"Luca will be here soon."

I knew that wasn't true. "Go now!"

We stared at each other, then finally he turned to my siblings. "Stay down and follow my orders."

Male voices screamed something in Russian, then more shots were fired. Cesare wouldn't be able to keep them at bay for long if the number of voices was any indication.

Romero shoved a gun at me. I grabbed it, then I ducked and ran outside. Umberto's blood covered the stone tiles, but I didn't look at his body. I hurried down the slope toward the bay when I noticed the vibrating of my phone. I pulled it out and pressed it to my ear as I scanned the beach for Gianna.

"Aria?" Luca's worried voice sounded. "Are you safe?"

"They killed Umberto," was the first thing out of my mouth.

"Where are you?"

"Searching for Gianna."

"Aria, where's Romero? Why isn't he taking you to the panic room?"

"I have to find Gianna."

"Aria," Luca sounded desperate. "The Bratva wants you. Get into the panic room. I'm taking the helicopter. I'll be there in twenty minutes. I'm already on the way."

Luca would need more than twenty minutes even with a helicopter and he wouldn't be able to take as many of his men with him, so there was no saying how long it would take him to fight his way into the mansion. There was the possibility that he would fail.

Gianna came running toward me, eyes wide.

"I can't talk anymore," I whispered.

"Aria—"

"What's happening?" Gianna asked, as she stumbled against me.

"The Bratva." I pulled her toward the dock where the boat was anchored. It would be safer to hide there than to go back inside and look for the panic room. The boards of the dock groaned under our weight as we walked toward the boat. But then Lily's scream pierced the night and I froze. Gianna and I exchanged a glance. Without a word, we turned around and hurried back toward the house.

My heart hammered in my chest when we arrived on the loggia. The living room was deserted. I knelt beside Umberto and took his knives even as I shuddered. I handed one of them to Gianna and put the switchblade into my back pocket.

"Come on," I whispered. I wasn't even sure what Gianna and I were going to do once we got inside. I'd shot a gun once, and I had handled a knife only when I'd sparred with Luca; that didn't bode well in a fight against Russian mobsters. Yet I knew I wouldn't be able to live with myself if I didn't find Lily and Fabi.

Gianna and I crept inside. It was dark. Someone must have turned the lights off in the entire house. I held my breath, but it was terrifyingly quiet. I approached the door that led into the lobby when an arm shot out and wrapped around my waist. I cried out, struggled, tried to angle the gun toward my attacker, but he twisted my wrist. Pain shot through my arm and the gun tumbled from my fingers. Gianna gasped behind me. I kicked out. A deep voice snarled at me in Russian. Oh God. My foot collided with his shin. He pushed me away but before I could catch my balance, his fist collided with my lips. My vision turned black and I dropped to my knees as blood filled my mouth and trickled over my chin, the warm, salty taste making bile rise into my throat.

Fingers twisted into my hair and I was wrenched to my feet, crying out from the pain in my scalp. My attacker didn't care. The lights came on as he dragged me into the lobby by my hair. I could see Gianna in the arms of another tall man. Her body was limp, a bruise already forming on her forehead.

I was thrown to the ground in front of jeans-clad legs and quickly peered up into a pockmarked face and cold blue eyes. "What's your name, whore?" he asked in heavily accented English. Didn't he recognize me? I supposed I looked different with blood all over my face. I stared back at him defiantly. He kicked me in the stomach and I toppled over, gasping for breath. "What's your name?"

My eyes darted to a body to my right. Cesare. He was making gurgling noises, clutching at a bleeding wound in his stomach. I didn't see Lily, Fabi or Romero anywhere, and I hoped they'd made it to the panic room. At least they would survive.

A hand gripped my chin and wrenched my head up. "Will you tell me your name, or do I have to make Igor hurt her?" He nodded toward Gianna, who lay on her side on the marble floor, blinking dazedly.

"Aria," I said quietly.

"As in Aria Vitiello?" the man asked with a cruel smile.

I nodded. There was no use denying it. He said something in Russian and the men guffawed. My skin crawled from the way they were looking at me.

"Where are the others? Your shadow and the children?"

It took me a moment to realize whom he meant by shadow. "I don't know," I said.

Igor kicked Gianna. She screamed. Her eyes met mine and I could see she didn't want me to say anything, but how could I watch them hurt her?

Voices and shooting carried over to us from outside. The leader of the Russians grabbed me and pulled my back flush against his chest before pressing a blade against my throat.

Fear paralyzed my body as I listened to the sound of fighting. I was dragged backwards closer to the living room. Igor was yanking Gianna by her hair. She didn't seem capable of standing. Another Russian mobster was flung back as a bullet tore through his throat. "We have your wife, Vitiello. If you want to see her in one piece, you'd better stop fighting and drop your weapons."

Luca walked in, a gun in each hand. Matteo was a step behind him.

"So this is your wife, Vitiello?" the man said, his breath hot against my neck. I squirmed, but he held me in a death grip. The blade sliced into my skin and I became still.

Luca's face was a mask of fury as he stared at my captor. Matteo twisted the knives in his hands over and over again, his eyes flickering to Gianna's trembling form on the ground. Cesare had stopped gurgling. This night could very well end with all of us drowning in our own blood.

"Let her go, Vitali," Luca snarled.

Vitali grabbed my throat. "I don't think so."

I could barely breathe in his hold, but all I could think about was that I could lose everyone I loved tonight. I hoped they'd kill me first. I couldn't bear the thought of watching everyone die.

"You took something that belongs to us, Vitiello, and now I have something that belongs to you." Vitali licked my cheek and I almost threw up. "I want to know where it is."

Luca took a step forward, then froze as Vitali raised the knife to my throat again. "Put your guns down or I'll cut her throat."

Vitali was stupid to think Luca would do that, but then I watched in horror as Luca dropped his guns on the floor.

"Your wife tastes delicious. I wonder if she tastes this delicious everywhere." He turned me around so I was facing him. His foul breath hit my face. From the corner of my eye, I could see Luca watching me, but I wished he'd look away. I didn't want him to see this. Vitali's lips came closer. I was sure I'd throw up.

I tried to lean back. He laughed nastily and gripped my hip but I barely noticed, because my shifting had made the switchblade dig into my butt. As Vitali trailed his tongue over my chin, I slipped my hand into my back pocket, pulled the knife out, released the blade and rammed it into his thigh.

He cried out, stumbling back, and then all hell broke loose. Luca practically flew through the room and pulled me against him as he sliced Vitali's throat open from one ear to the other. The man's head tilted back, blood spurting out, then he toppled over. Bullets tore through the air, and screaming filled the room. The ground was slippery with blood and only Luca's firm grasp on my arm kept me upright. He must have dropped the knife at some point, because he was shooting bullet after bullet out of a sleek black gun with a silencer. I picked up a gun lying in a pool of blood. It was slippery in my hand but its weight felt good. Suddenly Romero was there too. My eyes tried to find Gianna, but she was gone from her spot on the floor.

Luca shot another enemy and reached down for the gun of the dead guy as his own appeared to be out of bullets, when one of the Russian mobsters to our right pointed his gun at Luca. I cried out in warning, and at the same time stumbled forward and aimed my gun at the guy and fired. I didn't even think about it. I'd sworn to myself I wouldn't watch anyone I loved die tonight, even if meant I had to die first.

The bullet hit my shoulder and my world exploded with pain. My shot hit the guy in the head and he dropped to the ground, dead. Luca ripped me to the side, but my vision turned black.

When I came to my senses again, Luca was cradling me in his arms. It was silent around us except for someone's whimpers. It took me a moment to realize they were my own, and then the pain sliced through me and I wished I'd stayed unconscious, but I needed to know if everyone was all right. "You okay?" I croaked.

Luca trembled against me. "Yes," he gritted out. "But you aren't." He was pressing down on my shoulder. That probably explained the pain. The back and front of my shirt were slick with a warm liquid.

"What about Gianna, Lily and Fabi?" I whispered even as darkness wanted to claim me again.

"Fine," Gianna called from somewhere. She sounded far away, or maybe that was my imagination. Luca slid his hands under me and stood. I cried out in pain, tears leaking out of my eyes. The lobby was crowded with our men.

"I'll take you to the hospital," Luca said.

"Luca," Matteo said in warning. "Let the Doc handle it. He's been taking care of our business for years."

"No," Luca snarled. "Aria needs proper care. She's lost too much blood." I could see a few of Luca's men glancing our way before pretending they were busy again. He was their Capo. He couldn't show weakness, not even for me.

"I can do a blood transfusion," came a deep, soothing voice. The Doc. He was over sixty with snow-white hair and a kind face.

Luca's grip on me tightened. I clutched at his arm. "It's okay, Luca. Let him take care of me. I don't want you to take me to a hospital. It's too dangerous."

Luca's eyes showed hesitation, then slowly he nodded. "Follow me!" He carried me toward the staircase, but I lost consciousness again.

I woke in a soft bed, feeling battered and foggy. My eyes peeled open. Gianna lay beside me, sleeping. It was light outside, so several hours must have passed. The bruise on her forehead had grown, but I supposed I looked worse. We were alone and disappointment filled me. I tried to sit up and was rewarded with a fierce throbbing in my shoulder. Glancing down, I found my upper arm and shoulder wrapped with bandages.

Gianna stirred, then she gave me a relieved smile. "You're awake."

"Yeah," I whispered. My mouth felt as if it was filled with cotton.

"Luca has been guarding your bed almost all night, but Matteo forced him to come out and help him with the Russian mobsters they caught."

"They caught some?"

"Yeah, they're trying to extract information from them."

My lips twisted, but I couldn't bring myself to feel sorry for them. "How are you?"

"Better than you," Gianna said, then she closed her eyes. "I'm sorry I lashed out at you yesterday. I would have hated myself forever if that had been the last thing I said to you."

I shook my head. "It's okay."

She hopped off the bed. "I better tell Luca you're awake, or he'll rip my head off."

She disappeared and a couple of minutes later, Luca stepped in. He stood in the doorway, his expression unreadable as he let his gaze wander over me. Then he stepped up to the bed and pressed a kiss against my forehead. "Do you need morphine?"

My shoulder felt like it was on fire. "Yeah."

Luca turned toward the nightstand, picked up a syringe and slid the needle into the crook of my arm. When he was done, he threw the syringe into the trash but didn't let go of my hand. I linked our fingers. "Did we lose someone?"

"A few. Cesare and a couple soldiers," he said, then he paused. "And Umberto."

"I know. I saw him get shot." My stomach churned violently. It still felt surreal. I'd have to write Umberto's wife a letter, but I needed a clear head for that.

"What did that guy Vitali mean when he said you had something that belonged to him?"

Luca's lips thinned. "We intercepted one of their drug deliveries. But that's not important now."

"What is important then?"

"That I almost lost you. That I saw you get shot," Luca said in an odd voice, but his expression gave nothing away. "You're lucky the bullet only hit your shoulder. The Doc says it'll heal completely and you'll be able to use your arm like before."

I tried a smile, but the morphine was making me sluggish. I blinked, trying to stay awake. Luca leaned down. "Don't do that ever again."

"What?" I breathed.

"Taking a bullet for me."

chapter *eighteen*

Taking a shower was a struggle. I had to cover my bandages with a waterproof cap, which was a major hassle, but the feel of the warm water washing away the blood and sweat was worth it. Gianna, Lily and Fabi had left less than one hour ago. Father had insisted they leave. Not that they were much safer in Chicago. The Bratva was closing in on the Outfit as well. At least I'd had them with me a day longer than planned. They'd kept me entertained as I lay in bed while Luca had to take care of everything. As Capo he couldn't abandon his soldiers. He needed to show them he had a plan of action.

I was already feeling so much better. Maybe that was the lingering effect of the painkillers I'd taken two hours ago. I stepped out of the shower and awkwardly put on my panties. I could move both of my arms, but the Doc had said I should use my left arm as little as possible. Putting on the nightgown proved more difficult. I'd managed to slip one strap over my injured shoulder when I stepped back into the bedroom, where I found Luca sitting on the bed. He got up immediately.

"Done with business?" I asked.

He nodded. He came toward me and slid the second strap into place, then he led me toward the bed and made me sit down. We hadn't been able to talk alone since our first conversation, and then I'd been high on morphine.

"I'm fine," I said again because he looked like he needed to hear it. He didn't say anything for a long time before he suddenly knelt before me and pressed his face against my stomach. "I could have lost you two days ago."

I shivered. "But you didn't."

He peered up at me. "Why did you do this? Why did you take a bullet for me?"

"Do you really not know why?" I whispered.

He became very still, but didn't say anything.

"I love you, Luca." I knew saying it out loud was a risk, but I'd thought I'd die a couple days ago, so this was nothing.

Luca brought his face up to mine and cupped my cheeks. "You love me." He said it as if I'd told him the skies were green, or that the sun revolved around the earth, or that fire was cold to the touch. As if what I'd said didn't make sense, as if it didn't fit into his view of the world. "You shouldn't love me, Aria. I'm not someone who should be loved. People fear me, they hate me, they respect me, they admire me, but they don't love me. I'm a killer. I'm good at killing. Better probably than at anything else, and I don't regret it. Fuck, sometimes I even enjoy it. That's a man you want to love?"

"It's not a matter of want, Luca. It's not like I could choose to stop loving you."

He nodded, as if that explained a lot. "And you hate that you love me. I remember you saying it before."

"No. Not anymore. I know you aren't a good man. I've always known it, and I don't care. I know I should. I know I should lie awake at night hating myself for being okay with my husband being the boss of one of the most brutal and deadliest crime organizations in the States. But I don't. What does that make me?" I paused, staring down at my hands, the hands that had cradled a gun two days ago, at the finger that had pulled the trigger without hesitation, without a twitch or tremor. "And I killed a man and I don't feel sorry. Not one bit. I would do it again." I glanced up at Luca. "What does that make me, Luca? I'm a killer like you."

"You did what you had to. He deserved to die."

"There's not one of us who doesn't deserve death. We probably deserve it more than most."

"You are good, Aria. You are innocent. I forced you into this."

"You didn't, Luca. I was born into this world. I chose to stay in this world." The words of my wedding day popped into my mind. "Being born into our world means being born with blood on your hands. With every breath we take, sin is engraved deeper into our skin."

"You don't have a choice. There's no way to escape our world. You didn't have a choice in marrying me either. If you'd let that bullet kill me, you would have at least escaped our marriage."

"There are few good things in our world, Luca, and if you find one you cling to it with all your might. You are one of those good things in my life."

"I'm not good," Luca said almost desperately.

"You're not a good man, no. But you are good for me. I feel safe in your arms. I don't know why, don't even know why I love you, but I do, and that won't change."

Luca closed his eyes, looking almost resigned. "Love is a risk in our world, and a weakness a Capo can't afford."

"I know," I said even as my throat corded up.

Luca's eyes shot open, fierce and blazing with emotion. "But I don't care because loving you is the only pure thing in my life."

Tears brimmed in my eyes. "You love me?"

"Yes, even if I shouldn't. If my enemies knew how much you meant to me, they'd do anything to get their hands on you, to hurt me through you, to control me by threatening you. The Bratva will try again, and others will too. When I became a Made Man, I swore to put the Famiglia first, and I reinforced that same oath when I became a Capo dei Capi even though I knew I was lying. My first choice should always be the Famiglia."

I held my breath, unable to utter a word. The look he gave me almost broke me into pieces.

"But you are my first choice, Aria. I'll burn down the world if I have to. I'll kill and maim and blackmail. I'll do anything for you. Maybe love is a risk, but it's a risk I'm willing to take and as you said, it's not a choice. I never thought I would, never thought I *could* love someone like that, but I fell in love with you. I fought it. It's the first battle I didn't mind losing."

I slung my arms around him, crying, then whimpered from the twinge in my shoulder. Luca pulled back. "You need to rest. Your body needs to heal."

He made me lie down but I held on to his arms. "I don't want to rest. I want to make love to you."

Luca looked pained. "I'm going to hurt you. Your stitches could rip open."

I trailed my hands down over his chest, his taut stomach until I brushed the bulge in his boxers. "He agrees with me."

"He always does, but he's not the voice of reason, believe me."

I giggled, then winced as pain shot down my arm.

Luca still hovered over me but he shook his head. "That's what I mean."

"Please," I whispered. "I want to make love to you. I've wanted this for a long time."

"I've always made love to you, Aria."

I swallowed, and began stroking Luca's erection through the thin fabric. He didn't draw back. "Don't you want this?"

"Of course I want it. We almost lost each other. I want nothing more than to be as close to you as possible."

"Then make love to me. Slow and gentle."

"Slow and gentle," Luca said in a low voice, and I knew I had him. He moved down to the edge of the bed and began massaging my feet and calves. I opened my legs wide. My nightgown rode up, baring my thin white panties to Luca. His eyes traveled up and I knew he could see how much I wanted and needed this. Luca groaned against my ankle, then trailed his fingers up my leg, only dusting the skin until he brushed my center with his fingertips. My panties stuck to my slick heat. "You make slow and gentle really hard on me. If you weren't hurt, I'd bury myself in you and make you scream my name."

"If I wasn't hurt, I'd want you to do it."

Luca flicked his tongue across my ankle, then gently sucked the skin into his mouth. "Mine."

Then he covered my calves and thighs with kisses, saying the word "mine" over and over again as he made his way up toward my center. He slid my panties down, then settled between my legs and kissed my outer lips. "Mine," he whispered against my heated flesh. I arched and immediately jerked in pain.

"I want you to relax completely. No tensing your muscles, or your shoulder will hurt," he said, his lips brushing against me as he spoke and making me wet with arousal.

"I always tense up when I come," I said teasingly. "And I really, really want to come."

"You will, but no tensing."

I didn't say that I thought it was impossible. Luca could probably see it on my face, and his expression said that he accepted the challenge.

I should challenge him more often. As he began to pleasure me with ghost touches and kisses and licks that made my toes curl with need, I felt my muscles loosen and my mind drift into a cocoon of bliss. My quiet moans and the soft sound of Luca's mouth working my folds mingled with the silence of the room. A knot slowly formed deep in my core, and every brush of Luca's tongue tightened it, and then deliciously slowly the knot unraveled and my orgasm flowed through my body like honey. I released a long breath as Luca kept my orgasm going for what seemed like forever with feathery touches. I watched him get up through a haze that had nothing to do with painkillers. He slipped out of his boxers as I lay like a boneless heap on the bed. My body was humming as if every cell had been infused with sweet pleasure. He stretched above me, his tip at my entrance. Then he slid into me ever so slowly, stretching me. I let out a long moan when he filled me completely.

"Mine," he said quietly.

I stared into his eyes as he withdrew inch by inch until only his tip was in me before sliding back in. "Yours," I whispered.

The path stretching before us was one of darkness, a life of blood and death and danger, a future of always watching my back, of knowing every day could be Luca's last, of fearing that one day I might have to watch him receive a lethal injection. But this was my world and Luca was *my* man, and I would go this path with him until the bitter end.

As he made love to me, I touched my hand to the tattoo over his heart, felt his heart beating against my palm. I smiled. "Mine."

"Always," Luca said.

bound *by duty*

(Born in Blood Mafia Chronicles, #2)

prologue

"DON'T TURN YOUR BACK ON ME. LOOK AT ME. I THINK I deserve at least that small decency, Dante."

Tension radiated off of him when he turned to face me. He didn't move closer, but he was looking at me. For once, he didn't pretend I was invisible. His blue eyes wandered over my exposed body.

My nipples hardened in the cool air of his office but I didn't close my silk bathrobe, despite the overwhelming urge to cover myself against Dante's cold scrutiny. His gaze lingered on the apex of my thighs slightly longer than the rest of my body, and a small burst of hope filled me. "Am I your wife?"

His blond brows drew together. "Of course you are." There was the hint of something I couldn't place in his voice.

"Then claim your rights, Dante. Make me yours."

He didn't move, but his eyes slid down to my erect nipples. His gaze was almost physical, like a ghost touch on my naked skin.

I wasn't above begging. I knew I almost had him. I wanted to have sex tonight. "I have needs too. Would you prefer if I found a lover who relieved you of the burden to touch me?" I wasn't sure I could go through with it. No, I knew I couldn't go through with it, but this act of provocation was my last option. If Dante didn't react to this, then I didn't know what else to do.

"No," he said sharply, something angry and possessive breaking through his perfect mask. He pressed his lips together, jaw locked, and walked toward me. I shivered with need and excitement when he stopped in front of me. He didn't reach for me, but I thought I detected the hint of desire in his eyes. It wasn't much, but enough to embolden me. I bridged the remaining distance between us and curled my fingers over his strong shoulders, pressing my naked body against his front. The rough material of his business suit rubbed deliciously against my sensitive nipples, and I let out a small moan. The pressure between my legs was almost unbearable. Dante's eyes flashed as he looked down at me. Slowly he wrapped an arm around me and rested his palm flat against my lower back.

Triumph flooded me. He wasn't ignoring me now.

chapter *one*

Of course, I'd known it would happen. My father had made his standpoint clear the moment my first husband Antonio had been buried. I was too young to stay unmarried. But I hadn't expected my father to find a new husband for me so quickly, and I definitely hadn't expected my new husband to be Dante—the Boss—Cavallaro.

Antonio's funeral had taken place only nine months ago, which made my new engagement teeter on the brink of inappropriateness. My mother was usually among the first to pounce on anyone who committed a social faux pas, and yet she couldn't see anything wrong with the fact that today, less than a year after saying good-bye to Antonio, I was going to meet my next husband. I'd never loved Antonio as a woman loved a man, even if I'd believed I had at one time, and our marriage had never been real, but I'd hoped for more time before I was forced into another union—especially as I didn't even get to choose for myself this time.

"You are so lucky Dante Cavallaro agreed to marry you. It came as a surprise for many that he decided to take a woman who has already been married. He could have chosen from a line of eager young women, after all," my mother said as she brushed my dark-brown hair. She didn't mean to hurt my feelings; she was only stating the obvious. I knew it was true. Everyone did.

A man in Dante's position didn't have to content himself with the leftovers of another, a lesser man. That's what most people probably thought, and yet I was supposed to marry him. I, who didn't even want to marry someone as powerful and cunning as Dante Cavallaro. I, who wished to stay alone, if only to protect Antonio's secret. How was I supposed to keep up the lie? Dante was known as a man who could always tell when someone was lying.

"He'll be the Boss of the Outfit in two months, and when you marry him you'll be the most influential woman in Chicago and the Midwest. And if you keep up your good friendship with Aria, you'll have connections to New York as well."

As usual my mother was way ahead, already planning world domination, while I was still trying to wrap my mind around the fact that I was supposed to marry the Boss. This was too dangerous. I wasn't a bad liar. In the years of my marriage to Antonio I'd improved my skills continuously, but there was a big difference between lying to the outside world and lying to your husband. Anger toward Antonio resurfaced as it had so often in the past months. He'd forced me into this situation.

Mamma stepped back, admiring her work. My dark hair fell in soft glossy curls over my shoulders and back. I pushed to my feet. For the occasion, I'd chosen a cream-colored pencil skirt and a plum blouse that was tucked into my waistband, as well as modest black heels. I was one of the tallest women in the Outfit at five foot eight, and naturally my mother worried Dante would be put off if I wore high heels. I didn't bother to point out that Dante was still at least five inches taller than me; I wouldn't have been taller than him even with heels. And this wouldn't be the first time he saw me anyway. We'd met a couple of times at mafia functions and had even shared a brief dance at Aria's wedding in August three months ago. Still we'd never exchanged more than the expected pleasantries, and I'd certainly never gotten the impression that Dante was even remotely interested in me. But he was known for being closed off, so who knew what was really going on in that head of his?

"Has he dated since his wife died?" I asked. Usually that kind of gossip spread quickly in our circles, but maybe I missed it. The older women of the family often knew about others' dirty laundry first. To be honest, gossiping was the main occupation for most of them.

Mamma smiled sadly. "Not officially. Rumor has it he couldn't let go of his wife, but it's been more than three years and now that he's about to become the boss of the Outfit, he can't hang on to the memory of a dead woman. He needs to move on and produce an heir." She put her hands on my shoulders and beamed at me. "And you'll be the one to give him a beautiful son, sweetheart."

My stomach dropped. "Not today."

My mother shook her head with a laugh. "Soon enough. The wedding is in two months." If it were up to Mamma and Papà, the marriage would have taken place weeks ago. They were probably worried Dante might change his mind about me.

"Valentina! Livia! Dante's car pulled just up," Papà called.

Mamma clapped her hands, then winked. "Let's make him forget his wife."

I hoped she wouldn't say something that tasteless when Dante was around. I followed her downstairs and tried to put on my most sophisticated expression. Papà opened the door. I couldn't remember the last time he'd actually *answered the door*. Usually he let Mamma or me do it, or our maid, but even I could tell that he was practically bouncing with eagerness. Did he really have to make it so obvious that he was desperate to marry me off again? It made me feel like the last puppy of a litter that the pet shop couldn't wait to get rid of.

Dante's blond hair appeared in the doorway as my mother and I stopped in the middle of our lobby. It was snowing outside, and the soft veil of snowflakes on Dante's head made his hair look almost golden. I got why some people had been frustrated about Aria's marriage to Luca. Dante and she would have been the golden couple.

Papà opened the door wider with a broad smile. Dante shook my father's hand and they exchanged a few low words. Mamma was practically shaking with excitement beside me. She turned on her thousand-watt smile when Dante and Papà finally headed our way. I forced my own lips into a smile that was far less radiant.

As was tradition, Dante greeted my mother first, with a bow and a hand kiss, before facing me. He gave me a curt smile that didn't reach his blue eyes, then kissed my hand. "Valentina," he said in his smooth, emotionless voice.

From a solely physical standpoint, I found Dante more than a little attractive. He was tall and slightly muscled, impeccably dressed in a dark gray three-piece suit, white shirt and light blue tie, and had full blond hair that was loosely combed back. But everyone called him a cold fish, and from our short encounters I knew they were right.

"It's wonderful to meet you again," I said with a small tilt of my head.

Dante let go of my hand. "Yes, it is." He turned his blank gaze toward my father. "I'd like to talk to Valentina alone." As usual, no pleasantries were wasted.

"Of course," Papà said eagerly, taking my mother's arm and already leading her away. If I hadn't been married before, they would never have left me alone with a man, but as it was they thought they didn't have to protect my virtue anymore. And I couldn't tell them that Antonio and I had never consummated our marriage. I couldn't tell anyone, least of all Dante.

When Mamma and Papà had disappeared into my father's office, Dante turned to me. "This is acceptable for you, I assume."

He seemed so restrained and controlled, as if his emotions were bottled up so deep inside, not even he could reach them. I wondered how much of it was the result of his wife's death and how much was his natural disposition.

"Yes," I said, hoping he couldn't see how nervous I was. I gestured toward a door to our left. "Would you like to sit down for our talk?"

Dante nodded and I led him into the living room. I sank down on the sofa, and Dante took the armchair across from me. I'd have thought he'd sit beside me, but he seemed content to keep as much space between us as was acceptable. Apart from the brief hand kiss, he made sure not to touch me. He probably found it inappropriate as long as we weren't married. That's what I hoped, at least.

"I assume your father told you that our wedding is planned for January fifth."

I searched for a flicker of sadness or wistfulness in his voice, but there was nothing. I rested my hands in my lap, linking my fingers. There was less chance of Dante noticing my trembling that way. "Yes. He told me a few days ago."

"I realize that's less than a year after your husband's funeral, but my father retires at the end of the year, and it's expected of me to be married when I take over his place."

I lowered my eyes as my chest tightened with buried emotions. Antonio hadn't been a good husband, he hadn't been any kind of husband, but he'd been my friend and I'd known him all my life, which was why I'd agreed to marry him. Of course, I'd been naïve, hadn't realized what it would really mean to marry a man who wasn't interested in me, or women in general. I'd wanted to help him. Being gay wasn't something that was tolerated in the mafia. If someone had found out Antonio liked men that way, they would have killed him. When he'd asked for my help, I'd jumped at the chance, had secretly hoped I could win him over. I'd thought he could decide not to be gay anymore, I'd thought we could have a real marriage at some point, but that hope was quickly shattered.

That's why a nasty, selfish part of me had been relieved when Antonio had died. I'd thought I was finally free to find a man who loved me, or at least desired me. Thankfully, it was only a very small part, and I felt guilty whenever I was reminded of it. And yet, maybe this was my chance. Maybe my second marriage would finally provide me with a husband who saw me as more than a necessary evil.

Dante seemed to misunderstand my silence. "If it's too soon for you, we can still cancel our arrangements."

Mamma would kill me, and Papà would probably suffer a stroke. "No," I said quickly. "It's okay. I was lost in memories for a moment." I gave him a smile. He didn't return it, only regarded me with cold scrutiny.

"Very well," he said eventually. "I'd like to discuss the preparations as well as the time leading up to the event with you. Two months isn't a long time, but since this wedding isn't going to be a big affair, we should be fine."

I nodded. Part of me was sad that this wedding was going to be a quiet affair, but so soon after Antonio's death anything bigger would have been in bad taste, and since it was the second marriage for both Dante and me, for me to insist on a splendid feast would have been ridiculous.

"Why did you choose me? I'm sure there were many other viable options." I'd been wondering about this ever since Papà had told me about his agreement with Dante. I knew it was a question I wasn't supposed to ask. Mamma would have thrown a fit if she were present.

Dante's expression didn't change. "Of course. My father suggested your cousin Gianna, but I didn't want a wife who's barely of age. Unfortunately, most women in their twenties are already married, and most widows are older than me or have children, both unacceptable for a man in my position, as you will probably understand."

I nodded. There were so many rules of etiquette when it came to finding the right spouse, especially for a man in Dante's position, which was why so many were shocked when I was announced as his future wife. Dante had stepped on many toes with that decision.

"So you were the only logical choice. You are, of course, still quite young, but that can't be changed."

For a moment I was stunned into silence by his emotionless reasoning. Though I wasn't as naïve as I used to be, I'd hoped at least part of the reason Dante had chosen me was that he was attracted to me, found me pretty, or at least fascinating to some extent, but this cold explanation destroyed that small flicker of hope.

"I'm twenty-three," I said in a surprisingly calm voice. Maybe Dante's aloofness rubbed off on me. If so, I would be known as the ice queen in no time. "That's not young by our marriage standards."

"Twelve years younger than me. That's more than I would have liked." His deceased wife had been only two years younger than him, and they'd been married for almost twelve years before she'd died from cancer. Still, the way he said it made it sound as if I'd forced him into a marriage with me.

Most men in our world took on young mistresses once their wives got older, and yet Dante was displeased that I was too young.

"Then maybe you should look for another wife. I didn't ask you to marry me." The moment the words were out, I clamped a hand over my mouth, then met Dante's gaze. He didn't look angry; he didn't look *anything*. His face was as it always was. Stoic and emotionless. "I'm sorry. That was very rude. I shouldn't have said that."

Dante shook his head. Not a single hair moved out of line. There wasn't even a speck of dirt on his trouser legs, despite the snowy November weather. "It's okay. I didn't mean to offend you."

I wished he didn't sound so blasé, but there was nothing I could do about it, at least not until we were married. "You didn't. I'm sorry. I shouldn't have snapped at you."

"Let's get back on track. There are a few more things we need to discuss, and unfortunately I have a meeting scheduled for tonight and an early flight tomorrow morning."

"You're heading to New York for the engagement of Matteo and Gianna." My family hadn't gotten an invitation. As with Aria's engagement party, only the closest family and the respective heads of the New York and Chicago mob had been invited. I was actually glad. It would have been my first social event after my betrothal to Dante had been made public. Gossip and curious glances would have followed me everywhere.

A hint of surprise flickered in his eyes, but then it was gone. "Yes, indeed." He reached into his jacket pocket and held out a small velvet box. I took it from him and opened it. A diamond engagement ring was inside. Only a few weeks ago, I'd taken off the wedding ring and engagement ring that Antonio had gotten for me. They'd never meant much to me anyway.

"I hope you like the design."

"Yes, thank you." After a moment of hesitation, I took the ring out and put it on my finger. Dante hadn't given any indication that he wanted to do it for me. My gaze flickered toward his right hand and my stomach plummeted. He was still wearing his old wedding ring. Another strange burst of disappointment filled me. If he wore it after all this time, he must still be in love with his dead wife—or was it a simple matter of habit?

He noticed my gaze and for the first time his stoic mask slipped, but it was gone so quickly that I wasn't sure I'd actually seen it. He didn't give me an explanation or an apology, but I hadn't expected one from a man like him.

"Your father requests that we do a social outing before the actual wedding. As we all agreed that an actual engagement party is unnecessary..." I'd never been asked, but I wasn't even surprised. "...I suggest we attend the annual Christmas party of the Scuderi family together."

For as long as I could remember, my family had been at the Scuderi house on the first Sunday in Advent. "That sounds like a reasonable idea."

Dante gave me a cool smile. "Then that's settled. I'll let your father know when I'll pick you up."

"You can tell me. I have a phone and am capable of operating it."

Dante stared. There was a flicker of something like amusement on his face for a second. "Of course. If that's what you prefer." He pulled his phone out of his pocket. "What's your number?"

I needed a moment to suppress an unladylike snort of laughter before I could give it to him.

When he was done typing, he stuffed his phone back into his jacket, then he straightened without another word. I rose as well and took my time smoothing out the nonexistent wrinkles in my skirt to mask my annoyance behind schooled pleasantness.

"Thank you for your time," he said formally. I really hoped he'd loosen up after our wedding. He wasn't always so restrained. I'd heard the stories about how he'd established his position as the heir to his father's title and how efficient he was when it came to dealing with traitors and enemies. There was something dark and feral behind his ice prince demeanor.

"You're welcome." I walked toward the door, but Dante beat me to it and held it open for me. I said a quick thanks before I stepped into our lobby. "I'll get my parents so they can say goodbye."

"Actually, I would like to have a word with your father in private before I leave."

It was futile trying to get any information from his expression, so I didn't bother. Instead I strode to the end of the corridor and knocked at my father's office door. The voices inside died down and a moment later, my father opened the door. Mamma stood directly behind him. From the look on her face I could tell that she was eager to bombard me with questions, but Dante was close behind me.

"Dante would like to have a word with you," I said, then turned around to Dante. "Until the Christmas party." I considered brushing his cheeks with my lips but discarded that idea immediately. Instead I tilted my head with a smile before walking away.

My mother's heels clacked behind me, then she fell into step beside me. She linked our arms. "How did it go? Dante didn't look too pleased. Did you do something that offended him?"

I gave her a look. "Of course not. Dante's face is frozen in one expression."

"Shhh." Mamma looked behind us. "What if he hears you?"

I didn't think he'd care.

Mamma scanned my face. "You should be happy, Valentina. You won the husband lottery, and I'm sure there's a passionate lover hidden beneath Dante's cold exterior."

"Mamma, please." I'd suffered through two sex talks with my mother in my life so far: first the one where she tried to tell me about the birds and the bees when I was fifteen and already well aware of the mechanics of sex. Even in a Catholic girls' school that information got around at some point. And the second shortly before my wedding to Antonio. I didn't think I'd survive a third one.

But I hoped she was right. Thanks to Antonio's disinterest in women, I'd never had the chance to enjoy a passionate lover, or any lover really. I was more than ready to finally be rid of my virginity, even if that would pose the risk of Dante finding out my first marriage had been for show—but I'd cross that bridge when I came to it.

chapter
two

Dante picked me up at quarter to six as promised. Not a minute too late or too soon. I hadn't expected anything else. My parents had already left a few minutes ago. As the future head of the Outfit, Dante couldn't arrive too early to the party.

He was wearing another three-piece suit in navy blue with light blue pinstripes and a matching tie. I froze for a moment when I saw him. My dress was navy too. People would think we'd done it on purpose, but there was nothing to be done about it now. I'd followed a strict detox diet for three days to fit into the tight backless dress; I wasn't going to wear something else. Despite its long pencil skirt reaching my calves, the slit up to my thigh allowed me to climb stairs without too much trouble.

Dante's eyes did a quick scan. "You look beautiful, Valentina." He was being polite. There was absolutely no sign that he actually found me attractive.

"Thank you." I smiled and stepped up to him. He touched my lower back to lead me toward his black Porsche parked at the curb and tensed as his palm came into contact with my naked skin. I wasn't sure but I thought I heard him release a rushed breath, and the possibility that he might be affected by me, coupled with the feel of his touch, sent a shiver of delight down my spine. He planted his hand lightly on my back and gave no further indication that I'd taken him by surprise with my partial nakedness as he guided me toward the passenger door and held it open for me. I slid in, almost giddy with triumph over the fact that I'd managed to get a reaction out of the iceman. Once we were married, I'd try to do it more often.

The other guests had already arrived when we pulled up in front of the Scuderi mansion. We could have walked, if it weren't for the four inches of snow, safety concerns and my high heels. Dante hadn't bothered with small talk during our drive. His mind seemed far away anyway. When he put his hand on my naked back this time, he gave no outward reaction.

Ludevica Scuderi opened the door for us. Her husband Rocco, the current Consigliere to Dante's father, hovered behind her, his hands on her shoulders. They both smiled brightly as they ushered us into the pleasantly warm foyer. An eight-foot Christmas tree, decorated with red and silver baubles, dominated the space.

"We're delighted that you could make it," Ludevica said warmly.

Rocco shook Dante's hand. "I have to congratulate you on your excellent taste. Your future wife looks marvelous, Dante."

It was obvious that they were going out of their way to be nice. Although it was desirable for a new Capo to keep the Consigliere of his predecessor, it wasn't tradition, so Dante could nominate a new Consigliere when he took over from his father.

Dante inclined his head and returned his hand to my back. "That she is," he said simply while all I could do was smile.

Ludevica clutched my hands. "We were pleased when we found out Dante had chosen you. After all you've gone through, it's only fair that fate makes it up to you."

I wasn't sure what to say to that. Maybe she was being sincere. It was hard to tell. After all, they'd originally tried to marry Gianna off to Dante. "Thank you. That's very kind of you."

"Come on in. The party isn't happening in our foyer," Rocco said, gesturing for us to head for the living room. Laughter and voices were coming from inside.

"Aria is very excited to see you again," Ludevica said as we entered the living room. I had no time to express my surprise at Aria's presence because the moment we were spotted by the crowd, people flocked around us to congratulate us on our betrothal and upcoming wedding. In between shaking hands, I scanned the room. Aria stood at the other end of the vast room next to another massive Christmas tree and her no-less-massive husband Luca, who had a possessive hand on her waist. I didn't see Gianna and her fiancé Matteo anywhere. If my mother's gossip was to be believed, the Scuderis were concerned their middle daughter might cause a scene.

Dante moved his thumb over my back, startling me. My eyes snapped to him, then to the couple in front of us, whom I'd completely ignored because of my staring. I gave my brightest smile and pulled Bibiana into a hug. "How are you?" I whispered. She squeezed me briefly, then drew back with her forced smile. That was as much of an answer as I would get in the presence of other people.

Her husband Tommaso, who was thirty years her senior, bald and overweight, kissed my hand, which would have been fine except for the look in his eyes. Leering was the best word to describe it. Dante's fingers on my back tensed and I risked a peek at him, but his expression was the same aloof mask as usual. He fixed Tommaso with his eyes and the man quickly took off with Bibiana.

A waiter carrying a tray of drinks stopped beside us, and Dante gripped a glass of champagne for me and a Scotch for himself. Now that the onslaught of well-wishers had finally abated, Luca and Aria crossed the room toward us. Dante's demeanor changed ever so slightly, like a tiger that got wind of another predator in his territory. Instead of tensing, he relaxed as if to show that he wasn't concerned, but his eyes were alert and calculating.

Luca and Dante shook hands, both with those unnerving shark-smiles on their faces. Ignoring them, I grinned at Aria, honestly happy to see her again. It had been months. She looked much more relaxed than at her wedding. "You look amazing," I told her as I embraced her. She was wearing a dark red dress that set off her blonde hair and pale skin beautifully. No wonder Luca couldn't stop glancing her way.

"You too," she said as she stepped back. "Can I see the back?"

I turned around for her.

"Wow. Doesn't she look amazing?"

That question was directed at Luca and led to an awkward pause in which the tension skyrocketed. Dante wrapped his arm around my waist, his cold eyes on Luca, who took Aria's hand, kissed it and said in a low voice, "I have eyes only for you."

Aria gave me an embarrassed smile. "I need to look for Gianna, but I'd love to talk to you later?"

"Okay," I said, glad when she and Luca walked off. With the men around, Aria and I wouldn't be able to talk anyway.

I turned to Dante. "You don't like him."

"It's not a matter of like. It's about self-preservation and a healthy dose of suspicion."

"That's the Christmas spirit," I said, not trying to hide my sarcasm.

Again a hint of amusement made the corners of Dante's mouth twitch, then it was gone. "Would you like to grab something to eat?"

"Definitely." After the last few days of torturous dieting, I was starving. As we made our way through the crowd, I noticed that the current head of the Outfit wasn't present. "Where's your father?"

"He didn't want to steal the show from us. Now that he's as good as retired, he prefers to stay out of the public eye," Dante said wryly.

"Understandable." These social functions were exhausting. You had to be careful what you said and did, even more so as the head of the Outfit. From the hard looks that some of the women were throwing my way, I knew I was currently their favorite topic. I knew what they were saying behind their hands: Why had Dante Cavallaro chosen a *widow* instead of a young, innocent bride?

I glimpsed up into his emotionless face, the hard angles of his cheekbones, the calculation and vigilance in his eyes, and found myself wishing once more that the answer to that question was something other than pure logic.

The buffet was loaded with Italian delicacies. I took a slice of panettone for myself, as I was in desperate need of some sugary treats. As usual it tasted like heaven. I'd made it a few times, but it had never been as good as Ludevica Scuderi's.

"Dante," came a pleasant female voice from behind us.

Dante and I turned at the same time. His sister Ines, with whom I'd exchanged only a few words over the years as we were nine years apart in age, stood in front of us. She was pregnant, third trimester if my guess was correct. Across the room, her twins, a boy and girl, were busy playing with Fabiano Scuderi, who was their age. Ines had the same fair hair as Dante and she carried herself with the same cold aloofness, but as her eyes settled on me, they were not necessarily warm, but friendly. "And Valentina. It's good to see you."

"Ines," I said with a smile. "You look radiant."

She touched her belly. "Thank you. It's been a challenge finding nice dresses that fit me with my belly. Maybe you can help me go shopping for one for your wedding?"

"I'd love to. And if you don't mind, I'd be delighted if you would join me when I go looking for a wedding dress."

Her blue eyes grew wide. "You don't have one yet?"

I shrugged. Of course I still had the one from my last wedding, but I didn't intend to wear it again. That would mean bad luck. "Not yet, but I'll go looking for one next week, so if you're free?"

"Count me in," she said. Her eyes had become much warmer. She looked much younger than thirty-two, and even though she was pregnant she didn't seem to have gained an ounce of weight. I wondered how she did it. Maybe good genes. I definitely hadn't been blessed with those. Without the occasional detox day or week, and regular workouts, I'd be gaining weight in no time.

"Wonderful." From the corner of my eye, I saw Dante watching us with mild interest. I hoped he was happy that his sister and I got along. I knew his deceased wife and Ines had been friends. I'd often seen them laughing together at social events.

"Where's your husband?" he asked eventually.

"Oh, Pietro went outside for a smoke with Rocco Scuderi. They didn't want to disturb you and your future wife."

A muscle in Dante's cheek flexed.

"You can go after them, if you have business to settle," I said quickly. "I'll be fine on my own. I should probably talk to Aria. Maybe you'd like to join me, Ines?"

Ines shook her head, her eyes on her twins who were in a heated argument with each other. "I need to break this up or there will be tears and bloody noses." She gave me a quick smile, then rushed off toward her arguing kids.

Dante hadn't moved from my side yet. "Are you sure?"

"Yes."

He nodded. "I'll be back soon." I watched him head toward the terrace door and disappear outside. Now that he was gone, I could see that several women turned their attention more openly to me. I had to find Aria or Bibiana quickly before one of them engaged me in an awkward conversation. I meandered through the other guests, sparing them only the briefest smile. Eventually I found both Aria and Bibiana in the lobby in a quiet corner. "There you are," I said, not trying to hide my relief.

"What's wrong?" Aria asked with a frown.

"I feel as if everyone's talking about me and Dante. Tell me I'm imagining things."

Bibiana shook her head. "You aren't. Most widows aren't as lucky as you are."

"I know, but still. I wish they wouldn't act quite so shocked about my engagement."

"It'll pass," Aria said, then grimaced. "Soon Gianna will be back on the prime spot of daily gossip."

"Sorry. I heard there was a scene at Gianna's engagement party."

Aria nodded. "Yeah. Gianna has trouble hiding her unwillingness to marry."

"Is that why Matteo Vitiello isn't here?" Bibiana asked. I'd wondered that as well, but I didn't want to be nosy.

"No. But since Salvatore Vitiello's death, Matteo is second in charge and he has to stay in New York when Luca isn't there." I searched her face for a sign of the tension I'd heard in her voice, but she'd learned to hide her emotions. Was Luca having trouble in New York? He was young for a Capo. Maybe some forces in New York were trying to mutiny. Once Aria might have told me, but now that I was the fiancée of the future Boss of the Chicago Outfit, she'd have to be careful what she let slip. We might be trying to work together, but New York and Chicago definitely weren't friends.

"That makes sense," I said. Bibiana gave me a look. She too must have picked up on the strain in Aria's words.

Aria's blue eyes widened. "You didn't even show me your engagement ring yet!"

I held my hand out.

"It's beautiful," Aria said.

"It is. Dante chose it for me." My second engagement ring, and the second time that it wasn't a sign of love. "How long will you be staying in Chicago? Do you have time to come over for a coffee?"

"We'll be leaving tomorrow morning. Luca wants to return to New York. But we're coming over to your wedding a few days early so maybe we could meet for coffee then, unless you'll be too busy?"

"No, it won't be a big celebration, so I'll have time to meet you for coffee. Give me a call when you know more."

"I'll do that."

"What about you, Bibiana, do you have time to come over tomorrow? We haven't had the chance to talk in a while as well."

Bibiana bit her lip. "I think I can. Now that you're as good as the wife of the Boss, Tommaso can hardly say no."

"Exactly," I said before turning to Aria again. "Where's Luca?"

Aria looked around. "He wanted to talk to my parents about Matteo's wedding to Gianna. It's taking longer than expected."

Would they cancel the engagement? That would be the gossip of the year. I couldn't imagine they'd risk it, no matter how unwilling Gianna was.

Dante appeared in the doorway to the living room, eyes settling on me.

"I think I need to leave," I said. I hugged Aria and Bibiana before I moved toward Dante, stopping in front of him. "Are we leaving?"

Dante looked incredibly tense. "Yes. But if you want to stay, you can drive with your parents."

That would lead to more gossip. You couldn't appear at a party with your fiancé and leave without him. "I don't think that would be wise."

Understanding settled on Dante's face. "Of course."

Back in the car, I asked, "Is everything okay?" Now that we were engaged, I thought it was okay for me to ask him.

His fingers around the steering wheel tensed. "The Russians are giving us more trouble than usual, and it certainly doesn't help that Salvatore Vitiello died at this critical time and New York has to deal with a new Capo."

I stared at him, surprised. When I'd asked him, I hadn't expected a detailed reply. Most men didn't like to talk about business with their wife, and I wasn't even married to Dante yet.

Dante's eyes snapped toward me. "You look surprised."

"I am," I admitted. "Thank you for giving me an honest answer."

"I think honesty is the key to a functioning marriage."

"Not in the marriages I know," I said wryly.

Dante tilted his head. "True."

"So you don't think Luca is a good Capo?"

"He is a good Capo, or he will be once he's weeded out his adversaries."

He'd said it clinically. As if weeding out didn't mean killing other people because they were a risk to one's power.

"Is that what you are going to do once you become the Boss of the Outfit?"

"Yes, if necessary, but I've proven my claim to leadership in the last few years. I'm considerably older than Luca."

But still the youngest Boss in the history of the Outfit. People would test him too.

Dante pulled up in front of my parents' house. He killed the engine, got out and walked around the hood of the car before opening my door. I took his hand and stood, bringing our bodies so close for a moment that it would have been easy to kiss him. Then he took a step back, reestablishing the proper distance between us before he led me toward the door. I turned to face him. "I never see you with a bodyguard. Isn't it risky to be outside on your own?"

Dante smiled darkly. "I'm armed, and if someone wants to take me by surprise, let them try."

"You are the best shot in the Outfit."

"Among the best, yes."

"Good, I suppose then I can feel safe." It was meant as a joke, but Dante looked deathly serious. "You are safe."

I hesitated. Wouldn't he try to kiss me? We would marry in four weeks. It wasn't as if we needed to stay away from each other for decorum's sake. When it became clear that Dante wouldn't make the first move, I stepped up to him and kissed his cheek. I didn't dare look at his face; instead I unlocked the door, slipped in and let it fall shut behind me. I waited a few moments before I peered through the window beside the door. Dante's car pulled away. I wondered why he hadn't tried to kiss me. Was it because we weren't married yet? Maybe he thought it wasn't appropriate for us to get close physically before our wedding. Or maybe he was still in love with his wife? I hadn't even looked at his hand to see if he had taken off his old wedding ring. Was that why people had talked about me today?

chapter *three*

Bibiana came over the next afternoon, her eyes red from crying. I ushered her into the library and made her settle down on the leather sofa. "What happened?"

"Tommaso is angry that I'm not pregnant yet. He wants me to go to a doctor to see what's wrong."

They'd been married for almost four years now, but Bibiana had been taking contraceptives in secret. "Maybe it wouldn't be so bad to get pregnant. If you have a baby, you'd have someone to love and who loves you back." I wrapped my arm around her. The last few years of seeing Bibiana growing more and more depressed because of her marriage to Tommaso had been heartbreaking. I wished there was something I could do for her.

"Maybe you're right. And maybe Tommaso won't touch me if I have a big belly." She shook her head. "Let's not talk about this. I want to forget about my troubles for a bit. So what about you? How are the wedding preparations going?"

I shrugged. "My mother booked a ballroom in a hotel. The only thing I need to do is buy a wedding gown."

"Will you get a white dress again?"

"I don't think so. My mother doesn't think it's appropriate. Maybe cream colored. That should be fine."

Bibiana huffed. "I think it's ridiculous that you can't wear a white dress only because you've been married before. It's not like it was a real marriage."

"Shhh," I hissed, my eyes darting to the closed door of the library. I'd told Bibiana about the true nature of my marriage to Antonio a while ago. "You know nobody can know."

"I don't understand why you're trying to protect him. He's dead. And he used you as a means to an end. You should look out for yourself now."

"I am looking out for myself. I've helped Antonio betray the Outfit. Being gay is a crime, you know that."

"It's ridiculous."

"I know, but the mob won't change anytime soon, no matter how much we want it to."

"If you don't want to tell Dante about it, then what are you going to do about your wedding night? Aren't you worried he's going to realize you never consummated your marriage with Antonio?"

"Maybe he won't notice."

"If it's anything like my first time, then he will notice."

"Tommaso treated you horribly. You didn't want it, so of course you bled. I'm still so mad when I think about it."

Bibiana swallowed. "What's done is done. I really wish I'd have been married to a gay man." She laughed bitterly. I took her hand. "Maybe you'll get lucky and Tommaso will have a heart attack or get shot down by the Russians." It wasn't even a joke. I wanted Bibiana to be free of that man.

Bibiana grinned. "How sad is it that I'm actually hoping for that to happen?"

"Of course you want him gone. I get it. Everyone would."

She scanned my face. "So what about you? You want to sleep with Dante?"

"Definitely. I can't wait." My cheeks grew warm, but it was the truth and I didn't see anything wrong with wanting to have sex with your soon-to-be husband. Dante was an attractive man after all.

"Then maybe you should take preparations that ensure Dante doesn't realize your first marriage was for show."

"What? Find a guy to sleep with? I won't cheat on Dante. I think sex belongs in marriage." Despite my best intentions not to take everything my mother taught me to heart and not to let the strict words of my Catholic teachers worm their way into my brain, I couldn't imagine being close to someone I wasn't committed to.

Bibiana let out a choked laugh. "That's not what I meant." She lowered her voice, her skin turning red. "I thought you could use a dildo."

For a moment I didn't know what to say. I'd never considered something like that. "Where would I get a dildo? I can hardly ask my father's bodyguards to take me to a sex shop. My mother would die of embarrassment if she found out." And I would most likely die from embarrassment when I entered said shop.

"I wish I could get it for you, but if Tommaso found out, he'd be furious." The bruises on Bibiana's cheekbones from Tommaso's last outburst hadn't quite faded yet.

"It's probably for the best. I don't like the idea of having sex with an inanimate object anyway. I'll figure it out."

"Dante will probably be too wrapped up in his own needs to notice anyway. Men are like that."

That wasn't much of a comfort. I hoped Dante would be concerned about my needs too.

When January 5th, my wedding day, finally rolled around, I felt a flicker of nervousness—and not only because of my wedding night. I knew this was my second chance at a happy marriage. Most people in our world didn't get that. They lived their lives in miserable unions until death finally separated them.

As I walked down the aisle in my cream sequined dress, I felt more hopeful than I had in a long time. Dante looked sophisticated in his black suit and vest. His eyes never left me, and as my father handed me over to him, I was sure I saw a hint of approval and appreciation in my new husband's expression. His hand was warm around mine, and the small smile he gave me before the priest started his sermon made me want to stand on my toes and kiss him.

My mother was crying loudly in the first row. She looked like she couldn't be happier, and my father was practically beaming with pride. Only my brother Orazio, who'd arrived only two hours ago from Cleveland, where he had work to do for the Outfit, looked like he couldn't wait to leave. I preferred the sight of Bibiana's and Aria's encouraging smiles. While the priest spoke, I kept throwing glances at Dante, and what I saw on his face tore at my heart. Every so often sorrow marred his expression. We had both lost someone, but for Dante the person had been the love of his life, if rumors could be believed. Could I ever compete with that?

When it was time for our kiss, Dante bent down without hesitation and pressed his warm lips against mine. He definitely didn't feel like an iceman. Mamma's words popped into my mind and a thrill of excitement rushed through me. Maybe I couldn't make Dante forget his first wife—and I didn't want to—but I could help him move on.

After church, we all drove to the hotel for the following celebrations. It was the first moment of privacy Dante and I got as a married couple. He didn't hold my hand as he drove, but he probably wasn't the touchy-feely kind of guy. What worried me more were the tension in his jaw and the steel in his eyes.

"I think it went well, don't you think?" I said when the silence got too oppressive.

Dante's eyes snapped to me. "Yes, the priest did a good job."

"I wished my mother hadn't been crying so much. Usually she's better at composing herself."

Dante smiled tensely. "She's happy for you.'"

"I know." I paused. "Are you happy?" I knew it was a risky question.

His face closed off visibly. "Of course I'm happy with this union."

I waited for something more, but the rest of the drive passed in silence. I didn't want to start our marriage with a fight, so I let it drop.

When we got out of the car and headed toward the entrance, Dante touched my back. "You look very beautiful, Valentina." I peered up at him, but his gaze was directed straight ahead. Maybe he'd realized how cold he'd been acting in the car and had felt guilty.

The ballroom of the hotel was beautifully decorated with pink and white roses. Dante kept his hand on my lower back as we made our way to our table under the cheers of our guests. Most of them had arrived before us and had already settled at their tables. We shared a table with my parents and brother, and Dante's parents as well as his sister and her husband. I hadn't talked to Dante's parents, except for a few occasions of small talk. They'd been nice enough though. My brother Orazio pretended he was busy with something on his iPhone, but I knew he was only trying to avoid our father's questions.

Aria and Luca, and Matteo and Gianna, as well as the rest of the Scuderi family occupied the table to our right. Aria gave me a smile before she returned her watchful gaze to her sister and Matteo, who seemed on the verge of an argument. Those two would have one hell of a marriage. Matteo didn't seem to mind the glowers Gianna was sending his way.

"You look beautiful together," Ines said, drawing my attention back to our table.

Dante regarded me with an unreadable expression.

The servers chose that moment to enter the ballroom with plates.

After the four-course dinner, it was finally time for our dance. Dante led me toward the dance floor and pulled me against his chest. I smiled up at him. He felt warm and strong, and was a good dancer. He smelled perfect, like a warm summer breeze and something very masculine. I couldn't wait to share a bed with him, to see what he hid beneath the fabric of his expensive suit. If we had been alone, I would have rested my cheek against his shoulder, but everyone was watching us, and I didn't think Dante liked to show intimacy in public.

Of course our guests didn't care. Soon they started calling, *"Bacio, bacio!"*

Dante peered down at me with one cocked eyebrow. "Do we honor their wishes, or ignore them?"

"I think we should honor their wishes." I really really wanted to honor their wishes.

Dante tightened his hold on my back and firmly pressed his lips against mine. His blue eyes were fixed on me, and for a moment I was sure I saw something like warmth in them. But then the guests flooded the dance floor to join in the dancing, and our kiss was over. Shortly after, Fiore Cavallaro asked me to dance and Dante had to dance with his mother. I smiled at my father-in-law, unsure how to act around him. He had the same cold aloofness going as Dante. "My wife and I had hoped Dante would choose someone who wasn't married before," he said, and I had trouble masking my shock.

The smile on my face became difficult to maintain, but I didn't want people to realize that Fiore had said something that hurt me. "I understand," I said quietly.

"But his reasoning convinced us. Dante needs an heir soon, and someone not quite as young might prove a better mother to our grandchildren."

I nodded. Their cold logic was something I hated with every ounce of my being. Not that I could tell him that.

"I don't intend to sound cruel, but this is a marriage of convenience, and I'm sure you know what's expected of you."

"I do. And I'm looking forward to having children with Dante." It was true. I'd always wanted children. I'd even considered in-vitro fertilization when I'd still been married to Antonio, but I wanted the chance to get to know Dante better before I tried to get pregnant. Naturally, I couldn't tell his father that either.

When the next song started, my brother took over from Fiore as was expected. "I'm glad you could come," I told him as I looked up at him. He had my dark green eyes and almost black hair, but those were the only similarities between us. We'd never been close—not for lack of trying on my part, however. I wasn't sure if that would ever change. He resented our father for coddling me, and sometimes I thought he resented me for having had it easier than him.

"I can't stay long," he said simply. I nodded, having expected nothing else. Orazio avoided our father as much as possible.

I was glad when Pietro, Ines' husband, asked me to dance. He was a quiet man and didn't step on my feet, so I wouldn't have minded dancing with him until the end of the evening to avoid awkward conversation. Of course that would have been beyond inappropriate. After my dance with Pietro, hospitality dictated that I had to dance with the head of New York. While Aria looked perfectly comfortable around Luca now, I definitely wasn't. Nevertheless, I accepted his hand when he held it out for me. He wasn't smiling. I'd only ever seen glimpses of a real smile when he looked at Aria.

Dante was tall and muscled, but with Luca even I had to tilt my head back to maintain eye contact. I knew people were watching us as we danced. Dante's steely gaze in particular followed every move we made, even though he was dancing with Aria. Not that Luca seemed much happier about the fact that Dante was embracing Aria. Men in our world were possessive. Men like Dante and Luca were something else entirely.

When one song ended and the next began, I could hardly hide my relief. Luca had a knowing expression on his face. He was probably used to people being uncomfortable in his presence. My next dance partner was Matteo. I didn't know him very well, but I'd heard about his temper and his skill with the knife.

"May I?" he asked with an exaggerated bow.

I curtsied mockingly in turn. "Of course."

Surprise flashed in his eyes. He pulled me against him with a shark-grin. Closer than Luca had risked. Closer than any sane man would risk.

"I think I saw your husband twitch a little just now," he murmured. "That's the equivalent of an emotional outburst for a cold fish like him, I suppose."

I exhaled, trying to stifle laughter. "You don't like to beat around the bush, do you?"

His dark eyes twinkled with mirth. "Oh, I like bushes well enough, don't worry."

I burst out laughing. And not a ladylike, restrained chuckle. It was high-pitched laughter. "I'm pretty sure that was inappropriate."

I could feel a few heads turning our way, but I couldn't restrain myself.

"You're right. I was warned to behave myself around the wife of the Boss so as not to cause a rift between New York and Chicago," he said lightly.

"Don't worry. I won't tell on you."

Matteo winked. "I fear it's too late for that."

"I think it's my turn again," Dante said, appearing beside us, his hard glare fixed on Matteo, who seemed thoroughly unperturbed.

Matteo took a step back. "Of course. Who could stay away from such dark beauty for long?" He bent over my hand and kissed it. I stiffened, not because of the kiss, but because of the look in Dante's eyes. I slipped my hand into his quickly and squeezed, and suddenly Aria was at our side. "Matteo, you should dance with me now." He did and Aria cleverly moved them away from Dante and me.

"I thought you wanted to dance with me?" I said in a forced casual tone, peering up at Dante's hard face.

His blue eyes settled on me. He wrapped his arm around me and started to move us to the rhythm of the music. I wasn't sure what had been the source of his anger: jealousy, or Matteo's disrespect. "What did he say?" Dante asked eventually.

"Hm?"

"What made you laugh?"

Maybe jealousy was the major driving force after all. That made me unreasonably happy. "He made a joke about bushes."

Realization filled Dante's face. "He should be more careful." The threat was obvious. Good thing Matteo and Luca hadn't heard it.

"I think he's a bit tense because of the problems between Gianna and him."

"From what I hear, he's always been volatile, even before his engagement to the Scuderi girl."

"Not everyone is as controlled as you are," I said pointedly.

He raised his eyebrows but didn't say anything in return.

Shortly after midnight, Dante and I excused ourselves. The hotel had offered us their biggest suite for the night, but Dante preferred to return home and I was actually glad. I was eager to finally move into Dante's house. Although, I was also worried since he'd shared it with deceased wife. It was probably filled with many memories. Bibiana crossed her fingers as I walked past her, and I couldn't help but smile.

chapter *four*

I WAS GLAD IT WAS TIME FOR OUR WEDDING NIGHT. MY FIRST REAL wedding night. I'd waited too long.

On the drive to Dante's mansion at Chicago's Gold Coast, neither of us spoke. Silence seemed to have become a loathsome tradition for us. I busied myself watching traffic through the passenger window while I desperately tried to hide my rising nervousness. Was it possible to feel excitement and dread at the same time?

Dante slowed as we approached a huge light-brown three-story mansion. Wrought-iron gates swung open when he pressed a button in the dashboard and we drove through, then headed for the double garage. My family's mansion wasn't too far away. It was smaller than Dante's home, as was to be expected. The Underboss couldn't have a bigger house than his Capo.

After Dante had parked next to a Mercedes SUV, he got out. He walked around the car and opened my door for me, then held out his hand and helped me out of the car, which was difficult with my dress. His hand was warm and steady. I was always surprised not to find his skin as ice-cold as his persona. He released me the moment I stood, and I almost reached for his hand but stopped myself. I didn't want to push him. Maybe he could only ever let loose behind closed doors.

He led me through a side door into the lobby of the mansion. The floor and the staircase were dark hardwood, and a chandelier cast a soft glow down on us. It was strangely quiet. I knew Dante had a maid and a cook, who handled the household for him.

"I gave Zita and Gaby the day off," he said offhandedly. Could he read me that easily?

"That's good," I said, then cringed at how that might have sounded. It wasn't as if I thought we'd entertain the entire house with our bedroom noises, but I preferred to have total privacy for our first night together.

Dante headed straight for the staircase, then stopped with a hand on the banister to look back at me. I'd halted in the middle of the lobby but quickly rushed toward him and followed him upstairs. My stomach fluttered with nerves.

This was my second wedding night, but I was almost as inexperienced as I'd been all those years ago, something I really hoped would change tonight. Antonio and I had kissed occasionally at the beginning of our marriage, and he'd even touched my breasts through my nightgown a few times, but when it became clear to me that he wasn't into it, we abandoned those futile attempts at intimacy.

I wanted to become a real wife, a real woman, and unlike Antonio, I knew Dante was perfectly capable of consummating our marriage. But that was also my problem. What if Dante noticed I was a virgin? Could I hide it from him? Maybe if I asked him to extinguish the lights, I could hide my discomfort or blame it on nerves over being with someone other than Antonio. But what if he felt my hymen? What would I tell him then? I should have used a vibrator to get rid of it, but the romantic part of me didn't want to lose my virginity to a device. It was ridiculous.

My thoughts were interrupted when Dante opened the door to the master bedroom and made an inviting gesture for me to go in. I walked past him, my wedding dress swooshing gently with the movement. I flashed him a quick glance in passing to gauge his mood, but as usual his expression was unreadable. The king-sized bed was black wood with black satin covers. For a moment I wondered if he'd kept it black since his wife's death. And then a worse thought took its place: was it the same bed he'd shared with his first wife?

"The bathroom is through that door," Dante said with a nod toward a dark wood door to my right.

I hesitated. Did he want me to freshen up? He closed the bedroom door and started loosening his tie. Didn't he want to undress me? He headed toward the window and looked out, his back to me. I got the hint. Disappointed, I walked into the marble bathroom. It was black marble, so maybe Dante simply liked black. I strode toward the window that faced the same direction as the one in the bedroom, wondering if Dante saw the same view I did—the boisterous lake, the black clouds dotting the night-blue sky and blotting out the full moon—or was he far away, lost in memories? The idea made me uncomfortable, and so I turned away from the window and began to undress before I took a quick shower. I'd waxed my legs in preparation for the wedding as was tradition, so I didn't need to shave. After I'd dried off, I put on the plum satin nightgown I'd bought for the occasion and brushed out my hair. My stomach fluttered again with nerves and excitement. I took a few moments to gather myself, to look like the experienced woman I was supposed to be; then I stepped back into the bedroom. Dante hadn't moved from his spot at the window. I allowed myself a moment to admire him in his black suit. He looked strong and sophisticated, untouchable, with his hands pushed into his pockets. An iceman, cold, emotionless, controlled.

I cleared my throat nervously and he turned toward me. His cold blue eyes scanned my body briefly, but his expression didn't change. There wasn't even the flicker of desire. There was nothing. He might as well have been carved from stone. Antonio had at least complimented me on my beauty on our wedding night. He'd even kissed me, had tried to pretend he could desire me, but it had become obvious pretty quickly that the kiss had done nothing for him.

But what stopped Dante? I deflated inwardly at his reaction. I knew many men found me pleasant to look at and they had never seen me this scantily dressed, but Dante didn't seem to be interested in me. I knew his wife hadn't looked anything like me. Where I was tall and dark, she'd been petite with light brown hair.

"You can lie down. I'll grab a shower," he said. His gaze shifted for the barest moment, but then he stalked into the bathroom and closed the door after him.

Trying to fight my frustration, I walked up to the bed and slid under the covers. With Antonio, I'd known that he wouldn't react to my body the way I wanted him to, but I'd thought it would be different with Dante. Maybe he needed a moment to gather his thoughts. It couldn't have been easy for him today. He'd loved his wife, and marrying again must have been really tough for him. Maybe he needed a shower to prepare himself mentally for the wedding night.

The shower ran for a long time and eventually my eyelids became heavy. I tried to fight the tiredness, but at some point I must have dozed off because I jerked awake when the bed dipped. My eyes darted to the side where Dante was stretching out. His chest was naked and I wanted nothing more than to run my hands over his slightly tanned, firm stomach and chest. His cool eyes settled on me. It was impossible to say what he was thinking. Would he reach out for me now?

I lay on my back, waiting for him to do something, nervous and excited and scared. I had to stop myself from making the first move. That would have been too forward.

"I have an early day tomorrow," he said simply, and then he turned the light off and rolled away from me. I was glad the darkness hid my shock and disappointment. I waited for a few more minutes for him to change his mind, to claim his rights, but he didn't. He lay beside me quiet and unmoving, his back a few inches from my arm.

Hurt welled in me and I rolled over, away from him. Dante was into women, so why didn't he want to sleep with me? What was wrong with me that after two wedding nights, I was still as untouched as the virgin snow? I wasn't sure I could go through this again. I wanted to experience lust, wanted to be desired. With Antonio, I'd known trying to seduce him was a losing battle from the start, but with Dante I had to at least try. Even if he still loved his wife, he was a man. He had desires and I was perfectly capable of giving him what he physically needed, even if he kept his emotions locked away.

I listened to his calm breathing. Although we weren't touching, I could feel the heat radiating off of him. He wasn't an iceman. There had to be a way to crack his mask.

chapter *five*

Dante wasn't in bed when I woke the next morning. His side of the bed was cold as I pressed my palm against it. Forcing my anger down, I made sure the door was closed before I slipped my hand into my panties. Over the years with Antonio, I'd learned to give myself pleasure with my fingers. I buried my face in Dante's pillow, inhaling his musky scent, and imagined he was touching me as I stroked myself to an orgasm. Afterward, I lay on my back for a while, staring at the ceiling, wanting to cry and laugh at the same time.

I slipped out of bed, headed into the bathroom and took my time making myself presentable. I chose a form-fitting brown dress that ended above my knees and a cute red cashmere cardigan. Even if Dante didn't care, I felt more comfortable if I put an effort into my outfits. I left the bedroom, hesitated and looked down the long corridor, wondering what hid behind the other doors. I'd have to explore at another time. Instead I moved down the staircase. I wasn't sure if I was expected downstairs for breakfast. I didn't know my new home, didn't know the people who worked here, and worst of all: I didn't know the master of the house, my husband.

The double doors were ajar and I approached them, then lingered in front of them for a moment before I walked inside. I'd expected Dante to be gone already and was surprised when I found him sitting at the dining table in the vast living and dining room. As with the rest of the house, the floor was dark wood, the walls light beige, and the furniture dark and imposing.

The newspaper hid Dante's face, but he lowered it when he heard me entering. My brown heels clicked on the hardwood floor as I approached the table slowly, unsure of how to act around him. Antonio had been my friend first, and then my husband, but there was nothing between Dante and me. We were strangers.

The table was set for two people, but my plate wasn't next to Dante's—instead it had been set at the other end of the table. I stared at the distance between Dante and me, considered ignoring the set-up and sitting beside Dante, but then I lost courage and took my seat at the end of the table.

"I hope you slept well?" Dante asked in his smooth voice. He hadn't put down the newspaper, still held on to it, and I had a feeling it would come up as a barrier between us again soon.

Was he being serious? "Too well," I said, not able to stop the jibe. Didn't he realize I'd expected a bit more from our first night together?

"I still have to prepare for a meeting with Luca. He'll be here soon as he heads back to New York tonight, but I told him you'd be delighted to keep Aria company while we discuss business."

I doubted Aria was in need of my company. She had her family here. This was a way to keep me occupied, nothing else. If he'd wanted a naïve wife, maybe he should have agreed to marry someone younger. But I liked Aria and it would have been rude to retract the invitation, so I smiled tightly. "That's very considerate of you." Sarcasm tinged my words. Now that we were married, it would be more difficult to keep up the polite mask.

Dante met my gaze, and there was something in his that made me lower my eyes and grab a croissant. I wasn't hungry, but it was better than doing nothing. The rustling of paper drew my attention back to the other end of the table. As expected, Dante had disappeared behind his newspaper. Was this how he wanted our marriage to go? He hadn't even showed me around the house yet. "Will you give me a tour of the premises? I can hardly host guests without knowing my way around the house."

Dante lowered his newspaper again and folded it on the table. I felt the unreasonable urge to rip it into shreds. "You are right."

Excitement bubbled up in me but quickly dissipated at his next words. "Gaby!"

A moment later, a door half-hidden behind a massive cupboard opened and a short teenage girl entered the room and headed toward Dante. "Yes, sir, how can I help you?"

I had trouble masking my surprise. Gaby looked like she belonged in high school. How could she be the maid in this house?

"My wife," Dante said with a nod in my direction. Gaby turned toward me briefly with a shy smile. "—would like to get a tour of the house. I'm busy, so please show her around."

Gaby nodded and walked toward me. "Would you like to go now?" Her voice was hesitant, but I could see curiosity in her eyes. I swallowed the last crumb of my croissant and poured coffee into my mug. "Yes, please. I'm going to take my coffee with me if that's okay?"

Gaby's eyes grew wide and she darted a look toward Dante, who was back to reading his newspaper. He didn't look busy to me. If he had time to read the news, why couldn't he show me around? But I wouldn't cause a scene in front of Gaby. Dante must have felt Gaby and me watching him expectantly because he raised his eyes. "This is your home now, Valentina. You can do whatever you want."

So he had been listening to our conversation. And I wondered if what he said was really the case. I wished I were more courageous so I could test the theory. I turned back to Gaby and cradled my mug in my hands. "Then let's go."

She nodded and led me toward the door she'd come through earlier. "We could start in the kitchen and staff room?"

"Do whatever you think is best," I said. "You know the house better than I do."

Again a shy smile flitted across her face. Behind the door was a narrow corridor, which led into a vast kitchen. Pots hung from hooks attached to the ceiling. Everything was stainless steel, and it reminded me more of a canteen kitchen than a place where family meals were prepared. A round older woman stood at the oven and checked the temperature. Inside what looked like a lamb roast was cooking. I assumed this was the cook, Zita. She turned around as she heard us enter and wiped her hands on her white apron. Her black hair had gray streaks in it and was secured in a hair net atop her head; I guessed she was in her mid-fifties.

"I'm giving our mistress a tour of the house," Gaby said excitedly. I startled at the use of "mistress." That sounded like I was a whip-wielding dominatrix. Maybe Dante was comfortable being called "sir," but I definitely couldn't live with "mistress."

"Please call me Valentina," I said quickly. "Both of you." I smiled at Zita but she didn't return the gesture. Her lips were pursed and she was scanning me from head to toe with a look of disapproval on her face.

"It would have been nice to meet you before the wedding," Zita said haughtily.

I forced my face to remain calm even if I didn't like her tone. I didn't want to start off on the wrong foot with the staff in the house. "Dante never invited me, and I didn't think it appropriate to invite myself."

She huffed. "He introduced Mistress Carla to us before the wedding."

I stiffened at the mention of Dante's first wife, couldn't help it. I could hear the judgment in her voice. She thought me less worthy than Carla. I had a feeling she wouldn't let me forget it. I wasn't looking forward to a battle of wills with her, and I definitely didn't have the patience for it today. I looked around the kitchen instead, trying to pretend I wasn't bothered by her comment. "So did Carla cook here often?"

Zita gave me a shocked look. "Of course not. She was the mistress of the house. She didn't cook or clean. That's what I and Febe did, before Gaby took Febe's place."

Gaby shifted nervously. It was clear that she didn't know what to do.

"Well, you can expect me in the kitchen often. I love to cook," I said.

Zita straightened her shoulders. "I don't know if Master Dante will allow it."

I took a sip from my coffee, returning her gaze steadily. "Dante told me I could do whatever I want." She looked away from me with a frown. I knew it wasn't over yet.

"Why don't you show me the rest of the house, Gaby? I need to make sure I'm ready when Aria arrives."

Gaby bobbed her head quickly. "Of course, Mis…Valentina."

She led me into the room behind the kitchen. It seemed to be a sort of common room for the staff. There were two cots, a small TV and a couch. No chairs or table, but I assumed the staff usually gathered around the wooden table in the kitchen, since it obviously wasn't used for Dante's meals. There was also a small bathroom with a shower behind a white door. "Is this where you and Zita spend your time when you don't work?"

Gaby shook her head. "We stay in the kitchen. This is mostly for the guards because they spend the nights."

"Where are they now?" I hadn't seen any guards so far.

"They are outside. Either patrolling the grounds or in their guardhouse."

"Are there security cameras?"

"Oh no, Mr. Cavallaro didn't want them. He's a very private man." No surprise there.

She headed toward another door. "This way." We stepped into the back part of the lobby. Gaby pointed at the two doors in the hall. "This is Mr. Cavallaro's office, and that's the library. Mr. Cavallaro doesn't like to be disturbed when he's in his office." She flushed. "By us, I mean. He's probably happy to be disturbed by you." She bit her lip.

I touched her shoulder. "I understand. So are there other rooms on this floor?"

"Only the living and dining room, and the guest bathroom."

As Gaby led me upstairs, I asked, "How old are you?"

"I'm seventeen."

"Shouldn't you still be going to school?" I sounded like my mother, but Gaby's shy nature brought out my motherly side even though she was only six years younger than me."

"I've been working for Mr. Cavallaro for three years. I came into this house shortly after his wife died. I never met her but Zita really misses her—that's why she was rude to you."

My eyes grew wide. "For three years? That's horrible."

"Oh no," Gaby said quickly. "I'm thankful. Without Mr. Cavallaro I'd probably be dead, or worse." She shuddered, a dark look passing in her eyes. I could tell that she didn't want to talk about it. I'd have to ask Dante about her later. She quickened her pace and pointed at doors on this floor. "These are guest bedrooms. And beside your master bedroom, there's a room you could use for your own purposes. The nursery and two additional rooms are on the third floor."

My eyes rested on a door at the end of the corridor that Gaby had ignored. I headed in its direction. "What about this one?"

Gaby gripped my arm before I could turn the handle. "That's where Mr. Cavallaro keeps his first wife's things."

I had trouble keeping a straight face. I couldn't believe he still held on to the past. "Of course," I said instead of what I was really thinking. It couldn't be locked or Gaby wouldn't have stopped me from opening it. I'd have to return alone, and find out more about the woman who was casting such a huge shadow on my marriage.

One hour later I showed Aria into the living room. It felt strange to act like the mistress of the house; it was as if I was an impostor. Aria looked tired when she sank down on the sofa beside me. Dark shadows spread under her eyes. I supposed she'd had a longer night than I did.

"Coffee?" I asked her. Gaby had set up a pot on the table, as well as assorted cookies.

"God yes," Aria said, then smiled apologetically. "I didn't even ask you about your night. You probably got less sleep than me."

I poured her coffee and handed her the cup as I tried to come up with a reply. "I slept okay," I said evasively.

Aria watched me curiously but she didn't push the matter. "So have you and Dante had the chance to get to know each other better?"

"Not yet. There wasn't any time."

"Because of us?" Aria asked worriedly. "Luca and your husband have to discuss a few things regarding Matteo's and Gianna's wedding." I could hear the strain in her voice.

"Gianna's still not happy about it."

Aria laughed into her cup. "That's an understatement."

"Maybe she just needs a bit more time. I remember how scared you were before your marriage to Luca, and now you two seem to get along just fine." Of course I knew that appearances were deceiving. I didn't know what went on behind closed doors.

"I know, but both Luca and I wanted to make it work. Right now, I think Gianna's main goal is to make Matteo so sick of her that he cancels the wedding."

"Not every couple works well together," I said quietly.

"I'm sure you and Dante will manage just fine. You are both always so poised and controlled."

I snorted. "I'm not nearly as poised as Dante."

Aria smiled. "He is a bit cold on the outside, but as long as he thaws when he's around you, everything's all right."

"So Luca isn't always this scary?" I joked.

Aria's cheeks tinged red. "No, he isn't."

Seeing Aria's happiness gave me hope. If she could make it work with someone like Luca, then I could make it work with Dante.

Luca's and Dante's conversation lasted longer than expected and I was starting to worry. They weren't exactly friends, but eventually they emerged and we decided to have lunch together. That's why Zita had prepared a lamb roast, after all.

We settled down at the table. Unlike this morning, Dante didn't sit at the head of the table. Instead he and I sat on one side while Luca and Aria took the seats across from us. The tension between Dante and Luca was palpable, and I started to wonder if lunch was really the best idea. Fortunately, Zita served the food only moments after we'd sat down, so we were busy enjoying the lamb, which lifted everyone's spirits at least for a short while. But the moment our plates were empty, things went downhill quickly.

Dante's face was even colder than usual. He looked as if he'd been carved out of marble. Luca didn't look much happier, but the hardness of his mouth was accompanied by a fire in his eyes. I glanced between them, but it was obvious that they didn't have anything else to say to each other beyond what had been discussed during their meeting.

Aria gave me a beseeching look.

As the hostess, it was my job to salvage the situation. "So when's the wedding?"

Dante made a dismissive sound. "If things progress as they do now, never."

"If things progress as they do now, there will be a red wedding," Luca said sharply.

My eyebrows shot up, and Gaby, who'd come in with a new bottle of wine, froze.

"There won't be a red wedding," Aria said. She turned to Dante. "You could give Matteo another bride from the Outfit."

I almost choked.

"Aria," Luca said in warning. "Matteo won't accept another bride. It's either Gianna or no one." He turned his hard gaze on Dante, who looked unimpressed. "I'm sure the Boss has enough control over his Famiglia to make sure Gianna complies."

I waved Gaby toward the table. Maybe wine would distract the men from ripping into each other.

"I'm not concerned about the extent of my control. There are no members of the Outfit trying to overthrow *me*." Dante bared his teeth in a smile that sent a shiver down my back. The two men looked like they were seconds away from pulling guns. I wasn't sure who'd go out as the winner in such a fight. They'd probably both die, and plunge the Outfit and the New York Famiglia back into open war with each other.

Luca rose, pushing back his chair in the process. Gaby, who had been about to fill his glass, yelped and dropped the wine bottle, her hands raised protectively in front of her face. For a moment, nobody moved. Dante stood as well. Only Aria and I were still sitting, almost frozen on our chairs.

"Don't worry about New York. Just make sure you hold up your part of the bargain," Luca snarled. He held out a hand and Aria took it, rising from her chair, before he added, "We need to catch a flight." She gave me an apologetic smile.

I straightened, then glanced at Gaby. She still stood paralyzed beside the table, red wine pooling around her shoes. "I'll show you out," I said to Luca and Aria. As I led them into the lobby, Dante followed close behind as if he was worried Luca would do something to me, which was highly unlikely.

Dante and Luca didn't shake hands, but I hugged Aria tightly. I wouldn't let our husband's fighting get in the way of our friendship. Or at least I'd try.

If things really went downhill between Chicago and New York, I wouldn't even be allowed to talk to Aria anymore. I watched them drive off, then I turned around to Dante, who was still standing behind me. "What was that all about?"

Dante shook his head. "My father should never have agreed to marry the second Scuderi daughter off to New York. This won't end well."

"But things between Aria and Luca seem to be going well, and the Outfit has worked together peacefully with New York for years now."

"Theirs was a marriage of convenience, but Matteo Vitiello wants Gianna Scuderi because he's gotten it in his head that he needs to have her. That's not a good base for a decision. Emotions are a liability in our world."

I blinked. Again his cool reasoning. "Have you never wanted something so badly you would have done anything to have it?" I knew it was the wrong question the moment the words left my mouth, but I couldn't take it back.

His cool eyes met mine. "Yes. But we don't always get what we want." He was talking about his wife. He wanted her back.

I swallowed hard and nodded. "I should call Bibiana. I want to meet her tomorrow."

I turned around and headed up the stairs, feeling Dante's gaze on me the entire time. I was glad he couldn't see my face.

chapter *six*

After my short call with Bibiana, I'd retired into the library. It was stocked mainly with nonfiction and old classics, nothing I was usually drawn to, but I didn't want to go in search for Dante, nor did I want to ask my mother to come over. She would have thought something was wrong, and even though that was probably the case, I didn't want her to find out. She'd been so happy since she found out I was going to be Dante's wife. I didn't want to ruin it for her by admitting that Dante couldn't care less about my presence.

I grabbed a book that taught basic Russian. The only languages I spoke were Italian and English. I might as well get familiar with the language our enemies spoke, and it would keep me occupied in the hours Dante was busy ignoring me.

Eventually, the growling of my stomach lured me in the direction of the kitchen. It was already almost seven but nobody had called me for dinner. As I entered the kitchen, I found Zita, Gaby and two men gathered around the wooden table, eating dinner together.

I hesitated in the doorway, unsure if I should enter, but then Zita glanced my way and I couldn't back out anymore. I slipped inside, feeling acutely overdressed in my sleek brown dress. Everyone turned my way, and the two men rose immediately. They wore gun and knife holsters over their black shirts. Both were in their late thirties, and probably the guards.

"The master has already had dinner in his office," Zita informed me.

"I was busy reading anyway," I said, hoping I sounded indifferent. I focused on the two men still standing and watching me. "We haven't met yet."

I strode toward them and extended my hand to the taller man with a buzz cut and a scar in his eyebrow. "I'm Valentina."

"Enzo," he said.

"Taft," said the other man. He was a couple of inches smaller but much bulkier.

"Can I join you for a quick dinner?" I might just as well try to get familiar with the people I would see every day for the next few years, maybe longer.

Both men agreed at once. Gaby, too, seemed excited about the prospect of my presence; only Zita had trouble hiding her disapproval. "Are you sure this is what you want?" She gestured at the spread of cheeses, the Parma ham and the lovely Italian bread.

"I wouldn't have asked if I wasn't," I said as I took the seat beside Taft. He held up a bottle of wine. I nodded and took one of the rustic wineglasses from a tray at the end of the table. The wine was delicious and so was the food. I kept my eyes on Gaby, who thankfully wasn't drinking wine. Taft and Enzo didn't look at her in any way that would suggest they were interested in her, which calmed me further, but I couldn't forget the look of fear on her face when Luca had jumped to his feet. Of course he was a scary guy on the best of days, but there had been more. I had a feeling that Gaby had learned to fear men. I only needed to find out why. Taft and Enzo stopped after their second glass of wine; they still had guard duty until the morning and could hardly do their job drunk, but Zita and I emptied the bottle. With alcohol in her bloodstream, Zita seemed much nicer. Or maybe my own tipsiness made me blind to her rudeness. Either way, I enjoyed myself thoroughly. The men knew how to tell dirty jokes, and soon forgot that I was practically their boss.

After another particularly lewd joke that had Gaby hiding her face in her hands and me laughing like I hadn't laughed in a long time, the door to the kitchen opened and Dante stepped in. His eyes did a quick scan of the room until they settled on his men, then me. His jaw tensed as he glowered at Taft and Enzo. "Shouldn't you be outside keeping guard?" Dante asked in a dangerously quiet voice.

Both men stood at once. They fled the kitchen without another word.

"Gaby and I should head home too. We'll clean the kitchen tomorrow," Zita said as she grabbed her coat and put it on. "Come on, Gaby." Gaby shot me an apologetic look, although she'd done nothing wrong.

Two minutes later, Dante and I were alone in the kitchen. I had done nothing forbidden, so I had no intention of apologizing. I emptied my red wine, my eyes on Dante, who seemed to become perfectly still as he watched me. I rose from my chair. In a standing position, at least, I didn't have to tilt my head all the way back to look Dante in the eyes.

"Why did you eat with Enzo and Taft?"

I almost laughed. "Gaby and Zita were there too." Was he jealous? Or did he think I was distracting the men from work?

"You could have eaten in the dining room."

"Alone?" I asked in a challenging tone.

Dante advanced on me, and despite my best intentions I froze. "I don't play games, Valentina. If there's something you don't like, then say it and don't try to provoke me."

He stood so close, the spicy scent of his aftershave flooded my nose. I had to fight the urge to grab him by his lapels and pull him in for a kiss.

"I wasn't trying to provoke you," I said matter-of-factly. "I was hungry and I didn't want to eat by myself, so I decided to eat in the kitchen."

"You should keep your distance from the guards. I don't want people to misconstrue your friendliness with something else."

I took a step back. "Are you accusing me of flirting with your men?"

"No," he said simply. "We would have a different kind of conversation if I thought you were flirting with them."

I raised my chin, unwilling to let him intimidate me, no matter how intimidating he was. "I won't eat alone."

"Would you prefer we have dinner together every night?"

"Of course, I do," I said exasperatedly. There were many things I wanted to do together with him at night. "We are married. Isn't that what married people do?"

"Did you and Antonio eat together?"

"Yes, unless he was away for work." Or had a date with his lover Frank.

Dante nodded, as if he was filing away the information. I'd heard someone once say that he had a photographic memory, which made him a difficult opponent to outsmart, but I wasn't sure if it was true.

I softened my voice. "What about you and your first wife? Did you eat together?"

I could practically see his defenses coming up. A veil of cold impenetrability seemed to slide over his face. He pushed up his sleeve, revealing his gold watch. "It's late. I have an early morning with meetings in our casinos."

"Oh, sure."

"You don't have to go to bed if you're not tired."

"No, the wine's making me sleepy." We both walked out of the kitchen and headed upstairs. This time Dante disappeared in the bathroom first. I rummaged in my drawer for a skimpy satin camisole and matching panties that barely covered my butt. Maybe that would get Dante's cold blood boiling.

I nervously paced the bedroom, wondering if tonight would be the night. Maybe yesterday had been a sort of grace period. The door of the bathroom opened and Dante stepped back into the bedroom. Like yesterday he was naked from the waist up. I allowed myself a few moments to admire his body. Even the scars didn't make him any less gorgeous. If possible they added to his sexiness. Dante paused, and I quickly tore my eyes away and rushed into the bathroom.

I took a quick shower and brushed my teeth before I slipped into my lingerie. *Showtime.* I stepped out of the bathroom. Dante was already in bed, his iPad in hand and back propped up against the headboard. He looked up, eyes wandering the length of my body, lingering on all the right places. Anticipation mixed with nerves filled me as I slowly walked toward the bed, making sure Dante got a good look at me. He hadn't looked away yet, but he hadn't put down his iPad either. I stretched out beside him, my back against the headboard. I didn't bother pulling the covers up. I wanted Dante to see as much of me as possible.

I met his gaze. As usual his eyes were unreadable, but they weren't quite as cool as usual. He set the iPad down on his nightstand and I almost sighed with relief, but then he shifted and lay down. Confused, I did the same, but I rolled onto my side, facing his way. He hadn't turned the lights out yet. That had to be a good sign, and I knew he kept glancing toward my breasts. If I was more experienced, I would have initiated things, but I worried about revealing my inexperience to Dante if I risked it. If he made the first move, I could go along with him and would hopefully appear like the experienced woman I was supposed to be.

Dante tore his gaze away, closed his eyes and crossed his arms in front of his stomach. His jaw was locked tightly. Was he angry? He looked like he was on the verge of bursting. Maybe he didn't like that I was being so forward and practically shoving my breasts into his face. Maybe he preferred his women demure and scared of their own shadow.

Frustrated, I rolled onto my back as well. "What happened to Gaby?" If we didn't have sex, we might as well talk. Anything was better than the awkward silence.

Dante kept his eyes closed. "What do you mean?"

"She said she's been working for you for three years, but she's only seventeen. Shouldn't she be going to school?"

Dante's eyes peeled open, cool and blue, and firmly focused on the ceiling. "Three years ago we attacked two Russian clubs as retribution. They're making the majority of their money with human trafficking. The women in their clubs are mostly sex slaves. Women and girls who were kidnapped and then forced into prostitution. When we took over the two clubs, we had to figure out what to do with the women. We couldn't let them run around Chicago after what they'd witnessed."

My stomach turned. "You killed them?"

Dante didn't even twitch. "Most of them were illegals. We sent them back into the Ukraine or Russia. The others were relocated. Those who wanted to work in our clubs, we kept."

"So what about Gaby?"

"She was a child. The younger girls we found were sent to families, where they could work as maids or cooks."

"Or become mistresses," I said, because I had no doubt that some Made Men couldn't keep their hands off a helpless girl under their roof.

Dante frowned. "Even among Made Men, pedophilia isn't tolerated, Valentina."

"I know, but Gaby doesn't exactly look like a child anymore, nor do the other girls you captured, I presume."

Dante fixed me with a hard glare. "Are you suggesting I touched Gaby?"

"She almost died from fear today when Luca moved. Maybe one of your men..."

"No," Dante said firmly. "She hasn't been abused in any way since she came into this house. She's under my protection. My men know that."

"Okay." I believed him, and I also believed that none of his men dared to go against Dante's direct orders. If Gaby was under his protection, she was safe. "I bet those girls would have made you a lot of money. There's a reason why the Russians kidnap young girls. Why the qualms? It's not like the Outfit doesn't have its own clubs with prostitutes, and it's not like those women can just stop working for the mob whenever they want." I was honestly curious. Dante was a killer after all.

"The Outfit isn't in the business of sex slaves. The women in our clubs start working for us on their own free will, and they know that they'll be bound to us forever. We make enough money with our casinos and drugs, we don't need sex slaves or illegal racing like the Russians and the Camorra in Las Vegas."

"What about New York, do they deal in sex slaves?"

"No. That's really only the Vegas Camorra. I'm not saying that there aren't voices in the Outfit who would like to change that, but as long as I'm Capo that won't happen."

"That's good," I said.

Dante's eyes softened for a moment, but then he turned away and extinguished the lights.

"Good night," I whispered. I was still disappointed that Dante didn't touch me, but at least he'd talked to me as if we were equals, not like I was a brainless woman who didn't need to know anything about the business.

"Good night, Valentina," Dante said into the dark. There was something in his voice I couldn't identify, perhaps wistfulness, but I wasn't sure.

chapter *seven*

If I'd thought last night's chat with Dante would make him reconsider our seating arrangements during breakfast or even make him want to talk to me, I'd been horribly wrong. Like yesterday, he disappeared behind his newspaper after a quick greeting. I wasn't in the mood to fight for his attention. I was too confused and hurt by his continued disinterest in me. I only picked at some fruit and drank a cup of coffee before I decided to excuse myself. Dante didn't even look up from his newspaper when I walked out.

Usually I would have asked him if he wanted me to take one of his men as guard with me to Bibiana's house, but I was too angry. I had a driver's license. Antonio had wanted me to get one after we married, which sadly wasn't the norm for men in our world. After I'd put on a coat and grabbed my purse, I walked into the garage. Dante had given me keys for the house and the garage. Of the three cars parked there, the Mercedes GL was the least attention-grabbing. I took the car keys from a hook at the wall and slipped into the car. It took me a moment to find the button in the dashboard that opened the garage, but finally I steered the car outside and down the driveway. A guard I didn't know patrolled the fence but didn't try to stop me when I opened the gate with a press of another button. I drove off the premises and the gate closed automatically behind me.

It felt good to drive again, even if I didn't like Chicago traffic, but it had been too long since I had been allowed to drive by myself. My parents had been too determined to keep me under their watch after Antonio's death to let me go out alone. I knew the way to Bibiana's home by heart, had driven it countless times over the years, and it took me only ten minutes from Dante's mansion.

Bibiana's and Tommaso's house was much smaller than either Dante's or my parents'. They didn't have a long driveway where I could have parked. Instead I had to leave my car in the street. Not that I was worried someone might steal it. Streets where mob members lived were usually quite safe, unless you counted the risk of attacks from the Bratva or Triad. I walked up to their front door, noticing one of Tommaso's men sitting in a car on the other side of the street and watching the house. Tommaso wasn't as highly ranked as the men in my family or the Scuderis, but he wasn't a simple soldier either. He always kept a guard near the house to watch over Bibiana, or what I suspected: to make sure she didn't run away.

The guard didn't stop me, only tilted his head in a gesture of respect. I rang the bell. Bibiana opened the door, then glimpsed behind me. "Where are your guards?"

I shrugged. "I didn't take any. Dante never said I had to take guards."

"Won't you get in trouble?" she asked as she closed the door and led me into their living room. As usual her husband wasn't home. Bibiana, of course, didn't mind. She'd gained a couple of pounds since Tommaso had been forced to work long hours. Now she didn't look quite as emaciated anymore.

"Why would I?" I said. I wasn't even sure if Dante cared if I left the house without protection. He seemed too busy with God knows what.

Bibiana gave me a worried look. "You should be careful. Dante is a dangerous man. He always looks so calm and in control, but Tommaso told me Dante doesn't tolerate disobedience."

That didn't really come as a surprise, but I couldn't disobey him if he didn't give me an order in the first place. "I'm not one of his soldiers."

I sank down on the sofa. Bibiana took a seat beside me, curiosity filling her face. "So how was your wedding night?"

My lips twisted. "I slept well," I said sarcastically.

Bibiana blinked at me. "Huh? That's not what I meant."

"I know what you meant," I said, frustrated. "Nothing happened. Dante gave me the cold shoulder."

"He didn't try to sleep with you? What about last night?" I wished Bibiana didn't sound so stunned; it made me feel even worse. As if somehow it was my fault that I hadn't managed to make Dante want me. I knew she didn't mean it that way.

"He didn't even kiss me. He just lay down beside me and said he had an early day, and then he turned off the light and fell asleep. What kind of wedding night is that?" I leaned my head against the backrest. "I don't get it."

"Maybe he really was tired," Bibiana said tentatively.

I gave her a look. "Do you truly believe that? He looked fit enough to me. And what about yesterday? Was he tired then too?" I bit my lip. "Do you think it's still because of his wife?"

Bibiana twisted a strand of her brown hair around her finger nervously. "Maybe. I hear he adored her. They were the dream couple in Chicago."

I'd never paid much attention to Dante and his wife in the past, but I remembered seeing them together at social gatherings. I remembered thinking they looked like they belonged together. There were few couples in our world who appeared to love each other. Most of us married for convenience, but with Dante and Carla you had seen that they were meant to be together. Fate was cruel for ripping them apart, and even crueler for throwing me into the arms of a man who'd already found the love of his life once. "Maybe he hasn't been with a woman since his wife died. That could be the reason why he didn't try to consummate our marriage."

Bibiana avoided my gaze and reached for a macaron on the silver étagère on the table in front of us. She shoved it into her mouth and chewed as if it afforded all of her concentration. Dread filled my stomach. "Bibi?"

Her eyes darted to me, then they were gone again. She swallowed and reached for another sweet, but I grabbed her wrist, stopping her. "You know something. Did Dante have a lover since his wife's death?"

Bibiana sighed. "I didn't want to tell you."

The words hollowed me out. "Didn't want to tell me what?"

What if Dante had a steady lover? Someone he couldn't marry for social and political reasons. Maybe that's why he chose me, a widow, because he didn't want to screw over a poor innocent girl like that. My head started spinning.

Bibiana gripped my hand tightly. "Hey, it's not that bad. Calm down. You look like you're going to pass out any moment."

I reached for a green macaron and stuffed it into my mouth. The sweet taste of pistachio spread on my tongue and I relaxed slightly. "So spill before I come up with more horrible scenarios." I could tell Bibiana wanted to ask what kind of scenarios had popped into my mind, but thankfully she didn't. Bibiana knew me well enough to guess anyway. We'd been friends since we could both walk. She was the cousin closest in age to me and we'd always spent every free minute together. Even in school we'd been inseparable, except for the classes that we didn't share because I was a year ahead. But it was difficult to make friends among normal kids, so we'd stuck together. That hadn't changed after we'd married. If possible we'd gotten even closer, because we both could share our marriage troubles with each other without having to worry that anything would get out.

"My husband told me Dante frequented Club Palermo for a while."

I froze. Club Palermo was a mob-owned nightclub with pole dancing, striptease and prostitution. Bibiana's husband was the manager of the club. "What do you mean?"

Bibiana's cheeks turned red. She looked like she regretted ever having brought it up. "He used prostitutes for sex."

I pressed my lips together, trying to figure out why this hurt so much. Only last night we'd talked about prostitution; why hadn't he mentioned something? I could almost see how that conversation would have gone. "Not anymore, right?"

"Oh no, it happened a while ago. About a year after his wife's death, he had a rough stretch and came into the Club a couple of times per week to 'let off some steam,' as Tommaso put it."

It had been way before our marriage, and yet the knowledge that Dante had slept with prostitutes, but hadn't even tried to kiss me, hurt a lot. "So he has no problem sleeping with other women, he just doesn't want to sleep with me."

"No, that's not true. And like I said, he hasn't visited Club Palermo in a long time."

"Okay, but that doesn't change the fact that he didn't want to sleep with me. With Antonio, I could deal with it. I knew it was nothing personal. He wasn't into me because he wasn't into women, but what's the reason for Dante's disinterest? Maybe he doesn't find me attractive."

"Don't be ridiculous, Val. You're gorgeous. He'd have to be blind not to be into you. Maybe he didn't want to push you? You lost your husband less than a year ago, and Dante doesn't know that you and Antonio were never a real couple."

"It's not like I don't miss Antonio," I said defensively. "I miss our conversations, and that he confided in me."

"I know you do, but you don't miss him physically. Maybe Dante thinks you're not ready to be intimate with another man."

I pondered that. It seemed like a logical explanation, and Dante was nothing if not a logical man. On the other hand, Dante was also a Made Man, and they usually didn't suffer from excessive sensitivity. "How many men do you know who would care about that?"

Bibiana grimaced. "Tommaso definitely wouldn't."

"See," I said, feeling even more miserable. "It's unlikely that Dante's conscience is keeping him from sleeping with me. He's a killer, and a skilled one at that. He's the Boss for a reason."

"That doesn't mean that he doesn't have some scruples. I know that he strongly disapproves of rape."

I snorted. "He disapproves?"

Bibiana gave me a stern look. "I'm serious. Dante told his men that he'd castrate anyone who would use rape as a form of torture, punishment or entertainment. Tommaso hates it because he thinks he should be allowed to do whatever he wants with the women in Club Palermo."

I didn't doubt that for one second. I'd lost count of the times he'd raped Bibiana. Of course, nobody called it rape in our world because she was his wife and her body belonged to him. Thinking about it made me sick. "Okay, so he has qualms about a couple of things." It made sense after what he'd said about Gaby yesterday. Maybe he really didn't want to initiate anything with me because he thought I was still mourning Antonio.

"Maybe you should make the first move?" Bibiana said.

"I pranced around him half-naked yesterday; what else can I do?"

"You could kiss him. Touch him."

I knew how to kiss. Antonio had kissed me a few times. It had been nice, for me at least, so kissing Dante was definitely something I could do. "Touch him? Do you mean his you-know-what?"

Bibiana flushed. "I guess so? I never initiated anything with Tommaso, but he always wants me to touch him there and blow him." Bibiana took another macaron. I knew she hated talking about sex with Tommaso. Who wouldn't?

"Touching him can't be too hard."

"Oh, it'll be hard."

I laughed. "Dirty jokes already? The macarons really get you going."

Bibiana giggled and shook her head. "You will be fine. Even if you blow him, you can't do anything wrong. Use no teeth and you should swallow, those are the two most important things."

I had to hide a grimace. I wasn't so much disgusted by the idea of giving Dante a blow job, but the image of Bibiana having to swallow Tommaso's stuff made me want to hurl.

"The good thing about blow jobs is that most men love them, so if you're not into the actual sex, then you can keep them happy that way."

I really hoped it didn't come to that. I knew the only orgasm Bibiana had ever experienced was by her own hand, but I didn't want to share her fate.

"I'll give it a try tonight," I said, suddenly feeling more hopeful.

"Call me tomorrow. I want to know how it went."

"Don't worry, you'll be the first to know if something exciting happens."

That night when Dante joined me in bed I gathered all my courage, scooted over to him and touched his naked chest. It was warm and firm. Dante stilled under my touch, his brows drawn together as he watched me. I leaned forward and pressed my lips against his. Dante deepened the kiss immediately, his tongue slipping into my mouth. This kiss was much more intense than the ones I'd experienced with Antonio. Dante claimed my mouth, making me tremble with the need for more. I let my hand slide lower, down his stomach. He drew back and gripped my hand, stopping its descent. He shook his head, his eyes flashing with something dark and angry. "You should sleep now, Valentina."

I stared at him, uncomprehending. What had just happened? He'd kissed me as if he wanted to devour me, and then he stopped without an explanation. I snatched my hand out of his grasp, fighting the tears of anger rising into my eyes. Without a word, I rolled around, my back to Dante, and closed my eyes.

"I know you went to Bibiana without protection today. That won't happen again. You can go wherever you want. You can even drive yourself, but from now on I want one of the guards at your side when you leave this house. It's too dangerous for you outside these walls," he said as if he hadn't just kissed me, as if he wasn't the slightest bit affected by what we'd done.

I pressed my lips tightly together. I wanted to scream in frustration, but instead more tears pooled in my eyes.

"Understood?" Dante asked after a while.

I had to bite back a scathing comment. "Yes, understood."

We both fell silent again, not touching, as if we were two strangers forced into the same bed by accident. And that was actually closer to reality than I liked. The throbbing between my legs was almost unbearable, but it was clear that Dante wouldn't do anything about it. I wasn't sure what to do anymore.

chapter *eight*

DANTE WAS A VERY PRIVATE MAN. THAT'S WHAT EVERYONE always told me, which was why I knew how wrong it was for me to breach his privacy. But I needed to see the things Dante kept hidden behind the door Gaby had showed me. Maybe it would help me understand him better.

It was early afternoon, and Dante had left for a meeting at one of the Outfit's underground casinos. I wasn't sure when he'd be back, but if the last two days since my embarrassing attempt at seduction were any indication, probably not before eight. It was silent in the house. Today was Gaby's day off, and as usual Zita was busy in the kitchen and avoiding me.

I pushed down the handle and stepped into the room where Dante kept his dead wife's memorabilia. The curtains were drawn, casting the room in darkness. I fumbled for the light switch but when I pressed it, nothing happened. I switched it back and forth a few more times until I decided that it was futile. After a moment of guilt-induced hesitation, I carefully felt my way toward the window and pulled the curtains apart. Coughing from a billow of dust from the heavy fabric, I blinked against the sudden light, my eyes tearing up. I wiped them quickly before I dared to look around.

There wasn't a lamp attached to the ceiling, only a string of abandoned wires. No wonder the switch didn't do anything. Dust particles danced in the air and a musty smell penetrated my nose. A fine layer of dust had gathered on every surface and even the ground. My footsteps were clearly visible. Briefly, panic threatened to overwhelm me. There was no way I could hide my presence in the room if my footprints were all over the floor, but clearly nobody had set foot inside in a long time, not even Dante, so he'd never find out.

The room was cluttered with furniture and cardboard boxes. There was a dark wood wardrobe, two dressers and a king-sized four-poster bed. Slowly realization dawned on me. This must have been the master bedroom Dante and his wife had shared before her death. At least I wasn't sleeping in the same bed where Dante had made love to his dead wife. I tiptoed toward the wardrobe. I wasn't even sure why I was trying to be quiet, but it felt almost sacrilegious to be in this room. Opening the wardrobe, I was hit by the smell of disuse and old clothes. Two dozen dresses hung from padded pink hangers, everything from long ball gowns and pretty cocktail dresses to casual summer dresses. Some of them looked like they might have belonged in my wardrobe, but of course they were too small for me.

I brushed my fingers over the fabric. It was strange to think that the person who had worn them was long gone, buried in cold dark earth. With a shudder, I closed the door and stepped back, but my curiosity wasn't sated yet. I opened one of the drawers of the cupboard beside the wardrobe and found it stacked with underwear. I quickly closed it. That definitely felt too personal. I couldn't rummage through the lingerie of a dead woman, even if it might tell me something about Dante's preferences. Hesitantly, I approached the second dresser and opened the top drawer. It was empty except for two photo albums. I had a feeling the drawer had once belonged to Dante, stacked with his socks and briefs a long time ago. When he'd changed bedrooms, he'd left everything behind, even his own dresser.

Ignoring my qualms, I picked up the two albums and carried them over to the bed. A dark red duvet was spread out over it, which was also covered in a thin layer of dust. After a futile glance around in search for another option, I sat down on its edge with the albums in my lab. The first album was white except for the image of two entwined gold rings. With trepidation, I opened the album.

A much younger Dante and a young, small woman in a wedding dress were in the first photo. Dante wasn't looking into the camera. His sole attention belonged to his bride, and the adoration plainly visible in his eyes made a lump rise into my throat. The cold calculation and emotionless sophistication that were now ever-present were absent from his face. Maybe because he was still young, but I had a feeling it had just as much to do with the woman at his side.

It was a simple picture, and yet it conveyed everything a wedding should mean: love, devotion, happiness.

I hadn't seen the photos of our wedding yet, but I knew what I wouldn't find in them. Swallowing the rising emotion, I browsed the other photos, childishly hoping to find Dante with a look of the same indifference he always showed me. But even though his expression became more guarded and controlled in later photos, his feelings for his wife were hard to miss. They'd been married for almost twelve years, but they'd never had kids. I knew Carla had fought cancer in the last three years of her life, but I wondered why it hadn't worked before then. I'd never seen her with a baby bump, or heard rumors of a miscarriage. Not that it was my business.

Maybe I should count myself lucky that Dante didn't have kids with Carla, or I'd have them here to despise me as well. I hated the bitterness of that thought and quickly abandoned it. I didn't want to get petty, or act jealous toward a dead woman. She'd never done anything to me and it was horrible that she had died so soon.

I picked up the second album. At its end, there were a few photos that showed Carla with a wig and no eyebrows. Dante's arm was wrapped protectively around his thin, pale wife. Sorrow washed over me. How was it to lose someone you loved so much?

I had loved Antonio as a friend, but it didn't even come close to what Dante and Carla must have had, and if I was being honest I'd often resented Antonio in the end for keeping me in a loveless golden cage so he could hide the fact he was gay.

The door flew open, making me jump, and Dante stepped in, his expression thunderous. Before I could move, he was in front of me and ripped the photo album from my hand. He flung it onto the bed, his furious eyes burning into me. "What are you doing here?"

He grabbed my arm and pulled me to my feet, bringing us so close our lips were almost touching. "This room is none of your business."

I squirmed in his hold. "Dante, you're hurting me."

He released me, some of the anger replaced by cold disapproval. "You shouldn't have come here." His eyes darted to the album that lay open on the bed with the photo of his sick wife and him. He took a step back from me, the last of his fury gone and replaced by a frightening calm. "Leave."

I didn't need to be told twice. I quickly rushed into the corridor, scared by Dante's outburst, but honestly terrified by the odd calm that had taken over his face at the end. Dante stepped out of the room and closed the door. He didn't look at me again. I watched his back as he walked away and headed down the stairs. Wrapping my arms around myself, I closed my eyes. I didn't like to give up on things. I was stubborn—too stubborn, as my mother always pointed out—but I seriously considered accepting that the marriage between Dante and me wouldn't work. There was only so much rejection I could take.

We hardly spoke during dinner, and when we did it was about current news that was the last thing on my mind. Dante didn't mention what happened, and I definitely wouldn't. After Zita had cleared away our plates with a too-curious glance in my direction, Dante stood. "I have more work to do."

Of course he did. I nodded mutely and headed toward the library. If things kept progressing the same way they were now, I'd speak Russian in no time, I thought bitterly as I picked up the textbook. I couldn't focus. The letters swam before my eyes and eventually I gave up. I left the room and cast a glance in the direction of Dante's office. There wasn't any light spilling out from under the door. Maybe he had gone to bed?

I headed toward the staircase but stopped when I saw movement from the corner of my eye. The door to the living room was open, giving me a clear view of Dante, who sat in the wide armchair in front of the dark fireplace, drinking what looked like whiskey. I considered going to him and apologizing, but his brooding expression made me decide against it. Instead I quietly ascended the staircase and slipped into the bedroom.

Under the warm stream of the shower, my fingers found their way between my legs again, but I wasn't really into it and eventually abandoned my attempt to find release. Seeing those old photos had ripped open old wounds and created new ones. They had reminded me of the few times in the beginning of our marriage that Antonio had brought his lover Frank into our home to have sex with him. It was one of the safest places for them to meet, but despite my best attempts to be okay with it, I'd suffered because Antonio's interaction with Frank spoke of the love and desire he could never give me. Seeing Dante with his wife today had felt the same way. I hadn't stood a chance against Frank back then, and I was increasingly sure that I didn't stand a chance against Dante's dead wife either.

Once I told Bibiana what happened, she advised me to leave Dante alone for now and hope for the best, and during our call that had actually seemed like a decent solution, but after a day of crushing silence I couldn't take it anymore.

When I saw Dante sitting in front of the unlit fireplace that evening, drinking his whiskey, something snapped in me.

My first husband hadn't wanted me because he preferred men, and my second because he couldn't let go of a dead wife and because he preferred to brood over a glass of whiskey. I knew Dante had had sex with other women after his wife's death. Bibiana had confirmed that he'd frequented her husband's club for a while, so why didn't he want to have sex with me? Maybe something about me repulsed men. That was the only logical explanation, and if that was the case I needed to know and stop wasting my time on foolish hope and ludicrous seduction plans.

I stepped into the living room, making sure my heels made an audible sound on the hardwood floor. Dante kept his gaze on the dark fireplace. Of course, he ignored me. He almost always did.

My arms started to shake from restrained anger. "Is it true that you frequented Club Palermo?"

Dante frowned. He swirled the whiskey around in his glass, not looking up. "It belongs to the Outfit, but that was a long time before our marriage."

Bibiana had said the same, but his casual tone and dismissive body language were too much. He acted as if none of this was my business.

Anger burned through my veins. I could feel my temper bursting out of its cage, but I was too shaken to rein it in. "So you didn't mind the company of prostitutes, but you can't take your own wife's virginity?"

That got his attention, and now I wished it hadn't. His blue eyes shot up. I wished I could shove the words back into my mouth, wished he'd return his gaze to his whiskey. Maybe there was even a flicker of confusion on his face for a millisecond, before the schooled mask of calm slipped back on.

I turned around without another word, shocked by what I'd said, terrified of the consequences my outburst might bring down on me. The clink of a glass being set down on mahogany sounded behind me, followed by the creak of the armchair. My throat closed up, iciness filling my chest. My fingers clutched the banister as I made my way upstairs. His steps followed after me, calm and measured. I suppressed the desire to look back or even run. Dante couldn't see how shaken I was. What was I going to do?

He'd demand answers. Answers I couldn't give him, promised never to give anyone. But Dante was the Boss. Nobody got to that position without knowing how to acquire information. He wasn't going to torture me, or even raise a hand to me. But I was sure he didn't need to.

I slipped into the bedroom, then stopped in front of the window overlooking the premises. There was nowhere else to run. The bed was looming in the corner of my eye. I closed my eyes when I heard Dante enter the room and close the door behind him. His tall form appeared behind me in the reflection of the window. I lowered my gaze to my fingers, which were tracing the cool marble of the windowsill. Sometimes I felt like I could handle everything, like I was the sophisticated, controlled woman Dante probably wanted, but in moments like this I felt like a stupid girl.

"Virginity?" he said without a hint of emotion. The gift of all men in the Outfit. If you grew up with violence and death, you learned to seal your heart off from the world. Why didn't they teach the same to the women of the Outfit? "You and Antonio were married for four years."

I didn't turn around, didn't even dare to breathe. How could I have let that slip? My mistake could ruin Antonio's reputation, and mine for agreeing to his plan. Being gay was a punishable crime in the mafia, and I'd pretty much helped Antonio to commit it. I focused on breathing, on the feel of the marble against my fingertips, on the trees bowing down to the wind outside.

"Valentina." This time a faint hint of strain carried in the word.

"I shouldn't have said anything," I whispered. "It was just a figure of speech. I didn't mean it in the literal sense." I was a good liar, didn't have a choice but to become one. "As you said, Antonio and I were married for four years. Of course I'm not a virgin."

His hand touched my hip and I practically jerked forward a foot, colliding with the windowsill. I gasped in pain, then bit down on my lip to swallow the sound. I'd been longing for Dante to touch me for days, and now that he did I wished he'd go back to ignoring me.

Dante was watching me in the window. "Turn around," he said in a low voice. I didn't even hesitate. His voice, even without menace and danger in it, carried too much authority for me to resist. I steeled myself as I faced him, focusing on the buttons of his white dress shirt. His eyes would undo me. Every muscle in my body was tense like a bowstring. He put a finger below my chin and lifted it, forcing me to meet his gaze. Again the touch. Why would he touch me now, while before he'd gone out of his way to keep distance between us?

I swallowed. *Be strong, Valentina. The wish of a dead man is sacred. Don't break your promise.*

And it wasn't only Antonio I was protecting. I'd lived a lie, had as good as lied to Dante himself since our first encounter, had led him to believe one thing while the other was true. I wished there was emotion on Dante's face, even anger; I could have dealt with that, but he gave nothing away. Always the iceman.

"So your words downstairs were simply meant to provoke?" He sounded calm and curious, but I didn't let that fool me. I had all his attention.

I couldn't say anything. The way he'd worded it made it seem really bad. What was he thinking? I wished I had the slightest hint if he was in a good or bad mood.

He won't hurt you, Valentina.

He hadn't done anything to me so far, but we hadn't exactly interacted all that much in the few days of our marriage. And two days ago he'd been scary as hell when he'd found me with the photo albums.

The tension became too much and a tear slid out of my right eye, trailed down my cheek and caught on Dante's finger that was still pushing my chin up. He frowned, releasing my chin. I immediately tore my gaze away from him and took a step back.

"Why are you crying?"

"Because you scare me!" It burst out of me.

"Until today you never seemed scared of me." He was right. Except for a few brief occasions, I hadn't been scared of him, but I knew with a man like him I should be scared.

"Then maybe I'm a good actress."

"You have no reason to be scared of me, Valentina," he said calmly. "What are you hiding?"

"Nothing," I said quickly.

He closed his fingers around my wrist loosely. "You are lying about something. And as your husband, I want to know what it is."

Anger flared up. This time it was quicker than caution. "You mean as the Boss you want to know, because so far you haven't exactly been acting like my husband."

He tilted his head, scrutinizing every inch of my face. "Why would you still be a virgin?"

"I told you I'm not!" I said desperately, trying to slip out of his hold, but he tightened his fingers slightly, only enough so I couldn't escape. He pulled me against him, my chest pressed against his. Air left my lungs in a rush as I looked up at him. My heart pounded in my chest, my temples, my veins. And he felt it. That was why he was holding my wrist.

"So," he said in a curious tone. "If I were to take you toward our bed right now—" He took a step, forcing me closer to the huge four-poster bed. "—and make you mine, I wouldn't find out that you lied to me just now."

I'd wanted nothing more than for him to want to finally bed me, and now that he used it as a threat to find out the truth, I wished I'd never wanted anything from him in the first place. Would he feel that I had never slept with a man? I'd only talked with other women about their experiences, but I didn't know if men could feel if a woman was a virgin.

"You wouldn't because you won't take me to that bed now."

"I won't?" He raised one blond eyebrow.

"No, because you wouldn't take me against my will. You disapprove of rape." The words Bibiana had used still sounded strange coming from my lips, and it wouldn't even be against my will. I'd thrown myself at Dante for days now; he must have known that I wanted him. Still wanted him despite everything. My body was practically humming with longing for his touch.

He chuckled. I'd never heard him laugh. It sounded empty. "That's what you hear?"

"Yes," I said more firmly. "You gave the Underbosses direct orders to tell their men you'd castrate anyone who used rape as a means of revenge or torture."

"I did. I think a woman should never have to submit to anyone but her husband. But you are my wife."

"But still." My words were a bare whisper, filled with uncertainty.

He nodded once. "Yes, still." He let go of my wrist. Relief flooded me. "Now I want you to tell me the truth. I'll always treat you with respect, but I expect the same from you. I don't tolerate lies. And eventually, we will share a bed and then, Valentina, I'll know the truth."

"When will we ever share a bed like husband and wife, and not just sleep beside each other? Will that ever happen?" I snapped. My stupid mouth, always running free.

His expression flickered with something I couldn't place. "The truth," he said simply, but with authority. "And remember I will know eventually."

I lowered my face. Would the truth make things worse between Dante and me? It would definitely be much worse if he found out I'd openly lied to him, which he would if we ever consummated our marriage.

"Valentina," Dante said tersely.

"What I said in the living room was the truth." I was relieved and terrified when the words were out of my mouth. How much longer could I have kept up the lie anyway?

Dante nodded, a strange look on his face. "That's what I thought, but now I ask why?"

"Why is it such a surprising thought that Antonio didn't want me? Maybe he didn't find me attractive. You obviously don't, or you wouldn't spend most evenings in your office and your nights with your back to me. We both know that if you wanted me, if you found me desirable at all, I'd have lost my virginity on our wedding night."

"I thought we agreed on the fact that I wouldn't force you," he said. I searched his eyes because there had been a trace of anger in his voice.

"But you wouldn't have to force me. You are my husband and I want to be with you." Heat flooded my cheeks. "I've practically thrown myself at you for days now, and you didn't even notice my body. If you found me attractive, you would have showed some kind of reaction. I guess I'm just lucky to always end up with husbands who find me repulsive."

"You aren't repulsive to me," he said firmly. "Trust me, I find you attractive."

I must have looked doubtful, because he closed the distance between us. "I do. Do not doubt my words. Whenever I catch a glimpse of the creamy white skin of your thighs..." He traced my thigh through the high slit of my nightgown. I had to stifle a surprised gasp at his sudden proximity. Goose bumps erupted all over my body. "Or when I see the outline of your breasts through the little nothings you wear to bed..." He ran his finger gently over the lacy edge of my nightgown, right above my breasts. "I want to throw you onto our bed and bury myself in you." He dropped his hand, back to not touching me again.

My eyes widened. "You do? Then why—"

He cut me off with a finger against my lips. "It's my turn to ask questions, and you promise not to lie." I stared at him, nodding. Had he said the truth? Did he want me?

"Why did Antonio not sleep with you?" Dante asked, still standing so close that his warmth flooded my body. I could hardly focus.

"I promised him not to tell anyone ever."

"Antonio is dead," Dante said. He didn't sound sorry. "I'm your husband now, and your promise to me is more important."

I averted my eyes. He was right, but I'd carried the truth with me for so long, it had almost become a part of me. Dante would probably figure it out eventually.

"Valentina?"

"Antonio was gay," I blurted. Finally the burden of Antonio's lie didn't rest on my shoulders anymore. It felt freeing.

Dante seemed stunned for a moment. "I never suspected anything. Are you sure?"

I rolled my eyes. "He brought his lover home sometimes."

"Why didn't he sleep with you to create offspring? That would have fended off possible suspicions."

I hesitated. "I don't think that would have worked. You know..." I gestured in the general direction of Dante's groin.

"He was infertile?"

I flushed. "No, he mentioned once that he couldn't get one up with women." The words rushed out of me.

"Who was his lover?" he asked casually, but I knew better than to trust his outward disinterest. His eyes revealed a hint of his fervor to get an answer from me. I had a feeling that he was trying to use my emotional state against me, but I wasn't that easily thrown off my guard.

I shook my head. Frank was still alive and still very much not a member of the Outfit. If Dante found out that Antonio had dated an outsider... I didn't even want to consider the consequences. He wouldn't stop until he found the person, and I knew exactly what would happen to Frank then.

"I can't tell you. Please don't make me."

Dante touched my upper arms without any pressure. "If it's someone from the Outfit I need to know, and if he isn't...the Outfit comes first. I need to protect all those placing their trust in me."

He would kill Frank, and maybe even have him tortured first to make sure Frank gave away the names of all the people who knew about Antonio.

I wouldn't be able to live with myself if that happened. I wanted to close my eyes against Dante's piercing gaze, but I knew it would be a bad idea. "I can't tell you. I won't. I'm sorry, Dante, but no matter what you do, I won't give you a name."

Anger flashed across Dante's face, fiercer than yesterday. This was real fury, and for the first time it was directed at me. What had Bibiana said? Dante didn't tolerate disobedience. "You've lived a sheltered life, Valentina. I've had hardened men say the same to me, and in the end they gave up all their secrets."

"Then do what you have to do," I snapped, pulling away. "Cut off my toes and feed them to me. Beat me, burn me, cut me, but I'd rather die than be responsible for the death of an innocent man."

"So he's an outsider."

I stared at him agape. That's what he gathered from my outburst? God, he was good at this. He hadn't hurt as much as a hair on my head and had already gotten information out of me. "I didn't say that."

But it was too late. Dante smirked. "You didn't have to." His eyes were keen and eager. He looked like someone on the hunt. "If Antonio took his lover home, I assume you've met him and know his name and can describe him to me."

I pressed my lips together, glowering at him. Not in one million years would I tell him what he wanted to know. I'd already said too much. I'd have to be more vigilant in the future.

Dante came closer again. He touched my hips and despite everything, the simple contact sent tongues of fire through my belly. I wanted him, maybe more than ever before. What was it that made dangerous men so irresistible?

"Aren't you loyal to me?" he murmured. "Don't you think you owe me the truth? Don't you think it's your duty? Not only because I'm the Boss of the Outfit, but because I'm your husband."

"And you owe me a decent wedding night. As my husband, it should be your duty to take care of my needs. I suppose we both will have to live with the disappointment."

His mask cracked. Without warning, he gripped me and whirled me around so my back was pressed against his chest.

"I'm a patient hunter, Valentina," Dante said in a low voice that I could feel all the way to my core. "You will tell me what I want to know eventually." His hand slid down my side to my thigh, lingering there for a moment, making me hold my breath in anticipation and confusion. He pushed up my nightgown as he stroked his way up to my panties. I shivered and pressed myself even harder against his chest. The crisp fabric of his shirt rustled at the contact. It was a strangely erotic sound. Dante slipped a finger under the lacy fabric of my panties and brushed my folds. I whimpered, already wet and aching from our argument and his closeness. I wasn't sure why he was suddenly touching me or what had brought on that change of mind, and I didn't care as long as he kept touching me. He dipped his fingers between my lower lips and his breathing deepened. "You want this?"

"Yes," I hissed, rubbing myself shamelessly against his hand, but his other arm came around my waist and held me fast. "I want you, Dante."

"Tell me what I want to know." He stroked his fingers slowly back and forth. The slow sensual assault was making me breathe heavily. I was already so close. My body had waited too long for this. My legs started to shake and I threw my head back against Dante's shoulders. "Don't you want me?" I panted, instead of what he wanted to hear. His finger brushed my clit as if in answer, and I came apart with a small cry as ecstasy exploded through me.

Dante's arm around my waist kept me upright, strong and unyielding, as I trembled under my climax.

"I do. That's the problem," he growled. Suddenly, he let me go and stepped back. I gripped the windowsill to stop myself from falling to the floor. I whirled around, my pulse still pounding in my veins, but Dante was already on his way out of the room.

What had just happened?

chapter *nine*

DANTE DIDN'T COME TO BED THAT NIGHT. I WAITED FOR A LONG time, unable to fall asleep, too confused by what had happened. He'd admitted he wanted me, had touched me, but then he'd pulled back. Why? When I woke the next morning, his side of the bed was untouched, and when I walked into the dining room thirty minutes later, his newspaper lay discarded beside a clean plate.

Worried, I approached his office. It was silent behind the door but that didn't mean anything. I knocked, then entered without waiting for a reply. I didn't want to give Dante the chance to put up his defenses. Maybe if I caught him by surprise again we'd get somewhere. Dante sat behind a black wood desk and narrowed his eyes when I entered his office for the first time. Maybe he felt like I'd encroached on his personal space again by intruding.

My eyes settled on the silver picture frame on his desk. A picture of his smiling first wife. It sat in the middle of the desk as if he'd hastily put it down when I'd opened the door. There weren't any other photos in the room.

My stomach lurched violently. Trying to hide my hurt, I met his disapproving gaze. "What are you doing here?"

"This is my home too, isn't it?"

"Of course it is, but this is my office and I need to work."

"You always do. I wanted to see if you were all right."

He raised his eyebrows. "Why wouldn't I be?

"Why? Because you acted very strange yesterday. One moment you're touching me and the next you can't get away from me fast enough."

"You don't know anything about me, Valentina."

I interrupted him. "I know, and I want to change that, but you keep pushing me away."

Dante stood and ran a hand through his hair. "I never wanted to get married again. For good reason." Again he made it sound as if this marriage had been my idea, as if I had had any say in the matter.

"I didn't ask you to marry me!" I'd had enough. I turned on my heel and stormed out of his office, making sure I slammed the door as hard as possible.

It was a childish thing to do. I could hear it open again and Dante's steps behind me. He caught up with me and grabbed my wrist, pulling me to a stop.

"You have an impossible temper," he growled.

I glared at him. "That's your fault."

"This marriage has always been for practical reasons. I told you that."

"But that doesn't mean we can't try to make it a real marriage. There are no logical reasons why we shouldn't sleep with each other. You slept with prostitutes, so why can't you sleep with me?"

"Because I was angry and I wanted to fuck someone. I wanted it rough and hard. I wasn't looking for closeness or tenderness or whatever it is you want. I took whatever pleasure I wanted, and then I left. What you're looking for, I can't give you. The part that was capable of it died with my wife, and it won't come back."

"You don't know what I want. Maybe we want the same thing." My voice was a bare whisper.

He scoffed. "I can see in your eyes that's not true. You want to make love, but I can't give you that. I do want to possess you, want to own every part of you, but not for the reasons you want me to. I'm a heartless bastard, Valentina. Don't try to see anything else in me. The business suit and emotionless face is the thin layer covering up the fucking abyss that's my soul and heart. Don't try to glimpse beneath it—you won't like what you find."

I was too stunned for a comeback. Instead I watched him return to his office.

I spent the rest of the day considering my options. Dante didn't want emotional attachment. He didn't even want tenderness. Rough and hard, those were the words he used for the sex he'd sought from prostitutes. He was right. It wasn't what I wanted, but over the years I'd learned that sometimes you had to settle for the lesser evil to reach some form of happiness. I wanted to have sex with Dante, maybe not the same way Dante did, but who said I wouldn't like it? And he hadn't exactly said that he'd be rough with me. He'd only said that I shouldn't expect fluff and loving gestures from him. I could live with that, couldn't I?

I wanted to be desired by him. Maybe that would be as good as being loved by him.

It was almost time for dinner, but I was hungry for something else as

I undressed quickly in our bedroom before I could change my mind and slipped a bathrobe on. I couldn't walk naked through the house.

My stomach fluttering with nerves, I headed downstairs and toward Dante's office. I knocked, and this time I waited for him to call me in as I didn't want to start this seduction attempt with a fight, even if our argument in the bedroom yesterday had been a huge turn-on for me. He opened the door without a word. His cool eyes slid over my body. I wondered if he could tell that I was naked beneath the thin material of my bathrobe.

"Can I come in?"

He stepped back and I walked in. I could hear the door close, and then Dante headed back toward his desk and turned to me with an inquiring expression. "What's going on?"

"I made up my mind."

"About what?"

I opened my bathrobe. "About us. About sex."

Dante's eyes darkened. Clenching his jaw, he shook his head and began to turn away. "You should leave."

"Don't turn your back on me. Look at me. I think I deserve at least that small decency, Dante."

Tension radiated off of him when he turned to face me. He didn't move closer, but he was looking at me. For once, he didn't pretend I was invisible. His blue eyes wandered over my exposed body.

My nipples hardened in the cool air of his office but I didn't close my silk bathrobe, despite the overwhelming urge to cover myself against Dante's cold scrutiny. His gaze lingered on the apex of my thighs slightly longer than the rest of my body, and a small burst of hope filled me. How much control did he have? "Am I your wife?"

His brows drew together. "Of course you are." There was the hint of something I couldn't place in his voice.

"Then claim your rights, Dante. Make me yours."

He didn't move, but his eyes slid down to my erect nipples. His gaze was almost physical, like a ghost touch on my naked skin, but it wasn't nearly enough. I wanted to feel his fingers between my legs again, wanted to feel them on every inch of my body, wanted to come until I lost track of all my problems.

I wasn't above begging. I knew I almost had him, could see it in the tight set of his shoulders, in the unhinged look in his eyes. I wanted to have sex tonight. "I have needs too. Would you prefer if I found a lover who relieved you of the burden to touch me?" I wasn't sure I could go through with it. No, *I knew* I couldn't go through with it, but this act of provocation was my last option. If Dante didn't react to this, then I didn't know what else to do.

"No," he said sharply, something angry and possessive breaking through his perfect mask. He pressed his lips together, jaw locked, and walked toward me. I shivered with need and excitement when he stopped in front of me. He didn't reach for me, but I thought I detected the hint of desire in his eyes. It wasn't much, but enough to embolden me. I bridged the remaining distance between us and curled my fingers over his strong shoulders, pressing my naked body against his front. The rough material of his business suit rubbed deliciously against my sensitive nipples, and I let out a small moan. The pressure between my legs was almost unbearable. Dante's eyes flashed as he looked down at me. Slowly he wrapped an arm around me and rested his palm flat against my lower back. I wished he'd move it lower. I didn't think I'd ever been so desperate for someone else's touch, not even when I had to listen to Antonio fuck Frank in the room next door.

Sweet triumph flooded me. Dante wasn't ignoring me now.

I tilted my head up to look into his face. Whatever desire I'd thought I'd seen was gone, his walls up and impenetrable. I stood on my tiptoes, desperate for a real kiss, but Dante's hand on my back tightened and he didn't angle his face down, making it impossible for me to brush my lips against his. He didn't want me to kiss him. I couldn't take this anymore. I'd thrown myself at him naked, had offered him my body and myself, and still he refused me. I wrenched away from him, feeling dirty and cheap. Avoiding his eyes, I whirled around, clutched my bathrobe closed and hurried out of his office. I crossed the lobby and ran up the stairs. This was it. I wouldn't try again. I'd have to accept that Dante didn't desire me enough, that he wouldn't sleep with me until it was absolutely necessary to produce an heir.

I stumbled into the bedroom and flung myself on the bed. For a moment, a rush of despair and sadness gripped my body, but I didn't let it win. I'd survived a marriage with Antonio. I could survive a loveless marriage with Dante. Someday I would have beautiful children I could love and who would love me back, and until then I could deal. I wasn't the first woman in our world who had to live with a cold bastard as a husband, and I definitely wouldn't be the last. At least I wasn't trapped with an abusive asshole like Tommaso as a husband. That had to count for something.

And I would just have to take care of my other needs as I had done for the last few years. I rolled onto my back. I was still angry, still embarrassed and disappointment, but I was also still aroused. I closed my eyes and slipped my hand down my body and between my legs. I began stroking myself, imagining Dante's fingers were teasing me again, remembering the brief flicker of desire in his eyes that I'd probably imagined. My breathing came faster as I caressed my sensitive nub. I was getting closer. A moan slipped out of my lips, and there was a sharp intake of breath.

My eyes flew open and I stared at Dante; he stood in the doorway, hand on the door handle and eyes on me. For once they didn't look cold. God, how long had he been watching me?

I jerked my hand out from between my legs, mortification slamming through me like a wrecking ball. I clutched my bathrobe against my chest and scrambled for the edge of the bed. I couldn't stay in a room with Dante, not after what he'd just seen. I'd embarrassed myself enough today, but Dante was suddenly in front of me, barring my way. His tall form loomed over me. I threw my head back to meet his gaze. His eyes were more animated than I'd ever seen them. He looked almost angry. "No," he said quietly.

I wasn't quite sure what he meant. Then he leaned over me until I lay flat on my back again and he towered above me. His jacket fell open and encased me on both sides like a soft prison. I searched his face. I could feel myself getting more aroused from his proximity and the dominant look on his face. He braced himself on one arm and brought one knee between my legs, forcing them apart.

My heart pounded in my chest. Would he finally do what I'd been waiting for? For a long time he only glared down at me, and I almost expected him to pull away again, but instead he cupped my breast and I arched my back up with a needy moan. His eyes slid down to his hand, and he pinched my nipple, harder than I'd anticipated. Pleasure coursed like lightning through my body all the way down to my center. I needed him to touch me there, needed it more than food, than water, than air. Dante pinched and tugged my nipple, his eyes dark and intent as he watched me. I'd caressed my breasts a few times over the years, but it had never done much for me, yet Dante's firm touch sent sweet tingles through my core. He leaned down, the rough fabric of his jacket brushing my side, and captured my nipple between his lips.

I arched up with a mewl, pressing my breasts against his face, but Dante's hand gripped my hip and held me down. He sucked my nipple hard again, making arousal pool between my legs. I squirmed, trying to rub myself against his knee still wedged between my thighs, but his hand kept me in place. Not being able to move as I wanted to wasn't something I'd ever thought I'd find sexy, but boy had I been wrong.

Dante bit down lightly on my nipple, his teeth lightly scraping my sensitive skin, and I almost came. I'd already been so close before. He released my nipple, which was red and hard from his attention. His eyes on my face, he trailed his hand down my side. I couldn't look away from his beautiful cold face, mesmerized by the heat in his eyes, a stark contrast to the iciness of his features. There was something dark and feral and angry in them. He hooked his fingers under my thigh and pulled my legs further apart. I trembled with anticipation. "Tell me now if you want this," he said in a low voice. How could he even doubt my desire for him?

"I want this."

"Good." He drew my other nipple into his mouth with a dark smile and flicked his tongue over it as he slid two fingers over my mound and pressed down on my clit. Spears of pleasure shot from my core and through my entire body. It felt as if I was coming apart at the seams as my orgasm rocked through me. I rocked my hips desperately. Dante watched me calmly as I shivered beneath him, his fingers still pressed against my sensitive nub. Slowly I came down from my high. I was embarrassed that I'd come this fast, when he'd barely touched me, but I lifted my chin defiantly despite my embarrassment. If he hadn't made me wait for so long, I wouldn't be this easily aroused.

Dante released a long breath through his nose, his jaw flexing. Then he eased his fingers between my folds. His nostrils flared as he slowly pushed two fingers into me. My muscles tightened around him, and I sucked in a quick breath at the foreign intrusion. It wasn't painful, only slightly uncomfortable. I'd occasionally put one finger into myself but never understood the appeal. This, however, was amazing. Dante lowered his gaze and watched his fingers as they moved in and out of me. It felt incredible, better than I had ever made myself feel. His steady motion made me pant.

"You are incredibly tight. I can't wait to be inside you," he said roughly. I wished he'd keep talking in that sexy growl, but all I managed to bring out of my lips were whimpers and sighs.

I was close to a second orgasm, could feel it building deep in my core, could feel the familiar spikes of pleasure echoing through my body. Dante quickened his thrusting and flicked his thumb over my nub, and I dug my heels into the mattress as my climax hit me, this one even stronger than my first. I was still enjoying the last waves of my orgasm when Dante pulled out his fingers. I made a sound of protest, but Dante straightened with a look of utter desire in his eyes. I was startled by the intensity, by the resignation and darkness mingling on his face. He looked like a man who'd lost a battle with himself. He stood tall and regal, motionless except for the rise and fall of his chest as his eyes took in my naked body. Then he reached up and removed his jacket. It slid to the ground with a soft rustling. He didn't get rid of his vest and shirt, though. He unbuckled his belt with practiced ease, the movement drawing my eyes to his groin. My eyes were frozen on the bulge in his pants. Surprise washed over me, followed by intense triumph. "You're hard," I whispered.

Dante's gaze flickered to me and he paused with his hands on his fly. "I'm capable of getting an erection. I'm not impotent." There was a hint of amusement in his voice, but it was almost drowned out by the raspy desire in it.

"That's not what I meant. But I thought you weren't attracted by my body."

Dante gave me a strange look. "Don't worry. Your body would leave few members of the male species unaffected."

Still so in control, so poised, and yet…I glanced at his crotch. Dante unzipped his fly and pushed down his pants. His black boxers did little to hide the impressive bulge. I wanted to reach out and touch him, but I held back and watched instead as my nerves slowly started to rise. I'd waited so long for this. Finally, he pulled down his boxers. His cock was fully erect, thick and long, and a strange sense of satisfaction filled me. After years of being ignored first by Antonio and then by Dante, I finally got a reaction from the latter at least.

"Scoot up," Dante said in his Boss voice, a voice that brooked no argument, not that I would have dreamed of protesting. I crawled back immediately and slid my arms out of my bathrobe, then I lay completely naked in front of Dante. He made no move to remove his shirt and vest. He climbed on the bed and moved between my legs, pushing them apart, spreading me open for him. I wondered why he didn't undress fully. Was it some sort of barrier he wanted to keep between us? Or was I overthinking? He looked more than a little sexy in his vest, but still…

Any thought fled my mind when Dante guided his erection toward my center and nudged my opening. He felt hard and big, but I'd been waiting long enough for this. I was ready. Dante propped himself up on his arms, then shifted his hips and slid in a few inches until I tensed and cried out. I squeezed my eyes shut, and drew in a few harsh breaths through my nose to calm my racing pulse. The pain was already fading, but he wasn't all the way in yet. After another deep breath, I opened my eyes and found Dante staring down at me. His jaw was tight. For once he didn't seem quite so calm and in control, and I could tell how much he was struggling to keep still. I raised my arms and grabbed his shoulders, then I gave a small nod. Dante rocked his hips and pushed all the way in. I arched up, clamping my mouth shut to keep any sound in. I breathed out through my nose, as I forced my body to relax.

Dante peered down at me, his brows drawn together and a muscle in his cheek twitching. "Tell me when I can move," he gritted out, surprising me with that show of compassion.

I wiggled, impatient, desperate to have Dante move in me. There was still a slight discomfort but that too was getting better. "It's okay."

He nodded, then pulled almost all the way out before sliding back in. My muscles gripped his cock tightly, still trying to get used to the invasion, but I could feel a hint of pleasure behind the soreness as Dante fell into a slow rhythm. I wished he would come down on his forearms so we could be closer, but he braced himself on his palms. I guessed I shouldn't have expected anything else. He'd warned me, but at least he was careful and hadn't pounced on me.

I let out a small moan as he hit a delicious spot deep inside me. Dante sped up, his thrusts becoming more forceful. His face was filled with concentration. He didn't make loud noises, but his pants came quicker. I loved watching him, loved seeing the small twitches and flickers in his cold mask when his pleasure spiked.

"It's been a while for me," he warned in a rough voice. "I don't know how long I can last." I was surprised by his admission. I didn't think he was a man who readily admitted to anything resembling weakness in his mind. I was glad for that small flicker of humanness.

"It's okay." It wasn't as if I was going to come again. I could tell that I was close to the limit of what I could take.

His movements became even faster and less restrained, almost jerky and unhinged. And then he finally lowered himself to his forearms, bringing us closer than we'd ever been, our bodies pressed against each other as if we were one, and he really started to pound into me, hard and fast, and my soreness turned into an insistent twinge, but I didn't even care. I could feel his heat through his clothes. His vest rubbed my sensitive nipples, and I wished I could have felt his skin, but even that wasn't important right now. All that mattered was that Dante was finally making me a woman, finally allowing us to become close. Maybe this was a new beginning, the real start of our marriage. I clung to his back and buried my face in the crook of his neck as Dante thrust into me a few more times.

He groaned, his body tensing, and then I felt his erection expand in me, followed by the strange sensation of him coming inside me. I pulled back, wanting to see his face. For once the mask was gone. He looked disheveled, approachable, less unforgiving somehow. He shuddered once more before he lowered his face and brushed his lips against mine, his tongue sliding over my lips lightly. I eagerly opened my mouth for him. Our tongues met and I was in heaven. I'd waited for our first real kiss for so long, and now it was happening. He tasted perfect, and I loved the feeling of his weight on top of me, and the sensation of his softening cock inside me. Maybe everything would change now. I slipped my hands under his shirt and ran them up and down his back, my fingers finding every scar, mapping his body. He felt so warm and strong. He felt like he was mine.

Dante stopped kissing me, and our eyes met, and suddenly his walls went back up. I could see it happening. Like the curtains closing at the end of a play. He raised himself up to his palms. "Are you okay?" he asked, already pulling out of me in a swift motion. I gasped at the brief pain and Dante hovered over me for a moment, a hint of hesitation in his expression, but it was gone quickly and he straightened, holding up his shirt so it didn't get dirty. "I need to get cleaned up," he said matter-of-factly, as if he were telling me the weather forecast, as if we hadn't just slept together. He watched me an instant longer, then he disappeared in the bathroom. A couple of minutes later, the water started running.

I didn't move from my spot in the middle of the bed, desperately trying to sort out my emotions. There was relief over finally having gotten rid of my virginity, but there was also a strange sense of sadness. I wasn't someone who needed to be coddled, but I wished Dante would have stayed with me a bit longer after he was done.

Disappointment washed over me and I closed my eyes against the rising emotion. I wasn't sure how long I lay like that, but I was startled by Dante's cool voice above me. "Here."

My eyes fluttered open. He stood beside the bed, already dressed in his briefs again, and was holding a washcloth out for me.

I took it from him and pressed it against my sore flesh, ignoring the blush that crept up into my face. Wouldn't he lie down with me for a little while at least? I really wanted him to hold me, even if he had to pretend to care for me, but I couldn't bring myself to ask him.

"Would you like me to touch you, so you can come too?"

I stared at him. He sounded so matter-of-fact. I shook my head. I wanted his closeness, but not like this, not now. He nodded and grabbed his pants from the ground, then put them on. "I have some more work to do and I need to visit another of our casinos. I'll be home late. You don't need to wait up for me."

I nodded, couldn't have said a word if I'd tried.

After another lingering glance at my naked body, Dante walked out of the room. I listened to his retreating steps. When I couldn't hear him anymore, I sat up, and winced at the twinge between my legs. I stared down at the washcloth in my hand, which had a few pink spots on it, and a silly sense of accomplishment filled me. It banished the disappointment over Dante's coldness. For now, I wanted to be happy. I'd finally gotten what I wanted. Now that Dante had given in once, I was sure he would have a much harder time holding himself back. And I was determined to make it as hard as possible for him. I'd gotten my first real taste of pleasure; from now on I wanted to experience it over and over again.

chapter *ten*

I DIDN'T EVEN NOTICE DANTE SLIP INTO BED THAT NIGHT, BUT HIS side was rumpled, so he must have slept in it. I spent a few more minutes in bed, feeling somehow lighter now that I'd ripped down one barrier between Dante and me, but I wasn't kidding myself into believing that sex would change our relationship fundamentally. I didn't think Dante would suddenly act like the loving and caring husband I'd wanted when I was younger. It was strange. While Antonio had never been able to give me what I physically needed, he'd been my friend and confidante. We'd spent time together when he wasn't busy, and I'd never felt overly lonely in our marriage. I had a feeling the same wouldn't be true in my second marriage. Even if Dante now satisfied my sexual needs, it would take some time before we'd become partners.

After I'd showered and dressed in my favorite plum pencil skirt and a white blouse, I headed into one of the guest rooms that now harbored a few of my moving boxes that I hadn't unpacked yet. It took me a few minutes of rummaging before I found what I was looking for, a wooden case where I kept a few things from Antonio. Inside were our wedding bands, which I'd never much cared about. The most important thing in the case was a thin photo album that held mostly pictures of the time before Antonio and I had married. Back then we'd only been friends, without the added weight of having to pretend to be more. Antonio looked nothing like Dante. He had dark hair and dark eyes, and wasn't very tall. He'd always wanted me to wear flats so I wouldn't be taller than him. But appearances weren't the biggest difference between my first and my second husband; that was their aura. Where Antonio had been open and friendly, someone people perceived as a likeable albeit ordinary buddy type, Dante oozed cold power. Nobody would mistake him for a follower. If Dante hadn't been born into our world, he'd probably be a governor or senator. He would have done well in that arena. But as with all of us, our birth determined our fate. We were all bound to the mob.

I glanced down at a photo of Antonio and me on a horse. It had been the first time for me. We both looked young and happy, hopeful. Antonio hadn't been inducted into the mafia back then, had still thought he could find a way out of his duty.

I put the wooden case back down before I could dive deeper into sad memories. I straightened, took a deep breath and left the guest bedroom. There was no going back, but it wasn't always easy to move forward, especially if you didn't know which way to go. But I needed something that gave my life meaning and structure, something I could put my energy into, as long as Dante shut me out of his life.

I missed having a purpose, a daily task. I wasn't someone who could sit at home all day, or spent hours going over the newest piece of juicy gossip. I wanted a job, but even during my time with Antonio, people had found it strange that he'd allowed his wife to work. I worried that it would be a scandal Dante wasn't willing to risk.

My steps slowed as I headed toward the door he hid behind almost all the time. I wasn't only nervous because I wanted to ask Dante for a job. What if things would be awkward and strained between us now that we'd slept together? Though I really wasn't sure how our relationship could take a further nosedive. We were already barely being civil to each other. Apart from throwing dishes at each other's heads and bickering constantly, there really was no way our interactions could change for the worse. And to be honest, I wondered if I might prefer heated fights to the cold ignorance I was getting now.

Gathering my courage, I knocked at his door.

"Come in," Dante called after a moment.

I entered his office. My eyes immediately darted to the spot on the desk where the photo of his first wife had been, but he'd removed it. I didn't think he'd thrown it out. It was probably hidden away in one of the drawers in his desk, and I didn't expect him to forget her, to throw away every piece that reminded him of her, to banish her memory from his heart; I only wished he'd leave a little room in his heart for me.

Dante looked up from a pile of papers. "What do you need?" He didn't say it in an unfriendly way, but it was obvious that he was busy. His demeanor toward me hadn't changed at all, despite what we'd done yesterday. As my eyes took in his dark gray vest, my body remembered the way a similar vest had rubbed against my nipples yesterday, and I almost crossed the room and threw myself at Dante again. But I didn't want to appear too needy. Our next sexual encounter would have to be initiated by Dante. Of course, maybe he'd go back to not touching me again.

I pushed that worrisome thought aside as I closed the door after me and walked closer to the desk. "I have something I'd like to discuss with you."

Dante scanned my face. "Go on."

"I want to work. When I was married to Antonio I helped him run his family restaurants too." They'd only been a way to launder money, but I'd enjoyed the task. I'd greeted guests and organized arrangements when someone booked a wedding in our restaurants. After his death, his younger brother had taken over. A woman alone couldn't possibly handle the task. That's what our men thought anyway.

Dante leaned back in his desk chair with a frown. "Work? What did you have in mind?"

I was glad he was open to the idea and didn't shoot it down immediately. Emboldened by this, I walked around the desk and settled on its edge. Dante's eyes flitted to my legs, but too quickly they returned to my face. "I'm good at organizing and event planning. I'm also very good with people." I was also good at leading people, but I kept that to myself. Made Men didn't like women who enjoyed being in charge. Somehow most of them couldn't get it in their heads that a strong woman at their side didn't make them less of a man.

Dante nodded. "I need someone for one of our casinos."

I tried to curb my excitement. I didn't even know what Dante had in mind for me yet. "Riverboat or underground?" The casinos on land weren't official, of course. It was still illegal to run a casino in Chicago that wasn't situated on a riverboat, but the mob and Dante in particular were working to change that. He could be very convincing, and it certainly didn't hurt that a few senators were regular customers in the Outfit's casinos and brothels. Not that legalization would mean that the Outfit would make their secret casinos public. They'd lose too much money if they did.

"Underground. I don't want you in the public eye."

That made sense. People knew I was Dante's wife. It would attract too much attention if I worked in one of the riverboat casinos. "I know a little about gambling, and I'm sure I can learn everything else I need to know very quickly." Actually, the only knowledge about gambling I had was the rules of Texas hold 'em that Antonio had taught me, but Dante didn't need to know that.

There was a knowing glint in Dante's eyes. "The only thing you need to know about gambling is that the bank always wins."

I raised my eyebrows. "Really. What kind of job do you have in mind that requires next to no knowledge about the workings of a casino?" I assumed

Dante wouldn't let his wife be one of the girls behind the bar who encouraged men to drink more.

"I want you to manage one of the smaller casinos of the Outfit. The man who's been in charge for the last three years was laid off yesterday."

Was that what Dante had done after he'd slept with me? For a few moments, Dante and I stared at each other as if we'd been thinking the same thing, but now wasn't the moment to bring up sex. "Laid off?" I echoed his words, which I was fairly sure were a euphemism for something else, since it was hard to be fired from a position in the mob. If you messed up in one mob business, it was unlikely that you'd get a position somewhere else, unless you were someone's son, nephew, etc. And if you weren't…

Dante watched me closely when he said his next words. "I found out that he filled his pockets with Outfit money."

"So you killed him," I finished for him. I knew how things worked in our world. Maybe I'd never been allowed in the midst of it, but I heard the stories.

Dante nodded. "I did. And if you want you can have his job."

"I've never managed a casino before. Why are you giving such an important position to me?"

"The assistant manager can do the main work in the background. I need someone to make the high rollers feel welcome."

I stiffened. Dante, of course, picked up on it. "I think you misunderstand me." He stood and stepped in front of me. He rested his hands lightly on my thighs, making my skin tingle even through my tights. "You are mine, Valentina."

I had to bite back a smile at the possessiveness in his voice. "So what exactly am I supposed to do?"

He removed his hands and strode over to the window, hands in his pockets. "I want you to welcome the high rollers. Show them to their table. Introduce them to our complimentary girls."

"Complimentary girls, really?"

Dante turned. "Gambling and prostitution are our main businesses, and both can easily be combined."

"Okay. I can do that." Even if the words "complimentary girls" made me want to tear my hair out. "That doesn't sound like a lot though."

"Also, you'll organize special events. We have event nights once a month, and I think a female touch might make them more appealing. You'll also make sure that everything goes smoothly. I want you to be my eyes. I have a feeling I haven't weeded out all the rotten fruit yet."

"You want me to spy on your employees."

"Yes. I want you to keep your eyes open."

"Is it because you think they'll be less cautious around me, or because you don't have anyone else you trust with the task?"

"I have enough men I trust. But you are right, I think many men will underestimate you and be less vigilant around you." He leaned against the windowsill. "I don't trust anyone unconditionally."

"Not even me?" It was said in a teasing voice, but Dante's eyes became cool. "You haven't given me reason to. You lied to me about your marriage to Antonio, and you refuse to give me the name of an outsider who might be privy to compromising information about the Outfit."

The way he worded it made me sound like a notorious liar. "I didn't lie to you about the marriage. I told you that I've never been with Antonio."

"Yes, you did, but it was a truth I suspect you gave up only because you feared I'd uncover it eventually."

Of course he hit the nail on the head. I couldn't deny it. He would have known I lied and that wouldn't really have helped my situation. "Does it matter why I decided to tell you the truth?"

"It matters greatly, Valentina. Because I don't know if you'll be as forthcoming with future truths when you don't feel cornered. If I counted every coerced truth as redeeming, I would have to spare every traitor who gives away his knowledge under duress."

Under duress—what a mild word for what the Outfit did to traitors. "I know what you do to traitors, and that's exactly why I won't give you the name of Antonio's lover."

"You realize that by aiding Antonio in his deceit you became his accomplice and thus a traitor to the Outfit, and that you keep betraying the Outfit and me by withholding information."

I pushed off the desk, unable to sit still any longer. "I know. But no matter what you think of me, I am loyal to those I care about. I was loyal to Antonio. If he were still alive, I would have taken his secret to the grave with me to protect him."

Dante shook his head. "That's something you can't say for sure. You've never suffered through excruciating pain. Torture is a powerful motivator."

"I guess we'll never know, unless you intend to test the theory on me and try to coerce the name of Antonio's lover out of me," I said insolently.

Dante fixed me with a hard look. "Because you are my wife and because you are a woman, you are safe. You know that very well."

Because I was his wife, not because he liked me or even cared for me. "I know," I said, then because I couldn't bear the tension between us I added, "If you had a secret you needed to hide, I would keep it for you. I would try to brave torture, pain and death to hide it for you."

Dante didn't say anything, didn't even bridge the distance between us, only gazed at me with his unreadable eyes. I decided to take my exit before I said something sentimental, or before Dante could send me out. Dante didn't stop me, but I could feel his eyes on my back.

chapter *eleven*

After a dinner of almost silence, except for the few snippets of conversation about my visit to the casino tomorrow, Dante had returned into his office and I had gone to the library as was becoming habit. Instead of choosing the Russian textbook, I decided to read one of the books on gambling and casinos that crowded the shelves but was distracted by the sound of male voices through the walls. They didn't sound like Enzo and Taft, so I assumed Dante was having a meeting with other members of the Outfit.

When I went to bed hours later, the halls were dark and Dante was still in his office. I guessed that meant another late night. Would Dante really make me ask for a second round of sex?

Much later, I was woken by a hand on my hip. My eyes shot open but I stared into near blackness. The curtains were drawn and allowed only a sliver of moonlight to penetrate the room. My gaze found the pale glow of the alarm clock on the nightstand. It was almost midnight. I had been asleep for less than one hour. What was wrong?

I realized Dante was pressed up against my back, his fingers stroking my hip. "Dante?" I whispered, twisting my head to peer over my shoulder, but his face was covered by shadows. He was close though. His breath fanned over my shoulder, raising the little hairs on my arms. "What's the—"

He silenced me with a fierce kiss that made me gasp. He didn't hesitate; his tongue claimed my mouth. I tried to roll over so I was facing his way, but Dante's firm chest against my back and his tight grip on my hip kept me immobilized. His kiss sent waves of arousal down my center, but eventually I pulled back to draw in a deep breath and because my neck hurt from the awkward position. He pressed his erection against my butt. I exhaled audibly. "Tell me you're not sore," he rumbled against my shoulder before he bit down lightly.

I trembled. "Not sore," was all I managed, and it wasn't even the truth, but I'd be damned if I stopped Dante from having his way with me.

"Good," Dante growled before licking my throat. "Tell me to stop, or I won't."

I only whimpered in response, because Dante had dug his cock into my backside again. I couldn't wait to get out of my clothes and really feel him against me. I shoved my ass back for additional friction, but again Dante's hand on my hip stopped me. "No."

"Dante, I really want to—"

His lips swallowed my words again and his fingers tightened in warning. "I want you to be silent now unless you want to tell me to stop." He nibbled my neck. "You do what I tell you, Valentina, or you tell me to stop. There are only these two options."

I nodded, and he must have felt it because he couldn't possibly have seen it in the dark. I was glad Dante didn't know how turned on I was by his commanding tone.

"Very good," he said quietly. "You're still going to be very tight today; that's why we're going to go slow and take our time making you really wet."

I couldn't believe the same restrained and cold Dante I knew by day was saying these things to me. I wanted to ask him why he'd changed his mind. Did one time make such a difference? Maybe he'd accepted that I knew what I wanted. "I want you to undress now."

I felt an instant of disappointment that Dante wasn't going to do it himself, but then excitement drowned it out. He released my hip and I quickly sat up and tugged my nightgown over my head, then slid down my panties. I could feel Dante's eyes on me. I turned to him, wondering if I was supposed to give him some sort of sign, and that idea almost made me giggle, but then the bed shifted and I could see Dante getting up and starting to undress. Everything was in shadows, but I could make out his impressive hard-on. "Sit on the edge of the bed."

I scooted over to his side of the bed and perched on the edge, nervous and curious and excited, and almost bursting with lust. Dante moved closer until he stood in front of me, his erection on eye level with me. I gasped before I could swallow the sound, realizing what he wanted to do. Bibiana's advice shot through my mind, but I wasn't sure if Dante wanted me to act on my own accord. He cupped my cheek, his palm warm and slightly rough against my skin. "How far have you gone before me?"

I hesitated a moment, but I supposed he wanted me to answer, so I said,

"I kissed Antonio a few times and he touched my breasts a few times, but that's all I've ever done before you."

Silence filled the dark room. My heartbeat accelerated, the *thud-thud* seemingly louder by the second. I could hear Dante's rhythmic breathing, no sign that he was sexually aroused—except for the proof straining to attention before my face. "I want you to suck my cock, Valentina."

His thumb brushed my lips, then slipped between them, parting them slightly. He waited, and I nudged his thumb with my tongue before sucking on it lightly, hoping he'd take it as the confirmation that it was. He moved even closer until his tip grazed my lips. Dante's thumb stroked my chin, his palm still cupping my cheek. "Lick around the tip." I darted my tongue out and trailed it around his head. Dante's breathing hitched, but that was the only sign that my actions had an effect on him. "Now lick up to the top and dip your tongue into the slit."

I followed his orders and was rewarded by the quickening of Dante's breathing. His thumb on my chin tightened. "Open your mouth." I parted my lips without hesitation. I was glad for Dante's orders. That way at least I wasn't left to fumble around and embarrass myself. He slid the head of his cock into my mouth, so it rested lightly on my tongue. "Close your lips around me and suck lightly."

I did as he said and he stroked my chin, then trailed his thumb up until it brushed the spot where his cock disappeared between my lips. "I like my cock in your mouth," he said in a low voice. "And I love that it's the only cock you've ever sucked." He slid deeper into my mouth, but still not very far. "Let's see how much of me you can take." He eased himself into me inch by inch until he hit the back of my throat and I gagged. I reached out for his erection. There were still a couple of inches of him that I couldn't fit into my mouth. Dante pulled back slightly, then thrust a few times into me, his palm on my face keeping me steady. "With some practice maybe you can take all of me into your mouth, but for now this is enough." I quivered with arousal. Could someone come from giving someone else a blow job?

Dante withdrew his erection from my mouth and stroked my lips with his thumb again. "Lie back." I let myself fall back on the mattress. Dante knelt down and wedged his hands between my knees, then pushed my legs as far apart as they would go. "Put your heels on the edge of the bed."

God, I knew what he was going to do. I'd read so many things about it, but I couldn't even imagine how it would feel.

I was glad for the dark. That way I didn't feel quite so exposed. He eased his palms under my butt and lifted me slightly. I stopped breathing when I felt his warm breath on my wet folds. Dante licked around my outer lips slowly. I bucked my hips, but Dante ignored my silent pleading and kept up his torturous teasing. "Dante," I said pleadingly.

He squeezed my ass and pulled back. "No."

I pressed my lips together, and then finally he trailed his tongue along my slit in one long stroke. I moaned, not caring if that counted as speaking or not. He alternated between quick and light strokes, and firm but slow licks until I was panting and on the verge of climax. My hands shot out and I buried them in Dante's hair, wanting to press him tighter against me. Dante resisted. His thumbs trailed up my folds and parted them. With the tip of his tongue he lightly circled my clit until I started shaking, seconds away from tumbling over the edge. He sat back without warning. It took all my self-control to stay silent.

"Turn around and get on your knees."

My eyes grew wide with surprise, but I rolled over and knelt on the bed.

"Lower yourself to your elbows."

I did. Now my butt was raised into the air. The position felt strange, and even more exposed than the one before. Dante nudged my legs apart until I could feel the cold air on my opening from behind, and then his lips were back on my center. I cried out with pleasure as Dante dipped his tongue into me and started fucking me at a leisurely pace. I could feel every move of him in me, the slight roughness of his tongue, the way he curled the tip when he was deep in me. I dropped my face into the sheets to stop more embarrassing noises from escaping my lips, but when Dante slipped a hand around my front and began teasing my clit with his fingers, even the sheets couldn't stifle my moans and gasps. I jutted my ass out even more, my fingers scratching over the mattress as my orgasm exploded outward from my core, numbing and heightening my senses seemingly at the same time. I sucked in ragged breaths. My skin was damp with perspiration and my heart beat frantically in my chest. I lifted my head to breathe more easily.

Dante was gone from behind me, but before I could glance over my shoulder to see what he was doing, his fingers grasped my hips and pulled me closer to the edge of the bed. Then his erection pushed against my entrance, and my body seized up with surprise and nerves.

I'd read that doggy-style allowed men to go deeper than in other positions. I was still slightly sore, and the lack of intimacy this position allowed made it even less desirable for me. I wanted Dante's chest pressed against mine.

Dante stilled behind me, not trying to enter me. His hands slid to my backside and massaged it gently. I relaxed slightly but was still tight. I could feel how clamped up my inner muscles were. Dante bent over me and wrapped an arm around my waist before he pulled me up against his chest. I was still kneeling, but now my upper body was upright and Dante held me in his arms. He snuck one hand between my legs and started teasing me again while the other found my breasts and kneaded them lightly. I hung my head back against his shoulder, my breathing slowing. I was still tense but in Dante's embrace, I could slowly feel my muscles softening. Dante leaned forward with me a bit and guided his tip to my opening. I still clamped up, but not as badly as before. "What's the problem?" he murmured against my ear. He didn't sound impatient or frustrated, merely curious.

Embarrassment twisted my stomach. My seduction skills were obviously lacking, if I couldn't even do it doggy-style for my husband. "I don't know," I admitted quietly. "Can't you just push in?"

"Of course I can, but you're tight anyway and as tense as you are now, it'll be painful." His voice was calm, neutral even, no hint to what he was thinking about my suggestion. Dante's fingers were still between my legs, stroking and pinching lightly.

"Don't tell me you have a problem with causing other people pain," I teased in a breathy whisper as tingles of pleasure spread through my core.

"I don't," he said simply. I could feel the tension building as his fingers worked their magic between my legs. He increased the pressure on my opening, the tip of his cock sliding in, and at the same time I came hard, my muscles squeezing Dante's cock tightly. Dante leaned forward a bit more, pressing me down, and my arms shot out to support my body on the bed while I was still recovering from my climax.

Dante bit my neck. "But I don't want to cause you pain." He pinched my nipple, then pushed a couple more inches into me, making me quiver from the sensations of slight pain and pleasure. "At least not more than you enjoy."

He sheathed himself completely in me, then paused a couple of heartbeats before he started to thrust into me slowly. His movements became gradually faster until I had no choice but to lower myself to my elbows, or my arms would have given in. Dante straightened, robbing me of the warmth of his chest, and grabbed my hips. "Valentina, touch yourself," he demanded.

It took me a moment to understand what he meant. I brought an arm under myself and found my clit. I rubbed frantically as Dante's movements turned more forceful. He pulled out as far as he could go and slammed into me again, making me cry out his name and my fingers press down on my nub even harder. Sometimes my fingertips grazed his cock, slick with my juices, and he moaned every time they did. Encouraged by this, I angled my hand so I could stroke myself and brush his cock at the same time. As my muscles seized up under my release, Dante tumbled over the edge too with a loud groan.

He stilled behind me as his cock twitched in me a few more times, and I buried my face in the sheets. My forearms ached from propping myself up. The moment Dante pulled out of me, I rolled onto my back, my chest heaving. I could see Dante move away from the bed like he'd done last time, and then the light in the bathroom came on and he disappeared inside. He didn't close the door though. I scooted off the bed and quickly followed after him. He stood in front of the shower and turned the water on. "Are you taking a shower?" I asked hesitantly.

Dante glanced over his shoulder at me. I didn't bother covering my body. He'd seen it all. Dante didn't seem to be ashamed of his nakedness. "Yes. You can join me if you want."

Relieved, I hurried over to him. He held the glass door of the shower open for me and I slipped under the warm spray of the shower. Dante joined me after a moment. I took my time admiring his body. It was the first time I really got a good look at him without clothes on, and he was a sight to behold. His chest and stomach were lightly sculpted, and a fine trail of dark blond hair led down to his pelvis. Dante dipped his head under the water, then turned his back to me to reach for the shower gel. There was a tattoo on his shoulder. I was surprised to find him inked at all. Somehow Dante didn't seem the type. "There is no good on earth; and sin is but a name. Come, devil. For to thee is this world given," I read the quote written in cursive on his skin aloud. Dante faced me, an unreadable expression on his face.

"Isn't that a bit of a bleak outlook on life?" I asked.

He handed me the shower gel. A barrier had come up between us again now that we were no longer in bed, and I wasn't sure how to tear it down. I could see that Dante wouldn't allow it. "I'm a man of sin, Valentina. My experience has taught me that good seldom wins. If there is a devil, he's certainly the patron of the Outfit."

I leaned against the shower wall, frowning. "Nothing's holding you back from being a better man."

That cold smile was back. "Yes, something is—my nature."

chapter *twelve*

My mother called me early the next morning to invite me over for brunch. I knew she was eager to interrogate me how my marriage was going. I was actually surprised that it had taken her so long to contact me. Maybe she'd wanted to give Dante and me some alone time to get to know each other. I told her I couldn't make it to brunch but would be there for teatime. I wasn't sure how long my visit to the casino would take. I chose a chic beige outfit and modest heels for the occasion. I didn't want to look too sexy for my first impression. I had a feeling I would have trouble getting everyone's respect even without flashing my legs.

When I came down the staircase, Dante was already waiting in the entrance hall. As usual he was dressed impeccably in a dark brown three-piece suit and matching oxfords. His gaze flickered to me, and I hoped he'd approve of my clothes. "Is this okay?" I gestured at my body.

"You look like a businesswoman. That's the right choice for today," Dante said with a nod. I stepped up to him. I didn't try to take his hand or kiss him, even though I wanted to.

"Only for today?"

"When you welcome our high rollers, you can dress more casually. Most of them are traditionalists, so a dress or skirt would be a wise choice."

My eyebrows shot up. "I thought you didn't choose me for the job because of my looks."

Dante's eyes traveled the length of my body. "Valentina, only a blind man wouldn't notice you. It's always good to charm up the high rollers as you would entertain guests who were invited to a party in our house. They know who you are. They know you are mine, and you taking your time to welcome them and tell them about our newest amenities will make them feel special. Nobody will mistake your hospitality for inappropriate flirting."

I gave him a doubtful look, but I wasn't going to argue with him. I was too grateful that he'd allow me to work at all. I didn't have to listen to the rumors to know exactly what people would be saying about me once they found out the wife of the Boss wasn't satisfied with being a trophy wife.

We took Dante's Mercedes for our ride to the industrial part of Chicago because a snowstorm made the streets impassable for the Porsche. After thirty minutes, in which Dante explained what kind of gambling was most popular in our casinos and who the most important high rollers were, we pulled up in front of a gate barring the way down into an underground garage. Behind it loomed a massive storehouse with dirt-covered windows and graffiti-sprayed walls. A guard in a small cabin greeted Dante and opened the gate for us. We drove down the slope into a nondescript parking garage. Nothing hinted at the presence of a casino, but of course it made sense that the Outfit had to hide their illegal gambling endeavors. A few other cars were already parked in the garage. Dante steered the Mercedes into the spot between a sleek black BMW and a pretentious red Mustang with snow chains around its massive tires. I had a feeling I knew to whom the latter belonged.

Dante and I got out of the car. To my surprise, Dante put his hand on the small of my back as he led me toward a rusty elevator at the other end of the garage.

"Is it safe?" I asked suspiciously. That thing looked as if it was in desperate need of service.

Dante chuckled. "This is all make-believe." For a moment, his eyes met mine and unexpected warmth filled me. Dante pushed a small black button and the elevator doors slid open. The inside wasn't much better than the outside. This was a freight elevator with bare steel walls and a scratched-up floor. Dante took a keycard from his pocket and eased it into a slit I hadn't even noticed before. It wasn't anywhere near the obvious buttons of the elevator. Dante noticed my curious look. "We've never had a visit from Feds, but if they ever check the storehouse, this will make it more difficult for them to find out what's below us."

The moment Dante had inserted the card, the elevator started moving down. The ride was quick and when the doors finally glided open, I gasped.

We stepped into a vast underground area with plush red and gold carpets, chandeliers and dozens of massive tables for poker games, blackjack, roulette and whatever else was played down here. Flat-screen TVs on one wall of the casino showed everything from the Africa Soccer Cup over a darts championship in Scotland, to camel racing in Dubai and skiing tournaments in the Alps. Sofas were arranged around the wall for people who wanted to watch the athletes or teams they'd put a bet on. At the end of the room was a bar that took up almost the entire width of the room, with hundreds of bottles of liquors, wines and champagne.

Right now the casino was deserted except for two cleaning ladies who vacuumed the carpet. Several doors led to what I assumed were private rooms for VIP guests.

"In the back are the offices, as well as a welcome area for high rollers," Dante explained as he led me across the room toward a dark wood door next to the bar.

"Do I work daily?"

Dante gave me a strange look. "You can work whenever you want. Nobody will force you to work at all. But you'll always get notified when a high roller is expected so you can decide if you're going to be there to welcome them."

"Okay. You said there were special events. Is anything set up in the next few weeks? For Valentine's Day, for example?" The day was still four weeks away, but organizing an event took time.

Dante stroked my back lightly, surprising me with the gesture. I wasn't even sure he'd noticed what he'd done, since his face was still distant except for the wry smile directed at me. "Valentine's Day isn't really something the men coming here are interested in. Even if they're married, their wives probably don't know they're coming here. As I said, we always have at least a dozen prostitutes in the bar area, and the bedrooms in the back are never empty."

"So I'm not just going to manage a casino, I'll also be a bordello queen."

Dante laughed. A real laugh. I slanted him a look to make sure my ears weren't playing a trick on me, but the smile was already disappearing from his face. "You aren't their pimp. You can introduce our high rollers to their complimentary girls but apart from that, the prostitution part of the casino is in Raffaele's hand."

Raffaele was Aria's cousin. He wasn't related to me though. With satisfaction, I realized my guess about the car had been right. I'd heard rumors about his swanky persona. "Isn't he the one who got his finger cut off for gawking at Aria?" Everyone knew that tidbit of information, but I was curious about Dante's feelings toward the incident. I still remembered the huge stir it had caused years ago.

Dante's lips thinned. "That's him. Rocco Scuderi allowed Luca to punish Raffaele."

We stopped in front of the door. "But you wouldn't have?"

"I wouldn't have let someone from New York dish out punishment in my territory," he said in an unyielding tone. I wasn't sure why, but my body reacted immediately to Dante's steely fierceness, yearning to be alone with him, to let him have his way with me like last night.

Ignoring my body's needs, I said, "So you don't think Raffaele deserved it." Personally, I thought it was a bit extreme to cut someone's finger off for staring, but Luca was known for his cold-bloodedness, even in the Outfit.

"I didn't say that. But I would have insisted on punishing him myself, seeing as he is my responsibility. But what's done is done."

"So is Raffaele the assistant manager?"

"No, he's responsible for the hookers. He makes sure we have enough of them available at all times. He works together with Tommaso for that purpose."

My nose wrinkled, my standard reaction to hearing his name. Dante cocked one blond eyebrow. "Is this because of the prostitution, or because of Tommaso? I thought you were friends with his wife Bibiana."

"Bibiana is my best friend, which is why I can't stand that man. I don't suppose there's any chance that Tommaso might be a traitor, so you can get rid of him?"

Dante scanned my face. "You are being serious."

"Yes. He's treated Bibiana like dirt since they married. I wouldn't shed a single tear if you put a bullet in his head."

For a couple of heartbeats, our eyes locked and I got the impression that Dante wouldn't have minded a moment of privacy with me either, but then the moment was gone. "He's a loyal soldier. He's never given me any reason to doubt him. There's nothing I can do about him."

"Not even if I tell you that he's raping Bibiana?" I knew Bibiana didn't want people to know, but maybe Dante could help. It wasn't as if he would tell others about it.

He put his hand on the door handle, his eyes bleak. "She's his wife."

"That doesn't mean he can rape her," I hissed.

"I know, but I can't tell my men how they're supposed to treat their wives. Even a Capo can't interfere in a marriage. My decision to forbid rape as punishment or entertainment was already met with resentment."

I looked away to hide how emotional this topic made me. Sometimes it was easy to forget the horrible things happening in the Outfit.

"Are you ready to go in? Raffaele and Leo, the assistant manager, are waiting in your office to meet you."

I took a deep breath, then I nodded.

Dante opened the door, and, his hand still pressed against my back, he led me into a long corridor with five more doors.

"I assume these aren't for the public eye, unlike the doors branching off the main floor?"

"Yes. This is only for you and the other employees. The doors outside lead into several rooms that the prostitutes can use with their customers."

I nodded. It was surreal that I would soon work here.

Dante steered me toward the door at the end of the hallway and opened it. Behind it was a spacious windowless office with a desk, a meeting table with six chairs, a sofa, and two chairs facing the desk. Raffaele, who was a couple of years younger than me, and a middle-aged man with a mustache occupied the chairs. Both rose when Dante and I entered. My eyes were immediately drawn to Raffaele's hand. His finger had been re-attached by the Outfit doctor, but it stuck out and was obviously stiff.

"Raffaele, Leo," Dante said coolly, dropping his hand from my back to shake their hands. Then he gestured toward me. "This is my wife, Valentina. As I told you yesterday, she'll be taking Dino's place." I assumed that was the guy who'd filled his pockets with Outfit money.

I tilted my head, hoping to appear self-confident. I shook first Leo's hand, who was a few inches shorter than me, then Raffaele's. Both men greeted me in a friendly manner, but I could see in their eyes that they were unhappy with Dante's choice to involve me in Outfit business. They couldn't possibly like having a woman as their boss, even if Leo would still do most of the management work.

"Why don't you show Valentina around? You know the ins and outs of this place better than I do," Dante said to Leo, who nodded before facing me with a stiff smile. "This way," he said as he walked out of the room and headed back to the main floor. "Our opening hours are from six in the evening until six in the morning. Of course sometimes a group of high rollers wants to book the place for a different time slot. Then we open for them."

It wasn't even noon yet, so there was still plenty of time before the casino opened its doors. That explained why everything was still deserted. I pointed toward a booth. "Is that where customers exchange their money for chips?"

Leo nodded. "Yes. If a customer doesn't have any money, we offer them credits."

"At fair interest rates, I'm sure," I joked.

"Of course," Leo agreed with a toothless smile.

"And if they don't pay back our money, who takes care of it then?"

"The same soldiers who collect all of our money," Dante said. He was trailing behind us. I wasn't sure if he was making sure that the men were acting civilized, or if he wanted to see how I was handling myself.

"I assume this is a by-invitation-only place, so how does word get around? Do customers have to sign some kind of non-disclosure clause?"

Raffaele snorted, but fell silent when Dante shot him a glower.

"We don't need non-disclosure clauses. We tell customers that they can't tell people about this place unless they ask us for permission in advance and we do a background check on the person. Our customers know to keep their mouths shut."

"Nobody wants to mess with us unless they have a death wish," Raffaele said proudly.

Raffaele was starting to grate on my nerves. He was a bit too sure of himself. Losing a finger didn't seem to have diminished his self-esteem. "And you are responsible for the girls?"

"I make sure the whores make our customers happy. And I choose the sluts who sit at the bar to get the men horny, and I also decide who's going to be the complimentary girls. I test all of them to make sure they know how to suck a cock and can take it up their asses. Anal is a must. Most poor bastards don't get that at home."

Dante's eyes were burning with anger, but he wasn't interfering. Maybe he thought it would make me look weak. I was going to be the head of this casino, after all. "I hope you don't talk like that around customers," I said to Raffaele.

Raffaele's throat turned red—from anger or embarrassment, I couldn't tell. Probably a little of both. He opened his mouth then closed it after a glance at Dante. I had a feeling that Raffaele would give me more trouble than Leo.

"Are any of the girls in already? I'd like to talk to them."

Raffaele's eyes darted between Leo and Dante, as if he needed their approval before he could answer a simple question. "Most of them work in Club Palermo until five and then come over here after that."

The girls who worked here were from Club Palermo? Had any of them slept with Dante? I had to ask Bibiana if she knew the names of the women Dante chose when he frequented the club. "Then I'll talk to them tomorrow. Make sure they come in early so I can have a word with them before our doors open."

"What is there to talk about? They are brainless whores, nothing more than three-hole sluts."

"Raffaele, that is enough. I don't tolerate you talking to my wife like that," Dante said in a dangerously low voice.

Raffaele lowered his head, but not before sending me a scathing look. I decided to ignore him for now. "Are any important high rollers visiting today?"

Leo shook his head. "No. But tomorrow two senators and a few of their friends are coming in. They don't gamble that much. They mostly spend the nights with the girls."

"So we humor them because we want them to protect our interests in the Senate?"

"Exactly," Leo said, surprised, as if he couldn't believe a woman could come to such a conclusion by herself. Men in our world would be surprised how much their wives and daughters knew about the life the men were trying to protect them from. You can't grow up in a mob family and not figure out most of what's going on.

Dante nodded his head in approval, and a strange sense of pride filled me.

"Okay, then I'll be there tomorrow to introduce myself to them, and meet the rest of our employees. I hope we're going to work well together."

Leo nodded, but Raffaele obviously didn't think we would. Dante put his hand on my back and we headed back to our car.

"So what do you think?" he asked as he started the car.

"I think Raffaele will give me trouble. He obviously doesn't like me."

"He doesn't do well with women in general, unless they are prostitutes and have to do what he says. Don't take it personal."

"I don't. I couldn't care less what he thinks of me."

"No," Dante disagreed. "He should respect you."

"Because it would reflect badly on you if he didn't."

"That, and because you are his boss. You are going to make sure everything runs smoothly. Leo will hopefully help you."

"He seemed okay. But you don't trust him?"

"I don't trust either of them."

I nodded. "They seemed surprised when I said something clever. It really annoyed me."

"Most men in the mob prefer to think of their women as ignorant and clueless. I know the same men who disapproved of my ruling against rape will disapprove of you working in our casino."

"I think the mob should stop underestimating women."

Dante gave me a sideways glance. "Maybe you can convince them."

Did he really believe that? A question burnt on the tip of my tongue. "Did your first wife work?"

His expression darkened. "No. She kept busy with social engagements as most women in our world do."

"Oh, of course." I wondered if despite having offered me a job in the casino, he was unhappy with my desire to work. Would he prefer a trophy wife? Someone who looked good at parties, who warmed his bed and who kept the staff in check? I decided to change the topic. "My mother invited me over. I assume you have work to do?"

"Yes, I do. But I can drive you to your parents' house if you want. It's on the way. I can tell Enzo or Taft to pick you up when you're done."

"My mother will be delighted," I said, rolling my eyes.

"Would you rather we drive home and you drive to your parents without me?"

"No," I said quickly. "I wasn't joking. My mother will be giddy with pleasure over seeing you again."

"Your father is one of my underbosses. It's not like your mother hasn't met me countless times."

"But not as her son-in-law. I've never seen her happier than when she found out you were stooping to marry me."

Dante's brows drew together. "Because you were married before?"

"Of course. I was damaged goods by our standards. Not a pure, innocent girl like Gianna or the many other girls fawning over you at parties."

"Believe me, I'm more than happy that I didn't agree to marry Gianna. She's a troublemaker. I don't have the patience for someone like her. And I don't pay much attention to girls at parties."

I huffed. "You are a man. How can you not notice their smoldering glances?"

"Smoldering?" Dante asked with a hint of amusement. "And I didn't say I didn't notice. I make sure to always be aware of everything going on in a room around me, but I'm not interested in their silly attempts at flirting. They fawn over an image they have of me, but I'm not that man."

"I don't know. Girls think you're sexy because you are powerful and aloof. The ice prince whose heart they want to melt."

Dante shook his head, then something changed on his face and he slanted me another glance. "So your mother didn't know you never consummated your first marriage?"

"Of course not. I don't talk to her about things like that. And believe me, she would have found a way to tell you about my virginity because it would have increased my worth. She'd die from happiness if she found out you are the man who took my virtue." I froze. "You're not going to tell anyone about Antonio, are you?"

Dante narrowed his eyes in thought. "I don't see how that would help anyone. Of course, it would make my search for Antonio's lover easier if I could involve my men."

"I'm not going to tell you his name," I interjected, knowing where this was going, and really hoping he wouldn't get angry again.

chapter *thirteen*

DANTE PULLED UP IN FRONT OF MY OLD HOME AND TURNED OFF the engine before he faced me. "I assumed as much. I still don't understand why. That man you're protecting, he's not your blood and from what I gather you were never close. After all, he stole your husband, so why do you insist on choosing him over me?"

"I don't choose him over you," I said, honestly shocked. "But I know what you're going to do to him, what you *have to do* to protect the Outfit, and I can't condemn him to death. If you swear that he won't come to any harm, then I might change my mind."

"You know as well as I do that I can't swear it. There are rules for a reason. We have to protect the secrets of the Outfit. If details about our structures, our business, or traditions went public, many people you know would go to jail, me and your father included."

"He would never tell anyone about the Outfit. Antonio told him about our oaths."

"But he isn't bound by them. We all keep the silence because we're bound by honor and duty, and because we would all pay the price if we didn't, but that man has no reason to keep our secrets now that Antonio is dead. Not everyone honors a dead man's wish as much as you do."

"But he loved Antonio."

"How can you know that? But if it were the case, wouldn't that make him hate our world even more?"

"What do you mean?"

"Because of the rules of the Outfit, Antonio couldn't be open about his sexuality. He had to hide his desires and his lover, and ultimately he died because he was a Made Man. The Russians killed him because he was one of us. You see, the man you're protecting has a lot of reasons to despise our world and want it gone."

I'd never considered it from that standpoint, and was seriously freaked. What if Dante was right? I hadn't seen Frank since I'd told him about Antonio's death a year ago. He'd left quickly, silent and out of it. He hadn't tried to contact me, and I had only known his mobile number, but that had stopped working shortly after the funeral. I'd simply assumed Frank had wanted to cut off anything that linked him to the mob. Had he talked to anyone about Antonio? About the Outfit? I didn't want to believe it. He had reason to detest the Outfit and its ways. Not only had he been forced to hide his relationship with Antonio, but he didn't even get the chance to say goodbye to him. Neither had I. All that had been left of Antonio was a burned corpse. I'd never seen it—Father had forbidden me from doing so. He'd said there was nothing left for me to recognize. The Russians had even cut his head off before they'd set him on fire. The Outfit never found it.

Dante watched me closely. Or was he trying to manipulate me? Even so, what he'd said was the truth.

"Will you come to the door to say hi to my mother? She'll be disappointed if you stay in the car," I said to distract him.

Dante wore a knowing look but didn't try to push the topic of Antonio's lover. He got out of the Mercedes, walked around the hood and opened my door for me. His hand found its usual spot on my lower back as we walked to the front door. I'd barely rung the bell when the door was already opened and my mother beamed at us. She'd probably been spying on us through the windows.

"Dante, I didn't expect you to come. How wonderful of you to pay us a visit," she said with a wide smile. She pulled Dante into an embrace. He remained stiff but briefly patted her back. At least he was against public displays of affection in general, and not just with me.

"I'm only here to drop Valentina off. I don't have time to stay. There's still much work to do." He straightened and Mamma had no choice but to release him.

Her face fell. "Of course. Now that you're Capo, you have many responsibilities. How wonderful of you to take time out of your busy schedule to drive Valentina around town." Mamma smiled at me. "You got yourself a gentleman."

I gave Dante an I-told-you-so look. A flicker of something softer filled his eyes before he excused himself and headed back to his car. The moment he'd driven off, Mamma closed the door, gripped my arm and practically dragged me into the living room. "Giovanni! Valentina is here!" she screamed.

"Papà is here?"

"I told him you'd be coming over. He wanted to have a word with you as well."

I groaned.

"Don't be like that. Your father and I are worried about your well-being. We want to know if married life is treating you well."

"You mean you want to make sure I'm not messing up with Dante."

Mamma pursed her lips. "You are twisting my words in my mouth today."

Papà came into the living room, closing his cuff links, his checkered jacket slung over his shoulder. "I don't have much time. I'm actually having a meeting with the Consigliere and your husband later. So how are things between you and the Boss?"

"If you're meeting my husband anyway, then you could ask Dante how our marriage is going so far and if he's satisfied with me," I said in an overly sweet voice.

"Sometimes I think I wasn't strict enough with you. Your insolence was much more endearing when you were a little girl," he said affectionately. I stood and wrapped my arms around his middle. He pressed a kiss against my temple. I knew as Underboss Papà was almost as ruthless as Dante and probably had killed more men than I had fingers, but for me he'd always be the man who'd carried me on his shoulders when I was younger.

"Things are going well between Dante and me, don't worry," I said as I pulled back. "I think he's still not over his first wife though."

Papà exchanged a look with Mamma. "It took Fiore a long time to convince Dante to marry at all. I'm glad he chose you. Don't push him."

"Listen to your father, Valentina. Men don't like pushy women."

"I hear you convinced Dante to give you a job?" Papà asked.

"Don't pretend you don't already know everything about it. I bet half of the Outfit is already ranting about it."

"What do you expect? A woman of your status isn't supposed to work," Mamma said.

"Some people think women aren't supposed to interrupt their husbands either, and you do that all the time."

Mamma huffed. "I don't interrupt your father."

"You don't?" Papà said in mock surprise. Their marriage hadn't always been for love. Like Dante and me, they'd married for convenience, but over time they'd grown fond of each other. When I saw them, it gave me new hope for my own marriage.

I couldn't hold back a smile. "Dante doesn't mind me working. I think he likes that I want to do something useful."

"What could be more useful than raising beautiful children? When are we going to become grandparents?"

I sent Papà a pleading look, but he shrugged. "Fiore really wants an heir to his name. Dante has responsibilities. What if he got killed without having a son to inherit his title?"

"Don't say that. Nobody's going to get killed. I lost one husband already, I won't lose a second," I said desperately.

Papà patted my cheek. "Dante knows how to take care of himself, but what's wrong with having children?"

"Nothing's wrong with it. I want children, but not because it's my duty to produce an heir. I want children because I want something to love and that loves me back unconditionally." God, when had this conversation turned so horribly emotional?

"Val," Papà said carefully. "Did Dante do something?"

I gave him a shaky smile, grateful for his concern but knowing it was useless. Even if Dante had done something and I told my father about it, there was nothing he could do. He wouldn't go against his Capo, not even for me. "No, he's a gentleman." *Outside of the bedroom,* I added silently. Not that I minded. "He's just really closed off. I feel lonely, but working will keep me busy, so that should make it better."

"Give him time," Papà said. I could tell he was getting increasingly uncomfortable with my emotionality. Why were Made Men cowards when it came to expressing feelings, but didn't bat an eye when confronted with death? He glanced at his Rolex, then grimaced. "I really need to go." He pressed a kiss against my temple before he bent down to give my mother a proper kiss. Then he was gone. Mamma patted the spot on the sofa beside her, and I plopped down with a sigh. "I really need cake right now."

Mamma rang a bell and our maid entered the living room with a tray full of pastries and Italian macarons. I bet she'd been waiting in front of the door since I'd arrived. For as long as I could remember, she'd always been a bit too nosy. She gave me a quick smile, set the tray down and then disappeared again. I grabbed a delicacy made of marzipan, chocolate and puff pastry, and took a big bite. Mamma poured me coffee, never taking her eyes off me. "Careful with these. They are full of fat and calories. You have to make sure you take care of your body. Men don't like plump women."

I made a show out of finishing the rest of my pastry, then washed it down with coffee. "Maybe you should write a book about what men want, since you seem to know all about it." I opened my eyes wide to lessen the impact of my snippy words.

Mamma shook her head before taking a pastry for herself. "Your father is right. We should have been stricter with you."

"You were strict with Orazio and it didn't help."

"He's a boy. They are all boisterous. And he's really shaping up nicely. He said he's even thinking about settling down." I doubted that. He'd probably only said it to get my mother off his back. And given that he didn't live in Chicago but helped keep our business in line in Detroit and Cleveland, our parents didn't often get the chance to bother him. And he was a man, of course. Nobody cared if he slept with a new girl every night, as long as he didn't tell them who he really was.

"I've never gone against your wishes, so I don't know why you complain. After all, I married Dante because you wanted it."

Mamma looked offended. "He's the best catch we could hope for. Who wouldn't marry a man like him?"

I drank my coffee, not bothering to reply. It was a rhetorical question anyway.

"Does Dante seek you out at night?"

I almost spit out what was in my mouth. "I'm not going to talk to you about *that*, Mamma." My cheeks burned from embarrassment, and Mamma gave me a knowing smile.

I loved her, but she was the most infuriating woman on this planet.

Enzo picked me up in the SUV. Except for a bit of small talk, we didn't speak during the short ride. When we drove past Bibiana's street, I said, "Wait. Turn the corner. I want to pay Bibiana Bonello a visit." I'd promised her I'd tell her how things between Dante and me had progressed. She'd hopefully be happy to see me.

Enzo didn't argue. He steered the car toward Bibi's house and parked at the curb. "Do you want me to wait?"

I hesitated. "If you don't mind?"

Enzo shook his head. "That's my job." He reached behind his seat and pulled out a magazine about old-timers.

"It won't take long," I said even though Bibiana and I could spend hours chatting.

I climbed out of the car and strode toward the front door. I rang the bell, then waited. Nothing happened for a while, and I was about to return to the car when the door opened.

Tommaso stood in front of me. My eyes widened in surprise, then worry. "Hello, Tommaso," I said, forcing my voice to be pleasant. "I hope I didn't come at a bad time. I wanted to talk to Bibiana. Is she there?" *Is she okay* was the question that I really wanted to ask. Tommaso was sweaty, his skin red and his fly was still open. A feeling of dread cursed through me.

Tommaso bared his teeth in a wide smile. He took my hand in both of his. "She'll be down in a moment. We have always time for Dante's wife."

I fought the urge to pull away. His skin was clammy with perspiration, and the thought that the reason for his rumpled appearance had something to do with what he'd been doing with Bibiana made me want to scrub my palms raw until no trace of him was left on me. "Bibiana, hurry up. Valentina Cavallaro is here," Tommaso shouted. As if Bibiana didn't know who I was.

I gingerly pulled my hands out of his grip.

"I hear you're taking over the casino," Tommaso said curiously, his small beetle eyes keen as they watched me.

"Did Raffaele tell you that?"

Tommaso guffawed. "He didn't have to. Everyone's talking about it. I wouldn't allow Bibiana to work, but Dante has been trying to change things up in the Outfit for a while now, even before Fiore retired."

I tried to figure out if I could construe his words as traitorous, but sadly they were only mildly critical. Nothing that would cause Dante to put a bullet in Tommaso's head. "Even the Outfit has to keep up with the times," I said neutrally.

Bibiana appeared at the top of the stairs, her hair all over the place, her blouse dress buttoned wrongly and her feet bare. Tommaso winked at me. "Please excuse me. I have a meeting with Raffaele to discuss tomorrow night's girls."

Keeping up the smile was almost painful and the moment he was out of sight, I dropped the charade and hurried toward Bibiana, who'd come down the stairs. "Hey, everything okay?"

She swallowed. "Can we talk upstairs? I really need to shower."

"Of course," I said quickly. She gave me a tiny smile. I followed her silently upstairs, trying to suppress my fury toward Tommaso. I was already looking for ways to make Dante kill him, and that wasn't something I should ever consider. I'd never been responsible for someone's death. Even if Tommaso was the lowest scum on earth, I shouldn't want him dead.

Bibiana led me into their bedroom. I pretended I didn't notice the ruffled sheets as I followed her into the adjoining bathroom. Bibiana and I had seen each other naked before, especially when we were younger, so I wasn't surprised when she got undressed in my presence. I perched on the edge of the bathtub.

"If I'd known Tommaso was home, I wouldn't have come over."

"No," Bibiana said. "I'm glad you're here. This way, at least, Tommaso won't go for a second round right away." My eyes flitted over the bruises on her hips, inner thighs and upper arms. I lowered my gaze to my lap and blinked away angry tears. Bibiana stepped into the shower and turned the water on. "Val?"

I stood and approached the shower stall. Bibiana's expression was imploring. "I know I shouldn't ask you this, but is there anything you can do?"

"Is he doing anything that goes against Dante or the Outfit? Anything at all?"

Bibi shook her head as the water plastered her dark hair against her forehead. "He's loyal to the Cavallaros."

That's what I'd suspected. "Dante won't act unless he's a traitor, but maybe we can set him up."

Bibiana's eyes became huge. "You would trick Dante if we did that. You can't go against him, Val. I can't ask that of you." She put on a brave smile. "I'm being overdramatic. Women have been going through this for centuries, and they all survived."

Maybe, but that didn't mean Bibiana should suffer through it.

She stepped out of the shower and I handed her a towel. "Let's talk about something else. How are things going with Dante and you? Have you…?"

I nodded, a blush heating my cheeks. "Twice."

"And? Was it bad?"

"No, actually it was…" I trailed off, realizing what I was doing. I couldn't talk about how much I'd enjoyed being with Dante when Bibi had just been mounted by her pig of a husband. "…okay," I finished halfheartedly.

Bibi gave me a look. "I know you, Val. I can tell that you're lying. You don't have to hold back because of me. I know that there are women who enjoy sex."

"It was good," I said.

Bibi took my hand and squeezed. "That's good. You deserve some fun after the years with Antonio."

I wanted to throw my arms around her and hold her, wanted to have Tommaso killed for her, but instead I merely squeezed back. "One day Tommaso will be gone, and then it's your turn."

She nodded, but the hopelessness in her eyes gutted me. "He's fifty-two. With my luck, he'll live another thirty years. I'll be old and bitter then."

Twenty minutes later, I was back in the car with Enzo, heading home.

As we pulled up in front of the gate to the premises, my eyes were drawn to a man standing on the other side of the street, and I jerked in surprise. It was Frank.

chapter *fourteen*

Frank? I'd recognize his red hair and lanky stature anywhere. Enzo shot me a look, but I quickly tore my eyes away from Antonio's former lover before Enzo followed my gaze. What was Frank doing here? He should know better than to creep around the house of a mob member, especially the Boss of the Outfit. But then, Frank probably didn't know that's what Dante was, unless Antonio had revealed more to his lover than I was aware of.

I tried to keep a passive face as we pulled up the driveway, but I wasn't sure I was succeeding. Enzo definitely had picked up that something was wrong and kept looking my way. "Thanks for picking me up," I said and slipped out of the car the moment we came to a stop in the garage. Once inside the house, I strode upstairs into one of the guest bedrooms facing the street, but when I peered out of the window, Frank was already gone.

I had to figure out a way to contact him to find out what he wanted. But how?

I wasn't supposed to leave the house unguarded anymore. And I didn't even know where Frank lived, but I had a feeling he'd show up again soon. There must be something he needed to talk to me about. What if he wanted to blackmail me?

Great, now Dante's manipulation was making me paranoid. Next time Frank was around, I'd simply have to find a way to sneak out of the house to talk to him.

A knock made me jump. The door was ajar and Gaby poked her head in. "Dinner's ready," she said shyly. "Mr. Cavallaro is waiting for you."

"Couldn't he have told me that himself?"

Gaby flushed. "I'm sorry. He sent me to get you."

I touched her shoulder as I walked past her. "Don't worry. I'm not blaming you."

She followed a few steps behind me as we headed downstairs. Before I entered the dining room, I turned to her. "You don't have to trail behind me. We can walk side by side, Gaby."

She nodded before she disappeared through the door leading into the staff area. With a sigh, I stepped into the dining room. Dante was sitting in his usual spot at the end of the table. I crossed the living area and headed for him. My plate was placed at the other end of the table as it had been the other evenings. Somehow this made me unreasonably angry today. I stopped next to my chair, but didn't sit down. "Why am I supposed to sit so far away from you?"

Dante lifted an eyebrow. "Are you angry?"

"Of course I'm angry. I don't want to go through meals as if we're strangers. You never try to keep that much distance between us when you fuck me." The word made my skin crawl with discomfort, but I stood my ground.

Dante's eyes narrowed a fraction, always so cool and calculating. "I wasn't the one who insisted we have sex. If I recall, you were quite adamant about it."

I couldn't believe he acted as if he didn't enjoy it. Maybe I wasn't experienced, but I knew that he'd enjoyed himself tremendously. I grabbed my plate and cutlery and carried them over to the place beside Dante, where I sat them down with a bit too much force, making them clank loudly. I lowered myself into the chair, then stared at Dante defiantly.

"Please tell Zita to set the table like this from now on."

"If that's what you want," he said indifferently.

Just then Zita walked in, and I didn't get the chance to say something else. Her eyes flitted from Dante to me and a smile crossed her face. I really wanted to scream. She set down our plates. Homemade sweet potato gnocchi, sage butter and veal cutlets. She took her sweet time before she left again.

I speared a gnocchi and slid it into my mouth, then almost sighed because it was so delicious, but I didn't want Dante to think I'd already gotten over my anger toward him.

Dante cut his veal without hurry. My eyes took in his strong hands, remembering how they felt on my skin, and hating myself for wanting to feel them again, despite his frustrating behavior.

"How was the visit with your parents?" Dante asked eventually. He sounded so blasé, I couldn't even count the question as an attempt at making up for his rudeness.

"Didn't my father give you a report?"

Dante slid a piece of veal into his mouth before he leveled his gaze on me. "We talk about business in our meetings," he said, then a bit sharper, "I don't know why you're acting like a petulant child. If I wanted a wife who did that, then I would have chosen Gianna."

I dropped my fork with a clang. "Then maybe you should ask her. I'll marry Matteo. At least I hear he isn't a cold fish."

"Cold fish, hmm? That's what people call me?"

"They call you many things, but that's the most accurate description of your character I've come across so far."

"So are you interested in Matteo?"

"Excuse me?" The sudden question threw me off.

"You danced with him at our wedding, and you seemed to enjoy yourself more than usual."

"Are you jealous of Matteo?"

"I'm not jealous, no. I'm merely trying to protect what's mine."

That sounded an awful lot like jealousy to me. "I don't know why you even care. You don't seem to be interested in me outside of the bedroom, and even that was initiated by me, as you pointed out so helpfully. Right now, I think if you ever caught me in bed with Matteo, you'd probably give me one of your cold looks and then go back to work." I wasn't sure why Matteo was even a topic. I'd never been interested in him. He'd always been too unpredictable for my taste.

"I'd go back to work, yes," he said with a predatory smile. "After gutting Matteo and watching him bleed to death." He took a sip of his white wine.

I gave up. It was obviously not possible to talk to Dante like husband and wife. We ate the rest of our dinner in silence, only broken by the scratching of our knives on the plates and the occasional thud when we set out glasses down on the table.

I was half-asleep when Dante came into bed. The mattress dipped and then his warm body pressed up against me. I didn't stir. Dante brushed my hair off my back and pressed a hot kiss against my neck, then followed it with a gentle bite. I was glad I lay on my stomach and could stifle my gasp in the pillow. I didn't want him to know how much his touch affected me, how much my body craved his ministrations. I was still mad at him for his words during dinner, but my body had a mind of its own.

Dante didn't seem too put off by my unresponsiveness. He trailed his tongue over my shoulder blade, then along the bumps of my spine until the nightgown was in his way. He made his way back up and sucked the skin over my pulse point into his mouth, then left soft kisses up to my ear. He moved even closer, so I could feel his erection through the fabric of his pajama pants. It took all my self-control not to reach out and curl my fingers around his hard-on. His breathing was hot against my ear as he licked my earlobe, making me shiver with desire.

He brushed my neck with his knuckles, then moved lower until he reached the dip above my butt. My breathing was coming faster and I could feel my panties sticking to my center from arousal, but I still didn't move. This time I wouldn't be the one initiating anything.

Dante slid his hand over my ass before dipping between my legs. He groaned when his fingers brushed my panties. It took all my willpower not to press myself against his hand for some friction. His mouth found my ear. "I know you're ignoring me, but you should learn to control your body if you want to succeed in doing so."

That infuriating bastard.

Dante sat up and pushed my nightgown up before hooking his fingers under the waistband of my panties and sliding them down my legs. I lifted my face from the pillow and glimpsed over my shoulder. It was too dark in the room to make out much. The silvery moonlight streaming through the windows cast Dante into shadows, but I was certain he was watching me. Then his hands were back on me. He massaged my calves, slowly working his way up higher. His breathing was deep and calm in the dark. He slipped his hand between my legs and pushed them apart. I buried my face back in the pillow when his fingers found my folds and started stroking my clit. He shifted, and then his lips were on my butt. He bit my cheek lightly, then soothed the spot with his tongue and lips. I almost came right then. Instead I sank my teeth into my lower lip to hold on longer. This was too good to be over so soon. Dante repeated the motions until he'd worked his way back up to my throat and I was a boneless heap of desire.

I parted my legs even further for him, not caring that only hours ago I'd sworn to ignore him until he stopped treating me with cold detachment outside of the bedroom. As he rubbed my clit, need overtook my reasoning. He spread my wetness, then slid two fingers into me. I arched my backside up to give him better access to my opening. He started moving his fingers in and out slowly while his lips kept up their ministrations on my throat and shoulder, always alternating between nibbling, licking and kissing. He was panting too. This was affecting him. I moved my hand to the bulge in his pants and started rubbing it through the fabric. He released a harsh breath into my ear. "Every moment of the day I think of the things I want to do with you, catch myself remembering your taste, your smell. Sometimes I think I'll go insane if I don't bury myself in you."

I whimpered. Why couldn't he show me that during the day? Why did he have to act like I was nothing but a needy wife? He thrust his fingers faster into me and I moved my hips against them, wanting him deeper. He hit a sweet spot deep inside me; fire licked my belly and core, making me cry out as pleasure rippled through me. Dante kept pumping into me as I bucked my hips desperately, riding the waves of my orgasm. Finally I slumped against the mattress, not enough energy in me to keep my butt raised. Dante's fingers were still buried in me, but they were moving slowly, almost tenderly in and out of me now.

I sucked in a few deep breaths, trying to calm my racing heart, but Dante had other plans. He shifted and there was the rustling of clothes, then he was back beside me. He bent down and rasped into my ear. "I want to feel your hot mouth again."

Shivering, I twisted and braced myself on my elbows. In the shadows I could see Dante's outline as he knelt on the bed next to me. His cock was inches from my face, long and hard, and waiting for me. Dante tangled his hands in my hair and gently pushed me closer to his erection. He smelled clean, of soap, spicy and fresh. His erection brushed my lips and I parted them, and took him into my mouth, tasting the saltiness of pre-cum on his tip. It spiked my own arousal. The iceman was eager for me. I swirled my tongue around his cock, then dipped the tip into the small slit in his head. Dante's fingers in my hair tightened as he made a sound deep in his throat. His grip, rather than being painful, was oddly erotic.

Dante pushed slowly into me, and I took him deeper and deeper into my mouth until I almost gagged, then let him slide all the way out. Soon Dante seemed to want to take control of the situation and started thrusting in and out of my mouth, slowly at first, then faster. His hand in my hair kept me in place as he took my mouth. I hummed in approval. This was far hotter than I could have imagined. Having Dante fuck my mouth, having him above me, guiding my head the way he wanted… It was a huge turn-on, and I began moving my pussy against the sheets, hoping for some friction.

Dante's hand came down on my ass, keeping it in place. "Don't," he said roughly, squeezing my cheek. I made a sound of protest, though it was difficult with his cock in my mouth.

Dante pulled out abruptly, hissing when my teeth grazed his cock. He gripped a pillow and shoved it under my pelvis. Then he was behind me. He gripped my ass cheeks and his tip nudged my opening. "Fuck. You're so wet, Valentina." Without a warning, he slipped all the way into me, filling me completely. I gasped, arching up as pleasure and a trickle of pain shot through me.

Dante stilled for a moment as he rubbed my butt and lower back. He leaned down until his chest was pressed against my back, pinning me beneath his weight. Then he braced himself on his elbows to either side of me. I could feel every inch of him; I couldn't have moved even if I'd wanted to. I tilted my head to the side and found Dante's lips for a hard kiss. He slid out of me slowly until only his tip was inside before thrusting back into me. Soon he established a fast, hard rhythm. Every thrust of his cock made my nipples slide over the sheets, making me gasp from the added friction. His balls slapped my folds, sending lightning bolts of pleasure up to my clit.

Dante's pants came faster. His chest was slick against my back. The sound of his thighs hitting my butt with every thrust filled the darkness, and mingled with my desperate moans and whimpers as I spiraled toward my second orgasm. I tried to hold it back, but Dante snuck his hand under me and flicked his thumb over my clit. "Come for me," he whispered in my ear.

I shattered as pleasure shot through me in a torrent. Dante raised himself on his arm and really started pounding into me, harder and faster than ever before. I clawed at the sheets. He clamped his hands down on my hips and raised my butt higher as he thrust into me, his fingers digging almost painfully into my skin. I sunk my teeth into the pillow as I felt the treacherous signs of another orgasm rippling through me.

Dante thrust into me hard and let out a low groan, his fingers tensing against my hips. His erection expanded in my channel as he spilled into me, and the fire in my belly raged through my body as I tumbled over the edge again. Dante collapsed on top of me, leaving open-mouthed kisses on my shoulder and neck as he whispered words too low for me to hear. I closed my eyes as my chest tried to hammer its way out of my rib cage. I'd probably be sore tomorrow, but it had been worth it. I didn't even care anymore that I hadn't kept my promise to myself. Why should I deprive myself of a good time to punish Dante? I'd only be punishing myself.

Dante was getting heavy. I turned my head, hoping to breathe easier that way. I could ask him to get off me, but I knew the moment I did, he'd pull away again as he always did. I wanted to relish our closeness for a little longer, even if it meant being crushed by his weight. He felt hot and strong, and pressed up like this, it was hard to say where his body began and mine ended.

Dante raised his head and our lips met for another kiss, languid and unhurried, almost sweet, but then he rolled off of me. I turned around so I was facing him. He was lying on his back, staring at the ceiling. It was too dark to make out his expression. I cautiously moved closer and rested my head on his chest. He tensed and I braced myself for his rejection. My own body stiffened in anticipation of the rebuke, but it never came.

He relaxed, wrapped an arm around my shoulder, and I finally dared to snuggle closer against him. I drew in a deep breath, savoring his warm scent that was becoming increasingly familiar; it was mixed with the musky aroma of sex. My hand came up to his stomach and I stroked him lightly. Was it the dark that made him more approachable? That made him forget who he was, who he was bound to be?

chapter *fifteen*

I wasn't sure what woke me but when I opened my eyes, the sun hadn't risen yet. The sky was already lightening in the distance and provided enough light to make out my surroundings, but that was it. Dante was pressed up against my back, his face half-buried in my shoulder, his breath warm against my skin. It was uncomfortably warm but I didn't move away. This was the first time I woke with Dante still in bed, and he was actually holding me in his arms. Maybe his subconscious had accepted what he couldn't: that he wanted to be close to me.

I kept my breathing even, tried to appear asleep, so I wouldn't wake him. I must have dozed off again because I startled awake when Dante shifted away from me. I listened carefully, but he wasn't getting out of bed. He'd rolled away from me in sleep if his rhythmic breathing was any indication. I slowly turned on my other side, so I could see him. He lay on his back, an arm thrown up over his face. The sheets were pushed down to the delicious V of his hips. I propped myself up on one arm, careful not to make any sound. My fingers itched to stroke his blond hair back, to tickle the ridges of his taut stomach, to follow the trail of fine hair down to his erection.

I reached out hesitantly and lightly brushed my fingers over his hair. Dante's hand shot out lightning fast, grabbing my wrist in a crushing grip. At the same time he sat up and his eyes met mine. I pressed my lips together. He released my wrist in a jerk. I rubbed it, lowering my eyes to the bruises already forming. Dante touched my naked waist, his hand warm and light on my skin. "Did I hurt you?" There was real concern in his voice.

I peered up, surprised. "It's okay. I startled you."

He grasped my hand and inspected the marks his tight grip had left on my wrist. His thumb brushed over my skin in a featherlight touch. "I'm not used to waking up beside someone anymore."

It was the most personal thing he'd ever shared with me. I had to stop myself from digging deeper, from wanting more. "I know. It's okay. You'll get used to it."

He lifted his gaze, but his fingers kept up their light stroking on my wrist. "Did you and Antonio share a bed?"

"In the beginning, yes. It was for appearance's sake mostly. We still had a maid then and we didn't want her to get suspicious. At first it was like having a sleepover with a friend, but eventually it got awkward, especially when he came home smelling like his lover, so he fired the maid and we started sleeping in separate rooms."

His eyes lingered on my exposed breasts. "I can't imagine a man looking at you and not wanting to have you for himself."

I flushed with happiness, but I decided to keep the mood light, worried a more emotional response would make Dante retreat again. "I think Antonio would have said the same about you. I think you might have been his type."

Dante laughed and his entire face transformed. "That's not something I want to think about."

I smiled. "I imagine you don't." I paused, curious. "What would you do if one of your men came to you and admitted that he was gay?"

"I would tell him to keep his disposition a secret and to fight it."

"It's not like people choose to be gay. They are gay or they aren't. You'd force your men to live a lie."

"They can live a lie, or they will have to live with the consequences."

"You would kill someone for who they love."

"Society may have come a long way but the mafia is built on traditions, Valentina. If I declared I'd accept Made Men to be gay, all hell would break loose in the Outfit. That would be one change I wouldn't be able to push through. I wouldn't kill someone for confiding in me, as long as they kept it a secret. I don't doubt that there are soldiers in the Outfit who are attracted to men but who've learned to restrain themselves. They are probably married and live a lie, but as long as they do, they are safe."

We were still sitting close together, actually talking in bright daylight. I reached for Dante's chest, lightly brushing my fingertips over a long scar there. Dante gripped my wrist, gently this time, and pulled my hand away. He slid his legs out of bed and stood. I watched as he headed for the bathroom, completely naked, and yet encased by hundreds of invisible layers I could never penetrate.

I dropped my hand in my lap. With a sigh, I got out of bed as well. There was no sense in lying back down alone. I had a busy day. My first day in the casino without Dante. I was anxious and excited at the same time. After a quick shower, I took a ridiculously long time trying on different outfits. I didn't want to look too sexy, but I also didn't want to hide my femininity. I knew those men, especially Raffaele, didn't like that a woman was now working with them—and worse, was their boss—and I had no intention of making this easier for them. They had to learn to deal with strong women, and if they couldn't, that was their problem. I chose a knee-length dark-blue pencil skirt, matching sling-back heels and a white blouse with a round neck and long puff sleeves. After I'd tugged the hem of the blouse into my waistband, I put my hair up in a bun, letting a few wayward strands hang down.

When I entered the dining room, it was deserted. I stopped in the doorway, letting my eyes rest on Dante's usual place. His newspaper was folded beside his empty plate. With a sigh, I headed for my own chair. The door opened and Gaby walked in, carrying a carafe with fresh orange juice and a coffeepot. She smiled brightly at me. "Good morning, Mis…Valentina." She gave an apologetic look but I only smiled, happy to see a friendly face in the morning. "I hope you slept well?"

My cheeks warmed. "Yes, thank you."

She poured me coffee and orange juice. "Would you like some eggs or pancakes?"

"No, I'll only have a croissant and some fruit." I gestured at the array of pastries and fruit in front of me.

Gaby turned to leave. "Wait," I blurted, then flushed at how desperate I'd sounded. Gaby faced me with wide eyes, as if she worried she'd done something to offend me and would be punished. "Why don't you keep me company?"

Gaby froze.

"Only if you want to. I'd like to get to know you better."

A shy grin spread on her face, but she didn't sit down.

"You don't have to stand. Sit." I pulled out the chair beside mine. Gaby put down the carafe and the coffeepot before she lowered herself gingerly in the chair.

"Have you had breakfast yet?"

Gaby hesitated, then shook her head.

"Then have a Danish. There's more than enough food for the two of us." I grabbed the basket and pushed it over to her. She took a chocolate croissant with a mumbled thanks, her cheeks turning red.

I grabbed one for myself, took a bite, then followed it with a hot gulp of coffee. I wanted to give Gaby some time to get past her nervousness. "Where do you live? I've been wondering about this since you told me your story."

"Oh, I live with Zita and her husband. They took me in shortly after I started working for Mr. Cavallaro."

"Are they treating you well?" Whenever I saw Zita, she was glowering or frowning. She didn't seem like someone who should take care of a girl like Gaby, who'd gone through hell as a teen.

Gaby nodded her head vehemently. "Yes. Zita is strict but she treats me like family." She put the last crumb of croissant into her mouth and swallowed before saying, half-embarrassed, "She's starting to warm to you. Zita always needs some time to get used to new people."

"Really? She doesn't look like she's liking me any better."

Gaby gave a small shrug. "I'm sure she'll change her mind soon."

I couldn't help but like Gaby. She was kind. I peered at the watch around my wrist. "I need to leave now. I want to be early on my first day at work."

"Good luck," Gaby said, rising from her chair. "I think it's great that you want to work. You're the only woman of your status who doesn't only stay at home. I mean, there's nothing wrong with being just a wife."

I briefly touched her shoulder to show her I wasn't offended, then followed her back into the staff area where Enzo was drinking coffee. He got up at once when he saw me. "You can finish your coffee. There's no rush," I told him. Despite my words, he picked up his cup and downed it in one swallow. Zita was throwing disapproving glances my way. I definitely couldn't see her warming up to me. She hadn't said anything yet except for a curt "good morning," but I could tell that she wanted to.

"In my time, the wife of a Capo would never have lowered herself to work," she muttered as she wiped the counters, which were already spotless.

"Times change," I said simply.

"The deceased mistress, may God rest her soul, was happy with the role of mistress of the house. She spent her days trying to make her husband happy and make sure he had a beautiful home."

"Zita," Enzo said sharply. "That's enough."

Zita pointed a finger at him. "Don't talk to me like that."

"Maybe we should head out now," I said to Enzo. I didn't want them to fight because of me. He nodded, grabbed his gun holster from the chair, and we walked in silence toward the garage.

"Thank you for speaking up for me," I said as we sat in the car.

"Zita should show you respect. You are the Capo's wife. He wouldn't approve of anyone treating you like that." Would he really care? "You should tell him."

I shook my head. "No. I can handle myself, but thank you."

Enzo inclined his head and the rest of the drive passed in silence. To my surprise, Enzo didn't just drop me off at the casino. He followed me inside and didn't budge from my side. I had a feeling Dante might have told him to keep an eye on me. I wondered if it was because he didn't trust his men to treat me decently, or if he didn't trust me not to mess up. Neither option made me feel better.

Leo seemed surprised when he spotted me. "I didn't expect you yet. Raffaele and the girls aren't here yet. There's not much to do right now."

I headed straight toward the back where the offices were located. "I know, but I want to read up on our high rollers. I assume you have documents and statistics about them?"

Leo's eyes darted between me and Enzo, who had his arms crossed over his barrel chest, looking like he was waiting for a chance to crush Leo's head. No love seemed to be lost between them. "Yes, we do. Let me get them for you."

I settled in the plush chair behind my desk, feeling out of place, but when Leo returned with folders full of papers, I held my head high and gestured at him to put them on my desk. "I'll read them. Please let me know when Raffaele and the girls arrive so I can talk to them."

Leo nodded and left without another word. Enzo hesitated, then he too walked out and closed the door behind him. I slumped in the chair, and let my eyes take in my windowless office. I grabbed the first folder, determined to learn everything I needed to know to do a good job. I didn't want to disappoint Dante. I knew he was risking the wrath of many Made Men by letting a woman work this job.

My eyes were burning from the dry air-conditioned air, and I'd only gotten through two folders, when a knock sounded at my door. "Come in," I called hoarsely. I cleared my throat as the door opened and Enzo poked his head in. "Raffaele is here. Should I let him in?"

I stifled a smile. Was Enzo now acting as my secretary? "Yes, thank you."

Enzo held the door wide open. Raffaele strode in with a scathing look in Enzo's direction, who returned it with the same fervor. He closed the door and stood in front of it, arms crossed and hard eyes on Raffaele. "Can't you talk to me without your watchdog?" he asked with a nasty smile.

I straightened. With my high heels I was as tall as him and immediately felt more at ease. "I could, but I won't," I said, making it sound as if it was actually my decision, and not Dante's order.

Raffaele seemed taken aback, but he recovered quickly. "You wanted to talk to the whores. They are getting ready in their dressing room."

"Good. Lead the way."

Raffaele walked out without a word and headed toward one of the doors leading away from the main floor. Enzo was close behind us. Raffaele didn't bother knocking, he just ripped open the door. A few of the girls let out surprised gasps, but when they saw who it was they quieted. Apparently they were used to that kind of behavior from him. Raffaele made a mock sweeping gesture, inviting me inside the dressing room. "Careful," Enzo hissed, bringing his face very close to Raffaele's. "Or do you want to lose another finger? Dante won't let you stitch it back on."

Raffaele turned red but he didn't dare give a nasty retort, though it was obvious from his expression that he wanted to.

I took a step into the dressing room, then stopped. "Is it okay if I talk to you for a moment?" I asked the gathered girls. There were ten of them, varying in age from their late teens—that's what I hoped, at least—to their late twenties. Some of them catered to the girl-next-door, cheerleader taste, while others were more exotic. Almost all of them were sporting silicon breasts. Their expressions ranged from suspicious to worried to outright scared. As if choreographed, their gazes sought Raffaele, silently looking for his permission. I could tell by the self-satisfied grin and the way he seemed to get bigger how much he enjoyed it.

"I want to have a word alone with the girls," I told him firmly.

"But—"

"No but," I said at the same time as Enzo gripped Raffaele by the collar and shoved him outside, then followed after him and closed the door so I was alone with the girls. I turned my full attention to the women, who'd all stopped what they were doing and were watching me. "Maybe you can introduce yourself. Name, age, how long you've been working for the Outfit."

I pointed at a petite Asian girl in the corner when it became clear that none of them wanted to start. After that, they all seemed to relax and gave me their information without much prodding. To my relief, the youngest girl was already twenty, unless she was lying about her age.

"How are you being treated?"

Again silence.

"The Outfit treats us very well," a girl named Amanda said.

"I want the truth. Does Raffaele treat you with respect?"

A few of the girls exchanged amused expressions, and finally one of them said. "We're whores. Hardly anyone treats us with respect. Raffaele is no exception."

"He's not the worst."

"That's your opinion, not mine."

"Oh shut up."

I raised my arms and the girls fell silent. "Okay. Who's worse than Raffaele?"

"A few of the customers are into beating us up. And Tommaso wants some nasty stuff too." That didn't come as a surprise. Bibi didn't tell me everything, but the few things she'd shared with me about her sex life with Tommaso had made my stomach turn.

"I like it rough."

"You like everything, but I don't."

"Oh get over yourself. They buy your body so they decide what to do with it."

"You sound like Raffaele."

"Okay, okay," I said slowly. "What exactly is Raffaele doing?"

"He's like our pimp. He tests us before he decides if we're good enough to work here. And he makes sure we make the customers happy. And if we don't, he punishes us."

"I assume 'tests' mean he's sleeping with you?"

"Fucking us however he likes is more like it."

"And what exactly does he do to punish you?" I asked, but the bruises the girls had been about to cover up with makeup before I entered gave me a good idea.

"He slaps us, or fucks us really hard. Or he sends us to one of the whorehouses at the outskirts of town."

"The johns there are the worst. They are drunk, and brutal, and fat."

I took a deep breath. "Okay. Any good things you can tell me?"

"The money is great. I can buy nice clothes and rent an amazing apartment. That's something I could never do without this job."

Many girls nodded, and I tried to take comfort in it. They all had started working as prostitutes on their own free will, and they earned more money than most people with a college degree. I talked to them a bit more and asked them to tell me when a customer was too brutal. They promised to do it, but

I wasn't sure if they were only saying it to get me off their backs. I'd have to talk to Leo and Raffaele about the situation.

When I stepped out of the dressing room, Enzo was waiting for me. "Where's Raffaele?"

Enzo nodded in the direction of the bar. "He's gone off to sulk. That boy would have been removed from the Outfit a long time ago if it weren't for his father. Useless fucker." He shut his mouth. "I apologize for the crude language."

"No need. I've heard worse."

Surprise crossed his face. Happy that I was making progress with Dante's men, I headed toward Raffaele. He was perched on one of the barstools, drinking what looked like a martini. "Isn't it a bit early to start with the alcohol?"

Raffaele emptied his glass. "We're the mob, not a convent."

"I'd still appreciate it if everyone stayed lucid during work."

"Maybe one glass is enough to get you drunk, but I know how to hold my liquor. I'm not a pampered woman."

"Raffaele," Dante's voice sliced through the room like a knife. I whirled around as Dante walked toward us, his body brimming with angry energy. His cold eyes were focused on Raffaele, who quickly slipped off the barstool and stood, a flicker of nervousness replacing that self-satisfied arrogance. Enzo was grinning menacingly. I had a feeling he had kept Dante updated about the way things had been going so far.

Dante stopped right in front of Raffaele, fixing him with an expression of stark brutality. "If I hear one more word of disrespect from your mouth, I'm going to chop you into tiny pieces and feed you to your father's dogs. Do you understand?"

"Yes, Boss," Raffaele said hastily. He turned to me. "I'm sorry if I offended you." He sounded sincere, but there was something vengeful and bitter in his eyes.

Dante finally leveled his gaze on me. "I'd like to have a word with you."

I fell into step beside him as we headed toward my office and stepped inside. Dante closed the door. Before he could say anything, I muttered, "Did Enzo call you?"

"Enzo didn't have to call me. I'd intended on checking on you all along. I want to make sure your first day went well."

I gave him a doubtful look.

"Why are you so surprised?"

"Because so far you didn't strike me as the caring type of husband."

Dante didn't say anything, only watched me with that unnervingly cool gaze.

"I didn't need you to defend me. I can handle myself," I said when it became clear that he wouldn't say anything.

Dante narrowed his eyes. "This is my territory. These are my men, and it's my job to keep them in line. If they show disrespect toward you, it's only a small step until they dare to disrespect me as well. I won't allow it."

"You made me look incapable of doing my job. Raffaele will think I'm weak because I need you to protect me."

Dante came very close, engulfing me with his aftershave. "Valentina, the only reason why these men respect you is that you're my wife. I know you don't like it. I know you are strong, but you can't exact dominance over these men like I do because you don't have the same weapons as I do."

"What weapons?"

"Cruelness, brutality, and the utter determination to kill anyone who disputes my claim to power."

I held my breath. "What makes you think I wouldn't kill someone if I had to? Maybe I'm capable of the same brutality as you."

Dante smiled a joyless smile. "Maybe, but I doubt it." He traced a finger down my throat. "Maybe you would have had the potential to survive in the Outfit, if you'd been brought up the same way boys are raised in our world. My father had me kill my first man on his orders when I was fourteen. A traitor that my father had tortured in front of me before I put a bullet in his head. After that, my father had one of his soldiers torture me to see how long I could stand the pain until I broke down and pleaded for him to stop. I lasted less than thirty minutes. The second time, I lasted almost two hours. The tenth time, my father had to stop the soldier or I would have died. I didn't beg, not even to save my life. Be glad that you never got the chance to develop your cruelness, Valentina."

I had to swallow twice before I could speak. "That's barbaric. How can you not hate your father for what he did to you?"

Dante's finger lingered on the swell of my breast. The fabric of my blouse might as well not have been there; it felt as if he was touching bare skin. "I hate him. But I respect him too. Fear, hatred and respect are the three most important feelings a Capo must instill in other people."

"In your wife as well?"

Dante pulled away his hand. "Hatred and fear have no place in a marriage." He stepped away from me and casually walked over to my desk, which was piled with the folders I intended to read. "I see you're trying to familiarize yourself with our high rollers."

I had trouble handling the sudden topic change. My mind was still reeling from the horrible things Dante had told me about his youth. No wonder he was so good at shutting himself off after the cruelty his father had subjected him to. I wondered how many of the scars marring his body were from those torture sessions, and how many the result of an enemy's attack. "Yes. I want to memorize their faces, names and quirks."

"I thought I should stay until the high rollers arrive and introduce you to them. That way it'll appear more official. I had Leo send them invites for an early reception. You'll have the chance to talk to them without the usual chaos of the casino, and they get the chance to gamble in private for a while."

I was grateful to Dante for making sure things went smoothly for me. Of course, I realized at least part of it was because he liked things to be under his control. "Thank you."

He inclined his head, then looked at me for a moment longer before he checked his watch. "Why don't you prepare yourself some more? The first high rollers should arrive in one hour. I'll talk to Leo and make sure everything is set up for the reception."

When he tried to walk past me, I put my hand on his arm to stop him. Then I stood on my tiptoes and kissed his cheek before I strode toward my desk and picked up a folder. After a moment, I heard the door open and close.

Fifteen minutes before the reception was supposed to start, I headed toward the main floor where a few tables with glasses and ice buckets filled with champagne bottles had been set up. There was also a small buffet of canapés. Dante made his way toward me the moment he saw me and his presence set me at ease.

Soon the first high rollers arrived. Most of them were at least in their fifties. Old, rich men with expensive designer suits, tans from too many hours spent on the golf course, and smiles that spoke of overconfidence. These men thought the world was theirs for the taking. And yet I didn't miss the look of respect that crossed their eyes when they faced Dante. The way they shook his hand, you could tell they were trying to pay him deference. Dante always quickly turned their attention to me, introducing me as the new manager and his wife. The last part led to a wave of respectful compliments of my beauty. While I certainly didn't mind being praised for my appearance, it wasn't something that would help me keep the casino staff in check. I steered the conversation away from my looks and involved the men in small talk. Luckily they let me, only too eager to share their stories about tricking the IRS, their achievements on the golf course, or the selection in their wine cellars—and it was obvious they were used to women hanging on their every word.

I led them toward the roulette table, all smiles, and soon they began to throw away money with hardly a care, too busy bragging and impressing me. From the corner of my eye, I noticed Dante talking to Enzo before leaving the casino. I knew he was busy but I wished he'd stayed a little longer. I didn't have much time for that thought, however; I had to be the perfect hostess for another group of high rollers eager to schmooze the wife of the Capo.

It was past midnight when things had progressed enough for me to take my leave. Several of the high rollers had disappeared into back rooms with girls, or were too immersed in gambling to need my attention. I was exhausted, more exhausted than a few hours of talking and listening should make a person.

After I'd slipped into the passenger seat of the car, I let out a quiet sigh of relief to be finally off my feet. My legs ached from standing for so long, especially in my uncomfortable heels. Men had it easier. They could wear their oxfords or Budapest shoes, and not squeeze their toes into pointy heels.

I must have dozed off because the next thing I remembered was Enzo turning off the engine in the garage. I sat up, embarrassed. "I'm sorry I fell asleep. That was rude."

Enzo shook his head. "I don't mind."

I was too tired to analyze that statement. I made my way into the house, my eyes sliding toward the door to Dante's office, wondering if he was still in there. Deciding I was too exhausted to give him a recount of the evening's event, I headed upstairs, wincing every time my feet hit the floor. I needed to get out of my heels as soon as possible or I'd go crazy. I walked into the bedroom and froze. Dante was in bed, reading something on his tablet. As usual his upper body was naked, but now as my eyes raked over the scars marring his skin, I couldn't help but imagine Dante at age fourteen, being tortured by his father to toughen him up.

"Did everything go well after I left?" Dante asked, barely glancing up from whatever he was reading.

"Yes, the high rollers lost quite a bit of money." I slipped out of my heels and could have wept from relief. "I'm going to grab a quick shower." Dante only nodded distractedly. I was too exhausted to care about it. After the shower, I put on a satin chemise and matching panties, and returned to the bedroom where I sat down on the edge of the bed, my back to Dante. I wasn't in the mood to make an effort. I lifted my foot and started massaging it. Maybe next time I should switch to ballet flats. They would still look elegant but not hurt as much. The mattress shifted and then Dante's voice was at my ear. "Let me."

Before I could protest, he made me lie back and put my feet in his lap. His fingers started rubbing my tired feet and calves with just the right amount of pressure.

"Tonight was an exception. The high rollers needed to get to know you. You don't have to stay that long in the future. Just make an appearance, greet them, make them feel welcome and then leave. Leo is a capable man."

I hummed, my eyes closed as I relaxed under his massage. Now and then Dante's finger strayed higher, stroking my knees or even thighs, and my breathing deepened. Dante, too, wasn't unaffected. I could feel his erection pressing against my feet still resting in his lap. "Turn around," Dante ordered.

I rolled over so I was lying on my stomach, knowing exactly what Dante wanted. Tonight I wasn't even bothered by the fact that he never wanted to look at my face. I raised my butt when his fingers hooked under the waistband of my panties and slid them down my legs. Sighing into the pillow, I let Dante waken my exhausted body with his touch.

chapter *sixteen*

DANTE WAS RIGHT. THE NEXT FEW WEEKS I MADE SURE TO BE OUT of the casino by ten at the latest. I enjoyed the time I spent talking to the girls, the bartenders or the croupiers, but listening to most of the customers was strenuous. At least Raffaele had made sure to stay away from me, which was a huge plus.

When Enzo took me home at night, I always checked the street for a sign of Frank, but the only person I saw regularly on the sidewalk was an elderly woman walking her Yorkshire Terrier. By now, I'd almost convinced myself that I'd imagined seeing him. Maybe my mind was unconsciously missing Antonio, and conjuring up Frank had been a way to cope with it. Dante wasn't the presence I wanted him to be in my life. He took me every night, mostly in the dark, and always with my back to him, sometimes with me kneeling, sometimes lying flat on my stomach. Not that I was complaining. He always made sure I came at least once while he was in me, but I was starting to long for something else. This felt too much like mere fucking, almost like I was nothing more to him than a way to relieve tension; but whenever Dante's hand slipped between my legs at night, I promised myself to talk to him next time, too desperate for his touch.

As usual my eyes wandered over the sidewalk when Enzo steered the car through the gates to the house. But tonight I saw him again. Frank was strolling along the sidewalk across the street, trying to look as if he was only catching some fresh air. He wasn't succeeding. He looked suspicious to me, so I didn't dare to think how he would appear to Dante's guards. I would have to find a way to send him away. It was too risky for him to be here. I headed straight up to the guest bedroom that allowed me to view the street, but like last time, Frank seemed to have disappeared.

My phone rang and for a moment I was sure it was Frank, but he knew better than to call me. There was no saying who was tracking my calls, after all, and I'd changed my number a few months ago. The screen flashed with Bibiana's name. I picked up. "Hey, Bibi."

"Val," Bibi said in a whisper. Her voice was shaking. She sounded terrified. "Can you come over?"

I tensed, turning my back to the window. "What's wrong?"

"Tommaso, he..." She sniffed. "He was in a foul mood today."

"What did he do? Is he still there?"

"No, he left because of a meeting with Raffaele, but he'll be back soon. Can you come over? I'm scared of what he'll do when he comes back." My eyes darted to the clock that said it was almost nine.

"I'll be there in ten minutes, Bibi."

I rushed out of the guest bedroom and down the stairs. I wasn't sure where Enzo was. It probably would have been easy to find him, but I wasn't in the mood to explain myself. Instead I grabbed the keys from the hook in the garage and took the SUV. Before the doors had glided up all the way, I pressed the gas and shot out of the garage, the car roof missing the bottom of the door by inches. I slowed only as I waited for the gate to part for me. Dante would be furious.

As I turned around the corner at the end of the street, I spotted a familiar back and hit the brakes. Frank jumped, and threw a panicked look over his shoulder. He had his phone pressed against his ear but ended the call when he saw me. I checked our surroundings before I rolled down the window and gestured for him to come closer. "What are you doing here?"

He crept closer, eyes darting around nervously. I understood his anxiety only too well. He was risking too much by being here. "I need to talk to you in private."

I frowned. "About what?"

"About Antonio, about the Outfit, about everything."

I checked the rearview mirror again. "I can't talk right now. Meet me tomorrow around five thirty." I explained the way to the street where the storehouse was that hid the casino, but didn't tell him what was inside.

"That's where one of the underground casinos is, right?"

I stared. Antonio had told him? Damn it. Why couldn't Frank have stayed away? "We'll talk tomorrow." I let the window slide back up and pulled away. Nobody seemed to have followed me, or at least I didn't see anyone. I hoped I could sneak out of the casino tomorrow undetected. I needed to clear things up with Frank. But what if he really wanted to blackmail me somehow? I knew he'd leave me no choice but to tell Dante about it if he did.

Why did today have to turn into such a mess?

It took me less than ten minutes to arrive at Bibi's house. As always a guard was sitting in a car in front of it. He gave me a curt nod when he saw me getting out of the car. I almost ran toward the door, but Bibi opened it before I even got the chance to ring the bell. I had to stifle a gasp when I saw her face. Her lower lip was busted open, and dried blood stuck to her lower chin and her shirt. A bruise was already forming on her left cheek, and the eye above it was starting to swell shut. She ushered me in, then quickly shut the door. Before I had time to say something, she threw herself into my arms. I embraced her, but she winced when I touched her ribs and I loosened my hold on her. I pulled back to look at her face. "Why did he beat you up?"

Bibi shrugged, then winced. I didn't even want to know what her body looked like under her clothes. Finger marks bloomed bluish-red on her throat and her collarbone. "He's been in a foul mood all day and when I told him I still wasn't pregnant, he lost it." Something tickled at the back of my mind, but I pushed it aside for now.

"Maybe it's his fault. Maybe the old fool is infertile," I muttered. I didn't like the word "hate" or the sentiment behind it. Hate always led to more hate, but I definitely hated Tommaso. Dante wasn't sure I was capable of taking another person's life, but I was.

"He can't be. He got a few of the whores in Club Palermo pregnant."

My eyes widened. Bibi had never told me. "So he's got children with other women?"

"No, he forced them to get an abortion. Nobody wants to fuck a pregnant whore, that's what he said."

"I'm so sorry, Bibi."

"I feel so bad for calling you away from Dante on Valentine's Day."

I'd completely forgotten about that. Not that Dante had given any indication that today was special during our breakfast together.

"Don't be ridiculous. You know I'm always there for you. What can I do?"

A small sob escaped her and she clapped her hand over her mouth, her eyes huge and full of fear. She lowered her hand. "I don't know. I just don't know, but I was so scared and didn't know who else to call. You are the only one who seems to care."

"I do care, Bibi. You know that."

"I'm scared of when he returns. He told me it wasn't over. And he's always more brutal after he's spent time with Raffaele. They are both disgusting sadists. Oh, Val, the things Tommaso sometimes does to me, the things he forces me to do, I can't even tell you."

I grabbed her hand. "Come. Spend the night at my place."

"I can't run away from him. You know they'd never let me. They'll always force me to return to him no matter what he does."

I knew. How could I have felt self-pity for my loveless marriage when Bibi had it so much worse? "I know, and I didn't mean that you should move out. But you could spend the night with us so Tommaso has some time to cool off, and tomorrow after breakfast I'll take you back home."

Bibi nodded slowly. "Are you sure Dante won't mind? I don't want to impose on your time together."

I almost laughed. "He won't mind, don't worry," I said. "Do you want to leave now?"

She shivered, her thin arms coming up to wrap around her middle. There were bruises on her wrists too. If my fury alone could have killed Tommaso, he'd be dead now.

I helped Bibi pack a few things before I led her out of the house. The guard looked up, then started, obviously unsure of what to do. Tommaso had probably told him Bibi wasn't allowed to leave the house, but I was the wife of the Capo, who was his main boss. Bibi tensed in my arm but didn't stop walking. Not even when the guard picked up his phone and called someone, undoubtedly Tommaso. I felt the childish urge to give him the finger, but I'd passed the age where I would have considered acting on it. Bibi plopped down into the passenger seat and I slipped behind the steering wheel. "You are without a guard?"

I shrugged. "I didn't want to waste time looking for Enzo or Taft."

"I don't want you to get in trouble because of me," she said miserably.

I started the car and pulled away from the curb. Bibi's guard didn't try to follow us. He knew where we were going anyway. "I won't."

"Does Dante ever beat you or force himself on you?"

"No. He's not violent. Well, at least not in our marriage. Of course I know that he's perfectly capable of atrocious acts. He told me he doesn't believe fear or hatred belong in a marriage. That's probably why."

"He's a good man."

"I wouldn't say that. If you want a good man, you have to go looking outside of the Outfit."

"Remember when we were young and dreamed about finding our Prince Charming and marrying him? I was obsessed with Disney princes. They were all so gallant and good."

I smiled at the memory. "We were young and stupid. I'd give everything to be that clueless again, if only for a few hours."

"Yeah."

It was almost ten when we finally stepped into my home. "Do you want to grab something to eat, or would you like to try to get some sleep?"

"I'm not really hungry," Bibi said hesitantly. "But I don't think I can fall asleep right now."

"We could sit in the library and talk a bit. Or I could run you a bath so you can relax."

"I think I'd rather talk. I don't want to be alone."

"Okay, I…" I trailed off when I saw Dante heading our way. Bibi stiffened beside me, her terrified gaze darting to me. I wasn't sure why, but I positioned myself between Dante and Bibi. He noticed, of course, and gave me a searching look. "Good evening, Bibiana," he said politely.

"Evening," she said quietly. Dante's cool blue eyes scanned her bruised face and arms briefly before they fixed on me. "Tommaso called me to ask if his wife was here. He said you'd picked her up at their house without his permission."

"His permission?" I hissed. "She's not a dog. I don't need to ask him permission for anything."

"That's what I told him," Dante said calmly, startling me.

"You did?"

Bibi watched us with wide eyes.

"Of course, you are my wife. If you want to have a word with one of the wives of my soldiers, you have every right to do so."

We both knew that wasn't the reason why Bibi was here. Dante wasn't blind. I hoped he could see how grateful I was for his support. "So he's okay with her staying the night?"

"I didn't know that's what you'd planned, as you didn't inform me," he said simply. I could hear the hint of a reprimand in his tone. He knew I'd left without a guard—*again*.

"I didn't have the time," I said. "But I think Bibi should stay here, so Tommaso can calm down."

"If he comes here and asks for her, it would be against our traditions to deny him. She is his wife."

Bibi nodded. "He's right. I shouldn't have come." The defeat in her eyes and voice almost brought me to my knees. I shot Dante a pleading look.

Dante pulled his phone from his pocket and pressed it against his ear. After two rings, I could hear a deep voice on the other end but I couldn't hear the words.

"Yes, Tommaso. I want you to accompany Raffaele when he checks out the new goods. I trust your judgment, and Club Palermo could use fresh blood. I want your report tomorrow." Dante listened to something Tommaso said. "My wife and Bibiana have plans. Don't worry. She's safe here. I'll have my driver take her home tomorrow." Dante lowered the phone and put it back in his pocket.

"Thank you," Bibi said in a shaky voice. I stayed silent, overwhelmed by Dante's kindness.

"You realize I sent your husband out to sleep with our new prostitutes, but I suppose you don't mind."

"No, I don't. I'm waiting for the day when he finally finds a mistress he prefers to me." Bibi clapped her hand over her mouth, obviously shocked by her own words.

Dante inclined his head. "I understand, but you should be more careful what you say in public." Bibi gave a submissive nod. Then his eyes found mine. I tried to send him all the gratitude I was capable of with that one gaze. I was quite sure he could see it. "I'll return to my work. I'm sure you and Bibiana have a lot to talk about."

He turned around and strode back to his office, disappearing from our view. I linked arms with Bibi, who was gaping at me. "I can't believe he did that for you. He must really care about you."

"He tried to help you. He saw your bruises."

Bibi laughed. "He did it for you. It was written all over his face." She paused, then quickly added, "Not that I mind. I'm just glad that he got rid of Tommaso for now."

"Come on, let's go into the living room. I'll put in a movie and we'll have a glass of wine. You deserve it. Do you need some Tylenol with it?"

Bibi grimaced. "Yes, please. I feel sore. I think Tommaso bruised my ribs."

That was the last mention of what had happened with Tommaso today. We spent the rest of the night remembering our childhood and teenage years, laughing, and getting drunk.

I regretted last night's wine the next morning when a splitting headache woke me from sleep. I sat up, groaning. Pressing a palm against my forehead, I took a few deep breaths, hoping it would help with the nausea. Something red caught my eye. A small parcel lay on Dante's side of the bed. I snatched the card propped up against the parcel.

I would have given this to you last night but I didn't want to wake you, was written in neat script on the card. Delighted, I grabbed the present and unwrapped it. Inside the small velvet box rested a delicate white gold necklace with an emerald pendant. I stumbled out of bed and hurried toward my vanity, holding it up against my eyes. The emerald had almost exactly the same color. That couldn't have been a coincidence. I sank down on the chair and fastened the necklace around my neck with shaking hands.

I probably wouldn't have gone to work at all that day—Leo could take care of everything without me—if I hadn't told Frank to meet me there.

After we'd dropped Bibiana off at her house and I'd made her promise to call me the moment Tommaso was home, Enzo drove us to the casino and we went inside as we always did. Luckily for me Raffaele was screaming at one of the girls, which wasn't a one-time thing either, but today it was the distraction I needed. I turned to Enzo. "Could you please have a private word with Raffaele and make it clear that I don't appreciate him manhandling our girls?" Enzo looked only too eager to comply.

He headed straight for Raffaele and shoved him into one of the private rooms. Leo was making a beeline for me, but I shook my head and told him that I was busy. He seemed confused but didn't try to stop me when I stepped into the elevator. Guilt almost stopped me in my tracks a couple of times. My secret meeting with Frank could be construed as a betrayal of Dante's trust. After this morning's considerate gift, the idea of going against him like that made me feel even worse. He seemed willing to try, and I was risking it all because of Frank.

Three minutes later, I hastened away from the storehouse. I glanced around my surroundings nervously; not only because I worried about being followed, but also because this was a deserted and creepy area. It was already getting dark, which didn't help my anxiety at all. At least I was wearing ballet flats so I could run if someone attacked me. In the distance, leaning against the wall of another empty warehouse, I could make out a tall figure. I hurried toward him, then slowed because it was hard to make out much. "Frank?" I whispered. "Is that you?"

He took a step away from the wall, looking as nervous as I felt. "Hey, Valentina."

I bridged the remaining distance between us. "What's going on? Why do you keep showing up in front of my home? Do you want the Outfit to find out about you?"

Frank rubbed his hair, his eyes darting around. "Of course not." His obvious nervousness was making me anxious in turn. "I need to talk to you."

"Then talk. I don't have much time. Don't you realize what kind of risk we're taking by talking right now?"

"I think it's dangerous that you agreed to marry Dante Cavallaro."

I was taken aback. That wasn't what I'd expected when he'd told me he wanted to talk. "Why do you care? Your connection to the Outfit died with Antonio." I realized a moment too late how insensitive that sounded, but Frank didn't seem to notice. He was busy checking our surroundings, especially the darkness spreading out behind us.

"Can you stop that?" I asked impatiently. "You're making me nervous."

"Sorry. I'm not used to sneaking around in dark alleys. That's Antonio's thing."

Was he still not over him? His words made me believe it. Maybe that was why he was here. Maybe he couldn't let go of his former life and I was the only connection he had to it. "It wasn't my decision to marry Dante. You should know that marriages in our world are often decided by other people for reasons of power or strategy."

"You don't love him."

"I'm not going to discuss my feelings with you, Frank. What do you want?"

"Did you tell Cavallaro about Antonio and me?"

"I told him that Antonio was gay."

"Why did you do that?" Frank asked angrily, taking a few steps in my direction, startling me with his outburst, but not enough to back away. I was used to other kinds of men. Frank really wasn't scary enough.

"That's none of your business."

"But you promised Antonio to keep his secret!"

"I know, but he's dead, Frank, and I'm trying to move on. If Antonio were still alive, I'd take his secret to my grave, but the truth can't hurt him anymore. And Dante won't tell anyone in the Outfit anyway."

"He won't?" Frank asked hopefully. "What about me? You didn't tell him my name?" The anxiety returned to his face with full force.

"No. I won't. You are safe, but for it to stay that way, you need to stop hanging around on our street. It's only stupid luck that none of Dante's men have noticed you yet. And when they do, you'll be in huge trouble. So do us both a favor and move on."

"I can't," Frank said quietly. "Don't you miss him? Don't you want him back? Wouldn't you do anything to have him back?"

"You should really leave. This doesn't get us anywhere. I promise you are safe."

Frank gripped my arm, stopping me from walking away. "Valentina—"

"Hands off," a cool voice drawled from the shadows, and I let out a scream. Frank whirled around and tried to run away, but Enzo was there and pulled him into a headlock. Dante appeared beside me and grasped my arm in a steely grip.

He nodded toward the door to the warehouse. Enzo dragged Frank toward it, despite his struggling.

Dante glared at me. "So this is what you do when I'm not around? Meeting with other men?"

"No!" I protested, horrified that he would think that. "It's not like you think."

"He's been lurking around the house twice now, Boss," Enzo said, then grunted when Frank's knee hit him in the groin.

"Explain," Dante snarled. Enzo was still trying to stop Frank from kicking him. Frank was putting up a surprisingly good fight.

"It's Frank," I said quickly, self-preservation overriding my desire to protect Frank.

Dante's grip on my arm loosened. "Antonio's lover."

That caught Enzo's attention. He knew Antonio. The Outfit wasn't that big of an organization that Made Men didn't know each other.

Suddenly shots rang out from somewhere. Enzo cried out and clutched his arm, releasing Frank in the process. More shots rang out. One hit the wall two feet above my head. Dante pushed me to the ground and crouched in front of me, drew his own weapon, and fired into the direction where the shots were coming from. Enzo pulled his own gun, but his right hand was useless and it was obvious that he wasn't used to shooting with his left hand. Frank was running as fast as his legs could carry him away from us toward the shadows. Dante pointed his gun at him. I jerked his hand away when he pulled the trigger and the bullet hit the ground, instead of Frank. "Valentina," Dante snarled, taking aim again, but Frank had disappeared into the darkness. Dante glanced at Enzo, who was clutching his bleeding arm, muttering under his breath.

"What the fuck was that?" Dante asked, eyes blazing with fury as they held my own.

Shaking, I fought to calm myself before I could form a reply. "I don't know! I thought he was alone. Frank doesn't even know anyone who can shoot a gun."

"You should have let me shoot him. Never interfere like that again."

"He's innocent. He doesn't deserve death."

"Bullshit. That guy laid a trap and you fucking walked into it," Enzo muttered.

"What do you mean?" I asked carefully.

Dante shook his head. "Haven't you wondered why he wanted to meet you? Maybe he's been approached by the Russians and agreed to help them. They'd love to kill you."

"Frank wouldn't do that."

"Are you sure?" No, I wasn't. "The Bratva can be very convincing. Or maybe they offered him a substantial amount of money. Money makes sinners out of most saints."

Enzo held up his phone. "Called reinforcement."

"Come on," Dante said, straightening up and holding out his hand for me. I took it and let him pull me to my feet, but my legs wobbled and I leaned on him for support for a couple of seconds. He let me do it, despite his anger, his hand strong and warm against my waist.

Clearing my throat, I finally straightened. "Do you really think it was a trap? I got the feeling Frank was lonely and wanted to talk to someone about Antonio."

"Someone shot at us," Dante said simply. I couldn't argue with that. And Frank had definitely run in the direction of the shooters. Slowly I was starting to understand why Dante didn't trust anyone.

"I'm sorry," I said quietly, but Dante wasn't looking my way. More of his men were running toward us from the direction of the casino. He barked orders at them and they spread out in the area to search for our attackers.

"Take Enzo to see our Doc," Dante told another man, despite Enzo's protests. Then Dante turned to me. "We're going home now."

I shivered at the anger in his voice. Dante urged me forward with a hand against my lower back. He didn't talk as he led me toward the car, nor during the ride home. I kept glancing his way, trying to decide how much trouble I was in. "I'm really sorry."

He ignored me, but a muscle in his jaw twitched. I turned back toward the passenger window. Dante parked the car in our garage and got out immediately. I followed him toward the house. Once inside, I headed straight for the bedroom, his fury practically burning my back as he walked behind me.

"I'm really sorry," I tried again, then gasped when Dante threw the door shut and pressed me against it. I was sandwiched between his muscled body and the door, startled and confused but not scared. Dante was obviously careful not to hurt me.

"Why do you keep disobeying me, Valentina?" He shoved up my skirt and pulled my butt roughly against his groin, and his rock-hard erection. Wetness pooled between my legs. "I don't know," I said, trying to hide my excitement.

"That's the wrong answer." Dante pushed my panties—I wasn't wearing tights, only garters—aside and slipped two fingers into me. Before I had time to articulate another answer, Dante replaced his fingers with his cock, slamming into me in one fierce stroke before he started to fuck me against the door. I was pretty sure he realized that was as far from a punishment as it could possibly get.

chapter *seventeen*

I quickly figured out that Dante fucking me against the door wasn't his idea of punishment. That came in the days that followed. Dante treated me with even more coldness than before, and I barely got to see him because he was too busy looking for Frank and his accomplices. He didn't seek me out at night anymore, and though I was too proud to admit it to him, my body longed for him to touch me again.

One afternoon, about one week after my messed-up meeting with Frank, I encountered Rocco Scuderi in the lobby of our house. "Valentina, good to see you," he said on his way to the front door.

I smiled, although I was surprised. Scuderi always treated me with politeness and respect, but I didn't have a personal relationship with him like I had with his wife, or with Aria.

"I have a favor to ask of you," he said.

"Of course." It was unusual for a Consigliere to approach the wife of his Boss and ask her for a favor, but he was also my uncle, so maybe that changed things.

"You know my daughter Gianna is supposed to marry Matteo Vitiello, but she's still a bit hesitant about the marriage."

From what I'd heard, hesitant didn't even begin to cover Gianna's feelings about her wedding to Matteo, but I nodded anyway.

"I thought maybe you could talk to her?"

I'd never been very close to Gianna, so the request surprised me. "Wouldn't it be better if Aria talked to Gianna? After all, she's married to another Vitiello."

"Gianna won't listen to her sister. I think someone who isn't immediate family might have a better chance to get through to her." I was Gianna's cousin, but of course he had a point.

"I can try, of course, but I can't promise that she'll listen to what I have to say."

"Try is all you can do," he said, looking almost resigned.

"Is there anything in particular you'd like me to address?"

"Maybe you can tell her that marriage doesn't mean she'll be trapped in a golden cage? I mean, look at you, you're even allowed to work."

I did, but I was the huge exception. Gianna would know that as well. And even if Dante started pushing his men to let their wives work, that wouldn't help Gianna. She'd be living under the Vitiellos' rule in New York. "I'll do my best."

"Thank you."

"Why don't you and your family come to dinner tomorrow?"

"That's a great idea. That way Gianna won't get suspicious and you can breach the subject casually." We set up a time before he inclined his head in thanks once more and walked out.

I closed the door and headed toward the kitchen. Zita was preparing dinner—cannelloni filled with ricotta from the looks of it—when I stepped in. Gaby was ironing Dante's shirts in a corner of the kitchen, far enough from the cooking that there was no risk of the fabric absorbing the smell.

"Zita, I invited the Scuderis for dinner tomorrow."

Zita pursed her lips. "A bit more time to prepare would have been nice. I need to go grocery shopping, figure out a menu and then cook everything."

"I know, but you won't be cooking."

Zita's lips parted but no words came out. Gaby had stopped ironing to stare at me as well.

"I'm going to take care of everything. I used to cook frequently in my first marriage, and I want to prepare dinner for our guests."

"Are you sure that's wise? They expect a certain standard."

"Don't worry. I know what I'm doing."

"And what are you going to cook?" Zita asked skeptically.

I smiled. "That's a surprise. Now I'll let you get back to your work." With a wink toward Gaby, who was openly gawking, I left the kitchen and headed for Dante's office and knocked.

"Come in."

I slipped inside. Dante was busy cleaning his guns. They were arranged on a towel on his desk. "I invited Rocco Scuderi and his family for dinner for tomorrow night. I hope that's all right with you?"

He barely spared me a look. He was obviously still angry with me. "I assume this is so you can talk with his daughter Gianna?"

"He asked you first, didn't he?"

"I'm your husband. Rocco wanted to make sure it was okay to approach you."

Sometimes their unwritten rules and traditions drove me up the wall. "Of course."

"Don't forget to tell Zita and Gaby, so they can prepare everything for our guests." He rubbed a spot of grease at the barrel of his gun.

"I already did. But I will cook dinner myself."

That made him raise his eyes, surprise flickering across his face. "You can cook?"

"Yes. I used to cook often in my first marriage," I said, and that was obviously the wrong thing to say because Dante's expression darkened again. "You haven't found Frank yet?"

"No. We haven't. He's probably gone into hiding if he has any sense."

Hovering next to the door, I nodded. Though I could tell the discussion was over for Dante, I hated how strained things had become between us. I opened my mouth to say something, anything, but then I lost my nerve and left without another word.

I hadn't realized how much I missed cooking until I stood behind the stove again. Zita was a constant presence at my back, hawk-eyes watching my every move, but I was confident in what I was doing. I had cooked every part of today's meal countless times. Vitello Tonnato for starters, followed by Saltimbocca with homemade gnocchi and a green salad, and at last, Tiramisu. As I worked in silence beside Gaby and Zita, I could occasionally glimpse the hint of approval in the older woman's expression. I mixed everything for the sauce that accompanied the cooked veal for the starter before turning to Zita. "Would you try it? I'd like to know if it's good."

I *knew* it was how it was supposed to be, but I wanted to show Zita that I appreciated her input. She stopped chopping the endive for the salad and walked over to me, wiping her hands on her apron. I took a step back as she dipped a spoon into the tuna sauce. She nodded slowly before leveling her brown eyes on me. "Good." I knew then that things would turn out okay between us. I smiled and chanced a quick glance at the clock. "I have to change. I can't welcome our guests in stained clothes."

"We'll take care of the rest," Gaby assured me.

"Thanks," I said as I hurried upstairs, feeling better than I had in a while.

The Scuderis arrived forty minutes later. My aunt Ludevica stood in the front with her husband Rocco, who had a hand on nine-year-old Fabiano's shoulder. I greeted his parents before I turned to him. "You've gotten so tall."

He beamed up at me, straightening his shoulders even more. His father gave him a look that made the smile slip right off his face. Why did Made Men have to be so strict to their sons? My father had always coddled me, but my brother had never heard a word of praise from him. I ushered them inside as it had started snowing again. I couldn't wait for winter to be over. The darkness and cold made it even harder to be upbeat about my marriage.

"Girls, greet the wife of the Capo," Ludevica said sternly.

"I'm still their cousin. They don't have to treat me any different now that I'm married to Dante." I hugged Gianna, who looked gorgeous with her red hair that twinkled with stray snowflakes, then her younger sister Lily, who was getting more lovely by the day as well.

Dante chose that moment to join us. He shook hands with Rocco, then patted Fabiano's shoulder with one of his kinder smiles before he kissed the hands of Ludevica, Gianna and Lily. The latter blushed furiously while Gianna looked like she wanted to be anywhere but here. Dante walked ahead with Fabiano and Rocco. I hung back with the women of the family as we made our way to the dining room table.

During dinner, one topic wasn't mentioned: Gianna's wedding to Matteo. It should have been the focus of attention under normal circumstances, seeing that it was less than six months away, but I had a feeling the Scuderis were desperate to avoid a scene. After I'd received my fair share of praise for the first two courses, I rose and turned to Gianna, who was staring down at the table with a frown. "Will you help me with dessert, Gianna?"

Her head shot up, suspicion written plainly across her face, but she knew that manners dictated she must agree. She rose from her chair, sent a scathing look toward her mother, and then followed me through the door to our left. "Mother asked you to talk sense into me, didn't she?" she muttered as we headed toward the kitchen.

"No, it was your father."

"Wow. Shouldn't you have lied to me? That's what most people do."

I shrugged. "I think it's easier if you know the truth."

We stepped into the kitchen. Zita was cutting the Tiramisu into squares and setting them on plates while Gaby decorated them with fruit. "We'll take over from here," I told them. They seemed to understand. With a small bow toward Gianna, they slipped away toward their staff room. I grabbed the spatula and heaved another piece of Tiramisu on a plate, then motioned at Gianna to spread raspberries, strawberries, slices of mango and star fruit around it. "So talk," Gianna said.

"I know you don't want to marry Matteo."

Gianna snorted. "I'd rather chop my fingers off and eat them."

I gave her a look. "All women in our world face the same problem as you do. Very few are lucky enough to choose their husband. An arranged marriage doesn't necessarily have to be a bad thing."

"Why? Because love can grow over time?" Gianna said in what I assumed was an imitation of her mother's voice.

"Yes, that's an option."

Gianna glared. "Come on. I'm not blind. Don't tell me there's love between you and Dante. You act like fucking strangers." She snapped her mouth shut. "That was rude."

It was, but I couldn't blame her for speaking her mind, and the truth. "We haven't been married for very long."

"Shouldn't two months be enough to know if you can stand someone or not? I knew after my first encounter with Matteo that I didn't like that arrogant asshole."

I put down the spatula and leaned against the counter. "What about Aria and Luca? She seems happy with her arranged marriage."

"Aria is a pushover. If it had been me who had to marry Luca, either he or I would be dead by now. And Matteo is just as bad."

"Aria made the best out of a situation she couldn't escape. That's all we can do."

"No, it's not. She could have escaped, if she'd been braver."

I paused. Was she saying what I think she was saying? "Nobody escapes the mob."

Gianna shrugged. "Maybe nobody's really tried."

"Oh, there have been enough people who tried, but eventually your past always catches up with you."

"I know," she said softly, then she pointed at the plates. "Shouldn't we serve dessert now?"

"Yes, you're right." We loaded our arms with plates and returned to the dining room. Gianna's parents cast hopeful glances my way. Dante eyed Gianna, then met my gaze. He seemed to know what the Scuderis didn't:

nobody could get through to Gianna. Her words about Dante and me kept bothering me the rest of the evening. It made me realize just how far my marriage with Dante was from the relationship I longed for.

That evening I decided to help Gaby and Zita wash the dishes, desperate to keep busy. We were almost done when Dante walked in, eyes taking in the scene before him without emotion. I was up to my elbows in dishwater. "You can go home," he told Zita and Gaby, who didn't need to be told twice. They quickly took their leave. I withdrew my arms from the wash water and took the dishtowel Dante held out to me. "Thank you."

"You are a great cook."

I chanced a glance at him, wondering if he'd come here to tell me that. "I'm glad you enjoyed dinner."

He nodded. I blew a strand of hair out of my face, then stretched my tired muscles. Dante's eyes scanned my body. I became acutely aware of how close we were and how long it had been since we'd had sex. Had he changed his mind?

"I take it your conversation with Gianna didn't go well."

I sighed. "Of course it didn't. How can I possibly convince Gianna that an arranged marriage won't make her miserable? I'm the last person she would listen to."

Dante smiled tersely. "You are right." He took a step. "I'll get back to work then."

I didn't try to stop him. Maybe a few weeks ago I would have made an attempt at seduction, but today I lacked the energy. I slumped against the counter as I watched Dante stride out of the kitchen.

chapter *eighteen*

I peered at the clock again. It was past midnight, but I couldn't sleep. I longed for Dante's closeness, for his touch. It had been more than a week since the dinner with the Scuderis, and two weeks since Frank had run off and Dante had fucked me. God, I missed him.

I slipped out of bed and left the room, not bothering to put on a bathrobe. It was dark in the corridor. I felt my way toward the staircase, then slowly descended it. At the end of the hall, light spilled out from under Dante's office door. I knocked, then entered without waiting for a reply. Tonight I would take what I wanted. The silent treatment was over.

Dante sat in his leather chair behind the desk. His hair was disheveled as if he'd run his hand through it repeatedly. He'd thrown his jacket and vest over the sofa, unbuttoned the top two buttons of his white shirt and rolled up the sleeves, revealing his strong arms. He hadn't bothered to remove his gun holster. He was staring at something on his laptop but glanced up when I stepped in.

He looked tired. "Is something wrong?" His voice was gravelly from disuse, almost growly, and made me even more determined to distract him from his work and lure him upstairs. His blue eyes took in my skimpy silk nightgown as I walked toward him. "I was just wondering when you'd come to bed," I said casually as I walked around his desk and stopped beside him.

He leaned back in his chair, eyes flitting between my naked legs and my face. A couple of months ago I wouldn't have recognized the look in his eyes, but now I knew it was desire. Maybe he shut himself off emotionally, but my body definitely got his attention. I must have caught him at a good time: too tired to keep up his disinterested act.

"Las Vegas contacted me. They want a meeting."

I nodded, but I had something very different in mind than a conversation about mob business. I reached out for his laptop and shut it.

Dante raised his eyebrows. "Valentina, I really need to…" He trailed off when I leaned over him and slowly knelt down, running my hands over his thighs. I began massaging them as I looked up at Dante with big eyes. "Can't the work wait?"

Dante's eyes darkened with lust. A bulge was slowly forming in his black pants as he regarded me, and I had to stifle a smile. "What do you have in mind?" he asked matter-of-factly, trying to appear unaffected. Of course, the hard-on straining against his pants betrayed him.

I cupped his erection through the fabric. "I don't know."

Dante smiled darkly. "I doubt that." He reached for his zipper and dragged it down, then he pulled out his hard cock. He stroked it a few times, running his thumb over the tip already leaking pre-cum before he traced my mouth with his thumb. I licked my lips, tasting him on me, and Dante let out a low breath. "Stop teasing me, Valentina."

I leaned forward and licked his shaft slowly from the base to the tip before I dipped my tongue into the tiny opening. Dante gripped the back of my head and gently held me in place as I trailed my tongue around his tip over and over again, barely touching him.

His fingers in my hair twitched and he nudged me slightly forward. "Suck my cock, Val." It was the first time he'd called me by my nickname. I cupped his tip with my lips and began sucking, making sure to run my tongue around the rim now and then. Dante watched me through hooded eyes as he massaged my scalp.

I took him deeper and then started bobbing my head up and down how he liked it. Dante's eyes never left me. He bucked his hips and tightened his grip on my head as I sucked him harder. "I'm coming," he said in warning. I felt him tense as his climax overwhelmed him. His cock jerked and he erupted in my mouth. I tried to swallow while keeping up my sucking. Dante groaned, still rocking his hips, and his hooded eyes fixed on me. These were the moments he allowed me the occasional glimpse behind his guarded mask.

I could feel him softening in my mouth, and I released him from my lips. A defiant part in me wanted to ask him if that meant he'd forgiven me for the mess with Frank, but the reasonable side of me won.

Dante dropped his hand from my head and went limp, squeezing his eyes shut. I quickly wiped my mouth while he wasn't watching and checked my décolleté for stains. My own arousal was a throbbing between my legs. Dante shifted, drawing my attention back to him. He stared at me with an unreadable expression until I started to feel self-conscious. I stood but Dante did the same, towering over me in his posh white dress shirt, gun holster and half-open dress pants. I searched his eyes, but as usual I couldn't read him.

He cupped my neck and crashed his mouth against mine. I gasped in surprise and his tongue slid in. He used his body to back me up until my legs bumped into the edge of his desk. He gripped my hips, hoisted me on top of the cool surface, and stepped between my legs, still possessing me with his mouth and tongue, making my legs go numb and my heart slam against my rib cage. God, Dante could kiss. I wished he'd do it more often.

He grasped my shoulders, stopped kissing me and eased me down until I lay flat on his desk. I stared up at him, forcing myself to lie still and let him admire me, when all I wanted to do was rip the buttons off his shirt and have him inside me. Dante seemed to know what I wanted. The dark smile was back, and the cool sophistication had been replaced by something feral and hot. I bit my lip and spread my legs even wider, making my nightgown ride up.

I knew Dante could see what was below it: nothing. I wasn't wearing panties.

He released a harsh breath, but he still wasn't touching me and it was driving me to the brink of despair. I tried to grab his shirt but he stepped out of my reach. "No," he said with authority. The voice he only used when he was giving orders to his soldiers. It was the sexiest sound in the world, but I was burning up with need.

"Touch me."

"I'm still angry with you. Sex won't change that. You disobeyed my direct order."

He couldn't be serious. If this was another form of punishment, I'd lose it.

"Let's see if you learned your lesson. You will obey me now, won't you?"

I almost moaned at the timbre of his voice and dark look in his eyes. "Yes," I said quickly.

He took another step back, his eyes meeting mine. "Spread your legs wider."

I didn't hesitate. The air in his office felt cool against my heated flesh, but it did nothing to alleviate the burning need. Dante unfastened his gun holster without hurry, never taking his eyes off me. "Touch yourself."

My eyes widened, but again I complied. When he used that voice, I had a hard time resisting. I slid my hand down my body and between my legs. Part of me was embarrassed. This definitely wasn't something a respectable wife did, according to my mother. But the bigger part enjoyed the way Dante's eyes darkened as he watched my fingers slip between my folds and the way his lips parted. He let the gun holster drop to the floor with a clunk. He was growing hard again as he watched my fingers draw small circles over my clit.

"Put a finger into your pussy."

I shook with arousal as I followed his order. I dipped my index finger into my hot core. A muscle in Dante's cheek flexed, and his cock was standing to attention. I could see how much he wanted to touch me, to fuck me, but Dante was nothing if not in control of himself and others. He stepped between my legs, gripped my wrists, and I slid my finger out of my tight channel, hoping he'd do it for me now.

"No," he growled. "Keep fucking yourself with your finger."

How could he sound so dangerous and sexy at the same time? How could that cold man say such naughty things with the utmost authority? I pushed my finger back into myself, even though my clit practically screamed for attention. Dante stared down at me, his jaw tense. He pushed the top of my nightgown down, revealing my breasts. My nipples hardened from the cold and Dante's piercing gaze. He took my nipples between his forefingers and thumb, and started rolling them back and forth. I arched my back, but didn't stop fingering myself.

I reached for Dante's shirt, but he pinched my nipples in warning. "No," he rasped. I bucked my hips at the sensations rocking through my body, the sensual pain I started to enjoy more than I ever thought I could. Dante's fingers twisted and rolled my nipples relentlessly. My core quivered with the need to come. "Dante, please."

He fixed me with a stare, then he released one of my breasts and gripped my arm, stopping me from touching myself further. He pulled my hand away and put it beside me on the desk. He pushed my nightgown up so my pussy was bare to his eyes. "Don't come," he warned.

"What?" I gasped, but the sound turned into a moan when he slid his two middle fingers into me. My muscles clenched around him, gripping his fingers in an iron grip. He started fucking me slowly, his warning gaze on me. "Don't, Valentina."

I dug my nails into my palms, trying to fight off the climax. Dante pushed his fingers deep into me and kept them in place while his thumb brushed my clit. I gritted my teeth, my body starting to spasm.

"Do not come," Dante said huskily.

"Dante..." I shook my head back and forth, sure I was going to burst any moment. Dante curled his fingers in me and pressed down hard on my clit. "Now," he ordered harshly, and my release crashed down on me with blinding force. My butt arched off the desk as I cried out. My hands slid over the smooth surface of the desk, searching for something to hold on to.

"That's right," Dante said, his eyes on me. I stilled, feeling drained and sated. Dante slowly pulled his fingers out of me, sending another spike of pleasure through me. He unbuckled his belt, the only thing keeping his open pants in place, and let them drop to the floor. His cock was hard and red and glistening. "Turn around."

I slid off the desk, and stood on unsteady legs for a moment before facing the other way and bending forward. I braced myself on my elbows and jutted my butt out. Risking a peek over my shoulder, I found Dante taking in the sight of me. He kneaded my ass cheeks before gripping his cock and guiding it to my entrance. In one swift movement, he buried himself deep inside me. I exhaled and curled my fingers around the edge of the desk, trying to steady myself as Dante started pounding into me. I gasped as he drove himself deeper and deeper inside me, making my nipples rub against the cold, smooth desk.

"Am I forgiven?" I gasped out.

Dante growled. He leaned over me, his fingers finding my nub. "I shouldn't forgive you," he said between grunts, accentuating every word with a hard thrust. "But for some reason, I can't stay mad at you."

A grin tugged at my lips but dropped off my face when Dante hit my G-spot and made me shatter under the force of my climax. Dante tensed behind me as his own release overcame him. My legs were seconds away from collapsing, and my chest was probably chafed from rubbing over the desk. Dante wrapped his arm around my chest, pulling our bodies flush together and still pumping into me as he left a trail of kisses up my shoulder. He shuddered again and licked my ear. We stayed like that for a couple of moments before Dante stepped back. I pushed myself to my feet. "Will you come upstairs with me?" I asked as I gathered my clothes.

Dante hesitated but then he nodded. I walked ahead to hide my elated expression from him. This felt like a major victory.

After we'd showered, we slipped into bed. I snuggled up to Dante's back and slung my arm over his stomach. When I'd almost fallen asleep, his hand gently covered mine.

Several weeks passed as we fell into the same routine we'd established before the Frank fiasco. Dante fucked me at night, engaged me in talk about the casino during meals and otherwise mostly ignored me. Every morning I woke alone, no matter how long Dante had kept me up the night before.

This was also the case the morning I was woken from cramps. When I sat up, a violent wave of nausea hit me. I stormed into the bathroom and threw up what little I had in my stomach, gasping for breath and feeling dizzy. Gradually a suspicion wormed its way into my mind. My period was overdue at least a week. But then, my menstrual cycles had always been rather volatile, so I hadn't paid it much heed.

Was I pregnant? Slowly I straightened and walked toward the washbasin to rinse my face and mouth. It would be the logical explanation. Dante and I had been sleeping with each other for months without protection. When I was certain that my dizziness had passed, I took a shower before I dressed in casual chinos and a pullover, pulled my hair into a ponytail and made my way downstairs. I had to find out if I was pregnant.

I called for Taft and told him I needed to go to a pharmacy. Enzo still had his arm in a cast, so he couldn't work as my driver at the moment. Taft didn't ask why, for which I was glad. I didn't want anyone to suspect anything yet. I needed to know for sure before I told anyone. Taft waited in the car as I headed into the pharmacy and bought two pregnancy tests. Once back in the car, my purchase safely hidden in my bag, I turned to Taft. "Please drive me to Bibiana." Since I'd started working in the casino, I'd had less time for her, but this was something I wanted to share with her.

I texted her so she'd know I was coming and I wouldn't surprise her and her husband at a bad time again. Luckily, Tommaso wasn't home when I arrived at Bibiana's. There were no visible bruises on her body, and I hoped it was because Tommaso was treating her better and not because he targeted less visible places since Bibi had spent the night at my house. "Are you okay?" I asked by way of greeting.

Bibi nodded. "Tommaso has been in a good mood recently." She led me into the living room. "I'm so glad to see you again. Don't you have to work?"

"I don't think I'll go today. I'll give Leo a call later to let him know."

"Has something happened?"

I pulled the pregnancy tests out of my bag.

Bibi's eyes grew wide. "You're pregnant?"

"I don't know. That's why I bought these. I wanted you to be there when I found out."

"Wow. Does Dante suspect?"

I shook my head. "I want to know for sure before I tell him."

"I understand. He'd only be disappointed if you told him and then it wasn't true." She took one of the pregnancy tests. "So do you want to do it now?"

I nodded, nerves fluttering in my stomach. Bibi led me to their guest bathroom. I walked in alone. I'd never mastered the talent to pee with other people in a room with me. Once I was done, I set both tests down on the edge of the washbasin and opened the door. Bibi wrapped her arm around my waist, as we both stared at the tests.

"I think it's time," she said after a few minutes.

"Okay." I reached for the tests and with a deep breath, stared down at them. Both were positive. "I'm pregnant."

Bibi hugged me tightly. "That's wonderful! I'm so happy for you. Dante will be so proud when he finds out. He's waited long enough for children, and you're finally giving them to him. Will you tell him today?"

I considered that. "I think I should get confirmation from my gynecologist. As you said, I should be absolutely sure before I tell him." And the other reason was that I needed some time to get used to the idea myself. I'd always wanted kids, and Dante and I had never taken countermeasures, but now that I knew I would be having a baby in less than one year, I was hit by nerves.

"I couldn't keep it a secret. Especially since Tommaso is so desperate for me to get pregnant."

"Maybe we'll be pregnant together. That would be great."

She smiled. "Go on, call your doc."

"I will," I said with a laugh. She looked more elated than I did.

As usual I got an appointment for the next day. My gynecologist was associated with the Outfit, so I never had to wait long.

That evening when Dante and I sat down for dinner together, the truth was on the tip of my tongue. I was still feeling nauseous and didn't eat more than a few bites of Zita's delicious lasagna. My glass of wine stayed untouched and I could manage only few gulps of water. Dante peered at me over his wine. "Are you all right? You've barely touched your food."

"I don't feel well. Maybe I caught the stomach flu."

Dante's brows crinkled. "Should I tell Zita to make you tea and chicken soup?"

I couldn't help but smile. "Thanks, but I think I'll just go to bed early." I stood and had to grip the edge of the table as a wave of dizziness gripped me. Dante was beside me immediately. "Should I call the doc?"

I shook my head, then regretted the movement. "No. I'll feel better once

I lie down." Dante didn't budge from my side as he led me upstairs, his hand resting on my hip.

I changed into my pajamas as Dante watched me. Then I slipped under the covers. "Do you want me to join you?" he asked.

I hesitated. "I don't think I'm well enough for sex."

Dante perched on the bed. "Valentina, that's not what I meant. I'm not that kind of bastard."

"I just thought..." I trailed off. "You usually approach me only when you want to sleep with me."

Dante exhaled, then shook his head. "Would you like me to keep you company until you fall asleep?"

I didn't want to look needy, but even more than that, I wanted him to stay with me. His baby was growing in my body, and if my gyno confirmed what the tests had said, I'd tell him. "I don't want to keep you away from work."

Dante sat back against the headrest, his legs hanging over the edge so his shoes weren't touching the sheets. I moved closer to him and rested my head on his stomach. When his fingers started massaging my scalp, my eyes fluttered shut. Maybe a baby would bring us closer together. It had worked for some couples in the Outfit.

The next day my gynecologist confirmed my pregnancy and that I was seven weeks along.

I could barely contain my excitement and nervousness when I came home afterwards. Dante wasn't in his office. I called Bibi and grabbed a few pieces of plain toast from the kitchen before I stretched out on the sofa, hoping that way the toast would stay down. My gyno had said my nausea could last for several weeks, but I really hoped I was among the lucky ones who suffered from morning sickness for only a very short time.

I was woken by the sound of a door being slammed shut and sat up, disoriented. It took me a moment to realize I'd fallen asleep in the living room. Heavy steps passed the living room door, then retreated to the back of the lobby. I stood, and after I'd straightened my clothes and hair, I headed toward Dante's office. The door was closed as always. I knocked and stepped in.

Dante sat behind his desk, a thunderous expression on his face. I leaned against the doorway. He glanced up, but didn't say anything.

"What happened? Did the Russians give you trouble?" I didn't mention Frank, not wanting to remind Dante of my screw-up.

Dante leaned back in his chair and shook his head. "No, the Russians aren't the problem for once," he said coldly. "Our own people have taken up the task."

I frowned. "What do you mean? Did one of your men betray you?"

"It looks like there's not going to be a wedding."

"You mean between Gianna and Matteo? Why? Did they have another fight?"

"A fight wouldn't have prevented Matteo from making the Scuderi girl his wife. He's obsessed with her. No, the girl ran away."

I walked into the room and perched on the edge of the desk, stunned by the news. "Gianna ran away from home? But how did she manage to escape her bodyguards?" I doubted Scuderi would have let her out of sight for a second. She was way too volatile for that.

"I had a meeting with Rocco but I don't know all the details yet."

"New York won't be happy about it. Do you think it'll lead to war between them and us again?"

Dante's lips twisted into a wry smile. "I doubt it. Gianna ran off while she was visiting her sister Aria, so it's as much the Vitiellos' fault as ours."

"It's on them then. How can it be our fault if she was in their territory?"

"People are going to say Scuderi didn't raise his girls right. Some will start to wonder how a Consigliere can control his soldiers if he can't even control his own daughter. A few might even say it reflects badly on me that I'm taking advice from someone who lets his daughter go rampant."

"That's ridiculous. Gianna has always been boisterous. Her siblings are perfectly well behaved, so nobody can blame Scuderi or you." I remembered what Gianna had said about escape when I'd talked to her. Should I have taken that more seriously? I'd thought she was only letting off steam.

"I'm not so sure. And who says that Aria didn't help her sister escape?"

My eyes grew wide. "But Gianna's supposed to marry Aria's brother-in-law. She would have betrayed her own husband if she'd helped her sister run away."

Dante nodded, that same cold smile still on his face. "Things are going to get very unpleasant."

I rubbed my belly absentmindedly. "What will you do? Has Matteo cancelled the wedding yet?"

"Oh no. Matteo has no intention to cancel the wedding. He's

determined to find Gianna. He already started searching for her." He sighed. "Scuderi is sending two of his soldiers with Matteo. The three of them should be able to track down the girl. They are professionals, and she's a sheltered girl who doesn't know anything about the real world."

I could feel a new wave of sickness rising up in me, but I fought it. "Don't underestimate Gianna. If there's anyone who could do it, then it's her."

"Perhaps. But she's also hotheaded, and that will eventually lead her to make mistakes."

I sucked in a deep breath through my teeth as my stomach churned again. Dante searched my face. "You look pale. Are you still not feeling well? Maybe you should talk to the doc."

"No, I..." I didn't get to finish the sentence when another wave of nausea washed over me. I rushed out of Dante's office and toward the guest bathroom. I wouldn't make it to the master bathroom on the second floor. The moment I was bent over the toilet, I emptied what little I had eaten that morning. Bile burned in my throat. I closed my eyes for a moment as I clung to the bowl. It didn't help with the dizziness; if possible, it made things even worse.

My eyes popped open when I heard steps behind me, and Dante's black Budapest shoes appeared in my peripheral vision. I quickly flushed the toilet and staggered to my feet. Dante gripped my arm to steady me as I swayed. "Valentina?" His voice conveyed confusion.

I rinsed my mouth over the washbasin and washed my face. I could feel Dante's eyes on me the entire time. I faced him, smiling shakily. "I'm fine."

Dante didn't look convinced. He followed me into the lobby and then upstairs into our bedroom. I wanted to change my shirt. I couldn't help but think it smelled of vomit. I knew Dante was suspicious, but I didn't want to tell him about our baby when he was in such a bad mood because of Gianna. I'd rather keep it a secret a bit longer.

Dante touched my waist. "You know I hate it when you're keeping secrets. Don't make it a habit."

I met his gaze, and pressed my palm against my stomach. Dante followed the movement, his body turning tense.

"I'm pregnant," I said quietly, hopefully. I wasn't sure what I'd expected. I knew Dante wasn't the overly emotional type, but I'd hoped for at least some flicker of joy. But there was only suspicion on his face. He took a step back, eyes hard and calculating. "Pregnant?"

"Yes. We never used protection, so I don't know why you're acting so shocked. Wasn't an heir one of the reasons why you married me?"

"That was the reason why my father wanted me to marry again."

"So you don't want kids?"

Dante's mouth was set in a tight line. "Is it mine?"

Now it was my turn to stumble away from him, shock and hurt slamming into me. I couldn't even speak. Had he really just asked what I think he had? I was on the verge of an emotional breakdown.

"Answer my question," Dante said in a low voice.

"Of course it is your child. You're the only man I've ever slept with. How can you even ask such a question? How *dare* you?"

"I'm not keeping track of everything you do, and there are many men who frequent the casino that wouldn't say no to a night with you. You've made a habit out of keeping things from me. Do I have to remind you of Frank?"

I couldn't believe what I was hearing. I didn't want to believe it. Tears of disappointment and fury burned in my eyes. Being pregnant hadn't exactly helped with my temper and emotionality. "How can you even say something like that? I've never given you any reason to doubt me like that. I'm loyal to this marriage. There's a difference between not telling you about Frank and cheating on you."

Dante still didn't look convinced. "My first wife and I tried for years to get pregnant. It never worked. You and I have been married for less than four months and you're already pregnant."

"I don't know why you act as if that's impossible. If your first wife was infertile, then that's your explanation. Have you never consulted with a doctor? Or did you think it was you who was infertile?"

"We never went to a doctor to find out why we couldn't conceive. Not that it is any of your business. I won't discuss my first marriage with you."

I knew why he'd never consulted with a doctor. Stupid pride of Made Men. They'd rather live in ignorance than risk being told that they were shooting blanks. "Too bad. We're discussing it now. I know why you didn't want to find out. You didn't want to know the truth, because you worried it would make you less of a man if it was your fault that your wife couldn't get pregnant. But now we know it wasn't your fault. It was Carla who was infertile." I winced inwardly at my wording. I didn't want to badmouth a dead woman.

Dante shook his head. "I told you I didn't want to talk about Carla."

"Why not? Because you still love her? Because you can't move on?" He stiffened. "I'm sorry you lost Carla, but I'm your wife now." Suddenly everything I'd bottled up seemed to come to the surface.

I could see that Dante was teetering on the edge of losing control, and I wanted him to. I was so tired of his sophisticated calm, of his cold logic. "I'm so sick of you treating me like a whore. You ignore me by day and come to me at night for sex. And now you accuse me of cheating on you? Sometimes I think you hurt me on purpose to keep me at arm's length. When will you finally move on? Your wife has been dead for four years; it's time you stop pitying yourself and realize that life goes on. When will you stop clinging to the memory of a dead woman and realize there's someone in your life who wants to be with you?"

Dante was in front of me without a warning, his eyes flashing with fury and sorrow. "Don't talk about her."

I lifted my chin. "She's dead and she won't come back, Dante."

He clenched his hands at his sides. "Stop talking about her." There was a hint of warning in his voice.

"Or what?" I said, even though the anger in Dante's eyes sent a shiver of fear down my back. "Do you want to hit me? Go ahead. It can't possibly be worse than the knife you thrust into my back by accusing me of carrying another man's child." It wasn't exactly the truth. If he raised his hand against me, this marriage would be over once and for all. I knew some women in our world accepted physical abuse—many didn't have any choice but to do so, and Bibiana was one of them—but I'd sworn to myself that I'd never bow down to a man like that. Stupid tears made my vision blurry, but I forced them back. I wouldn't cry in front of Dante.

"You're so busy honoring her memory and protecting the image of her you have in your mind that you don't realize how badly you're treating me. You lost your first wife through no fault of your own, but you will be losing me because you can't let go of her."

Dante stared at me, completely frozen. The myriad of emotions in his eyes were impossible to read, and I was too tired to bother. I walked past him and he didn't try to stop me. He didn't move at all. "I'll move into the guest bedroom. There isn't enough room in our bedroom for me and the memories of your past. If you ever decide you want to give this marriage a chance, then you can come to me and apologize for what you said. Until then, I'm done with us."

I hurried up the staircase. Dante didn't try to follow me. The guest bedrooms were always prepared for visitors. I slipped into the first, glad when the door shut behind me, and crept into bed. Maybe I'd sealed the fate of my marriage today, but I couldn't go back to how things had been. I'd rather have a clean cut. Of course I couldn't divorce Dante and he would never allow it, not that I wanted to, but we could lead completely separate lives despite being married. Many couples in our world did it. We'd go about our days like before, sleep in separate beds and play the married couple in public. We'd have to raise our children together, but most men took a back-seat in these matters anyway. Eventually Dante would start frequenting Club Palermo or find a mistress like so many Made Men did, and I would focus all of my energy on taking care of our children. Many women had it worse, and yet the idea that I'd just painted my future made me sick; but I couldn't pretend Dante hadn't said those horrible things to me.

It was out of my hands now. Dante had to decide if he wanted to live in the past or move on into a future with me.

chapter *nineteen*

Dante didn't apologize. Not the day after our fight, and not in the weeks after it. Maybe it shouldn't have come as a surprise. I went to my ten-week checkup at the gynecologist with Bibi. I didn't even tell Dante about it. If he wanted to ignore the fact that I was pregnant, that was his problem.

One week after the appointment, Dante's sister Ines and her husband Pietro came to visit us. I had only seen Ines twice since the wedding, as she'd given birth to her third child four weeks ago. Zita had made dinner, as I was too tired to cook most of the time now, and only barely managed to drag myself to work for appearance's sake.

"Can I hold her?" I asked when Ines lifted her daughter out of the car seat. She searched my face, then handed the baby to me, who had little spittle bubbles in front of her lips and looked too adorable for words. The twins were bickering in the background, but I couldn't take my eyes off the squishy girl in my arm. I carried her into the living room, cooing to her. When I glanced up, Dante was watching me with something close to warmth in his eyes. I lowered my gaze immediately.

Later, after dinner, Ines and I went into the library to talk while the men and the twins stayed in the living room. Ines began nursing her daughter, then fixed me with a knowing look. "You are pregnant, aren't you?"

"How did you know? We didn't tell anybody yet." Not that I didn't want to, but it was Dante's decision if he wanted to make it public.

"You didn't drink any wine during dinner, and you kept touching your stomach."

I flushed. "I wasn't aware it was that obvious."

"Probably not to a man. You aren't showing yet."

"Please don't tell your parents about it. I don't think Dante wants people to know."

Ines shifted her daughter because she was too fussy to latch on properly. "Why not?" It was strange to think that this would be me in less than a year.

I shrugged.

"Are you two having problems? Isn't he happy that you're pregnant?"

"I think he needs time to get used to the idea."

"He did something stupid, didn't he? He's my brother. I know he can be stubborn."

"Stubborn doesn't even begin to describe it. Has he ever apologized to you when he did something wrong?"

Ines laughed. "No. Sometimes I think he can't speak the actual words. Most of the time he tries to ignore the problem until I give up and don't expect an apology from him anymore."

That sounded familiar.

"The anniversary of Carla's death is in one week."

"Oh," I said, freezing. I'd completely forgotten about that.

"I just thought you should know. Dante is always in a particularly bad mood on that day. Maybe you should try to avoid him."

That wouldn't be a problem.

My morning sickness had finally stopped, and physically I felt perfect. When I left the guest bedroom on June 1st, the day of Carla's death, I expected Dante to be either out of the house or hidden away in his office. I jerked to a halt when I found the door to the room where he kept Carla's old things ajar. I could hear rummaging. Was he in there looking at old photos of them together? I remembered what Ines had said—that I should leave Dante alone—but it had been more than five weeks since I'd moved out of our bedroom. I missed our moments of intimacy. Yet pride rooted me to the spot. The door opened and Dante stood in the doorway, carrying a moving box.

I smiled apologetically. "Sorry. I didn't meant to…" I trailed off, not sure what to say to him.

My eyes darted to the moving box. "What are you doing?"

"I'm moving these boxes out of the house."

"All of them?"

He nodded. "Enzo and Taft are going to dismantle the furniture later and throw it away."

I swallowed. "Why?"

"We can put the room to better use. It would make a good nursery."

A lump rose into my throat. "That's true. But we don't have furniture for a nursery yet."

Dante cleared his throat. "You could go shopping in the next few weeks."

"Alone?"

"I could come with you."

I nodded. "If that's what you want."

He didn't say anything. Why couldn't he make this easier on the both of us? Did he think I'd fall on my knees from relief? He hadn't even apologized. This was the first time he acknowledged that we were going to be parents, and only indirectly. He hadn't even admitted that he was the father of my child.

"Do you need my help carrying boxes?" I nodded toward the boxes piled behind him in the room.

"No. You shouldn't carry anything heavy."

"I'm not that far along." Again silence, and an expression I couldn't read. I turned around, ready to go downstairs and have breakfast.

"I want you to move back into our bedroom, Val."

I stopped. It was a request worded like an order. He hadn't apologized. Despite all that, I heard myself saying, "Okay."

That evening I returned to our bedroom and when Dante's hands started rubbing my back and butt, and he whispered, "I want you," I nodded and relaxed under his touch.

A few days later, after I'd left Bibi's house, I let Enzo drive me to the pharmacy for something against my nausea that had flared up again in the last couple of days. As usual Enzo stayed in the car to give me privacy. Bibi had also asked me for a pregnancy test because she suspected she was pregnant, but she didn't want Tommaso to find out; he'd only get furious when her suspicions didn't prove right. That man didn't deserve her. I strolled toward the aisle with the pregnancy tests.

"Val," someone whispered. I turned slowly, knowing that voice from somewhere.

Shock rooted me to the floor as I stared into the face of my first husband. His hair was shoulder-length, and much lighter than it used to be. He was wearing glasses that he couldn't possibly need and had gained some weight. He was almost unrecognizable, especially with the way he dressed. Like a college student who'd rolled out of bed without much thought for what he was going to wear. It was a good masquerade.

"Antonio?" I asked shakily, starting to feel faint. I couldn't believe he was actually in front of me, alive and in one piece. How was that even possible? They'd found his body; a badly burned body without a head. "Shhh," he said quickly. "Not so loud."

Antonio approached me and pulled me into a tight hug. At first I was board stiff, but then I sank into the embrace. "We need to hurry. I saw your bodyguard outside in the car. I don't want him to get suspicious and come in."

Tears burned in my eyes. I drew back, my eyes tracing the familiar lines of his face. "You are alive."

He smiled. It was slightly off. "I am."

"Does Frank know?"

"Yes, that's why he wanted to meet with you. I sent him."

"Why didn't he tell me?"

"Because I wanted him to figure out your loyalties first."

My loyalties? Had Antonio worried that I would tell Dante about him? I frowned. "Okay…why did someone try to kill me when I met with him?"

Antonio laughed. "I didn't try to kill you. I aimed a couple of feet above your head. I had to help Frank. Dante would have killed him if I hadn't done something."

I still didn't like that he'd aimed anywhere near me. The bullets had hit the wall less than two feet above my head. "So you were there the entire time and didn't tell me?"

"Dante and his bodyguard showed up when I was about to step out. He ruined everything."

"How did you even manage to follow me here without Enzo noticing anything?"

"I was one of them once. I could outsmart that guy any day."

My head was spinning. I took a step back from him. "I cried at your grave! I mourned you for months."

"I know," he said. "But I couldn't tell you about my plan."

"Why not? You didn't have a problem telling Frank."

Antonio gave me a pleading look. "I didn't want to involve you in this. It would have been too dangerous."

"Who was the body they found? He had your favorite knife with him."

"He was just a homeless stranger," he said dismissively.

"You killed him and made it look as if the Russians killed you?"

Antonio nodded, a proud glint in his eyes. "I cut off his head so they couldn't try to identify me through my teeth."

I stared. "The Outfit sought revenge after they found you! They attacked the Russians and killed several of them."

"The Russians deserve death. The world is a better place without them."

The world would be a much better place without many of the people I knew. "I can't believe you didn't tell me. I married you to help you, and you didn't trust me enough to involve me in your plan. Have you ever considered that maybe I wanted out of this life as well?"

"I did trust you. I still do, Val. There are few people I trust more, but I couldn't involve you in this. And how could I have taken you with me? It would have looked suspicious if we'd faked your death as well."

I couldn't see how that would have looked more suspicious. We could have staged a crime scene in our house and burned two bodies. But I wouldn't have wanted an innocent to die so I could follow Antonio. It wasn't as if I loved Antonio like I had at the beginning of our marriage.

"And be honest, would you really want to leave this life behind?"

I shook my head. This was the only life I knew. I wouldn't even know how to function in normal society. I scanned his face. "But why are you here? If you wanted to leave this life behind, meeting with me isn't exactly clever. Why are you even still in Chicago? Shouldn't you be somewhere in the Caribbean or in South America, enjoying your newfound freedom from the mob?"

"I heard about your marriage to Dante Cavallaro."

I scoffed. "You didn't come back here because of that. Why would you get out of hiding for that? You were safe."

Antonio looked away. I could tell that he was reluctant to answer my question. "I tried. Frank and I tried a different life, a normal life. I had enough money to live comfortably in Mexico for a while, and then the plan was to find jobs, to live as normal people do."

"And?"

"I couldn't do it, Val. I tried to work but it was degrading to work as if I was a nothing, to work for peanuts, to live without money. I was bored out of my mind. I tried for a while for Frank's sake, but he realized I was unhappy, and so we decided to return to Chicago."

"But why?" I asked. "You can hardly waltz into Dante's office and tell him you're alive. You broke your oath by leaving the Outfit. You betrayed them. They won't welcome you with open arms."

Antonio nodded grimly. "I know. Don't you think I know that?"

Something dawned on me. "You want me to talk to Dante so he pardons you? You want me to come up with some crazy lie that will save your life?" I wasn't sure there was anything I could do or say that would stop Dante from putting a bullet in Antonio's head. He'd broken the mob's cardinal rule. You couldn't just leave the Outfit. It was for life.

Antonio grabbed my shoulder, eyes imploring. "If I could, I would undo what I've done. I wouldn't leave you behind as a widow. You know I love you, Val, right?"

I exhaled slowly. "I know, Antonio. You told me more than once that you loved me like a sister."

Antonio brought us even closer. "Maybe I could love you more than that. Maybe if we tried again, we could be more than a fake couple."

"What are you saying?"

"I want to return to my old life, to you. I want to try for real this time."

I was more confused than ever before in my life. "Antonio, you have Frank. What about him? You are gay."

Antonio avoided my eyes. "I know. But you could be the exception. Frank wouldn't mind if I acted as a husband should. He doesn't mind sharing."

I blinked, on the verge of laughter. "You want what...a love triangle?" I wasn't sure what else to call this. It was too ridiculous to even consider.

Antonio gave me his most endearing smile. The one that brought back memories of our youth together, the one that had manipulated me countless times before.

"I'm married to Dante now. You aren't even my husband anymore. You were declared dead."

"But you can't be married to Dante if I'm not dead, because our marriage is still valid."

"You realize that Dante might be reluctant to agree to your insane suggestion, right?" I said. This was surreal. Maybe this conversation wasn't happening. Maybe I was asleep and dreaming.

"Yes. He wouldn't allow it, and he would kill me if he found out I'm alive. That's why I need your help."

Dread settled in my bones like a leaden weight. "What kind of help?"

"I know you didn't want to marry Dante. He's always been a cold bastard. You can't be happy with him."

"Antonio," I said imploringly. "Spit it out."

"When I decided to return to Chicago, I contacted a couple of my former friends who aren't too fond of the way the Cavallaros run the Outfit, especially Dante with his new rules. I told them I had faked my death because I was sick of serving under the Cavallaros' rule. They welcomed me with open arms. They want change as much as I do. Dante hasn't been Capo for very long. This is the perfect moment to force a change."

I swallowed, worrying where this was going. "Who are those friends?"

Antonio shook his head. "I can't tell you, but they want what's best for the Outfit. Once they are in power, I can safely return and be a part of the Outfit again."

"Did you tell them you were gay?"

"Not yet, but I will eventually."

"They won't accept you."

"That's for me to worry about when the time comes. What matters is that I will get the chance to live in Chicago again, to return to you."

"What is it you want me to do?" I asked quietly.

"It's too risky for us to attack Dante in the open. We don't want an open war. Once Dante is out of the way, things will fall into place. Old Fiore Cavallaro will be easier to dispose of once his son is dead. But we need you for our plan to work." Antonio pulled a small vial out of his pocket and checked the aisle, but we were the only customers, except for an elderly lady at the counter chatting up the pharmacist. He held out the vial in front of him. "You are the only one I trust enough to ask and who has direct access to Dante."

"What's that?" I whispered, even though I knew.

"It's poison, Val. All you have to do is sneak it into Dante's drink, and you'll be rid of him."

I backed away, out of Antonio's hold. My stomach was churning. "You want me to kill my husband?"

"I'm your husband, Val." Antonio grabbed my hand and pulled me toward him, eyes imploring. "Does he love you like I do? Does he even care about you? We've known each other all our lives."

I couldn't breathe. I searched Antonio's eyes for a sign that he was joking, but found none. He held out the vial. "Take it."

I grabbed the vial, stared at the colorless liquid inside of it.

"He won't notice. It's tasteless and odorless, don't worry."

I still didn't pocket the vial. I seemed unable to move a muscle.

"It works quickly. It's a muscle relaxant, and causes the lung and heart to stop working. A quicker death than he deserves."

"You really want me to kill someone?" My voice was almost toneless. "If something goes wrong and I'm found out, they'll kill me." Or more accurately, Dante would probably kill me himself after such a betrayal.

"You are too clever to be caught, Val. And once he's dead, we'll be taking over power in no time. You'll be under my protection. Everything will be fine." Antonio leaned down and brushed my lips lightly with his. I was too stunned to pull back. Slowly I eased the vial into my bag.

"You should do it tonight. The sooner we move, the better. I don't want to risk staying in Chicago like this for much longer."

"Does Frank know about all this?" I had to ask, had to know. I fought the tears that wanted to rise into my eyes.

"Yes. It was actually his suggestion. He thinks it's safer than risking a gunfight. Dante is a damn good shot, and the bastard never lowers his guard, except when he's home." Antonio smiled brightly at me. I was a means to an end for him—again. Once before he'd used my feelings for him to lure me into a fake marriage, and now he wanted to manipulate me into killing my husband. Maybe I should have tried to talk him out of it, but the moment I'd tried, he would have gotten suspicious, gone into hiding again and attacked Dante another time. It was too much of risk.

"I'd really feel more comfortable if I knew the names of your friends. I trust you, but what about them?"

"I trust them."

I gave him a pleading look.

Antonio brushed a strand of hair from my face. The gesture was so tender and loving that it made me choke up with emotion. Antonio must have seen it because he nodded. "I can give you one name, but the others will stay a secret until things have settled down."

"Okay."

"Raffaele, you know him from the casino, right?"

Oh, I knew Raffaele. And he was the last person in the Outfit who'd ever accept Antonio's homosexuality. "Yes, I do."

I was close to bursting into tears. To hide it from Antonio, I pretended to look at my watch. When I was sure I was in control of my emotions, I raised my face.

"So will you do it tonight?" Antonio asked almost eagerly. "For me, *for us?*"

I patted my bag where the vial was hidden, then I reached up and cupped Antonio's cheek. "I've loved you since I was fourteen. I was so happy when we married."

Antonio smiled, eyes brimming with satisfaction. "I know, Val. I should have been a better husband to you."

Yes, you should have been.

"But soon things will change. And this time everything will be better."

I nodded. *No, it won't.*

I drew back. "I need to return to the car before Enzo gets suspicious."

"Here's my number. Call me once it's done, okay?" He slipped a piece of paper into my pocket.

I nodded again.

"Say goodbye to Dante from me," Antonio said with a wink. He was still so very confident in the power he'd once held over me, but I wasn't the doting, naïve girl I used to be.

I turned around and slowly walked out of the pharmacy and back to the car.

Goodbye.

chapter *twenty*

I TWISTED THE VIAL IN MY HANDS OVER AND OVER AGAIN. THE TEARS had dried by now, and my face felt hot and sticky from crying, but my decision was made. There was only one thing I could do. Dante's step rang in the corridor, and I quickly pocketed the poison. The door opened and Dante stepped in, then stopped with a surprised look on his face when he saw me standing in front of the window.

"Valentina, what are you doing here?" His gaze swept over my teary face. "Did something happen? Are you all right?"

"We need to talk."

Dante closed the door slowly, every motion deliberate and calculated. He knew something was up. I didn't have to see my face to know it gave everything away, not only because of my swollen eyes. I had never been so shaken in my life as I was today. He approached me carefully, then stopped out of reach. I searched his face for something, some kind of gentleness, but he was only alert. This was the man who'd accused me of having cheated on him, who'd rejected our unborn child because he thought it wasn't his. A man who never let me get close. Would he ever love me? Would I ever find in this marriage what I so desperately wanted?

Dante's cold scrutiny was such a stark change from Antonio's tenderness and easygoing smiles. Antonio had promised me to give me what I wanted, to be a husband I deserved. Three years ago I'd have done everything to hear those words from him, even slipped poison into the glass of someone who wanted Antonio dead. But somehow in the last months of my marriage to Dante, something had changed. My heart had moved on from one unattainable man to the next. Despite everything Dante had said and done, he was my husband and I had come to love him, no matter how stupid that made me. He was the father of my child, even if he didn't want to believe it.

"Valentina?" A hint of impatience crept into Dante's voice.

"I saw Antonio today."

Dante frowned. "You went to his grave?"

"No," I said with a hysteric note. "I saw him in person. He isn't dead."

Dante became still. I could tell that he wasn't sure if he should believe me. He probably thought I was losing it. "What do you mean?"

Tears spilled out. "What I said. He isn't dead."

Dante's face hardened but he remained silent.

"That's why Frank contacted me. Antonio was there that night at the warehouse. He shot at us to save Frank. It wasn't the Russians."

"Why did you meet him without telling me after he tried to kill you once already?"

"I didn't! He followed me into the pharmacy today."

Suspicion was edged into Dante's face. "Why didn't you call Enzo? Where was he?" He didn't sound like a husband; he sounded like he was my Boss and I was one of his soldiers.

"I don't know. I was shocked. I thought Antonio was dead and then suddenly I'm staring at his face. I wanted to hear him out. He told me he faked his death to escape the Outfit and live with Frank."

"And now he's back. Does he want my forgiveness? I don't have any to give. I hope he doesn't expect me to give him a warm welcome. The only thing he can have is a quick death."

I wrapped my arms around my middle. "He doesn't want to ask for your forgiveness."

Dante searched my face.

"He wants you dead. He and a few others want you and your father gone so they can take over power."

Dante's jaw flexed. "Do they now? And how do they intend to do that?"

"Antonio asked me to poison you."

Dante's eyes bored into mine. "Why would he think you'd agree?"

"Because he's certain I still love him. Because he trusts me. Because it's probably obvious to everyone how unhappy I am." My hand unconsciously moved to my still mostly flat stomach. There was only the slightest bump visible when I was naked. Dante's eyes followed the movement, and some of the hardness around his eyes lessened. "And what did you tell him?"

I made an exasperated sound. "Would I be telling you about all this if I wanted to kill you? It was bad enough that you accused me of cheating and didn't believe me when I told you I was pregnant with your child, although you are the only man I've ever been with. But this? Thinking I'd agree to kill you, this is too much, even for me."

Dante walked up to me and touched my upper arms lightly. "I didn't ask what you decided. I didn't think you'd kill me. I asked what you told Antonio. There's a difference."

"I pretended to agree with his plan. I worried he'd find another way to kill you."

"Probably. And I bet he would have tried to kill you too."

I sucked in a breath. "Antonio would never harm me."

"Are you sure? This is a man who goes to great lengths to get his way, from what I know."

"I don't know. I don't know anything anymore."

Dante kept his hands on my arms. "Did he tell you who else is involved?"

I nodded numbly. "He mentioned Raffaele, but he didn't want to tell me the other names."

"Okay," Dante said gently. "Do you have a way to get in contact with him?"

"You are going to kill him."

"I'm going to kill them all, Valentina. I have to."

I stared into his determined blue eyes. No hesitation, no pity, no mercy. "I have his number."

"You will send him a text saying you gave me the poison, and now you're panicking because you don't know what to do with my dead body. Ask him to meet you at the warehouse again."

A tear slid down my cheek. Dante wiped it away with his thumb. "You know what's strange?" I whispered thickly. "At one point, I thought I could never love someone as I loved Antonio, no matter how unrequited that love was. And today I'm condemning him to his death for another man who will never love me back."

Dante's fingers froze against my face. His gaze flickered, and some tiny part of me hoped he'd say that he loved me. It would have made things easier. He cleared his throat. "We shouldn't wait too long. Maybe he'll realize it was stupid to contact you and he'll decide to go back into hiding. We need to reach him before that."

I drew away from his touch, and nodded. I reached into my bag for my phone, my fingers brushing the vial with the poison. I should tell Dante about it. I pulled out my phone and opened a text. I quickly typed what Dante had told me and sent it off. Afterward, I anxiously stared down at the screen. Less than a minute later, I got a reply.

Meet me in 30 minutes. Bring the body. I'll take care of everything.

"How am I supposed to get your body into my car?"

"I suppose dragging would work," Dante said dryly.

I laughed, then choked up. "What now? You will need reinforcements."

Dante shook his head. "I don't know who to trust right now. Not until I've talked to Antonio."

I knew he wouldn't just talk to him, and the thought sent a stab through my heart. "But what if Antonio isn't alone? Isn't it too risky for you to go by yourself? Maybe you should ask one of the guards. They have access to this house. If they wanted you dead, they'd probably have figured out a way to kill you by now."

"I'd rather get a picture of the situation before I involve anyone else. It's crucial that I don't look vulnerable in front of my men. I need to be in control at all times. I will handle this alone. Once I know more, I'll call my soldiers. They'll need to see what I do with traitors anyway."

I swallowed. "Can you kill Antonio quickly? You can get the information you want from Raffaele."

"Raffaele might get suspicious and disappear, or he might not know everything Antonio does. I'll have to make sure I find out exactly who's involved in this."

I touched his arm. "What if you get shot?"

"I can handle myself. I've fought many battles in my life. I wouldn't be Capo if I hadn't."

"I should come with you."

"No," Dante said immediately.

"What if Antonio doesn't come out until he sees me in my car? If they have binoculars they'll see it's you behind the steering wheel. They'll run off and we'll never find out who's behind this coup."

Dante regarded me with respect. "I won't risk your life."

"I won't get out of the car. It's bulletproof, remember? I'll be perfectly safe."

"You want to be there when I handle Antonio?"

I hesitated. That was the last thing I wanted. "No," I said honestly. "But there's no other way. Once the situation is under control and you call your men, I'll leave."

For a long time, Dante and I stared at each other. "You shouldn't risk your life for me. And it's not only your life on the line."

"Nothing will happen to me or our baby. I know you will protect us."

Dante didn't say anything. I wished he'd say he believed it was his baby, wished he'd take back the hurtful things he'd said. "Let's go then."

Dante hid under the backseat of the car while I drove. As we passed the gate, Enzo gave me a strange look but didn't try to stop me. Dante had two guns strapped into his gun holder and another one in his hand. There were also knives in the legroom, and I had a gun in the glove compartment. Not that it would do me much good. I'd never handled a gun in my life.

My pulse picked up when I steered the car toward the deserted parking lot in front of the abandoned storage facility. "We're almost there," I said.

"When you're in sight of Antonio, try not to speak to me unless it's absolutely necessary. He can't know you're not alone."

The meeting point came into sight. Antonio stood beside his car. From what I could make out, Frank wasn't with him, but he wasn't alone. My heart picked up its pace and my hands became clammy as I clutched the steering wheel tighter. There was a second car. Raffaele and two men I didn't know were inside.

"Antonio isn't alone," I whispered, barely moving my lips.

"How many?"

"Three others. Raffaele, and two men I don't recognize."

Dante pulled out his phone and brought it to his ear. "Enzo, prepare the crew. I need to dispose of some rats. Take only the inner circle with you." He quickly gave Enzo the address, then he hung up.

I slowed the car and forced a shaky smile onto my face when I came to a stop a few feet from where Antonio stood. He looked anxious and kept glancing toward Raffaele, who was getting out the car, followed by the man from the backseat. Why had Antonio brought Raffaele to a meeting with me? Raffaele hated me. He'd rather see me dead than see me at Antonio's side.

What if Dante was right, and Antonio wanted to get rid of me too? I didn't want to believe it. I turned off the engine. After another look toward Raffaele, Antonio headed toward my car. I tensed but forced my face to give nothing away. When he'd almost reached me, his eyes settled on the backseat and he jerked to a stop. His gaze darted to me for the briefest moment before his lips opened, probably to shout a warning. It was too late.

Dante pushed open the door and pointed his gun at Antonio. My stomach shriveled with sadness and guilt when the first bullet hit Antonio in the stomach. The second went straight through his right hand, which had been about to pull his gun. Antonio dropped to the ground, clutching his middle, face contorted with pain.

I clawed at the steering wheel with all my might. Part of my brain screamed at me to grab the gun from the glove compartment to have some kind of protection, but the other, the louder part was just screaming. Screaming in anguish and horror and guilt.

Dante was shielded by the bulletproof car door as he fired his next shot. The bullet tore through the throat of the man who'd gotten out of the car after Raffaele.

Raffaele was trying to reach the safety of his own car, firing bullet after bullet in our direction, but none of them could burst through our protective windows.

When Raffaele dove for the passenger door of his car, Dante stepped out from behind the door that had been shielding him. My heart pounded wildly in my chest as he squared his shoulders and aimed calmly. In quick succession Dante pulled the trigger, hitting Raffaele first in his left, then in his right kneecap. Raffaele dropped to the ground, face twisted in agony. The man behind the steering wheel of the car hit the gas, not even bothering to close his passenger door, as he tried to escape and save his own life. Three other cars, Dante's reinforcement, were already heading our way at dizzying speed, but Dante didn't let the enemy car get away. He aimed his gun at the tires and hit them one after the other, causing the man to lose control of the car, which started spinning and finally collided with the abandoned warehouse. Airbags shot open, filling the car and hiding the driver momentarily from view.

Now that silence fell over the area, I released a harsh breath and kept my eyes straight ahead. If I looked back, toward where Antonio was slowly bleeding to death, I'd lose it. He shouldn't have come to me, shouldn't have asked me to kill Dante. He should have known better. Now there was nothing I could do for him, except hope that Dante wouldn't prolong his agony for too long. Tears blurred my vision, and my knuckles were stark white and throbbing from my grip on the steering wheel. From the corner of my eye, I could make out Raffaele. His legs useless, he was dragging himself forward with his arms, leaving behind a streak of blood on the dusty asphalt.

The cars with Dante's reinforcement came to a halt next to me. Enzo shot me a short glance before he jogged toward Dante. I didn't know what they were saying, but Enzo walked toward Raffaele, grabbed him by the scruff of his neck and yanked him upright. Of course Raffaele's legs gave way again, and Enzo started dragging him behind despite Raffaele's cries of pain. With the help of Taft, they loaded Raffaele into the car beside mine.

Dante appeared at my window. I couldn't even move to open it. My fingers, my body, my entire being seemed paralyzed. After a moment, Dante opened the door. He squatted beside me. It was an unusual enough gesture for him that my eyes settled on his face. "Valentina," Dante said carefully. "Are you capable of driving yourself home, or do you want one of my men to do it?"

I want you. I need you, now more than ever. "No, I'm okay. I can drive."

Dante scrutinized me. His hair was still perfectly combed back, his suit as impeccable as ever. Nothing that indicated he'd just killed one man and wounded three others. "I'll send Taft with you," he said firmly. "It'll be a while before I'll be home." He didn't need to say more. I didn't want to hear more. I nodded simply. Dante stood and waved Taft over, who slipped into the passenger seat without a word. He slanted me a quick look. I probably looked as if I was close to losing it. And that was exactly how I was feeling.

Dante hesitated before he shut my door and took a few steps back from the car. As if in a trance, I pressed my foot down on the gas. I didn't look back, couldn't. I'd said my goodbye to Antonio this afternoon. No, actually I'd said goodbye to him a long time ago.

Taft kept looking my way. I was driving too slow, but he didn't comment. My throat was tight and I was feeling sick, but not the sickness I'd experienced as part of my pregnancy. This was something that seemed to take hold of my entire body, but I fought it. I needed to keep up appearances. Dante was a proud and strong man, and I was his wife. I wouldn't throw up in front of one of his men.

I wasn't sure how long it took to reach the manor, but if felt like eternity. When I finally parked the car in the garage, I was on the verge of a nervous breakdown. I opened my door and stepped out. As I headed for the door leading into the house, my legs buckled. Strong hands grabbed me under the arms and stopped me from hitting the floor hard. Driven by pure determination, I forced my legs to stop shaking. "Are you all right?" Taft asked. "Should I call the Boss?"

"No," I said quickly. "He's got to take care of business." Of Antonio. A new wave of sickness crashed down on me. I stepped forward, out of Taft's hold, my head high and back stiff. Barely breathing, I made my way into the house and, clutching the banister in a death grip, I dragged myself upstairs. I stumbled into the master bedroom and straight into the bathroom, where I emptied my stomach into the toilet. My abdomen constricted painfully and for a moment I froze in fear, but then the sensation was gone.

I stood and slowly, shakily began undressing, letting my clothes lie strewn about on the floor. I turned the shower on and stepped under the stream of hot water, closing my eyes and finally letting sobs wrack my body. I leaned against the shower stall and slowly glided down until I sat on the cold marble floor. I pulled my legs tightly against my chest, and cried. Cried for Antonio, for the boy I'd grown up with, for the man I'd once loved, for someone I'd betrayed the Outfit for once before. But today I'd made a decision, and it had been against Antonio. I'd known what it would mean for him, had known I'd signed his death warrant the moment I told Dante about the plan. And yet I hadn't even hesitated. I'd chosen Dante, and I'd choose him again. He was my husband, he was the father of my unborn child, he was the man I loved even if he'd never given me reason to. I buried my face against my legs, hurting, hurting so much I couldn't stand it. There was blood on my hands now. I cried even harder.

That's how Dante found me. I wasn't sure how much time had passed, how long he'd been gone. I was shivering, skin shriveled and red from the hot water. Dante stood in the doorway for a couple of moments, watching me, before he strode toward the shower. He wasn't wearing the same clothes he'd worn when I'd last seen him. He'd changed. Had to change. My throat closed up. I stared up at him, shaking and crying silently. He reached into the shower, still fully dressed, and shut the water off. His cool blue eyes settled on me as I cowered on the ground. There was concern and sympathy, riddled with something raw and dark in his face. I didn't move, couldn't.

He bent down, slid his arms under me and slowly straightened with me pressed against his chest, soaking his expensive shirt. My fingers clawed at his shoulders almost desperately. He set me carefully down, but didn't let go of me. I wasn't sure I could have stood on my own. He grabbed a towel and started drying me unhurriedly, his eyes following his hands as they rubbed the fluffy fabric over my skin. I pressed my face into the crook of his neck, soaking in his familiar scent, now mixed with gunpowder and blood. Blood. Sweet and metallic. Blood, so much blood.

"Oh God," I gasped, and gasped, and gasped but couldn't breathe. Dante lifted me into his arms again and carried me into the bedroom, where he lowered me on our bed. He took off his shoes and lay down beside me, cradling my face until my frantic gaze settled on his intense eyes. "Shh, Val. It's okay."

But it wasn't, couldn't be. "I killed him." I squeezed my eyes shut against the images my mind created, but they were even more colorful against the black canvas of my closed eyelids. "I killed him," I repeated over and over again, until I wasn't sure if the words still left my lips or if it was an echo in my ears.

"Val," Dante said firmly, his fingers on my face tightening. "Look at me."

I peeled my eyes open, staring at the beautiful face of my husband. Beautifully cold. Not a flicker of regret.

"You did what was right."

Did I? Sometimes it was hard to see the line between right and wrong from all the death and blood plastering the mob's paths.

"You did what you had to do to protect me." His fingers stroked my chin. "I won't ever forget it. Never."

"I told you that you could trust me," I whispered.

"I know, and I do."

I wanted to believe him, but he still hadn't said anything about our child, still hadn't admitted that it was his, that he'd been wrong to accuse me of cheating. Too proud, too stubborn. He must have known he was wrong all along, because if he'd ever really thought I had cheated on him he would have moved heaven and earth to find the man who touched me. I didn't want to think about it, but as my mind shied away from one hurtful topic, it latched on to the next. "Did you get the names of the other traitors?"

Dante nodded grimly. "Yes. I'm fairly sure. Enzo and a few others are taking care of the less important rats right now."

"What...what did you do to Antonio?" I knew I shouldn't ask. It wouldn't make things better. It would only add fuel to the fire that was my guilt.

Dante shook his head. "He's dead, Val."

"I know, but what did you do to him?"

"If it's any consolation for you, I focused my main attention on Raffaele. Antonio got a quicker death than any other traitor."

Tears pooled in my eyes. "Thank you." What kind of twisted world did we live in that I thanked my husband for killing my first husband quickly, for keeping the torture to a minimum? A world of blood and death. A world our child would be born into and grow up in, and maybe one day, if he was a boy, he'd follow in Dante's footsteps and kill and torture others to stay in power. An endless circle of blood and death.

Dante searched my eyes. "Val, you're worrying me."

I raised my head and pressed my tear-slick lips against Dante's. He didn't pull back, only watched me with furrowed brows. I drew back a couple of inches, my fingers curling in his hair, my eyes pleading. "Please," I said quietly. "Make love to me. Just today. I know you don't love me. Pretend, just for tonight. Hold me in your arms for once."

Tumultuous wasn't the right word to describe the look in Dante's eyes, but it was the only thing that came to my mind. "God, Val." He released a harsh breath, then he pressed his lips to mine, parting them and tasting me, tasting my tears, my sorrow, and somehow taking some of it away with every brush of his mouth. His hand ghosted over my collarbone, my arm, my side, my hip, like a whisper of a touch, barely there and yet the only thing I was aware of. He sat up and quickly unbuttoned his shirt before throwing it mindlessly to the ground, and then his bare chest was pressed up against me, so warm and solid. He left cotton-soft kisses on my temple, forehead and cheek before he found my lips again for a kiss that took my breath away.

His hand discovered my breast as if for the very first time, fingertips laying featherlight touches on my skin, laying claim to me without the usual burning possessiveness. I moaned against his mouth as his fingers traveled the length of my body to slip between my legs. He nudged them apart and then he lightly explored my folds, gentle and unhurried. I whimpered softly, but Dante silenced me with another kiss before he nuzzled my neck and collarbone. When his lips finally closed around my nipple, I was already panting. Dante slipped one, then two fingers into me before he got off the bed and stood. He made quick work of his remaining clothes, and then he was on the bed, gloriously naked and hard. He settled between my legs and lowered himself to his elbows, molding our bodies together like we were one. He didn't enter me. Instead his hand caressed my leg and raised it until it was curled over his back. His erection pressed against my inner thigh, but Dante didn't seem in any hurry. He kissed me, his eyes dark and probing as they watched me. He lightly petted my breast, making me ache for him to finally claim me.

He must have seen the need on my face because he reached between us and lined his erection up with my entrance. His claim didn't come in one swift, hard move as so often in the past. It was a slow conquest, and my walls yielded to him as they always did. I gasped when he was buried completely inside me. Dante cradled the back of my head, his forearms braced to both sides of my face, and then he started to move in me. Time seemed to stand still as our bodies glided against each other. Was this lovemaking?

I wrapped my arms around Dante, trying to bring him even closer. Dante didn't resist. He brought his face down to mine, kissed my lips, then my cheeks until his mouth brushed my ear. "I should have made love to you before," he said in a low voice.

And I cried in response. I wasn't sure if this was part of his pretense, and I didn't care. In this moment, it felt real, and that was all that mattered to me. When Dante shuddered under his release, he took me with him, and even afterward as he started to soften inside me, he didn't pull away.

He lay on top of me, still buried in me, his breathing fanning over my cheek. I knew many women in our world preferred a beautiful lie to the harsh truth any day, and for the first time, I understood. After all that had happened today, I allowed myself that weakness. Tomorrow would be the time to face reality.

chapter *twenty-one*

When I left the house before breakfast the next morning, Dante wasn't there. I hadn't expected him to be—he hadn't lain beside me when I'd woken either. Yesterday I'd forced him to let me closer than he was comfortable with, and now he would be pulling away until we were barely civil again. I waved Taft over and he approached me at once. "I need you to drive me to Bibiana," I said as we walked into the garage. He grabbed the keys, slid into the car and then we were already off. Time was important. "Hurry," I added when we pulled away from the house. Taft didn't ask why.

The moment we parked in front of Bibiana's house, I got out of the car and hurried toward the entrance door. I rang the bell. I knew Tommaso was still home because there wasn't a guard sitting in a car in the street. I'd hoped for that.

I could hear Tommaso shouting angrily, and then there were quick steps and Bibiana opened the door, still in her bathrobe. Her eyes widened with confusion when she saw me. "Val? Tommaso told me what happened yesterday. Are you okay?" There was a hand-shaped bruise on her cheek, and it made my decision easier.

I pulled her against me in a hug and pushed the vial with poison into her palm. "Nobody knows I have this. It's poison, Bibi. If you really want to be free, then slip it into his breakfast today. Tomorrow it'll be too late. Today we can still blame it on the traitors. Nobody will ask questions." I straightened with a smile, my face the mask I'd learned from Dante. Bibi smiled back, but there was surprise and incredulity and gratitude in her eyes.

"Bibiana, what's taking you so long?" Tommaso bellowed as he trudged down the staircase. He paused when he spotted me. Bibiana quickly hid the poison vial in her bathrobe.

"I'm sorry for disturbing you," I said. "I only wanted to make sure Bibiana knew I'm all right. I don't have much time though. I need to get back home."

"Dante called for a meeting of the entire Outfit. Just got the email. I suppose you can't give me details about what went down?"

I shook my head. "I should really go." I gave Bibiana a smile, then I turned on my heel and walked back to the car. The last thing I heard was Bibi telling Tommaso she would make him a quick breakfast before he left.

This was the second man I'd condemned to death. This time, however, I felt no guilt.

"Valentina, I'd like to talk to you," Dante said before disappearing back in his office. I hesitated. This was the first time that Dante had actually asked me into his office for a conversation. All the times before, I had to seek him out.

Worry gnawed at my insides as I stepped into his office and closed the door behind me. Dante was facing the window but turned to me. For a long time his blue eyes searched my face. "Tommaso didn't show up at the meeting I'd called."

I forced my face to stay expressionless. "So?"

"The men I sent over to get him found him dead in his living room. Poisoned."

"What about Bibiana?" I asked, trying to sound worried and shocked. She hadn't sent me a text or tried to call me. It would have been too risky anyway.

"She's with her parents now, but I'll have to drive over there now to question her."

I froze. "Why?"

"Because as Capo, I need to investigate when one of my men gets killed." Dante slowly advanced on me. "Of course, I'm fairly sure I know what happened."

I raised my chin as he stopped in front of me. "You do?" I held his gaze—anything else would have looked guilty, even if it was probably too late for that anyway.

"You are best friends with Bibiana and you wanted to help her." I didn't say anything, but he didn't seem to expect me to. He continued in the same quiet, smooth voice. "Antonio gave you poison when he asked you to kill me, didn't he?"

I considered lying to him, but I needed him on my side, and he wouldn't take being lied to kindly. "Yes," I said softly.

"You didn't tell me about it because you knew it was your chance to help Bibiana, so you took it to her and told her to blame it on Raffaele."

"Did she say that?"

"She mentioned Raffaele visited them yesterday when my men took her to her parents, but she was too hysterical to say much."

Was Bibi regretting what she'd done? Or had her breakdown been for show? "So why don't you believe it was Raffaele?"

Dante's eyes narrowed. "Because he would have mentioned it when I interrogated him."

I nodded. "So what now?"

Dante shook his head. "Goddamnit, Valentina. You should have come to me."

"I did come to you. I asked you if there was something you could do against Tommaso, but you said there wasn't."

"You asked me to kill him and I told you I couldn't because he wasn't a traitor."

I scoffed. "As if that matters. You are a killer, Dante. You can kill whoever you want. Don't tell me you've never killed for other reasons than protecting the Outfit."

Dante gripped my shoulders, bringing us even closer. "Of course, I have. But I told you 'no' and you should have listened to me."

"Because your word is law," I said mockingly.

"Yes," Dante said in a low voice. "Even for you."

"I would do it again. I don't regret freeing Bibi of that cruel bastard. I only regret that I had to go behind your back, but you left me no choice."

Dante's eyes flashed. "I left you no choice? You can't go around killing my men!"

"He deserved it. You should have seen what he did to Bibi. You should have wanted to kill him for how he treated an innocent woman, wife or not."

"If I killed every man in the Outfit who treated women badly, I'd be left with half of my soldiers. This is a life of brutality and cruelty, and many soldiers don't understand that as Made Men we should protect our family from it, and not unleash our anger on them. They know I don't approve of their actions. That's all I can do."

"But I was handed the chance to do something, and I did."

"You helped a wife murder her husband. Some men in my position would find it unsettling to be with a woman who doesn't hesitate to use poison."

My eyes grew wide. "I gave Bibi a chance, a choice. That doesn't mean I would kill you. I would fight you if you ever treated me like Tommaso did with Bibi. Tommaso preyed on Bibi's weakness. She was given to that old bastard when she was only eighteen, and she never knew how to defend herself against him. He's had four years to be a better man, to treat her decently. He failed. Our marriage has nothing to do with theirs. You don't need to beat and rape me to feel like a man, and I wouldn't let you. And anyway, I'm not vengeful, or I wouldn't have swallowed how you treated me the last few months, how you accused me of cheating. And Bibi never loved Tommaso, so…" I trailed off, clamping my lips shut. The last part wasn't supposed to slip out.

Dante's fingers on my shoulders loosened. I looked away from his penetrating gaze, unable to stand it.

"I'm not worried that you'd poison me. As I said before, I trust you," he said after a while, dropping his hands from my shoulders. "But I'll have to investigate Tommaso's death."

"You won't punish Bibi, will you?" I asked, terrified. "Please, Dante, if you care about me at all, you'll rule that Tommaso's murder was related to the traitors and that Bibi is innocent. She's gone through too much already."

"There might be people out there who won't believe Bibiana wasn't involved in Tommaso's death, for exactly the reasons you stated before. She had reason to hate him. She had reason to kill him."

"Then blame it on me. I could have done it behind Bibi's back to help her."

"And then what?" Dante asked quietly.

"Then you punish me and not her."

"And what if punishment for such a crime would be death in turn? Eye for an eye, Valentina."

I stared, tears brimming in my eyes. "Don't hurt Bibi. Just don't. Without me, she would have never found a way to kill him. It was as much my fault as it was hers. I will share whatever punishment you inflict on her."

"I fear you're saying that because you know I won't punish you," Dante said, a dark smile on his lips.

"You won't?"

Dante kissed me hard, then pulled back and lightly brushed my abdomen. Was it because of our baby? Or was I reading too much into the gesture? Or maybe he'd touched my stomach by accident. "As long as I rule the Outfit, you won't be harmed."

He stepped back. "I need to go talk to Bibiana now."

"Let me go with you," I said hastily.

"Your father and my Consigliere will be there as well, so don't interrupt. I don't want them to suspect you. Your father would overlook it, but I would hate to have to force Rocco into silence over this."

It had been a while since I'd been at Bibiana's childhood home. I never liked her parents much. That hadn't changed when they'd forced Bibi into a marriage with an old man. My father and Rocco Scuderi were waiting in front of the door for us. When we walked up to them, Papà pulled me into a hug, kissed my temple and pressed his palm against my abdomen. "So how are you?"

I could feel Dante's eyes on us. Scuderi, too, was watching with hawk-eyes. I wasn't sure if he knew about my pregnancy. It wasn't public knowledge yet, but soon it would be hard to hide. A closer look was already enough to raise suspicions. "I'm good," I said in a whisper.

Papà nodded, then stepped back. "Are you here to support Bibiana?"

I gave him a nod, but was distracted when the door opened and Bibiana's parents welcomed us into their house. Bibiana was in the living room, wrapped in a blanket. I rushed over to her and pulled her into a tight hug. "I did it. I really did it," she whispered into my ear.

"Shhh," I murmured, patting her back. When I pulled away, Dante, my father and Rocco Scuderi stood beside us. Bibi stiffened, eyes fearful as they darted between us. Her parents hovered in the doorway. If Bibi had been my child, I wouldn't have left her side in a moment like this.

"They're here to question you because of Tommaso's death. It's standard procedure. Everything will be fine," I told her.

Dante approached us. "It would be best if we could have a word alone with Bibiana," he said to me. Bibiana's parents left without a word of protest. I stood but didn't move. Dante's imploring gaze made me back away a few steps. Bibiana rose, then looked at Dante fearfully as he stood before her. She was practically cowering and it brought out my protective side, but Dante shot me a warning glare. He wanted me to trust him, to let him handle this, and I knew I had no choice. After an encouraging smile at Bibi, I left the living room, but I didn't go far. I pressed my ear against the door, trying to listen in on their conversation. They spoke too quietly, which would have been a good sign under normal circumstances. No raised voices should have been a positive thing, but Dante was his most dangerous when he was quiet.

Fifteen minutes later, I heard steps approaching the door and quickly backed away. Papà opened the door and beckoned me in. "Everything's okay," he said when he saw my worried expression. I walked in. Bibi sat on the sofa, her cheeks wet with tears, while Dante and Scuderi stood near the window, talking in quiet voices. I hurried over to her and sat. She gripped my hand immediately and I squeezed.

Her parents came in when Dante turned to us. "The men most likely responsible for Tommaso's death are dead. There's no punishment to dole out, so I rule the case closed." I almost sagged with relief.

"Does that mean we are allowed to look for a new husband for our daughter? Recently the habit of waiting a year has been loosened," Bibiana's father said and was of course referring to me. That bastard. Bibiana had barely been freed from one husband they had chosen for her, and they were already eager to find someone new.

Dante's answering glower made the other man lower his head. "Bibiana is pregnant with Tommaso's child."

My eyes flew to Bibi, who gave me a small happy smile. "I suspected for a while, but I got confirmation this morning," she whispered.

Her parents looked like they'd been punched. They could hardly marry off a pregnant widow. That would be in bad taste. Bibi met their disappointed glares head-on. "I'm not going to move back in with you."

"I give you my word that your daughter will be safe in the house she shared with Tommaso," Dante said.

I had to hide a smile. Bibi's parents couldn't argue with that. After that, Dante and I drove Bibi back to her house. Although we didn't talk about what had really happened, Bibi's relieved expression left hardly any doubt. She tried to look solemn whenever she remembered herself, but most of the time her relief spoke too loud.

I was glad Dante knew the truth. He would have figured it out anyway. When Bibi had gotten out of the car and we were on our way home, I put my hand on his leg.

Dante's eyes registered surprise. I usually honored his reluctance for public displays of affection. "Thank you for helping Bibi."

"I did it for you," he said simply. That was probably as close to a declaration of what—Love? Affection?—I'd ever get from him.

"Thank you." I pulled my hand away again and rested it in my lap, but Dante took me by surprise when he reached for my hand, brought it up to his face and pressed a kiss against my knuckles. My breath caught in my throat, and immediately tears gathered in my eyes. Such a small gesture shouldn't have meant so much, but it did, and pregnancy hormones didn't help. Dante didn't let go of my hand and sent me a questioning look. "Valentina? Are you all right?"

"It's the hormones. I'm sorry. Just ignore me."

Dante rested our linked hands on his thigh and drove with one hand. He didn't comment as I wiped my eyes and pressed my free hand against the small bump of my stomach.

chapter *twenty-two*

In the weeks following Tommaso's death, Bibiana blossomed to new life. She seemed to thrive in the solitude of her home. I wished I could handle loneliness as well. Dante was busier than ever. He wanted to make sure that the rest of his men were behind him one hundred percent. That didn't leave much time for me, except for the nights he woke me with caresses and kisses. Since I'd asked him to make love to me after Antonio's death, he'd allowed more closeness during sex, had often held me in his arms, but I had a feeling he still preferred to be behind me as it allowed him to keep his distance.

I spent my days either working in the casino, or with Bibiana or Ines, who'd become a stronger presence in my life as my pregnancy progressed. Today Bibiana, Ines and I had agreed to go shopping together. Of course baby clothing was the number one item on our agenda for the day.

When we walked into our first baby store, Ines asked the question I knew she'd been dying to ask for hours. "So how's Dante dealing with the pregnancy?"

"He's not dealing at all," I said casually. I didn't want Ines to know how much it bothered me that he hadn't asked me about our baby directly once. He always inquired about how I was and was increasingly careful when we slept together, but the word "baby" never left his mouth. He hadn't even asked if it was a boy or girl yet. "Most of the time he pretends there is no pregnancy."

Ines eyed my protruding stomach. It still wasn't too obvious when I wore a loose-fitting blouse, as I was only twenty-six weeks along, but of course Dante saw it all the time. "He's being impossible. Do you want me to talk to him?"

"God, no," I said quickly, then sent Ines an apologetic smile. "But thank you. Dante would be furious if you interfered."

"You're probably right. I still don't like it. Sometimes I don't understand men. Why can't they admit when they messed up?"

I shrugged. It was something I'd wondered so often, but it never got me far. Bibiana held up a cute onesie with "Lock up your boys, my Dad owns a gun" written across the front. "Not that anyone needs the reminder, but why not? You should get something like this." She grinned, then sobered. "Is something wrong?"

I wasn't sure. There was a strange twinge in my lower abdomen. Maybe my little baby was lying in an awkward position and pressing down on my kidneys. "I'm fine," I said. I picked up the same onesie. "I don't even know if it's a girl."

"I really hope it is, then our girls can play together." Bibiana was only eighteen weeks along, but she had already asked the doc about the gender. She'd been relieved when she found out it was a girl because she worried a boy might remind her too much of Tommaso.

"I want to be surprised." That wasn't true. I was curious. I'd been from the moment I'd found out I was pregnant, but I wanted Dante at my side when the doctor told me the sex of our baby. I wasn't sure that was ever going to happen though.

"I don't know how you do it. I'm way too curious," Bibiana said.

Ines nodded. "That, and Pietro desperately wanted to know if he was getting an heir. I guess with twins we really had the perfect result for both of us." She laughed, then quieted when she saw my face. "Did my parents bother you? I know my father is eager for Dante to have a son who can become Capo in the future. Don't let them pressure you."

"I don't see them very often," I said. "But of course they asked me about the gender. Your father didn't seem very happy when I told him I didn't want to know."

"Men. I'm really surprised Dante isn't more interested in finding out if he'll have an heir soon. But he's always been laid-back about these things. Many men would have found a way to produce an heir elsewhere if their wife was infertile, but Dante never blamed Carla. He stood by her even when our father urged him to find a mistress to impregnate."

"That's horrible," I said. There was still an odd pressure in my lower abdomen, but it seemed to get better now that we weren't walking so much anymore.

"It is. Father suggested Dante and Carla could bring up the child as their own, but Dante refused to do it."

"Maybe because he worried it was him who didn't deliver," Bibiana said quietly. I shrugged. I didn't want to talk about this in public. Dante wouldn't be happy if he found out. Of course, now we knew that it must have been Carla who was infertile, even if Dante and I hadn't talked about it again since our major fight.

"So what do you say?" Bibi asked with a bright smile, still holding up that onesie with the cute quote.

I nodded with a resigned smile. "Okay. I'll get it. Even if I'm having a boy, maybe next time it'll be a girl, so it's not like I'm wasting money."

Ines touched my belly lightly. "I can't wait. Nothing's better than the scent of a newborn and those tiny toes and fingers."

"True," I said as I peered into the stroller where Ines' little girl was sleeping deeply.

Bibi and I both bought the onesies. Then we said goodbye to Ines, who headed back to her car with her own bodyguard, while Taft trailed after me and Bibi as we walked back to the Mercedes. He pretended he wasn't there. For which I was grateful. When I was married to Antonio, I often went out of the house on my own, but that was a thing of the past now.

Taft drove us back to my house. Bibi and I wanted to spend the rest of the afternoon together, browsing books with baby names and eating the delicious Italian almond cake Zita had baked this morning.

The slight discomfort in my belly I'd felt all day increased as we walked up the few steps to the front door and entered my home. Taft excused himself quietly and would probably return to the guardhouse now that he was no longer needed. It was quiet in the house, except for the distant rumble of male voices. Dante was probably still in a meeting.

"Come on. Let's take our purchases upstairs. I want to show you the lamp I bought for the nursery," I told Bibiana.

I put my foot on the first step and froze. A sharp pain shot through my belly. I dropped the bags I'd been carrying and clutched my stomach immediately as my other hand shot out to hold on to the banister. Something warm trickled down my legs. I looked down my body in horror. My beige pants were quickly turning darker. Did my water just break? It was too soon. Way too soon. It didn't seem like enough water, but what did I know?

Bibiana let out a shocked cry. I was too stunned to utter a word. "Valentina? Talk to me."

"It's too soon," I said quietly. Fourteen weeks too soon. I began shaking as I clutched my belly.

"You're bleeding," Bibiana whispered. She was right. My pants had a light red tinge. My vision swam.

"We need an ambulance," Bibiana said. Then she shook her head. "We need to call Dante."

My legs started shaking, and I had to lean against the wall or risk falling. Dante was in an important meeting. And I wasn't even sure if he wanted this child. He probably still thought I'd cheated on him to conceive. "No, Dante is busy."

Bibi gave me an incredulous look. "The hell he is. Help! Help!" she started screaming.

I was busy staying on my feet, so I didn't try to stop her. The door to Dante's office was ripped open and Dante charged out, gun in hand. My father and Rocco Scuderi were behind him, their own weapons drawn. Dante's fiery eyes settled on me, and the fury slid off his face and was replaced by panic.

"Valentina?" Dante said as he rushed toward me, already putting his gun back in his holster. "What's happening?"

"It's nothing. I didn't want to disturb your meeting."

Dante wrapped an arm around my back as my legs gave away. His gaze traveled down my wet pants. I'd never seen that look on his face. Was he really worried about me? I gasped as pain sliced through me again. My father appeared in front of me. "Valentina?"

"We need to get her to a hospital," Bibiana said sharply.

Dante nodded and lifted me up.

"Your shirt. You're getting it dirty."

Dante held me even tighter and carried me outside. At once, Taft and Enzo stormed in our direction. "I want you to make up the front," Dante ordered. The calm efficiency was replaced by something urgent in his voice. They nodded before they rushed off. My father held open the passenger door of the Mercedes and Dante gently sat me down.

"I'll get your mother," Father said as he touched my cheek. "We'll be in the hospital soon."

He closed the door, and the moment Dante slipped behind the steering wheel, he revved up the engine and we shot out of the garage and down the driveway. The car with Enzo and Taft waited at the front but shot onto the street when we'd almost reached them.

Dante drove well over the speed limit. Every bump in the street made me wince. The pain wasn't as strong anymore, now there was only a dull ache, but what if that was a bad sign? "We should have put a towel on the seat. I'm getting it wet," I said.

Dante glanced my way. "I don't give a fuck about the seat, or the car, or anything right now. You are all that matters." He reached out and took my hand, which was resting on my belly. "We're almost there. Are you in pain?"

"It's not as bad as before," I whispered. Then, because I just couldn't let it drop, "It is your baby, Dante. I never cheated and I never will."

Dante sucked in his breath. "Is that the reason for this?"

"You think my water broke because I was upset with you?"

"I don't know." There was something close to despair on his face. "I'm a fucking bastard, Val. If you lose this child..." He shook his head and focused back on the windshield as we pulled up in front of the hospital entrance. The car with our guards was already there, and so were a doctor and a nurse with a stretcher. Dante jumped out of the car and jogged around the hood to help them get me out of the car. Once I'd lain down on the stretcher, I was rolled into the hospital. Dante never left my side. And he only let go of my hand when he got in the way of the doctors and nurses.

After hours of ultrasounds, blood work and all kinds of other checkups, I was finally rolled into a room. I was tired and scared, though not as badly as before. Dante settled on the edge of the mattress and brushed a few strands of hair from my face. My eyelids were heavy but I didn't want to sleep. Dante had talked to the doctors, as I didn't feel like my brain could follow their explanations right now. "What did they say?" I asked.

"He said you had a preterm rupture of membranes. That's why you lost some of your amniotic fluid."

"What does it mean? Do they have to deliver our baby early?" Fear felt like a vice around my throat. It would be too soon. What if I lost our child?

Dante settled himself against the pillow and pulled me against his chest. "No, they don't. It didn't rupture completely, but of course there's a higher risk of an infection now, which is why you'll have to take antibiotics for a while. You didn't go into labor, so that's a plus. They hope to delay the birth until week thirty at least. You'll have to stay in bed as much as possible and aren't allowed to exert yourself in any way."

"Okay," I whispered. "I just want our baby to be safe."

"It will be. We won't let anything happen to her," Dante said in his calm, soothing voice.

I startled. "Her?"

Dante nodded. "I asked the doctor. They could see it when they did the ultrasound. It's a girl."

I wanted to be happy, and I was. I would love our child no matter if it was a girl or a boy, but I knew what was expected of me. I licked my dry lips, searching Dante's eyes. "Are you angry because it isn't a boy? I know you need an heir. Your father—"

Dante cupped my cheek, stopping me from saying more."I'm happy. I don't care if it's a boy or a girl. And my father will eventually see reason."

He sounded honest, but I knew the realities of mob life, and the need for a Made Man to have a boy who could follow in his footsteps, be inducted into the mafia and guarantee the success of the Outfit. A man needed a son to be fully respected by his fellow Made Men. "You don't have to sugarcoat things for me, Dante. I know how things work in our world."

Dante pulled back a few inches, eyebrows raised. "I'm not sugarcoating anything. I told you the truth. I'm happy that we're having a daughter. I'll be happy about every child we have. I'm not going to lie—many people in the Outfit will see it as something less desirable. They will only really congratulate me once you're pregnant with a boy, but I don't care about them. You're still young, and we have time. We'll have more children and maybe there'll be a boy among them. But for now let's be happy about our daughter."

"Are you happy?" I asked, already getting teary again. That was the one thing I hated most about being pregnant: my loss of self-control when it came to my emotions, especially my tears. "Since I told you I was pregnant, you never once asked about the baby. You pretended it wasn't there. You made me feel horrible for something that should have been cause for joy. Why did you change your mind? Because I almost lost our baby?"

"I didn't change my mind. I've been happy about your pregnancy for a while now."

I gave him a doubtful look. "That's not what I saw."

"I'm good at hiding my thoughts and emotions," Dante said regretfully. "But I shouldn't have done it in this case. You are right, I ruined your first weeks of pregnancy for you. All because I was too proud to admit I'd been wrong."

I waited patiently for him to say more. I wasn't ready to accept his unspoken apology yet.

Dante rested his palm lightly on my stomach. "You were right during our fight after you told me about your pregnancy. I never wanted Carla to see a doctor about her inability to conceive because I didn't want to find out it was me who was infertile. I'm a proud man, Val. Too proud, and somehow I had convinced myself that I couldn't become Capo if I found out I was incapable of getting my wife with child. I would have been half a man."

"No, you wouldn't. But I understand where you're coming from. But if that's the case, then why weren't you elated when I told you I was pregnant with your child? After all, that meant you weren't infertile. Shouldn't you have been proud?"

Dante's smile was solemn. "Yes, I suppose I should have been." He paused, and I gave him the time he needed to figure out his next words. I had a feeling he'd share something very personal with me. "But when you told me about your pregnancy, it almost felt like an attack on Carla's memory, as if you were blaming Carla for her inability to give me children by getting pregnant so quickly."

"I never wanted to attack your wife," I said, horrified. "I know you loved her more than anything. I knew it before we married, and you never let me forget it in all the time we've been together." The last part came out more accusatory than intended.

"I know," Dante said, his cool blue eyes tracing my face. "I treated you badly. You did nothing to deserve it. When you gave yourself to me for the first time, I should have held you afterward. It would have been the decent, the honorable thing to do. Instead, I left. I didn't want to allow myself to be close to you. I'd allowed myself to love once, and after I had to watch Carla die a slow, horrible death, I'd sworn to myself that I wouldn't let a woman into my life again."

I nodded slowly. "I'm sorry for what happened to Carla. I'm sorry you had to watch her die."

Dante's eyes were distant. He wasn't crying. I didn't think he'd ever allow himself to do so in front of anyone, but there was a deep sadness in his eyes that tore at me. "I killed her."

I jerked in his embrace, my eyes wide. "You did what? But I thought she died from cancer."

"She would have, yes. The doctors said there was nothing they could do for her. She was home, drugged up most days so she wasn't in too much pain, but even the morphine eventually didn't help anymore. She asked me to help her, to free her from the horror that her life had become. She didn't want to spend more weeks bound to her bed, unable to get out and wracked by pain." He paused, and I was openly crying, even if he couldn't. I pressed my hand against his chest, trying to show him that it was okay, that I understood. "She wanted me to shoot her because she thought it would be easier for me, less personal. I couldn't do it. Not like that. Not the same way I dealt with traitors and scum that wasn't even worth the dirt under her feet. I injected her insulin, and she fell asleep in my arms and never woke up again."

"I didn't know. I was always told that she died because her organs failed in the end."

His eyes settled on me, dark and haunted. He brushed his thumb under my eyes, wiping away my tears. "That's what I wanted. I never told anyone."

I shivered against him, too overwhelmed to say anything. I buried my face in his neck, seeking his warmth and scent. His hand rubbed gentle circles on my stomach. "If I'd known, I wouldn't have pushed you so much."

"Val, you didn't push me. When I married you I made a vow to take care of you and try to be a good husband, and I don't take my vows lightly. I'm a man of honor, and yet I didn't fulfill the promises I made to you."

"Why did you ever agree to marry if you knew how hard it would be for you?"

"My father wanted me to marry, and I knew I was starting to look weak because I couldn't move on from Carla, so I did what I thought would be best for my claim to power. You seemed like the perfect choice."

The way he said it made it sound as if I wasn't, but I didn't interrupt him.

"I thought you'd be reluctant to allow closeness so shortly after your first husband died."

The mention of Antonio tightened my throat, but I swallowed past it. "I would have if we'd been in love, or had had anything resembling a real marriage."

"I'm not blaming you for wanting something real after how Antonio used you. Which makes it even worse that you married another man who used you for his own purposes." He let out a low breath.

"So when you decided to marry me, you never intended to sleep with me?"

Dante laughed darkly. "I'm not that honorable. No, I thought I'd consummate our marriage and then sleep with you whenever I felt like it, without any kind of emotional attachment."

"Then why didn't you sleep with me on our wedding night or in the days after?"

"I wanted to. When I brought you into my bedroom on our wedding night, I wanted nothing more than to rip your gown off and bury myself in you. I was angry. I wanted to fuck you until I got that anger out of my system, but then you stepped out of the bathroom in that modest silk nightgown looking every bit the lady, and you were my wife, and you had that fucking hopeful and insecure look in your eyes, and I knew I couldn't use you like that."

My lips parted in surprise. "Did you suspect that I had never slept with a man?"

Dante shook his head. "No. I could tell you were unpracticed in your advances and attempts at seducing me, but I guessed your first husband had been dominant in the bedroom and didn't let you take the initiative, although it didn't match up with my assessment of Antonio."

"Was I that bad at trying to seduce you?" I asked with a small, embarrassed laugh. It felt incredible talking to Dante like this, so openly, and being in his arms without him trying to pull back was even better.

Dante's lips curled into a wry smile. "I'm a man who prides himself on his self-control. Believe me, most men wouldn't have been able to resist your charm. To be honest, when I found out I would be your first, I had an even harder time holding back. It's probably a male thing, but I wanted to put my claim on you."

"That sounds very animalistic."

"It is. Before I married you, I didn't want an inexperienced bride, but once I knew the truth about you, I had a hard time thinking about anything else other than making you mine." Dante's eyes darted to my round belly where his hand was still resting. "And the knowledge that you're carrying my baby makes me proud, though it really isn't something that should cause that notion in me. After all, it's not a great achievement to impregnate your wife."

I shook my head with a smile that slowly died on my lips as my eyes sought out Dante's. "I love this. I love talking to you like a real husband and wife. Please don't pull back from me again. I can't go back to being lonely."

Dante cupped my cheek. "I won't. Today was the wake-up call I needed. I'll try to be the best husband I can possibly be, which probably is still much less than you deserve. I'm not an emotional man, and I hate public displays of affection, but I won't go back to ignoring you. That I can promise."

I kissed him. "Thank you."

We lay in silence beside each other until I felt our daughter move. I quickly shifted Dante's hand so he could feel it too. He stilled.

"Do you feel her moving?"

Dante nodded. He didn't say anything, but I knew this time it wasn't because he was unaffected by what was happening. Smiling, I put my head back down on his shoulder.

"When can I return home?"

"Tomorrow. They want to keep you overnight."

"Okay." I wasn't really happy about this. I worried about being separated from Dante for that long, but not because I was clingy or couldn't be alone; no, I was worried that despite his promise, Dante would find reasons to retreat from me once more if we were separated so shortly after we'd come to an understanding.

"I'll stay with you. I won't let you alone in this place," he said as if he knew about my worries, and my heart swelled with gratitude. "And I already told Leo that he would have to handle the casino alone for a while."

"You don't want me to work anymore?"

"The doctor said you need to stay in bed as much as possible, so you won't be able to work. Once our child is born and you're feeling well enough, we can still talk about finding you a new job."

"That's reasonable," I said, then pulled back and kissed him again. Now that he let me, I wanted to do it over and over again. Soon my breathing quickened, but Dante drew back with a small shake of his head. "We shouldn't. You need rest."

"Did the doctor say something about sex?"

"Because of the rupture sex is too risky. It could lead to an infection or cause the rupture to widen."

"So we can't have sex for three months if I'm going full-term?"

"Yes. That's right."

I knew some men started using mistresses when their wives got pregnant. I didn't think Dante was the type, but it still worried me. And it wasn't as if I didn't enjoy sex. Three months, and possibly longer, without any kind of relief sounded like a challenge.

Dante smoothed out the furrows between my brows. "What are you thinking?"

"Will you be okay with it?"

"You mean with no sex?" he asked with a hint of amusement. "Yes. As I said, self-control isn't my problem."

"I hope you have enough for both of us."

Dante kissed a spot below my ear. "I'm not saying it's going to be easy. I always want you, Valentina. You drive me insane with desire, but I won't do anything that could endanger our child."

"I know. Me neither." I smiled. "I still can't believe that we'll have a little girl soon. When we're back home tomorrow, I'll have to show you something I bought today." I couldn't wait to see his face when he saw the onesie. I hated that something as horrible as a rupture of membranes had finally brought us closer, but I was glad it had. Now we could look forward to the birth of our daughter together.

Dante kept his arm around my waist as he led me into our house, though I was perfectly capable of walking on my own. I felt good. Maybe the medication was helping. Or maybe our little girl had decided she liked it in my belly now that her parents had figured things out. Of course I knew I had to be careful. I couldn't risk going into labor in the next couple of weeks. Our girl still had quite some growing to do.

Dante was about to lead me into the living room, but I shook my head. "I really want to take a shower." Instead of guiding me toward the staircase, he picked me up and began carrying me upstairs. I was tall, and it couldn't have been easy for Dante to manage the stairs with my added weight. When he set me down at the top, I said, "You don't need to carry me. You won't always be around when I need to take the stairs."

"I don't want you to use the stairs, Valentina," he said, his voice not brooking an argument. "If I'm not around to carry you, then you'll call for one of the guards."

I could tell that he wouldn't budge on the subject, and I was glad that he was trying to take care of me. "Okay. I promise."

As we stepped into our bedroom, I saw that someone, probably Gaby, had carried up the bags with my purchases and set them down on the chair in front of my vanity. With a smile, I walked toward it and pulled out the onesie I'd bought yesterday before things had taken a turn for the worse. I held it up for Dante to see. "So what do you say?" My voice brimmed with excitement. I almost felt bad for feeling so exuberant after what had happened yesterday and what could still happen to our baby girl, but I was too hopeful to let worries overshadow my other emotions. Dante raised one eyebrow. "I doubt anyone will need the reminder."

I laughed. "That's what Bibi said. But it's cute, don't you think?"

His arm snuck around my waist. "It is. I thought you didn't know if it was a girl or a boy?"

"I didn't, but Bibi wanted to buy matching onesies. She was really hoping for a girl, so her daughter and ours could be best friends. She'll be beside herself with excitement when I tell her." I paused. "Have you told your parents that it's a girl yet?"

Dante frowned slightly. "I talked to my mother last night after you fell asleep. She's excited for us."

"But your father isn't?"

"He didn't contact me yet. He's probably trying the silent treatment as a way to show me his displeasure."

"Really? It's not like it was our choice to have a daughter. And I hate this fixation on boys anyway. A girl is worthy too."

"You don't have to convince me," Dante said. "But boys are seen as something that strengthens the Outfit, while girls only mean a weak link the men need to protect. It's the way it's always been. I can't see it changing anytime soon."

"Do you know if there's ever been a woman inducted into any of the Famiglias in North America and beyond?"

Dante smiled wryly. "That would be news to me. And it won't happen. I wouldn't want my daughter to be part of the Outfit. I want her safe and protected. I don't want blood on her hands and death in her dreams."

"But you want that for our future son?" I asked softly. Dante brushed a strand of hair back from my shoulders. "It's the way things are, Val. I will protect all of our children for as long as I can, but eventually our son, at least, will have to brave the dangers of our world. But he'll be strong."

"My father always treated my brother Orazio with brutal harshness, and your own father tortured you to toughen you up. Sometimes I don't want a son because I worry that he'll have to suffer through the same things." I didn't think I could stand back and watch Dante treat our son like that. Even my mother had protected Orazio occasionally when Papà had been too strict. Not that he'd ever abused Orazio as Fiore had done with Dante.

"I will have to be stricter with our son, but I won't be like my father, I swear."

I nodded. I believed him.

I could tell that I was starting to tire already, although I'd hardly done anything. "I should grab a shower now. I'm supposed to lie down again soon."

Dante followed me into the bathroom, his eyes on me as I stepped out of my shoes. I reached for the zipper in the back of my dress, but Dante beat me to it. His thumb traced the bumps of my spine as he pulled the zipper down, and I could feel it all the way down to my toes. The dress pooled at my feet. Now there were only my tights. Dante eased them down my legs, then let his gaze slowly travel up my body as he knelt before me. I wanted nothing more than to fall in his arms and feel him inside me.

Licking my lips, I whispered, "This is going to be hard."

Dante straightened, his expression confirming my words. "Take a shower. I'll wait here in case you feel faint."

"You could shower with me," I said.

Dante looked hesitant, then he nodded. He got out of his clothes, and when he turned to me I could see he was already half-erect.

"I thought you had self-control," I teased.

Dante steered me toward the shower, steadying me. "I do, or my fingers would already be delving into your wet heat."

He turned the shower on, letting the warm water rain down on us before he closed the shower stall and turned to face me, hands on my hips. "How do you know I'm wet?" I asked in a challenging tone.

Dante picked up the sponge and rubbed it lightly over my breasts and stomach. Then he leaned close until his mouth was against my ear. "Because I could see it when I knelt before you. You were wet for me."

I was. I didn't think I'd ever wanted him as much as I wanted him now that we weren't allowed to sleep with each other. We washed each other with the sponge, occasionally kissing, and our breathing was coming faster with every passing moment. Dante's erection was hard and red. "Do you want me to blow you?" I whispered as I was pressed up against him. He groaned as my fingers curled around his shaft, but then his hand stilled my motions and he pulled my hand away from his hard-on.

"No," he rasped. He didn't sound very convincing. "I'm fine."

He turned me around so my back was pressed against his chest and his erection was sandwiched between his stomach and my back. His arms came around my belly, palms pressed against my skin, and he kissed my neck lightly. "I think we should get out. You need to lie down."

I didn't protest. All the naked kissing was making it more difficult to suppress my desire for him. Dante helped me dry myself, and he looked almost relieved when I was finally dressed in comfortable satin pajamas and stretched out on our bed. Dante and I would have to deal with our desires in the next few weeks. Our baby was more important than anything else.

Dante cradled me in his arms as his fingers raked through my hair. "Thank you for never giving up on me, Val."

"I knew my stubbornness would come in handy one day," I said with a small laugh.

Six weeks later, the doctors decided to perform a C-section. It was still eight weeks too early, but the risk of an infection had become too great. Dante didn't budge from my side as they cut open my belly. His presence, his steady gaze, the utter control and strength he emanated helped me tremendously. With Dante at my side, I knew nothing would go wrong. As if by the sheer power of his will he could make things turn out okay. Dante could make you believe that he was in control of the situation even when he wasn't.

He held my hand throughout the C-section and when the first cry sounded, he sought out my eyes before we both turned toward our daughter, wrinkled and smeared with blood as the nurse presented her to us. I let go of Dante's hand. "Go to our daughter. Go." He seemed reluctant to leave my side, but after he'd brushed a kiss against my forehead, he straightened and headed toward the end of the operating table. Dante didn't even twitch at the amount of blood, but I hadn't expected him to. If the nurses and doctors were surprised by his calm, they hid it, or maybe they believed the rumors about Dante: that he was a high-ranking mafia boss. Of course, nobody would ever confirm these suspicions.

After a few moments, the nurse handed him our daughter, wrapped in a blanket. She looked tiny in Dante's arm as he peered down at her with the softest expression I'd ever seen on him. There was something fierce there too, and it replaced the gentleness when he glanced up to find the nurses and doctors watching him. I knew our daughter would be safe.

Dante's eyes spoke of protectiveness, of pure determination to destroy anything and anyone that meant her harm. Turning his gaze away from the hospital staff, Dante approached me with our daughter and lowered himself to the chair beside my head so he could show me our little girl. I knew the doctor would have to take her away soon. She'd have to spend some time in the incubator before she could come home with us. "She's so beautiful," I whispered. I didn't even care that the doctors were busy stitching me back together, or that Dante and I weren't alone.

"She is, just like you," Dante said quietly. I ran a finger over her cheek. She blinked at me with her glassy eyes. Her hair was blond like Dante's, albeit still matted. She was tiny, and I wanted nothing more than to protect her.

"Anna," I said, for the first time calling her by the name Dante and I had chosen only days before. "Your dad will always love you and keep you safe."

Dante kissed Anna's, then my forehead. "You and Anna, both."

I searched his eyes, and the tears I'd successfully held back up till that point finally found their way out.

epilogue

I LOWERED MYSELF INTO THE HOT WATER IN OUR BATHTUB WITH A sigh. Anna had finally fallen asleep in her crib, and Gaby would spend the night with her in the nursery to make sure she was all right. Dante had a meeting with my father down in the office. Though I suspected the sudden increase in short meetings was the result of my father's eagerness to see Anna as often as possible. He definitely didn't share Fiore Cavallaro's disappointment over having gotten a granddaughter instead of a grandson. It had been only five weeks since I'd given birth to our daughter, and I could already hardly imagine how it had been before her. But tonight I needed some time for me…and Dante. Luckily, Anna had hit a phase of long stretches of uninterrupted sleep. She sometimes slept for up to five hours without a hitch.

I leaned back in the tub and closed my eyes, relaxing for the first time today. My fingers itched to slip between my legs to alleviate the tension there, but I didn't. It had been months since Dante and I had been intimate, and tonight I wanted that to change. Dante had been nothing but patient, but I didn't miss that he always took a long time in the shower. I didn't have to guess what he was doing. Now that my scar had healed, I couldn't wait to be with him again. Only this time it would be different. For the first time, I'd know he loved me while he made love to me, even if he'd never said the words aloud. The way he looked at me and Anna was worth more than all the spoken declarations of love in the world.

"Val?" Dante called as I heard him enter the bedroom and a moment later the bathroom. His eyes lingered on the swell of my breasts, mostly covered by bubbles. He looked devilishly handsome in his dark gray vest and pants. The top two buttons of his white shirt were open and the sleeves were rolled up, revealing lean muscle. "I checked on Anna. She's asleep. Gaby is singing to her."

"That's great," I said with a smile. Like Dante had suggested, we'd moved the nursery to the room he'd shared with his first wife a long time ago. Considering that it was three doors down from our bedroom, I wouldn't have to worry that Gaby might hear us. Dante's eyes were practically transparent with lust, but he just stood in the doorway. His self-control was marvelous, and a bit frustrating.

"You look tired," he said carefully. "Do you want to get some rest?" His body said something very different. The growing bulge in his pants was hard to miss.

I shook my head with a smile and straightened, letting water and bubbles trail down my naked body as I stood before Dante. His gaze left a scorching trail on my skin as it slid down to the apex between my thighs. My hand came up to cover the narrow but angry red C-section scar marring my lower belly. I'd always found a way to hide it from Dante's view so far. The doctor had said it would fade to white in time, but it would never go away completely.

Dante stalked toward me and gently pulled my hand away, revealing my scar to him. "Don't hide yourself from me."

"I wasn't sure if you'd be turned off by the sight of my scar."

Dante laughed, a rough sound deep in his throat. He gripped my waist, eyes hungry and possessive. "You look like a goddess, Val. Your scar doesn't make you any less desirable for me. Or do you find my scars repulsive? I have plenty of them."

"No, of course not. But you are a man. It's different for women."

Dante lightly stroked my scar. "This makes you even more beautiful to me because I know why you have it."

I put my hands on his shoulders, soaking his shirt, but Dante didn't seem to mind. His eyes kept roaming over my body. I leaned forward and kissed him. "I need you, Dante. I need you so much."

Dante's eyes flashed with desire. "Are you sure? Have you recovered enough? I don't want to hurt you." My heart pounded with love for him. It meant a lot that he asked me when I could tell how much he wanted to throw me on the bed and take me. One of his hands had already found its way to my butt, stroking the globes in a gentle but very distracting way.

"You won't," I said. "As long as we take it slow, we should be okay." The last thing I wanted to do was take things slow. I wanted to rip off Dante's clothes, lick every inch of his skin and have him slam into me over and over again.

Dante didn't say anything, but he helped me out of the tub and wrapped me into a fluffy bathrobe. He massaged me through the thick fabric until my skin was dry and my breathing was coming in quick puffs. Dante lifted me into his arms and carried me toward the bedroom, where he lowered me on the bed. My toes curled in anticipation as he looked down at me. He slowly crawled on the bed and reached for the belt holding my bathrobe closed. With a tug it came apart, laying me bare to his eyes. "So beautiful," he said roughly. "I missed your taste."

His words alone made arousal pool between my legs, and I bucked my hips in silent invitation. A smirk curled his lips before he lowered his head and kissed my breasts, first the left, then the right before he kissed his way down to my stomach. I stiffened when his lips brushed my scar, not because it hurt, but Dante didn't retreat. My flinching seemed to make him even more determined to pay special attention to this part of my body. His gaze flitted up to me as he pressed another kiss against the scar. His eyes were unrelenting until my muscles finally loosened under his lips.

After another quick kiss, he moved lower, pushed my legs farther apart and then dipped his tongue between my folds. I cried out, already so close to the edge that I could feel my leg muscles tense in anticipation. After a few more strokes and gentle nips, my release gripped me. "Dante!" I shoved my fingers into his hair, holding him against me as I succumbed to the pleasure he was giving me. Dante lifted his face and pressed a kiss against my inner thigh before sitting up. I did the same, my hands going for his vest, pushing it down his shoulders before moving on to unbuttoning his shirt with shaking hands.

"Get up," I ordered in a breathless whisper. Dante complied, a surprised twinkle in his eyes. I half tore his pants down his legs, letting his hard length spring free. I peered up at Dante as I took him into my mouth, tasting the salty pre-cum on the back of my tongue as he slid to the back of my throat. Dante groaned. He glided in and out of my mouth a few times before he took a step back, out of my reach.

"As good as that feels, I'm going to come if you keep it up. You don't know how much I fucking want you."

Dante held out his hand and I took it without hesitation, letting him pull me to my feet. Dante pushed the bathrobe off my shoulders; it pooled at my feet, and then I was already in Dante's arms, pressed up against his firm, warm body. He moved us back until the back of my legs hit the bed and I fell down onto the soft mattress. Dante lowered himself beside me. My brows scrunched together in confusion as he turned me on my side. "What are you doing?"

He slid up behind me, pressing his chest against my back, his erection digging against my thigh. "We're going to try a new position. It'll make things easier for you, and my weight won't rest on you."

"Okay," I said, my voice shaky with excitement.

"Your pill is already working?"

I nodded quickly.

Dante nuzzled my neck as his hand traveled over my breast, then trailed down my stomach until it slipped between my legs. He dipped one finger, then a second into me, making me moan.

"You're ready," Dante growled. I was more than ready. I needed him desperately. My entire body ached for him. Dante moved his hand along my inner thigh before hooking his palm under my knee and lifting my leg until my foot was flat on the bed and my legs opened in a wide V. He pulled me even tighter against his body, spooning me, and guided his erection toward my opening. He slowly eased his tip into me, and I squeezed my eyes shut at the stretching feeling. Dante's palm cupped my breast as his lips kissed the spot beneath my ear and he pushed inch by inch into me. My breath caught in my throat when he filled me to the brim. He let out a harsh breath. "God, you're so tight, Val."

It had been too long, and I had to get used to his size again. Dante paused, our bodies merged together, his cock stretching me. He stroked my side and stomach. "Are you all right?"

I glanced over my shoulder at him, then claimed his lips for a kiss before pulling back and whispering, "I missed this." Dante trailed his fingers down to my folds and gently started drawing circles on my sensitive nub. "Please move," I half begged in between moans. And Dante did. He eased almost all the way out before sliding back in. When my inner muscles relaxed he settled into a slow, delicious rhythm. It felt like we were one as we moved against each other. Our breathing quickened and so did Dante's thrusting, but he kept me in his embrace, his lips nibbling on my throat. I wasn't sure how long we made love like that, the pleasure slowly building until I dug my toes into the mattress, desperate for release. When it finally claimed me, my clenching muscles took Dante right with me, and he spilled into me with a hoarse cry.

Afterward he didn't immediately pull out. Instead he wrapped me even tighter in his embrace, our bodies still joined together. My breathing was slowly coming down as Dante left a trail of kisses along my neck until he cupped my earlobe between his lips. I moaned and arched against him as his fingers took up their playing between my thighs again.

"How about another round?" he said huskily. I couldn't do more than nod as his other hand tweaked my nipple, and I felt his cock starting to grow hard in me again. He pulled out of me, causing me to glance at him in confusion. He rubbed my ass lightly as he sat up and opened his arms in invitation. "Another new position?" I asked excitedly. Dante's cock was so hard it rested against his firm stomach. I crawled toward him and squatted over him before I slowly eased myself down on his length. I wrapped my arms around Dante's neck, bringing our chests close together, and pressed my mouth to his.

Dante's hands cupped my butt and guided me up and down his erection. "Look at me," he demanded hoarsely. My eyes flew open, meeting his heated gaze. "I love seeing your eyes when I'm in you."

We kept our gazes locked as our breathing quickened and my movements turned jerky, and even when I cried out my release, followed by Dante's own raspy groans. His gaze was all the declaration of love that I needed as we clung together, unwilling to separate even now that we were spent and satisfied.

Dante slowly lay back, taking me with him so I was stretched out on top of him. A silly smile spread on my face as I peered down at Dante. His messy hair, the shadow of stubble, his unguarded expression. I buried my face in the crook of his neck, whispering, "I love you."

Dante's arms around me tightened, and he pressed a kiss against the side of my head. I closed my eyes, listening to the cacophony of our pounding hearts.

We lay like that for a long time. I never wanted to move, but eventually we slipped under the shower.

Afterwards, we crept into the nursery. Gaby was sitting in the rocking chair reading a book, but quickly got up when she saw us.

"You can go," I whispered. "We're going to watch her the rest of the night."

Gaby nodded and slunk away, closing the door without a sound. Anna lay in her crib, her tiny hands curled to fists and her face peaceful. She was still small, but she'd grown a lot since we'd been allowed to take her home from the hospital two weeks ago. I tiptoed toward her bed and rested my hands on the edge, itching to stroke her rosy cheek, but I didn't want to wake her. I loved watching her in these quiet moments. I never felt more peaceful. Dante came up behind me and wrapped his arms around my waist, leaning his head against mine. "I'll never let anything happen to you or Anna. I'll protect you until my last breath." I knew he would.

It had taken a while and we'd encountered some bumps along the road, but finally I had what I'd always wanted: a husband who cared deeply about me, and a beautiful baby we both loved more than anything else in the world. It felt as if I'd finally arrived where I was supposed to be.

bound *by hatred*

(Born in Blood Mafia Chronicles, #3)

prologue

Gianna

MY REFLECTION COULD HAVE BEEN THE OPENING SCENE OF A horror movie. Blood covered my chin and more blood dripped from the cut in my lower lip and onto my white shirt. My lip was already swelling, but I was happy to find my eyes dry, no sign of a single tear.

Matteo appeared behind me, tall frame towering over me, his dark eyes scanning my messed-up face. Without his trademark shark-grin and the arrogant amusement, he looked almost tolerable. "You don't know when to shut up, do you?" His lips turned into a smirk, but it looked somehow wrong. There was something unsettling in his eyes. The look in them reminded me of the one I'd seen when he'd dealt with the Russian captives in the basement. Something dark and twisted lurked in their depth.

"Neither do you," I said, then winced at the pain shooting through my lip.

"True," he said in a strange voice. Before I had time to react, he gripped my hips, turned me around and hoisted me onto the washstand. "That's why we are perfect for each other."

Back was the arrogant smile. The bastard stepped between my legs.

"What are you doing?" I hissed, sliding back from the edge of the washstand to bring more distance between us while pushing against his chest.

He didn't budge, too strong for me. The smile got bigger. He grabbed my chin and tilted my head up. "I want to take a look at your lip."

"I don't need your help now. Maybe you should have stopped my father from busting my lip in the first place."

"Yes. I should have," he said darkly, his thumb lightly touching my wound as he parted my lips. "If Luca hadn't held me back, I would have plunged my knife into your father's fucking back, consequences be damned. Maybe I will still do it. I'd fucking love it."

He released my lip and pulled a long curved knife from the holster below his jacket before twisting it in his hand with a calculating look on his face. Then his eyes flickered up to me. "Do you want me to kill him?"

God, yes. I shivered at the sound of Matteo's voice. I knew it was wrong, but after what Father had said today, I wanted to see him begging for mercy and I knew Matteo was capable of bringing anyone to their knees, which excited me in a horrifying way. That was exactly why I'd wanted out of this life, why I *still* wanted out. I had the potential for cruelty regardless of how I tried to convince myself of the opposite, and this life was the reason for it.

"That would mean war between Chicago and New York," I said simply. Not that I gave a damn about peace. The men would find a reason to tear into each other soon enough. Someone always managed to insult someone else's honor and then all bets were off.

"Seeing your father bleed to death at my feet would be worth the risk. You *are* worth it."

chapter *one*

Matteo

The first time I saw Gianna, she was a scrawny fourteen-year-old with a too big mouth, a splattering of freckles on her face and untamed red locks. She was everything a proper Italian girl wasn't supposed to be, which was probably why I found her entertaining. But she was a kid, and though I was barely four years older, I had already been a Made Man for five years, killed several people and fucked my fair share of women. The moment Luca and I were back in New York, busy with mob business and easy society girls, I didn't give the rude redhead a second thought. We had enough trouble with the Bratva trying to sabotage our drug labs, and our father had grown too old to handle things as they needed to be handled: with unrelenting brutality. It was time for the old man to die and hand the job over to my brother. Luca was the perfect man for brutality.

I'd pretty much forgotten all about Gianna when Luca and I returned to New York three years later for his wedding to Aria.

Luca had gotten it into his head that he wanted to see Aria before the wedding. The official explanation being that he wanted to make sure she was on the pill—which was bullshit. I knew it was because he was eager to see how she'd grown up. And damn, the girl had filled up nicely. When she appeared behind her younger sister Liliana in the doorframe to their suite in the Mandarin Oriental, my eyes didn't know what part of her to check out first. Long blonde hair, stunning blue eyes, narrow waist, lean legs, nice butt and tits. She was smoking hot. She was also Luca's fiancée and so firmly off-limits. Not to mention that she was a bit too demure for my taste. The way she cast down her eyes whenever Luca looked at her would have driven me insane. Luca was an intimidating fucker, and the girl had been dealt a heavy blow for having to marry him, but she needed to grow a spine if she wanted to stand a chance against Luca. He was used to bossing people around.

Of course, the moment I entered the suite, Aria was the last thing on my mind. My gaze settled on the girl with the flaming red hair who lounged on the sofa, long legs casually crossed and propped up on the coffee table. At once the long-forgotten memory of her rudeness resurfaced and with it my interest in her. She wasn't the awkward, scrawny girl she used to be.

Definitely not scrawny.

She had developed all the right curves in all the right places, and her face had gotten rid of her freckles. Unlike most girls I knew she didn't seem impressed by me. To be honest, she looked like I was a cockroach she wanted to squash under her boots. With a grin, I headed straight for her, never one to shy away from a challenge. Especially a hot challenge. What was life without the thrill of getting burned?

Gianna straightened in a jerk, her black boots landing on the ground with a thud, and then she narrowed her eyes at me. If she thought that would stop me, she was thoroughly mistaken. Unfortunately, the youngest Scuderi girl stepped in my way and gave me her version of a flirty smile. "Can I see your gun?" she asked in that voice caught somewhere between girl and woman.

Had Gianna asked that question, a myriad of inappropriate replies would have been on the tip of my tongue, but Liliana was a bit too young for them. What a waste of opportunity.

"No, you can't," Aria said before I got the chance to come up with a reply fit for younger ears. Always so proper, that girl. Thank God, Father had chosen her for Luca and not for me.

"You shouldn't be here alone with us," Gianna muttered, her eyes moving from Luca to me. Damn it. She was something else, really. "It's not appropriate."

Luca didn't seem too impressed with her. It was obvious that she grated on his nerves, already something she and I had in common. "Where is Umberto? Shouldn't he be guarding this door?" he asked.

"He's probably on a toilet or cigarette break," Aria said.

I almost laughed. What kind of idiots worked for Scuderi? Things in Chicago seemed to follow very different rules. I could tell that Luca was on the verge of an outburst. He'd been on edge for days, probably because his balls were bursting. He'd fucked Grace far more often than usual to bridge the time before he could fuck Aria.

"Does it happen often that he leaves you without protection?" he asked.

"Oh, all the time," Gianna snapped, then rolled her eyes at her sister.

"You see, Lily, Aria, and I sneak out every weekend because we have a bet going who can pick up more guys."

Big words for a girl who'd never seen a cock in real life. From the look Luca gave me, he thought the exact same thing. Gianna really didn't know anything about my brother if she thought it was a good thing to taunt him like that.

Luca stalked toward his little fiancée who flinched as she always did when he acted like a berserk. "I want to have a word with you, Aria."

Gianna jumped to her feet like a tigress determined to protect her young. "I was joking, for God's sake!" She actually tried to get in between Luca and Aria, which was a fucking bad idea. Before Luca could lose his shit, I grabbed her wrist and dragged her away.

Gianna's blue eyes flashed with fury. I'd been wrong. Her face hadn't gotten rid of all of her freckles. This close up I could see the soft dusting of freckles on her nose, but somehow they made her look even more beautiful.

"Let go of me, or I'll break your fingers," she hissed.

I'd love to see you try. I released her with a grin that seemed to enrage her only further if the narrowing of her eyes was any indication.

Luca started leading Aria away. "Come on. Where's your bedroom?"

Gianna's gaze flitted between Luca and me. "I'll call our father! You can't do that."

Of course, Luca didn't give a fuck. Scuderi would have given Aria to him years ago; he definitely wouldn't care if Luca sampled her goods a few days before the wedding. The door fell shut and Gianna stalked toward it. I gripped her hand again before she could piss off Luca even more. This girl really didn't know what was good for her. "Give them some privacy. Luca won't rip Aria's clothes off before the wedding night."

Gianna shook me off. "Do you think that's funny?"

"What are they talking about?" Liliana asked.

The door to the suite swung open and Umberto stepped in, sending a glare my way. The old man still hadn't forgiven me for insulting his wife three years ago.

"Gianna, Liliana, come here," he said sharply. I cocked one eyebrow at him. Was he worried I'd hurt them? If that were my intention, they definitely wouldn't be standing next to me unscathed. Romero rolled his eyes behind Umberto's back as he stepped in behind the man, and I smirked. Of course, the old man caught it and his fingers moved a bit closer to his knife holder.

Do it, old man. It's been too long since I had a good fight.

Liliana obeyed at once and walked toward her bodyguard. As expected, Gianna stayed beside the door to her sister's bedroom. "Luca dragged Aria into her bedroom. They are alone in there."

Umberto started to head toward the door but I blocked his way. Romero was close behind him. Not that I would need him to stop the old guy. Umberto tried to stare me down. He was at least four inches shorter than me, and no matter how good of a knife fighter he was, I'd cut him open with my blade before he could even blink. My fingers actually itched to do it.

"They aren't married yet," he said like that was news to me.

"Her virtue is safe with my brother, don't worry." It wasn't a lie. Luca wouldn't dishonor Aria.

Umberto's lips thinned. I had a feeling that he wanted to start a fight as much as I did. Before things could get entertaining, the door to the bedroom opened and Aria walked out. She looked as if she'd seen a ghost. I gave Luca a look. Did he really have to scare the shit out of his fiancée a few days before their wedding?

"What are you doing here?" Umberto asked.

"You should pay better attention in the future and keep your breaks to a minimum," Luca told him.

"I was gone for only a few minutes and there were guards in front of the other doors."

Bored by their argument, I turned my attention back to the redhead.

Gianna put her hands on her hips, somehow pushing her chest out. She really had a body to die for. I wondered if Scuderi had already set her up with some loser from the Outfit. That would be a pity.

Gianna met my gaze. "What are you looking at?"

I let my eyes wander the length of her. "At your hot body."

"Then keep looking. Because that's all you ever get to do with my *hot body*."

"Stop it," Umberto warned.

Gianna really shouldn't have said that. I'd always enjoyed the hunt. While Luca didn't bother once a girl proved to be work, I'd always preferred going after a difficult conquest. It kept things interesting. Getting a girl into our beds had never been a problem for either of us. We were good-looking and rich, not to mention the kind of bad boy many bored society girls needed to spice up their boring lives, but there was no fun in always getting what you wanted without having to fight for it.

Gianna's narrowed eyes followed me when Luca, Romero, and I left the suite. I smiled to myself. The girl had fire.

Luca sighed. "Don't tell me you've set your sights on the redhead. She's a major pain in the ass."

"So what? She'd definitely make my life more interesting."

"What? Killing off Russians and having a new girl in your bed every other night isn't doing the deal for you?"

"I like to change things up now and then."

"You can't have her. She's off-limits. I won't tell Father you brought war with the Outfit down on us because you pawed at Scuderi's daughter. There's only one way you could have the redhead in your bed and that's if you marry her, and that's not going to happen."

"Why not?"

Luca paused. "Tell me you're joking."

I shrugged. I didn't really want to marry yet, or ever for that matter, but Father had been on my case for months. Every woman he'd suggested so far had been boring as hell.

Luca gripped my shoulder. "You won't ask Scuderi for his daughter's hand tonight."

"Is that an order?" I asked quietly. Luca would be my Capo very soon and he was above me in the hierarchy of the Famiglia but I wasn't good at following orders.

"No. A piece of advice." Luca smirked. "If I ordered you, you'd do it just to annoy me."

"I'm not a hotheaded teenage boy," I said, then grinned because Luca knew me too well.

"I just want you to take your time. You might find Gianna's bitchiness fascinating now, but I doubt that'll last more than a few days. I know you. The moment the hunt is over and you got what you wanted, you'll lose interest. But this time you'd be stuck with her forever."

"Don't worry. I have every intention of scoring tonight. That'll make me forget all about Gianna."

chapter *two*

Aria & Luca's wedding
Gianna

THIS WEDDING WAS A FARCE. ARIA LEANED AWAY FROM LUCA AND clutched my hand the moment we sat down at the table. It was obvious how unhappy she was. She was trying so hard to hide it, but for me it was plain as day. Of course nobody gave a shit. It was pretty much standard that the bride was forced into marriage, so unhappiness was a given. Nobody ever asked what we wanted. Nobody ever cared. Not even the other women.

It was then that I made a promise I was determined to keep: I wasn't going to end up in a loveless marriage. I didn't care if it was my duty or if honor dictated it; nothing in this godforsaken world could make me marry for anything but love.

Matteo kept glancing my way from across the table, that annoying cocky grin on his face. He'd pretty much ogled me throughout the entire wedding. I had to admit that he didn't look too shabby in his light gray vest, white shirt, and dress pants. Somehow his tall muscled frame stood out even more dressed up like that. Of course, I'd have bitten my tongue off before admitting to anyone that I found Matteo's looks tolerable, especially when his personality wasn't anywhere close to being sufferable.

Aria clutched my hand under the table even tighter because of something Luca had said to her. She was oblivious to Matteo's flirting with me. Oblivious to anything but her distress.

I squeezed her hand but then the dance floor was opened and soon we were ripped apart as Luca led her to their first dance as a married couple. I quickly pushed to my feet, desperate to sneak away toward the bay where I could be alone, but Matteo cornered me at the edge of the dance floor, that same cocky grin on his striking face. Why did the bastard have to look so good?

His dark hair was intentionally messy and his eyes were so dark, they were almost black. It was impossible not to check him out. Of course, he was perfectly aware of the effect he had on most women and obviously expected me to fawn over him as well. Hell would freeze over before that happened.

He bowed without taking his eyes off me. "May I have this dance?"

My stomach did a stupid flip at the sight of his grin. He was more easy-going than most Made Men, but I had a feeling that was only a cover-up. Maybe he'd perfected the boy-next-door routine, but beneath it a predator was lying in wait, ready to pounce. I wasn't going to be his prey.

Father watched me from his spot at the table, so I had no choice but to nod in response to Matteo's question, or risk a huge scene. Not that I would have cared but I didn't want to add more stress for Aria. She was already on edge.

Matteo took my hand and rested his palm on my lower back, the warmth of his skin seeping through the thin fabric of my dress. My stomach lurched but I forced my face into a mask of boredom. I hated how my body seemed to react to Matteo. If I'd be allowed to interact with other guys, I'd probably be unimpressed by Matteo, but like Aria this dance was the most action I'd ever gotten.

I peered up at him. This close up I could see that his eyes were dark brown with an almost black outer ring. He had thick black lashes and the shadow of stubble ghosted his cheeks and chin. His smile widened and I turned my head away, focusing on the dancing guests around us. Everyone was laughing and smiling, enjoying themselves. From the outside it looked like a marvelous feast. It was easy to be taken in by the mansion's garden that was decorated to perfection. It was *so damn easy* to let the breeze drifting over to us from the ocean carry away reality. The unique atmosphere only a place in the Hamptons could offer could convince anyone that life was a dream.

I knew better.

Matteo pulled me even closer, pressing our bodies together so I could feel every inch of muscle as well as the weapons hidden beneath his vest. I squirmed, though part of me wanted to lean in, get closer, and claim his mouth for a kiss. That would have been the scandal of the wedding, no doubt.

Father would blow a gasket. That was almost enough to make me want to do it. Why should girls be forced to wait with their first kiss until they were married? It was ridiculous. I pitied Aria for having to experience her first kiss in front of the entire wedding party. That wouldn't happen to me. I didn't care whom I had to bribe to kiss me.

Matteo leaned down, a teasing smile curving his mouth. "You look gorgeous, Gianna. The pissed-off look goes really well with your dress."

Before I could stop myself, a laugh burst out of me. I tried to cover it up with a cough but Matteo didn't buy it judging from the look on his face. Damn it. I narrowed my eyes—in vain. I decided to ignore Matteo for the rest of our dance, hoping that my body would do the same, but then the bastard started moving his thumb back and forth on my back, and every nerve ending in me seemed to jerk to life.

I wanted to kiss him, and not just to spite my father and every other male in our world who thought it was okay to keep women on a leash. I wanted to kiss him because he smelled delicious, and that was exactly the reason why I needed to get away from him quickly.

Sadly, Matteo seemed intent to drive me crazy, because after our first dance he managed to steal two more dances from me, and to my utter annoyance my body didn't stop reacting to his closeness. I had a feeling he knew, and that was why he kept stroking my back ever so lightly, but I couldn't ask him to stop without admitting that it was bothering me, and somehow part of me didn't want him to stop.

It was almost midnight when people started to shout for Luca to bed Aria. She didn't manage to hide her panic. When she stood and took Luca's offered hand, her eyes met mine but then Luca was already leading her away, followed by a crowd of shouting men. Anger surged through me. I pushed to my feet, determined to follow and help her. Mother gripped my wrist, jerking me to a stop. "This isn't your business, Gianna. Sit down. Aria will do what's expected of her and so should you."

I glowered at her. Wasn't she supposed to protect us? Instead she watched without a flicker of compassion. I wrenched away from her, disgusted by her and everyone around us.

Father stood beside Salvatore Vitiello, who shouted something that sounded like "We want to see blood on the sheets, Luca!"

I almost tackled him. What a bastard. New York and its sick traditions. Despite Father's warning glare, I turned and followed after the men. Luca and Aria were almost at the house, and I had trouble fighting my way through the male guests to get to them. I wasn't even sure what I was going to do if I reached them. I could hardly pull Aria into our shared bedroom and lock the door. That wouldn't stop anyone, least of all Luca. That guy was a beast.

A few of the men made lewd comments in my direction but I ignored them, my eyes firmly focused on Aria's blonde head. I'd almost reached the front of the crowd when Aria disappeared into the master bedroom and

Luca closed the door. My breath caught, worry and anger taking center stage in my body.

I was wavering between storming into the bedroom to kick Luca's ass and run as far away as possible so I didn't have to hear what was going on behind that door. Most of the male guests were on their way back outside to resume drinking, only Matteo, who was shouting disgusting suggestions through the door, and a few younger Made Men from New York were still around. I backed away, knowing there was nothing I could do for Aria, and hating it more than anything else. So often in the past Aria had protected me from Father, and now when she needed protection, I was unable to help her.

Instead of returning to the party, I decided to go to my bedroom. I wasn't in the mood to face my parents again. I'd only get into a huge fight with Father, and I really didn't need that on my plate today. Before I could head down the corridor toward my room, two guys stepped in my way. I didn't know their names. They weren't much older than me, maybe eighteen. One of them still sported some baby fat and acne. The other was taller and looked like more of a threat.

I tried to sidestep them but the taller guy blocked my way. "Piss off," I said, glaring at the two idiots.

"Don't be a killjoy, Red. I wonder if you are red down there too?" He pointed between my legs.

My lips curled in disgust. *As if I hadn't heard those words before.*

The acne guy snorted with laughter. "We could try to find out."

Suddenly Matteo was there. He gripped the tall guy in a headlock and held a sharp long knife to the guy's crotch. "Or," he said in an eerily calm voice. "We could try to find out how long it takes for you to bleed out like a pig after I cut your dick off. How about that?"

I used the moment to ram my knee into acne guy's balls. He cried out and dropped to his knees. I probably shouldn't have enjoyed it as much as I did.

Matteo raised his dark eyebrows at me. "Wanna have a go at this one too?"

I didn't need to be told twice. Instead I landed a good kick and sent the second guy to his knees as well. Both guys looked up at Matteo with fear-widened eyes, ignoring me completely.

"Fuck off before I decide to cut your throats," Matteo said.

They scrambled off like dogs with their tails between their legs.

"Do you know them?" I asked.

Matteo sheathed his knife. He didn't look as drunk as he'd seemed at the party. Maybe it had all been for show. A quick glance around made me realize that we were alone in this part of the house, and from the way my heartbeat quickened and my stomach fluttered, I knew this really wasn't a good idea.

"They are the kids of two of our soldiers. They aren't even Made Men yet."

Inducting them into the mafia probably wouldn't turn them into nicer human beings. "I could have handled them myself," I said.

Matteo scanned my body again. "I know."

That wasn't the answer I had expected, and I wasn't entirely sure if he was pulling my leg or not. "It's funny how you can act like a knight in shining armor one second and the next you're encouraging your brother to sexually assault my sister."

"Luca doesn't need encouragement, believe me."

"You make me sick. All of this does." I turned and stalked away but Matteo caught up with me and barred my way with an arm against the wall.

"Your sister will be fine. Luca isn't cruel to women."

"Is that supposed to reassure me?"

Matteo shrugged. "I know my brother. Aria won't get hurt."

I searched his face. He seemed serious. I wanted to believe him but from what I'd witnessed, Luca was anything but a kind man. He was brutal and cruel and cold, and I wasn't sure if Matteo's definition of not being cruel to women matched my own.

"I really want to fucking kiss you," Matteo said in a rough voice, startling me.

My eyes widened. He didn't move, just stood in front of me with his arm propped up against the wall and his dar eyes boring into mine. We weren't engaged, thank God, so speaking to me like that was more than inappropriate. Father would have gone nuts if he'd heard. I should have been anxious, embarrassed at the very least, by his words, but instead I found myself wondering how it would be to kiss someone, to kiss Matteo. The girls in my class had all kissed and done far more already. Only Aria, the other girls from mob families, and I were sheltered from the outside world, always guarded by bodyguards. How would it be to kiss someone forbidden? To do something a good girl didn't do?

"Then why don't you?" I heard myself say. Alarm bells went off in my mind but I ignored them.

This was my choice. If we weren't who we were, if we hadn't been born into this screwed-up world, if Matteo wasn't a Made Man and a killer, maybe then I could have fallen for him. If we'd met as two normal people, then maybe we could have become something.

Matteo moved closer to me. For some reason I backed away until I bumped into the wall, but Matteo followed and soon I was trapped between cold stone and his body. "Because there are rules in our world and breaking them has consequences."

"You don't seem like a for rules." I wasn't sure why I was encouraging him. I didn't want his attention. I wanted out of this fucked-up world and its fucked-up people. Getting involved in any way with someone like him would make that impossible.

Matteo smiled darkly. "I'm not." He reached for my face and slowly raked his fingers through my hair. I shivered at the light touch. I didn't even like Matteo, right? He was annoying and arrogant and never knew when to shut up.

He's like you.

But my body wanted more. I grabbed his vest, my fingers crinkling the soft material. "Me neither. I don't want my first kiss to happen with my husband."

Matteo let out a quiet laugh and he was so close that I could feel it more than hear it. "This is a bad idea," he murmured, his lips less than an inch from mine, his eyes dark and devoid of the usual playfulness.

My insides seemed to burn with need. "I don't care."

And then Matteo kissed me, lightly at first as if he wasn't sure if I was being serious. I tugged at his vest, wanting him to stop being careful, and Matteo crushed his body to mine, his tongue slipping between my lips, tangling with mine, giving me no time to wonder what I was doing. He tasted of whiskey and something sweeter, like the most delicious whiskey truffle I could imagine. His body radiated heat and strength. His hand cupped the back of my neck as his mouth set my body alight with need.

God, no wonder Father didn't want us to be around men. Now that I knew how good kissing felt, I never wanted to stop doing it.

There was a gasp, and Matteo and I pulled apart. I was still dazed when my eyes settled on my sister Lily who stood frozen in the hallway, probably on her way to her room. Her eyes were wide. "Sorry!" she blurted, then took a few hesitant steps in our direction. "Does this mean you're going to marry?"

I snorted. "No, it doesn't. I won't marry him. This means nothing."

Matteo shot me a look, and I almost felt bad for my rude words, but it was the truth. I had no intention of marrying a Made Man, no matter how good he could kiss, or how much he could make me laugh. The men in our world were killers and torturers. They weren't good men, they weren't even decent men. They were bad, rotten to the core. Nothing could change that. Maybe they occasionally managed to imitate normal guys, especially Matteo had that act down to a T, but in the end it was only a mask.

Matteo turned to Lily. "Don't tell anyone what you saw, okay?"

I slipped away from him, needing to bring some distance between us. How could I have let him kiss me? Maybe I was lucky and he was more intoxicated than he let on. Maybe he wouldn't remember a thing tomorrow morning.

"Okay," Lily said with a shy smile.

Matteo gave me a knowing look before he walked past Lily and turned the corner. The moment he was gone, Lily rushed toward me. "You kissed him!"

"Shhh," I said as we walked down the hall.

"Can I sleep in your room tonight? I told Mother I could."

"Yeah, sure."

"How was it?" she asked in a hushed whisper. "The kiss, I mean."

At first I wanted to lie but then I opted for the truth. "Amazing."

Lily giggled and followed me into my room. "So are you going to kiss him again?"

I wanted to, but I knew it would be a majorly bad idea. I didn't want to give him any ideas. "No. I won't ever kiss Matteo again."

I should have known that wouldn't be the end of it.

The next day, a couple of hours before my family had to leave for Chicago, Matteo caught me alone in front of my bedroom. He didn't try to kiss me but he stood very close. It would have been easy to bridge the distance between us, to grab his shirt and pull him against me. Instead I put my guards in place and glared. "What do you want?"

Matteo clucked his tongue. "Last night when we were alone you didn't give me the cold shoulder."

"I'd hoped you were too drunk to remember."

"Sorry to disappoint you." If he didn't stop smiling that arrogant smile

I'd wring his neck, or kiss him, I hadn't decided yet. Choice number one was the better option, no doubt.

"It was a one-time thing. It didn't mean anything. I still don't like you. I only did it because I wanted to do something forbidden."

His dark eyes lingered on my lips before they slid lower. "There are plenty of other forbidden things we could do," he murmured, stepping closer, too close, and enveloping me with his scent.

"No, thanks."

He rocked back on his heels, smile getting impossibly wide. "Why? Losing your courage? I could ask your father for your hand in marriage if you're tired of forbidden things."

"*Right*," I said sarcastically. "I will never marry you, that's a promise. And now that Aria's already trapped in New York, Father wouldn't send me away anyway."

Matteo shrugged. "If you say so."

His overconfidence made me snap. I jabbed my finger against his muscled chest. "You think you are irresistible, don't you? But you aren't. You and Luca and all the other men in the fucking mafia think you are oh-so-great. Let me tell you something: if you weren't fucking rich and didn't carry a fucking gun wherever you went, you wouldn't be better than anyone else out there."

"I'd still be good-looking and I could still kill most of the wimps out there with my bare hands. What about you, Gianna? What would you be without the protection of your family and your father's money?"

I sucked in a deep breath. Yes, what would I be without all that? Nothing. I'd never had to do anything by myself, never had been allowed to do so, but not for lack of wanting. "Free."

Matteo laughed. "You won't ever be free. None of us are. We are all caged in by the rules of our world."

That's why I want out of this world.

"Maybe. But a marriage to you won't ever be my cage." I stalked off, not giving him another chance for a comeback.

chapter *three*

Matteo

Maybe Gianna didn't understand it yet but marriage would be her cage no matter if she wanted it or not.

Last night after our kiss, I'd returned to the party to drink myself into a stupor when I'd come across my bastard of a father and Rocco Scuderi, talking about Gianna and his plans for her to marry some old geezer who was known for his hard hand with women. I hadn't said anything then because I knew Father. If he thought I wanted Gianna because I desired her, liked her or wanted to protect her from a worse fate, he'd never agree to set me up with her.

Now in the morning after the presentation of the sheets, I searched for Luca and found him on his way to the master bedroom with Aria at his side. "You two lovebirds will have to postpone your mating session. I need to have a word with you, Luca," I said.

Luca and Aria turned around to face me. Aria's cheeks turned bright red and she peered up at my brother with a mix of worry and embarrassment. He glared at me before lowering his gaze to his wife. "Go ahead. Check if the maids packed all your stuff. I'll be back soon." She quickly disappeared in the bedroom.

"The sheets were fake, weren't they? My big bad brother spared his little virgin bride."

Luca glowered as he stepped close to me. "Keep your fucking voice down."

"What happened? Did you have too much to drink and couldn't get it up?"

"Fuck off. As if alcohol ever stopped me," he said.

"Then what?"

Luca glared. "She started crying."

I chuckled. I reached for the knife holder around his forearm and pushed it up, revealing a small wound. Luca snatched his arm away.

"You cut yourself."

Luca looked like he was considering slicing me up into bite-sized pieces. Since I still needed his help, I decided to keep my taunting to a minimum.

"I knew it. I told Gianna last night that she didn't need to worry about Aria. You have a soft spot for damsels in distress."

"I don't—" He frowned. "You were alone with Gianna?"

I nodded, then led him away from the bedroom, in case Aria was trying to eavesdrop. She'd only tell her sister everything. "I kissed her, and she tastes even better than she looks."

"I can't fucking believe you got more action than me on my own fucking wedding night," Luca muttered.

"The ladies can't resist my charm."

He clamped his hand down on my shoulder. "This isn't a joking matter, Matteo. The Outfit won't find it funny if you go around deflowering their girls."

"I didn't deflower anyone. I kissed her."

"Yeah, as if that's ever the end of it."

"I want to deflower her. But I'm not an idiot."

"Really?" that's what Luca's expression said.

"I want to marry her."

Luca stopped abruptly. "Tell me you're kidding."

"I'm not. That's why I need your help. Father won't talk to Scuderi on my behalf if he thinks I want Gianna for any other reason than spite or revenge. You know him."

"So what do you want me to do?"

"Help me convince him that she hates me and insulted me and that I want to marry her to make her miserable."

"Isn't that the truth? The girl can't stand you, and you want her because of it. How is that any different from the story we're going to tell Father?"

"I don't want to make her miserable."

Luca looked doubtful. "The end result might be the same. That girl is going to drive you insane, you realize that, don't you? I'm really not sure if I want her in New York."

"You'll deal with it. And Aria will be happy to have her sister with her."

"You really think you thought that through, don't you?"

"I did, and Father will choose some bitch that'll make me miserable for me soon enough."

"So you rather choose your own bitch who'll make you miserable."

I shook off his hand. "Gianna isn't a bitch."

"You want to hit me because of her," Luca said with a twisted smile.

"I want to hit you for a lot of reasons."

Luca shook his head. "Come on. Let's find Father."

We headed down the corridor and down the stairs toward Father's office. He was on his way out of the room. I forced my face into a mask of fury. "I can't believe her fucking nerve."

"There's nothing you can do," Luca said to me, then he turned to Father. "The Scuderi redhead provoked Matteo."

Father raised his brows in mild interest. "How so?" He gestured for us to move into his office, then closed the door.

I pretended to be seething while Luca made up some ridiculous story that ended with Gianna telling me that her father would never give her to New York, and that nobody could convince him otherwise.

"She made it sound as if I was beneath her, as if we were beneath her. I want the bitch to pay. I don't care what she wants. I want her in my bed."

Excitement flashed in Father's eyes. The sadist actually believed that bullshit, because in his twisted, power-hungry, sadist mind, it made sense. "I suppose I can talk to Scuderi. He'll be glad to be rid of her. She's a handful." His smile widened. "You'll have to teach her manners, Matteo."

"Don't worry," I said. I'd teach her a lot of things.

Two days later my father and Scuderi came to an agreement and Gianna was mine. Now I just had to figure out a good time to tell her.

Gianna

Sometimes at night when I relived our kiss, I wondered if maybe Matteo and I weren't such a bad idea, but then Aria called and told me about how she'd found Luca cheating on her, and that was the wake-up call I'd desperately needed. Made Men would always kill, always cheat, always ruin anything they touched. I wouldn't let anyone treat me like that. I wouldn't even give them the chance to try. No matter how much my body wanted to kiss Matteo again, I swore to myself that I would push him away. One kiss had already been too much. If I let him close again, he'd never leave me alone.

Of course when I visited New York a couple of weeks after Aria's wedding, Matteo was there in Luca's apartment to have dinner with us. The grin he gave me when Aria led me toward the table made my blood boil. Had he told anyone about our kiss? I hadn't even told Aria about it, and I'd always told Aria everything. This would be a long dinner.

The next day I convinced Aria to take me to a club dancing, desperate to forget Matteo. It was my first taste of freedom, and boy, did it taste good. Not as good as Matteo, an annoying voice reminded me, but it was soon blasted away by the beats filling the dance floor of the Sphere. It was an exhilarating experience to have strangers check me out, to have them want me. I'd never dressed this sexy before, had never been allowed to, and couldn't help but feel strangely empowered. I was dancing with a tall guy when he was suddenly shoved away from me by none other than Matteo *fucking* Vitiello.

"What the fuck are you doing?" he snarled.

"What the fuck are *you* doing? This is none of your business." My dance partner had found his balance again and stepped up to us but before he could say something Matteo punched him below the ribs, sending him to his knees, and then two bouncers were there and dragged the guy away.

I stood in stunned silence. "Have you lost your fucking mind?"

Matteo brought his face close to mine and gripped my upper arm. "You won't ever do this again. I won't let you mess around with other guys."

"I wasn't messing around, I was dancing." Then his words really sank in. "With *other* guys? So you think because we kissed once you can tell me what to do with my life? Newsflash: you don't own me, Matteo."

He smirked. "Oh, but I *do*." His dark eyes roamed over my skimpy outfit, lingering on my naked legs. "Every inch of you."

I shook off his grip. "You are insane. Get away from me." He followed Luca without another word, but left one of his stupid baboons-slash-bodyguards with me. I was so angry, I wanted to run after him and pummel him to dust.

Instead I went over to Aria who looked lost as she stood unmoving in the center of the dance floor. "That asshole," I muttered.

After a moment, her eyes settled on me. "Who?"

"Matteo. The guy has the nerve to tell me not to dance with other men. What is he? My owner? Fuck him." Aria looked as if her thoughts were miles away. "Are you okay?"

She nodded. "Yeah. Let's go to the bar." Luca's two lapdogs, Romero and

Cesare, followed us and Aria lashed out at them. "Can you watch us from afar? You're driving me crazy."

Stunned, I watched as she rushed toward the bar and ordered drinks for us. Romero and Cesare were watching us with hawk eyes from afar. So much for feeling free and having fun. Anger at Matteo resurfaced again but I swallowed it. I wouldn't let him ruin the evening.

"You can go dancing," Aria said with a shaky smile, clinging to her drink like it was her lifeline.

"In a few minutes. You look pale."

"I'm okay."

She didn't look okay, and I wasn't sure why she didn't want to tell me what was bothering her. Although, I really had no right to complain. After all, I still hadn't told her about the kiss.

"I really need to go to the restroom," I said after several minutes of silence.

"I need to sit for a few more minutes."

I hesitated, wondering if it was a good idea to leave her, but it wasn't like she was alone. After all, Romero never let her out of his sight, thanks to Luca's possessiveness.

I made my way toward the back of the bar where the restrooms were, trying not to lose my shit on Cesare who was like an annoying shadow. When I returned to the bar a few minutes later, all hell had broken lose. Aria was swaying and Cesare had to hold her up while Romero had his knife buried in some sleezebag's leg. "You will follow us. If you try to run, you'll die," Romero growled.

"Aria?" I whispered, my heart pounding in my chest. She didn't seem to hear me.

"Take her drink. But don't drink," Cesare told me. I picked up the glass, too shaken to be annoyed by his patronizing tone.

We made our way to the back and then down into a basement. Aria's legs barely supported her. I stayed beside her the entire time. When we stepped into a sort of office, my eyes settled on Matteo who lounged in a chair. His gaze zoomed in on me before taking in the rest of the scene. He pushed to his feet. "What's going on?"

"Probably roofies," Romero said.

Roofies? I narrowed my eyes at the asshole who'd drugged my sister. I wanted to hurt him, but the expression on Matteo's face made it clear that I would get my wish. His eyes held a promise to me. I knew it was sick, but somehow this made me want to kiss him even more.

Something was so wrong with me.

Aria and I were sent away before Luca and Matteo started dealing with the bastard, and Romero led us out the back door toward an SUV. My heart clenched when I settled on the back seat with Aria's head on my lap. She was so helpless. I stroked her blonde hair as I listened to her rambling. The idea that someone wanted to hurt her scared the shit out of me. This was probably the first time that I was glad for our bodyguards. Without them that sick fuck would have kidnapped Aria and raped her. But I knew he'd get what he deserved, and I was oddly okay with it. I hated the mob and what it stood for, but right now I couldn't bring myself to feel bad for Aria's attacker. Maybe this was a sign of how much this life had shaped me, a sign of how messed up I was. I couldn't get the look on Matteo's face out of my head. That flicker of excitement as he pulled out his knife before Aria and I left the room. He and Luca were both monsters. I wasn't sure yet who was more dangerous of the two. But the worst thing was that part of me felt attracted to Matteo's monstrous side.

Almost one month had passed since I'd last seen Matteo. Somehow his words about owning me still wouldn't leave my mind. Every time I relived our kiss, I brought them to the forefront of my brain to let my anger wash away any kind of longing my body felt. The only reason why I even still remembered that stupid kiss was because things at home were so bad. I was constantly fighting with Father, most of the time about my habit of saying whatever crossed my mind, just like today. "I don't give a damn what's expected of me."

Mother shushed me, her eyes shock-wide, but I was beyond listening. If Father told me one more time that I should behave like a decent lady, I'd lose my shit. "Why is it so difficult to get into your head? I don't want to be a lady, definitely don't want to be a good little wife to some mob asshole someday. I'd rather cut my own throat than end up like that."

I saw it coming but didn't even try to avoid it. Father's palm hit my face. It was one of his lighter slaps, which usually wasn't a good sign. He hit hard when he had no words to break my spirits. If he went easy on me, I wouldn't like what he had to say. He gripped my shoulders hard until I met his gaze. "Then maybe you should go looking for a sharp knife, Gianna, because Vitiello and I decided to marry you off to his son Matteo."

My mouth fell open. "What?"

"You must have made quite an impression because he asked his father to make this arrangement."

"You can't do that!"

"I can. And it wasn't my idea. Matteo seemed very adamant about marrying you."

"That bastard."

Father's grip tightened and I winced. Lily only stared with huge blue eyes. She and Aria had only occasionally experienced Father's rougher side. He usually reserved his slaps and cruelness for me, the bad daughter. "This is exactly the reason why I'm glad to have you out of our territory. If I married you off to one of our soldiers, I'd have to punish one of our own for beating you to death for your insolence, but if Matteo Vitiello tortures some sense into you, I'll be off the hook because I can't risk war with New York."

I swallowed my hurt. I knew Father liked me least, and it wasn't as if I needed his approval or affection, but his words stung anyway. Mother, of course, didn't say anything, only stared down at her plate while folding and unfolding her stupid napkin. Lily's eyes were brimming with tears but she knew better than to open her mouth when Father was in a mood. She and Aria had always been better at self-preservation than me.

"When did you make the decision?" I asked firmly, trying to mask my feelings.

"Matteo and his father approached me right after Aria's wedding."

And suddenly I knew when Matteo had decided to marry me: when I'd told him the morning after our kiss that I would never marry him. The arrogant asshole couldn't take the hit to his pride. He was marrying me to prove a point: that he got whatever he wanted, that he had the power while I was a marionette in the hands of the mafia. "I won't marry him or anyone else. I don't care what you say. I don't care what the Vitiellos are saying. I don't *fucking* care."

Father shook me hard until my ears started ringing. "You will do as I say, girl, or I swear I will beat you until you forget your name."

I glared. I'd never hated anyone as much as I hated the man in front of me, and yet part of me, some hopeful, stupid, weak part loved him. "Why do you do this? It's not necessary. We already gave them Aria to make peace. Why do you force me to marry? Why can't you let me go to college and be happy?"

Father's lips curled in disgust. "Go to college? Are you really that stupid?

You are going to be Matteo's wife. You are going to warm his bed and bear his children. End of story. Now go to your room before I lose my patience."

Lily sent me a pleading look. What had once been Aria's job was now Lily's: keeping me out of trouble. If it hadn't been for her, I would have continued the fight. I didn't care if Father beat me over and over again, it wouldn't change my mind.

I turned on my heel and ran up to my room where I grabbed my phone and flung myself on my bed. I speed-dialed Aria and after the second ring she answered. Hearing her voice, the tears I'd been holding back, slipped out. At least, our bastard of a father couldn't see them.

"Aria," I whispered. The tears were coming faster already.

"Gianna, what happened? What's going on? Are you hurt?"

"Father's giving me to Matteo." The words sounded so ridiculous. Nobody in the outside world would even understand them. I wasn't a piece of furniture that could be handed over to someone and yet that was my reality.

"What do you mean he's giving you to Matteo?"

"Salvatore Vitiello spoke to Father and told him that Matteo wanted to marry me. And Father agreed!"

"Did Father say why? I don't understand. I'm already in New York. He didn't need to marry you off to the Famiglia too."

"I don't know why. Maybe Father wants to punish me for saying what I think. He knows how much I despise our men, and how much I hate Matteo. He wants to see me suffer." That wasn't exactly the truth. I didn't really hate Matteo, at least not more than I hated every other Made Man. I hated what he stood for and what he did, hated that he had asked Father for my hand like my opinion didn't matter.

"Oh, Gianna. I'm so sorry. Maybe I can tell Luca and he can change Matteo's mind."

"Aria, don't be naïve. Luca knew all along. He's Matteo's brother and the future Capo. Something like that isn't decided without him being involved."

"When did they make the decision?"

After I was stupid enough to kiss him. "A few weeks ago, even before I came to visit." I couldn't tell her that it had happened at her wedding. Aria would only figure out a way to blame herself for my misery.

"I can't believe him! I'm going to kill him. He knows how much I love you. He knows I wouldn't have allowed it. I would have done anything to prevent the agreement."

Aria sounded remarkably like me in that moment, and while my heart swelled with love for her because of her willingness to protect me, I couldn't allow it. Maybe Aria didn't see it, but Luca was a monster and I didn't want her to get hurt, not for me, not when it was already too late. "Don't get in trouble because of me. It's too late anyway. New York and Chicago shook hands on it. It's a made deal, and Matteo won't let me out of his clutches."

And I knew it to be true. Even if he decided he didn't want me, he would never admit it. I'd always thought I could evade marriage, had always thought I could figure out a way to go to college, to find a life away from the mob world.

"I want to help you, but I don't know how," Aria said miserably.

"I love you, Aria. The only thing that stops me from cutting my wrists right now is the knowledge that my marriage to Matteo means I'll live in New York with you." I'd never considered suicide a valid option, had never felt miserable enough to do it, but sometimes it felt like the only choice I had left in my life, the only way to decide my own fate and to ruin Father's plans was actually when to end it. But I'd never actually go through with it. I couldn't hurt my siblings like that, and regardless of my hopeless future, I clung to life too much.

"Gianna, you are the strongest person I know. Promise me you won't do anything stupid. If you hurt yourself, I couldn't live with myself."

"You are much stronger than me, Aria. I have a big mouth and flashy bravado, but you are resilient. You married Luca, you live with a man like him. I don't think I could have done it. I don't think I can." I'd seen glimpses of Matteo's darkness in New York when he'd offered to kill Aria's attacker to make me happy, and afterwards in his eyes when he'd been covered in blood like Luca. There hadn't been regret or guilt in his gaze then. Sometimes I thought he was the more dangerous of the two because he was less in control. Sometimes I thought he hid how messed up he was with his outgoing personality.

"We'll figure it out, Gianna," Aria said.

I knew she couldn't do anything.

That evening Matteo fucking Vitiello actually dared to call my phone. I ignored him. There was no way in hell that I'd talk to him. Not after what he'd done. If he thought this was over, if he thought he'd won, then he had another thing coming.

chapter *four*

Matteo

I WAS READY FOR THIS FUCKING DAY TO BE OVER. FIRST FATHER'S funeral, and now hours of discussion with the Cavallaros and Scuderis about ways to keep the Russians at bay and to show them who was boss. It wasn't like I needed time to grieve. Luca and I hadn't harbored any feelings except for contempt and hatred for our father in a very long time but I wasn't a fan of funerals and everything they entailed. Especially seeing my stepmother cry her fake tears had grated on my fucking nerves. Did she really think anyone believed she actually missed her sadistic husband? She'd probably spit on his carcass when nobody was looking. It's what I wanted to do.

The only good thing about this whole ordeal had been Gianna who had to attend the funeral with her family. She'd ignored my calls ever since she'd found out about our marriage a week ago, but she couldn't avoid me forever. I was actually looking forward to our first private encounter. I loved when she was angry.

After the meeting, I was on my way to my motorcycle when I heard steps behind me. I turned, finding Luca running my way, the phone pressed against his ear and a thunderous look on his face.

Before I could ask him what had crawled up his ass, he lowered the phone and said, "Cesare called. The Russians are attacking the mansion. Romero is trying to get everyone to safety, but there are too many attackers."

"Where are Gianna and Aria?"

"I don't fucking know. We'll have to take a helicopter."

I followed Luca toward his car. He floored the gas the moment we both had sat down. We should have never let Aria and Gianna leave for the Hamptons without us. We'd thought they'd be safer there. We'd thought our enemies would attack in the city where so many members of the Outfit and the Famiglia had gathered to honor my father. We'd been fucking idiots.

Luca hit the steering wheel. "I'm going to hunt down every fucking Russian if they hurt Aria."

"I'll be at your side," I said. I didn't care how many Russians I'd have to cut into tiny pieces to get to Gianna. Damn it.

When we finally landed near our mansion in the Hamptons, Luca and I didn't speak. We both knew we might be too late. "They are fine," I said to Luca.

We got out of the helicopter and shot our way free until we reached the lobby of the mansion. I pulled my knife out of the throat of some asshole and straightened when one of the Russian bastards shouted from inside.

"We have your wife, Vitiello. If you want to see her in one piece you better stop fighting and drop your weapons."

Luca glanced my way. "Don't do anything stupid, Matteo."

"You aren't the only one with something to lose," I said grimly. "Gianna is in there too."

Luca gave a nod then slowly walked forward. I followed a few steps behind him. My eyes found Aria first. One of the Russian underbosses, a fucker named Vitali, was holding a knife against her throat. Luca would kill the bastard.

"So this is your wife, Vitiello?" Vitali asked, but I barely listened.

Gianna was sprawled out on the floor, a huge bruise on her forehead. I could tell that she was trembling, from fear or pain, I wasn't sure. Her blue eyes met mine. A huge Russian asshole towered over her. Bloodlust filled my body. I twisted my knives in my hands, trying to decide which part of the Russian's body I'd slice off first, probably the hand he'd used to hit her.

Gianna didn't take her eyes off me, like she knew I was going to make this all okay. I wouldn't let any of those fuckers hurt her now that I was here. And by God, I'd make them pay, make them regret the day they'd laid eyes on Gianna, make them regret the day they were fucking born.

"Let her go, Vitali," Luca snarled.

"I don't think so," Vitali said in that fucking annoying accent. "You took something that belongs to us, Vitiello, and now I have something that belongs to you. I want to know where it is." I wasn't sure what the Bratva bastard did because I kept my eyes on Gianna's captor and the assholes behind him but Luca took a threatening step forward, then stopped.

"Put your guns down or I'll cut her throat."

When pigs learn to fly, motherfucker.

There was a thud, then another. My eyes flew to Luca, who'd dropped his fucking guns to the floor. I couldn't believe it. He narrowed his eyes at me.

Was he serious? From the look on his face, he was. I put my knives down slowly. Gianna closed her eyes as if she thought everything was over. It wasn't over, far from it. Not before I'd killed every fucking asshole in the room and made them regret the day they were born.

"Your wife tastes delicious. I wonder if she tastes this delicious everywhere," Vitali said as he pulled Aria against him like he was going to kiss her. I could tell that Luca was seconds away from attacking.

The Russian asshole behind Gianna nudged her butt with his shoe and grinned. His foot would be the second thing I'd cut off, and I'd take my fucking time killing him.

Vitali licked Aria's chin. She looked like she was going to be sick. Then she reached into her back pocket and pulled a switchblade out. Where the hell had she found it? The moment she rammed it into Vitali's thigh, I fell to my knees, gripped my gun with my left hand and one of my knives with my right hand. I shot four times in quick succession. Two bullets tore through the calves of the asshole who'd kicked Gianna, the third broke every bone in his right hand, the fourth smashed the skull of another bastard. I flung the knife at the same time. It pierced the eye socket of Russian number three.

I stormed toward Gianna, slipped my arms under her body and carried her over to the side where she was shielded by a massive wooden sideboard. I knelt in front of her and shot another Russian, then another. Gianna's face was pressed up against my knee, and I put my palm down on the top of her head, stroking her unruly red hair.

A woman cried out. My eyes darted around until they settled on Luca who was cradling an unmoving Aria in his arms. I froze, my heart slamming against my chest.

"No!" Gianna cried hoarsely. She tried to sit up but her arms gave away and she fell against me. "Aria!"

I wrapped my arm around her and she stared up at me with terror-stricken eyes.

"Help Aria! Help her!" she whispered.

She tried to stand again. I helped her up, one arm around her waist, but didn't let her go to her sister. Luca looked like he would kill anyone who dared to approach. There was an expression on his face I'd never seen before. Leading a life of brutality, Luca and I had the potential to snap. But until now I hadn't thought there was anything on this planet that could actually bring Luca to the brink.

Gianna started crying. I touched her cheek. "Shh. Aria will be fine. Luca won't let her die."

For everyone's sake I hoped I was right. Gianna leaned against me, hands clutching my shirt. I peered down at her.

When Aria finally opened her eyes, Gianna let out a sob and pressed her face against my chest. I cupped her head, then brushed a kiss against it. She didn't react. She was probably in shock.

"What about Gianna, Lily, and Fabi?" Aria asked in a weak voice.

Gianna lifted her head but didn't let go of me. "Fine."

Luca lifted Aria into his arms and after some discussion carried her upstairs to one of the bedrooms. The doc was already on his way.

Gianna tried to stand on her own but swayed and had to grip my arm. Her eyes lost focus for a moment before they settled on me again. She didn't say anything, only stared up at me. I lightly brushed my fingertips over the bruise on her forehead. "Is this the only place you're hurt?"

She shrugged then winced. "My side hurts, and my ribs."

"Hey, Matteo, what about this asshole?" Romero asked, nudging the Russian who'd kicked Gianna.

"Is he the only survivor?"

"There is at least another one," Romero said.

"Good. But that one is mine. I'll question him."

"That's the guy who hit my head," Gianna said quietly.

"I know."

She searched my face but I wasn't sure what she was looking for. Her eyes fluttered shut for a moment but she quickly opened them again.

"You need to lie down," I said.

She didn't even try to protest, which was a bad sign. I tightened my hold on her and led her toward the staircase.

"Matteo?" Romero called.

I glanced over my shoulder at him and the other men. "I'll be back in a moment. Get rid of the bodies, and take the two living Russians down into the basement."

Romero nodded. "Okay." Then his eyes slid to Cesare's body on the ground. There was nothing we could do for him. I'd known him for a long time. He'd been a good, loyal soldier. The time to mourn him would come, but it wasn't now.

I helped Gianna up the stairs, and pretty much carried her down the corridor toward one of the guest bedrooms. I really wanted to take her to the room I slept in when we were in the mansion but I didn't want to have a fucking fight, not until Gianna was fit enough to be an equal contestant. She lay down on the bed, and closed her eyes with a groan.

I bent over her. "I want to take a look at your ribs. Don't punch me."

Her eyes fluttered open, and the hint of a smile tugged at her lips. I wondered if it was because she had a concussion or if she'd finally come to terms with our impending marriage.

I pushed her shirt up, revealing inch over inch of creamy skin, but before my mind could come up with any ideas, I found the first bruises. A big one on her waist and two slightly smaller ones over her rib cage. Gently, I pressed down on the bruise on her waist but she flinched away from my touch with a hiss.

"Fuck. That hurts."

I gritted my teeth. I couldn't wait to go down to the basement and have a word with the asshole who'd hurt her. I slid my hands higher, lightly tracing her ribs.

She shivered. "What are you doing?"

"I want to see if your ribs are cracked," I told her.

"You want to use your chance to grope me, admit it." Her attempt at humor was ruined by her shaky voice but I decided to play along. She didn't need to know that I was thinking of a way to prolong her attacker's suffering.

I smirked. "We'll be married in less than a year, then I can grope you whenever and wherever I want."

Her smile died and she turned away, closing her eyes. Maybe she hadn't come to terms with our marriage yet…

I straightened. "I need to go back down. I'll send the doc to you when he's done with your sister. You should catch some rest. Don't walk around the house."

She didn't open her eyes, didn't give any indication that she'd heard me at all.

I walked out, and closed the door. The doc was heading my way, one of his assistants, a young woman whose name I kept forgetting, a few steps behind him. "Where's Aria?" he asked in his raspy, chain-smoker voice.

I pointed toward the master bedroom. "When you're done with Aria, take a look at Gianna. I don't think she's seriously injured but I want to be sure."

He gave a curt nod, not even slowing. Nobody wanted to make Luca wait.

"Call me before you go in. I want to be there when you check on Gianna."

The doc was over sixty but that didn't mean I wanted him alone with Gianna, not after almost losing her.

He paused briefly, pale eyes settling on me. "She's yours?"

"Yes."

He nodded simply then he continued toward the master bedroom. I turned and headed downstairs.

When I stepped into the basement, the two Russian survivors were tied to chairs. Tito, one of our best enforcers, leaned against one wall, his arms crossed. Romero stood beside him. Another soldier, Nino, attached a drip to the asshole I was going to tear apart. The other Russian was in slightly better shape and didn't need a transfusion—yet. Once Tito got his hands on the poor bastard that would change too.

Tito straightened and inclined his head.

"I hope you didn't start yet," I said.

"We waited for you," Tito said.

"Does it look as if Tito started his work yet?" Nino asked eagerly. The kid had a sick fascination with torture.

"Good." I stalked toward Gianna's attacker. He glowered at me. "What's your name?" I asked.

"Fuck you," he said in heavily accented English.

I smiled at Tito, Romero, and Nino. Then I unsheathed my knife and held it out for the Russian bastard to admire. "You sure you don't want to tell me your name?"

He spit in front of my feet. "Where's that red-haired whore? Her pussy was calling for me."

Nino nudged Romero with an eager smile. Tito had pulled his own knife and was wiping it on his jeans.

"Tough words for a dead man," I said lightly.

"I won't tell you anything."

"That's what they all say." I stepped closer. "Let's see how tough you really are. Twenty minutes is the longest it ever took me to get someone's name."

I slammed my fist into his side, right over his left kidney. While he gasped for breath, I nodded at Tito to start his work on the other Russian bastard.

Twelve minutes later I'd learned that the man in front of me was called

Boris and had been working for the Bratva in New York for six years, before that he'd been in Saint Petersburg. He was still reluctant to give me more than the basic information. I paused, staring down at his blood-covered face. "You sure you don't have an answer to my question?"

He coughed, blood dripping down onto his shirt. "Fuck you."

"I can do this all night, but I can promise you, it won't be pretty."

Gianna

I grew tired of waiting for the doc to show up. I didn't feel very dizzy anymore, and I barely winced when I straightened. And to be honest, being alone freaked me out after what had happened today. I'd been sure we'd all die, and my body still wasn't convinced otherwise. My pulse was fast and occasionally I broke into a sweat. All because the mob had a bone to pick with the Bratva.

I walked out of my room, then hesitated in the corridor. My eyes darted to the end of the hallway where the master bedroom was. Luca and the doc were probably still taking care of Aria. They'd send me away if I tried to walk in, or worse lock me into the guest bedroom so I couldn't wander the house. I decided to go in search for Lily and Fabi instead. I yanked my phone out of my pocket and sent my sister a text.

Where R U?

Instead of replying, a door opened and Lily's dark blonde head poked out. Her face was puffy from crying and her eyes were huge and fearful. When her gaze settled on me, she ran in my direction and threw her arms around me.

"Where's Fabi?" I asked when I could breathe again. My ribs were throbbing fiercely from her hug but I didn't want her to know I was hurt. She looked terrified as it was.

"Asleep. They gave him some kind of sleeping pill because he was having a meltdown." She looked up at me. "I was so scared, Gianna. I thought we were all going to die, but Romero protected Fabi and me."

Her cheeks turned red. Her crush on Romero had been growing rapidly over the last few months. I didn't have it in me to tell her what kind of man he must be if Luca chose him as Aria's protector. Lily would realize soon enough that we were surrounded by the bad guys, not knights in shining armor.

"What about Aria? Romero only said she was fine before he left Fabi and me alone in that room and told me not to walk around the house because it was too dangerous."

"She was shot in the shoulder, but the doc is taking care of her. She'll be alright."

That's what I hoped. My eyes darted to the master bedroom again. I'd have to try to sneak in later when the doc and Luca were gone.

"Go back to your room, I'll be back soon." I turned to leave but Lily followed me like a lost puppy.

"Where are you going?" she asked.

"Downstairs. I want to see the damage."

"I'm coming with you."

I sighed. Aria would have told our sister "no," but it was hypocritical of me to tell Lily to behave when I'd rarely followed orders in my life. Lily wasn't a small kid anymore. "Okay, but be quiet and stay away from the men."

Lily rolled her eyes. "I'm not interested in them."

"I didn't say you were, but they might be interested in you."

I really didn't want to have to explain to Luca that I had to kill one of his men because they touched Lily. Of course, I'd first have to figure out a way to kill them. We headed downstairs. The entrance hall was a mess. Blood and broken glass littered the floor. At least the bodies were gone, but a trail of blood led outside to a pile of dead Russians. I really hoped they didn't treat Umberto's body like that. My chest tightened but I fought the sadness. Umberto had chosen this life. Death was part of the game.

I blocked Lily's view of the corpses and dragged her toward the living room, which wasn't in much better shape. The white couches would definitely have to be replaced. I didn't think any bleach in the world could get out the stains. Lily made a small distressed sound and I pulled her further along, already regretting that I had allowed her to come with me. A couple of men were taking a smoking break on the terrace, and glanced our way as we passed. They didn't seem bothered by the blood. I walked faster.

"Hey," Lily protested but I ignored her. If I'd been on my own, I wouldn't have cared but I didn't want to put my sister in danger.

We headed to the back of the house where the kitchen was, and almost bumped into another man. "Watch where you're going," he said, then paused and actually checked us out. I didn't know him and I had no interest of finding out more about him.

I pushed Lily past him. His eyes followed us all the way to the back of the corridor. When we turned the corner, we came face-to-face with a steel door, which was left ajar. A cry of pain carried out from below and made me shiver.

Lily clutched my arm, blue eyes wide. "What was that?"

I swallowed. I had a pretty good idea what was going on but I wasn't going to tell her that. "I don't know." I took a step closer to the door, then hesitated. I couldn't take Lily with me, but I couldn't leave her alone in the hallway when there were so many creepy fucks running around. I opened the door and peered down a long, dark staircase. Light spilled out from somewhere in the basement. Lily was almost pressed against my back, her breath hot against my neck.

"You don't want to go down there, right?" she whispered.

"Yes, but you will stay on the stairs."

Lily followed me a few steps down before I gave her a warning look. "Stay there. Promise me."

Another cry sounded from below.

Lily flinched. "Okay. I promise."

I wasn't sure if she meant it but she looked freaked out enough that I was willing to take the risk. I crept down the remaining steps, but halted on the last step, scared of what I might see. Exhaling, I stepped down and found myself in a huge basement. Bile shot up my throat. I wasn't stupid. I knew what the mob did to their enemies, especially if they wanted to get information out of them, but hearing stories and actually coming face-to-face with the horrendous reality of it were two very different things.

I braced my hand against the rough wall, my fingers curling around the hard edge. Two men were bound to chairs. Matteo and a tall, heavily muscled guy seemed to be in charge of pressing information out of them, while Romero stood back, but he must have had some part in their torture too because his hands were covered in blood, and so were his clothes. But it was nothing compared to the sight of Matteo. His white shirt was covered in blood, his rolled-up sleeves revealed blood-covered skin. There was red and red and red, so many different shades of it. But the worst, God the worst thing, was his face. There was no pity, no mercy, no nothing. There wasn't excitement or eagerness either, that was what I tried to cling to. At least he didn't get off on what he was doing. He didn't seem to feel anything judging from his expression.

I'd always known his easygoing, playful, flirty attitude was a mask to cover up the ugly truth, but again knowing and having that knowledge confirmed in such a brutal way were two very different pair of shoes. Maybe if I'd been more naïve I could have convinced myself that Matteo was doing this because he'd had to bury his father today, because he was grief-stricken and needed an outlet for the pain, but I knew better. This was common mob business. Grief had nothing to do with it.

One of the tied-up Russians was the man who'd hurt me and I knew that was why Matteo had chosen him as his victim.

I'd always wanted out of the world I'd been born in, this fucked-up brutal world I knew, but in this moment I made the decision to actually try to flee. No matter the cost, no matter what it took and what I had to do, I would escape this hell. How could anyone want to stay when they saw this?

I knew people got used to these things, but I didn't want to get used to them. I could already tell that I had less trouble with blood every time I saw it. How much longer until the sight of someone being tortured would do nothing to me? How much longer until the voice in my head that said the Russian bastard deserved it and would have done the same to me if given the chance wasn't a quiet whisper but a roaring shout?

Something brushed my arm and I jerked back, barely stifling a cry of surprise. Lily stood beside me, and then everything went very quickly. I opened my mouth to send her back up but at the same time her eyes settled on the scene in the center of the room, and I knew things would get very ugly. I'd heart Lily scream before but that had been nothing in comparison to the sound breaking free from her lips when she saw the blood and the men who'd lost it. I supposed it was close to the sound fluffy lambs made when they were being slaughtered.

I actually flinched away from Lily. Her eyes went wide, then dilated scarily, her face taking on an expression that scared the shit out of me. All eyes jerked toward us. Matteo released the Russian, narrowed his dark eyes at me, as if I was the one doing something wrong. Lily kept up her screaming, a high-pitched wail that made the hairs on my neck rise.

"Romero!" Matteo snarled, nodding toward my sister. "Take care of Liliana."

Romero advanced on us. Tall and imposing.

Lily had always fawned over him, but now even she couldn't see anything but the killer in him. His hands were red. Red from blood, and Lily completely lost her shit. I could only stare. I was unable to move. Somewhere in the back of my mind a voice was telling me to talk to my sister, to try to calm her, to do something, *anything*, but that voice was drowned out by the terrified static filling my head.

The steel door slammed against the wall above our heads and then Luca was suddenly there. "What the fuck is going on here?"

Nobody replied.

Romero spoke to my sister in a soothing voice. "Calm down, Lily. Everything is okay."

Really? The scene in front of us told a very different story. Nothing about this was okay.

Of course, Lily wasn't to be calmed. Romero gripped her arm and Luca went to help him, but she was fighting them like an animal. How could such a skinny girl fight off two men?

Romero slung his arms around her chest, trapping her arms against her sides, but that didn't stop Lily from kicking out at him and everything around her, and she still didn't stop screaming at the top of her lungs.

"Shut her up! Aria will hear," Luca growled. He tried to catch her legs but she lashed out and kicked his chin. He stumbled back, more from surprise than anything else. Of course they could have subdued her easily if they hadn't been so careful not to hurt her. I took a step in their direction, worried that they might give up the gentle approach soon, but the ground tilted under me and I had to grip the wall again.

"Lily," I said. "Lily, stop."

She didn't even hear me.

The tall, muscled guy took a few steps toward them as if he was going to interfere, but Matteo pushed him back. "No. Stay out of it."

I'd forgotten about Matteo, but while I had watched Lily, he'd managed to clean his hands. They were still pink but at least not smeared with blood. His eyes settled on me but I had to look away. I couldn't return his gaze right now. I had a feeling I wasn't far from pulling a stunt like Lily and going bat-shit crazy on them. The coppery scent of blood hung like fog in the air, clogged my throat and nose, seemed to sink into my skin, bury itself deep in my body together with the horrible images.

Lily managed to kick off the wall, causing Romero to stumble back, lose his balance and land on his back with Lily on top of him. He grunted and lost his hold on my sister. She pushed to her feet, a look like a hunted animal on her face. Her gaze passed right through me.

"Lily, calm down," I tried again.

She tried to storm past Matteo but he was too quick. He grabbed her wrist, and wrapped an arm around her waist. Then she was suddenly on her back and he was kneeling on her legs and had her hands pinned above her head. Luca headed toward them with a syringe in his hand. That was the final straw.

I stumbled toward them despite my wobbly legs. "Don't hurt her!" I hissed. "Don't you fucking dare hurting her!"

"I'm trying very hard not to hurt her, but she's making it difficult. Luca, now!" Matteo growled from his spot on top of my sister.

I blocked Luca's way. "What is that?" I pointed at the syringe.

"Something that will calm her down," Matteo said.

"Get out of the fucking way." Luca brushed past me, knelt beside my sister who was still struggling against Matteo's hold, and pushed the needle into her arm. It didn't take long for her to grow quiet and stop struggling. Matteo released her wrists and sat up. Lily whimpered before curling into herself and starting to cry silently.

"I hope you all burn in hell," I whispered harshly as I knelt beside her and stroked her hair. Matteo watched me with unreadable dark eyes. There were a few specks of blood on his throat; they seemed to be all I could see.

One of the Russians started to laugh. For a second I considered punching him in the face. I wasn't even sure how he was still capable of any sound the way he looked.

Matteo shot to his feet and got right into his face. "Shut the fuck up, or I swear I'll cut your dick into pieces while you watch."

"Romero, take Liliana into her room and tell the doc to check on her," Luca ordered, his voice already back to business.

Romero lifted Lily into his arms, and she actually pressed her face into his chest and sobbed. He was the last person she should seek out for comfort. He was one of the fucking reasons why she'd freaked out in the first place. Maybe she didn't even realize who held her.

I stood as well to follow after them. I wouldn't leave my sister alone with any of them. Luca gripped my wrist. "I want to have a word with you first."

"Let me go!" I snarled but he didn't budge.

Matteo grasped Luca's forearm. "Let her go."

Luca and he stared at each other for a moment, then I was finally free but now Matteo was blocking the stairs. I still couldn't look at his face. I glared at Luca instead. "I need to go to Lily. Maybe you didn't notice but she had a breakdown because of you sick fucks."

"She'll get over it," Luca said dismissively.

"Do you hear yourself? You make me sick. Lily won't ever get over what she saw today. She'll probably have fucking nightmares for years, only because of you."

Luca smiled coldly. "If you want to blame someone, blame yourself, because I have a feeling she was only down here because she followed you."

"Luca," Matteo said in warning. "It wasn't Gianna's fault."

It was my fault, at least partly, but I would never admit it in front of them. If it weren't for their sick business, nothing of this would have happened. I decided to switch to attack-mode. "I wonder what Aria will say when she finds out what happened."

Luca narrowed his eyes. "You won't tell her."

"Oh, I won't?" I asked. I had absolutely no intention of telling her. She didn't need the extra baggage, but Luca didn't need to know that. Matteo stepped between his brother and me, and touched my arms. I jerked back as if he'd burnt me. "Don't touch me ever again."

"I really don't get what you see in her," Luca said.

"Luca, stop provoking her," Matteo hissed, then he turned his dark eyes on me. "You can't tell Aria. It won't serve any purpose, only make her miserable."

"Maybe she'll decide to leave him." I nodded toward Luca.

"Aria won't ever leave me," Luca said quietly. "She took a fucking bullet for me today. I almost lost her. I won't ever lose her again. And I won't let you ruin things between us."

The worst thing was that I knew he was right when he said Aria wouldn't leave him, not even when I told her what I'd seen today. It wasn't as if she didn't know what kind of man Luca was and what kind of things his men did on his orders. He'd killed and tortured for her before, and she still loved him. Somehow she could forget the monster and only see the man when she was with Luca. I was pretty sure I couldn't do it. I could hardly meet Matteo's gaze.

"I won't tell her," I said eventually. "But not for you. I'm doing it for her. I want to see her happy." And for some fucked-up reason Luca was making her happy, happier than I'd ever seen her. For her sake, I would pretend.

Luca turned to Matteo. "Take her to her room and make sure she stays there until Scuderi comes to pick them up. I don't want her to make another scene."

I bit back a snarky comment. "I want to see Aria. She needs me."

I could tell that Luca wanted to tell me "no" but he surprised me when he said, "You can stay with her when I'm not around."

"It's not like I'm eager to be in a room with you."

"Come on, Gianna." Matteo gripped my arm and didn't even release me when I protested. He led me up the basement stairs, then along the long hallway and up the stairs. We didn't speak until we reached my room and I jerked free of his grip.

My eyes darted to his pink hands and blood-covered shirt. Matteo followed my gaze, grimacing. "I'll go change."

"Don't bother. I won't ever forget what I saw."

Matteo walked up to me and I stood my ground, despite my body's desire to flee. "You are clever, Gianna. Don't tell me you didn't know what we were doing behind closed doors. Believe me, the Outfit doesn't handle enemies with kid gloves either."

"I know. That's why I despise everything about the fucking mob. And you are right, I wasn't surprised about what I saw today. It only confirmed what I'd known all along."

"And what is that?"

"That you are a sick fuck and that I'd rather die than marry you."

Matteo pulled me against him, his dark eyes practically scorching me with their intensity. "Maybe you think you could live in the normal world, maybe you think you could date a normal guy, but you'd get bored, Gianna. Maybe you don't want to admit it, but it excites you to be with someone like me. If a normal guy tells you he'd kill and torture to protect you, he'd be lying, exaggerating at best, but I'm making a promise I can keep."

"Let me go," I gritted out.

He did, then gave me his fucking shark-smile and headed for the door. "I'll lock the door. Luca will unlock it when he takes you to Aria."

"So you're going back to torturing that guy?"

Matteo's gaze flickered with an emotion I couldn't place. "Maybe. I'm a sick fuck, remember?" He slipped out. "But maybe I'll let Luca have some fun with the Russians first." His gaze lingered on me for another moment before he closed the door and locked it. I reached for a vase on the sideboard and flung it at the door where it shattered and tumbled to the floor.

I squeezed my eyes shut, making a promise I was determined to keep. I would escape before my wedding to Matteo. I would leave this life behind and never return. I would try to live a decent, honest, ordinary life.

Afterward I felt calmer, even if I knew it would be close to impossible to escape from the mob. It would take a plan and help, but I still had ten months until my wedding. Plenty of time.

Later when Luca picked me up and took me to Aria, I didn't even provoke him. I ignored him, even when he warned me again not to tell Aria about the basement. He didn't have to worry. I couldn't burden Aria with the truth, not when she still had to live in this world and with Luca.

chapter *five*

Gianna

"You look so pretty," Lily said from her spot on my bed in the guest room of the Vitiello mansion in the Hamptons. At least, it wasn't the same room I'd had last time. I had to suppress a shiver when I thought of that day and all the blood I'd seen.

I glared at my reflection. Mother had chosen the dress for me because I'd refused to go shopping with her for my engagement party. It was a surprisingly nice dress, which didn't make me look like a tramp. I still shuddered when I remembered the slutty dress they'd chosen for Aria when she'd gotten engaged to Luca.

My dress was dark green, my favorite color. I was surprised Mother knew that much about me, or maybe Lily had helped secretly. The skirt was flared and reached my knees. Definitely modest. Maybe Father thought I was bad girl enough and didn't need a slutty outfit to emphasize that further.

"I don't know why they bother," I said. "They know I don't want to celebrate my engagement to Matteo. I don't want to marry him."

"It's tradition."

Lily was wringing her hands nervously in her lap. Pushing my own feelings aside, I walked toward her and sat down. She didn't even look up but her lower lip was trembling.

"Hey, are you okay?"

She gave a small shake of her head. "I know it's stupid but I'm kind of scared."

"Of Luca, Matteo, and Romero?"

"I'm sorry."

I wrapped my arm around her. "Why are you apologizing? It's perfectly natural for you to be afraid of them after what you saw in September."

She shuddered. "I can't get it out of my head. I dream about it almost every night."

Two months since that day, and almost every night she woke me with her screams before she slipped into my bed. "They would never hurt you, Lily.

We are girls, they will always want to protect us from harm." It was laughable that I was singing their praises, but I would have done anything to calm Lily down.

"I know." She took a deep breath. "I hope I don't freak out like last time. Father would be so mad if I made a scene."

I kissed her cheek. "You won't. I'll be at your side. And Aria will be there too. Everything will be okay."

Someone knocked at the door but before I could reply, Fabi poked his head in, his eyes darting between Lily and me. "Are you having a girl talk?"

"Yes," Lily said at the same time as I said, "No."

Fabi narrowed his eyes and slipped into the room. He looked too cute in his tuxedo. "Father sent me to tell you everyone's waiting." He straightened his shoulders, his little chin lifting a little higher. Fabi had turned ten a couple of days ago and in a few years, he would already start his initiation process. I was glad that I probably wouldn't get the chance to see my sweet, good-natured brother become a killer.

"You ready?" I asked Lily, who nodded quickly but her eyes told a different story. I understood her only too well.

Fabi tugged at his collar, which looked tight even from afar. "Lily is supposed to come with me, so you can enter alone."

Lily stiffened beside me. She had clung to me when we'd first stepped foot into the mansion this morning. I wasn't sure why Luca and Matteo had insisted on celebrating in New York, and worse in the very place where Lily had seen Romero and Matteo torture a Russian, but it was too late now. So far we'd managed to avoid them all. I hadn't even seen Aria yet.

"No. I don't care what Father wants. Lily and I will go down together."

Fabi gnawed on his lip. "Father will be angry."

I stood, pulling Lily with me. "He'll get over it." He wouldn't make a scene in front of New York. He'd wait with his punishment until we were back in Chicago. Lily, Fabi, and I headed downstairs together and Lily's grip on my hand tightened with every step we took. As we passed the front hall her eyes darted to the back where the entrance to the basement was. She shivered. Voices were coming from the living room and we headed toward the door, our shoes clicking on the marble floor; a floor that had been slick with blood two months ago. I tried to forget what I'd seen that day. I needed to focus on today if I didn't want things to end badly.

It wasn't a big celebration, but the most important members of the New York Famiglia and the Outfit had been invited. I was determined to be on my best behavior today. I didn't want Father to think I was thinking of ways to escape and up the number of my bodyguards.

The moment we entered the living room, I knew I could kiss that plan goodbye. Lily let out a small sound in the back of her throat, her nails digging into my palm. Father was talking to Dante Cavallaro, Luca, and Matteo, while the other men, as well as Aria, my mother, and Matteo's stepmother, Nina Vitiello, stood around them. Father's eyes narrowed immediately when he saw me with Lily. Fabi quickly rushed toward him and Father scowled at him, probably giving Fabi a lecture under his breath.

Matteo's gaze captured me with its intensity. He was dressed in black pants and a white shirt.

"Gianna," Father said in a tight voice. "We've been waiting for you."

Everyone expected me to walk over to my father, so he could hand me over to Matteo, and I would have if Lily hadn't started shaking beside me at the sight of Matteo, Romero, and Luca.

Her eyes darted to me. There was a flicker of fear on her face. I didn't want Father, much less anyone else, to know that she was terrified. Father would be furious. Maybe he'd even hit her, and Lily really didn't need another bad experience. She'd been struggling enough in the last few months.

She was frozen beside me.

"Gianna, stop the nonsense and come over here," Father growled.

Aria came toward me. "What's wrong?"

Lily and I exchanged a look. So far we hadn't told Aria anything, but it would be hard to explain Lily's strange behavior.

"Long story," I said. "Can you take Lily's hand?"

But Father had had enough. He stalked toward me and grabbed my wrist in a crushing grip before he dragged me toward Matteo. "I've had enough of your insolence." I almost stumbled on my heels as I hurried after him.

Matteo pulled me against him, forcing Father to release me. The look on Matteo's face bore a remarkable resemblance to the one he'd had when the Russian had kicked me. I was glad to escape Father's wrath for now and didn't pull away from Matteo. Aria was hugging Lily to her side and both were whispering quietly. I hoped Aria could calm our sister down. I hated seeing Lily so distressed.

"I know what you did there," Matteo murmured in my ear once he'd put the engagement ring on my finger.

"And what would that be?"

"You helped your sister."

I slipped out from under his arm. "I wouldn't have had to help her if she wasn't terrified of you."

Matteo didn't look sorry. Maybe he wasn't capable of guilt. "I'll have a word with her."

"Stay away from her," I hissed, but he seemed to find my threatening tone funny, and I blew. My voice rose. I was beyond caring if the others would hear. "And while you're at it, stay away from me too. I don't want anything to do with your fucked-up world."

Unfortunately Father heard, and so did probably everyone else in the room, and while Matteo didn't seem to take my outburst to heart, Father's scowl promised punishment. I had a feeling Matteo would have stopped him, if I'd asked for his help, but I didn't want to be indebted to Matteo. I'd rather bear Father's beatings.

I couldn't stop staring at the yellow gold ring with the huge diamond in the center. Father had made it very clear what would happen if I took it off.

In our world it was like a cattle brand. Everyone would know whom I belonged to.

chapter *six*

Gianna

I HATED HAVING TO INVOLVE ARIA IN ANY OF THIS, BUT SHE WAS MY last option. The biggest problem was actually asking her. I didn't trust the phones. I wouldn't put it past our father to rig them so he could keep an eye and ear on me. I had to ask her in person but as a punishment for my misstep at the engagement party I hadn't been allowed to see Aria since our family's Christmas party. But after weeks of begging, Lily and I finally managed to convince Father to let Lily and me fly to New York for Lily's birthday in April.

Lily was practically bouncing with excitement during our flight. I was still surprised how quickly she'd recovered from the horrible events of last September. I really hoped she wouldn't be set back by being back in New York. She'd been avoiding Matteo and Luca the last few times we'd seen them but this time we'd be staying at Luca's penthouse, so there was no way she could do it.

The moment we walked into the waiting hall buzzing with voices, I wanted to groan. Matteo stood beside Aria and Luca. I should have realized he would come. He seemed determined to ignore my antipathy. Sometimes I almost considered to give up on running away and to try to come to terms with my marriage to Matteo, but then there were the moments when he gave me that cocky grin like now, and then I wanted to run away as fast as my feet could carry me because I actually wanted to kiss him, despite what I'd seen him do in September.

Lily kept close to me. It was the only sign that she hadn't forgotten what had happened almost seven months ago. She didn't take my hand like she might have done a couple of years ago but her arm brushed mine as we walked toward Luca, Matteo, and Aria. "Are you okay?" I whispered.

She jumped, flushing. "Yeah." She squared her shoulders. "I'm fine." She almost managed to hide her nerves from me. Aria ran toward us when we'd almost reached them and threw her arms around both of us. "I missed you so much."

"We missed you too," I whispered, kissing her cheek.

Lily beamed at both of us.

Aria shook her head. "You're as tall as me now. I still remember when you didn't want to go anywhere without holding my hand."

Lily groaned. "Don't say anything like that when Romero is around. Where is he anyway?"

I rolled my eyes, and Aria laughed. "He's probably at his apartment." Lily must have managed to get over her anxiety around Romero at some point. Puppy love turned you blind.

"Come on," Aria said. "Let's go."

As expected, Lily turned shy again the moment we stood in front of the guys. My protective side made me want to step in front of her and shield her from everything, but I knew she'd be embarrassed if I did something like that. My gaze found Matteo's eyes; they were warm; they were a normal guy's eyes, and for an instant I wanted to believe the lie he was so good at telling, but I forced myself to break our staring contest.

"The birthday girl," Matteo said with a smile at Lily, arms crossed over his chest. He looked so approachable and harmless, and I knew he was doing it on purpose because of Lily. Despite my best intentions not to, I felt grateful, and at the same time couldn't help but wonder how he could be so kind and funny one moment, when he was capable of the horrible things I'd seen in September.

"Not yet," Lily said, biting her lip. "Unless you have an early present for me." I almost exploded with relief. I'd worried Lily would be as nervous as last time when she'd see Matteo, but he was a master manipulator and had her wrapped around his finger again.

"I like the way you think," Matteo said with a wink. He took her suitcase then held out his arm for her to take. She glanced between Matteo and me. "Won't you carry Gianna's luggage?"

"Luca can take care of it," Matteo said, eyes dancing with mirth as they settled on me. Why did he have to be so…tolerable? If I didn't know any better, I'd say he had a suspicion I was trying to figure out a way to run away from our impending marriage.

I narrowed my eyes at him before turning to Lily. "Go on."

She linked arms with Matteo and they walked ahead. Luca took my suitcase without a word before following after his brother and my younger sister. I fell back with Aria. "Maybe Father should have married Lily off to Matteo instead of me," I said, only half-joking. She seemed to have no trouble getting along with him.

"Matteo needs someone like you, someone who talks back to him. I don't think she could handle him."

I snorted. "But you think I can?"

Aria searched my face. "There's something you're not telling me."

"Later," I whispered, and she nodded with a glance toward Luca and Matteo.

I didn't get the chance to talk to Aria until much later that day, and only because Luca and Matteo had business to conduct in their dance club "Sphere." Romero was still there but Lily had convinced him to play Scrabble with her in the living room so he was occupied as I led Aria out onto the roof terrace despite the cold. Once we stood at the edge of the roof, she turned to me. "You're up to something, aren't you?"

I hesitated, suddenly feeling guilty for even considering to involve Aria. "I can't do this, Aria. I want out. Out of this world. Out of my arranged marriage. Just out."

Her face became still, blue eyes wide. "You want to run?"

The wind had picked up and tore at my hair, but I wasn't certain if that was the only reason why I shivered. "Yes."

"Are you sure?"

"Absolutely," I said, though sometimes doubt kept me awake at night. This was a huge step. "Ever since the Bratva attacked the mansion and I saw what Matteo is capable of, I knew I had to run."

"It's not just Matteo, you know that, right? He isn't any worse than any other Made Man."

"That makes it even worse. I know that pretty much all the men in our world are capable of horrible things, and one day even Fabi will be, and I hate it, hate every second I'm trapped in this messed-up world."

"I thought you and Matteo were getting along better. You didn't try to rip each other's head off today."

"He's trying to manipulate me. Didn't you see how easily he could make Lily forget her nervousness around him?"

Aria shrugged. "It could be worse. Most men wouldn't have forgiven you for giving him such a hard time, but he really seems to like you."

Did he? I was never sure with Matteo. He was too good at hiding his emotions, at choosing the mask he wanted to show to the world. "Are you on his side?" I asked with a bit more force than I'd intended.

"I'm not on his side. I'm just trying to show you an alternative to running away."

Stunned, I said, "Why? You know I've never wanted this life. Why are you trying to make me stay?"

Aria glared, gripping my wrist. "Because I don't want to lose you, Gianna!"

"You won't lose me."

"Yes, I will. Once you've run away, we can't ever see each other again, maybe not even talk unless we figure out a way to do it without risking the mob tracing you."

Of course, in the back of my mind, I'd known that would be the result of my escape, but I'd pushed it aside, not able to bear the thought. "I know," I whispered. "You could come with me."

Aria parted her lips in surprise and even before she spoke I knew her answer. "I can't."

I nodded, facing away from her and letting my gaze wander over New York. I blinked a few times. "Because you love Luca."

She put her hand on mine. "Yes, but that's not the only reason. I can't leave Fabi and Lily behind either, and I've made peace with this life. It's all I've ever known. I'm okay with it."

Guilt crashed down on me. "Do you think I'm abandoning them if I leave?"

"They'll understand. Not everyone is cut out for a life in this world. You've always wanted to live a normal life, and they'll still have me. You have to think of yourself. I just want you to be happy."

I wrapped my arms around her, burying my face in her hair. "I don't think I can be happy here."

"Because you don't want to marry a killer, because you can't live with what Matteo does."

"No," I said quietly. "Because I can see myself being okay with it."

Aria drew back, pale brows drawn together. "What's wrong with that?"

I wanted to laugh and cry at the same time because I had a feeling that Aria wouldn't have asked that question before Luca. "Are you okay with what Luca does? Don't you ever lie awake at night feeling guilty for being married to a man like him?"

"We come from a family of men like him." She stepped back, her arms dropping to her sides. "Do you want me to feel guilty?"

"No. But normal people would feel guilty. Can't you see how messed up we are? I don't want to be like that. I don't want to spend my life with a man who carves up his enemies."

Aria stared but didn't say anything. She looked so horribly sad and hurt that I wanted to kick myself hard for ever opening my stupid mouth.

"I'm sorry. I didn't want to make you feel bad. I just…" I trailed off, not sure how to explain my conflicted emotions to Aria. "I know I have to risk it. I have to try to get away from all this and live a life without all the violence and messed-up morals. I'll always regret it if I don't."

"You know you can't ever come back. There's no going back once you've run. Even if Matteo would forgive you for insulting him like that, the Outfit would be responsible for your punishment until your marriage. And running away from the mafia is betrayal."

"I know."

"The Outfit punishes betrayal with death. Because you aren't a Made Man they might decide to go easy on you and throw you into one of their whorehouses or marry you off to someone far worse than Matteo."

"I know."

Aria gripped my shoulders. "Do you really? Few people risk running from the mob and there's a reason for it. Most people get caught."

"Most people but not all of them."

"Have you ever heard of someone who escaped the mob successfully?"

"No, but I doubt anyone would tell us about them. Neither Father nor Matteo or Luca have any interest in putting ideas in our heads."

Aria sighed. "You are really determined to go through with this."

"Yes."

"Okay," she said. This was the perfect moment to ask her for help but I realized I couldn't do it, couldn't ask that of her.

Of course Aria being Aria didn't need to be asked.

"You can't do it alone. If you want any chance at succeeding you'll need my help."

I stared at my sister, my beautiful, brave sister. I'd often thought we were twins who'd been born apart by some cruel twist of fate. She was the one person I'd die for. And if she'd asked me to stay, told me she couldn't live without me, I wouldn't even have hesitated. I'd have stayed, would have married Matteo. For her. But Aria would never ask that of me. Aria was the one thing that reminded me that there was good in our world too, and I hoped she'd never let the darkness around us corrupt her. "No," I said firmly. "I can do it on my own."

But Aria ignored my comment.

"If I help you to run, I'll betray the Famiglia and by doing so my husband," she said with a distant look in her eyes.

I shook my head. "You are right. And I can't let you take that risk. I won't let you risk it."

She linked her fingers with mine. "No, I will help you. I'm your only choice. And if anyone can make it, then it's you. You never wanted to be part of all this."

"Aria, you said it yourself, what I'm doing is betrayal and the mob deals harshly with people who betray them. Luca isn't the forgiving type."

"Luca won't hurt me." There wasn't the hint of doubt in her voice. Sadly, I didn't share her conviction. I opened my mouth to object but she raised her hand.

"He won't. If Salvatore Vitiello were still alive, things would be different. I'd have been under his jurisdiction, but Luca is Capo and he won't punish me."

How could she trust that cruel bastard like that? What must it be like to love someone so much that you would put your life in their hands without hesitation? "Maybe his men won't leave him a choice. He's a new Capo and if he looks weak, his men might revolt. Luca won't risk his power, not even for you. The Famiglia comes first to Made Men."

I was talking to a wall from the impact I was making on Aria. "Trust me," she said simply.

"I trust you. It's Luca whom I don't trust."

"And if you think about it, I wouldn't really be betraying the Famiglia. You are still part of the Outfit until you marry Matteo. That means what I'm doing is a betrayal of the Outfit at most, but I'm not bound to them, so I can't betray them."

"Be that as it may. Luca might not see it that way. Even if you aren't betraying the Famiglia, you're still going behind Luca's back. Not to mention that Matteo will probably move heaven and earth to find me."

"True," Aria said slowly. "He'll hunt you."

"He'll eventually lose interest."

Aria looked doubtful. "Perhaps. But I wouldn't count on it. We have to make sure he can't find you."

Above us the sky was turning dark gray, the first signs of an impending rainstorm. If I were superstitious, I'd probably see it as a bad omen. "Aria, I shouldn't have come to you with this. You can't get involved."

Aria rolled her eyes. It was such a me-thing to do that I couldn't help but smile despite the severity of our conversation.

"Don't try to talk me out of it. I'd feel guilty if I didn't help you and you got caught," she said firmly.

"And I will feel guilty if you get in trouble for helping me."

"I'm helping you. End of story."

"How can I ever make it up to you?"

"Just be happy, Gianna. Live the life you want, that's all I want."

That was so typically Aria. If anyone deserved a life outside of this fucked-up world, it would be her. I pressed my lips together, fighting tears. "Shit."

Aria smiled. "Come on. We need to figure out when and how to get you away."

"I suppose it's a bit too late to give it a try during this visit?" I forced a smile, wanting to get rid of the heavy feeling in my chest.

"Yeah. But you'll definitely have to run when you are in New York. You'll never escape from Father's men."

Sadly, she was right. Father didn't let me out of his sight for a second. He didn't trust me. The only thing missing from my prison was leg irons. "But Romero is always around."

Aria and I both glanced toward the living room where Lily was laughing at something Romero must have said. She looked so happy. "I think we can get him off our back," Aria said.

"Next time Lily won't be around to distract him. I don't want her to know about this."

Aria nodded. "I'll figure something out. I tricked him once before. I can do it again. Luca trusts me. Romero doesn't follow me as much as he did in the beginning."

Guilt twisted my insides again but I ignored it. "I have to get a passport so I can leave the country. I'll never be safe in the States."

"You should go to Europe."

"I've always wanted to visit Sicily," I joked.

Aria cracked up. "Yeah, that sounds like a foolproof plan."

"I need money. Maybe I can find out where Father keeps his stack of cash."

"No, he'd notice. We'll have to take Luca's money. If we wait until the last minute before we take it, he won't notice until it's too late."

"Are you sure?" I asked.

Aria nodded but there was a flicker of hesitation in her eyes.

"Maybe we can get money from somewhere else. I could ask one of the credit sharks for a loan. It's not like I'll be around for them to get it back," I said quickly.

Aria shook her head at once. "All the credit sharks either belong to the Famiglia or to the Bratva. That would be the quickest way to get caught."

"I know I can't ask the Famiglia, but what about the Russian credit sharks? I don't have to announce to them who I am. I could pretend I was some random girl with financial troubles."

Aria seemed to consider that but then she shook her head. "It's too risky. Those guys are dangerous."

Memories I'd tried to bury resurfaced like a tidal wave. I'd been terrified when the Russians had attacked the mansion. I'd been sure we'd die a horrible death, sure we'd be raped and tortured. I really didn't want anything to do with the Bratva ever again but Aria didn't need to know how much the images of that day still bothered me. Most of the time I managed to lock them away, and once I was in Europe, away from this world, they'd hopefully disappear for good. "Aria, you are married to the man all those dangerous guys are scared of."

"And you are engaged to the man who cuts those dangerous guys up," she said. "But the Russians are worse than our men. They don't have any honor."

I wasn't sure if that was possible, but I wasn't in the mood for that argument. "Okay, so no loan sharks, but what about a forged passport? I'll have to get that from somewhere. Is there anyone we could bribe?"

Another gust of wind tore at us, raising goose bumps all over my body. Aria moved closer to me until we huddled together. "No one will go against Luca."

"Except for us," I said with a snort. "Tell me this isn't crazy."

"It's crazy, but we'll figure something out." She paused, scrutinizing me.

I raised my eyebrows. "What?"

She smiled. "I have an idea. You know how people always say we look alike?"

"Not if you look closely. I'm a couple of inches taller than you and then there's this." I lifted a strand of my hair.

"Yeah, but if we dye your hair blonde, nobody will doubt that you are me. Luca has a few forged passports with different names in the same place where he stashes the money, in case we ever need to leave the country fast. You could use one of them."

"Luca will be able to track them."

"Yes, but you'll already have landed in Europe by then. You can throw away the passport once you're there and travel around without a passport until you figure out a way to get a new one. They don't have border control in the EU, so you should be fine to cross over to other countries within Europe."

Hope kindled in my body. "That could actually work."

"It will."

We stared at each other. "So I'm really running away," I whispered.

"Yes," Aria said quietly.

"When?"

"Next time you visit, so we have time to really think every detail of our plan through."

I couldn't believe I was really going to do this, but now I wouldn't back out, even if part of me wondered if this was really what I wanted.

I was allowed to visit Aria again in May; pretending that I had finally come to terms with my marriage to Matteo had made my father more lenient with me.

Lying had once been hard for me but I was getting better at it.

I hugged Lily and Fabi before I left Chicago, knowing it might very well be the last time I saw them, but I didn't allow myself to linger on that thought. It would make things only more difficult. If I started to cry, someone might get suspicious.

When I arrived in New York, Aria picked me up from the airport with a new bodyguard. There was something bittersweet about our reunion. The new guy gave me a quick nod after Aria and I had pulled apart. "Who is he?" I whispered.

"That's Sandro. He's one of Matteo's men." So Matteo had already chosen a bodyguard for me, for a future life as his wife, someone who would cage me in whenever Matteo wasn't around to do it.

Once we were in the penthouse, my new bodyguard retreated to the kitchen under the pretense of giving us privacy. As if there was ever such a thing under his constant surveillance. Aria and I lingered near the sofa, out of earshot. "Does Luca still have Romero guard you all day?"

Aria shrugged. "I don't mind having Romero around, especially when Luca is busy. Sandro has taken Cesare's place mostly, but he's never watched me before."

"You need to ask Luca to let you go to college or do something else before you go crazy over here. I want you to be happy too, Aria. I want to know that you'll be okay once I'm gone."

"Don't worry. And the last few weeks I've been pretty busy planning your escape," Aria said with a teasing smile but there was a hint of wistfulness in her voice.

We both glanced at Sandro who was making coffee. "Why is that Sandro guy really here?"

"Because of you."

"Because I'm the troublemaker?"

"No," Aria said with a laugh. "Because Matteo wants you to get to know the guy who'll be your bodyguard once you move to New York."

"Oh great, how thoughtful of him." Again a decision about my life that no one had bothered to discuss with me. With a nod toward Sandro, I asked, "How are we going to get rid of him?"

"I have a plan." Aria opened her bag and pointed at a small syringe. At my confused look, she explained, "I remembered how you'd told me that Luca found the tranquilizer he used on Lily in a drawer in the basement. Last time I was in the mansion, I sneaked down there and took what we needed."

My eyes widened. "You are a genius, Aria."

"Not really."

Our eyes darted toward our bodyguard once more. He was busy with his phone. "How are we going to inject him with the tranquilizer?" I asked. "He's tall and strong, and probably a skilled fighter."

Aria bit her lip. "We have to distract him. Maybe I can talk to him and you ram the needle into his thigh?"

"What if I break the needle by accident or if he smashes it?"

"I have a second syringe, but that's it, so we should try to get it right the first time."

Aria could be so badass if she tried. "Are you sure the dosage is right?"

"I don't want him to get hurt so I reduced the dosage they listed on the packaging."

"Okay. It still should be enough to knock him out for a while, right?"

Aria nodded. "We should probably tie him up. I found duct tape in the gun cupboard."

She knew where her husband kept his guns? "Luca must really trust you."

Aria didn't say anything and I felt bad for bringing him up. Did I have to remind her how she was risking her marriage for me?

"Come on," she said after a moment. "Let's do this. Matteo and Luca will be back in a few hours. We should be gone by then."

After another look toward Sandro who was still reading something on his phone, she quickly handed me the syringe. I hid it behind my back as we strolled toward Sandro who finally looked up from his phone and set it down on the counter.

"Would you like some coffee?" he asked with a nod toward his own cup. He was polite and his brown eyes were friendly. He didn't *look* very threatening, but I didn't let that fool me.

Aria leaned next to him against the counter and pressed a palm to her stomach.

Sandro frowned. "Are you okay?"

"I'm not feeling so good," she said, then her legs buckled. It was a bit over the top if you asked me, but Sandro must have acted without thinking because he reached for her. *My chance.*

My arm shot out and I rammed the syringe into the back of his thigh and injected the tranquilizer. Sandro hissed, let go of Aria and lashed out instinctively. He caught my arm and I was thrown against the kitchen island, my back colliding painfully. I swallowed a cry.

"What the fuck?" he gasped, eyes furious as they darted between Aria and me. He reached for his phone but Aria shoved it away. It flew off the counter, crashed to the ground and skidded over the marble. Sandro staggered toward it, his movements already less coordinated than usual. I quickly rushed toward the phone and kicked it away. "Where's the stupid tape?"

Aria nodded and rushed away.

Sandro glared at me. "What are you doing?" he growled. He advanced on me, his hand fumbling for the gun in his chest holster. Did he want to hold us at gunpoint?

He didn't get very far. His legs gave away and he fell to his knees. He shook his head like a dog then tried to stand again.

"Aria!" I screamed. What if this didn't work? What if our plan was over before it had really begun?

"I'm coming!" She ran toward me with the tape. "Grab his arms."

I tried to pull Sandro's arms behind his back, but he was too strong even in his dazed state. He shook me off.

"It's not enough tranquilizer!"

"I don't want to hurt him," Aria said panicky.

I tried to grip his arms again but he managed to stagger back to his feet, pushing me out of the way. Aria moved quickly and thrust the second syringe into his leg. This time he dropped to his knees almost instantly, then fell to his side. Aria and I made quick work out of tying him up then she touched his throat.

"Is he okay?" I asked.

"Yeah, it seems so. I hope we didn't give him too much."

"He's a tall guy. I'm sure he'll be fine." I got up. Aria did the same and then she rushed off again. A few minutes later she returned with a huge stack of dollar notes as well as two passports. For a moment I thought she'd decided to go with me and that was why there wasn't only one passport, then I realized how ridiculous that thought was.

"Here." She handed me everything. "That's about ten thousand dollars. That should get you by for a while, and two passports just in case. But you should really get rid of them once you're in Europe."

I stuffed everything into my bag then grabbed my suitcase.

"Ready?" Aria asked, hesitating.

"As ready as I'll ever be." She didn't return my smile, only glanced at Sandro again before setting her phone down on the counter. I did the same to prevent them from tracking us.

We took the elevator down and hailed a taxi. Traffic was on our side and we pulled up in front of the JFK airport after forty-five minutes.

After we'd entered the departure area, I headed straight to the ticket counter to buy a one-way ticket to Amsterdam while Aria stayed back; the photo in the passport looked more like her than me and if we stood beside each other nobody would have been fooled.

I gingerly slid the fake passport across the counter. The woman barely glanced at the photo, despite the fact that I didn't have blonde hair like the girl in it. She probably thought I'd dyed it red. Twenty minutes later, I walked over to Aria with the ticket to freedom in my hand. I'd have thought I'd feel more excited, instead nerves twisted my stomach so tightly I worried I'd throw up, but I couldn't let Aria see it.

"So how did it go?" she asked nervously.

I waved the ticket in response. "She didn't even ask about my hair."

"That's good, but once you're in Amsterdam, you need to change your appearance."

I smiled, touched by her concern and at the same time wondering if I was really doing the right thing. This could be the last time I ever saw Aria. I couldn't even imagine a year without her, much less the rest of my life. "Don't worry."

A small part of me wondered how Matteo would feel once he found out. I didn't think my disappearance would do more than bruise his pride. This wasn't about love, or even feelings.

Aria peered toward the main entrance again. "When does your flight leave?"

"In two hours. I should probably go through security."

"I will rent a car and drive it out of town as a red herring. Luca will think you and I ran away together. Maybe it'll buy you additional time. Once you're off the plane, go to a restroom and put on the wig, in case there's already someone looking for you at Schiphol airport."

Aria was talking fast but it didn't stop me from noticing the way her voice was shaking. She was trying to be strong for me.

I wrapped my arms around her. "Thank you so much for risking so much for me. I love you."

"Create the blog we talked about and post an update the moment you get the chance. I'll worry if I don't hear from you tomorrow at the latest," she said, her fingers digging into my shoulder blades. "Promise me you'll be happy, Gianna. Promise."

"I promise." Could you even promise something like that? My eyes burnt furiously but I fought the tears. This was hard enough without me turning into a blubbering mess. I pulled back, and ran a hand over my eyes.

Aria had lost her fight with tears. "If you ever want to come back, we'll figure something out."

"You said it yourself, there's no going back," I said, and finally the truth sank in. This was it. This was goodbye to the life I'd known, to my family, to my home, to everything. I took a step back from Aria, dropping my arms. She gave me an encouraging smile. I quickly turned around and hurried toward the security check. If I didn't leave Aria now, I'd lose my courage. Doubt was already eating away at my resolve, but this was my only chance. I had to take it. I needed to live my own life, needed to make my own decisions, needed to get away from the horrors of our world.

The security guard didn't stop me. Nobody did. Once I was through security, I risked another peek over my shoulder to where Aria stood. She raised her arm in a wave before she walked away quickly, wiping her eyes.

I watched her back disappear. My heart felt heavy, my throat tight. It wasn't too late yet. I could still go back. We could figure out some ridiculous explanation for drugging Sandro. Nothing was lost yet.

I peered down at my ticket to Amsterdam, my ticket to freedom, before I headed to the terminal where boarding would start soon.

As I waited, I kept checking my surroundings nervously, but nobody showed up. And why would they? Nobody suspected anything. When Sandro finally woke in a couple of hours and called Luca and Matteo, I'd be on the plane.

~

My heart was beating in my throat when I boarded the plane. It was my first time traveling in economy class. Father had always bought business or first-class tickets when we hadn't used a private jet. I was wedged between a stranger, who insisted on using my armrest, and the window. I barely dared breathing until we were finally up in the air, and even then I kept looking for a familiar face among the other passengers. It took a while before I finally settled back into my seat and relaxed. Now that there was no going back, a flicker of excitement mixed with my anxiety. This was my life and I was finally taking it into my own hands, finally taking back control from those who had ruled every aspect of my existence until now. I was going to be free.

Matteo

Luca's phone rang. "Yes, Romero?" Silence. "Repeat that."

I was checking last month's earnings for our clubs in Manhattan but looked up at the strain in Luca's voice. His expression made me close the laptop. "What's going on?"

Luca pushed to his feet. "Romero found Sandro drugged and tied up on the floor of the penthouse. Aria and Gianna are gone."

I straightened. "You're fucking kidding."

"Do you think I would joke about something like that?" he snarled into my face.

I glared right back. "I thought Aria was in love with you."

For a moment Luca looked like he was going to punch me. Then he whirled around and stormed out of the basement of the Sphere. I hurried after him. "This is Gianna's fault. This girl is the root of every problem. Why couldn't you stay the fuck away from her like I told you?" he muttered.

If only I fucking *knew*. For some reason, I couldn't get her out my head. And now she'd run. From *me*.

"I'm sorry, boss," Sandro said again, half hunched on Luca's sofa, eyes bloodshot.

I wanted to fucking kill him for letting her get away. I should have never let her out of my sight. I got up and started pacing the room again, my eyes darting up to the bedroom door. Luca had disappeared with Aria behind it more than twenty minutes ago. *She* hadn't run away. That had all been for show. She'd helped my fiancée run, but she'd come back to Luca. She'd come back.

Normally I wouldn't doubt Luca's skill to get information out of anybody, but this was Aria, and Luca wouldn't hurt her. Not even for me, not even when she was the only one who could help me find my fiancée.

"I shouldn't have taken the morning off," Romero said from his spot on the armchair.

"One bodyguard should have been enough. I should have been enough. They were only girls," Sandro muttered.

I didn't say anything. I was too pissed. My pulse was pounding in my temples. I wanted to smash every fucking piece of furniture into tiny bits. The bedroom door finally opened and Luca came down the stairs. From the look on his face I knew I wouldn't like what he had to say.

"Don't tell me you couldn't get anything out of her," I snarled.

Luca scowled. "The only thing I know is that Gianna took a plane from JFK. Aria won't tell me anything, but our informants will let me know which plane Gianna took soon."

"Great," I muttered. "And then what? Aria knows Gianna's plan. They told each other everything. The only way to find Gianna is through your wife."

"She won't tell me anything."

I tried walking past him. "Then let me have a word with her."

Luca grasped my arm and pushed me back. "You will stay away from her, Matteo."

"*You* let her steal *your* money, *your* passports. You let her attack our men, let her make a fool out of you and betray you. You should want to punish her. You are Capo."

Luca's eyes flashed. I was walking on thin ice but I didn't give a fuck.

"Aria is my wife. It's none of your business how I deal with her. I told you that Gianna meant trouble but you didn't want to listen. You should have never asked for her hand," he growled.

My fingers longed to grip my knives. I turned my back on him and stalked out onto the roof garden. I needed to cool off before I lashed out at my own brother. Luca and I had fought occasionally when we were younger but it had never been for real. I had a feeling that a fight between us wouldn't end well today. We were both royally pissed and out for blood.

I braced my arms against the banister and let my eyes wander over New York. Gianna was slipping through my fingers. With every second that passed she was bringing more distance between herself and me. Once she landed wherever she was going, she wouldn't stop running until she was sure she was safe. She'd be alone, unprotected. What if something happened to her?

Steps crunched behind me and I tensed but didn't look over my shoulder. Luca stopped beside me. "I called Scuderi. He's furious and blames us of course."

"Of course," I said quietly.

"He's sending two of his men after Gianna."

"I will go with them."

"I figured you would. I told Scuderi as much. You will meet them in Amsterdam."

I turned. "Amsterdam?"

Luca nodded. "I got word that she took a plane to Schiphol."

"When do I leave?" I asked, the thrill of the impending hunt spreading in my veins.

"Four hours."

"I need to leave sooner."

"Impossible. I tried everything I could."

"Damn it. Gianna will be long gone when I arrive."

"You'll find her. You are the best hunter I know. She doesn't stand a chance."

I clapped his shoulder. "You let me go, even though you need me here."

"You aren't of much use to me if all you can think about is Gianna."

"It could take weeks," I said. "I won't return until I've caught her."

"I know. If Aria had run, I would have done the same."

I nodded. I wouldn't stop until Gianna was mine. I didn't care if I had to search the entire world, if I had to turn every single stone, if I had to squeeze information out of every fucking person in Amsterdam, I would find Gianna.

chapter *seven*

Gianna

I BARELY GOT ANY SLEEP IN THE SIX HOURS IT TOOK THE PLANE TO reach Amsterdam. Worry for Aria had taken the place of worrying about getting caught. She was sure Luca wouldn't see her actions as betrayal, but what if she was wrong? God, what had I done? I shouldn't have involved her, shouldn't even have told her about my intention to run away.

When I finally got off the plane and had successfully passed through immigration, I slipped into the first restroom I found and locked myself into one of the small stalls. At the bottom of my bag was the wig Aria had given me. It was long and blonde. Nobody would be fooled by it close up, but it would only have to do until I dyed my hair later today.

Fear clogged my throat when I headed into the waiting area, half expecting someone from New York or the Outfit to wait for me, but that was impossible. Even if Matteo had figured out where I was by now, I was fairly sure that the Famiglia didn't have close relations to any crime syndicates in the Netherlands, and it would take some time for mobsters from Sicily to travel up all the way to Amsterdam. For now I was safe. At least, until the next plane from the East Coast landed in Schiphol, which would be the case in a few hours.

I quickly left the airport with my suitcase, overwhelmed by the sound of people speaking in languages I didn't understand. I knew a few words in Dutch but hadn't bothered learning the language; the Netherlands had never been intended as more than a stopover.

I hailed a taxi and let it take me to a non-descript middle-class hotel in the city where I booked their cheapest room. Despite feeling tired from jet lag and the flight, I only deposited my suitcase in the room before venturing out again to buy a few items I needed.

Two hours later I was back in my small hotel room with light brown hair dye, scissors, a couple of new outfits that helped me fit in better than my super expensive designer clothes, as well as a pre-paid cell phone and a small laptop. After I'd connected my laptop with the wireless internet of the hotel and set up the blog Aria and I had talked about, I wrote a short post, saying that a new journey had begun and that I'd safely arrived at my destination. It was all a bit cryptic and nobody would probably read my blog except for Aria. I resisted the urge to write something more personal, or worse use my new phone to call her. I wanted to hear her voice, wanted to know if she was okay, but I couldn't risk it. Even this blog was already risky. Instead I slipped into the bathroom and changed my hair.

Two hours later I stared at my new reflection. My hair was caramel brown and I'd cut it into a bob that reached my chin. Of course that wouldn't stop people from recognizing me from close up but unless I paid a surgeon to redo my face, which I had no intention of doing, a new haircut would have to be enough. I'd just have to move from city to city until I was sure that Matteo had moved on to another target and I was safe. That would probably take a while. Matteo had told me numerous times that he wouldn't give me up and I had a feeling he meant it.

I wouldn't give him a chance to catch me. Tomorrow, I'd leave Amsterdam and head for Paris, and who knew where I'd be the day after that? This was a new beginning with endless options.

I stared up at the white ceiling of my hostel room. I'd been living in twenty different places in the last three months, never staying anywhere for more than a week at a time. Sometimes when I woke in the morning I wasn't sure where I was, sometimes I even thought I was back in Chicago, and sometimes I found myself longing for it. Not for my father and the rules of our world, but for Fabi and Lily and Aria, and sometimes even for Mother.

I sat up, groaning, and went through my usual morning habit of reminding myself of my current pseudonym and everything that encompassed her before I got out of bed. It was almost noon. I still hadn't figured out any kind of routine. Most days I spent exploring the city where I stayed while always checking my surroundings. This fear of being followed, of being hunted, would that ever stop? I doubted it. Whenever I saw men in dark suites, panic filled me. I'd lost count of the times I'd imagined I'd seen Matteo from the corner of my eyes.

I hadn't made any real friends yet, which wasn't all that surprising; I never stayed anywhere long enough to build a connection. Which was better anyway. I couldn't risk getting close to anyone yet, maybe never. That didn't mean I was alone. I always stayed in youth hostels wherever I went, and met people from all over the world. Of course I couldn't tell them anything about me, not even my name. Currently I was calling myself Liz, short for Elizabeth, and was spending my year before college abroad road-tripping through Europe. That was pretty much my cover story wherever I went, only my name changed.

Lying to everyone 24/7 made any kind of friendship hard. I opened my laptop and checked my blog, which I still updated almost every day, even though I hadn't gotten a comment from Aria in weeks. In thirty-one days to be exact. My eyes darted to my cell phone on the nightstand. As so often recently I felt the almost irresistible urge to call her and find out what was keeping her from visiting my blog. I had a feeling it was for my safety. In her last comment she'd warned me "not to waste time in one spot because there was too much to explore in Europe." I'd taken that as a hint that Matteo might be after me and had jumped from city to city in the last few weeks, never staying anywhere more than one or two days, but I was growing tired of running constantly. I'd lost weight, and most of my clothes hung off me like they belonged to someone else. I wanted to belong again, to find a place to call mine.

I got dressed and stuffed my clothes into my backpack. I'd gotten rid of my suitcase four weeks into my journey. It wasn't practical lugging a heavy suitcase wherever I went. I didn't need most of my old belongings anyway. When would I ever wear evening dresses and high-heeled Louboutins again? That life was over. I stared down at my shabby backpack, at my cheap sneakers and jeans, and for a moment longing for something I'd thought I'd never miss came up in me. When I'd decided to run away from the mob, I'd known I'd miss my siblings horribly, and so far not a single day had gone by that I hadn't considered returning to Chicago just to see them again, to talk to Aria again, to have a steady home again, but so far I'd managed not to miss the luxuries my former life had afforded me, at least not this insistently. So why was I suddenly missing the things I'd despised?

Everything I'd ever owned had been paid for with blood money, and even my flight up till this point had been financed that way. But I was scarily low on cash and would have to find a job in the next place I stayed, though that would mean staying longer than just a couple of days unless I tried my hand at pickpocketing, which wouldn't really be a big improvement over mob money, except that nobody got killed for it.

I swung my backpack over my shoulder and exited my small room.

Fifteen minutes later, I'd checked out and left my alter ego "Liz, short for Elizabeth" behind. I'd become someone new for my next destination. Maybe a Megan. It was August but heavy clouds draped over Vienna as I headed toward the train station. I'd loved the regal buildings but it was time to move on from Austria. I'd been living in the same country for almost two weeks and was getting antsy.

After I'd boarded my train to Berlin, I checked my cell-phone, a stupid habit I still hadn't dropped. I never got a message from anyone. The date caught my eyes. August, 15th. The day I was supposed to marry Matteo.

Unwantedly the kiss we'd shared flashed in my mind and a small shiver ran down my back. I'd kissed three guys in the time since I'd arrived in Europe, all of them cute foreigners who weren't interested in anything lasting, just like me, but none of those kisses had come even close to what I'd felt while kissing Matteo. Maybe it was because he'd had more practice than any other guy. Matteo was a gigolo, there was no doubt about it.

But what worried me most was that I found myself comparing every guy I met to Matteo, and they always fell short. They weren't as good-looking, as interesting, they didn't have a six-pack, and most importantly being in their proximity didn't give me a thrill. It annoyed the hell out of me that despite being thousands of miles away from Matteo, he still held some power over me. I wished I'd never let him kiss me then I wouldn't have that problem.

I'd just have to find a nice guy who could make me forget Matteo and his annoyingly sexy and arrogant smile. Maybe my next destination, Berlin, would help with that.

I only stayed four weeks in Berlin before I decided to move on. Something hadn't felt right, or maybe I wasn't used to staying in a place for a longer period of time anymore. At least I'd worked as a waitress for the last three weeks and managed to earn some money. It wasn't much but enough to buy me my train ticket to Munich and food for the next couple of days. I didn't have anything left for a hotel room however, so that was a major problem.

I had spent too much at the beginning of my flight, never having learned to be economical. Money had never been an issue growing up. If there was one thing that women in the mob never had to forego, then it was money. I was a spoiled brat, that much I'd come to realize.

The moment I arrived in Munich I knew this could work. I loved everything about the city, but there was still the problem that I didn't have any money to pay for a room. I didn't want to spend the night on the streets. I wasn't sure how safe it would be. As I walked through the city center, I noticed a few people singing and playing instruments, and they seemed to make a fast buck with it. There was always a heap of Euro coins in the hats they'd put on the ground.

I could play the piano. Father had forced Aria, Lily, and me to take lessons from the moment we could talk but I had neither a piano nor a keyboard I could use to make music. I had a decent singing voice, definitely nothing to get excited about but at least it didn't make people want to hold their ears. Maybe it was worth a try.

A group of three girls with colorful hair was singing and playing the guitar at the next corner, and I headed for them. When they finally took a break, I approached them. I really hoped they spoke English. They looked to be my age. "Hey. I was wondering if you know of any places where I could do what you do and sing for people? I'm out of money and this is pretty much my only shot at paying for a room tonight."

The girls exchanged a look and I was half convinced they hadn't understood me when the girl with short blue hair said in an accent I couldn't decipher, "You need a permission. The authorities are pretty strict in Munich. They'll fine you if you make music or any kind of other art in the streets without permission."

"Damn. Is it easy to get a permission?"

The pink-haired girl shook her head. "No. They only hand out a few permissions and they make sure you can sing and actually play instruments before they allow you to make music here."

I sighed and slumped against the wall of the building. The three girls exchanged another look then whispered in a language that definitely wasn't German before they turned to me. "We're sharing a small apartment. If you want you can sleep on the couch in the living room until you find a job and can afford your own place."

My eyes widened. "Really?"

Blue-haired girl nodded with a smile. "You're a backpacker, right?"

"Yes. Traveling through Europe before college."

"We're all from Croatia, but we've been spending the last few months in Munich. You'll love it." Pink-haired girl stood. "So what's your name?"

I hesitated a moment before deciding who I wanted to be. "Gwen."

Maybe Munich would finally become a place I could stay and figure out what I'd do with the rest of my life.

What was meant to be for a few days only had turned into two months. I was still sharing an apartment with the three crazy girls from Croatia. We'd become friends and I paid rent for my spot on the sofa, albeit not much. Of course every part of my life was built on lie after lie, but sometimes I almost forgot that I wasn't who I pretended to be. I'd even found a job as a waitress in a café that catered mostly to tourists and my German had improved greatly.

Now that I'd finally found a place where I wanted to stay, I'd decided to give dating a real shot. When my flat mates introduced me to Sid, a fellow musician from Canada with long dreadlocks, I knew he was someone I could get used to, and maybe even make me forget that stupid kiss I'd shared with Matteo.

Sid was nothing like Matteo. He was nothing like men in the world I'd grown up in. He was a vegan, peace-loving idealist, and he never hesitated to convince others of his ideals. He could spend hours talking about the horrors of dairy farms and the dangers of the NRA. Sometimes I wondered what he'd say if he knew who I was.

This idealistic world-improver was his mask, I'd realized. Maybe everyone wore some kind of mask. What had been a novelty and endearing in the beginning, quickly started to annoy me. Still I couldn't break up with Sid because it would seem like the ultimate failure. If even someone like Sid couldn't stop me from thinking about Matteo, who could?

Sid's hand crept under my shirt then unhooked my bra. I made a sound of protest. We were in the living room of my shared apartment, so if one of my flat mates returned she'd get a show. His fingertips were rough from playing the guitar. He pushed me down until I lay flat on my back and he was half on top of me. His tongue seemed to take up too much space in my mouth and he tasted of stale smoke. Why had I thought a smoking guy was hot? Maybe in theory, but the taste and stink weren't something I was too excited about. He started unbuttoning my jeans and kept rubbing his bulge against my leg like a horny dog.

"I want you, Gwen," Sid rasped, already trying to shove my pants down my legs. Gwen. For the first time, the name didn't make me pause. Two months using the same name seemed to be the magic barrier for getting used to a new identity. Pity that I got the feeling I wouldn't use it for much longer. Munich was getting too comfortable, and Sid was simply getting too much. He was being too pushy.

"Not yet," I gritted out, trying to hide my boredom and annoyance. It wasn't his fault that I wasn't into our make-out sessions. We'd been going out for almost four weeks, so it wasn't really all that surprising that he wanted to sleep with me. And I wasn't even sure what the hell was stopping me. Sid wasn't a bad guy. He could be funny after he'd drunk a couple of beers or had a few drags of pot, and his guitar play and singing weren't even half bad. And yet I didn't want to commit to this relationship fully, didn't want to go another step. Before I'd run off from home, I'd thought I'd jump into bed with every guy I met once I was free of my bodyguards; to spite Matteo and my father, more than anything else, so what was stopping me?

"Come on, Gwen. I'll make it good for you," he said as he tried to shove his hand into my panties.

I clamped my legs shut and pushed his hand away. I didn't want him to touch me *there*. For some reason the idea that he'd be the first to do that made me sick. "I'm really not in the mood. And I'm getting my period," I said to stop him from bitching around anymore. It was a fucking lie. The stress of the last few months had pretty much stopped me from having much of a period at all.

But he didn't know that. I just wanted this make-out session to be over, so I could grab my laptop and figure out where to run off to next. Sid would find a new girl quickly. His cute Canadian accent, laid-back nature and dreadlocks were a huge hit among German girls.

He didn't even bother hiding his annoyance, which in turn really made me want to push him off and tell him it was over. "You're never in the mood," Sid grumbled. "Jerk me off at least."

Anger shot through me at his demand. When I didn't react, he grabbed my hand and pressed it against the bulge in his pants. Where was the peace-loving idealist now?

With a bang, the door flew open. Before either Sid or I could move, three men stalked in. Matteo was one of them. Oh holy shit.

chapter *eight*

Gianna

MATTEO WAS FIRST TO ENTER, HIS DARK HAIR MESSY AND WET from the rainstorm raging outside, his white shirt plastered to his upper body. In that moment, I almost felt silly for thinking I could ever forget him. He was more man than all the guys I'd met combined. His dark eyes settled on me, then on my hand, which was still pressed against Sid's crotch. There really was no question what he'd walked in on, and his face twisted with fury.

"What the fuck, dudes?" Sid shouted.

"Shut up, shut up," I wanted to scream. I didn't get the chance. Matteo crossed the room in a few steps, grabbed Sid by the arm and hauled him off me. Sid landed on the floor hard, face twisting with pain, then anger. Matteo towered over me, nostrils flaring, eyes almost black, and a look in them that made me want to hide. I met his gaze straight on. He wanted to scare me. My fear was something I'd never give him.

Sid stumbled to his feet and almost lost his fucking pants. He must have unzipped them at some point to make it "easier" for me. He headed for Matteo. I jumped to my feet, knowing I had to intervene before things got even worse.

"Get out of this apartment or I'll call the fucking cops," Sid said.

God, no.

Matteo sent me a look that made me realize just how dangerous this situation was. Not for me, but for someone who should have never gotten dragged into the fucking misery that was mob life.

"He doesn't mean it," I blurted.

Sid glared. "The fuck I do." For the moment, he seemed to have forgotten about his peace-loving ideals.

Matteo hadn't pulled his weapons yet. I wanted to convince myself that it was a good sign but a glimpse at the two men with him made my heart plummet into my shoes. They were both my father's men and they had already closed the door and were standing beside it with expressionless faces. A closed door was never a good thing. Nothing I could say would change their minds because they were acting on my father's orders. They would do what he'd told them. There was only one person who could help me now.

Sid got right into Matteo's face as if he wanted to punch him. Matteo didn't even twitch, only stared down at Sid with the scariest look I'd ever seen in anyone's eyes. Even without knowing who Matteo was, Sid must have sensed just how dangerous the man in front of him was. Sid took a step back, his eyes darting between Matteo and me. I jerked into motion and stepped between Matteo and him. "He doesn't know anything. Please, just let him leave."

My father's men laughed and one of them murmured something that sounded remarkably like "slut." Matteo's expression darkened even further. My father's men were watching him expectantly. I'd insulted Matteo by running away, and worse by being with another man. In our world there was only one thing a man in Matteo's position could do to protect his honor. I'd only ever seen Matteo with some variation of an arrogant smile on his face, but there was no trace of amusement now.

"I should probably go," Sid said suddenly, backing away. "This got nothing to do with me."

Coward. The moment the thought crossed my mind, I felt bad. Running was really the only sensible thing for him to do. He couldn't protect me from Matteo or my father's men, but that he wasn't even going to try was something I could and would never understand.

One of my father's men, Stan or something like that if I remembered him correctly, grabbed Sid by the arms. Sid started struggling like a madman, but it was obvious he'd never had a fight in his life. Stan laughed, ripped Sid's arms back sharply then rammed his knees into Sid's back. With a cry, Sid fell to his knees, only held upright by Stan's grip.

"Hey! Stop it," I shouted, wanting to rush toward them, but Matteo snatched my arm, jerking me to a stop. I whirled on him, on the verge of snarling into his face but stopped myself. He was Sid's only chance, regardless of how ridiculous that sounded.

"Please," I said, even though begging left a bitter taste in my mouth. Matteo's dark eyes didn't even flicker as he peered down at me. Expecting him to help me after what I'd done was preposterous. "Don't kill him. Just let him go. He's not a danger."

"You want me to spare the fucker who had his fucking hands all over you? You let that sucker have what's mine and want me to let him walk away? That's what you want from me?" Matteo asked in a dangerously quiet voice.

I swallowed down a nasty retort. I wasn't his, would never be. Nothing I had done with Sid was Matteo's business. Even if I had fucked Sid, that still wouldn't have been his fucking business. Even if I'd fucked every single guy I'd met that still wouldn't have been his business. I needed to tell him that I hadn't slept with Sid. Maybe it would placate him if he knew I hadn't given everything away. His ego would love that there was still something he could take from me. Pride kept my lips sealed.

"We should head out. Someone might have heard when we kicked the door in. Let's get rid of this asshole and move on," Stan said, knocking his knee into Sid's back again. Sid's eyes were huge as they flitted back and forth between us.

"Silence," Matteo said sharply and Stan snapped his lips shut.

I reached for Matteo's arm, my fingers digging into the damp material of his dress shirt, feeling the hard muscles beneath. I had to swallow my fucking pride if I wanted to save Sid's life. "Matteo, it's not—"

My words were cut short by the sonic crack of a suppressed gunshot. I froze, eyes flying to the source of the noise. The other Made Man was pointing a Glock with a silencer at the spot where Sid's head had been moments before. He was slumped forward, head hanging limply and blood dripping to the ground. Stan let go of Sid's arms. The body toppled over and landed on the ground with a resounding thud. I stared and stared. Slowly my hand slid down Matteo's arm.

"Did I give you the fucking order to kill him?" Matteo snarled.

"This was Outfit business. As long as she isn't married to you, she falls under our jurisdiction and so did the asshole here." Stan kicked Sid's lifeless form. I flinched. Inside a beast was raging, wanting to claw Stan's fucking eyes out, wanting to kill them all, but I was paralyzed.

Blood spread out around Sid's head, soaking his dreadlocks. My stomach constricted. I'd seen that much blood only three times before. The first time when Luca cut off Raffaele's finger; the second time on Luca's shirt after he'd dealt with the guy who'd drugged Aria; and the third time when the Russians had attacked us. It didn't get easier as some people said, as even *I* had suspected. I had a feeling it never would.

Stan nodded toward me. "What about other witnesses? You don't live here alone."

I blinked, terror gripping me so hard I could barely breathe. I couldn't let them kill my flat mates as well. The girls had been nothing but kind to me. They didn't deserve that. My eyes found Matteo. His gaze searched my face before he turned to my father's men. "We're done here."

Stan looked like he wanted to protest but the other guy nudged his shoulder. With a glare at me, Stan opened the door and checked the corridor. "Clear. Let's go."

I turned to Sid's body again. Matteo wrapped an arm around my waist. I didn't look his way. I couldn't avert my eyes from Sid as if my attention was the only thing that anchored him to life. He was long gone. Pieces of his brain dotted the red sea on the ground.

Matteo steered me toward the door, then down the corridor. Stan was in front of us, while the other man made up the rear. Surrounded. I was surrounded. I should have tried to run away. The odds had always been against me. It had never stopped me before. Maybe this was my last chance to escape. Once back in the States, I'd be trapped. Giving up wasn't in my nature. I'd always fought my own battles, but so far only I had to pay the price for my courage. Tonight, an innocent, someone who'd never been sullied by the darkness of my world had paid with his life for my dreams, for my wish for freedom, for my selfishness. I'd thought I could evade fate, could outrun a world of blood, but had inadvertently dragged innocents into that world.

Could I live with that?

I wasn't sure.

Maybe it was in our nature to bring misery and death to everyone around us. Maybe that was why it was best for us to stay among ourselves. Hadn't Aria said something along those lines a long time ago?

Aria. I'd finally see her again. That was the good news I was clinging to right now. She'd get me through this. She always did.

Matteo's grip on my wrist was painful. His eyes held a clear message, now that he'd caught me, he would never let me get away again.

Everything seemed to happen behind a fog. I was pushed into the back of a car and Matteo slipped into the back seat beside me then we drove off with squealing tires. I watched the place I'd called home for the last two months disappear. I pressed my forehead against the cold window. I hardly dared to blink. Every time I closed my eyes, crimson flashed behind my eyelids. Sid was dead because of me.

I could hear Matteo talking to someone on the phone in the background but I couldn't focus. Everything was over. He'd take me back to my father now, and I had no doubt that I couldn't expect any kind of mercy. I had betrayed not only the Outfit but also New York, had made my father and Matteo lose face. I would be punished. I glanced at Matteo who was glaring at the back of the front seat. I quickly fastened my bra again and put it back in place. Of course Matteo noticed.

I could tell he was furious. I wondered what kind of punishment he had in mind for me. I'd been on the run for six months. He couldn't possibly want me for any other reason than revenge. I knew the rules. I wasn't worthy of marriage anymore. Matteo probably already had a new fiancée and once he'd dealt with me, he'd move on with his life. If he'd wanted to kill me, he would have done so already. That didn't mean Father wouldn't do it the moment I set foot on Chicago ground.

We pulled up in front of an airport hotel, and Matteo turned to me, his eyes holding a clear warning. "We'll spend the next few hours until our flight here. If you try to ask anyone for help, this will end in a bloodbath, understood?"

I nodded. Then Matteo pulled me out of the car with him and led me inside. Nobody paid us any attention as we headed toward the elevators and rode up to the fourth floor.

Matteo led me through the long hallway until we arrived in front of a simple white door.

Stan and the other Outfit man stopped too. "She should come into our room with Carmine and me. She's still part of the Outfit," Stan said, his eyes sliding over my body. I knew what he and the other guy would do to me if I came into a room with them.

"She's mine. I won't let her out of my eyes again. Now fuck off. Gianna and I have matters to discuss," Matteo growled. He slid the keycard into the slot and opened the door.

Stan and Carmine exchanged a look but didn't protest. Then Stan sent me a cruel smile. "Teach her some manners."

Matteo dragged me into the room, kicked the door shut and fixed me with a terrifying expression. "Oh, I will."

chapter *nine*

Gianna

MATTEO FLUNG ME ONTO THE BED. THEN HE WAS ON TOP OF ME. He pressed my arms into the mattress above my head, his knees beside my thighs. His eyes were almost black with fury. Did he want me to beg for mercy? Ask him for forgiveness? Then he had a long wait coming.

"You let someone have what's mine," he growled, his eyes scorching my body with their possessiveness. He leaned down as if he was going to kiss me. Our noses almost brushed but he only scowled. "Your father gave me his permission to do with you as I please. He doesn't care if you live or die. He doesn't care what I do to you. I think he'd even approve of me punishing you harshly."

I wasn't surprised. Father had already barely tolerated me before I'd brought shame to our family by running away. Now he probably hated me like the devil. I almost wanted Matteo to hurt me. I deserved it for getting Sid killed. I knew Matteo would have no trouble hurting me. I'd seen what he was capable of. Maybe physical pain would finally drown out the anguish I felt deep inside.

Matteo

Gianna didn't say a fucking thing as if she couldn't care less what I did to her.

I tightened my hold on her wrists to see if she would finally show some of that fire I was used to from her, but despite a small wince she didn't react.

I hated what she'd done to her hair. It was light brown, no longer the fiery red I loved. At least, she hadn't cut it off.

My eyes were drawn to the sliver of naked stomach that peeked out where her shirt had ridden up. The thought that someone else had touched her there, had touched her everywhere made me want to tear everything down.

She was supposed to be mine. *Mine alone.*

For a moment, the fury was so blinding I wanted to hurt her, wanted to show her that she belonged to me, wanted to fuck her so hard that she forgot everything else. I gripped her waist, my fingers brushing over her soft skin. Mine. Only mine from now on. Her father had told me I could use her as I saw fit before I took her back to him. Nobody would blink an eye if I took from her what had been mine for the taking in the first place. She tensed under my touch but still didn't say anything. Her eyes were resigned. No hint of her usual temper.

She didn't fight me, didn't do anything. She reminded me of a ragdoll. She probably waited for me to do what everyone expected me to do, to fuck her even if she was unwilling, to hurt her until she begged me for forgiveness. And I could have done it but I didn't want to. Despite what she'd done and how bad she'd made me look, I still wanted her, and not just her body.

"Being submissive isn't like you," I said quietly. Her pulse sped under my fingertips. It was the only sign that she wasn't as indifferent as her expression made me want to believe. Maybe she didn't care what happened to her because she was heartbroken over the bastard I'd found her with.

The idea sent a new spike of wrath through me and I quickly released her before I lost control. I slid off her and sat on the edge of the mattress, trying to ignore the look of surprise and shock crossing her face. I glared at the floor, clenching and unclenching my hands. If Carmine hadn't killed the fucker, I would probably have done it. I still wanted to do it, wanted to slice the part of his brain out that harbored the memory of Gianna's body under him.

Gianna sat up slowly, carefully as if she thought I might attack if she moved too fast. "Aren't you going to rape and torture me?"

I almost laughed. That's what everyone expected. Most men in our world even thought she deserved it. I turned to her, my gaze tracing her beautiful face. Even more beautiful than my memory had made me believe, even now when she was pale and her eyes were puffy from tears.

"Did you think I would?" I asked in a surprisingly calm voice. Some of my anger was suddenly gone now that she was watching me with her wide blue eyes.

"Yes. My father's men definitely thought you would. Didn't you see their expressions? They probably hope that you'll give them a go at me once you're done with me."

Of course, they'd told me so numerous times while we'd been on the hunt. I knew what they thought was happening right now. Fuck, part of me wished they were right. I wasn't a good guy. "I don't give a fuck about your father's men, and I don't give a fuck about your father. And if they lay a single finger on you, I'm going to kill them. They won't hurt you, nobody will."

Her brows crinkled. "Once I'm back in Chicago, Father will punish me."

Did she really think I'd hand her over to her asshole of a father? I hadn't hunted her for sixth months only to give her up. I smirked. "You aren't going back to Chicago, Gianna. You are coming to New York with me."

Hope and relief crossed her face. "To Aria? Is she alright? Did she get in trouble because she helped me?"

Somehow her response annoyed me. "Aria is fine," I said, before I stood and walked toward the window. I kept my back to her when I asked, "That guy, did you love him?"

I wasn't sure what I'd do if she said "yes." I couldn't hurt that fucker anymore, and I didn't want to hurt her, so what could I do? Kill someone else, preferably the two assholes from the Outfit who'd been grating on my nerves for too long, and maybe while I was at it, I'd kill her fucking father the next time I saw him.

"Sid?" she asked in a shaky voice, and I almost lost it right then. I scowled at her over my shoulder. Her eyes were actually moist with fucking tears.

"I don't care what his name was," I growled.

Fuck, I wanted to kill that guy so badly. I'd have paid a billion dollars if there were a way to resurrect the asshole, only so I could kill him again. Slowly, painfully.

"His name was Sid," she said stubbornly, a familiar glint returning to her eyes.

She still hadn't answered my question. "Did you love him?"

"No," she said without hesitation. "I barely knew him." I would have rejoiced if she hadn't started biting her lower lip like she was fighting tears. She looked fucking sad and then a tear slid out of her left eye. She blinked a few times.

"If you didn't love him, then why are you crying?"

She glared. Glared, as if she was the one with reason to be angry. "You really don't know?"

"I'm a Made Man, Gianna. I've seen many people die, have killed many myself." And right now I wanted to kill again more than anything else in the world.

"Sid didn't deserve to die. He died because of me. He never did anything wrong."

What the fuck? Really? "He touched the wrong girl. He died for touching what wasn't his to touch."

Gianna shook her head. "You wanted to kill him yourself, didn't you? That's why you stopped Stan? Not because you wanted to spare Sid's life."

Did that really come as a surprise to her? For someone who was convinced I and every other member of the mob were monsters, she seemed oddly surprised by my desire to kill the asshole who'd pawed at my fiancée.

Before I could reply, my phone rang. Luca's name flashed on my screen. I had only sent him a short text while I was in the car. He'd tried calling me but, except for a quick talk to the pilot of our private jet, I hadn't been in the mood to speak to anyone, but knowing Luca he wouldn't give up. Stifling a groan, I picked up, turning away from Gianna again.

"A text with 'I got her,' that's all I get from you?" he said angrily.

"I was busy."

I could hear Aria's high voice in the background, but thankfully Luca didn't put her on. I really wasn't in the mood to talk to a hysterical woman, least of all the woman who'd helped my fiancée escape in the first place. It was early morning in New York, couldn't Luca have let his wife sleep in for once?

"With what?" He paused. "No, don't tell me. I don't want to fucking know."

"Did he hurt her?" Aria asked loud enough for me to hear.

I didn't say anything.

Luca lowered his voice. "Is she alive?"

"Fuck you."

"I take that as a yes."

Aria was still speaking in the background.

"Tell your wife that her sister is fine."

"Gianna is fine," Luca said in a muffled voice, then to me. "When will you be back?"

"The flight leaves in less than two hours."

"You're flying directly to Chicago to meet Scuderi. Right?"

"He already called you, didn't he?" I said. Stan and Carmine had definitely sent their boss a message after we'd caught Gianna. That meant, of course, that he knew about Sid too.

"Of course, he did. His daughter has been on the run for six months. This is big news."

"Don't tell me he's happy to have her back."

"No, at least not for the same reason Aria is. He wants to see her punished. She made him lose face and you too. From what I heard you caught her with another guy. You realize the news will spread like wildfire. Scuderi is eager to make a public show out of punishing Gianna. He expects you to help him with it."

I gritted my teeth. "I don't give a fuck. I'm not taking her to Chicago. If he wants to talk to her, he can come to New York."

"You want to protect her after what she did?"

"Yes."

"Matteo, this is Outfit business. She isn't your wife, and nobody expects you to marry her after she went around fucking with half of Europe."

"Careful," I hissed.

"Damn it. Can't you just get over her? Fuck her, it's not like it matters anymore, and then hand her back to her father."

"Is Aria still around to hear you talk about her sister like that?" I asked.

"No. I need to think about the Famiglia. Gianna brought this upon herself. You have to take her to Chicago, Matteo. I won't risk war over her."

"Fuck you, Luca. You are my fucking brother. Shouldn't you be on my fucking side?"

"Not when you've lost your fucking mind."

"Fuck you."

Luca sighed on the other end. "Listen, I'm not saying that you should abandon her. Take her to Chicago and pretend you're delivering her to her father. Then make a deal with him. She's still promised to you, so he won't refuse you. He'll probably be glad to have her off his hands. Aria and I will be flying over there too. I'm emailing our pilot right this moment. You won't have to deal with this alone."

"Okay, I'm taking her to Chicago. But I'm not leaving without her, no matter what Scuderi says. She's mine."

"Alright, but I doubt there will be any problems. And believe me, I have no interest in letting Gianna get hurt by her father. Aria loves her sister, and I want Aria to be happy, so I won't let Scuderi kill or hurt her. We will bring her back to New York with us, even as your wife if that's really what you want."

"You'll go against Scuderi if he disagrees for some reason?"

"I will. For you and for Aria."

"Swear it."

Luca sighed again. "I swear it. You and Aria are going to be the death of me."

I almost smiled but hung up. When I turned back around to Gianna, she was watching me with an anxious expression, which she tried to mask the moment I looked at her but she didn't quite manage. Sometimes in the last few months I'd been sure I wouldn't find her, that she was too clever; I was glad that I'd been wrong. "Tradition dictates that I hand you over to the Outfit and your father."

Fear flashed across her face. Gianna wasn't stupid; she knew what might happen to her if her father got his will. I wasn't sure if Dante Cavallaro would intervene, and I didn't give a fuck. Protectiveness washed over me. They had no right to decide about her fate. This was my chance to show her that she'd been wrong to run away, that I was the right guy for her. For a long time she stared at me, her face unguarded and vulnerable. This was a side of her I'd only seen twice before: when Aria had been drugged and when Gianna had been in the hands of the Russians. I was still angry at her, still fucking furious, especially because I knew she'd run away again if I gave her the chance, but part of me was simply glad to have her back.

"I will take you to Chicago, but I won't leave your side, Gianna. I won't give you the chance to run from me again."

Gianna

After what had happened today, I wasn't sure I'd ever risk another escape.

Matteo's phone rang again and he cursed. I was glad for the distraction. The intensity of his gaze had spoken to a part of me I'd tried to fight ever since the kiss. I lay back down, but the moment I closed my eyes, images of Sid's body flashed through my mind. Even if Matteo hadn't killed him, that didn't mean it wasn't his fault. He'd have done the same if Carmine hadn't acted first.

I must have dozed off because I jerked violently when something touched my arm. My eyes flew open and I found Matteo hovering over me. He straightened with a wry smile. "Sid's death doesn't seem to bother you too much if you can fall asleep like that."

I sat up, glaring, knowing he was being cruel on purpose, but at the same time wondering if it was true. Was I that callous? Was I more like Matteo than I wanted to admit? No. I had dreamed about Sid's death, and my chest felt like it was in a vise when I thought about him.

"We need to get going. Our flight leaves soon." Matteo grasped my wrist to pull me to my feet but I wrenched it away, suddenly angry. Matteo reached for me again, jerked me to my feet and against his body. "Careful, Gianna. Less than two hours ago I saw you messing around with another guy. I pride myself for my control but there is a limit to what I will take from you."

I swallowed my words and let Matteo lead me out of the room. Stan and Carmine were already waiting in the corridor. Their eyes scanned me from head to toe then Stan said, "She's still surprisingly unscathed. If my fiancée had gone around fucking other men, I'd have beaten her to a bloody pulp."

"Do I look like I care about your fucking opinion?" Matteo asked dangerously. I chanced a look at him, wondering why exactly he wasn't doing what Stan had suggested. I decided to keep my mouth shut for now. Self-preservation wasn't my strong suite, but I wasn't completely suicidal, even if death might be preferable to what Father had in mind for me.

Twenty minutes later we boarded the private jet of the Outfit and I took a seat next to the window. Matteo sat across from me but he didn't make conversation. Nobody tried to speak to me throughout the entire flight. I had a feeling Matteo was using the time to calm down. Occasionally I'd catch him watching me but I couldn't read the look in his eyes. When I rose halfway through the flight to go to the toilet, Matteo stood as well.

I swallowed a comment and walked toward the toilet in the rear. When Matteo didn't back off even as I opened the door, I couldn't hold back any more. Self-preservation be damned. "Are you going to watch me pee? It's not like I can escape by jumping off the plane."

"I wouldn't put it past you to try and kick a hole into the wall of the plane to kill us all."

Was he being serious? The corner of his mouth twitched but then his expression hardened again. For a moment our eyes were locked, then I quickly stepped into the small toilet and closed the door. Matteo didn't stop me but I knew he'd be waiting for me and probably listen for strange noises.

I leaned against the wall and closed my eyes. Fear and sadness raged in my body, and it was getting increasingly difficult not to break down into a sobbing mess. I almost wished Matteo had manhandled me. Why did he have to act like a decent human being?

"What are you doing? Don't force me to kick in that fucking door," Matteo muttered.

Not even caring that he would hear me, I took care of business before I stepped back out two minutes later. Matteo's eyes wandered over me as if he was looking for a sign that I was up to something. I would have laughed if I thought I could.

We returned to our seats and resumed our silence.

My stomach was in knots when we landed in Chicago. I hadn't gotten a minute of sleep while we were in the air. The knowledge that I would have to face Father soon kept me wide awake. Only yesterday, I'd eaten pizza with my flat mates and made plans for a trip to Croatia in the summer, and now my life was once again out of my control. Even worse, I might very well face harsh punishment from the Outfit. Matteo really had no reason to protect me from Father's wrath. And even if he tried, why would Luca allow him to risk a conflict with the Outfit over me? I was less than vermin in their eyes.

The private jet came to a stop and Matteo got to his feet and motioned for me to do the same. My legs shook as I followed him toward the door, which was already gliding open. Cold air blasted against my face. Snow dusted the landing strip and the surrounding buildings. It was around 4 p.m., but I felt as if it was the middle of the night. Matteo grabbed my wrist, giving me a warning look. "Don't run. Don't do anything stupid. Your father's men are looking for a chance to hurt you. I'd kill them of course but that won't help you."

Was he actually worried about me? Matteo was an enigma. I wasn't sure why he was so interested in me. I had a feeling it was his pride. He couldn't accept that I didn't want him, so he'd force me to marry him even if I didn't want it, even if *he* didn't want me anymore. If he really cared about me, he would let me go. No, this was a power play. Emotions had nothing to do with it.

"Don't worry. I want to see Aria."

He shook his head. "This isn't the right moment for your snark to return. Your father won't appreciate it."

Then why was he almost smiling if he thought it was such a bad idea? The door was fully down and Matteo led me down the few stairs, his fingers around my wrist unwavering. I felt like a toddler who did her first steps. Annoyance battled with worry in my body, but before I could decide if I wanted to risk a retort I spotted a familiar blonde head. Aria. She stood beside Luca, and when she saw me she started running.

I peered up at Matteo pleadingly but he didn't let me go and kept leading me toward Aria in unhurried steps. When my sister had almost reached us, he released me and I rushed toward Aria. We collided almost painfully. I crushed Aria against me, hugging her as tightly as possible and she did the same in return. "Oh, Gianna, I was so scared for you. I'm so glad you're here." She was crying and my own face was wet with tears. God, I'd missed her.

After a moment, she pulled back, her eyes doing a quick scan, lingering on my new hair color. "Are you okay? Did they hurt you?"

I brushed a few strands of her blonde locks away from her face, suddenly feeling like breaking down sobbing. Regret weighed heavy on my mind. I should have never run. Seeing Aria's worried face was another reminder. If I'd stayed, if I'd married Matteo, then Sid would still be alive, and Aria wouldn't have had to worry for months. Why did I have to want the freedom to make my own decisions?

"Gianna?" Aria lowered her voice. "Did Matteo do something?"

"Matteo didn't do anything," Matteo said in a hard voice, making Aria and me both jump.

"I didn't ask you," Aria said quietly. My eyes darted between them. I had a feeling they weren't on good terms. Also because of me. Luca arrived beside us and clapped his brother's shoulder. "Good to see you again."

I hadn't even considered that Matteo had been gone from home for a long time because he'd been after me. Luca barely glanced my way, not that I cared.

"I'm fine," I told Aria who seemed reluctant to believe me.

"The boss is waiting," Stan barked. "Let's go. It's not like the whore deserves a big welcome."

Aria gasped. I stiffened but managed not to show my shock. I didn't give a damn what Stan thought of me. But Matteo was the fastest to react. He pulled a knife and hurtled it at Stan who cried out when the blade nicked his ear.

"Next time my blade will split your fucking skull if you don't keep your mouth shut," he said.

Stan rested his hand on the gun in his holster but didn't pull it. Blood was dripping from his cut ear down onto his shirt. There was murder in his eyes. Carmine stood very still, but he hadn't pulled his gun either. When I turned to Luca, I knew why. He had both of his guns aimed at my father's men and behind him Romero whom I hadn't even seen before was doing the same.

"We don't want this to end badly, do we?" Luca asked in a very low voice. "Your boss wouldn't appreciate it."

Carmine nodded and relaxed his stance but Stan looked like he didn't care if my father punished him as long as he got to kill Matteo first. For several moments neither of us moved, then Luca put his guns back into their holsters. "Let's go."

Carmine picked up the knife Matteo had thrown and handed it back to Matteo, who didn't take his eyes off Stan.

"She'll drive in a car with us," Stan said.

Matteo's lips pulled into a cold smile. "This is the last warning you get. Stop pissing me off or I'll carve a smile into your throat."

Carmine grabbed Stan's arm and pulled him toward a black Outfit car while the rest of us headed toward two BMWs.

Aria moved to sit in the back with me, but Luca held her back. "No. I want Matteo to keep an eye on your sister." Aria gave me an apologetic smile before she sat shotgun beside Luca.

Matteo gave me a knowing look when he settled beside me on the back seat. "You'd probably jump out of the moving car if I gave you the chance."

I huffed. "I'm not completely crazy. Do you think I'd risk running around Chicago unprotected when my father's men are obviously out to hurt me?"

"So you trust me to protect you but still don't want to marry me."

Surprise shot through me. "You still want to go through with the marriage?"

"You could probably ram a knife into his back and he'd still want to go through with it," Luca said from the front. "He's a stubborn fucker."

"I didn't hunt you for six months only to let you go."

I searched his face, but I couldn't look past his arrogant mask. He wouldn't let me. "Maybe you shouldn't have wasted so much time hunting me." Then I'd still be in Munich, and Sid would still be alive. But I had to admit that part of me had missed my former life. Not all of it, mind you, but definitely my siblings and maybe even some other aspects that I didn't want to admit to myself yet.

Matteo didn't say anything but his lips tightened. The rest of the drive passed in tense silence.

I tried to hide my nerves as we pulled up in front of my old home. What would Father do to me?

chapter *ten*

Matteo

The Outfit car came to a stop in front of the Scuderi villa and Luca parked the rental BMW right behind it. Luca and Aria exited the car immediately and I pushed the door open to follow them but paused when I realized Gianna hadn't even unbuckled her belt yet. She was staring intently down at her hands resting in her lap. Annoyance flared up in me. Couldn't she ever go the easy route? Did she have to be so damn stubborn?

"I'm not in the mood to argue with you, Gianna. You really shouldn't let your father wait right now. He's pissed as it is. Get out of the car or I'll carry you."

I waited for a clever comeback. Instead she reached to unbuckle herself. Her hands were shaking and suddenly I realized what was going on. Gianna wasn't stalling to annoy me. She was nervous about being back here. Her fingers struggled with the seat belt. I pushed them away and did it for her. Her eyes shot up, brows drawn together as she searched my face. She looked fucking anxious. She didn't even push my hands away, which were still resting on her thigh.

"We need to get out," I said again, this time without the previous annoyance.

She nodded slowly, her eyes darting toward the window. I could see Luca and Aria watching us, and behind them Stan and Carmine were waiting. Romero lingered next to our second car, scanning the surroundings. I didn't think this was a trap, but you could never know with the fucking Outfit. Things hadn't exactly been peachy between us in the last few months.

"I'm scared," she said quietly, then laughed harshly. "Isn't it messed up that I'm scared of my own father?"

"Your father is Consigliere and a huge asshole. There are plenty of reasons to be scared of him."

She was still staring at her lap. "He hates me. He wouldn't even hesitate to put a bullet through my head after what I did."

He'd have to go through me, and I had no doubt that I could take him down with one arm tied to my back. I hooked a finger under her chin and turned her face around to me until her blue eyes met mine. "I won't allow it."

For a moment she softened and her eyes darted to my lips but then Gianna became her usual self and pulled back. I almost groaned. She opened the door and slid out. When I caught up with her, there was no sign of fear on her face. She held her head high and sent Scuderi's men the most scathing look I'd ever seen from her. That was the Gianna I knew. The only indication that she wasn't as relaxed as she pretended was that she didn't argue when I rested my hand on the small of her back as I led her toward the front door. I couldn't wait to run my hands over every inch of her body, to finally claim her. Images of Sid with his paws on her slipped into my mind again and I had to resist the urge to hit something.

Luca raised his eyebrows, impatience written all over his face. "What took you so long for fuck's sake?"

I ignored him because the door opened in that moment and Scuderi appeared in the doorframe, a scowl on his face. Gianna shrank against me. I didn't think she even noticed because her face remained perfectly unimpressed.

Scuderi talked to his men briefly before sending them away and turning to Luca. They shook hands and then he hugged Aria. He hadn't spared Gianna a single look so far. It annoyed the hell out of me. His cold eyes zoomed in on me and I sneered at him. I hated everything about that man, even his stupid face and slicked-back hair. He looked like the worst cliché of a mobster.

"I see you found her," he said.

"I always get what I want."

He still didn't even glance Gianna's way but his expression turned cruel. "What you wanted was a reputable Italian girl. What you get are the ruins of God knows how many men."

Gianna stiffened under my hand, her eyes widening a fraction before she regained control over her face, but her father wasn't done yet. No wonder he and my father had gotten along so well.

"I can't see why you even bothered wasting your time on her. My men could have caught her without you."

His men would have done a lot of things with Gianna. Luca narrowed his eyes at me in warning. Could he tell how much I wanted to bury my knife in Scuderi's ugly mug? I glared back at Scuderi, wanting to wipe that superior grin off his face.

"I think we should go inside to discuss matters," Luca said, using his Capo voice. It usually grated on my nerves when he did that, but this time it was probably for the best. I had a feeling that my knife would accidentally find its way into Scuderi's eyeball if I had to bear his stupid expression another second.

Scuderi nodded and opened the door further. Gianna was practically pressed up against my side as we walked past him. Protectiveness burned through my veins. Maybe she didn't realize it but that she sought my closeness when she was scared was all the confirmation I needed for her feelings for me, even if she wasn't aware of them yet.

"How can you even touch her after what she's done? After what you saw her doing. I'd be disgusted," Scuderi said as he closed the door. He obviously didn't expect a reply because he turned to Luca. "If my wife had done something like that, I would have killed her, and I have a feeling you would have done the same, Luca."

Aria shot Luca a shocked look but he was busy staring Scuderi down. "I'm not here to discuss what-ifs with you. I want to have this settled once and for all. You promised us something and I expect you to deliver."

"What I promised isn't available anymore." Scuderi nodded toward Gianna. "But if you want damaged goods, I'm sure we can come to an agreement. Dante is waiting in the living room for us. This is foremost Outfit business, and Dante will have the last word on the matter."

Luca met my gaze, warning clear in his eyes. "Then let's go. I have better things to do than chitchat with you. And I'm sure we can come to an understanding that will benefit all of us."

I didn't give a damn about Dante or Scuderi. I was taking Gianna back to New York with me, even if I had to gut every single Outfit asshole in the process.

Gianna

I was trying very hard to keep a neutral expression but it was incredibly hard. To my embarrassment, Matteo's hand on my back really helped me focus. His expression on the other hand only fueled my own anxiety. He looked like a man out for blood. I chanced a look at Luca and my father, who weren't bothering to dish out pleasantries either.

Things had taken a definite turn for the worse since I'd left. If Luca was acting barely civil toward my father, relations between the Outfit and New York couldn't be good right now.

Aria gently touched my arm, eyes full of worry. I forced a smile, but it must have been off because she only frowned in return. Damn it. Matteo nudged me forward. Father and Luca were already heading toward the living room, but at the sound of hurried footsteps I froze, my eyes darting to the staircase. Lily and Fabi were storming toward me, their faces alight with happiness. Tears sprang into my eyes as my little brother tackled me, burying his head against my sternum. God, he'd grown since I'd last seen him. How was that even possible? I'd been gone for only six months. And then Lily threw her arms around me as well. "We missed you so much," she whispered tearfully. Fabi's hold on me was making breathing difficult but I didn't care.

I hugged them back just as tightly. While I'd been on the run, I'd barely dared thinking about my family because it had felt like a chasm was ripped into my chest every time I did.

"Didn't I tell you to keep them upstairs?" Father hissed, causing me to look up and find Mother coming down the staircase hastily.

"I'm sorry. They were too quick," she said in a meek voice. Her eyes flitted over to me briefly before she returned her gaze to Father without a word to me.

I swallowed. So this was it? Because I hadn't done what they wanted I was dead to them? I'd known Father would condemn me but I'd hoped at least Mother would be happy to have me back.

"Lily, Fabi, back to your rooms."

"But, Father, we haven't seen Gianna in forever," Fabi grumbled. Father crossed the distance between us in two quick strides and wrenched my brother and sister away before shoving them toward Mother. "Upstairs now."

Fabi jutted his chin out, and even Lily didn't move. Father's face was turning red in anger. "It's okay," I told them. "We can talk later."

"No, you can't. I won't have you around them. You are no longer my daughter, and I don't want your rottenness to rub off on Liliana," Father said, eyes hard.

I wasn't even sure what to say to that. He didn't want me to see my own sister and brother anymore.

"That's bullshit," Matteo said.

"Matteo," Luca warned. He was already gripping Aria's wrist to keep her from interfering. "This isn't our business."

Father glared. "That's right. This is my family, and Gianna is still subject to my rule, don't you ever forget that."

"I thought I wasn't your daughter anymore, so why do I have to listen to a word you say?"

Matteo gripped my waist tightly. What? He could provoke my father but I wasn't allowed to?

"Careful," Father said. "You are still part of the Outfit."

"We shouldn't let Dante wait any longer," Luca said.

This time we actually moved into the living room without incident. Dante Cavallaro was waiting in front of the window, talking on the phone. He hung up and turned to us. I had to suppress a shiver when his cold eyes settled on me. The iceman indeed. Suddenly I was really scared. This was serious.

I couldn't remember the last time I'd felt so horribly helpless.

"Luca, Matteo, Aria," Dante Cavallaro said in his emotionless voice. "Gianna."

I jumped in surprise. I'd figured he'd pretend I was beneath a greeting like my father had done. "Sir," I said, bowing my head slightly. I hated doing it but I knew what was good for me.

"You realize that what you did was betrayal?" Dante asked.

I wasn't sure what to say. If I agreed I'd be screwed, and if I didn't I'd infuriate the man who could decide to have me killed.

"Gianna is my fiancée, and if she hadn't run she'd be my wife by now. I think it should fall upon my brother as Capo of New York to determine if she deserves punishment."

My eyes flew from Matteo to Luca whose hard eyes sent another shiver down my back.

"That's ridiculous," Father muttered.

Dante didn't look offended though. "I take it you still want to go through with the wedding?"

"Yes," Matteo said without hesitation.

Nobody bothered to ask what I wanted of course, but I knew better than to open my mouth. Not when things could end really badly for me.

Dante gestured Father closer and they talked quietly for a moment. Father didn't look pleased in the least.

"I won't make this an official Outfit matter. I won't stop you from going through with the wedding. If you don't, however, I won't have a choice but to punish you," Dante said to me. He nodded toward Matteo before turning to my father once again. "I'll hand this over to you since Gianna is your family, and I hope at the end of this day there'll be an agreement that allows us to work together peacefully." With that he stepped back and motioned for Father to take over.

"Can you really afford to welcome someone like Gianna to New York? As a new Capo your people expect you to protect traditions and treat traitors without mercy," Father said to Luca.

"My men accept my decisions," Luca said, but there was a hint of warning in his voice. "Whatever that decision will be."

Suddenly I wondered if Luca would really burden himself with me. It wasn't like I wanted to become part of the Famiglia, but if the choice was between staying in my father's territory and living in New York with Aria, then I knew what I'd choose.

Looking like he was on the verge of pulling his knives, Matteo walked over to Luca to discuss something quietly and Aria used the moment to join me. I gave her a grateful smile.

"My brother will take your daughter off your hands, despite her transgressions. I think that's a very generous offer on our part. You should be glad that you don't have to look for a new husband for her."

Father scoffed. "As if I'd find someone. I wouldn't waste my precious time like that."

My blood was boiling, not only because of Father's words, but Luca's offer didn't sit well with me either. They acted like I was a piece of scum. Listening to them made me realize I had been right to run. This world was majorly messed up.

"So what do you say?" Luca asked, lips tight.

Father glanced at his boss but Dante seemed intent to stay out of it. He looked like he couldn't care less about the result.

"I hope you don't intend to have a wedding celebration. I want this matter to be dealt with as quietly as possible. She has caused me and the Outfit enough embarrassment already. I won't give her a chance to shame us further," Father said eventually.

I gritted my teeth so hard I was surprised my jaw didn't snap.

Matteo shook his head. "I don't need a wedding party. I prefer getting drunk without the old spinsters of the family around anyway."

A laugh tickled the back of my throat but I swallowed it. Matteo shot me a look as if he wanted to see if I found him as funny as he obviously found himself. Everything he did was calculated. That was something I could never forget. Matteo masked his deadliness with humor and smiles, but I wouldn't let that fool me. Not now, not ever, especially not when it was obvious he thought he was being generous by taking me back.

"The old spinsters wouldn't have come anyway. Nobody wants to be associated with someone like her," Father said with a glare in my general direction.

Aria's grip on my wrist was steely as if she still didn't trust me not to viciously attack our father.

"There will be a church service as is tradition," Luca said. "There's no need for guests beyond the closest family."

"Tradition," Father huffed. "Gianna spat on our traditions. The presentation of the sheets your Famiglia is so adamant about will have to be cancelled. And a white dress is out of the question too. I won't have her make a mockery out of our values."

Luca nodded. "That's reasonable."

Aria gave her husband an incredulous look, but I wasn't surprised that I wouldn't be allowed to dress in white. As if I gave a damn. For all I cared I would marry naked. I didn't want any of this. And I didn't give a fuck about their stupid traditions. They acted like they were doing me a favor, as if I was a criminal on death row who was handed a pardon on a silver platter. I'd done nothing wrong, nothing compared to what each of the men in this room had done.

"She's probably let every man in Europe have her, and you still want her?" Father asked again. I knew he was doing it to shame me and hurt me, and I hated it that he wasn't entirely unsuccessful.

I stared at the man who was my father, and felt nothing. I'd always known he didn't like me much, but I'd never realized how much he despised me. I sunk my nails into the soft flesh of my palms.

Matteo stood tall with that twisted smile on his face. "I hunted her for six months. If I didn't want her, do you really think I would have wasted so much time on her? I've got better things to do."

If I heard that one more time, I'd completely lose it.

"I thought you were looking for revenge, but my men told me you didn't lay a finger on her." Father directed a hard look at me. "Then again, you probably didn't want to get your hands dirty. I don't think a simple shower is going to wash my daughter clean again."

Aria gripped my wrist even tighter, and I halted. I hadn't even realized I'd taken a step toward our father to do…I wasn't even sure what I would have done. Hit him? Maybe. His words and expression made me actually feel dirty, and I hated that he had that power over me. At the same time I'd have rather thrown myself off the roof of this house than admitted that I hadn't slept with any guy while I was on the run. That was a secret I'd protect with all my might.

"Who says I'm not still out for revenge?" Matteo asked in a dangerous voice. His dark eyes met mine. The bastard. So the concerned looks in the car had been all for show? He knew I didn't want to marry him. He knew this was a punishment for me. Who knew what else he had in mind for me once I was in his clutches?

"I won't marry anyone," I snapped. "This is my life."

Father looked livid as he stomped toward me and slapped me hard across the face. My ears rang and the taste of copper filled my mouth. A long time and many slaps ago, I would have cried.

"You will do as I say. You soiled our name and my honor enough as it is. I won't tolerate your insolence a day longer," he growled, his face bright red.

"What if I don't?"

My wrist was almost numb from Aria's crushing grip. She'd managed to position herself halfway between Father and me, despite Luca's obvious disapproval but he was busy holding Matteo's shirt in an iron grip.

I tried to tug Aria back but never took my eyes off Father. Aria was still trying to protect me but this was a battle she couldn't fight for me.

Father's hand was still raised, ready to hit me again. What would he do if I hit him back? I wished I were brave enough to find out.

"For your betrayal nobody would blink an eye if I gave you to one of the Outfit's sex clubs, so we can make use out of your promiscuity."

Despite my best intentions, shock widened my eyes. Dante frowned but I wasn't sure if that was a good sign or not.

Matteo's eyes were burning with so much hatred that the hairs on the back of my neck rose. Luca was still gripping his shoulder, stopping him from what? I wasn't really sure. "That won't happen. Gianna will become my wife. Today," Matteo said.

"What? I—" I blurted but Father's slap silenced me again. It was harder than before and his ring caught my lower lip. Pain burst through my face and warm liquid trickled down my chin.

"That's enough," Aria said, and suddenly Luca was pulling her back and Matteo was gripping my arm tightly and leading me out of the room and down the hall toward the bathroom. I wasn't sure if it was the shock of what had happened or the speed in which Matteo dragged me away, but I didn't fight him, only stumbled along, not even bothering to stop blood from dripping onto my shirt from my split lip. Matteo shoved me into the bathroom, then entered after me and locked the door.

I stared at my image in the mirror. Blood covered my chin and more blood dripped from the cut in my lower lip and onto my shirt. My lip was already swelling, but I was happy to find my eyes dry, no sign of a single tear. Matteo appeared behind me, towering over me, his dark eyes scanning my messed-up face. Without his trademark shark-grin and the arrogant amusement, he looked almost tolerable.

"You don't know when to shut up, do you?" he murmured. His lips turned into a smirk, but it looked somehow wrong. There was something unsettling in his eyes. The look in them reminded me of the one I'd seen when he'd dealt with the Russian captives in the basement.

"Neither do you," I said then winced at the pain shooting through my lip.

"True," he said in a strange voice. Before I had time to react, he gripped my hips, turned me around and hoisted me onto the washstand. "That's why we are perfect for each other."

Back was the arrogant smile. The bastard stepped between my legs.

"What are you doing?" I hissed, sliding back from the edge of the washstand to bring more distance between us while pushing against his chest.

He didn't budge, too strong for me. The smile got bigger. He grabbed my chin and tilted my head up. "I want to take a look at your lip."

"I don't need your help now. Maybe you should have stopped my father from busting my lip in the first place." The taste of blood, sweet and coppery, made my stomach turn and reminded me of darker images.

"Yes. I should have," he said darkly, his thumb lightly touching my wound as he parted my lips. "If Luca hadn't held me back, I would have plunged my knife into your father's fucking back, consequences be damned. Maybe I still will."

He released my lip and pulled a long curved knife from the holster below his jacket before twisting it in his hand with a calculating look on his face. Then his eyes flickered up to me. "Do you want me to kill him?"

God, yes. I shivered at the sound of Matteo's voice. I knew it was wrong, but after what Father had said today, I wanted to see him begging for mercy and I knew Matteo was capable of bringing anyone to their knees, and it excited me. That was exactly why I'd wanted out of this life. I had the potential for cruelty, and this life was the reason for it. "That would mean war between Chicago and New York," I said simply.

"Seeing your father bleed to death at my feet would be worth the risk. You *are* worth it."

I wasn't sure if he was joking or not, but this was getting too…serious.

I wanted to kiss him for his words, but it was wrong. Matteo was wrong. Everything was. Not too long ago I'd watched Sid getting killed and I knew it might just as well have been Matteo who'd pulled the trigger. I couldn't let him mess with my mind. He was too good at it.

I shoved his shoulder again. "I need to take care of my lip. If you have nothing better to do than to stand around, get out of my way."

He still didn't budge and he was simply too strong to move him. His muscles flexed under his shirt, making me wonder how he would look without it. *Wrong. So wrong.*

He set his knife down on the counter beside me.

"You shouldn't leave sharp objects in my reach when I'm pissed."

"I think I'll take the risk," he said, bracing his palms to both sides of my thighs, leaving me no choice but to lean back to bring some distance between us.

"Stop it," I growled because he smelled too nice and I felt my body wanting to move closer then winced again. I brought my hand up and felt my lower lip. It seemed to have swollen even more and it still hadn't stopped bleeding.

Matteo pulled my hand away. "You'll make it worse. It needs stitches. Should I call for a doctor?"

"No," I said quickly. I didn't want any more people to find out, and most of all I didn't want my bastard of a father to find out he'd managed to split my lip. "I'll do it myself."

Matteo raised his eyebrows. He took a step back and did a quick scan of the cupboards before he came up with a medical kit. He threaded a needle and handed it to me. I shifted on the washstand to see myself in the mirror then brought the needle up to my lip. I'd never stitched anyone up, least of all myself. I hated needles. I even had to close my eyes when I got a shot. Matteo was watching me and I didn't want to look like a wimp to him, so I nudged my lip with the tip of the needle, jumped from pain and pulled back again.

"Fuck. That hurts like hell." I flushed then glared at Matteo. "Go on. Laugh."

Matteo snatched the needle out of my hand. "This isn't going to work."

"I know," I muttered. "Can you do it?"

"It'll be painful. I don't have anything against the pain."

"Have you ever stitched yourself up?"

"A few times."

"Then I can handle you stitching me up. Just do it."

He handed me Tylenol. "Pop a few of them. They won't help with the immediate pain but they'll be good later."

"Vodka works too."

"I guess you found out in your months as a fugitive," he said with a grin that bordered on scary. He hadn't asked too many questions yet. Not even about other guys besides Sid. Maybe he didn't want to know, and I wouldn't tell him anyway. It was bad enough that one innocent had lost his life because of me. I wouldn't tell him the names of the other guys I'd kissed so he'd kill them too. Death was too harsh a punishment for a kiss, for anything really, but that wasn't something a man like Matteo would agree on.

"Among other things," I said because I never knew when to shut my mouth. And what better moment to choose for provoking someone than before they were going to poke you with a sharp needle.

"I bet," he said, the scary smile getting a bit scarier. Matteo cupped my chin. "Try to hold still."

I braced myself as he touched the needle to my lip. Despite my taunting, Matteo was careful when he stitched me up. It still hurt like hell every time the needle pierced my skin and my eyes filled with stupid tears. I fought them for as long as possible but eventually a few trailed down my cheeks. Matteo didn't comment for which I was glad. For him this was probably nothing. When he set the needle down after what felt like forever but had probably been less than five minutes, I quickly wiped the tears off my cheeks, embarrassed that I'd shown weakness in front of him like that.

"It'll swell even more. Tomorrow morning you'll have a fat lip," Matteo said.

I checked my reflection. My lip had already swollen considerably since I'd last seen it, or maybe that was my imagination. I pulled down my lower lip to check the stitches. You couldn't see them from the outside. At least I wouldn't have an ugly scar. "You can't possibly want to marry me looking like this." I pointed at my face. "We should postpone the wedding."

Matteo shook his head with a small laugh. "No chance in hell. You won't slip out of my hands again, Gianna. We will marry today. Nothing will stop me."

chapter *eleven*

Gianna

After my lip was taken care of, Aria and I were allowed to go to my old room while the men discussed how to proceed with the wedding. Two bodyguards were ordered to keep watch on me. One waited in front of the door, the other below my window, in case I decided to climb out of it. The moment the door of my room closed I leaned against it and let out a shaky sigh.

Aria touched my cheek. "How's your lip?"

"Okay. Matteo stitched it up for me."

"I'm so glad he decided to marry you."

My eyebrows shot up. "Not you too, Aria."

Aria pulled me toward the bed and made me sit down. "Father would have given you to one of his soldiers as punishment, Gianna. And you can be sure he would have chosen the least appealing option. Someone really nasty. He's really mad at you. Matteo isn't a bad choice. He must care for you if he went to such great lengths to find you."

"He's a proud man. Pride made him pursue me, nothing else."

"Maybe," she said uncertainly. She picked up a brush from the nightstand. Everything was still as I'd left it six months ago. I was surprised Father hadn't burnt all of my things. I was so tired I could barely keep my eyes open. It was almost seven in the evening. It would have been past midnight in Germany. I couldn't believe how much had happened since I'd woken in Munich this morning.

"Was it worth it?" Aria asked softly as she combed my hair. I couldn't remember the last time she'd done it. Her fingers felt good on my scalp and I had to resist the urge to burry my face against her stomach and cry.

I met her compassionate gaze, and for some reason her understanding infuriated me. "Was the chance at freedom worth pissing off Father and being called a whore and slut? Yes, absolutely. But was my silly wish for something more worth the life of an innocent guy? Then fuck no. My entire existence isn't worth that much. Sid paid the ultimate price for my selfishness. There is nothing I can do to redeem myself." Tears sprang into my eyes.

"Luca told me," Aria said. "I'm so sorry."

I brushed the tears off my face. "Maybe I should let Father marry me off to one of his sadist soldiers. It would serve me right."

"Don't say that, Gianna. You deserve happiness as much as anyone. You couldn't have known what would happen. It's not your fault that they killed Sid."

"How can you even say that? Of course it's my fault. I knew who was hunting me. I knew what Matteo and Father's men were capable off. I knew I was putting anyone whom I let close at risk. That's why I never dated any guys in all the other places I stayed. I flirted and kissed, but then I moved on. Your words from long ago always echoed in my mind. That being with another guy when you're engaged to a man like Luca would mean that guy's death."

"I wasn't talking about you. That's been a long time ago."

"But Matteo is just like Luca and I knew that. I knew that he'd kill any guy he would find with me, but I still went out with Sid. I might as well have pulled the trigger myself!"

"No. You didn't think he'd catch you. You wanted to feel at home and start a new life like you deserved after being on the run for so long. You felt safe and wanted to give love a chance. That's okay."

"No. No, it isn't. You don't get it, Aria. It wasn't even about love. I didn't even really have a crush on Sid. I didn't even like him all that much at the end because he could be a jerk, and that makes it even worse. I risked too much for sloppy kisses and awkward groping, and Sid died because of it."

"Please don't blame yourself. Blame Father and his men. Blame Matteo. I don't care, but don't blame yourself."

"Oh, I'm blaming all of them, don't worry, but that doesn't change that, without me, Sid would still be playing his crappy guitar and flirting with Munich girls."

"You can't change the past, Gianna, but you can make the best of your future."

I couldn't help but smile. "I missed your optimism." I rested my head in her lap and closed my eyes. "I missed you so much."

She stroked my hair. "I missed you too. I'm so happy that you'll live in New York with me."

"First I have to marry Matteo. How am I going to be a wife, Aria?"

"He and Luca work a lot. You won't have to see him very often."

"But still. I'll have to sleep with him and share a bed with him and try to be civil to him for God knows how long. It's not like he'll give me another chance to run."

"You're thinking about running again?" she asked in a small voice.

"I don't know. Maybe."

"Maybe it won't be as bad as you think. Matteo can be funny and he's good-looking, so on a physical level at least it shouldn't be too bad. I'm sure he's a good lover considering how many girls he's had in the past."

I cringed. "Right. If we return to New York tonight, he'll probably expect to sleep with me."

Aria searched my face. "Are you worried he'll let his anger out on you for sleeping with other guys before him?"

"I never did."

Aria blinked. "You never did what?"

"I never slept with any guy. I would have if I'd had a bit more time to get to know a guy but that was never the case."

"Why didn't you say anything? Father treated you horribly. Maybe he would forgive you if you told him the truth." She moved as if she wanted to head downstairs to tell him herself, but I pulled her back down on the bed.

"Don't," I said firmly. "I don't want anyone to know. I don't care if they call me a slut. I don't want to give them the satisfaction of knowing."

Aria gave me a look that made it clear she thought I'd lost my mind. "You have to tell Matteo at least. You have to."

"Why? So he can pride himself on being my first? Fuck no. He's already acting like he's my savior. It'll be only worse if he finds out."

"No, you have to tell him so he can be careful."

I snorted. "I don't need him to be careful. I don't want him to know."

"Gianna, if your first time is anything like mine you'll be thanking your lucky stars if Matteo is careful, trust me."

"I'll survive." But Aria's words were starting to make me nervous.

"That's ridiculous. If he thinks you're experienced, he might take you without much preparation. That'll really hurt."

I shook my head. "Aria, please. I've made my decision. I don't want Matteo to know. It's none of his business."

"What if he finds out anyway? There would have been no way I could have hidden it from Luca."

"I'm good at hiding pain. Maybe I'll bite into a pillow."

Aria laughed. "That sounds like the stupidest idea I've ever heard."

Someone knocked. I quickly sat up, my stomach in knots. What if Father and Dante had changed their minds and I was to stay in Chicago?

When the door opened and Mother walked in, I exhaled. She didn't smile and didn't try to come closer. She was the image of a perfect Italian wife, always properly dressed, always submissive and polite, and incredibly skilled at hiding bruises whenever Father lost it and slapped her. She was everything I never wanted to become. If Matteo ever slapped me, I'd hit him back, no matter the consequences.

"The priest is on his way. He'll be here in fifteen minutes. We need to get you ready for the ceremony," she said matter-of-factly.

My eyes widened. "So soon?"

Mother nodded. "The Vitiellos want to return to New York as soon as possible, which is probably for the best."

I rose from the bed, then slowly walked toward Mother. "Father will be glad to see me gone."

"What about you?" I wanted to ask but didn't dare to.

Mother lifted her hand and brushed my cheek for the barest moment before taking a step back. "You shouldn't have run. You ruined your reputation."

"I don't care about my reputation."

"But you should." She turned to my wardrobe and opened it. "Now let's see if there's a dress you can wear for the ceremony. Of course I wish I could have seen you walk down the aisle in a beautiful white wedding dress." She sighed. Was she trying to make me feel guilty? Because it was working.

Aria moved to my side and squeezed my shoulder before helping Mother look for a dress. Eventually she chose a backless cream-colored floor-length fitted gown that I'd worn for New Years. Aria helped me with my makeup, though it didn't hide my fat lip.

"I'll see if the priest has arrived," Mother said, before hesitating in the doorway with a wistful expression. She opened her mouth but then turned and closed the door.

I tried not to take it to heart. I'd known my parents and most of the people in my world would condemn me for what I'd done, so why was it hurting so much?

"Do you think Lily and Fabi will be allowed to watch the ceremony?" I asked in an embarrassingly hopeful voice.

"Let me talk to Father. I'm sure I can convince him," Aria said.

I didn't protest as she walked out. If someone could convince Father, then it was Aria. I faced the mirror. My eyes were sad and tired. I didn't look like the blushing happy bride. Not that anyone expected me to. This wasn't even a real wedding. Despite my best intentions, regret gripped me once again. How could my life have become such a mess? All I'd ever wanted was to be free to make my own decisions. Maybe I would have married Matteo if he'd ever bothered to ask me instead of ordering me to do it. And now I wouldn't ever get a real wedding or a beautiful dress. I'd always thought I didn't care about these things but now that they were lost to me I felt saddened.

Aria returned. "It's time. The priest is waiting in the living room. Fabi and Lily are there too."

I mustered a smile. "Then let's get married."

Matteo

Even without a wedding gown, Gianna was a fucking sight to behold. The dress hugged her curves; curves I'd take my time exploring when we were back in New York. I couldn't wait to lay claim to every inch of her body. I'd make her forget everything that was before me.

Gianna met my gaze as if she knew what I was thinking. And I really didn't bother to hide my want for her. I'd fuck her tonight, no matter how tired and jet-lagged I was. I'd waited too long for this. Gianna stopped beside me and I took her hand. The priest was looking down his nose at her. I couldn't wait to leave Chicago behind. Not that people in New York would look upon Gianna more kindly, but at least they were too scared of me to show their disdain openly.

Gianna's hand was cold in mine and she avoided my eyes as the priest spoke the wedding vows. When it was her turn to say "I do" I half expected her to say "no" and I really wasn't sure what I would have done then but she didn't. Gianna was a clever girl; she'd hide her hatred for our bond until she was a safe distance away from Chicago and her bastard of a father.

When it was finally time to slip on the wedding ring, she actually shivered. Somehow that annoyed the crap out of me. She should be grateful I wanted her as much as I did. Her stupid actions could have cost her everything. She could at least pretend to be grateful.

"You may kiss the bride," the priest intoned.

I didn't hesitate. I cupped her face and pressed my lips against hers. Gianna stiffened, making my blood boil even more. When I pulled back, she met my gaze head-on. She was really intent on provoking me. If she liked to play with fire, fine. I didn't mind getting burned. I'd walk through flames for her.

Less than sixty minutes later we were back in the air on our way to New York. My body was humming with desire as I watched Gianna in her sexy dress. She and Aria huddled together in the last row on the plane.

Luca sank down beside me and handed me a glass of Scotch. I swallowed it in one gulp. "An espresso would be better. I need to be awake."

Luca followed my gaze toward the girls. "You intend to have your wedding night once you're home."

"Damn right."

"From what I know about Gianna, she probably won't make it easy for you. What are you going to do if she fights you?"

I hadn't considered that. In every fantasy I'd had about Gianna, she'd been a willing participant. I wanted her to scream my name in pleasure, wanted to make her wet. Would she really refuse me? "She won't," I said with more conviction than I felt.

Luca's eyes were practically x-raying me. "Nobody would blame you if you took what you wanted against her will. It's not like she hasn't already done the deed."

My hands curled to fists but instead of following my first impulse and punching Luca, I counted to ten in my mind. Luca often said things like that to gauge someone's reaction. I didn't think he was being serious. Maybe before Aria I would have doubted him more.

His eyes took in my balled fists then scanned my face before smirking. "You are like an open book to me."

"Shut up," I muttered. My eyes found Aria and Gianna once more. They seemed to have an argument, an unusual sight. I'd never seen the two not getting along.

"What's that about?" I asked after a moment.

"How should I know?"

"You and Aria are practically soulmates, haven't you mastered the art of reading each other's mind yet?"

Luca gave me the finger. "I know your wife will make your life hell, so I'll cut you some slack."

"How considerate of you." I wondered how life would be with Gianna. Today she'd been mostly subdued, except for a few occasions but I had a feeling she'd recover quickly and return to her old snarky self. I hated seeing her quiet side, especially when it meant she was sad about that fucker Sid. I tried to forget the bastard but somehow he'd anchored himself in my brain. And then I couldn't stop thinking about him with Gianna. How many more guys had seen her naked? Had been in her? I really needed to find out their names and kill them all.

When we finally landed in New York, I was back to being royally pissed again. I barely glanced at Gianna as we took my Porsche Cayenne back to our apartment building. Every time I caught a glimpse down her shirt to the soft swell of her breasts, I almost lost my shit. I needed to get a grip on myself. It didn't matter what Gianna had done before today. Now she was mine, and if I didn't put a stop to my rising wrath, I'd only do something that I'd regret later on.

Gianna

Matteo had a strange look on his face whenever he glanced my way. I couldn't really put my finger on it, but somehow it made me nervous. Of course I pretended I didn't notice anything.

Aria had tried to talk me into telling Matteo the truth throughout the entire duration of our flight, and even now that we were pulling into the underground garage of the apartment building, she was still giving me meaningful looks. I was worried that she'd take it into her own hands to share my secret with Matteo, but she knew I'd see it as a breach of my confidence and so I hoped she'd hold herself back.

Matteo took my hand when I got out of the car and practically dragged me toward the elevator. Aria and Luca had trouble keeping up with our pace. I had a feeling I knew why Matteo was so eager to reach his apartment. We all piled into the elevator. It started moving and Matteo's dark eyes watched me in the mirror, something hungry and furious gleaming in their depth. The hunger was inexplicable to me. I looked a mess. Shadows under my eyes, fat lip, pale skin.

Maybe I should have felt more anxious, but I only wanted to get this over with. Maybe Matteo would even lose interest in me once he'd had me, though part of me wondered if I'd really be happy if Matteo suddenly started ignoring me.

The elevator stopped with a bling and the sleek doors glided open. Without another word, Matteo pulled me into his apartment. I threw a glance over my shoulder and caught sight of Aria's worried expression moments before the closing elevator doors hid her from my view. Matteo led me toward a door to our right. I barely had time to take in the modern furniture and stunning view of New York before we rushed into the bedroom and Matteo flung the door shut. The desire in his eyes made it clear that he wouldn't take no for an answer tonight.

chapter *twelve*

Gianna

NOBODY HAD EVER LOOKED AT ME LIKE THAT, LIKE I WAS THE ONLY source of water in a time of drought. And by God, I enjoyed it. Part of me at least, the other part, the stubborn part, wanted to hang onto my anger and sadness and indignation, and not give a damn about Matteo's desire for me.

In the last twenty-four hours my dreams had been crushed and an innocent life had been taken. I felt like it was my duty to fight this marriage, and the tingling that flooded my body whenever Matteo touched me. I owed it to Sid, and to my own self-respect. I'd fought too hard and long to be free.

Before I could make up my mind about what I was going to do, Matteo jerked me against him and claimed my mouth in a fierce kiss that made me gasp, then tense. His tongue slipped between my lips, and without wanting to I opened up for him, parted my lips, wrestled his tongue with mine. My hands found their way into his hair, tugging, raking, wanting him closer and at the same time wanting to shove him away.

Matteo gripped my butt and hoisted me up. My legs wound themselves around his waist, but our lips never parted. My body was aflame with lust. No kiss before had even come close to this. Matteo started walking, carrying me toward his bed.

Fight him, Gianna. Fight this. You owe it to Sid.

But I was sick of fighting for today, sick of my emotions. Today I only wanted to feel, let my body take control, forget everything for a few hours at least. There would be plenty of time for resistance later in this marriage.

Matteo threw me down on the bed and the air left my lungs in a rush, but I didn't get much time to recover because suddenly he was on top of me and his lips were back. His hand slipped under my shirt, fingertips gracing my stomach, then the sensitive skin over my ribs. He cupped my breast through my bra and I arched against him. He pulled away, and I barely managed to suppress a sound of protest. He seemed to know it though. He smiled in that arrogant way as he pushed my shirt up over my head and unhooked my bra. My nipples hardened and his smile widened even more.

Annoyance shot through me. He seemed so damn sure of himself, certain of his victory over me. He had another think coming.

"What would you do if I told you 'no'?" I asked in a challenging tone.

I'd expected fury or annoyance in return.

"You won't," he said without a hint of doubt in his voice. I glared but he didn't give me the time for a nasty retort. He lowered his head over my breasts and sucked one erect nipple into his mouth. A moan slipped out before I could stop myself and Matteo didn't allow me any time to gather myself, to raise my defenses. His mouth was relentless. The sensations rippling through my body were almost too much. How could he make me feel like that? His tongue circled my nipple before moving on to the other, leaving a wet trail between my breasts. I shivered. Matteo's eyes were glued to my face. He wanted to see me surrender to him, wanted to enjoy this victory to the very last. I resisted the urge to close my eyes. He would have seen it as another victory. I wouldn't give him that as well. He gently bit down on my nipple and I moaned, even louder than the first time.

With a self-satisfied grin, he moved lower, dipping his tongue into my belly button. I squealed like an idiot girl and tried to squirm away from him, but his hands came down on my hips, holding fast, as his tongue found every ticklish place on my stomach and hips. I was laughing so hard, tears were pooling in my eyes. I had expected him to be rougher after what he'd witnessed, had almost wished for it, but this playful side? That scared me because he seemed likeable, even loveable. I pushed at his forehead. "Stop it!" I gasped between laughter.

"What's the magic word?" he murmured against a particularly ticklish place right above my hip bone.

"Fuck you," I said sweetly. I braced myself but it didn't stop the squeals and laughs when Matteo traced his tongue over my hip bone. I was on the verge of begging when suddenly he stopped his assault. He unbuttoned my pants and pulled them down. His eyes traveled over my legs, and his hands followed the same path, barely brushing my skin. His motions were almost reverent; I didn't get it. Disgust and fury, those I would have understood.

When he kissed me through my panties, I became very still. I knew what he wanted to do. Nobody had ever done that. It felt very personal, as if I had to bare myself to him in more than just the physical sense, and I couldn't do it, wouldn't do it, no matter how much my body craved the experience. Matteo gripped my panties and slid them down my legs. He sat back for a moment, admiring me. "I'd wondered if you were a redhead."

I rolled my eyes, despite the flush spreading in my cheeks. "Isn't that what every man wonders?"

I realized a moment too late that mentioning other men wasn't the best idea in my current situation.

"How did you explain that to the other guys you've been with? Brown on top and red down below?" His voice and eyes had become harder, *dangerous*.

Nobody's ever seen me like this. The words lay on the tip of my tongue. "I thought you wanted to fuck me. I'm not in the mood for chitchat."

Matteo shook his head. "Oh, I will fuck you, don't worry." He crashed his lips down on mine and I kissed him back just as fiercely. "Feel, don't think" became my mantra. His hands roamed my body until they found their way between my legs. I forced myself to relax despite my nerves. When his fingers brushed over my folds, I gasped against his lips. The sensations were delicious. His thumb found my bundle of nerves and started rubbing. Two of his fingers slid back and forth the length of my slit while his thumb pressed down on my clit. Maybe my mind didn't want Matteo, but my body was so eager for him it was ridiculous.

My toes curled as he drove me higher with his fingers. I gripped his neck, bringing him even closer, wrangling his tongue with mine, as my orgasm crashed down on me. My nails dug into his skin but that seemed to turn him on even more judging from the growl deep in his chest. Suddenly two of his fingers moved lower and brushed my opening. Fear spiked. Clamping my legs together, I shoved at his chest and wrenched my lips away from his.

"Stop with the foreplay," I said breathlessly. What if he could feel something with his fingers? I doubted his cock would be as sensitive as his fingertips.

The hint of a frown crossed Matteo's expression but then he slid off the bed with a wicked grin. He stood tall in front of the bed. The bulge in his pants was unmistakable. He didn't give me much time to wonder what lay below the fabric. His hands made quick work out of unbuttoning his shirt and then he slid it off his strong shoulders and let it drop to the ground. This was the first time I saw him without a shirt. I'd caught glimpses of his six-pack through his white shirt before but it couldn't compare to seeing him barechested. My core tightened with desire. Even if Matteo's personality grated on my nerves, my body definitely reacted to his looks. His hands moved on to his pants, and in one swift motion he dropped both his pants and his boxers on the ground. When he straightened, it took all my acting skills to mask my embarrassment and nerves at the sight of him fully erect.

I really should have listened to Aria, but even as the thought crossed my mind I knew I was too proud to tell Matteo the truth. My eyes took their time taking in every inch of him, not even caring that he smirked at my obvious admiration.

And, boy, was he gorgeous. Everything about him was, his chiseled chest and six-pack, even his cock. I hated him for it. Hated how my body reacted to him so quickly and easily when it had never reacted to Sid or the other guys I'd made out with. He advanced on the bed, every move lithe and calculated. Every move aimed to show off his muscles and strength. God, I wished it wasn't making an impression on me. He put one knee on the bed, fixing me with a gaze that made me shiver.

"Stop playing around," I hissed because my nerves were getting the better of me and that was the last thing I needed.

And he did as I asked. He moved onto the bed and climbed between my legs, grabbing my hips with a dark smile. "I'm going to make you forget every fucking guy you've ever been with."

I glared, and was about to give him a nasty comeback, when he pulled at my hips sharply and slammed into me in one hard thrust. I arched up with a cry as pain shot through me. Damn it. Aria hadn't been kidding. This was fucking painful. So much for keeping it a secret. I sucked in a few quick breaths through my nose, my eyes clenched shut. "Oh fuck," I gasped out when I could speak again. This was much worse than I'd thought. I opened my eyes slowly, dreading what I would see. I should have bitten into a fucking pillow, or even my stupid tongue.

Matteo had frozen above me as he stared down at me in surprise. "Gianna?"

My face turned hot. "Shut up," I muttered. I loosened my fingers, which had clawed at the bedsheet.

Matteo's eyes were soft. "Why didn't you tell me?"

I decided to play dumb. Maybe I could convince him this wasn't what it looked like. "Tell you what?"

A sly grin twisted his lips, and I wanted nothing more than to wipe it off his face. Of course he didn't buy my lie. He wasn't an idiot. He was a master manipulator and I obviously had a lot to learn before I could trick him.

"That I'm your first," he said. Did he have to sound so…relieved and proud?

If I hadn't been worried that getting his cock out of me would hurt as much as getting it inside had, I would have shoved him away. Lying beneath him made a fair argument difficult.

I narrowed my eyes. "I thought we were going to fuck? I'm tired of talking to you."

Matteo braced himself on his hands, bringing us closer. I tensed at the twinge the movement caused.

"First I want you to answer my question. Why? You could have spared yourself a lot of pain, if you'd told me," he said calmly. He looked like this was the easiest thing in the world for him, being buried deep inside of me, and having a chat.

When it became clear that he would wait until I gave him what he wanted, I said, "Because I didn't want you to know."

His grin got even cockier. "Because you didn't want to admit that you waited for me."

"I didn't wait for you. Now stop talking and fuck me, damn it." This was getting too personal, and I hated how vulnerable I was, naked inside and out. How was I supposed to stop feeling if Matteo kept asking me things I didn't want to think about?

Matteo didn't take his eyes off me. They were dark and possessive, and seemed to stare right through me. If it hadn't felt like a defeat, I would have looked away. He pulled out slowly before sliding back in and I tensed from the pain. My body was a horrible traitor. At least, I managed to hold back a gasp this time. Matteo moved slowly and carefully, his muscles flexing with every thrust.

I hated that he was being considerate. I hated that he wasn't acting like a total asshole, hated that hating him wasn't as easy as I'd thought. If he wasn't an asshole, then somehow Sid's death was even more my fault, because my running away was unnecessary and selfish and unfounded.

I gripped his shoulders. "Stop holding back."

Matteo's brows drew together but he still didn't move faster.

I dug my fingers into his skin and jerked my hips despite the soreness between my legs. "Stop holding back!"

This time he listened. His eyes flashed and then he slammed into me harder and faster. I closed my eyes as I held onto his shoulders. I probably left marks with my nails. I didn't care and Matteo didn't seem to mind if his quick breathing was any indication.

The pain felt good, gave me something to focus on beyond the crushing guilt. But there wasn't only pain. Soon the stretched feeling turned into an exquisite pressure, a low hum of pleasure I'd never felt before. Matteo lowered himself, changing the angle in which he pushed into me, hitting an amazing spot deep inside me. Matteo's mouth found my throat and then he bit down on my skin lightly. A moan slipped out of my lips. My eyes shot open, meeting Matteo's intense gaze. I couldn't look away. I wanted to pull him closer and push him away at the same time, wanted to hide and open up to him, wanted and not wanted. "Are you going to come?" Matteo rasped.

I shook my head "no," not trusting my voice. Maybe I could have come. It felt increasingly good, but I needed to bring space between Matteo and me, needed time to get a handle on my emotions before they overwhelmed me. I was confused and tired and sad.

Matteo raised himself on his arms again and sped up even more, slamming into me over and over again, and then he tensed above me, his face twisting with pleasure, and damn he looked magnificent, like something even Michelangelo couldn't have created better. Matteo's movements became jerky and then he stilled, eyes closed, a few strands of dark hair stuck to his forehead.

My fingers itched to brush them away, to touch his lips and jaw. Instead I dropped my hands from his shoulders and rested them on the bed beside me where they couldn't do something stupid, something I'd regret later.

Matteo's eyes peeled open slowly and I sucked in a quiet breath. Why couldn't he stop looking at me like that? He didn't smile, only pierced me with his dark gaze.

I pushed against his chest. "You're getting heavy. Get off."

The corners of his mouth twitched, then he slowly pulled out and plopped down on the bed beside me and reached for me as if he was going to embrace me. Panicking, I sat up and slid off the bed. If he hugged me now, if he acted like we were a real couple, one that cared about each other, I'd lose my shit. I headed for the bathroom, not bothering to cover myself. Matteo had seen all of me already, and I wouldn't give him the satisfaction of thinking I was embarrassed to be naked in front of him.

I didn't hear him coming after me but suddenly Matteo grabbed my hand, stopping me from disappearing into the safety of the bathroom. Our eyes met. His were almost…regretful. "I shouldn't have gone so hard on you, but you know how to push my fucking buttons, Gianna. Did I hurt you?"

Concern, there it was again. Damn it. Why couldn't he stop acting like he was a normal guy? Did he really think that would make me forget who and what he really was? "Don't pretend you didn't like it."

"I don't. I loved every fucking second of it. I've waited a long time for this moment. I've spent almost every waking moment of my search for you imagining having your hot body under me. But in my imagination you were moaning my name and having multiple orgasms. You definitely weren't in pain."

That arrogant bastard. "Keep imagining that. It won't happen."

Matteo braced himself against the doorframe, trapping me between his arms. "Your body reacted to me, Gianna, even if you don't want to admit it. Next time you will come when I fuck you, trust me."

"What makes you think my body was reacting to you? Maybe I was imagining I was with someone else. The mind is a powerful tool." I tried to slip away under his arm but he pushed me against the doorframe. "Maybe I was imagining it was Sid and not you fucking me."

Matteo didn't even blink. He didn't believe a word I was saying. Damn it!

"If you'd really wanted Sid to be your first, you would have let him fuck you. So why didn't you?"

"Because you killed him!"

Matteo smiled. "We both know that's not the reason why, but let's just pretend it were true. Then I'm glad he's dead. That wimp didn't deserve the privilege."

I couldn't believe him. "You asshole. I knew you'd get a kick out of it, that's why I didn't tell you."

Matteo leaned close until there was less than an inch between our lips. "But I know and I won't ever forget. You are mine now, Gianna, and I fucking love that I caught you before you found a loser to pop your cherry."

I tried to slap him but he caught my wrist and actually kissed my palm with a self-satisfied grin. I wrenched my hand away from him. A myriad of insults flitted through my mind, too many to choose only one.

Matteo nodded toward the bed. "Maybe I should tell everyone that we can have a presentation of the sheets after all."

My eyes grew wide. That was the last thing I wanted, and Matteo knew it. He was taunting me. I pushed past him and this time he let me, and rushed toward the bed. There was a small pink smudge on the sheet. Men had it so much easier. Women had really been screwed over when it came to anatomy. We got our period, we couldn't pee standing up, we had to squeeze something the size of a melon out of our vagina and our first time sucked majorly. "You wouldn't dare," I said.

Matteo crossed his arms over his chest. He was still gloriously naked and was getting a boner again. The bastard was turned on by our fight. "You shouldn't tempt me."

I shrugged. "Even if you showed the sheets to your family, nobody would believe you anyway. They think I'm a slut, remember? They'd probably think you faked the stain with your own blood like Luca did on his wedding night." I tensed. This was a secret I was supposed to keep. Nobody knew. Why couldn't I ever keep my stupid mouth shut?

chapter *thirteen*

Matteo

Gianna's eyes widened when she let Aria and Luca's little secret slip. Did she actually think I didn't know? Luca and I would die for each other. He knew he could trust me with every secret, even one that revealed he wasn't quite the cruel bastard he and everyone else thought he was. Somehow by some stroke of luck our sadist of a father had made the right decision when he'd chosen Aria for Luca. I didn't think he'd known how well those two would get along, or he wouldn't have agreed to the match. He'd always strived on the misery of others. "Don't worry. Luca told me. Your sister has warmed his cold heart. You Scuderi women have a talent for it."

Gianna relaxed. No matter how tough she thought she was, her body gave her away. She wasn't very good at hiding her emotions, which would make it easier for me. Her gaze returned to the stain on the sheets. Seeing it actually gave me a sick kick, so had the fine smear of blood on my cock. I wasn't like some men in our world who would have refused to marry Gianna because she might have messed around with other guys during her flight. Not that I didn't hate the thought that any guy had ever laid a fucking finger on her beautiful body, but I wanted Gianna too much to care, and I found the whole obsession with purity in our world ridiculous anyway. The best sex I'd had in my life definitely had been with women who knew what they were doing, but I had a feeling Gianna was a quick learner. Still after the initial shock when Gianna had cried out in pain, I'd felt a rush of possessiveness and fucking joy.

Gianna glanced at me, suspicion tightening her kissable lips. Her hair covered her pale skin like a veil and I couldn't resist brushing the strands from her shoulder, marveling at their silkiness. Only Gianna's skin was even smoother. I didn't think I'd ever get enough of touching her. My fingers found her pulse before I started stroking her throat lightly. For a moment Gianna held her breath and actually leaned into my touch before she seemed to catch herself. She took a step back so I had no choice but to drop my hand. I had to stifle a smile. She was so very predictable. At least, in her reactions to me. Sometimes in the past she'd managed to surprise me, which wasn't something other people managed often.

Gianna narrowed her eyes at me. If she knew how hot she looked when she was angry, she'd smile more often. I was already hard again and wanted nothing more than to fuck Gianna. Her eyes flitted down to my cock and she huffed. Shaking her head, she brushed past me and disappeared in the bathroom before slamming the door shut with an audible bang.

I released a small laugh before heading back to the bed, dropping on my back and crossing my arms behind my head. I couldn't keep the grin off my face. After months of frustration, I had been rewarded, even more than I'd hoped for. I waited for the sound of running water but silence reigned in the bathroom. I sat up, suspicion filling me. There wasn't any way Gianna could escape from the bathroom, but what if she decided to end her life rather than spend it with me?

Gianna seemed to love life too much for such an action, but I wasn't sure she wouldn't do it to spite me. I moved toward the bathroom door, ready to tear it down when it opened. Gianna stepped out, her eyebrows shooting up when she spotted me right in front of her. Her eyes weren't puffy, so at east she hadn't been crying, which was a relief.

Her nose crinkled. "What? Don't tell me you've been spying on me while I was in the bathroom?"

I crossed my arms over my chest with a smirk. I definitely wouldn't tell her what I'd thought. "We both know you need supervision."

With a sigh, she walked past me and climbed under the covers. After a quick scan of the bathroom, which looked the same as it had before, I joined Gianna. She had her back turned to me, and the blankets pulled up to her chin. I pressed myself against her back, my arm sliding around her naked waist. Having her naked body so close to mine was giving me all kinds of ideas and my cock was digging insistently against her butt. I couldn't wait to take her like this, to have her in front of me on all fours, to have her riding me. I wanted to fuck her in a thousand different ways.

"Don't even think about it," Gianna said quietly, warningly. "I'm tired and I don't owe you more than one go on our wedding night."

I laughed against her neck before pressing a kiss to her soft skin. "You are such a romantic, Gianna. Your words always warm my heart."

"Oh shut up," she muttered.

I tightened my hold on her. She didn't try to pull away, which surprised me, and again raised my suspicions, but I blamed her demureness on the long day both of us had had. It had been more than twenty-four hours since I'd slept.

Still, I fought off sleep until I heard Gianna's breathing deepening and her body softening against me. I didn't trust Gianna, not after what she'd done. I wasn't sure if I'd ever trust her completely. I knew she'd run the moment I let her out of my sight. I wouldn't give her another chance to evade me. I didn't care what I had to do to keep her in New York.

Luca had thought I'd lose interest in her once I'd fucked her. Part of me had hoped for it, but I could already tell that it wasn't the case. I still wanted her, probably more than before.

I was completely and utterly screwed.

Gianna

The next morning I woke to Matteo moving around in the bedroom. I didn't give any indication that I was awake, instead I listened to his sounds. I didn't want to face him. He'd be smug about last night, definitely intolerable. Before a long shower and a strong coffee I wasn't in the mood for that particular kind of confrontation. When his steps finally moved away and the door clicked shut, I exhaled and opened my eyes. The skyline of New York was hung with heavy clouds. Maybe I could simply stay in bed, but I had a feeling Matteo might try to join me if I did. My traitorous body tingled with excitement at the idea of having his hands on me again, maybe even allowing him to go down on me for real.

I quickly sat up, slid out of bed and hurried into the bathroom to splash cold water into my face. I winced at the burning in my lip. I peered at myself in the mirror. My lower lip was swollen dramatically and the skin below it was bruised. I looked like I'd been in a fight, which wasn't that far from the truth. I opened my mouth to take a look at the stitches. Disgusted, I quickly snapped it shut again. The events from yesterday flashed through my mind.

I hadn't even had nightmares about what happened to Sid. I still felt horrible for his cruel death, but my dreams had been empty, a black void of nothingness. Maybe I did belong into this world after all.

My eyes slid down to a spot on the side of my neck where Matteo had left a hickey. The bastard had marked me like I was his property, and to him that was probably the case. I touched the bruise.

Grimacing, I turned away from my reflection, and took a quick shower. When I returned to the bedroom, I found my bags on the floor. Matteo must have carried them in while I was getting ready. Sneaky bastard. How could he move so quietly?

I quickly put my clothes into the drawers that Matteo must have cleared for me. Somehow it annoyed me that he'd made space for me as if he'd known all along that I'd eventually move in. He must have done it long ago. There hadn't been any time last night or this morning. Putting away the clothes that I hadn't worn in six months also made me realize that I desperately needed to go shopping. My old clothes felt like a relic from an old life. In our rush to leave my apartment in Munich, I hadn't been able to grab any of my new clothes.

Afterward, fully dressed I headed out of the bedroom, pausing briefly to listen for Matteo. It was silent in the apartment and as I walked through the living room toward the open kitchen I didn't encounter anyone, not even a bodyguard. Suspicion flared in me. Matteo would never leave me unsupervised after what I'd done. My eyes scanned the ceiling, the corners and every other possible place for security cameras, but I found none. I hesitated in the middle of the kitchen for a moment, eyes darting to the massive coffee maker. Screw it. I needed caffeine. If Matteo wasn't there, for which I was grateful, I'd pretend this was my home.

And I didn't even need to pretend. This was my home now, or it was supposed to be. Of course it didn't feel like it. It had been a long time since any place had felt like home. In the last few months of my living there, even my parents' house hadn't felt like one anymore. There was no use thinking about it now. I'd never forgive Father for how he'd treated me, nor Mother because she'd let him. Maybe I was dead to them, but they were dead to me too.

My finger hovered in front of the button that would turn the coffee maker on. This eerie silence was driving me crazy. Scolding myself for my ridiculous caution, I finally pushed it. I grabbed a cup and selected a cappuccino. I wasn't on the run anymore. The worst had already happened.

With a satisfying fizz, the hot liquid shot out. The moment it was done, I cradled the cup and took a long sip, feeling how the warmth and familiar taste cleared my mind further. I leaned against the counter, letting my eyes wander through the apartment. I actually liked the puristic design, the sleek black leather couches, black hardwood furniture and white walls. I wondered if Luca and Matteo had hired the same interior designer because their furniture was so similar. I could see myself looking for art pieces that would fit in, could see myself shop for pillows that would bring some color in, could see myself decorating a large tree for Christmas. I walked around the counter, perched on the stool and turned my back on the place I could so easily see myself living in.

This wasn't what I wanted. Or at least something I hadn't wanted six months ago, something I shouldn't want, not after risking so much to escape it. I closed my eyes and inhaled the comforting scent of my coffee. I needed to see Aria again, but was I even allowed to go one floor up to her penthouse? The idea that I had to ask Matteo and maybe even Luca for permission whenever I wanted to see my sister drove me up the walls. It was a good reminder of why I'd run in the first place, something I could never allow myself to forget.

A warm breath ghosted over my neck, followed by a low, "Good morning."

I cried out in surprise and sent my coffee cup flying off the kitchen bar. It broke into dozens of sharp pieces and spilled coffee everywhere. My head whirled around and I found myself face-to-face with a smirking Matteo.

"Fuck. Why the hell are you creeping up on me like that? You scared the hell out of me," I hissed.

He shook his head with an amused expression. "All those nasty words pouring out of your sweet mouth, is that really appropriate?"

He was making fun of me. His eyes took their sweet-ass time wandering over my curves, lingering on the hickey before moving a bit lower again. And the worst thing was the way my body was reacting to his closeness, his scent, his muscled chest. Thankfully, my face didn't feel hot, so maybe I hadn't blushed.

"Since when do you care about being appropriate?" I muttered. I slipped past Matteo and knelt beside the broken remains of my cup. I hoped Matteo didn't suspect what his proximity was doing to me. I picked up the pieces but Matteo came to my help. I wasn't sure if he was doing it to be nice or if he knew about his effect on me and was trying to play with me. From what I knew about him, I guessed the latter. I was trying not to look his way as he squatted beside me. He was giving me a good view of his perfectly shaped ass. Goddammit, why did he have to look like that?

Without warning, he brushed his finger over my swollen lip. "I really should have killed your father."

His touch was so gentle, it made me want to nuzzle my face against his neck and have a good cry. "Do you have a mop?" I asked casually.

He shrugged, dropping his hand. "I've seen Marianna run around with one on occasion."

I rolled my eyes. Of course he had no clue. He probably had never even done his own laundry. "Do you at least know where Marianna keeps the cleaning stuff?"

His gaze lingered on my cleavage. With a sigh, I rose to my feet and stalked off in search of a storeroom. When I finally returned to the mess in the kitchen, mop in hand, Matteo was talking on the phone. He was leaning against the counter, legs casually crossed.

I tried to listen to the conversation as I wiped the floor. I had a feeling it was about me.

"Come over now. I want this done ASAP."

With that he hung up, and turned back to me. I leaned the mop against the wall, then asked, "Who was this? A new bodyguard you hired to keep an eye on me?"

"Something like that. I'm going to put an ankle bracelet on you."

"What? Have you lost your mind?"

"On the contrary, but we both know you'll use the next chance you get to escape again, so until I can trust you to stay with me, you'll have to wear the bracelet."

I stared, completely stunned and so angry I was worried my head would explode. "So you admit I'm your prisoner. You're treating me like one after all."

Matteo advanced on me. "Without the bracelet I would have to lock you into this apartment, but with it, you can spend time with Aria, walk around New York, and live an almost normal life."

"I guess you want me to thank you for your kindness?"

The asshole actually chuckled. "No. Knowing you I didn't expect you to like the idea."

"Nobody would like that idea! And you don't know me, Matteo."

He moved very close and without warning he slipped his hand under my shirt, pushed aside my bra and twisted my nipple. At once, my core tightened with need. "I know that you love it when I do this with your perfect little nipple," he growled.

I wanted to deny it, but the way his thumb and forefinger teased me, I couldn't find the words. Matteo's dark eyes bore into me as he leaned very close. "I know you are wet. I know your pussy wants me even if you won't admit it."

He dropped to his knees and shoved down my tights and panties.

"What—"

I didn't get farther. He leaned forward and kissed my heated flesh. I sucked in a startled breath. Matteo freed one of my legs from my tights and panties before he lifted it and draped it over his shoulder. His eyes found mine as his tongue parted my lower lips and licked slowly. I shivered, pressing my mouth together from fear of making an embarrassing sound.

Matteo pulled back a couple of inches. "See, I knew it. Wet for me," he said in a rough voice. He pressed a few kisses against me before suckling lightly. My eyes wanted to roll back in my head from the sensation.

"Has anyone ever done this to you?" he asked fiercely.

I couldn't even find the power to lie. I merely shook my head "no."

"Good." He rewarded me with a mind-blowing kiss, his tongue tracing my opening, then darting back up to my clit.

"Oh God," I whispered.

Matteo released my throbbing labia. "You taste perfect, Gianna." He parted me and brushed a kiss over my clit. "Do you want me to stop?"

I gritted my teeth. I had never wanted anything less. It took all my self-control not to grab him and shove his face against me.

"The silent treatment?" Matteo asked in a teasing voice before he nudged me with his tongue, sending spears of pleasure through me before he captured my clit between his lips and suckled lightly.

I gasped and gripped the counter behind me, needing something to support me. My head fell back as Matteo did the most amazing thing with his tongue. With slow strokes he brought me closer and closer to the edge. I could tell this time it would be even more intense than yesterday. Without intending to, my hand gripped Matteo's head and my fingers tangled in his dark hair. Matteo rewarded me with a flick of his tongue against my clit.

"Yes," I whispered. I didn't even care anymore that I was admitting how good this felt. My entire body screamed for release. I was so close, my legs started shaking, my breathing quickened. And then the bell rang. I jerked in surprise and my eyes flew to the elevator. Nobody could come up without Matteo granting them access.

Matteo pulled back from what he was doing. My fingers on his head tightened. "Don't stop," I demanded. I couldn't hide the need in my voice.

Matteo straightened and wiped his mouth with an annoyingly cocky grin. He leaned in to kiss me but I turned my head so his lips brushed my cheek.

"Patience, Gianna. I've had six months to practice patience, now it's your turn, but don't worry, I'll eat you out later. You taste too good to resist," he murmured before stepping back and heading toward the elevator. "You should get dressed. We don't want to give Sandro a show."

I couldn't believe him. I quickly scrambled to put my panties and tights back on, before I washed my hands and straightened my skirt. My blood was boiling with fury. Matteo smirked as he pressed the button that allowed the elevator to stop on our floor.

This wasn't the end of it. Two could play this game.

chapter *fourteen*

Matteo

GIANNA WAS TRYING TO KILL ME WITH HER EYES. NOT THAT I wasn't used to that look from her by now, but I had to admit it was still turning me on. I wished Sandro had waited a few minutes longer to show up, even if his early appearance gave me the chance to teach Gianna a lesson. Unfortunately I was punishing myself as much as Gianna with my little lesson. She'd tasted fucking perfect. I couldn't wait to lick her again, to have her screaming my name and rake her fingers through my hair. I was already getting a fucking boner again. Fuck this.

The elevator doors slid open and Sandro stepped in, holding up a black case. "Morning, boss. Hope I didn't interrupt anything," he said, his eyes sliding past me to Gianna. Despite his mess-up six months ago, he was still a good soldier. The best one next to Romero.

"You didn't," I said with a grin at Gianna, whose eyes narrowed even further. It was a good thing that Sandro didn't look anywhere near my crotch area because there was no way I could have hidden the bulge. Not that I fucking cared. "Let's do this now," I said eventually.

Gianna crossed her arms over her chest, somehow managing to push her breasts up in a delicious way. Was she doing it on purpose? She didn't move as we walked toward her. She looked like she couldn't care less but I knew her better than that. She was probably trying to figure out a way to make me pay for teasing her, not to mention for the ankle bracelet. But she'd brought this upon herself.

Sandro watched Gianna suspiciously as we stopped beside her. I couldn't blame him. His pride had taken quite a bruising when she and Aria had drugged him and tied him up. He was too clever to show his dislike though.

I pointed toward the barstool. "You need to take off your tights and sit down."

"Thanks for the heads-up. You could have mentioned the tights thing before and spared me a whole lot of trouble," she muttered. Fuck, her glare made me want to bend her over the kitchen counter and fuck her brains out.

Sandro pretended he was busy with the ankle bracelet in the case as I leaned close to Gianna. "But I loved watching you put on your sexy tights, and I'll love watching you take them off again."

Gianna almost tore her tights down this time before she perched on the stool, her long lean legs crossed. She pressed her lips together in anger, then flinched from pain. Fury for her father burst through my rising lust. Damn Luca and his determination to keep peace with the Outfit.

Sandro hesitated, ankle bracelet in hand, and darted an inquiring look my way.

I'd never put an ankle bracelet on anyone, so even if I fucking hated the thought of Sandro touching Gianna's leg, it was the logical choice. I nodded. "Go on."

"Extend your left leg."

Gianna sent me a scathing look but she raised her leg without protest. Maybe she'd decided it was the better option than being locked into the apartment all the time, or maybe she was coming up with torturous things to do to me as retribution. I had a feeling I might enjoy whatever she had in mind, even if that wasn't her intention.

Sandro bent over Gianna's leg and started fastening the small black monitor around her ankle. I leaned against the kitchen bar next to Gianna. She didn't glance my way.

"Will this monitor my alcohol intake as well?" she asked Sandro. He raised his eyes to her, then me.

"I don't care if you're getting drunk as long as you do it in New York," I said. Her blue eyes fixed me with another scowl before she turned back to Sandro, who was checking the bracelet for its functionality.

With a nod, he straightened. "All done. You can trace her with your laptop, phone or any other internet-ready device."

"Great," Gianna muttered.

"Thanks, Sandro."

"Do you need anything else?"

I shook my head. "Not today. Romero is upstairs. You can return to your other tasks."

Sandro gave Gianna a curt nod before he turned around and headed for the elevator. After I'd let him out, I returned to Gianna.

"So how long am I going to have to wear this thing?" she asked, lifting her leg to take a closer look at the small black device around her ankle. I hated seeing her with that thing. It seemed wrong to shackle her like that, but Luca had suggested the bracelet and it was a neat solution. Gianna was too volatile for her own good.

"Until I decide I can trust you enough not to do something stupid."

"So forever." She dropped her leg back down.

I chuckled. "No. I like your gorgeous legs better without the ankle monitor, believe me. I'll relieve you of that thing as soon as possible." I traced my fingers over her bare knee, then higher until I reached the edge of her jeans skirt. She swatted my hand away and hopped off the barstool.

"Hands off," she said sweetly.

I raised my eyebrows. "I thought you wanted to continue where we left off before?" I really wanted to fucking continue where we left off.

She walked past me toward the coffee maker, swaying her hips in a way that turned me hard again. "I'm good," she said with a shrug. "All I need is a cup of coffee." She grabbed a new cup and put it under the coffee maker before peering over her shoulder at me. "What about you? Is there anything you need?" Her eyes wandered down my body toward my hard-on. I could tell that she was fighting a smile.

Oh, fuck. She really knew how to give me bedroom eyes. And obviously she thought she could play my game better than I did. "I'm good too."

She brought her cup to her mouth, took a sip, then ran her tongue slowly over her upper lip.

I stifled a groan. I had to meet Luca to discuss what I'd missed in the last few months while I'd been hunting Gianna, but I really wished I could watch her all day and maybe convince her to run her tongue over my cock. I strolled toward her and twisted a strand of her hair around my forefinger. "I hate your new color. I liked you better red."

Gianna pulled back and set her cup down with a clang. "Well, looking good wasn't my main concern while I was on the run. Maybe you didn't notice but a notorious mobster was hunting me."

I grinned. "Notorious?"

She rolled her eyes. "If you are fishing for compliments, then you're talking to the wrong person."

I didn't tell her to dye her hair back to her natural color, even though I wanted to. I knew she wouldn't do it if I tried to push her. Maybe admitting that I liked her red hair was already enough to make her want to stay a brunette forever. "I'm meeting with Luca. You can spend the day with Aria upstairs if you want."

Her eyes widened. "I'm allowed to spend the day with Aria?" After a moment, her mouth twisted and she added, "Not that I should need your permission to see my sister…"

"You and Aria haven't seen each other in a long time, I suppose you have a lot to talk about." I wondered if Gianna would tell Aria about last night and what exactly she would say. Normally I'd ask her what she'd enjoyed but I knew Gianna wouldn't give me an honest answer. Women had never complained about my sexual skills, but I wanted to hear it from Gianna. Maybe Luca was right and I was a vain asshole.

"Can we go up now?" Gianna asked, excitement lighting up her face. It was the first real emotion she'd shown me all morning.

"What about a kiss to convince me?"

She surprised me by grabbing my shirt, jerking me toward her and pressing her lips to mine. Her sexy body leaned up against me and her tongue slipped into my mouth. I didn't need any more encouragement. I grabbed her ass cheeks, squeezed, relishing in her gasp as our tongues danced with each other. I pushed my hard cock against her. She needed to know what she was doing to me. Fuck. I was so fucking hard, it was a wonder that I hadn't come in my pants yet like an idiotic teenage boy.

Without warning she drew back and I growled in response, my grasp on her ass tightening, but she pushed my arms down and stepped out of reach. "You wanted a kiss, you got your kiss. Now let's go to Aria."

That vixen. I knew by her rapid breathing and flushed cheeks that she was as affected by our kissing as me, but she seemed determined to suppress her lust. I'd simply have to up my game, show her what a mind-blowing orgasm really meant. After that, she'd hopefully be putty in my hands.

I walked toward the elevator as if I didn't give a damn. I had more than enough experience at hiding my emotions, so I had no trouble masking my arousal. I pressed the button that made the elevator doors slide open and motioned for Gianna to walk in. She frowned but then she headed into the elevator and leaned against the wall.

Hiding my smile, I joined her and jabbed the button that would take us up. It took several moments before Luca approved our going up. Before he'd married Aria, I had been allowed to take the elevator up without his approval, but since then he'd installed the manual override again. Not that I blamed him. I didn't want him or Aria barging in when Gianna and I were desecrating every available space of the apartment either. The elevator started moving and within a few seconds stopped again.

Aria was already waiting in front of the doors when they slid open. She barely spared me a glance before she pulled her sister into a hug and dragged her away toward the living area.

Luca stood with his arms crossed against the wall. "No kiss goodbye for you from your lovely wife?" he asked wryly.

Aria and Gianna had settled on the sofa, and were whispering among themselves. Romero raised his hand in greeting from his spot in the kitchen. He'd keep watch over Aria and Gianna while Luca and I were busy in Sphere. He knew what the two girls had done to Sandro, so he wouldn't let his guard down, and even if he did, the ankle bracelet would alert me of Gianna's whereabouts.

"Aria doesn't really look too sad to see you gone either," I said when Luca joined me in the elevator.

He smirked. "We already said goodbye twice this morning. What about you? How was your wedding night?"

I couldn't stop the grin. "Better than yours."

Luca's eyebrows rose in silent doubt. "So did she put out?"

"She did," I said. "And I was her first."

"Did she tell you that?" Luca asked doubtfully.

"No, she didn't. She was furious that I found out. But there was no way she could have hidden it."

"Good for you," Luca said, clapping my shoulder. "So are you still into her or have you come to your senses now that your cock isn't ruling your thinking anymore?"

I gave him the finger. "What makes you think my cock isn't still in charge?"

Luca sighed. "Suit yourself, but don't come bitching to me when she starts to annoy you." The elevator stopped and opened to the underground garage. "Now let's focus on business. You've wasted enough time. I need your full attention now."

"Don't worry," I said, but I had a feeling it wouldn't be easy to get Gianna out of my head. The image of her naked body beneath me had burned itself into my brain and I wasn't too keen on letting it go.

Gianna

Aria dragged me toward the sofa, away from Luca and Matteo. We sat down and Aria reached for my fat lip with a frown. "I can't believe Father hit you so hard."

"He's done it before," I muttered.

Romero was watching us from the kitchen. I really wondered how he could stand being trapped in this penthouse with Aria all day. I doubted many soldiers had vied for the job.

After a moment, Aria leaned toward me, whispering. "Are you okay? How was last night?"

I glanced in the direction of Luca and Matteo but they had already disappeared in the elevator and were off to God knew where.

"Gianna?"

"I'm fine," I said, sending my sister a comforting smile. She looked like she hadn't slept much last night. Had worry for me kept her awake?

"And? How was it? Did you sleep with Matteo?"

I laughed. Aria reminded me of myself after Aria's wedding night. I had been so terribly worried for her. "Don't sound so anxious. I'm really fine." I was oddly fine. Maybe even too fine. It had been too easy finding my way back to my old life, as if the life I'd tried to lead in the last few months had never really fit. This morning I hadn't wondered where I was, hadn't had to remind myself of my current pseudonym. I was me again.

"You don't look fine. Please tell me what happened. I drove Luca crazy with my anxiety last night."

That made me smile. Everything that soured Luca's mood did. "I slept with Matteo." My mind returned to the feeling of him inside me, of his intense gaze, his strong body, his touch, and my core tightened again. I wasn't sure how I could stop my body from being so eager for Matteo's attention but I knew I had to figure out a way if I ever wanted to hold some sort of power in this marriage.

"You look like you didn't mind," Aria said with a teasing smile.

"Like you said, Matteo is good-looking, and he knows what he's doing, so it wasn't bad."

"Did he notice that you hadn't slept with anyone before?"

"Yeah. You were right. It hurt like hell. He was so damn smug about it. I really wish he hadn't figured it out. I feel like he's got more power over me now that he knows."

Aria shook her head. "You need to stop thinking like that. You and Matteo need to find a way to get along now that you're married. It's a good thing that he knows the truth."

"Matteo doesn't exactly make it easy for me either. He's always so arrogant. And he's the one who started with the games. And do you know what else he did?" I lifted my leg with the stupid ankle bracelet. I still couldn't believe Matteo had actually put that thing on my body, like I was a dog who needed a collar. Of course from his standpoint it was probably the normal thing to do. He was a controlling, possessive, power-hungry killer after all, but that didn't mean I liked it.

Aria grimaced. "I know. Luca mentioned it to me this morning. It was his idea." She paused with an apologetic expression. "I tried to talk him out of it, but he said he won't risk any more conflicts with the Outfit by letting you roam free."

"As if Father or anyone else in the Outfit would care if I ran off again. I'm not their problem anymore, remember?" I wiggled my fingers, showing off my wedding ring.

"Luca and Matteo would look weak if you managed to get away again, and that would weaken their position. Things between New York and Chicago haven't exactly been going smoothly in the last few months."

"Because of me?"

"Not just because of you," Aria said. "Luca and Dante don't get along very well. They are both alphas who aren't used to working with equals."

"I don't suppose you know of a way how to get rid of this thing?" I tipped my finger against my black shackle.

"No. Is it very uncomfortable?"

I shrugged. "Not really, but I hate it. And I can kiss short skirts and dresses goodbye unless I want everyone to think I'm a criminal."

Aria touched my arm lightly. "I'm sure Matteo will take it off soon."

"I doubt that." If I were him, I wouldn't trust me anytime soon. Probably never.

Aria's eyes darted to my hair again. She'd been doing it since she'd first seen me with the new color.

I smoothed a hand over my hair. "You hate it, right?"

"I'm not used to it. Maybe it'll grow on me. But I miss your red hair."

"Me too," I said. "Matteo hates my brown hair as well."

"Don't tell me you're going to stay a brunette because you want to annoy him?" Aria asked with a knowing look.

I wasn't that childish. Maybe six months ago that would have been my reaction but being on the run had helped me grow up. I wouldn't keep my hair in a color I didn't like to annoy Matteo. There were other ways I could make his life harder and I hoped to explore as many of them as possible. "I'll change it back to my natural hair color as soon as I get the chance.

Do you think Matteo will freak out if we leave the apartment in search for a hairdresser?"

"Probably. You've been married for less than a day. Maybe you should try to stay on your best behavior for today at least."

"I'll do my best," I said sarcastically.

Aria got up. "It's almost lunchtime. Let's grab something to eat and I'll give my hairdresser a call and ask her to come over to do your hair, okay?"

I pushed to my feet. "Perfect. I'm starving." I followed Aria toward the kitchen area. Romero put his phone down on the counter, eyes and posture alert as we approached. Sandro had probably warned him of us. That reminded me of something I'd wanted to ask Aria ever since I'd run off. I waited until she'd finished her call with her hairdresser and fixed us a salad before I bridged the topic.

"Did you get into a lot of trouble with Luca for helping me?" I asked quietly. I didn't want Romero to overhear us. He seemed busy enough talking on his phone, probably to Matteo or Luca who were checking up on us.

Aria's face tightened. "He was angry at first, but he's forgiven me. I think he realized that I would never leave him."

She and Luca seemed happy enough but sometimes outward appearances were deceiving, and I wasn't entirely sure if Aria was telling the truth. She wouldn't say something that might make me feel guilty.

"You sure?"

"Isn't that my line?" she asked teasingly.

I grinned. "You taught me a thing or two."

"Good to know."

"There's something else I've been wondering about," I said quietly. "How did Matteo find me?"

"Luca didn't really talk to me about the search. He knew I'd warn you. Do you think it could have been the blog? I think Luca checked my laptop. I tried to warn you."

"I tried not to mention locations in my blog posts. But maybe they could track my location through my blog. Who knows?"

The bell rang. Romero walked toward the elevator before either Aria or I could move. "Will he ever leave us alone?" I asked when he was out of earshot.

"Not anytime soon," Aria said with a shrug. She rose from her chair to greet the woman in her mid-forties who entered the penthouse with two huge bags. Aria introduced me to her hairdresser and five minutes later we'd set up a chair in the bathroom and my hair was being smothered in cream that was supposed to turn my hair to its original color, not immediately but after several treatments.

Luckily I was allowed to walk around while the color reacted with my hair. Aria lent me her laptop and I settled at the dining room table. With dread, I searched the German websites for any homicide news in Munich. It didn't take me long to see the article mentioning Sid's death. The police didn't have any leads. My former roommates had to move for the time being, and I doubted they'd return to an apartment where Sid had found his end. The newspaper mentioned me, or rather my pseudonym Gwen, and that the police were looking for her because she was a witness. There wasn't a photo of me, thank God. I'd always been careful that I didn't appear in any pictures. But there was a photo of Sid with his guitar.

My stomach tightened with sadness and regret. Aria put a hand on my shoulder. "You shouldn't read that. There's nothing you can do, Gianna."

I shut the laptop slowly. There was one thing I could have done. I could have told the police who was responsible for Sid's death, so his family could find peace, but that was something I would never do. There were certain rules even I wasn't going to break. I wasn't stupid, or suicidal.

Aria's worried gaze didn't leave me as I returned to the bathroom to wash my hair. "I'm fine," I whispered, but she didn't seem to buy it, neither did I. The last twenty-four hours had been a whirlwind of emotions and change. I'd hardly had any time to reflect on everything that had happened, and I wasn't sure I wanted to. Maybe Aria was right and I should try to move on and leave the past behind. The problem was I wasn't sure I could. Didn't I owe it to my conscience and Sid that I showed some defiance, that I didn't just settle in my new life with Matteo as if nothing had happened?

chapter *fifteen*

Matteo

When Luca and I returned to his penthouse that night, I felt like a fucking train had run me over. I hadn't gotten more than four hours of sleep in the last three days. The moment I spotted Gianna any thought of tiredness vanished into thin air. Her hair wasn't brown anymore. It wasn't the red she'd had before she'd run away but it was close and she looked fucking amazing even with her swollen lip.

I sensed something was off though. After dinner with Aria and Luca, we returned to our own apartment. Gianna hurried into the bedroom as if she couldn't wait to get away from me; unfortunately for her that was the room I wanted her in anyway. I followed and closed the door with a bang. Gianna sent me an annoyed look but didn't say anything. Instead she turned her back to me and rummaged in the drawers. I walked up to her, slipped my arms around her waist and pulled her against me. "You are thinking too much. Why don't you let me distract you?" I sucked the skin over her pulse point into my mouth. At first she tensed but then she relaxed against me.

"How do I know you're not going to play with me again?" Her voice had a strange quality to it but I wasn't in the mood to talk emotions.

I kissed my way down to her collarbone and slipped my hand lower, cupping her pussy through her clothes. She arched into me. I smirked against her skin. She smelled of flowers and her very own delicious scent. "Don't worry. I want to taste you all night long. I want to make you come over and over again."

She trembled against me, then her hand clamped down on mine, pressing me harder against her. She made a greedy sound in the back of her throat. I licked her shoulder as my fingers slipped under her skirt and panties, brushing her wet folds. I stifled a groan at the feel of her arousal. It took all my self-control not to dip my tongue into her pussy right away. I parted her velvety lips, brushing my fingertips over her slick skin before slipping a finger into her. She leaned her head back against my shoulder at the same time as she reached back and grasped my cock through my pants. I growled, then thrust against her palm.

I slid another finger into her. Fuck, she was so tight. Her inner walls clamped around my fingers like a vise. I couldn't wait to replace them with my cock. I was too fucking horny to take things slow or be gentle. I fucked her with my fingers, relishing in the feel of her juices on my skin, and the sounds coming from her mouth. She moved her hips in rhythm with my thrusting and her grip on my cock tightened almost painfully. It felt fucking fantastic. I rubbed my thumb over her slick nub of pleasure.

"God, yes," she gasped, her body stiffening against me. I kept thrusting as her orgasm rippled through her. When she relaxed, I lifted her into my arms and carried her over to the bed. I didn't give her time to recover. I pulled down her skirt and panties, and climbed between her legs, shoving them apart. My eyes took in her glorious pussy, glistening and perfectly pink. Unlike some girls Gianna wasn't shy about her body. She didn't try to shield her breasts or pussy from me. She let me admire her, returned my gaze without hesitation. She was fucking perfect.

Never taking my eyes off her, I lowered my head. She tensed when my lips almost touched her folds but I stopped to draw in a deep breath of her intoxicating scent. Gianna bucked her hips, a silent demand that made me grin. I didn't need convincing. I took a long lick all the way from her tight hole up to her perfect pink clit. My dick twitched in response to her heady taste. Fuck. I dove in, licking and nibbling. She rewarded me with breathless moans. Her fingers dug into the blankets when I sucked her inner lips into my mouth, gently teasing them until she squirmed on the bed. I took my time, bringing her close only to pull back over and over again. Gianna's moans turned into cries. Watching her body arch up in ecstasy was the best sight in the world. My hard-on was almost painful. When Gianna came down from her high, I released her and quickly scrambled off the bed.

I needed to fuck her now or I'd lose my mind. I got out of my pants and briefs but didn't bother with my shirt. Gianna surprised me by kneeling on the bed and wrapping her fingers around my cock. Her blue eyes were almost challenging when she brought her mouth down and closed her lips around my length. I groaned and my fingers brushed her hair from her face to have a better view of her mouth taking in my cock. I almost shot my cum right then, but a few mental tricks brought me back in line. Slowly at first, then faster, Gianna sucked me, her pink lips stretching around my width. I wanted to come in her mouth with her looking up at me like that, but even more than that I wanted to feel her tight pussy again. She circled my tip with her tongue before she took me almost all the way in until I hit the back of her throat.

Then she pulled back abruptly and wiped her mouth. She raised her eyebrows. "How do you like it when I stop like that?"

I chuckled. Was she trying to make me pay for this morning? She'd chosen a bad time. I climbed on top of her with a wicked grin and pressed my erection against her hot opening. Her eyes grew wide, but I didn't give her time for a reaction. I hooked my hand under her leg and parted her further before I started to slide into her. She was still tight and her face flashed with discomfort at my intrusion. I slowed further, easing into her and giving her time to grow accustomed to my cock. Yesterday I hadn't been careful because I hadn't known the truth but today I wanted to make her come with me in her. I watched her face closely until I'd sheathed myself completely in her tight channel. I paused for a moment. She gripped my shoulders, the challenge returning to her gaze. "Are you going to stay like that, or are you ever going to start moving?"

"Oh, I'll move." I punctuated my words with a short experimental thrust to see how she'd react. There was no sign of discomfort this time and I was fucking glad. I needed to fuck her now, and I didn't want to hold back. Keeping my eyes on her face, I established a hard fast rhythm, not as hard as I'd have liked but Gianna was probably still sore even if she wouldn't admit it. She was tight, clenching around my cock in a mind-blowing way. Every moan I drew from her lips felt like a fucking victory because it was obvious she was trying to keep them in. I changed the angle and drove even deeper into her. Another moan slipped out.

I reached between us, pressing my fingers to her clit. I needed her to come. My own orgasm was already close and there was no fucking way I'd come before her.

I thrust hard and deep, and Gianna's eyes grew wide, her face twisting with pleasure. She grasped my back, fingernails scratching my skin and I lost it. I fucked her even harder, losing every shred of control. Lust clouded my vision as I spilled into her. I growled against her slick throat, drawing in her scent as I spent myself in her pussy. Gianna breathed heavily when my body stilled. I raised my head and smiled down at her flushed face, even when she scowled. It was almost adorable that she was still trying to keep up the show.

Slowly I pulled out of her. She winced, then quickly masked it.

"Sore?" I asked as I stretched out beside her. I touched her stomach. She didn't push me away, only shrugged in response.

I moved closer and kissed a spot right below her ear. "Has sex turned you mute?"

"You wish," she muttered, her voice slower and more relaxed than usual.

"No, that would be boring. The things coming out of your mouth are more entertaining than you think."

She gave me a look. "I'm glad I amuse you."

"Me too."

Like last night I waited for her to fall asleep before I relaxed. I wasn't sure if that would ever change.

The next few days followed the same routine until one night when Gianna's breathing didn't slow like it usually did. I was fucking tired and quickly losing my fight against sleepiness.

"You always wait for me to fall asleep first," she said into the dark, startling me awake.

Of course she'd noticed. "Sometimes I forget how observant you are."

She turned around, facing me in the dark. I could make out the white of her eyes and the contours of her head but not much more. "Why?"

"I'm a wary bastard."

"Do you think I'd kill you in your sleep?"

It was hard to gauge her emotions without seeing her expression and I fucking hated it. "Have you been thinking about it?" It was meant to sound like a joke but came out way too serious.

"No, I can't stand the sight of blood."

"That's the only reason I don't have one of my own knives stuck in my back?"

"No. Killing you wouldn't get me out of this apartment. I don't know the code for the elevator."

"That's a relief," I muttered. I wasn't sure if she was teasing or not. "You don't seem that unhappy in our marriage."

"We've been married for only a few days, and you're never around, that's a plus. And maybe I'm a good actress."

"I guess it's good that I don't trust you then."

"Yes," she said seriously.

"I suppose you want to scare me?" I asked in a low murmur, leaning so close to her that I could feel her breath on my cheek.

"I don't think there's anything or anyone that could scare you," she whispered back.

"Everyone's scared of something. Why would I be different?"

"Because you are the scariest person I know."

I paused. She didn't sound like she was kidding. "Are you scared of me?"

Silence was my answer.

I reached for her arm. "Gianna?"

"Yes," came her sleepy reply.

"Why?"

But her breathing had calmed. She had fallen asleep. What was I supposed to do with her admittance? I'd never given her reason to fear me. Okay, she'd seen me do some scary shit, but I'd never done anything to her. It took me a long time after that to fall asleep.

The next day Gianna didn't mention our conversation from the previous night. I had a feeling she hated that she'd been honest. I'd never shied back from a topic but I didn't ask her again why she was scared of me. I wasn't sure I wanted to know.

Gianna kept touching her lip during breakfast. It wasn't swollen anymore.

"Let me take a look," I said, pushing her hand away. "I think we can pull the stitches."

She grimaced. "Now?"

"Scared?" I asked because I couldn't help myself.

"No, of course not," she said. I wondered if she referred to more than the stitches. I got up and led her into the bathroom where I kept my medical kit. Gianna didn't protest when I lifted her onto the washtable and stepped between her legs this time.

I took small scissors from the kit. "Open your mouth."

She did, but gave me a warning look as if she thought I had something naughty in mind. I grinned and kissed her ear. "Do you know how kids always get a treat as reward after they see the doctor?"

She rolled her eyes but didn't push my hand away when I pressed it against her center through her jeans.

"Be a good girl and you shall be rewarded."

I drew back, enjoying the scowl on Gianna's face. She didn't get the chance for a retort because I started working on her stitches. It didn't take long and Gianna winced only twice. "Done," I said, setting down the scissors and tweezers. "Do you want your reward now?" I rubbed her pussy.

She glared.

"You just have to say the words." She pressed her lips together. "No?" I said, taking a step back, and stopped touching her.

"As if I need you for that," she said snidely, and then she opened her jeans and shoved her hand inside.

I exhaled as I watched her fingers move under the fabric. "Fuck." I stepped up to her and ripped her jeans and panties down her legs.

Gianna didn't stop caressing herself. Her slender fingers rubbed her clit nimbly while she watched me through narrowed eyes. It was the hottest thing I'd ever seen.

"Open your legs a bit wider," I ordered. To my surprise, Gianna obeyed. Her eyes were clouded with lust as she teased herself. Damn, I could see how wet she was.

I leaned back against the wall, tugged down my zipper and pulled out my cock. Gianna stroked herself even faster when I wrapped my hand around my hard-on and started jerking off.

"This is messed up," she whispered. She didn't take her eyes off my cock and I couldn't take my eyes off her fingers that worked her pink nub.

"Who cares?" I growled. "Put a finger in your pussy."

She slipped one finger into her tight opening.

"Another one," I demanded.

She barely hesitated. But I couldn't fucking take any more. I staggered forward, shoved her hand away and buried myself deep in her. She shuddered around me as her orgasm rippled through her. After a few thrusts, I came too.

"This is so messed up," she said again, her voice heavy with sex.

I didn't pull out of her yet. Instead I rested my forehead against her shoulder and caught my breath. "Messed up is good."

"I knew you'd say that."

"This thing is fucking annoying," she said after another round of sex that evening, wiggling her leg with the ankle monitor in the air. It had bothered me too the few times I'd come into contact with it during sex, but I wouldn't risk taking it off. Not only would Luca blow a gasket, I'd also have to supervise Gianna myself 24/7 without the monitor.

"You'll get used to it." I tried to pull her against me but she slipped away, moving to the edge of our bed.

"No cuddling as long as I have to wear this thing," she said.

I laughed. "As long as you don't ban sex."

"Maybe I will do that."

I moved my hand down from her stomach and ran a finger over her clit. "Why would you want to punish yourself like that?"

"You are an arrogant bastard. Maybe you think your cock is magic, but let me tell you something: it isn't." She didn't shove my hand away from where it was stroking her. Maybe she didn't notice but she'd even parted her legs a bit more to give me better access. I lightly traced her soft folds. I loved her silkiness and the way her body responded to me. I didn't increase the pressure, only lightly brushed my fingertips over her pussy. She was probably still oversensitive so I needed to be careful if I wanted to guide her toward another peak. Her lips parted and her breathing quickened ever so slightly. I leaned over her and sucked her nipple into my mouth. Pushing her over the edge this time was ever better because I wasn't busy with my own lust. I could completely focus on Gianna, her labored breathing, hooded eyes, hardening nipples as she succumbed to her orgasm.

I didn't even care when Gianna turned her back to me afterward, trying to punish me by not reciprocating. I'd gotten what I'd wanted.

"You realize that sex is all there is between us, right?" she said angrily.

"Sex is important."

"Sure, but it's not all there is."

"It's not all there is," I said, annoyed.

"Yes, it is, and there won't ever be more. Don't think I like you just because I like to fuck you."

"Thanks for the heads-up," I growled.

Gianna

I was still annoyed at myself during breakfast, especially because Matteo's expression was far too smug despite my harsh words. Maybe he thought I'd been joking, or maybe he didn't care.

My body had a mind of its own, always eager for his touch. It didn't help that Matteo looked like a male model with his tight white shirt and messy black hair. He was sex on legs, and knew it.

"We are invited to dinner at one of the leading families this week, so Aria and you should probably go dress shopping."

I dropped my spoon with the yogurt. "You want me to attend a social event with you?" I couldn't believe he'd drag me into public so quickly. We'd been married for two weeks and the gossip mills were probably still going strong. "Everybody will be talking behind my back."

Matteo shrugged. "I don't give a damn what they think and they know better than to say anything in front of you or me."

"I know those women, they won't miss an opportunity to talk trash about someone, especially me."

"Ignore them. It's not like their opinion matters. They will always talk shit about you. That's all they can do."

I didn't care what they said, but I'd never enjoyed myself at social functions and I doubted that would change any time soon. "I know, but I hate these gatherings. Everything about it is false. People who wouldn't hesitate to thrust a knife into your back smile into your face if they hope to gain something from it."

For a long time I'd thought I was anti-social and just didn't like to be around larger groups of people but during my time on the run, I'd attended several parties and I'd never felt out of place. Even though I'd been pretending to be someone else then, I'd still felt truer to myself than I ever did around the people in our world.

"You'll get used to them."

"I don't want to. That's why I ran away."

Matteo searched my face with a curious expression, then his lips twitched. "So you didn't only run from me?"

"Don't get your hopes up. You were definitely one of the main reasons," I said.

"But not the only reason."

I rolled my eyes and took another sip from my coffee. "Do I really have to attend the dinner?"

Matteo rose from his chair and startled me with a quick kiss on my mouth. "Yep. I won't suffer through it alone now that I have a wife who can share my anguish. Just do what I do when I have to talk to idiots, imagine how it would feel to slice their heads off."

Despite how often I'd pushed him away, Matteo seemed intent on making it work between us. Why did he have to be so stubborn? Couldn't he finally grow tired of me and give me the chance to get away? "That's easy for you to say, but not all of us make a habit out of killing people."

Images of Sid wanted to anchor themselves in my brain again, but I couldn't bear them right now and forced them away.

"Then imagine how it would be to watch me kill the people that annoy you. As your husband it's my duty to kill your enemies after all." Matteo smiled his cocky grin, his eyes lit up with humor. My stomach fluttered in a scary way and I quickly tore my gaze away from him and emptied my cup.

"I'll go up to Aria and talk to her about going shopping. I need to be a good wife after all," I said mockingly but somehow it felt wrong. My emotions were confusing me, everything about my new situation did.

"You should probably buy some new clothes for you," Matteo said as he put his gun holster on.

"Is that an order?"

"I didn't know it was necessary to order a woman to buy clothes. Isn't that your favorite hobby?"

"Really?" I almost laughed. "Not all women are the same."

"Oh, I know." There was that smile again.

My eyes lingered on his gun, trying to remind myself that this was who he really was. The smile that made my stomach do flips was only a mask.

I stood abruptly. "You and Luca will be gone all day again?"

"Why? Do you and Aria have another escape planned?"

"Haha," I muttered, then raised the leg of my jeans, revealing the black ankle bracelet. "I can't, remember?"

"It doesn't stop you from making plans. Don't tell me you're not still thinking about escaping?"

I considered lying but instead opted for the truth. "Of course I am thinking about it. Did you think good sex and a ring around my finger would suddenly make me change my mind?"

"Only good, hm?"

I snorted and headed toward the elevator. Matteo joined me inside, his eyes resting on my hand.

"You are wearing your ring. I thought you'd throw it away the first chance you got."

I peered down at the gold band with the fine line of diamonds. "Did you carry it the entire time you were hunting me?"

Matteo smirked as if he knew I was avoiding his question, and I was. I hadn't even considered throwing the ring away. It seemed like such a waste. At least I hoped that was the only reason.

"Of course," he said. "I always knew I'd catch you eventually and I knew I would have to make you my wife before you ran off again."

His confidence was exasperating. It was also incredibly sexy. I was glad when the elevator doors slid open and I could walk away from Matteo's smile and my own unwanted thoughts. Luca passed me with barely a nod and joined his brother in the elevator.

Aria's welcome was much warmer. She was beaming all over her face as she headed my way and hugged me. "I still can't believe that you're living so close to me. I really missed having you as my confidante."

"I suppose there aren't many trustworthy women around here," I said, my blood boiling when I remembered how Luca's cousin Cosima had tricked Aria into walking in on Grace and Luca.

"Now that you are here, I don't care." Aria peered down at her elegant gold watch. "How about we head out for coffee now and then go shopping. Luca said we were all invited to the Bardonis' Christmas party."

I sighed. "Yeah. Matteo told me I had to attend."

"At least we can suffer together. Believe me, Luca isn't too excited about that invitation either. Bardoni wants his son to become Luca's Consigliere because in the past the Consigliere has always been one of the Bardonis, but Luca wants Matteo and nobody else."

"So this party is going to be even more awkward than I thought. Everyone is going to scheme against Matteo and me. Oh, joy."

Aria smiled apologetically. "It won't be too bad. Now let's go shopping. I need some fresh air."

Of course Romero accompanied us as we headed out to buy dresses. Maybe I would have enjoyed myself more if I didn't have to be careful not to flash my stupid ankle monitor whenever I tried a dress on. From the look on the face of one of the vendors, I was fairly sure I didn't manage to cover the bracelet with the hem at all times. I realized I'd barely thought about escape in the last few weeks. Too many things had happened. And then there was Romero's constant surveillance whenever I went somewhere with Aria. Moreover, the ankle monitor was making it entirely impossible. I'd have to figure out a way to convince Matteo to take that thing off. Once that was taken care of, my desire to run away would probably return with full force.

chapter *sixteen*

Gianna

I'D KNOWN ALL ALONG THAT THE CHRISTMAS PARTY AT THE Bardonis' house was going to be a huge flop, but it was even worse than I'd thought. The only good thing about this ordeal was that Matteo had Sandro take off the ankle monitor so I could wear my cocktail dress without flashing that thing at everyone. That would have been the talk of the evening, no doubt.

The Bardonis lived in a townhouse, which had been decorated to an inch of its capacities. They'd even set up a massive angel, which had been carved from ice, in their front yard. The decoration was white and gold, expensive crystal baubles adorned the massive tree. It screamed money, and felt so impersonal that I was sure an interior designer had arranged it. Mrs. Bardoni didn't appear as if she'd ever moved a finger for anything. She was also at least twenty years younger than her husband.

She and her husband greeted Aria and Luca first, and while their smiles hadn't been exactly warm or honest, they turned positively fake and condescending when it was time to greet me.

I shook Mrs. Bardoni's hand with a polite smile, or at least I hoped it looked polite. Her expression was as if an untalented sculptor had tried to carve a smile into a statue. The smile of the ice angel outside had been warmer than hers. When Mr. Bardoni turned to me, I had to suppress a shudder. He reached for my hand but while he'd barely brushed Aria's skin, his lips pressed firmly to my hand and then his tongue darted out and licked my skin. The accompanying leer he sent my way almost made me punch him. I quickly retracted my hand, only barely managing not to wipe it on my dress, and only because the silk was too beautiful to come in contact with that asshole's slobber.

Matteo was in conversation with Mrs. Bardoni who was introducing him to a young woman my age. It was obvious that the old hag was trying to set Matteo up with her daughter. Anger bubbled up in me but I knew better than to show my emotions. When I finally turned my eyes away from the scene, I found Aria watching me with a worried expression. I gave a small shake of my head. Matteo tore himself away from Mrs. Bardoni and her daughter, and wrapped his arm around my waist. He scanned my face as he led me into the living room where the remaining guests had gathered. "You look pissed."

I shrugged. If I told him what Mr. Bardoni had done, things would become ugly. "Looks like you have a fan," I said instead, nodding in the direction of the Bardoni daughter whose eyes followed Matteo.

"Jealous?" he asked, smirking.

"You wish." But was I?

We didn't get the chance to talk more, because other guests approached us, and while most of them were acting polite, I could see in their eyes that they despised me. I had a feeling that they would show me what they really thought of me the moment Matteo wasn't around. They soon got their chance. While Matteo and Luca joined the other men, Aria and I strolled toward the buffet. Of course we weren't alone for long. Soon the bitch Cosima, Matteo's stepmother, Nina, as well as Mrs. Bardoni, and a few other women joined us. Aria's presence still offered me some protection from direct insults, but none of the women bothered talking to me. It was as if I wasn't even there. Even Aria's attempts to include me in the conversation failed. I didn't care. I hated these women, hated their fake smiles and nasty personalities. But the worst was watching Aria being polite to Cosima despite what that bitch had done.

Eventually I excused myself and headed toward the terrace door, which allowed a view into the small snow-covered garden. My reprieve was very short-lived however.

"Beautiful, isn't it?" a high female voice said.

Nina Vitiello stood beside me, her mouth stretched wide in the imitation of a smile. She no longer wore black. Her husband's funeral had been more than a year ago. She linked our arms to my utter disdain and led me outside despite the cold. I knew this wasn't going to be pleasant. Even though she was Luca and Matteo's stepmother, she'd never come to visit. I had a feeling she was scared of her stepsons.

The moment we were away from privy ears, she turned her back to the windows and faced me with a face devoid of any pleasantness. She reminded me of an ugly toad. "You might be parading around like you are one of us, like you belong in our circles, but if it weren't for Matteo, nobody would invite you."

I raised my eyebrows. Did she really think I gave a damn? I'd never wanted to be part of this world, that was why I had run away. It took immeasurable control on my part not to say what I wanted. Instead I tried to return to the party but Nina Vitiello held my arm, obviously not done. "A decent girl would have died from shame after being caught with another man. The only reason you're still alive is Matteo's good-heartedness. That boy is too dutiful. Although nobody would have blamed him if he'd discarded you like a dirty rag after what you did. If my husband were still alive, he'd have fed you to our dogs."

Dutiful and good-hearted? That didn't sound like Matteo.

Deep breaths, Gianna. Don't cause a scene.

Again I tried to leave, but her fingers dug into my skin. "Aren't you ashamed of yourself? You've dishonored your family, and now you are bringing shame to the name Vitiello. Your mere presence is an insult to every honorable woman in this house. Your existence is sin."

I couldn't help but laugh. "Sin? You want to talk to me about sin?" I pointed toward the windows, behind which New York's worst criminals were gathered. "That room breathes sin."

Nina Vitiello lifted her chin. "Do us all a favor and kill yourself."

I wrenched my arm away, shocked. "I won't ever do any of you a favor." I turned and headed back inside. Matteo spotted me from across the room where he was talking with a younger version of Mr. Bardoni, Luca, and a couple of other men. I quickly looked away, hoping he wouldn't approach me. I wasn't in the mood to talk to him now. Aria was still where I'd left her, completely entrenched in conversation.

I crossed the room as quickly as possible, pretending I didn't hear the whispered "whore" a couple of people called me. Despite my best attempts not to let those insults get to me, I felt relief when I finally left the living room and found myself alone in the front hall. I needed to find the bathroom to freshen up and clear my head before I entered that room again. I was seriously worried that I'd attack someone if I didn't get a grip on myself. Taking a deep breath, I went in search for the restroom. I hoped I'd come across someone leaving the bathroom so I didn't have to open every single door. I definitely wouldn't ask Mrs. Bardoni to point it out to me. Unfortunately the only thing I found was Mr. Bardoni who must have been following me. The leer the bald idiot sent my way made me want to puke.

Matteo

If Bardoni thought I hadn't noticed the way he'd eye-fucked Gianna when we'd arrived, he was even more stupid than I thought. If it weren't for Luca, I would have plunged my knife into the fucker's face right away. But Luca was a new Capo and couldn't use any more trouble, so I had promised him to stay on my best behavior. As the party progressed I slowly came to the realization that I might have to break my promise.

Gianna was trying to put on a brave face but I could see how upset she was after a talk to my bitch of a stepmother. I didn't want to know what the old goat had said to Gianna. She would never dare say something to my face. She was scared of Luca and me, had been for as long as I could remember.

Unfortunately, it took me a few more minutes before I could finally follow Gianna after she'd fled the living room. Luca's warning glance almost made me want to laugh. I had no intention of doing something stupid, except for having a quickie with my wife to lift her spirits. What was wrong with that?

When I stepped out into the lobby, I didn't see Gianna anywhere. I paused, listening closely, but the sounds of the party behind me were drowning out everything else. What if she'd run? I should have told Romero or Sandro to keep an eye on her at all times, but I hadn't wanted to embarrass her further. People had enough to gossip about as it was.

I headed in the direction of where I remembered the bathroom to be, hoping I'd find her there. A deep voice made me quicken my steps and when I came around the next corner I found Gianna alone with old Bardoni. One look at her face and I knew she was on the verge of a freak-out. She didn't see me as I approached, her narrowed eyes directed at Bardoni.

"Why don't you show me what you learned in Europe. I bet you're very talented with your lips. That's why Matteo was so eager to marry you, hm?" Bardoni said and reached for Gianna's arm. Before she or I could react, he pulled her against him and fucking kissed her while groping her breast. My blood boiling, I stormed toward them, pulled my knife, shoved Bardoni away from Gianna and slammed my blade into the soft spot below his chin, piercing his fucking brain. Gianna gasped and stumbled back against the wall, her eyes darting from my knife to my face.

"Fuck," I muttered. I chanced a quick glance around, then dragged Bardoni's body toward his office, leaving my knife in his chin so blood didn't shoot out.

"You killed him," Gianna whispered harshly.

"He shouldn't have touched you." I nodded toward the door. "Open that for me." After a moment of hesitation, she stumbled forward and pushed the door open for me. I dragged Bardoni inside and Gianna quickly followed me inside before closing the door.

I put Bardoni down in his desk chair, then took a step back. This was bad. Luca would kick my ass when he found out.

"What are we going to do?" Gianna asked in a toneless voice from her spot near the door.

"We are going to make it look like I didn't kill him."

"Your knife is in his head."

I grinned but sobered when I saw Gianna's expression. It reminded me of the look she'd had after Sid had been shot. Sometimes I forgot that not everyone was as used to blood and death as me.

Slowly she came closer, gaze frozen on the body. "Why did you kill him?"

"Because he was an asshole."

Gianna stopped beside me and dead Bardoni. She looked like she couldn't quite believe what she saw. She raised her arm as if she was going to touch the corpse to convince herself of its existence.

"Don't touch anything," I ordered a bit too harshly, gripping her wrist to stop her.

She stared up at me with huge eyes. After another moment, she nodded almost robotically. She looked like she was going into shock. That was the last thing we needed.

Ideally I would have gone in search of Luca but I couldn't leave Gianna alone with the body. If someone came in, she'd have more trouble dealing with that person than I did.

I touched her cheek to bring her attention back to my face. "Go and get Luca," I told her.

She hesitated.

"Go."

"Okay." She whirled around, crossed the room in a rush and slipped out. She closed the door silently. I really hoped she wouldn't give everything away because she was so freaked out.

I lowered my eyes to Bardoni. I really loved the sight of my knife in his skull.

"Matteo?" I heard Luca's quiet voice a couple of minutes later. I jogged toward the door and opened it a crack. When I saw Luca standing in the corridor, I ushered him in.

"What do you want? Gianna didn't say anything," he said, but shut up when his gaze settled on Bardoni behind the desk. "Oh fuck."

"Bardoni had an accident," I said with a shrug.

Luca gave me a look. "Fuck, Matteo, what did you do?"

"If you ask me, I think good old Mr. Bardoni killed himself," I said.

Luca circled the body, then he glared at me. "It's because of Gianna, isn't it? Bardoni did or said something that annoyed you and you lost your shit. I knew the girl would bring nothing but trouble."

"The asshole has been on your death list for a while. He's been stirring up shit. You are glad he's gone, admit it. We've discussed having him killed countless times. I decided to finally act."

"Of course I wanted him dead, but not in his own fucking home at his Christmas party. Damn it, Matteo. Can't you think first and shoot second for once?"

Luca was right. I should have chosen a better time to kill Bardoni, but he shouldn't have talked shit to Gianna, and he most certainly shouldn't have touched her. He'd dug his own fucking grave.

"I'll call Romero. He's keeping an eye on Aria and Gianna but we'll need him here to deal with this fucking mess." Luca ran a hand through his hair, sent me another glower, then picked up his phone and called Romero.

A couple of minutes later, someone knocked. Luca held up his hand to stop me from opening it. Instead he went and let Romero in. Romero's eyes scanned the scene before him before focusing on me. "You killed him?"

I raised my arms. "Why did it have to be me?" It was a rhetorical question. It was almost always me doing the killing at improper times.

"Because you're the crazy one," Luca muttered, then said to Romero, "Can you make this look as if Bardoni killed himself?"

We all looked toward the dead asshole, hanging limply in his chair, lifeless eyes still expressing surprise at his early demise.

Romero grimaced. "Few people stab themselves in the brain."

"There's always a first time for everything." I chuckled but fell silent at a look from Luca. "Oh, come on," I said. "It was funny."

Luca's lips twitched but he was too stubborn to admit I was right. I knew he was more than a little glad that I'd gotten rid of Bardoni for him. "Search the room for a gun that could have blown his fucking head off. I don't need the Bandonis on my back right now. I want this matter dealt with quietly."

"No matter how we make it look, the Bardonis will suspect something. They won't believe it was suicide. Bardoni was far too narcissistic to end his own life," I said.

"Maybe I should put a fucking ankle monitor on you, too," Luca growled. "You are a ticking time bomb."

Romero stopped searching the drawers of the desk. "Even if the

Bardonis suspect something, they won't say it aloud. If they don't have proof, they won't seek retribution."

"I wouldn't count on it," I said. "But we'll make sure they won't get a chance for revenge."

"Maybe you should pull your knife out of Bardoni's head. Nobody will believe it was suicide with your blade stuck in his chin," Luca said.

I walked toward the body and slowly pulled my knife out, then quickly took a step back before blood could get on my clothes. I checked my white shirt for any specks. My black trousers and jacket would hide blood better, but luckily I was clean. The same couldn't be said for Bardoni's clothes. Blood was quickly soaking his shirt and trousers.

Romero pulled a high-caliber Smith & Wesson from a drawer in the cupboard behind the desk. "This could do."

"Good," Luca said with a nod. "Matteo and I will return to the party. Wait about five minutes before you blow his head off, then get the fuck out of here. Matteo and I will hopefully be here first and in the commotion nobody will notice you are gone."

Romero was already busy figuring out the best angle to shoot Bardoni and barely reacted when Luca and I slipped out of the room quietly and closed the door. The corridor was deserted except for Gianna who was lingering at the end, looking anxious.

"Make sure she doesn't let something slip," Luca ordered. "And we'll have a talk about this fucking matter later."

"Don't worry. Gianna can lie if she has to."

"Oh, I don't doubt she can lie very well if she wants to. But she's not exactly the most trustworthy person."

"She's my wife," I reminded my brother with a bit too much force.

"That's the problem." He walked off back to the party before I could reply, and I headed toward Gianna.

Gianna

I couldn't believe Matteo had rammed his knife into that man's chin. It had been a horrible sight, seeing Bardoni with dead, shock-widened eyes. He had been an asshole, and I certainly wasn't sad to see him gone, but seeing my own husband kill him without a second thought had been horrible. Matteo had acted so quickly, no hesitation, no preparation. Every move had spoken of experience. I'd known he was good with the knife of course. Even in Chicago people had talked about his skills but it hadn't prepared me for watching him actually use a knife on someone like that.

After I'd told Luca to find Matteo, I waited in the corridor. Aria had gone back into the living room; it would have looked suspicious if all of us had suddenly disappeared. And people were very eager to talk to Aria so her missing would definitely have drawn attention. Nobody would mind my absence however.

I'd barely waited for a minute, when Romero hurried past me toward the office. People always said I was unpredictable. I had nothing on Matteo.

I wrapped my arms around myself. My heart was still pounding in my chest, and I couldn't stop checking my surroundings nervously.

I was still trying to come to terms with my feelings for what happened when the door to the office opened and Luca and Matteo stepped out without Romero. Luca passed me without a glance. He probably blamed me for the mess his brother had caused. I didn't think Matteo needed much of an incentive to kill, but naturally I realized that I had been the reason for Bardoni's death.

Matteo had acted out of jealousy and possessiveness. Seeing another man touching me had made him snap. Matteo scanned my face as he approached me. I probably looked pretty upset. The problem was I didn't feel nearly as upset as I knew I should. I couldn't bring myself to be sad about Bardoni's death, no matter how much I tried.

Matteo's movements were so lithe, so self-assured. And somehow, despite everything, I felt myself drawn to him, even to that dangerous side he'd showed me today. Matteo wrapped an arm around my waist and led me toward the front hall. Instead of returning to the living room, he steered me into a small guest bathroom near the front door.

"What the hell are you doing?" it burst out of me. "I won't make out with you after you killed someone."

Matteo gripped the back of my neck and pulled our bodies flush against each other before pressing his mouth to mine, kissing me hard. I panted for air when he drew back. His lips brushed my ear. "You look so fucking sexy. I could fuck you in a room with a dead body and wouldn't care."

"I don't doubt it," I muttered, but I didn't try to pull back. His warmth and strong body steadied my trembling limbs. Maybe the events were affecting me more than I thought.

"But that's not why we are here," he murmured.

A loud shot carried through the house. I jumped. "What—"

"That's why," Matteo said calmly. "We're going to pretend we had a quickie. We don't want people to think we had something to do with Bardoni's unfortunate end, right?"

He ruffled my hair, then his own before unbuttoning his top two buttons. He raised his dark brows. "Ready?"

I nodded.

"Remember we don't know anything. We are shocked, and surprised."

Matteo ripped open the door, and headed out, pulling his gun. The lobby was filled with other guests, most men with their weapons drawn. Confused looks were exchanged. Luca and Bardoni's son ran toward where the gunshot had come from. Several people gave me and Matteo disgusted looks. They seemed to believe the lie Matteo wanted them to. It probably helped that they all thought I was a whore.

"Stay here," Matteo said. "I'll have to see what's going on." He looked so honestly worried and alert as if he really didn't know why a shot had sounded. Nobody would doubt him. If I didn't know better, even I would have believed in his innocence after that show.

He hurried toward the crime scene. I could only watch in stunned silence. Matteo was a master manipulator.

chapter *seventeen*

Gianna

IT WAS WAY PAST MIDNIGHT WHEN WE FINALLY GOT HOME. MOST OF the other guests had left long before us, but Luca and Matteo had to stay as heads of the Famiglia and pretend they were trying to figure out what had happened. Nobody had suspected them, at least not openly. To be honest, neither Bardoni Jr. nor Mrs. Bardoni had looked too distraught. Their tears had been crocodile tears if I'd ever seen any. Maybe he'd been as unpleasant to them as he'd been to me in the short time I'd spent with him.

I couldn't believe my life had changed from waitressing in Munich to covering up my husband's crimes. After a quick shower, I slipped into bed. Matteo was still arguing with Luca in our living room. This was one of the few instances where I understood Luca's anger completely.

I lay on my back, staring at the ceiling as I listened to their voices. The ankle monitor lay on my nightstand, mocking me. Maybe I should have used tonight's confusion to escape. Luca, Matteo, and Romero had been busy cleaning up their mess, and I had been without my stupid ankle bracelet. It had been the perfect opportunity. Then why hadn't I run? I doubted anyone would have stopped me.

Because of Aria? I wished that was the only reason, but as I'd stood in the lobby waiting for Matteo to return, I hadn't even considered escape. Why wasn't it at the forefront of my brain anymore? Six months ago it had been all I could think about, had been an obsession that had consumed me, and now it sometimes felt that I only thought about running because I felt that I was supposed to do it.

It was confusing. I wasn't as miserable as I'd worried I'd be living with Matteo. Of course, he was a crazy-ass killer, but it wasn't as if I wasn't used to that kind, and it actually made life exciting even if I hated admitting it. Living life as a normal person, doing normal things, earning money with normal jobs, had been an incredible experience, but for some reason it had never felt like more than a distraction.

The door opened and Matteo strode into the bedroom. He wasn't wearing his jacket anymore and half of his shirt buttons were already unbuttoned. He flashed me his usual grin before he disappeared in the bathroom.

I could have pretended to be asleep to avoid talking to him but for some inexplicable reason I wanted to talk to him. When he emerged from the bathroom in his boxer shorts, flashing his lean muscled torso, I almost cancelled my plans. But that would really have felt too wrong. A man had died, albeit a horrible man, and having sex so shortly after his death would have felt utterly wrong.

Matteo slid under the covers and reached for my waist, pulling me toward him. His eyes were hungry. There was no sign that he even still remembered what he'd done not too long ago. His lips claimed mine and I let his tongue in, let the kiss consume me until my body was humming with pleasure and I forced myself to push him away before I did something for which I'd despise myself tomorrow morning.

Matteo flung himself on his back with a groan. "This is because of Bardoni, right?"

I glared. "Maybe I'm just not in the mood. You aren't that irresistible."

"If you say so," he said in a low voice that sent a traitorous shiver down my spine. The bastard was way too manipulative.

I decided to steer this conversation toward safer grounds. "So will Luca punish you?"

Matteo chuckled. "Luca has never punished me for anything. He's used to my proactivity."

"Proactivity?"

Matteo winked and I almost reached for him again. Instead I pulled the blankets up to my chin as another barrier between us.

"Luca looked furious."

"He'll get over it. He always does. He would have had Bardoni killed anyway. It was only a matter of time."

I had a feeling this wasn't ordinary bedtime talk. "When did you kill your first man? Kindergarten?"

Matteo propped his head up on his arm, smirking. He ran a finger down my arm in a very distracting way. "No. I was a late bloomer in comparison to Luca."

"Really? That seems unlikely."

"Not really. Luca made sure I didn't get in trouble when I was younger. He was a protective big brother."

"I can't even imagine Luca being a kid, much less him making sure you stay out of trouble."

"He did. Is that really that surprising? Didn't Aria try to protect you when you were younger?"

"She still does," I said with a grimace.

"See. Luca's the same way. Of course now I'm making it harder for him to keep me in check, just like you make it hard for Aria."

"I think there's a huge difference between the kind of trouble I stir up and the trouble you cause."

"Give it some time. I have a feeling you haven't reached your full potential yet."

A laugh bubbled out of me. Damn it. Why did he have to say things that made me laugh? "You didn't answer my question. When did you kill the first time?"

"It was a few weeks after my thirteenth birthday."

"That's what you call a late bloomer? Most guys that age worry about their sprouting pubic hair and not killing someone."

"Oh, I'd come to terms with my pubic hair a long time before," he said in a teasing voice. "And most guys aren't the second son of the Capo of the New York Famiglia."

"Good point. But Luca can't really have protected you very well if you had to kill when you were still so young."

Matteo's gaze became distant. "He did what he could. Our father wanted me to kill one of the boys Luca and I had been hanging out with occasionally because he'd tried to get out of the mob."

My stomach tightened. "And?"

"Luca pulled his gun and killed the guy before I could. Father was majorly pissed. He beat Luca within an inch of his life."

The idea that Luca had done something so considerate for his brother was strange, but it wasn't all that surprising if you watched how those two interacted. It was obvious they cared for each other, cold-hearted bastards or not. "Luca is huge. How could anyone beat him?"

Matteo smiled wryly. "Luca could have wiped the floor with our father if he'd tried, but he never fought back. Father was Capo and would have put Luca down like a rabid dog if he'd raised his hand against him."

I sometimes forgot that things weren't all sunshine and rainbows for men. They had more freedom when it came to promiscuity and going out but they had their own burdens to bear. "I guess your father found someone else for you to kill pretty quickly after that." I'd barely known Salvatore Vitiello but he'd seemed like a creepy fuck.

Matteo nodded. "He found out about another traitor a couple of months after that. He made me slice his throat."

Girls weren't given many details about the induction ceremony, but Umberto had often let something slip when he'd guarded us. Usually the first kill of an initiate happened from afar with a gun. "He didn't let you shoot him?"

"No, it was probably meant as additional punishment because I'd wormed my way out of killing the first time. Shooting is easy, it's less personal. Using a knife is dirty work. You have to get close to your victim, have to get blood on your hands."

I held my breath. His voice had become very quiet. Slowly I raised myself up on my arm. I wanted to touch him but I didn't. "That sounds horrible. Could you do it?"

"What do you think?"

There was the scary shark-grin. The one that made me believe Matteo was capable of anything.

"You killed him."

"I did. It was messy. He was tied to a chair, so he couldn't fight back but it still took me three tries to cut his jugular. I was covered in blood from head to toe. I still found blood under my nails the next day."

"Then why do you prefer knives to guns? You really don't seem to mind getting your hands dirty anymore."

"In the beginning it was to prove to my father that I was tough and that he hadn't broken me like he'd probably intended. And once I got really good with the knife and everyone admired me for my skills, it seemed like a waste to give it up."

I searched his face but it was blank. I couldn't tell if it was the whole truth, or if he was keeping the worst of it to himself: that he'd come to enjoy the more personal kill. For a moment we stared at each other until it became too personal again and I lay back down and turned on my back.

"Did you ever consider killing Luca? If he were dead, you'd become Capo. You wouldn't be the first Made Man to kill a family member to climb the career ladder," I asked.

Matteo's expression hardened. "I would never kill my own brother. I don't care about becoming Capo, and even if I did, I still wouldn't get rid of Luca to improve my position. Luca's got my back and I've got his. That's the way it's always been."

"That's good. It's important to have people you can trust," I said honestly. Loneliness was a big problem in our world. You had always people around you, but you could trust no one. There was only one person I trusted absolutely and that was Aria. Lily was too fragile and young for many of my secrets, and Fabi was a boy and Father's influence on him was growing by the day. And I couldn't even talk to them anymore.

"What will it take for you to trust me?" Matteo asked curiously.

"A miracle." I turned my back to him and shut off the lamp on my nightstand. The look in his eyes had stirred something in my chest that terrified me.

Matteo shut off the other lights, then leaned over to me, kissing my ear. "Who doesn't like a good miracle?"

Matteo's arm was heavy around my waist, his breath hot against my neck, and the leg that was thrown over mine was cutting my blood flow off; then why did it feel strangely good to wake next to him?

I pushed his arm off and slipped away, and quickly got up. Matteo didn't wake. His hair was a complete mess and his face looked honest and almost gentle in sleep. I reached out but stopped myself before I could actually brush my fingers over his forehead. What was wrong with me?

I took a step back. My eyes landed on the discarded ankle monitor on the nightstand and an idea crossed my mind. I snatched up the monitor and rushed into the bathroom with it. The thing couldn't be destroyed with water. After all, you could shower with it, but maybe I could flush it down the toilet. Not that Matteo couldn't ask Sandro to bring a new monitor, but the gesture would send a nice message. I plunged the monitor into the toilet and flushed. Unfortunately it got stuck.

"Did you just flush down your ankle monitor?" Matteo asked in a voice raspy with sleep.

I whirled around. He was leaning in the doorway, arms crossed over his naked chest and an amused expression on his arrogant face. Heat rushed into my cheeks. "I tried, but it got stuck."

Chuckling, Matteo advanced on me and we both stared down into the bowl. "And who's going to get it out of there now?"

"You?"

Matteo reached down but I grabbed his arm.

"Aren't you going to put on gloves or something like that?"

"It's clean and I can wash my hands afterward," he said with barely disguised amusement. "My hands have been covered with worse, believe me."

I released him with a shrug. "Do what you want."

He retrieved the ankle monitor and put it on the washstand, then shoved down his boxer shorts and strode toward the shower, presenting his firm butt to me. He turned on the water and stepped under the stream before facing me again with a raging hard-on. "Wanna join me?"

I grabbed my toothbrush. "No, thanks."

It took a lot of restraint not to watch Matteo while he showered. I had a feeling he was taking his time on purpose. The water shut off and Matteo stepped out, drying himself with his towel. He nodded toward the ankle monitor. "You realize that it's still working, right?"

"Oh, come on. I didn't run away last night. You don't need to put that thing on me again. I'll behave."

"Really?" Matteo asked, dropping the towel and stalking toward me. "That doesn't sound like you."

I rolled my eyes. Two could play this game. I pulled my shirt over my head, then slid my panties down my legs before straightening, completely naked. Let Matteo deal with that.

As expected, Matteo's eyes traveled over my body and his cock twitched in response.

I smiled smugly. "I really hate the monitor. I don't want to wear it again."

Matteo leaned against the washbasin, so close that our bodies were almost touching and I could smell his minty shower gel.

"How about a little bet?"

I had a feeling I wouldn't like what he was going to suggest, but I motioned for him to keep talking.

"If I manage to give you an orgasm today, then we put the ankle monitor back on. If you manage to resist my skills, we throw that thing in the trash."

"Only one?"

"Greedy girl," he said teasingly, his dark eyes sparkling with excitement. "I thought you weren't attracted to me? Are you worried your body won't be able to resist me?"

I wished he was wrong, but my body really was a horrible traitor. I'd lost count of the times we'd had sex in our short marriage. "No, of course not. But one orgasm seems setting the bar very low for you, don't you think?"

"Oh, I don't know. We both know how stubborn you can be, and I promised Luca to put that ankle monitor on you. I can't make it too easy for you to get rid of it again." His eyes were drawn to my breasts, then lower. "So what do you say? Resist an orgasm until midnight and you'll be free of the monitor."

I backed away from him to be safe. "Okay."

"Of course you can't just avoid having an orgasm by not letting me touch you. You have to give me a fair fighting chance."

I huffed. "A fair chance? What is fair about this?"

Matteo shrugged. "Deal?"

"Deal," I said grudgingly before dashing into the shower and closing the door. It wouldn't stop Matteo, but he didn't try to follow.

Grinning, he walked toward the bedroom. "I'll be waiting for you."

Okay, I needed to put myself in a mindset of complete calm, needed to figure out a way to make me immune to whatever Matteo was going to do. Problem was my pulse was pounding with excitement when I thought of what he was going to do. Damn it. I closed my eyes and turned the water on cold. Gasping for breath, I started shivering and slowly my arousal abated. After a couple more minutes, I stepped out of the shower, frozen to the bone and hopefully turned off enough to resist Matteo at least for the moment. I headed into the bedroom. Matteo lay on the bed in all his naked glory with his arms crossed behind his head.

I was actually glad for his self-assured smile because it only strengthened my resolve to resist him. Straightening my shoulders, I walked past the bed, determined to head toward the dressing room. "Shouldn't we get up?"

Matteo's grin widened. "We have some time. Or are you scared of losing our bet?"

I walked toward the bed without another word. Matteo's eyes followed every move I made. I should have made a bet that he wasn't allowed to come. That bet I would have won without trouble judging from the hunger in his gaze. Matteo pulled me down on top of him and kissed me. He took his time, his hands only lightly stroking my back, and yet the pressure between my legs was already close to unbearable.

I tried to think of something else. Anything really, and somehow Matteo seemed to sense that I was drifting away. He flipped us over so he hovered over me, and then my torture began. His mouth closed around my nipple, nibbling and licking, before moving on to my other breast and lavishing that one with the same amount of attention. I lay my palms flat against the bedspread, trying to calm my breathing and racing pulse.

Matteo cupped my other breast, and squeezed harder than expected. I arched up at the intense sensation, then quickly relaxed again. I couldn't make it too easy for him. He'd be even more smug if he got me aroused so fast. Peering up at the ceiling, I focused all my attention away from Matteo's teasing lips. He chuckled against my sternum, then licked a trail down to my navel. "So stubborn."

I knew the moment Matteo parted my legs, he'd see how much my body craved his touch. There was nothing I could do about it. Maybe there was a way I could have an orgasm without Matteo actually noticing? By now that was almost my only hope because I was fairly sure my body was going to betray me.

With a wicked grin, Matteo moved between my legs and pushed his palms below my butt and then he pressed his mouth to my heated flesh. I bit back a moan at the feel of his tongue. His eyes were on me, so possessive and hungry that it turned me on even more.

I closed my own eyes tightly, trying to block out what Matteo was doing, but he was making it difficult.

"Delicious," he murmured, then took another lick. "You taste so good, Gianna. I want to eat you out every day." He dipped his tongue into my opening before drawing the softest circles with the tip of his tongue, only to enter me again. I pressed my lips together to hold back a moan. His hands pushed my legs even further apart and then his fingers gently opened my lips to give him even better access. His tongue barely brushed me, so soft my toes curled from the intense sensations. "You can pretend this isn't doing anything to you, Gianna, but your body betrays you."

Damn it, as if I didn't know it.

"Are you going to keep your eyes closed the entire time?" he asked in a mocking tone.

My eyes shot open and I glared at him.

He lifted his head with his damn shark-grin, his chin glistening with my juices. "That's better," he murmured before he lowered his gaze back down to my center and rubbed his thumb lightly over my clit. His tongue slid over my inner thigh before lightly biting down. More wetness pooled between my legs and Matteo's smile widened even more. "See, you like this." He slid his thumb between my folds, then lifted it to his lips and licked off my juices. "Hmm." I knew I should close my eyes again but it was impossible. Instead I braced myself on my elbows to get a better view. This was a losing battle anyway, I might as well enjoy it fully.

Matteo raised his eyebrows. "Upping the ante?" He dove back down and I threw my head back, not even bothering to keep the moan in. Fuck the stupid bet and the stupid ankle monitor. My calves started spasming and the tremor spread through my entire body as pleasure coursed through me. There was no thinking of hiding my orgasm. No chance in hell.

I arched off the bed, letting pleasure consume me. Loud cries fell from my lips and I let them out without restraint.

Eventually, I caught my breath. Matteo pushed himself up on his elbows. The look on his face made me regret my weakness. "Maybe one orgasm was really unfair," he said in a raspy voice.

"You think?" I whispered breathlessly. "How about an additional bet? All or nothing?"

"I'm listening."

"If I manage to make you come, you lose and I won't have to wear the ankle monitor again. If you resist, I'll put that thing back on without protest."

Matteo sat back on his haunches, presenting his rock-hard cock. I leaned forward and curled my fingers around his length with a challenging look. "So what do you say?"

"Why should I risk losing if I can only win the same thing again."

I licked my lips and squeezed his cock once. "Are you scared of losing?" I repeated his earlier words.

He chuckled. "Of course not. The bet's on. I'm in your hands."

"Lie down," I ordered, not wasting any time. I'd win this bet no matter what.

Matteo

I flopped down on my back beside Gianna and crossed my arms behind my head. Gianna looked pretty confident. My cock was already hard from licking her, and she probably thought I wouldn't last very long. She didn't know me very well.

She knelt beside me, then lowered her head very slowly, her eyes glued to me, challenging and sexy as fuck. Did she know how much her gaze turned me on? That look alone made my cock twitch. Gianna curled her fingers around my base and swirled her tongue around my tip before she took all of me into her fucking hot mouth. I loved seeing my cock disappear between her pink lips. When I hit the back of her throat, I almost groaned.

Gianna smiled around my width as if she knew exactly what she was doing to me. And then she started to hum, and the vibrations went straight to my balls.

"Fuck," I growled, which only seemed to spur her on more. She bobbed her head up and down, eyes on me, and massaged my balls in the best possible way.

"You're so good at this," I said.

She rolled her eyes at me, and damn, if that didn't make her even sexier. Her red hair stuck to her forehead and cheeks as she took me deep into her mouth.

I wasn't going to last forever. I'd never really thought I could win this bet, never actually wanted to win. All I wanted in this moment was to come in Gianna's hot mouth. I raked my hands through her gorgeous locks. The muscles in my thighs tightened but I fought the sensation off. It was too fucking amazing to be over so soon, and knowing Gianna I might have to wait a while before she gave me another blowjob. She looked like a sex goddess. Fuck. I'd wanted to see her like that for a long time, had fucking daydreamed about it. I jerked my hips, and felt my balls tightening. Gianna sucked even harder. Not that I needed any more convincing. All I wanted was to spill into her. And then I fucking exploded. Gianna didn't pull back. Fuck, she kept sucking even as I shot my cum down her throat. With a long moan, I let my head fall back and my body became slack. Gianna lifted her head and wiped her mouth with a wide smile. "I win."

I laughed quietly. "You did. Congratulations."

"So I won't have to wear the ankle monitor ever again?" she asked with a hint of suspicion.

"That's the bet." I didn't tell her that I felt like the real winner. I'd never liked seeing her with the ankle monitor; it had always felt like a sacrilege to cage her in like that. I was glad that she wouldn't wear it anymore, even if that meant I had to keep a close eye on her, and that Luca would probably punch me.

chapter *eighteen*

Gianna

The next morning after I'd showered and dressed, I enjoyed my newfound freedom, even if it was small. Matteo had kept his promise and stashed the ankle monitor in a drawer. I didn't have to wear that stupid thing, at least for now. I doubted Matteo would still keep his promise if I tried to run again.

We'd both lost our bets and yet we both felt like winners. Life with Matteo was an enigma. He was already leaning against the kitchen counter, drinking coffee when I came out of the bedroom. His smile was so smug I had trouble stopping myself from wringing his neck. I grabbed a cup for myself, then leaned across from him. "Do you ever feel regret or guilt?"

Matteo's eyebrows climbed his forehead. "Regret?"

"Yes, you know that feeling normal people have when they've done something wrong?" I took a sip. I wasn't even sure why I was asking, except to wipe that annoying smugness off Matteo's face.

For a long time Matteo only looked at me until I couldn't stand it anymore and pretended my coffee was really interesting. Why did I suddenly feel guilty for asking that question?

"There's little time for guilt and regret in my life," Matteo said. His voice was quiet and devoid of humor; I couldn't help but look up, trying to gauge his mood, but as usual he was making it difficult.

"So you *do* feel it sometimes?"

"Occasionally. But I've learned a long time ago that it's not clever to dwell on the past. I prefer to focus on the future." With that, his usual charm was switched back on. He strode toward me, set his cup down on the counter, and braced his arms beside me. "Do you ever regret running?"

I opened my mouth to say "no" but for some reason I hesitated. That moment of hesitation was all the answer Matteo needed.

"Why?"

"Because it got someone killed," I said quietly. I'd managed to forget Sid and his horrible end, but now it all came back. I could have kicked Matteo for bringing the memory back. Especially because I'd come to realize that the life I'd run from wasn't as horrible as I'd wanted it to be.

Matteo's expression said he didn't give a fuck about that, and it was pretty much what I'd expected. "I can tell you without a doubt that I don't feel guilt over that guy's death," he murmured. He ran a hand down my side. "I would have killed every guy that touched you. But we both know I don't have to because despite plenty of opportunity you were a good girl."

The way he said "good girl" made my blood boil. I was still trying to come up with a clever comeback when the elevator rang, announcing a visitor. Matteo pecked the tip of my nose with a superior expression before staggering off toward the elevator. I couldn't believe him.

I was still glaring at his back when the elevator doors slid open and Aria walked into the apartment. She was talking on the phone. To my surprise Matteo moved into the elevator, leaving us alone. I suspected he could lock the elevator from the outside, so I couldn't leave unless I took a dive out of the window and ended up as a blood splatter on the sidewalk down below.

"Who are you talking to?" I asked as Aria headed toward me.

She gave me a bright smile and held the phone out to me. "Lily and Fabi want to talk to you but Father forbid them from calling you, so..." She trailed off. Of course, I'd suspected something like that. Father had made it pretty clear that he didn't want me around them anymore.

"Thanks," I mouthed to Aria before taking the phone from her and pressing it against my ear. "Lily?" My voice was shaky and I had to clear my throat.

"Oh, Gianna! I was so sad when Father didn't let me say goodbye to you. I've been begging him to let me talk to you but he got really mad and now I'm grounded."

Grounded had always felt like a strange term for our punishment. We had never been allowed to go anywhere alone anyway, so being grounded only meant that we had to stay in the house even more.

"I'm sorry," I said, trying to keep my anger for our father back. Lily still had to live under his rule. She didn't need to get in trouble because of me. I walked over to the living area and sank down on the sofa. Aria perched on the edge beside me. "How's school?" I asked.

"Boring. But at home is even worse. Since you and Aria moved out, nothing fun ever happens anymore," Lily murmured. My heart ached for her. I'd always had Lily, and for a long time Aria, but Lily would have to survive for years without that kind of support. Of course she still had Fabi but he was a boy and would soon face very different challenges. "What about Fabi?"

"He's being a pain in the ass," Lily said. In the background I could hear my brother say something. "You are!" Lily retorted. "Oh shut up. It's my turn now. You can talk to her later." There was the sound of grappling and then there was Fabi's voice in my ear. "Gianna!"

"Shhh, you fathead," Lily hissed, obviously taking the phone back. "Nobody can know that we're talking to her." For a moment there was silence as if they were both listening for sounds, then Lily spoke again. "Is Romero there with you?"

I laughed. "That's why you're calling? I thought you wanted to see how I was doing," I said in a mock hurt voice.

"Of course I want to know how you're doing."

"I'm fine." There was a pause. Deciding to stop torturing her, I added, "And Romero isn't here." I glanced at Aria and she whispered "upstairs." "He's at Aria's place, discussing important mob business with our husbands." Sarcasm dripped from the words. "Do you want me to go upstairs and ask him to talk to you?"

"No!" Lily blurted. "He'll think I'm in love with him."

"Aren't you?"

Silence. Poor Lily, I didn't have the heart to tell her that there was no chance in hell that Father would ever allow an alliance between my sister and a mere soldier, especially one from New York. Love just wasn't something that mattered.

"How do I know if I'm in love?" Lily whispered after a while.

Yes, how? I hadn't been in love with Sid or anyone else. I wasn't in love with Matteo.

Right?

"I don't know," I admitted.

"Aren't you in love with Matteo?"

"Why would you think I was? I ran away, remember?"

"But you're married now."

"Marriage doesn't equal love."

"It did for Aria," Lily said. My eyes darted to Aria who was frowning at me.

"You're right. Maybe you should ask her then." Before Lily could say another word, I handed the phone to Aria. "Lily wants to know how it feels to be in love."

Aria took the phone from me, her blue eyes full of concern. She listened to Lily for a moment before she said, "That's hard to put into words. Love is when you feel safe in someone's arms, when he's the first thing you want to see in the morning, love is surrendering. You risk getting hurt but you don't care. You are willing to give someone the power to break your heart. Love means seeing someone at their worst and still seeing the good in them, love means someone is perfect for you despite their imperfections." She grew quiet, eyes distant.

I didn't have to ask; I knew about whom she was thinking. I swallowed hard. I could have never said what Aria had just said. Unwantedly an image of Matteo's cocky grin flashed in my mind. I'd definitely seen him at his worst that day he'd tortured the Russians.

"But how do I know when I'm in love?" I heard Lily's whine through the phone.

Yes, how?

"It's a gradual process. I don't really know when exactly I started loving Luca. For a long time I thought I hated him."

I pushed to my feet, suddenly restless. This wasn't a topic I felt comfortable with. It made my chest feel tight, made me start to panic in an odd way. I hurried into the kitchen and made myself another cup of coffee. After a couple of sips, I returned to Aria who gave me a questioning look. I raised my cup as a way of explanation. "Here," she said, handing the phone back to me.

"So what else is new?" I asked lightly.

I could practically hear Lily roll her eyes. "Are you going to come to our Christmas party?"

I opened my mouth to say yes, because I'd always been there, then I realized I probably wasn't wanted anymore. "I don't know. Things are difficult at the moment."

"You mean Father doesn't want you to come."

"The only reason I would want to come is you and Fabi. I don't care about anyone else. And maybe you and Fabi can come visit New York in the New Year."

Lily was silent. "Father said he won't ever allow us to go to New York again after what you did."

That shouldn't have shocked me as much as it did, I suppose. Of course he wouldn't let Lily out of his sight. He couldn't risk another one of his daughters turning into a slut. "We'll figure something out. I'll ask Matteo if we're going to Chicago."

Facing Father again was the last thing I wanted to do. For all I cared I would never set foot on Chicago ground again, but the idea of never seeing Fabi and Lily again was even worse.

"Promise?"

"I promise," I said. "Now give me Fabi before Father realizes you're talking to me and not Aria."

"Hi," came Fabi's voice.

"I bet you've grown another two inches since I last saw you."

"When I grow up I'll be at least six feet tall," he said proudly.

"Six feet four at least. You'll probably be taller than Luca."

"That would be so cool. I could kick everyone's ass. Everybody would have to be nice to me and respect me."

I smiled wistfully. Soon enough people would do that anyway. The cute boy would be replaced by a ruthless killer. "That would be cool," I agreed. "So do you have any new knives?"

Fabi had a huge collection of knives. A bigger collection of knives than a ten-year-old should have. Of course Father supported my brother's fascination with weapons.

"No," Fabi said, sulking. "Father is angry at me."

"Because of me?"

Fabi didn't say anything at first but I knew he was shrugging in that cute way he had. "I don't like how he screamed at you."

"I don't like it either, but you have to try not to make Father angry too often, Fabi. I don't want you to get punished." Now that I wasn't available as Father's favorite punching bag, I worried Fabi might have to bear the brunt of his anger.

"Okay," he said. "I miss you."

"I miss you too."

We hung up and I handed the phone back to Aria.

"Are you okay?" she asked.

I nodded half-heartedly. "The party is next weekend, right?"

"Yeah."

"I guess I'm not invited?"

Aria grimaced. "Even Luca and I aren't sure if we should be going."

"Why?"

"Things are really bad right now. Luca has enough trouble in New York. And he doesn't want to deal with Dante Cavallaro or Father in addition to that."

"Fabi and Lily will be really sad if you don't come to visit."

"I know," Aria said with a sigh, leaning against the backrest. "That's what I've been telling Luca. I even suggested I could fly over alone with Romero, so Luca could take care of business here."

"Let me guess. He hated that idea."

Aria laughed. "Yeah. He doesn't trust the Outfit and won't let me go there without him."

"I kind of have to agree with him. I wish we could go together though."

"Maybe next year. Father can hardly stay mad at you forever."

"Father will still be mad at me when he's roasting in hell."

As expected, I wasn't invited to my family's Christmas party. Officially, Father couldn't have denied me entrance as Matteo's wife, but not only would that have been very awkward but Matteo also didn't want to risk taking me back to Chicago so soon. That night after my body had won over my brain once again and succumbed to Matteo's charm, I lay naked in his arms, his chest pressed up against my back. I wasn't sure why I always fell asleep with his arms around me, and worse why I was sometimes longing for his closeness during the day too. So far I'd managed to resist that second notion at least.

"Will I ever see Fabi and Lily again?" I whispered into the silence.

Matteo's arms around my waist tightened. "If they were part of the Cosa Nostra, Luca could do something, but your father only has to listen to Cavallaro."

"I know," I said almost angrily. I knew how things worked in our world. "But can't we invite my family over for some kind of gathering? Father wouldn't reject a direct invitation, right?"

Matteo propped himself up and stared down at my face. "Your father would definitely follow the invitation, but he wouldn't have to take your sister and brother with him. Many men keep their families out of it for security reasons."

I nodded.

Matteo watched me for a long time and it was starting to make me feel naked in a very different way. I shot him a glare. "What?"

"Luca is very convincing. Maybe he can ask your father to allow Liliana and Fabiano to come for a visit after Christmas. Your father could send his own guards with them if he doesn't trust us."

"Why would Luca do that? He and Aria are still welcome in Chicago."

"If I ask Luca, he'll do it."

"And why should you ask him? Aren't you in enough trouble already because of Bardoni and getting rid of my ankle monitor?"

Matteo twirled a strand of my hair around his finger. "I'd do it for you. You are my wife and I want to make you happy." His smile was teasing and yet what he'd said had sounded sincere.

My heart thudded dangerously, and new panic rose up. What was happening? Fear of my own emotions got the better of me. "If you really care about me and want to see me happy, let me go. All I've ever wanted was freedom and a normal life."

The moment the words left my mouth, I realized I wasn't sure if they were still the truth.

Matteo's expression shut off, something hard and cold settling in his eyes. He lay back down and extinguished the lights. I almost apologized and reached out for him.

His lips brushed my ear. "I guess then that means I don't care enough. Because letting you go? That's the one thing I'll never do."

After that conversation, our interactions in the next few days were reduced to sex once again.

To my surprise, I missed our banter. I even missed Matteo's stupid cockiness and that annoying shark-grin, but most of all I missed falling asleep with his fingers tracing the soft skin of my inner forearm.

Christmastime was definitely turning into my own personal nightmare. Matteo and I were invited to three more parties, all of them either hosted by high-ranking mobsters, or business men with close connections to the mob. All of them too important to offend by not attending. I really hoped Matteo wouldn't kill any more hosts though. The Bardoni debacle so far had been without consequences but I still wasn't entirely sure it would stay that way. At some point people would undoubtedly get suspicious.

Now that I wasn't wearing an ankle monitor anymore, Sandro was my shadow, and when Aria and I went anywhere together, Romero was always there as well. It was ridiculous. Even without a technical device every aspect of my life was out of my control. Married bliss, my ass.

I fixed a wayward strand, which had fallen out of my updo, and brushed my hands over my new dress. With all the social events looming in my future, Aria and I had done another big shopping trip. I was starting to feel like one of those trophy mob wives I'd despised all my life. Shopping, social events, and warming their husband's bed was their whole world, and also mine. I glared at my reflection. I even looked all the way like a trophy wife with my hair in that elegant updo and the gorgeous dark green cocktail dress that hugged my curves. Even my huge wedding ring and the diamond necklace screamed trophy wife. It took all my self-control not to rip the dress off my body and cut my hair off. How could I have become what I'd hated for so long? And how could I be okay with it?

"Aria and Luca are here," Matteo shouted. "We need to get going." This was more than he'd said to me outside of the bedroom since that night. With a sigh, I turned away from the mirror and headed toward the living room where Aria, Luca, and Matteo were waiting. Matteo looked marvelous in a slim-fit black suit, white shirt, and black tie. It was so cliché mobster, but he pulled it off with ease. That man always looked good. His eyes did a quick scan of my outfit and my body responded with a familiar shiver. I'd read about looks that were like sex, but I'd always considered them urban legend. But Matteo had that look down to a T.

I kept my face unaffected as I walked toward them. Aria was an apparition in her dark red dress and with her golden curls. In the past I'd often felt like I could never compete with her but I'd come to realize that I didn't have to. Luca towered over my sister in a similar suit like Matteo, but it did nothing for me. I stopped beside Matteo and his hand immediately went to my hip. Did he even notice how possessive those small gestures were? In the past, my first reaction to them would have been annoyance followed by a rebuff, but now it seemed almost natural. I wasn't sure why this was the case, why I molded so easily into the life that had been cut out for me even before my birth. Some people would probably seek an explanation in fate or faith. I'd never considered either option to be valid. I didn't like the idea that some bigger outer thing controlled who I was and how my life would develop.

"Hey, where are you?" Matteo asked, squeezing my hip lightly. I blinked, focusing on him. I hadn't even realized we'd stepped into the elevator.

I shook my head. "Thinking of all the ways this evening could end badly," I lied.

"As long as Matteo keeps his knife in his holster and you keep your mouth in check, things should go smoothly," Luca muttered, sending both

Matteo and me a glare. "Tonight is important. Several of the attending businessmen are under pressure from the Russians. I want to show strength and make a good impression. It would be even better if you could manage not to offend the wives."

"Why me? What about Aria?"

"Aria knows how to behave herself. She's the perfect lady whereas you are anything but."

Aria touched Luca's chest. "Be nice to my sister."

"I'm not rude to everyone. Only people I don't like," I said pointedly.

"Which will be everyone at the party," Matteo interjected. "They are insufferable, believe me." We exchanged a grin, then as if remembering our "kind of" fight from a few nights ago, looked away from each other. I could see Luca give Aria one of those secret looks they always shared.

"Just behave yourself," Luca said. "Both of you. It's like God's sent you two to me to test my patience."

Aria giggled and hit Luca's shoulder lightly, but her eyes were sparkling with adoration. Would I ever look at someone like that? I wasn't sure if I wanted to. It seemed like she was baring her soul for everyone to see and she didn't even mind.

Together we stepped out of the elevator and into the freezing cold parking garage. I shivered. I hadn't taken a coat with me because I only had to walk from the elevator to the car and then from the car to wherever the party was taking place, but now I regretted it. It was mid-December after all. One month since Matteo had caught me. Sometimes it was hard to believe so much time had passed already.

Matteo let go of me, removed his jacket and put it over my shoulders. His warmth and scent enveloped me, and I caught myself drawing in a deep breath.

"Thanks," I said half-embarrassed.

Luca had done the same for Aria despite the short way to the car. Aria and I settled in the back of Matteo's Porsche Cayenne while Luca and Matteo sat in the front. It seemed the men weren't worried anymore that I'd try to jump out of the driving car to escape. Maybe they, too, had noticed how easily I'd settled in.

Aria leaned over to whisper in my ear. "I know you don't want to see it but you and Matteo are like you were made for each other."

I shot her a look, ignoring the way my pulse sped up with an emotion I didn't even want to think about. "Don't even start."

Aria shrugged. "It's the truth. And he's really trying. They aren't perfect but they are trying to be good to us. You don't look unhappy."

I wasn't exactly unhappy, but I tried to attribute it to Aria's constant presence in my new life. It was the convenient explanation. I didn't say anything, couldn't come up with a witty reply that wouldn't sound utterly fake.

We sat in silence after that and yet I felt like my silence was more of an answer than I liked. I was actually relieved when we finally pulled up in front of a luxury apartment building not unlike the one Matteo and I lived in. A doorman rushed toward our car and opened my door. Good thing he didn't see both Luca and Matteo reach for their weapons, always ready for an attack.

I thanked the guy who looked like he was barely my age, and got out. Aria followed quickly. We handed the jackets back to our husbands before walking into the brightly lit lobby. Another doorman waited next to the elevator and clicked the correct button for us.

As we rode up toward the top floor, Matteo leaned close and murmured, "Don't forget to behave yourself." He winked at me when he pulled back and I knew we'd be in trouble. Matteo's expression promised that he had absolutely no intention to be good tonight.

The party took place in a huge penthouse overlooking the city. It was not quite as big as Luca's but definitely showy. The walls were covered with drawings by Picasso, Warhol, and Miró, all of them originals, and I had a feeling the furniture was as pretentious, but everything had been removed to fit two long tables for eighty guests into the room as well as a dozen bar tables where guests could mingle before dinner.

The noise level was overwhelming despite the size of the penthouse and there wasn't anything Christmas-y about the decoration except for an abstract glass Nativity scene on the mantle and an even more abstract glass Christmas tree in one corner. Aria and I looked at each other and almost burst into laughter.

My mood dropped the moment the host and hostess, a middle-aged couple that looked even more fake than their tree, approached us. I braced myself for the disgusted once-over, but the woman smiled at Aria and me the same way.

The hostess who introduced herself as Miriam practically *beamed* at me, though it looked almost scary because her face was frozen from too many Botox treatments. "You must be the beautiful new bride," she said, and kissed me on both cheeks.

"Yes, thank you," I said, startled.

I darted a confused look at Matteo. He must have read it right because he leaned toward me while the host and hostess spoke to Luca and Aria. "They aren't part of our culture. They don't give a crap about our rules and morals," Matteo whispered.

The hostess turned back to us. "Dinner starts in thirty minutes. But please help yourself to our delicious hors d'oeuvres and champagne." She pronounced champagne in an odd French accent, which almost made me laugh again, but I pulled myself together and smiled politely instead. The woman had been kind to me, so I had to act accordingly, even if Luca thought I was incapable of pleasantness.

I glanced around, only spotting one familiar couple, that I assumed must be part of the mob or I wouldn't have recognized them. Apart from that, we were blissfully surrounded by strangers, who didn't call me slut under their breaths, or look down their noses at me. This was a straight-up social event that normal people, *well* normal *rich* people attended. I relaxed. Maybe this wouldn't be too bad.

"Come on. Let's fill up on some champagne. We'll need the buzz to carry us through the boredom," Matteo said. Luca shot him a scowl, but Matteo merely grinned and led me toward an unoccupied bar table. I grabbed a glass and took a deep gulp. That was the one good thing about living in our world; nobody gave a damn if I was of legal age to drink. The bubbles prickled delightfully on my tongue. It had been a long time since I'd had good champagne. The last time was at Aria's wedding.

Matteo smirked.

"What?" I asked, checking my dress for any stains.

"You look like a sophisticated lady."

"I'm not a sophisticated lady," I said quickly and was about to take another gulp of champagne but stopped with the rim against my lips. With a glare, I set it down. "I'm not."

"I didn't say you were. I only pointed out that you look it."

He was right. I fit in, which brought me back to my earlier problem. Why was I becoming more like a trophy wife every day? I downed the rest of my champagne in one large gulp, not at all ladylike, making Matteo laugh, and I couldn't help but do too. It felt good to laugh with him, and even better to see mirth banish some of the darkness in his eyes.

Miriam called for everyone to settle around the tables, and asked us to sit next to her with other important guests. Unfortunately Aria had to sit across from me, so I couldn't even talk to her in case I got bored. I was wedged between Matteo and a woman I didn't know. Luckily the first course was served almost immediately, so I had something to do. Miriam as well as the other women around us were more interested in Aria anyway, probably because she was Luca's wife and knew how to do proper small talk.

Suddenly I felt Matteo's hand on my knee. I shot him a look but he was immersed in a conversation with Luca and the host. I took another bite of my carpaccio but stopped mid-chew when his hand began its ascent higher, toward the lacy edge of my hold-ups. I had to suppress a small shiver at the sensations his light touch sent straight to my center. I clenched my legs together and tried to focus on the conversation Aria was having with the other women. The corners of Matteo's lips twitched in reaction. Of course that wasn't the end of it. When was it ever?

Matteo's fingers slipped between my legs despite my attempts to lock him out, and then his fingertips slipped under the edge of my panties and lightly stroked the crevice between my leg and vulva. I reached for the glass and took a deep gulp of the wine.

"What do you think, Gianna? Would you be interested?" asked the hostess Miriam. Her eyebrows were raised but due to all the Botox, the rest of her face was static, and her expression resembled one of mild boredom.

My eyes darted to Aria, hoping she'd help me out. I had no clue what Miriam was talking about. Matteo's fingers had distracted me completely.

"I know you love modern art, and it's not easy to come by a private tour through the Guggenheim. I'm sure Matteo can spare you for a few hours," Aria said with a meaningful look.

I could have kissed her. She always saved the day. "Yes, I'd love to—" Matteo's fingers slipped between my lower lips, gently nudging them apart, finding me wet and aching, the stupid bastard. He was still talking to Luca and the other men as if nothing of interest was going on under the table.

Aria and the other women were watching me expectantly. I cleared my throat and kicked Matteo's leg hard, before I said, "I'd love to take you up on that offer." Could I sound any more sophisticated? Trophy wife all the way.

Matteo's finger traveled up my slit until it reached my clit where he started to draw small circles. I pressed my lips together to stop a moan from slipping out. Thankfully, Miriam went on another monologue about a trip to the Caribbean and I was back to pretending to listen. Only Aria gave me the occasional odd glance, as if she thought I might not be feeling well.

If only she knew. The waiters entered the room with our main course, but I hardly cared.

Without even intending to, I parted my legs a bit more, giving Matteo more room to explore my wet folds. His fingers slipped up and down, teasing my opening, before they returned to my throbbing clit. I clutched my wine glass. It wouldn't have surprised me if I'd broken it in two from my tight grip. My breathing was shallow. Matteo kept up the slow rhythm, driving me closer and closer toward release. I should have pushed his hand away, should have stopped this madness before this turned into the most embarrassing night of my life, but need had taken over and banished any hint of reason. After a few bites of veal, I put my fork down. I was hungry for only one thing.

Matteo slipped a finger into me and I barely managed to keep in my whimper. I was getting so close. Could I even be silent?

But I was too far gone to care. Matteo still wasn't looking at me. Instead he was completely focused on the conversation, or at least he pretended to be. I hated him for his acting talent. He brought me closer and closer, taking his time. God, this was the most delicious torture.

His skilled fingers became the whole center of my being until suddenly, without a warning he pulled them away. Shocked, I stared at him, only to realize that the waiters had returned with our dessert, chocolate mousse. Matteo gave me a grin.

I wanted to rip his clothes off and have my way with him, bring him to the brink, only to deny him release. Matteo dipped a finger into the mousse, the finger he'd used to finger me, and slid it into his mouth, licking it clean. "Hm. Delicious."

My body was humming with desire, but in that moment I wanted to push Matteo's face down into the stupid mousse. He picked up his spoon and calmly started eating. Aria gave me a questioning look when I didn't move.

I grabbed my own spoon a bit too tightly and tasted the mousse. It was delicious, creamy and very chocolaty, but now all it did was remind me of Matteo's fingers and what they had done mere moments before. Two could play this game. Once I was done with my dessert, I slipped my hand under the table and reached between Matteo's legs. I found him already hard and that knowledge made me ache even more. I considered stroking myself instead of teasing Matteo, but banished the idea. If I wanted to win this game, I needed to play. My fingers closed around Matteo's erection. He sucked in a quiet breath before his eyes met mine, one corner of his mouth lifting. I massaged him through the fabric of his pants, feeling him grow even harder and bigger. Unfortunately my own body responded too.

Matteo turned his head to an older guy across from him who'd asked him a question and I used the moment to find his tip and start rubbing that. Matteo had had it easier. He didn't have as many barriers between his fingers and their goal, but as I worked the head of his cock, I could see from the flexing of his jaw that Matteo wasn't completely unaffected. And unlike me, he would have a hard time hiding his arousal if he got up, and an even harder time if he came in his pants. The thought made me smile.

Aria leaned across the table toward me. I really hoped she wouldn't notice anything. "What's the matter with you? You're acting strange," she whispered.

I shook my head and mouthed "later," but my hand never stopped its work under the table. I hoped Matteo was getting close. It was hard to tell. He'd angled his face away from me and was actually conducting a coherent conversation with the old man. I squeezed a bit tighter, getting annoyed, and finally got another, albeit small reaction. Matteo tensed briefly but then visibly forced himself to relax. I could have screamed in frustration.

I was about to squeeze again, even harder when his hand found mine under the table and pulled it away. I would have clung to his erection if I hadn't been worried about injuring him. Even if I'd never admit it to anyone, I loved Matteo's cock, and particularly the things he could do with it. I chanced a look at Matteo and met his gaze. There was hunger in there, but also something else, something that made me want to go running for the hills, because I had a feeling I knew what it was and I was pretty sure I was starting to feel the same. I wrenched my hand away from his hold, pushed my chair back and straightened.

With a small smile at the other guests, I said, "Excuse me." Without another look at Matteo, I headed straight toward where I hoped to find the restrooms.

It took all my self-control not to run down the long corridor branching off from the main area of the apartment. When I entered the restroom, I released a harsh breath. My cheeks were flushed, but not so much that anyone would suspect anything. That was what I hoped at least. I gripped the edge of the washbasin and squeezed my eyes shut. My heart was slamming against my rib cage. Suddenly someone gripped my hips. My eyes shot open and I stared into the mirror. Matteo towered over me, his gaze practically burning with want. He pressed his hips against my butt. "You left too soon." His hand slipped under my dress while his other hand pulled down his zipper.

"What are you doing?" I hissed with a glance toward the door. "What if someone comes in?"

"Who gives a fuck? Let them get the show of their lives. It's probably been years since those bitches got to see a cock." He pushed my panties aside and thrust two fingers into me. I jutted my butt out, giving him better access. My body seemed to be acting on its own accord even when my brain was screaming at me to push Matteo away.

"Matteo," I gasped. "Lock the stupid door."

He moved his fingers in and out in a deliciously slow rhythm. My hips moved against him, forcing his fingers deeper into me.

"Do you really want me to stop so I can lock the fucking door?" He licked my spine from the edge of my dress up to my hairline, then met my gaze in the mirror. I shivered. He slammed his fingers into me again, hitting a sweet spot deep inside of me. His eyes seemed to bore into me, trying to reveal my darkest deepest secrets. My heart lurched, and I knew I'd be doomed if I didn't stop this madness soon. Sex, that I could deal with, but these moments of silent understanding, these long looks full of too much meaning, they were starting to chip away at the walls I'd taken years to build.

Matteo cupped my breast through my dress, kneading and pinching my nipple in an almost painful way that made me grow even wetter. I closed my eyes to avoid his eyes and soaked in the sensations. Matteo thrust his fingers into me over and over again. I bit down on my lip to keep the sounds in. Matteo's lips clamped down on my pulse point, sucking the skin into his mouth. I arched, pushing my butt against his hand with all my might as my orgasm jolted through me.

"Look at me," Matteo ordered, and my eyes flew open, meeting his. "Yes, like that. Fuck, you are so fucking wet and hot."

I dropped down to my forearms with a shuddering breath, enjoying the last waves of pleasure while Matteo slowed his fingers. He lifted my skirt even higher. I heard him unbuckle his pants and then he wrapped his arms tightly around my chest, pulled me against him and rubbed his tip over my opening. Then he slipped in inch by inch. I tried to jut my butt out, needing to feel him all the way in me, but he didn't let me. If possible, he slowed even more, edging into me.

"Fuck me," I whispered harshly.

He reached up and tilted my head to the side before claiming it with his mouth, his tongue taking possession of me. He had finally sheathed himself completely in me and then after a moment of stillness, he started slamming into me. My hands shot out to grip the edge of the washstand. Matteo drove my body against the cold stone as his cock thrust into me, deep and hard.

"Fuck, you feel so good," Matteo rasped. I moaned in response. It did feel better than anything ever had. Everything about this did. God, what was happening?

I tried to shut my brain off and only focus on the way Matteo's cock filled me up, how he removed himself almost completely to drive me insane only to slam back into me. The edge of the washbasin dug into my palms as I clung to it. Matteo's hands moved down, clasping my hips. I threw my head back, gasping and whimpering as I tumbled over the edge again with Matteo close behind. The sound of his moans spurred me on even more. A moment before we both slumped forward, our gazes met in the mirror again. And then I knew why I'd hardly considered running in the last couple of weeks, and it terrified me like nothing ever had.

I quickly looked down, trying to catch my breath, and calm my pounding heart and pulse.

Matteo kissed my shoulder blade. "I'm fucking glad that you are mine."

I stiffened and would have pulled away if I wasn't trapped between the washstand and Matteo's body.

When Matteo eventually pulled out of me and we straightened our clothes and cleaned up, I couldn't meet his gaze. I wasn't embarrassed by what we'd done. That ship had sailed. I was confused and terrified by what I'd seen in my own eyes.

Matteo

During sex there were moments when I was certain Gianna was falling for me, but then always came the time afterward and I wasn't sure if I'd imagined it. In the past I'd always had girls crushing on me even when I never gave them reason to, but Gianna was a difficult nut to crack, and sometimes I caught myself wondering if maybe she'd never fall for me and was only fucking me to get on my good side. Gianna was clever, maybe she was trying to wrap me around her finger with sex so I'd grant her more freedom and she could run away again.

Gianna put a few strands that had fallen out during our quickie back into her updo. She was frowning at her own reflection and pretending I wasn't there.

When we left the bathroom, she still ignored me. Then she stopped suddenly. "We can't enter together. Everyone will know what we did."

I shrugged. I didn't give a fuck. Gianna was my wife and I'd fuck her whenever I felt like it. "We've been gone for a while. They're probably suspecting already."

"Great," Gianna muttered but then she squared her shoulders and headed back to the tables with the other guests without another glance in my direction. So we were back to playing games?

That night I woke to an empty bed. I jumped to my feet, and searched the room for a sign of Gianna, but she wasn't there. How could she have run? I didn't bother putting on pants. Grabbing my gun holster on the way I stormed out of the room and into the living room.

I had to call Luca and tell him. He'd be furious. He hadn't been happy when I'd removed Gianna's ankle monitor. My eyes made out a slender figure in an armchair close to the window. Gianna.

I relaxed and discarded my gun holster on a sideboard before I crossed the room toward her. She must have pushed the armchair closer to the window so she could look out. Her legs were pressed up against her chest and her face rested on her knees. She was fast asleep. But even in sleep her brows were drawn together. I wasn't sure but she looked as if she'd cried. I stopped beside her, staring down at her sleeping form. She must have moved very quietly for me not to hear her. I was a light sleeper. She'd even managed to put on pajamas. My gaze darted to the elevator console. Had she tried to crack the code and escape? The alarm would have alerted me to any attempts, and yet the suspicion remained. I hated that I didn't trust her. It wasn't as if I was used to trusting people, except for Luca, but I wanted to trust my wife. Of course it was difficult to develop trust when Gianna didn't even have the chance to prove herself.

If I gave her more freedom, and she didn't try to run, then I could start trusting her, but I had a feeling I'd never see her again if I did. I was too selfish and possessive. I didn't want to lose her, even if that was what was best for her. My eyes returned to her face and the sadness that seemed to be edged into it.

I slipped my hands under her body and lifted her into my arms. She didn't wake as I carried her back into our bedroom, back where I wanted her and where she belonged, but where she didn't want to be.

I put her down on the bed, but I didn't lie down next to her. I was too angry at myself for my wimpy thoughts. What did it matter if Gianna wanted to be my wife? What did it matter if she'd rather return to Munich and find some other idiot like Sid? She was mine and I wasn't a good guy. I didn't give a damn about other people's feelings. I felt on the edge, like I needed to hit something to get a grip. With a growl, I grabbed my gym clothes, put them on, grabbed my car keys and left the apartment.

I punched the code into the elevator panel and rode it down into the parking garage. I mounted my motorcycle, shot out of the garage and raced through the city toward our gym. Apart from a guard, it was deserted, which was a pity because I would have loved to actually spar with someone, instead of a fucking dummy.

I didn't bother with boxing gloves. I wanted to feel every hit. Facing the dummy, I started pummeling it, alternating between kicks and punches.

I was still at it when the gym started filling up with familiar faces. Nobody disturbed me. Apart from a short nod, they stayed the fuck away from me. They all knew what was good for them.

"Trying to kill a poor dummy?" came Luca's drawl.

I landed another hard kick against the head before I turned around to my brother. He wasn't wearing gym clothes. "What are you doing here?"

"Looking for you."

"Why?"

"Because you weren't there when I came to pick you up in your apartment this morning."

"You went into my apartment while I wasn't there?"

Luca rolled his eyes. "I didn't touch your wife, but I left Aria and Romero with her."

I nodded, trying to calm the fuck down. I was still on edge. I wasn't even sure why.

"Take a shower and get dressed. You look like you need a drink," Luca said in his Capo voice.

I didn't protest. I felt like a truck had run me over. I must have been in the gym for hours. It was already light outside. Luca and I went to one of our dance clubs. Except for the cleaning ladies, it was still deserted. I grabbed a whiskey bottle from the shelf, and Luca and I settled at the bar. In most social circles it was probably considered too early for alcohol. Luckily we didn't have to obey those stupid rules.

Luca and I emptied our glasses, then he fixed me with his big-brother stare. "So what's going on? Are you already growing tired of your obnoxious wife?"

I downed another glass of whiskey, waiting for the familiar burning to turn into warmth that spread in my chest. "Why do you ask?"

Luca cocked one eyebrow. "Maybe because you prefer spending the night in a sweaty gym than in bed with your young wife."

"I couldn't sleep."

"And you couldn't come up with something more entertaining to do than kickboxing a dummy?"

"You're starting to grate on my nerves," I said.

Luca ignored my warning tone. "To be honest I'm surprised you lasted this long with her. If I spend more than ten minutes in a room with Gianna, I want to seal my ears with hot wax."

"I'm not tired of her. I actually like Gianna's *obnoxious* personality. She spices things up. Life would be boring if she were like the other trophy wives."

Luca narrowed his eyes. "Aria isn't just a trophy wife."

Of course he was allowed to get angry when I even remotely insulted Aria but he could talk shit about Gianna all the time. "I didn't say anything about Aria. But I prefer my women..."

"Annoying and foulmouthed," Luca finished for me, before he took the whiskey bottle out of my hand. "Then what's the problem? Why are you sulking like a whiny bitch?"

I was waiting for one of my usual clever comebacks to pop into my mind, but I drew a fucking blank. That was serious bullshit. "I'm starting to think that Gianna might always hate me. I thought it was her way to be interesting and a challenge, a sort of game at the end of which she'd come to her fucking senses and fall for me like all the girls I've pursued before her, but I'm pretty sure Gianna is a challenge I'm losing. She won't come around. I think she hates this life a bit more every fucking day."

Luca scanned my face. "This is really bothering you."

He said it as if that was the biggest fucking surprise of his life, as if I was a fucking robot that wasn't capable of emotions. "That, coming from you," I said with a smirk. "Before Aria I wasn't even sure you were capable of liking anyone, least of all a woman."

"You make it sound like I'm a fag. It's not that I didn't like women. They were just not something I considered useful outside of the bedroom."

I shook my head. "How the hell did you get Aria to love you? It's like the fucking eighth Wonder of the World. Are there any new drugs you're not telling me about?"

"You're wasted, Matteo."

"I'm not. If you'd stop hogging the fucking whiskey, I might get the chance to be in a couple of hours." I ripped the bottle from his hand and took a swig.

"Gianna is like a tiger in the fucking zoo, caged in. It's fucking depressing to watch her look for a way to escape captivity."

"Did she try to run again?"

"How could she? I'm keeping her on a tight leash."

"You're not thinking about letting her go, are you?"

I didn't think I could, and I didn't want to. I was selfish and that wouldn't change any time soon. I still wanted Gianna. I wanted her gorgeous body in my bed every night, and my cock in her tight pussy. I wanted everything from her, most of all the things she was refusing to give me. "Would you let me?"

"No. The Famiglia is already displeased as it is. You'd look even weaker if you'd let her run away again. I really don't need the additional trouble. Not to mention the fucking Outfit would probably declare fucking war on us if we managed to lose Gianna again. Her father is being a real pain in the ass." He gave me his Capo look, which was meant to intimidate the rest of the world, but was useless on me as he fucking well knew. "You won't let her get away. You're stuck with her until the bitter end, and she with you. I don't care if she's fucking unhappy and if she hates you, she'll just have to deal."

"Wow, you're full of sunshine and rainbows today, aren't you?" I knew he was right, and really it wasn't like I'd tell Gianna she could go but somehow his words managed to piss me off anyway. "You realize the only thing stopping Gianna from slicing my throat at night is that she can't see blood. Do you know how reassuring it is to fall asleep beside someone who's probably fantasizing to see you dead so she can be free." She'd never said it in so many words but sometimes I thought I saw it in her eyes. Or maybe I was so fucking messed up that I was always thinking the worst of others.

"I hope you're joking," Luca said dryly.

"Who knows?" I emptied the whiskey bottle. I could feel the first treacherous signs of a nice buzz. I grinned. "Sometimes she's definitely trying to kill me with her eyes."

"Maybe then you shouldn't sleep in a room with her. She might get over her fear of blood at some point."

"Nah. Not anytime soon. And she isn't the violent type, not really."

"I wouldn't count on that. She can be really unhinged."

"You weren't worried about sleeping beside Aria when she still despised you so why should I?"

"You can't compare Aria to Gianna. They are like two different species. And I trust Aria absolutely. She caught a fucking bullet for me."

"Must be nice," I muttered. "Gianna would probably applaud my shooter."

chapter *nineteen*

Gianna

Matteo was in a strange mood, had been ever since he'd found me in the living room two nights ago. He hadn't said much, which was unusual for him. I wasn't sure if he was angry at something I'd done, and I didn't really care. That night I'd promised myself that I'd have to stop whatever was going on between him and me. I'd sworn to myself that I'd never become one of those women, that I'd never marry a Made Man, and much less develop feelings for him.

Christmas was only five days away but we both definitely hadn't caught the holiday spirit yet. There wasn't a single piece of Christmas decoration in our apartment. I'd considered asking Matteo to buy a tree and decorate it together, but then the panic had set in again and I hadn't said anything. Instead I'd accepted the strange mood between us almost with relief.

Matteo was gripping the steering wheel in a steel grip as we drove away from the last Christmas party of the season. The hosts had rented a deserted warehouse and turned into a winter wonderland with fake snow and a real ice bar. Aria and Luca were still there but Matteo's bad temper had caused Luca to send us away early. He'd probably worried that Matteo would end up killing someone again. I couldn't blame him.

The road was covered with a fine sheen of frost which glittered in the glare of our spotlights.

"You know what's funny?" Matteo asked in a tight voice.

I glanced toward him, his tense body and dark expression.

"Whenever you think I'm not watching, you look like you might be happy and then the moment our eyes meet, it's like 'poof' and the happiness is gone."

I wasn't sure what to tell him.

"Why do you insist on being miserable?"

Before I could formulate an answer, Matteo suddenly floored the gas. I was pressed into the seat. "What are you doing? You don't have to kill us because you're pissed."

Matteo peered into the side mirror. "I'm not trying to kill us. I'm trying to save our lives."

Something collided with our trunk. I glanced over my shoulder. Headlights of another SUV filled the rear window.

"Who are they?" I asked.

"Russians would be my guess. I noticed them too late. Fuck. This happens when I get distracted by other shit."

We were the only cars in this part of the industrial area. Matteo twisted the steering wheel and we shot around a corner into a narrow street between two high storehouses.

"Head down," Matteo barked.

I obeyed at once. Struggling against my seat belt, I leaned forward. A second later, our pursuers shot at us. The rear window exploded and shards rained down on us. Matteo didn't react, he kept driving like a madman. He'd somehow even managed to pull his own gun.

I clutched the seat, my head pressed against my legs as I jerked back and forth with every twist and turn of the car. The tires were screeching, gunshots whistling through the air, glass bursting. A new shower of shards rained down on me as the side window in the back exploded as well.

"Fuck," Matteo snarled while he tried to get a connection with his phone, probably to call Luca. Fear was clogging my throat tightly. Fear for my own life was only a small part of it. Seeing Matteo in clear line of fire terrified me even more. He couldn't duck his head. One bullet and everything could be over.

We turned another corner and I slammed against the door. I squeezed my eyes shut, fighting my rising sickness.

More shots rang out and Matteo let out a hiss. I peered to the side. Matteo was still driving and shooting at our pursuers, but he was bleeding from wounds in his arm and shoulder. That moment another bullet grazed his head, blood spurting everywhere, even on my face. Matteo didn't even seem to care; he fired another round of shots. Suddenly we were spinning, the car out of control. I wrapped my arms around my chest as I was thrown around in my seat. Through half-closed eyes I saw our car shooting toward a massive wall and then there was an earsplitting crash as we smashed into it. My body jerked forward, the air rushing out of me as I was flung against the safety belt. It cut into my collarbone, and my vision turned black. Then something soft exploded in my face, stopping my impact.

I didn't know how long I hung limply in my seat belt, my face buried in the deflating airbag as I tried to catch my breath. My ears were ringing but eventually that faded and silence greeted me. With a groan I sat up, ignoring my throbbing headache. Smoke was rising from our crushed hood, slowly filling the car through the broken windows. I blinked to get rid of the dots dancing in and out of my vision. My entire body was sore but nothing seemed to be broken. At least I could move.

I turned to the driver's side and stilled. It was dark in the car. Our lights were smashed but from somewhere a distant glow illuminated what was around me. Matteo was slumped over the steering wheel. Like many mafia cars, the driver didn't have an airbag because it was a bother during car chases. Blood plastered his dark hair to his forehead, soaked his shirt and dripped down on his pants. So much blood. He must have hit his head against the steering wheel or maybe the dashboard when we'd collided with the wall.

Was he dead?

He wasn't moving, and I couldn't see if he was breathing. I held my breath, listening for a sound. There was nothing. I blinked, then peered over my shoulder to see where our pursuers were. Their car had smashed into another building and had already caught fire. They were definitely dead. Was our car going to start burning too? I needed to get out.

Wasn't this the chance I'd been waiting for? Matteo and I were alone. Nobody was here to stop me from running. I could leave and be free. I unbuckled myself, then glanced at Matteo again. I needed to check if he was dead, but somehow I couldn't. What if he was really gone? What if he was dead? My throat felt tight and raw. My lungs refused to work as panic settled in my body. God, what if he was dead? What was wrong with me? Hadn't I wanted him out of my life six months ago? This was my chance, probably the only chance I'd ever get. The smell of gas drifted into my nose, and the smoke inside the car was starting to burn in my eyes. Matteo was a killer. He wasn't a good man. If you asked most people, they'd say he deserved death.

With shaky fingers I reached out and touched Matteo's shoulder. He still felt warm but that didn't mean he was alive. Slowly I inched my hand up until I brushed his blood-slick throat. My fingers ghosted over his skin, finding nothing, pressing and searching, until finally a soft pulse beat against my fingertips.

I exhaled, relief slamming into me like a hammer. Still alive. He was still alive. Thank God. With a sizzle and a pop fire shot out under the hood of the car. I gripped the door handle and pushed but it didn't budge, distorted from the crash. Panic spread in my chest as smoke and heat filled up the car, and I started clawing at the door. I shifted, tugged my sleeve down my hand and roughly cleaned the window frame from broken remains before I climbed out of the car headfirst. When I finally felt solid ground under my feet, I almost dropped to my knees because my legs were shaking like crazy. The entire hood was burning now and Matteo was still in the driver's seat. I rushed around the car, toward his door, praying that it wasn't stuck like mine. I didn't think I could drag Matteo through a narrow window without his help. I gripped the car door and tugged as hard as I could. With a screech it flew open and I landed on my butt. I caught my breath, then stumbled to my feet and grabbed Matteo's arm. He hadn't been wearing a seat belt so I could pull him out of the car without trouble. He plopped down on the asphalt a bit too hard and I winced, then quickly hooked my hand under his armpits and pulled him away from the car that was catching fire way too quickly.

Matteo was heavy and dragging him away from the car with my aching body hurt like hell, but I didn't stop until I was sure he was a safe distance away in case of an explosion. I let go of him before I straightened and wiped the blood from my palms on my pants. Matteo's eyes were closed, his face turned to the side, showing his striking profile. Strands of hair stuck to his bloody forehead and a puddle of red was quickly spreading around his head, trickling from his head wound. I could see his chest rising and falling. My eyes searched our surroundings. The car of the Russians was already a flaming mess, dark plummets of smoke rising into the sky. We were in the middle of nowhere, an abandoned industrial area nobody set foot in without reason. But the smoke would certainly attract attention. Somebody would find Matteo before it was too late.

Right?

I should run. I should *want* to run. I started backing away from Matteo's unmoving form on the ground, ignoring the way guilt corded up my throat. He'd forced me into a marriage I'd never wanted. He knew I would use the first chance I got to escape. I took another step back. Matteo had chosen a path of danger and death. Even if he died today, it was what he'd chosen for himself.

This wasn't the life I wanted.

I turned around, then paused. I closed my eyes. Distantly flames crackled. Someone would find Matteo in time. And even if they didn't, I shouldn't care.

I didn't care about him. I *didn't*. And I definitely *shouldn't*.

I should hate him. I should hate what he was and what it meant for me. I should that he couldn't give me up no matter how often I pushed him away. Why couldn't he give up?

I started walking away, one small step after the other. Once I was out of town, I would call Aria and ask her about Matteo.

It will be too late for him then.

Maybe.

Or maybe not.

Matteo was tough. A head wound wouldn't kill him.

I chanced a look over my shoulder, my eyes finding Matteo's unmoving body, sprawled out on the concrete. Behind him the cars were burning, tinge-ing the illuminated city sky black with their smoke.

Funeral black.

The pool of blood around Matteo's head looked black from my vantage point, and it had grown even more. "I don't want to love you," I whispered as I jerked to a halt, clenching my eyes shut. But I did. I did love Matteo.

My eyes flew open, I whirled around and began walking back, then started running, getting faster and faster, until I was racing. I dropped to my knees beside Matteo, fumbling in my pockets for my phone but coming up empty. It was in my bag. My gaze went to the burning car where I'd left my stuff. Stupid Gianna.

I reached into Matteo's pocket and exhaled a shuddering breath when I grabbed his phone. Not wasting time scrolling through his contact I hit speed dial.

"I'm not in the mood to talk to you, Matteo. You acted like a major ass-hole tonight," Luca's sharp voice rang in my ear.

I let out a sob.

"Gianna?" I could hear Aria in the background but couldn't hear what she was saying.

"He's dying," I said after a moment, sounding flat and voiceless.

"What are you talking about? Give me Matteo."

"I can't. Russians attacked us. There's so much blood, Luca, so much blood."

"Is Matteo alive?" For the first time since Aria almost died, Luca sounded worried.

My eyes darted to the body beside me. To my husband.

Was it my imagination or had Matteo's chest stopped moving? I pressed my palm against his blood-soaked shirt. There was nothing. "He's not breathing. He was a moment ago, but he's not anymore." Hysteria found its way into my voice.

"Gianna, you have to do CPR. I'll be there soon. I have your GPS coordinates. But you'll have to get him breathing or it'll be too late."

I didn't say anything, only stared at the man I loved. I'd wanted to hate him, had given it my all, and in the beginning there had been hate, so much of it, but not all of it had been directed at Matteo, and now hardly any seemed left, and it felt ridiculous to hold onto what little I still harbored.

"Gianna?" Luca's voice sliced right through me. I could hear commotion in the background, the sound of a car springing to life. I put Luca on loudspeaker and cupped Matteo's face, then pressed my lips against his and blew air into his lungs. I tried to remember how often to press as I rested my hands against his rib cage. I didn't know the first thing about CPR except for what I'd seen on TV. Why had I never paid better attention? What if Matteo died because I was doing something wrong?

Luca's next words tore through my thoughts. I'd forgotten he was on the phone. "I know you feel like Matteo trapped you, that he ruined your life, but no matter what you think, he didn't do it to make you miserable. For some unexplainable reason Matteo loves you. You don't have to believe me. You can keep hating him but don't leave him alone, not now. If you help me save his life, I'll grant you freedom. I swear it on my honor and my life. Aria is here. She's witness. You will get money, a new identity and even protection from the Outfit if you want. It's all yours if you save his life."

"Okay," I said as I pressed down on Matteo's chest again. I wasn't even sure why I said it.

"You have to do chest compressions. Hard and fast. Don't worry about breaking his ribs. Thirty pushes, two breathes. *Fast.*"

I sped up my compressions, then bent over Matteo to breathe into his mouth twice. "He's not reacting!" I gasped as I started everything from the beginning.

"Keep doing it."

And I did, even as my fingers cramped. They were red and sticky with blood. I couldn't even see through my eyes anymore. They were blurry with tears. Why couldn't I stop crying? I cried over a man like Matteo but had hardly shed a tear over Sid.

"We'll be there in ten minutes," Luca said. "How's Matteo?"

I didn't reply. I pushed harder against Matteo's chest and then he drew in a shallow breath. I froze, almost scared I'd imagined it. I quickly leaned over his face and felt the gentle breeze of his breath against my cheek. I brushed shaky fingers over his throat, finding his pulse. It wasn't as fast and strong as usual, but it was there. I closed my eyes for a moment, squeezed a few annoying tears away and then I opened them. I sank down on my butt and stretched out my legs. I wanted to cradle Matteo's head in my lap but worried about hurting his neck, so I merely rested my palm against his chest to reassure myself of his steady heartbeat. His blood was starting to soak my pants but I was beyond caring.

"Gianna? Are you still there?"

"Yes. Matteo is breathing again."

There was a pause. "Good," Luca said quietly. "Stay where you are."

"Don't worry." I tilted my head back and stared up at the sky littered with stars and hazy with smoke. The gentle rise and fall of Matteo's chest was almost like a lullaby and my eyes started to droop. My headache had gotten even worse. I probably had a concussion.

The roar of an engine made me turn my head. Two cars were racing in our direction. The one in the front was Luca's Aston Martin and the one in the back belonged to his crony Romero. I quickly pulled my hand away from Matteo's chest and rose to my feet, even as my vision swam.

The Aston stopped with fuming tires and Luca jumped out. He stormed toward Matteo, barely sparing me a glance as he knelt beside his brother and felt his throat. He did a quick scan of Matteo's injuries and then Romero and Sandro were already beside him.

Someone touched my shoulder and then Aria appeared in my field of vision. She wrapped her arms around me and I sagged against her, feeling drained. "Are you hurt?"

"Maybe. Probably. I don't know."

"Get her away," Luca said. "Take my car and drive her to our apartment."

I pulled back to look down at him. "Where are you taking Matteo?"

"To the hospital. This is too serious for our doc," he said, then smiled coldly. "Don't worry. I'll honor my promise. When I return to the apartment, we'll make the necessary arrangements to ensure your freedom." His eyes were hard. I had a feeling he wouldn't have minded much if I'd died in the crash.

"Maybe Gianna wants to go to the hospital with Matteo," Aria suggested softly as Luca and Sandro lifted Matteo carefully and carried him over to the jeep. Romero was talking to soldiers on the phone, making arrangements to keep the police out of this.

"She doesn't," Luca said firmly. "Help her gather her things from Matteo's apartment, so we can get her settled in her new life before my brother returns home."

Why didn't I protest? Why couldn't I admit my feelings even now?

Aria gave me a searching look but I shrugged, ignoring the heat behind my eyeballs and the tight feeling in my chest as I watched them take Matteo away. "We can follow them in our car," she whispered.

I swallowed, then shook my head. "No. Luca's right. I need to pack up my things."

Frowning, but without protest, Aria led me toward the Aston Martin.

Matteo

Every inch of my body hurt and my head felt like it was filled with cotton. Groaning, I tried to open my fucking eyes, which seemed to be glued shut. Resisting the urge to peel them open with my fingernails, I slowly opened them a tiny bit, then finally fully. Luca was sitting in a chair next to my bed. A fucking hospital bed. "Don't tell me you took me to a fucking hospital?" I rasped, then coughed. Fuck. I felt like death warmed over.

Luca leaned forward, a wry smile on his face. Did he have to look so damn worried? I wasn't a kid who needed his protection anymore. "Now that you're swearing again, I'll consider moving you to my penthouse. Romero is already looking forward to playing nurse."

I was reaching for the needle in the back of my hand to pull it out but paused when his words sunk in. "Your penthouse?"

"You'll need to rest a few days. And I know you, so there needs to be someone to keep an eye on you."

He was watching me carefully. As if he was trying to gauge if I could take the bad news. "Did something happen to Gianna?"

"No. She's fine." He paused.

"Spit it out. Damn it!"

"I made a deal with her."

"Stop fucking around. Tell me the fucking truth. I can take it."

"When she called me, you weren't breathing. I was worried she'd use her chance to run."

"My life against her freedom," I said with a dark laugh.

"She agreed. Now she's home with Aria, packing her bags."

"We need to protect her from the Outfit. Her father won't accept it."

"You want to protect her?" Luca asked incredulously.

"She's still my wife. And I'll protect her as long as she'll let me."

"She'll leave as soon as I've set everything up. You better forget about her sooner than later."

I glared. "Would you just forget Aria because someone told you to?"

"Aria wouldn't need bribing to save my fucking life."

I jerked the needle out of my hand and sucked the blood away that welled up before I swung my legs out of the bed, despite my splitting headache. My eyes scanned the table beside my bed for my knives and my gun holster. They weren't there. Damn it. I felt fucking naked without them.

"Fuck," Luca muttered. The bastard grabbed my shoulders to stop me from standing. "I didn't mean to get you all riled up. You're supposed to stay in bed."

"I don't give a damn. I'm not a fucking toddler. Stop patronizing me. I've dealt with worse shit than a headache." I shrugged his hands off and slid off the edge of the bed. Big mistake. The moment my bare feet hit the floor, I swayed. Luca steadied me. With a groan, I sank back down on the bed. "What did they give me? I feel as if someone put roofies in my drink."

Luca gave me his most patronizing expression. "I told you to stay in bed."

"Shut up." I blinked a few times. It did nothing to banish the dots from my vision. "I want to get the hell out of here. I'm fine."

"You're fine when I tell you. I'm your Capo."

I opened the drawer in the bedside table, but my weapons weren't in there either. "Where are my knives?"

"In the car. I could hardly roll you into the hospital armed to the teeth."

I clenched my jaw, then pushed myself to my feet again. This time I hardly swayed at all.

Luca glowered at me. "Goddammit, Matteo. Why can't you listen for once?"

"Don't give me that bullshit. If our situations were switched, you'd be out of the fucking hospital already." He didn't bother denying it. I knew him. "Let's go."

Luca thrust a bag at me. "Sandro picked up a few clothes for you. The ones you were wearing during the crash have to be burnt."

I got out of the embarrassing hospital gown and slipped into clean jeans. "What about underwear? Maybe Sandro likes it if his junk jiggles around in his pants, but I prefer another barrier between my balls and the zipper."

Luca snorted. "I wonder what it will take to shut your big mouth. Almost getting killed and having your wife leave your sorry ass obviously isn't enough."

I stopped buttoning my shirt. I knew he was joking. And he was right. Nothing ever got me down. Not when our mother died, not when Father beat the crap out of me, not when I was bleeding like a pig. Then why the fuck did mentioning Gianna feel like a fucking punch to the gut? Damn it. I was turning into a pussy. I sent Luca a forced grin, but he was already scrutinizing me with a frown.

"Don't tell me you're so eager to get out of the hospital because you hope to walk across Gianna and talk her into staying with you. She won't. The selfish bitch wants freedom."

I stalked toward him, getting right in his face. "Don't call her a bitch." Then I fucking swayed and had to grab Luca's shoulder to stop myself from making a faceplant. So much for being threatening. Damn it.

Luca only stared.

"I swear if you don't stop giving me that fucking pitying look I'm going to beat you to a bloody pulp," I muttered.

"I don't pity you. Pity is for people who got into a bad situation with no fault of their own, but you chose Gianna. You saw how volatile and fucking annoying she was and you still wanted her. You were turned on by her bitchiness. You got yourself into this mess. Now you have to deal."

"Cold-hearted bastard," I said, glad he didn't try to console me.

Luca smirked. "Always."

I shoved my shirt into my jeans and slipped into my shoes. "Sandro is a fucking asshole. No socks either? Is he a nudist or what?"

"He probably thinks you are."

I headed for the door, trying to walk as tall as possible despite my wobbly legs. Luca walked too close. He probably thought he might need to catch me if I fainted. "Stop hovering. People will think you're my sugar daddy."

Luca ignored my comment. "What do you remember before you woke up?"

Back to business, thank God. "A bunch of cock-sucking Russians chased Gianna and me. I got rid of the first car pretty quick. A bullet between the brows got rid of the driver and the resulting crash of the other fuckers. The second car was more trouble. I don't remember what happened to them."

"They burnt in their car. Charcoal all of them."

"What about my car?"

"Charcoal."

"Great."

"Could have been worse. You didn't look good when I first saw you."

I reached for the tender spot on top of my head. A few nurses watched us as we passed them, but they didn't stop us. Luca had probably already settled everything in advance.

"You're lucky they didn't shave your entire head. Knowing how vain you are, you wouldn't have stopped bitching about it."

"You know how to cheer me up," I said.

Luca was busy texting someone. He barely glanced up.

"You're warning Aria that we're coming, aren't you?" I couldn't help but wonder if Gianna was still with Aria, if they were making plans for Gianna's future without me. Luca had offered Gianna freedom on a golden platter. She'd be stupid not to go through with it. A life away from the mafia was something she'd always wanted. Away from me. She'd finally get her wish.

Luca spared me the barest glance. "It's for the best, believe me."

Annoyance zipped through me. Luca had always tried to dictate my life—look out for me as he called it—and it had only gotten worse since he was also my Capo. "I can handle Gianna. I'm not a pussy, Luca. I won't break down and cry because my wife wants to run as far away from me as possible."

"I know." He stuffed his phone back into his jacket. Of course I knew he'd already told Aria everything she needed to know.

We arrived at Luca's car. He opened the door for me. "Don't think I'll put out just because you're being a gentleman," I told him as I half fell into the seat. I hoped Luca thought I had done it on purpose and not because my legs had gone on strike.

"Don't worry. Your back door is safe." Luca shut the door in my face before he rounded the car and slipped behind the steering wheel. He started the car and slid out of the parking lot. "Do you want me to organize someone who can distract you? Maybe not today because of your head. But in the next couple of days."

I snorted out a laugh. "You mean a hooker?"

Luca gave a one-shoulder shrug, not taking his eyes off the street. He had his poker face on and it annoyed the crap out of me, because I wasn't sure if this was a test or if he was being serious. A few years ago, I'd have said he was dead serious. Luca had never had trouble moving from one woman to the next, but that had been before Aria.

"First of all, I might have a concussion but I'm not dead, and that means

I don't need a pity fuck. If I want a woman, I can find one myself and don't need to pay someone."

"You haven't seen yourself in the mirror yet."

I checked my reflection in the rearview mirror. "Okay. Maybe I'd have more trouble than usual." I had two black eyes, both of them swollen and bloodshot, and there was a bluish lump below my hairline. Not to mention that my hair was a matted mess.

"You'll scare the shit out of every woman you approach."

"So what? It always worked for you."

Luca chuckled. "So is that a no?"

"A big fat one. I don't want to fuck anyone but..." Realizing the fucking trap I'd just walked in I snapped my mouth shut. Damn it.

"You're not going to give her up, are you?" Luca said in a resigned tone.

"No."

"I swore on my honor to grant her freedom but I can break my promise if that's what you want. It's not like I haven't done worse before."

"No. I don't want you to break your oath. And it would only make her hate me more. You can't force Gianna to do anything. She needs to come back to me freely. That's the only way."

Luca shook his head. "Matteo, even you must realize how futile it is to hope for that. She'll run and never come back. Are you willing to risk that?"

"Yes."

"Then you're a better man than I am. I would never let Aria go."

I glared out of the window. It sounded easy: letting her go, giving her the chance to find her way back to me, but I wasn't sure I could go through with it. I wasn't better than Luca. But I was a hunter and sometimes a chase was useless, sometimes you had to wait for the prey to come to you. I wasn't a patient hunter, but this time I would try.

chapter *twenty*

Gianna

Aria kept throwing glances my way, her pale brows drawn together in concern. "Are you sure you don't need to see the doc?"

"I'm fine, really," I snapped, then felt bad for it. Aria was always on my side. She'd done so much for me in the last year, even gone against Luca. "Sorry. I'm exhausted." The smell of smoke and blood lingered in my nose, a vivid echo of the earlier events.

"It's okay. You've gone through a lot," Aria said gently.

My thoughts drifted back to Matteo. I hoped he'd be fine. He was tough, but he'd lost a lot of blood. Maybe I should have let Aria drive me to the hospital to make sure he was alright. I wanted to be with him, wanted to be there when he woke and hold his hand while he was unconscious. I wanted to tell him that I was tired of the games, tired of pretending that I didn't care for him, when I'd already lost my heart to him. It was futile trying to lie to myself. I knew I'd come to love Matteo, even his arrogance and shark-smile. He was still a bad man, a murderer and criminal, but I knew now that I wasn't much better. I had no doubt that I would have been like Matteo if I'd been raised like him and not sheltered from life like all the women in our world. It was an ugly truth, one I'd prefer to deny, but it was the truth, and it was time to admit it and own up to the life I was obviously meant to live. The words lay on the tip of my tongue.

"You can take a quick shower, and then I'll help you pack everything."

"Oh, sure," I said distractedly. Pride had always been my problem, even now when I knew it was only hurting me, and Matteo.

Aria glanced my way. "Luca will keep his word. You don't have to worry. He's never broken his promise. And he knows I'd never forgive him if he'd lied. You'll be free."

Free? What was freedom worth if it meant ignoring what my heart wanted? "I know."

"You don't look happy."

I wasn't happy. But why? For months I'd wished for nothing more than to figure out a way out of this marriage, out of this life, out of this world, and now that I finally got my wish, I didn't feel anything. How could I have been lying to myself for so long? And why couldn't I admit it, especially not to the outside world? Why did it feel as if admitting I loved Matteo was the ultimate defeat? "I'm still recovering from the crash. That's all," I said on autopilot. I wondered how long that lie would work.

Aria didn't look convinced but she didn't push the matter. I leaned my head against the window and closed my eyes, not in the mood for conversation. I needed to sort through my emotions as soon as possible, but the splitting headache definitely wasn't making it an easy feat.

I must have dozed off because suddenly Aria was nudging me awake and we were parked in the underground garage. She gave me an encouraging smile, and for some reason it made me feel horrible. I quickly scrambled out of the car, unable to meet Aria's compassionate gaze. I rushed toward the elevator, a few times almost tripping over my feet. Aria caught up with me and called the elevator down with a press of the button. "What's the rush? You don't have to worry that Matteo will come home while we're still packing. They'll probably keep him in the hospital overnight. He looked really bad."

I leaned against the cool wall of the elevator. Did Aria really think that would cheer me up? Was I such a horrible bitch that people thought I'd be happy that someone was seriously injured?

Of course they did. Luca had thought he had to offer me a ticket to freedom so I didn't let his brother die. I was nothing but a heartless, selfish bitch in his mind. And judging from Aria's words, she agreed with him.

My throat corded up. Maybe they were right. "I'm not worried," I said calmly. It was easier to play the part they all expected me to play.

Aria nodded, but she didn't stop watching me. We were leaning across from each other and I could see my reflection behind her in the mirror. We couldn't have been more different. Aria with her kind expression, angel-like hair, porcelain skin. and baby-blue eyes; the epitome of pureness. And I looked like I'd risen from hell with my messy red hair, blood-covered clothes and skin, and dark shadows under my eyes. When we stepped into the apartment that I'd shared with Matteo since our wedding, I quickly rushed into the master bedroom, and from there into the adjoining bathroom. Maybe a quick shower would help me get a grip on my heart. Luca's offer was my last chance, I knew that. If I followed my heart instead and stayed with Matteo, then that would be it. I had to let my brain make this decision.

After my shower, I still didn't feel better but at least I'd made up my mind. Aria was sitting on the bed, typing on her phone, when I entered the bedroom.

"Did Luca tell you about Matteo?" I asked immediately, my throat already tightening and panic flooding me. I should have gone with Matteo. Suddenly I couldn't breathe.

"He's doing fine. Apparently it's only a concussion and a few cracked ribs." She finally looked up and quickly walked over to me. "You look pale."

I swallowed. Matteo would be fine. Slowly my panic settled down.

"You are really worried about him, aren't you? Why don't you admit it? You can trust me, Gianna, you know that."

"Of course I worry. I'm not made from stone. I don't want anything to happen to him. I care about him, believe it or not."

"But not enough to stay?" Aria asked.

I wasn't sure what to say. All my well-laid plans in the shower seemed to crumble before me again. "I need to lie down for a while, I think. Or do we have to leave soon?"

Aria shook her head. "No, Luca will take Matteo to our penthouse when he wakes, so you won't cross his path if you stay here. And it's late anyway. Catch some sleep."

I grabbed clean clothes and put them on before I lay down on top of the covers. I could hear Aria closing the door and then silence reigned around me.

It was already light out when I woke. I was alone in the bedroom. I quickly scrambled off the bed and left the room, half expecting to find Matteo in the kitchen. He wasn't.

Aria was there. She typed something into her phone before handing me a cup of coffee. "How do you feel?"

"Where's Matteo? Is he okay? Is he still in the hospital?"

"He's fine. He's in the penthouse, sleeping off his concussion."

"Oh, right. He's at your place. That makes sense."

"Gianna, you don't have to leave, you realize that, right? It's okay to stay with Matteo."

I stared at her. It was okay, wasn't it? Okay to love a man like him, okay to accept life in the mob.

The elevator stopped with a bling and Luca walked out, his cold gaze settling on me. I had to suppress a shiver. That was what hatred looked like, and I supposed he had every reason to hate me. Sandro was a couple of steps behind him like a good lapdog.

"I hope your bags are packed. I want you out of this apartment as soon as possible."

"Luca," Aria hissed. "That's not fair."

For once she couldn't warm his cold heart. "No. That bitch needs to get as far away from my brother as possible. I want her gone. She's been ruining his life for long enough."

I glared, but deep down I wondered if he was right. Of course, I'd never admit it. "I know you think Matteo deserves better than me. But let me tell you one thing. Aria deserves better too. She's too good and pure and kind for you. You aren't even worth the dirt under her shoes. She's too loving and nice to see it, but I do. You think I destroyed Matteo's life, but I never got a choice in the matter. I didn't want to marry him. You on the other hand chose to marry Aria. You chose to destroy her life with your darkness. So get down from your high horse, you bastard. You don't deserve her and never will."

Aria's knuckles turned white from her grip on Luca's wrist. He could have shaken her off with ease but he didn't move. "I know," he said in a steely voice. "But the difference between you and me is that I'm trying to be a better man for her. But you never tried. You were always content with being a bitch."

Aria gasped. "Luca, please."

"No. He's right. I'm a bitch, and I'm leaving now. Tell Matteo goodbye from me." Wow, spoken like a true bitch. It was too late to take the words back, and I knew I would be too prideful to do it anyway. I took two of my bags that Aria must have carried down before I'd woken, and headed for Sandro who picked up my other bags and followed me toward the elevator. I stepped inside and faced Aria and Luca, my head held high. Luca's gaze was unrestrained hate, but Aria was crying. She was pleading me with her eyes and eventually I couldn't take it anymore and lowered my gaze to the floor. The doors slid shut and the elevator started moving. Sandro didn't try to make conversation. Every look he gave me spoke of disapproval. I wondered if Luca would have had me killed if it weren't for Aria.

Sandro drove me to a hotel where I would stay until I'd found an apartment. I wasn't even sure if I would stay in New York. Returning to Chicago was definitely out of the question. I'd be dead within a week.

"Here. That's five thousand dollars. Luca will contact you with more details soon," Sandro said as he parked in front of the hotel. A doorman opened my door. Sandro didn't follow me as I got out of the car, only gave the doorman information about the reservation. The moment the doorman had lifted my luggage out of the trunk, Sandro drove off, leaving me alone. I stared after the car. Nobody was watching me. I was free.

Then why did freedom feel like my new prison?

Matteo

"I don't think this is a good idea," Luca muttered as he followed me into my apartment.

"This is my home. I'm not an invalid. I won't have another sleepover at your place," I said. I was still feeling fucking dizzy but I wasn't going to admit it to Luca. I walked into my bedroom, Luca close behind me. If he didn't stop it soon, I'd kick his ass.

I stopped in the middle of the room. The drawers were ajar. I didn't have to look into them to know they were empty.

"She moved out this morning," Luca said.

"I know."

I could feel Luca's eyes on me. "You should stay with Aria and me. It's almost Christmas. Do you want to spend the holidays sulking?"

"I don't care about Christmas. And I'm not sulking. I'm supposed to rest, remember?" I pointed at my head, then walked over to the bed and lay down. "And I don't want you to watch me while I sleep."

"You will have dinner with Aria and me tonight. I don't care if I have to drag you into my penthouse, but you will be there."

I nodded. "Let me sleep."

He finally left. Of course there was no way I could sleep. My eyes darted toward the dressing room with its empty shelves. Gianna was really gone, and this time I wasn't going to hunt her.

chapter *twenty-one*

Gianna

I stared out of the window of my hotel room. It was dinnertime but I wasn't hungry. I hadn't left the room since I'd checked in this morning. Did freedom always feel this lonely?

My phone beeped with a message. It was from Aria.

Matteo broke down again. He's unconscious.

I called her immediately, my heart hammering in my chest. She picked up after the first ring. "Where is he?" I asked.

"At our place. He's in the guest bedroom. The doc says he needs to stay in bed. He overexerted himself too soon after the crash."

"I'm coming over."

"You are?" Aria asked in a hopeful voice.

"Yes. Tell Luca he should get used to my presence again."

I could practically hear Aria smiling. "I knew it." She paused. "I'll send Sandro over."

"No, I'm taking a cab. I'll be there soon."

When I arrived in the apartment, Luca barred my way. "What is she doing here?"

"I want to see Matteo," I said. And I didn't care if I had to knock out Luca to do it.

Luca glared. "Get the fuck away."

"Luca, please," Aria whispered.

I tried to walk past Luca but he didn't let me. "Let me see my husband."

"Matteo can't use the emotional stress right now. You leaving and then returning won't help with his recovery," Luca growled. I had a feeling his words would have been much worse if Aria weren't standing beside him. "If you stay now, you'll stay for good. I'm done with your games."

"I'm not leaving again."

Luca sent me a doubtful look but he stepped back. I didn't hesitate. I rushed toward the guest bedroom and stormed inside. Matteo was asleep. I lay down beside him, determined to keep watch over him until he opened his eyes.

Matteo

A soft hand held onto mine. I opened my eyes, blinking a few times to clear my vision. I felt like a total wimp for having passed out. Fuck. I'd been shot and stabbed and even burnt before, and a stupid hit to the head brought me down to my knees. It was a disgrace. I turned my head. Gianna was curled up beside me, her hand clutching mine. Her clothes were wrinkly and her hair a complete mess as if she'd been at my side for a while.

Her face was mostly covered by her unruly hair. I felt the irresistible urge to see her expression. Slowly, carefully I sat up and brushed a few strands away with my free hand. Gianna looked like a fucking angel in sleep. Too beautiful to be real. Her thick lashes rested on her pale skin. I trailed a fingertip over her high cheekbone, enjoying the softness of her skin. Her eyes fluttered beneath her lids and then they peeled open. She blinked sleepily until her gaze finally focused on me.

I waited for her to let go of my hand and jump off the bed like it had caught fire. At the very least I expected some ridiculous excuse for why she was here, holding my hand. I doubted Luca had dragged her back. He knew I didn't want him to.

She didn't do any of those things however. Instead she sat up slowly, blinking away sleep and rubbing her eyes with the hand that wasn't holding mine. She searched the room for something. "What time is it?"

I had no fucking clue. I wasn't even sure what day it was. "You are asking me?"

She laughed once, then her expression tightened. "You scared me."

"I did? I suppose I'm a scary guy."

Gianna didn't smile. She was looking at me with an expression I'd never seen on her face, vulnerable and open. "I should have never agreed to Luca's offer. I was being stubborn. I didn't want to admit my feelings to myself. But when Aria called to tell me you'd broken down again, I was terrified that I'd lose you." She paused, her fingers on my hand tightening. I didn't say anything, wasn't sure what to say. My general solution in emotional situations was humor but it felt wrong to make a joke and I didn't want to stop Gianna from saying whatever else she had to say.

She stared off toward the window, guilt marring her beautiful face. "All I could think about when I wasn't at your side after you'd broken down was 'what if you die and all I've ever done was treat you badly and push you away.' I've been acting like a major bitch. I'm sorry."

I touched her cheek and moved closer. "You don't need to apologize for anything, Gianna. I actually enjoyed most of our arguments. They added entertainment to my days." I grinned and this time I got a smile in return.

"You should be pissed, Matteo. You know what Luca offered me in exchange for saving your life and that I agreed. Why aren't you sending me away? I would deserve it."

I shrugged. I didn't like the idea that Gianna had eagerly accepted Luca's offer, but she was here now. It had taken a while but eventually I'd realized that Gianna had to come to me on her own. Gianna would never let anyone force her to admit her feelings. I touched the back of her head and pulled her toward me. She didn't resist and when her mouth touched mine, she wrapped her arms around my neck and deepened our kiss. My hand found its way under her shirt, feeling the soft skin of her stomach and moving higher.

Gianna stopped my hand's exploration. "You need to rest. You passed out yesterday. I won't let you overexert yourself again."

I chuckled. "Come on. If you ride me, I won't have to exert myself at all. You'll do all the work."

"Yeah, right," she said. "No way am I going to risk your recovery. Luca would be so pissed if I did something stupid. He hates me anyway. I don't want to give him another reason to keep me away from you."

"Luca wouldn't stop you from seeing me."

She raised her eyebrows. "He tried to stop me from coming here yesterday."

"Why the fuck did he do that?" Annoyance shot through me. Luca always had to play the Capo and order people around.

"I suppose he was worried about you," Gianna admitted grudgingly. There was no love lost between my brother and her, so I was surprised by her admittance. "He didn't want me to play with you. He thought it was better if there was a clean cut between us and I left your life for good."

"So what made him change his mind?" I asked.

"Aria, I suppose."

"Of course," I said, though I'd hoped for another reason. I leaned back against the headboard, ignoring the slight twinge in my head at the movement. I crossed my arms over my chest, trying to look fucking relaxed when I was anything but. "I'm fine now. I won't die. You could leave now without feeling guilty."

Gianna looked at me for a long time without saying anything. "I don't want to leave."

"You agreed to Luca's offer, you said it yourself."

"I did, because Luca took me by surprise with it. You were dying right in front of me. We'd barely survived a crash and the crazy Russians, and suddenly I was offered something I'd thought I wanted. I didn't even really think before I said yes."

I nodded, but didn't say anything. I was tired of making the first move, of always pursuing Gianna. This time I wanted to hear something from her.

She sighed, her blue eyes tired. "You think I would have let you die if Luca hadn't offered me a ticket to freedom, don't you? That's what everyone thinks, probably even Aria."

I kept my expression neutral. "Isn't it the truth?"

She glared. "No, it's not the truth. When Luca mentioned his stupid offer, I had already started chest compressions. I didn't know what I was doing and probably made every mistake possible, but I wasn't just letting you die. I was doing everything I could even before Luca offered me freedom for your life. I would have never let you die, never. I know you don't have to believe me. There's no reason why you should. I could be lying for all you know."

But I did believe her. I knew how to read people and Gianna wasn't lying. I could tell how upset she was, more upset than I'd seen her in a long time. "I don't think you are."

Gianna didn't even seem to hear me. She was scowling in the direction of the window, her cheeks flushed with emotions. "I knew the moment I saw you lying in your own blood that I didn't want to lose you. I knew it, but I still didn't want to admit it to anyone. I was so stupid and stubborn. I was being bitchy Gianna like usual. And once I'd agreed to Luca's offer, I was too proud to tell him that I didn't even want his stupid freedom. I didn't want to leave you, didn't want another life. I probably would have been miserable alone but too proud to admit it if you hadn't broken down. It felt like I was giving up, like I was admitting defeat, which is so idiotic. How can love ever be a defeat?" She fell silent, eyes widening.

I had become very still, like a hunter who didn't want to startle its prey.

She licked her lips nervously. I wished I knew what she was thinking, but I had a feeling I knew. She was probably regretting ever bringing up the "L-word" and everything else that had bubbled out of her. That was who she was. Maybe she was waiting for me to say something first, to tell her I loved her, but I wasn't going to open my fucking heart to her and risk her stomping on it. I knew what I was feeling, had known it for a long time but I'd never said it to her. I'd never said it to anyone. Admitting something like that made you vulnerable and so far Gianna had given me little reason to risk that. I'd hunted her long enough. Now was her turn. I wouldn't push her in either direction. Everything from this point on would have to come from her.

"Luca's offer still stands. You are a free woman. You can walk out of this building and nobody will stop you."

"No," she said firmly. "I've run from my emotions for too long." She braced herself on her palms and leaned forward. "I want to be with you, Matteo. By God, I know I shouldn't want it, but it doesn't matter anymore. I'm sick of ignoring my heart. I love you."

She kissed me almost desperately, her hands finding their way into my hair. My head was still tender but I'd have rather cut my own throat than told Gianna to be careful. I wanted to feel her lips, her fingers, her body. I wanted all of her. "You sure you mean it?" I asked in a teasing voice when she pulled back.

She nodded. "Yes. There's no fucking doubt in my mind. I love you, Matteo. I don't care what that makes me. I don't care what other people think about me, about us. I don't even care what Aria and Luca think. All I care about is us."

I kissed her again. I'd never get enough of tasting her. "I love you, Gianna. I've fucking loved you for a long time."

Gianna

Hearing Matteo say that he loved me set my heart aflame. I couldn't remember the last time I'd felt so happy. I'd thought admitting my feelings to anyone would give that person more power over me, but instead I felt freer than I had in a long time. I'd fought my emotions for so long, had held myself back for no good reason. Now that I'd said everything that needed to be said I felt relieved. Maybe all this had started as something that had been forced upon me, but today, this life, Matteo, my marriage, were my choices, and I said yes to all of them.

Matteo's kiss was demanding. There was no restraint, no sign that not too long ago he'd been unconscious. I knew it was stupid, but I wanted to feel him, wanted to show him with more than just words that I loved him. I pulled back and let my eyes wander down Matteo's body. He was dressed in only a tight white shirt and boxer shorts that did little to hide his erection. When I looked back up into his face, his gaze was transparent with lust. I'd never listened to other people's advice, so why should I start now?

Matteo wouldn't overexert himself. I would take care of him. I knelt on the bed, and gripped his waistband. Matteo smiled his shark-smile. "I thought you didn't want to risk my health."

"Oh shut up," I said quietly. "Or do you want me to stop?"

"No. Don't stop." He made himself comfortable against the array of pillows.

I smiled as I pulled down his boxer shorts, revealing his hard length. I moved between his legs so I could watch him while I sucked his cock. I cupped his balls, gently massaging them, but I didn't touch his shaft yet. Instead I watched it twitch and grow even harder under my ministrations.

"You tease," Matteo growled. "I thought you wouldn't torture me today."

He was right. This wasn't about me. I leaned forward and ran my tongue all the way from his balls up to the top, then swirled it around his tip before sucking him into my mouth. I took inch after inch of him in until he hit the back of my throat before I let him slide out again. Matteo watched me through half-lidded eyes. He gently pulled my hair back, which always got in the way, and stroked my cheeks as I licked and sucked his tip, knowing that it was where he was most sensitive. I traced the tip of my tongue along the ridge of his tip slowly. Matteo's breathing quickened, his abs tightened but he didn't take his eyes off me or stop touching my face. It felt like he was revering me while I was revering him.

I sucked a bit harder, feeling him getting closer. His fingers against my scalp tightened occasionally and he released a harsh breath every time my teeth scraped him lightly. He started pumping his hips, pushing his length deeper into my mouth and I let him. I was growing wet and the pressure between my legs had mounted to almost unbearable proportions but I was determined to ignore my own needs for today.

Matteo's motions grew frantic. I clamped my lips tightly around his cock as he thrust into me over and over again. "I'm coming," he rasped. I didn't pull back. Instead I cupped his balls tightly and met his gaze. The muscles in his shoulders flexed and his body seized up with his orgasm. Eventually he stilled. I pulled back and wiped my mouth with a self-satisfied grin.

Matteo chuckled, a low sound from deep in his chest. He reached for my shoulders and pulled me on top of him, claiming my mouth in a firm kiss. His hands glided down my back to cup my butt and squeezed. My core tightened with arousal. Before I could make up my mind, if I should allow Matteo to exert himself even more, a knock sounded. I tensed, my eyes darting toward the door, which was already opening.

Luca stood in the doorway, his gaze taking everything in without an expression. It wasn't hard to guess what we'd done. After all, I was lying on top of a bottomless Matteo who was groping my butt.

My face flamed with embarrassment.

"You really shouldn't barge into someone's bedroom like that," Matteo said in amusement. He didn't look embarrassed at all, but after everything I knew about him that didn't surprise me anymore.

I stayed exactly the way I was, even though Matteo wouldn't have cared if I'd moved away and bared his cock to his brother.

"You should be resting," Luca said dryly, gray eyes piercing me with an unreadable look. Was he angry? It was hard to tell. Recently he'd always been pissed around me. Not that his presence made me much happier.

Matteo gave my butt a firm pat, his grin turning annoyingly smug. "I feel very well rested."

Luca shook his head. "I give up," he said. "You two do whatever you want. I don't even want to know what's going on or not going on." He turned around and closed the door behind him.

I pushed away from Matteo and slid off the bed, trying my best to straighten my wrinkled clothes, but now there were also stains on them. They were an absolute mess.

"Hey, I thought we weren't done yet. I didn't even get to touch your pussy."

"And you won't. Luca was right. You should rest. You've had enough excitement for the day," I said sternly. Matteo was already growing hard again and he didn't bother to hide it.

I huffed. "I'm going to change and clean up, and then return with something to eat for you. In the meantime, please pull your mind out of the gutter."

Matteo winked. I stifled a smile and slipped out of the room. Aria and Luca were in the dining area, talking in hushed voices. Of course, I knew exactly what they were discussing.

Aria noticed me first and fell silent. After a couple of seconds of silent scrutiny, she smiled brightly at me. Luca didn't share her enthusiasm though. I ignored him. "Could you give me some of your clothes? I really need to change and shower."

Luca raised his eyebrows. "Do you need to make yourself presentable so you can leave?"

I met his gaze. "I'm not leaving. Not ever again."

Aria was practically bouncing when she stepped up to me and linked our arms.

"We'll see," Luca said simply. Aria shot him a glare before she led me upstairs toward their dressing room.

"Don't listen to him. He's protective of Matteo," Aria murmured. She pulled jeans and a long-sleeved shirt from her drawers and handed them to me.

Luca's protectiveness of Aria and Matteo was one of the few things I liked about him. "I know. I haven't given him any reason to trust me with his brother."

Aria watched me curiously as I undressed. "So will you move back into Matteo's apartment?"

I paused on my way to the bathroom. It wasn't as if I had already settled somewhere else. I hadn't even started considering where to live after I'd moved out. "Yes. I will move back in and be his wife. Probably not a good wife, but it's not like Matteo didn't know that when he married me."

"Matteo doesn't expect you to be a perfect wife. He likes you for who you are, flaws and all."

It was the truth, even if I'd been blind to it for so long. I stepped into the shower but didn't immediately turn the water on.

Aria sank down on the edge of the bathtub. "Are you sure you can do the same? Accept all of him, even the bad?"

There was plenty of bad in Matteo, in every Made Man really, but I'd come to realize that there was in me as well. Maybe not as much, but it was there. It was in all of us. I'd tried to become someone else, some kind of ideal I'd thought I needed to be, but that had never been me and never would. Matteo had held up a mirror to my face and showed me who I really was and where I belonged. I'd hated it, had fought it tooth and nail, but it was time to be brave.

"Yes. I love him, the bad and the good," I said firmly. Aria smiled as if I'd given her some huge present. Smiling back, I turned the water on, and really let the words sink in, their truthfulness.

I'd never be okay with everything Matteo did, would never do even half of the things he had done and was going to do in the future. But I'd realized I didn't have to be happy about every aspect of his life. As long as Matteo treated me with care and respect, as long as he loved me, and I loved him, things would work out.

I'd stand by him and support him as best as I could, because he was mine and I was his.

epilogue

Gianna

It was late April and today was the first warm day of the year. The temperature had finally climbed over 70°F. The ocean was still too cold to swim in it, but I didn't care.

I wasn't sure what it was about the beach and the ocean breeze that made me feel free. I stormed down the vast lawn of the Vitiello mansion toward the bay. Matteo was close behind me, and catching up judging from his steps. I sped up even more, not daring to throw a glance over my shoulder to check.

My feet hit the sand. It wasn't exactly warm; the water would be worse, but I didn't slow. I stormed right toward the soft waves. The moment my calves hit the water my breath caught in my throat and I stumbled to a stop. This was definitely still too cold to swim. I almost fell forward because of my momentum. Teeth chattering, I was about to back out again when warm hands gripped my waist and lifted me up.

"No! Don't you dare!" I screamed.

Matteo chuckled and then I was thrown through the air and landed with a splash in the freezing water. My muscles seized for a moment, then I burst through the surface and panted for breath. I scowled at Matteo who was grinning at me. He was up to his stomach in the water and didn't seem to mind the cold. "You bastard," I brought out through my chattering teeth.

My entire body started shaking. I wrapped my arms around my chest to make a show out of my freezing. Matteo's brows drew together and he came toward me, actually looking worried. The moment he was in arm's reach, I attacked. I lunged at him, grasping his shoulders and trying to dunk him under the water.

I should have considered how used Matteo was to physical fights. He used my momentum to catapult me up and swing me over his shoulder. "Hey!" I shouted in protest but he only clapped my butt and started carrying me out of the ocean. "Where are you taking me?"

"We need to warm you up," he said wickedly.

Excitement jolted through me but I made a show out of kicking my legs and hammering my fists against his back. He carried me to the right toward a corner of the lawn that was shielded from the mansion by bushes. A blanket had been set up. He had planned this!

He laid me down on the blanket and hovered over me. My body was covered in goose bumps, and not just from the cold.

"How about I lick every drop of water off your skin?" Matteo murmured as he leaned down and licked a hot trail up from my belly button to my collarbone.

"What if Aria or Luca come down here?" I whispered as he pushed my bikini top down, baring my breasts to the cold. My nipples hardened even more, and then Matteo's hot mouth closed around one. I cared less and less if someone caught us.

"They won't," he whispered against my skin. And that was the last time we spoke in a long time. His lips and hands found every place on my body, banishing the cold and leaving only heat and want. When he finally entered me, our bodies pressed together, it felt like everything was falling into place.

Even without the breeze and the blue sky, I would have felt free. It had taken a long time but I realized I could feel free, be free, even when I was bound to Matteo.

In the evening, Matteo and Luca set up a barbecue on the patio. The weather was holding up and we could eat outside. Aria went inside to grab the salad she'd prepared while Matteo headed toward the wine cellar for something to drink. That left me alone with Luca who was manning the barbecue grill. I set the table, pretending he wasn't there. Things between Luca and me were tense; they'd never been not tense, but they'd gotten worse since I'd accepted his offer months ago.

I took a deep breath. This had to stop. Luca was not only Matteo's brother, he was also Aria's husband. We had to make a truce at some point. I put down the last plate, wiped my hands and then strode over to Luca who was turning the marinated lamb chops around on the grate. As if he could sense my attention, he glanced up. It was futile trying to read his expression. I bridged the remaining distance between us. Most of our interactions hadn't exactly been civil. My go-to response to him was usually snarkiness, but I was doing my best to keep my expression open and as friendly as possible.

Luca raised one dark eyebrow when I stopped beside him.

Suddenly I felt ridiculously nervous. "I know you don't like me," I began. "But I think we should try to get along better for Aria and Matteo."

I managed not to squirm when he scrutinized me. What was he thinking?

"I didn't like you because I hated how you treated Matteo."

"Okay," I said slowly, not sure where to go from there.

"But I'm starting to change my mind."

"You are?"

He turned another lamb chop. "I'm starting to think that maybe Matteo was right and you two aren't the worst match."

"Thanks?" I said, unsure if it was meant in a positive way. "You are really bad with compliments."

"I'm not in the habit of handing them out. And don't tell my brother I said he was right. He's cocky enough." His eyes went to something behind me and I turned and spotted Matteo heading in our direction, his arms loaded with several bottles of wine.

"He is," I agreed with a smile. Luca gave me what could be considered his version of a smile, and some kind of silent understanding passed between us.

Matteo set the wine bottles down on the table before joining us and wrapping his arm around my waist. "What are you two gossiping about?"

"You," Luca and I said at the same time.

"Is that so?" Matteo lifted one eyebrow.

Aria came back from the kitchen, eyes darting between us. She pressed up against Luca with a confused look. "What's going on?"

"Your husband and my wife are discussing my many wonderful traits," Matteo said.

I nudged his side. "You are way too cocky."

Matteo kissed my ear. "Admit it, you love my cockiness."

"Done."

"Your declarations of love still make my knees go weak," he joked.

I stood on my tiptoes. "Your cockiness isn't the only thing I love about you." I let my eyes wander the length of him.

"I need some bloody lamb to cancel out this disgusting display of sweetness," Luca muttered, but I didn't miss the tender look he'd given Aria when he thought no one was paying attention.

Matteo swept me into his arms and kissed me. Luca grumbled something else but I didn't listen. All that mattered was Matteo.

bound *by temptation*

(Born in Blood Mafia Chronicles #4)

prologue

Liliana

I knew it was wrong. If someone found out, if *my father* found out, he'd keep me locked up in Chicago. He wouldn't even let me leave the house anymore. What I was doing was inappropriate and unladylike. People were still bad-mouthing Gianna after all that time. They'd jump at the chance to find a new victim, and what could be better than another Scuderi sister getting caught in the act?

And deep down I knew I was exactly like Gianna when it came to resisting temptation. I simply couldn't. Romero's door wasn't locked. I slipped into his bedroom on tiptoes, holding my breath. He wasn't there but I could hear water running in the adjoining bathroom. I crept in that direction. The door was ajar and I peered through the gap.

Romero was a creature of habit so I found him under the shower as expected, but from my vantage point I couldn't see much. I edged the door open with my foot and slipped in.

My breath caught at the sight of him. He had his back turned to me and it was a glorious view. The muscles in his shoulders and back flexed as he washed his brown hair. My eyes dipped lower to his perfectly shaped backside. I'd never seen a man like this, but I couldn't imagine that anyone could compare to Romero. He was all muscle and tanned skin. Strong and tall.

He began to turn. I should have left then, but I kept staring, fascinated by his body. Was he aroused? He tensed when he spotted me. His eyes captured my gaze before they slid over my nightgown and naked legs. And then I found an answer to my question. He hadn't really been aroused before. *Oh hell.*

My cheeks heated as I watched him grow harder under my unwavering attention. It was all I could do not to cross the distance between us and touch him.

Romero slid the shower open with unhurried movements and wrapped a towel around his waist before he stepped out, all naked glory and dripping wet. The scent of his spicy shower gel, peppermint and sandalwood, wafted into my nose. Slowly he advanced on me, long legs sure of every step. "You know," he said in a strangely rough voice. "If someone found us like this, they might get the wrong idea. An idea that could cost me my life, and you your reputation."

I still couldn't move. I was stone, but my insides seemed to burn, to liquefy into red-hot lava. I couldn't look away. I didn't *want* to.

My eyes lingered on the edge of the towel, on the fine line of dark hairs disappearing beneath it, on the delicious V of his hips. Without realizing what I was doing my hand moved, reaching for Romero's chest, for the Famiglia tattoo over his heart, needing to feel his skin beneath my fingertips.

Romero caught my wrist before I could touch him, his grip almost painful. My gaze shot up, half embarrassed and half surprised. What I saw on Romero's face made me shiver.

He leaned forward, coming closer and closer. My eyes fluttered shut but the kiss I wanted never came. Upon hearing the creak of the door, I peered up at Romero. He'd only opened the bathroom door wide. That's why he'd moved closer, not to kiss me. Embarrassment washed over me. How could I have thought he was interested in me like that? He was a Made Man.

"You need to leave," he murmured as he straightened. His fingers were still curled around my wrist.

"Then let me go."

He released me without hesitation and took a step back. I stayed where I was. I wanted to touch him, wanted him to touch me in turn. He cursed and then he was upon me, one hand cradling the back of my head, the other on my hip, the touch hot, warning and promise. I could almost taste his lips they were so close. His touch made me feel more alive than anything ever had.

"Leave," he rasped. "Leave before I break my oath." It was half plea, half order.

chapter
one

Four years before:
Liliana

I STILL CRINGED WHEN I REMEMBERED MY FIRST EMBARRASSING attempt at flirting with Romero. Mother and my sister Aria had always warned me not to provoke men, and I'd never been as daring with anyone as I'd been with Romero. He'd seemed safe, like there was no way he could possibly hurt me no matter the provocation. I'd been young and stupid, only fourteen and already convinced I knew everything there was to know about men and love and everything else.

It had been in the days leading up to Aria's wedding to Luca and he'd sent Romero to protect my sister because he didn't trust Father's men to do a good enough job—which was ridiculous, considering that Umberto had guarded my sisters and me since our births. It was a big deal to choose a bodyguard for your future wife; only someone who was deserving of your absolute trust could be allowed that close, but that knowledge wasn't even why *I* trusted Romero.

Romero had looked terribly handsome in his white shirt, black slacks and vest that hid his gun holster as he stepped into the suite my sisters and I shared in the Mandarin Oriental Hotel. And for some reason, his brown eyes had looked kinder than what I was used to from men in our world. I couldn't tear my gaze away from him. I wasn't sure what I'd been thinking, or what I'd expected to achieve, but the moment Romero sat down, I'd sauntered over to him and settled in his lap. His body was muscled, strength hidden beneath a sophisticated exterior. He'd tensed under me, but something in his eyes had made me fall for him that day. Often in the past, when I'd flirted with my father's soldiers, I'd seen in their eyes that they wouldn't hesitate to have their way with me if it wasn't for my father. But with Romero I knew I would never have to worry that he'd take more than what I was willing to give. His eyes filled with confusion and worry as I sat on his legs. He didn't push me off, didn't move at all. His fingers rested on the armrest. He was a man in control. He'd seemed like a good guy, like the guys I ever only got to admire from afar because you couldn't find them in the mafia. Like a knight in shining armor, someone dreams of silly girls were made of—girls like me. Aria had lost it and sent me off, but before I'd left I'd risked one more look at the man that had captured my heart and would never let it go: Romero. Soldier of the New York Famiglia.

Only a few months later, I found out that Romero wasn't whom I thought he was, who I wanted him to be and had made him out to be. That day still haunts me after all this time. It could have been the moment that my crush on Romero disappeared for good.

My parents had taken Gianna, Fabiano, and me to New York with them to attend Salvatore Vitiello's funeral, even though I didn't know Luca and Matteo's father. I'd been so very excited to see Aria again, but that trip turned into a nightmare, my first real taste of what it meant to be part of our world.

After the Russians attacked the Vitiello mansion in the Hamptons, I was alone with my brother, Fabi, in a room where Romero had taken us after the Famiglia under Luca's lead had come to our rescue. Someone had given my brother a tranquilizer because he'd completely lost it after he'd seen our bodyguard getting shot in the head. I was oddly calm, almost in a trance as I huddled beside him on the bed, staring at nothing and listening for noises. Every time someone walked past our room, I tensed, prepared for another attack, but then Gianna texted, asking me where I was. I'd never moved as fast in my life. It took me less than two seconds to jump off the bed, cross the room and rip the door open. Gianna stood in the corridor, her red hair all over the place. The moment I jumped into her arms, I felt better and safer. She winced because of the bruises the Russians had inflicted on her. Since Aria had moved, Gianna had taken over the role as substitute mother while our own mother was busy taking care of her social responsibilities and catering to Father's every whim.

"What are you doing?" I asked, my eyes darting left and right.

"I want to have a look downstairs."

Panic overcame me. I didn't want to be alone again and Fabi wasn't going to wake for another couple of hours so, despite my fear of what we'd find on the first floor, I followed my sister downstairs. Most of the furniture in the living room was ruined from the fight with the Russians and blood covered almost every surface. I'd never been very queasy about blood, or anything really. Fabi had always come to me to show me his wounds, especially when there was pus because he hadn't properly cleaned them. And even now, as we strolled past all the red on the white carpets and sofas, it wasn't the blood that made my stomach turn. It was the memory of the events. I couldn't even smell blood anymore because my nose was clogged from crying. I was glad when Gianna headed for another part of the house but then I heard the first scream from the basement. It was an agonized, high-pitched cry. It was a man, and I hadn't thought it possible *for a man* to make that kind of sound. I would have turned on my heel and pretended there was nothing. Not Gianna though.

She opened the steel door, which led to secret underground rooms. The staircase was dark but from somewhere in the depth of the basement light spilled out. I shivered. "You don't want to go down there, right?" I whispered. I should have known the answer. This was Gianna. When had she ever done what was reasonable?

"Yes, but you will stay on the stairs," Gianna said before she started her descent. I hesitated only a second before I went after her. Nobody had ever said I was good at following orders. In that regard we were very much alike.

Gianna glared. "Stay there. Promise me."

I wanted to argue, I wasn't a little kid anymore, but then someone cried out in the room below, and the hairs on the back of my neck rose. "Okay. I promise," I said quickly.

Gianna turned and moved down the remaining steps. She froze when she reached the last step before she finally stepped into the basement. I could only see part of her back but from the way her muscles tensed I knew she was upset. There was a muffled cry and Gianna flinched. Despite the fear pounding in my temples, I crept downstairs. I needed to know what my sister saw. She wasn't someone who freaked out easily.

Even as I did I knew I'd regret it but I couldn't resist. I was tired of being left out of everything, of always being too young, of being reminded every day that I needed protection from myself and everything around me.

The moment my feet hit the basement floor, my eyes settled on the center of the room. At first, I couldn't even comprehend what was going on. It was as if my brain was giving me a chance to leave and be none the wiser, but instead of rushing off, I stayed and stared. Kept staring as my mind went into overdrive, soaking in every detail, every *gruesome* detail before me. Details I still remembered vividly years later.

There were two of the Russians who'd attacked us, tied to chairs, and then there was blood. Matteo and another man were beating and cutting them with gleaming knives, *hurting* them. My vision tunneled, and terror rose up my throat, and then my gaze settled on Romero and his kind brown eyes, which weren't as kind as I remembered them. His hands, too, were covered in blood. The good guy and knight in shining armor I'd fantasized about? He wasn't *that guy*. A scream ripped from my body, but I could only tell because of the pressure in my chest and throat. I didn't hear anything beyond the rushing in my ears. Everyone stared at me like *I* was the crazy one. I wasn't sure what happened after that. I remembered fragments. Hands grasping me, arms holding tight. Soothing words that did nothing. I remembered a warm chest against my back and the smell of blood. There was a brief burning pain when Matteo injected me with something before my world transformed into eerie calm. The terror was still there, but it was blanketed. My vision was blurry but I could make out Romero kneeling beside me. He picked me up and straightened with me in his arms. The forced calm won out and I relaxed against his chest. Right in front of my eyes a red blotch disfigured his white shirt. Blood from the men that had been tortured. Terror tried to rip through the medication, but it was futile and I gave up the fight. My eyes fluttered shut as I resigned myself to my fate.

Romero

As Made Men it was our task to keep those safe that we were sworn to protect: the weak, children, women. I, in particular, had devoted my life to this goal. Many tasks in my job involved hurting others, being brutal and cold, but keeping people safe always made me feel like there was more to me than the bad. Not that it mattered; if Luca asked me, I'd do every bad thing imaginable. It was easy to forget that despite our own ethics and morals and codes, we Made Men were what most people perceived as evil. I was reminded of our real nature, of my real nature when I heard Liliana's scream. The screams of the Russians hadn't moved me. I'd heard those, and worse, before. But that high-pitched, not-ending scream of a girl we were meant to protect was like a fucking stab in the gut.

Her expression and eyes were the worst; they showed me exactly what I was. Maybe a good man would have sworn to be better, but I was good at my job. Most days I *enjoyed* it. Even the terror-stricken face of Liliana didn't make me want to be something other than a Made Man. Back then I hadn't realized that this glimpse of brutality wasn't even the worst way I would fuck up her life.

Liliana didn't stop screaming.

"Romero!" Matteo snarled. "Take care of Liliana."

I headed toward her but her eyes didn't even register me. Gianna made a move as if to step in my way but then she allowed me to pass.

The steel door slammed at the top of the stairs, and Luca stormed in. "What the fuck is going on here?"

I was right in front of Liliana but she hadn't stopped screaming. "Calm down, Lily. Everything is okay," I murmured. She didn't seem to hear me.

I reached for her, my fingers closing around her thin arm, but the touch sent her into flight mode. She jerked, tried to lash out but I slung my arms around her chest, trapping her arms at her side. Her back was heaving against my chest as she struggled against my hold.

She screamed and kicked. For a girl her size she put up a hell of a fight.

"Shut her up! Aria will hear," Luca growled. He tried to catch her legs but she managed to kick his chin. He stumbled back, more from surprise than anything else.

Fuck. I had fought men twice Liliana's size, experienced fighters, but with them I had been ruthless, intend on killing, but with Liliana I had to make sure to subdue her without harming her. Luca faced the same problem. Aria would go off on him if he hurt her baby sister, and even though he was Capo, Aria held that kind of power over him.

"Lily," Gianna tried to calm her sister. "Lily, stop."

Tito made a move as if to help us but Matteo shoved him backwards. "No. Stay out of it."

Liliana twisted in my arm. It was like holding a wiggling cat. She raised her leg and kicked the wall. I stumbled backwards, not having expected that kind of move, and fell to the ground. Liliana was still pressed up against my chest but my grip had loosened. She pushed to her feet before I could grab her and tried to storm past Matteo but he was too quick. He grabbed her wrist, and wrapped an arm around her waist. A moment later she was sprawled out on her back and he was kneeling on her legs and had her hands pinned above her head. I jumped to my feet, not comfortable with what I saw. A fourteen-year-old girl shouldn't be here, shouldn't experience these kinds of horrors. Luca headed toward them with a syringe in his hand.

"Don't hurt her!" Gianna shouted. "Don't you fucking dare hurt her!"

"I'm trying very hard not to hurt her, but she's making it difficult. Luca, now!" Matteo growled from his spot on top of Liliana.

Gianna blocked Luca's way. "What is that?"

"Something that will calm her down," Matteo said.

"Get out of the fucking way," Luca said as he brushed past her, knelt beside Liliana and pushed the needle into her arm. She stopped struggling. Matteo released her wrists and straightened. Freed from his hold, Liliana whimpered, curled into a small shivering ball and started to cry. Luca sighed as he ran a hand through his hair, regret on his face.

"I hope you all burn in hell," Gianna said. She knelt beside her sister and stroked her hair.

The Bratva asshole dared to laugh but Matteo got right into his face. "Shut the fuck up, or I swear I'll cut your dick into pieces while you watch."

"Romero, take Liliana into her room and tell the doc to check on her," Luca ordered.

I nodded. I bent over Liliana, slipped my arms under her petite body and lifted her in my arms.

She pressed her face against my chest and sobbed. It was an image that would haunt me for a long time.

Liliana

I woke to something warm and soft below my body. My mind was sluggish but the memories were clear and focused, more focused than my surroundings when I finally dared to open my eyes. Movement in the corner attracted my attention. Romero leaned against the wall across from me. I quickly did a check of the room I was in. It was a guest bedroom, and I was *alone* with Romero behind a closed door. Without the lingering effects of whatever Matteo had injected me with earlier, I would have started screaming again. Instead I watched mutely as Romero walked toward me. I wasn't sure why I'd ever thought of him as harmless, now every move he made screamed danger. When he'd almost reached the bed, I cringed, pressing myself against the pillow. Romero paused, dark eyes softening, but their kindness couldn't fool me anymore, not after what I'd seen. "It's okay. You are safe."

I'd never felt *not safe* in my life—until now. I wanted my blissful ignorance back. I didn't say anything.

Romero took a glass of water from the nightstand and held it out to me. My eyes searched the skin of his hands for blood but he must have cleaned them thoroughly. There wasn't the slightest hint of red, not even between his fingers or under his nails. He probably had a lot of practice cleaning up blood. Bile crept up my throat at the thought.

"You need to drink, kiddo."

My eyes flew up to his face. "I'm not a *kid*."

The ghost of a smile crossed Romero's face. "Of course not, Liliana."

I searched his eyes for mockery, for a hint of the darkness that had been there in the basement, but he looked like the good guy I wanted him to be. I sat up and took the glass from him. My hand shook but I managed not to spill water on myself. After two sips I handed the glass back to Romero.

"You can go to your sisters soon, but first Luca wants to have a word with you about what you saw today," he said calmly.

Fear speared me like a cold blade. I slid out of the bed when someone knocked, and Luca entered a moment later. He closed the door. My eyes darted from him to Romero. I didn't want to break down like I had before, but I could feel another panic attack pushing through the drugs in my bloodstream. I'd never been alone with them, and after today's events, it was too much.

"Nobody will hurt you," Luca said in his deep voice. I tried to believe him. Aria seemed to love him, so he couldn't be bad, and he hadn't been down in the basement torturing Russians. I risked another look at Romero, whose eyes rested on me.

I lowered my face. "I know," I said eventually, which probably sounded as much a lie as it felt. I took a deep breath and leveled my gaze on Luca's chin. "You wanted to talk to me?"

Luca nodded. He didn't come closer, nor did Romero. Maybe my fear was plain as day to them. "You can't tell Aria about what you saw today. She'll be upset."

"I won't tell her," I promised quickly. I'd never intended to talk to her. I didn't want to remember the events, much less to tell anyone about them. If I could, I'd wipe my memory clean of them instantly.

Luca and Romero exchanged a look, then Luca opened the door. "You're much more reasonable than your sister Gianna. You remind me of Aria."

Somehow his words made me feel like a coward. Not because Aria was. She was brave and so was Gianna, both in their own ways. I felt like a coward because I agreed to keep my silence for selfish reasons, because I wanted to forget, and not because I wanted to protect Aria from the truth. I was pretty sure she could have handled it better than I did.

"You can take her to Gianna, but make sure they don't walk around the house again," he said to Romero.

"What about Aria?" I blurted.

Luca tensed. "She's asleep. You can see her later." With that he left.

I wrapped my arms around my waist. "Do my parents know what happened?"

"Yes. Your father will pick you up once he's done with business and then take you back to Chicago. Probably in the morning." Romero waited but I didn't move. For some reason my body bristled at the idea of going closer to him, which was ridiculous considering that not too long ago I'd fantasized about kissing him.

He opened the door wide and stepped back. "I'm sure your sister Gianna is eager to see you."

Taking a deep breath, I forced myself to walk in his direction. His body was relaxed and his face kind, and despite the terror and fear still simmering deep in my body, my stomach fluttered lightly as I brushed past him. Maybe it was shock. I couldn't possibly have a crush on him after today.

chapter *two*

Liliana

WHENEVER I THOUGHT I'D GOTTEN OVER WHAT HAD happened last September, something would remind me of that day and my stomach would tie itself into a hard knot. Like today. Gianna and I were on our way to visit Matteo, Aria, and Luca in New York. Father had finally given in and allowed us to leave Chicago again to celebrate my fifteenth birthday. After what happened with the Bratva, he'd kept us on a short leash.

"Are you okay?" Gianna asked quietly when our plane landed, startling me out of my rising nervousness. Only being back in New York and seeing Matteo and Luca again was enough to fill my nose with the sweet stench of fresh blood.

"Yeah," I said quickly. I wasn't a little girl anymore who needed her big sisters for protection. "I'm fine."

The waiting hall of JFK was crowded when Gianna and I stepped through the doors. Aria ran toward us when we'd almost reached them and threw her arms around both of us. "I missed you so much."

Being reunited with my sister, I couldn't help but smile. I would have walked straight down into that basement if that meant I could see Aria again.

Aria gave me a once-over. "You're as tall as me now. I still remember when you didn't want to go anywhere without holding my hand."

I quickly looked around, but thankfully nobody was around to overhear her. "Don't say anything like that when Romero is around. Where is he anyway?" I realized a moment too late how idiotic I sounded, and flushed.

Aria laughed. "He's probably in his apartment. He got the day off but he'll work the night."

I shrugged, but it was too late. It wasn't that I'd forgotten the blood on Romero's hands but for some reason I wasn't as scared of him as I was of Matteo, or even Luca. And I realized just how much they terrified me when we walked toward them. My heart sped up and I could feel a panic attack rising up. I hadn't had one in weeks, so I fought it desperately.

"The birthday girl," Matteo said with a smile. How could that charming guy be the same person whom I'd seen covered in blood in the basement?

"Not yet," I said. I could feel my panic start to abate. In real life Matteo wasn't as frightening as in my memories. "Unless you have an early present for me."

"I like the way you think," Matteo said with a wink. He took my suitcase, then held out his arm. I glanced at Gianna. "Won't you carry Gianna's luggage?" I didn't want Gianna to think I was flirting with her fiancé even though she didn't seem to like him very much, regardless of the fact that I'd caught them kissing on Aria's wedding day.

"Luca can take care of it," Matteo said.

Gianna glared at him before she sent me a smile. "Go on."

I accepted Matteo's arm. I wasn't sure why Gianna despised him so much because it had started before the basement so it wasn't that. But it wasn't any of my business and Gianna didn't talk about her emotions with me anyway. That was what Aria was for. In their minds I was always too young to get it. But I knew more than they thought.

Fifty minutes later, we arrived at Luca and Aria's apartment building. I checked my reflection in the mirrors of the elevator, making sure my makeup was in place and I didn't have anything between my teeth. It had been months since I'd last seen Romero and I wanted to make a good impression. But when we walked into Aria and Luca's apartment Romero wasn't there yet. My eyes darted around and eventually Aria leaned toward me, whispering, "Romero will be here soon, don't worry."

"I wasn't looking for him," I said quickly, but she didn't buy it. I looked away before she could see my blush.

"Of course," Aria said with a knowing smile. "He'll come over around dinnertime to guard us when Matteo and Luca have to leave for business."

Excitement bubbled up in me, but it was mixed with something queasy and nervous, too. I'd had the occasional nightmare about that night in the basement, not about Romero in particular but I wondered if a live encounter would bring more of the bad stuff up. But that wasn't even the main reason why I was nervous. So far Romero had always ignored me, well not me, but my flirting. He'd treated me like a kid. Maybe he'd finally show more interest, or any interest at all. After all I was turning fifteen and it wasn't as if I hadn't caught many of my father's soldiers checking me out. Maybe I wasn't Romero's type, no matter my age. I didn't even know if he was dating someone or promised to someone.

During dinner I could tell that Aria and Gianna were exchanging the occasional glance. I wasn't sure what it meant. Were they talking about me?

The elevator made a bling sound and started its descent to whoever had called it.

"That's Romero," Aria said. Luca gave her an odd look but I didn't react at all, merely nodded as if I didn't care, but I did, and I was glad for Aria's warning.

"I need to go to the bathroom," I said, trying to sound casual. Gianna rolled her eyes. I snatched my purse from the floor and rushed toward the guest bathroom. When I closed the door, I heard the elevator doors slide open. A moment later Romero's voice rang out. It was deep but not rough. I loved the sound of it.

I faced the mirror and quickly refreshed my makeup and fluffed up my dark blond hair. It wasn't as bright and pretty as Aria's and not as eye-catching as Gianna's red hair but it could have been worse. The others would notice that I'd gone into the bathroom to make myself presentable, my sisters at the very least, but I didn't care. I wanted to look nice for Romero. Trying to look relaxed, I stepped out of the bathroom. Romero had taken a seat at the table and was loading a plate with the remains of our dessert: tiramisu and panna cotta. He was sitting on the chair right beside mine. I glanced at Aria wondering if she had something to do with it. She merely smiled at me, but Gianna didn't even bother hiding her amusement. I really hoped she wasn't going to embarrass me in front of everyone. I strolled over to my chair, hoping I looked grown up and relaxed, but apart from a quick smile Romero didn't pay me any attention. Disappointment settled heavily in my stomach. I sat down beside him and took a sip of my water, more to have something to do than because I was actually thirsty.

If I'd thought Romero's obvious disinterest in me was the full extend of my embarrassment today, I was sorely mistaken. Once Matteo and Luca had left for some kind of business meeting, it became obvious that Gianna and Aria were looking for a chance to be alone. They could have just asked me to leave but apparently they needed to get rid of Romero as well. Aria leaned in to whisper in my ear. "Can you distract Romero for a while? It's important." I didn't get the chance to refuse or ask any questions.

"Romero, why don't you play Scrabble with Lily? She looks like she's bored out of her mind, and Aria and I need a moment for girl talk," Gianna said pointedly.

My face burned in shame. Gianna usually knew better than to embarrass me like that. She made it sound like Romero needed to babysit me while she and Aria discussed important stuff.

Romero walked over from the kitchen where he'd been checking his phone and stopped beside me at the dining room table. I could barely look at him. What did he think of me now? I peered up through my lashes. He didn't look annoyed but that didn't mean he actually wanted to spend his evening entertaining me. He was a bodyguard, not a babysitter. "Your sister looks like she'd rather spend time with you," he told Gianna. Then his brown eyes settled on me. "Are you sure you want to play Scrabble with me?" he asked, and I couldn't help but smile. Few people ever asked what I wanted; even my sisters occasionally forgot that I was a person with her own opinions and wants.

Aria and Gianna gave me a meaningful look. I needed to convince Romero that I wanted it or I'd ruin things for them. "Yes, I really want to play Scrabble with you. I love that game, please?" I said with a bright smile. I didn't even remember when I'd played it last. Our family had never played board games.

Romero glanced toward my sisters. There was a hint of suspicion on his face. "You could join us," he said.

"I'd rather play alone with you," I said in a flirting tone. Gianna winked at me when Romero wasn't looking. "My sisters hate Scrabble and so does everyone else I know. You are my only hope."

A grin tugged at Romero's lips and he nodded. "Alright, but be patient. It's been a while since I played."

Playing Scrabble with Romero was actually a whole lot of fun. It was the first time we really spent time alone together. I looked up from the word I'd just put down, debating if I should ask the question that was burning a hole in my stomach. Romero was busy figuring out his next word. His dark brows were drawn together in an adorable way. I wanted to lean across the board and kiss him. "Do you have a girlfriend?" I blurted when I couldn't hold it in anymore. And then I wanted to die on the spot. Apparently, I didn't need my sisters to embarrass me. I was doing just fine on my own.

Romero glanced up. There was surprise and amusement on his face. I could feel a blush traveling up my neck. *Way to go, Lily.* I'd sounded like a moron. "Is that your way of distracting me from the game so you can win?"

I giggled, glad he wasn't angry with me for asking such a personal question. He returned his attention to the letters in front of him, and my amusement faded when I realized he hadn't answered my question. Did that mean he had a girlfriend? I couldn't ask him again without sounding desperate.

I sank deeper into my chair, annoyed. My eyes darted toward the rooftop terrace where my sisters were having their girl talk.

Aria and Gianna probably thought I wasn't sure they were up to something. They thought I was oblivious to everything going on around me. Just because I was flirting with Romero, however, didn't mean I didn't notice the secretive looks they shared. I didn't ask them because I knew they wouldn't tell me anyway, and I'd feel even more like the fifth wheel. They weren't doing it to be cruel but it hurt anyway. Aria looked upset over something Gianna had said. I had to resist the urge to go to them and ask them what was going on.

"It's your turn."

Romero's voice made me jump.

I flushed and did a quick scan of the words on the board, but my concentration was frayed.

"Do you want to stop?" Romero asked after a couple of minutes. He sounded like that was something he *wanted*. He was probably bored out of his mind.

Pushing my disappointment down, I nodded. "Yeah. I'm going to read in my room a bit." I rose to my feet, hoping my face didn't give my emotions away, but I needn't have worried. Romero gave me a distracted smile and picked up his phone to check his messages. I backed away slowly. He didn't look up again. I needed to figure out a way to get his attention, and not with stupid games.

Aria had decorated the entire apartment with balloons for my birthday, as if I was a kindergarten kid. I'd thought we might be allowed to head to one of Luca's clubs but he and even Aria had refused to take me there. The amount of food on the table made it look as if a huge party was planned, but it was only Romero's two younger sisters and us. Aria had asked him to bring them. I felt like the loser kid without friends who needed her big sister to find friends for her. Maybe I should have stayed in Chicago, then at least I could have spent the day with my friends.

When Romero arrived with his sisters, I put on my brightest smile. "Happy birthday, Liliana," he said, handing me an envelope. It was a voucher for a bookstore. "Aria said you love to read."

"Yes, thank you," I said, but somehow I'd hoped for a different gift from Romero. Something personal, something that showed I was special.

"These are my sisters." He pointed at the taller girl with thick brown curls. "This is Tamara, she's fifteen like you." I smiled and so did Tamara but she seemed as embarrassed as I felt. "And this is Keira, she's twelve. I'm sure you'll get along fine." It was obvious that I was supposed to spend time with them because I was still too young to hang with Aria, Luca, and the others. It annoyed me, even though Tamara and Keira seemed nice enough, but I hadn't come to New York for a kid party. With another smile, Romero headed for Luca and Matteo, and I led his sisters toward Aria and Gianna, and the buffet.

I tried my best to enjoy the evening and be nice to Romero's sisters but I wanted something special for my birthday, something I'd been dreaming about for a very long time. When I noticed Romero heading out onto the roof terrace for a call, I snuck out as well. The others were hopefully busy enough not to miss me for a couple of minutes. Romero talked on the phone and didn't notice me at first. I followed him quietly and watched as he leaned against the banister. His sleeves were rolled up to his elbows, revealing muscled forearms. I wondered how it would feel to run my hands over them, to feel his skin and strength.

When his eyes settled on me, his brows drew together in a frown and he straightened. I moved closer and positioned myself beside him. He hung up and put his phone in his pocket. "Shouldn't you be inside with your guests?" he asked with a smile, but I could tell that it wasn't as honest as usual.

I moved a bit closer and smiled up at him. "I needed some fresh air."

Romero's eyes were alert as he watched me. "We should return."

"There's something I want for my birthday," I said quietly. "Something only you can give me." I'd repeated the words in my head countless times but aloud they didn't sound half as flirty as they had in my imagination.

"Liliana," Romero began, his body brimming with tension.

I didn't want to hear what he was going to say. I quickly stood on my tiptoes and tried to kiss him. He gripped my shoulders before my lips reached his and held me away from him like I had an infectious sickness.

"What are you doing?" He let me go and took a few steps back. "You are a child, and I'm a soldier of the Famiglia. I'm not a toy you can play with whenever you're bored."

I hadn't expected that kind of reaction from him. Surprise and shock, yes, but anger? No. "I only wanted to kiss you. I don't want to play games. I like you."

Romero shook his head as he gestured toward the glass door. "Go back inside. Your sisters will start to wonder where you are."

He sounded like a big brother, and that was the last thing I wanted him to be. I whirled around before I walked back in a rush. My heart shriveled in my chest. For some reason I'd never considered a rejection from Romero. I'd fantasized about our first kiss so often that the option of it never happening had never crossed my mind. The rest of the evening, I struggled to keep a happy face, especially whenever I saw Romero. I was actually glad to return to Chicago. I wouldn't get to see Romero for a long time, enough time to get over him and find someone else to crush on.

Romero

I'd known Liliana had a crush on me. Aria had mentioned it before, but I'd never expected the girl to act on her feelings. She was a pretty kid. *A kid.*

I didn't have the slightest interest in her and the sooner she understood the better. She'd looked fucking hurt when I'd lashed out at her, but I had no choice. Even if she weren't still a child, I couldn't have let her kiss me. I was a soldier of the Famiglia and she was the daughter of the Outfit's Consigliere.

When I returned to the living area, Luca walked up to me. "What was that? Why was Liliana outside with you?"

Of course he'd noticed. Luca never missed anything.

"She tried to kiss me."

Luca's eyebrows rose. "I assume you pushed her away."

"Do you really have to ask? She's my sister's age."

"Her age isn't even the main problem. At least in her father's eyes."

"I know." I was a soldier, and girls like Liliana were supposed to stay in their own social circles.

Luca sighed. "That girl will be as much trouble as Gianna, if not worse."

I had a feeling he might be right.

chapter *three*

Liliana

"THE NERVE OF THAT GIRL! FROM THE DAY SHE'D BEEN BORN she's been nothing but trouble!" Father's words echoed through the house. Fabiano peered up at me with his big blue eyes as if I knew the answers to his questions. My own mind was a huge question mark. I wasn't exactly sure what had happened but I got the gist of it. Gianna had disappeared while she'd been in New York with Aria. Now everyone was looking for her. No wonder Aria hadn't asked me to visit as well. Not that I would have been too keen on returning to New York after my last embarrassing encounter with Romero four weeks ago, but it still stung that Aria and Gianna had made plans behind my back, behind everyone's back.

I walked down the stairs, motioning for Fabi to stay where he was, as I inched toward Father's office. Mother was there, crying. Father was on the phone, from his still angry but more restrained tone I assumed with his boss, Dante Cavallaro. Cavallaro was the only person that Father truly respected. Mother spotted me in the doorway and quickly shook her head, but I took another step forward and into the office.

I knew it was better to stay away from Father when he was in a mood like this, even though he usually lashed out at Gianna and not me, but my sister was gone now.

Father hung up, then narrowed his eyes at me. "Did I allow you to come in?"

His voice hit me like a whip but I stood my ground. "What happened to Gianna?"

Mother sent me a warning look.

"Your sister ran off. She'll probably get herself knocked up by some idiot, and ruin her and our family's reputation."

"Maybe she'll come back," I suggested. But somehow I knew she wouldn't. This wasn't a spur-of-the-moment thing. She'd planned this, for months probably. That explained all the secrecy with Aria during our last visit in New York. Why hadn't they told me? Didn't they trust me? Did they think I'd run to Father the first chance I got? And then another thought buried itself in my brain. If Gianna was gone, if she didn't marry Matteo, who else would? Fear washed over me. What if Father made me marry Matteo? I'd hoped I could marry for love now that my sisters had already been married off for tactical reasons. Maybe it was a selfish thing to think in a situation like this but I couldn't help it. An image of Romero popped into my head. I knew it was silly to think of him when it came to marriage. Even if Gianna returned and still married Matteo, it would be almost impossible to convince Father to give me to a mere soldier, especially one from New York. And then there was the problem that he didn't even want me and that I'd promised myself to get over him.

I knew all that but that didn't mean I couldn't hope and dream, sometimes it felt like that was all I could do.

"How many men will have had Gianna by then? She'll be worth nothing even if she returns," Father spat. I winced, horrified by his harsh words. Worth nothing? Surely we were more to him than a commodity to sell off. More than a thin piece of flesh between our legs?

Father gripped my shoulders, his eyes burning into me. I shied back but he didn't release me. "Don't think I don't see how you're making eyes at my soldiers. You're too much like Gianna for your own good. I won't have another daughter make a fool out of me."

"I won't," I whispered. Father had never talked to me in that tone before. His expression and words made me feel cheap and unworthy, like I needed to clean myself of my impure thoughts.

"That's right. I don't care if I have to lock you into your room until your wedding day to protect your reputation and honor."

This wasn't about my honor or reputation. I didn't care about it. This was all about my father. It was always about the men in the family, what they wanted and expected.

"Rocco, Lily is a good girl. She won't do anything," Mother said carefully. That wasn't what she usually told me. She always warned me that I was too flirty, too aware of the effect that my body had on men. But I was glad for her support because too often she'd remained silent when Father had attacked Gianna in the same way.

Father let go of me and turned on her. "It was your job to raise decent girls. For your sake, I hope you're right and Liliana won't follow after Gianna." The menace in his voice made me quiver. How could he be so horrible toward his own wife?

Mother blanched. I backed away and nobody tried to stop me. I quickly ran upstairs. Fabi waited for me, his eyes wide and curious. "What happened?" he asked fearfully.

I shook my head in response, not in the mood to recap everything for him, and stormed toward my room.

I'd never been at the center of Father's anger like that. But now that Gianna was gone, he'd keep an extra eye on me, making sure I was the perfect lady he wanted his daughters to be. I'd always felt free, never understood why Gianna felt so restrained by our life, but now it started to dawn on me. Things would change now.

In the months since Gianna's escape, things at home had been tense at best. Father had lost it over the smallest things. He'd hit me only twice, but Fabi hadn't been as lucky. But worse than the violence was his constant suspicion, the way he watched me like I was another scandal in the making. My golden cage had become a bit smaller, even though that had seemed hardly possible before. I hoped things would change now that Matteo had caught Gianna and was bringing her back to Chicago. Maybe that would appease Father, although he'd seemed far from appeased when I'd last seen him. I wasn't quite sure what exactly had happened but from what I gathered Gianna had been caught with another man, and that was the worst-case scenario in our world. Father would probably put me in shackles to stop me from doing the same.

"When will they be here?" Fabiano asked for the hundredth time. His voice had a whiny tinge to it and I had to stop myself from lashing out at him in frustration.

Fabiano and I had been waiting on the first floor landing for the last twenty minutes, and my patience was running thin.

"I don't know," I whispered. "Be quiet. If Mother figures out we're not in our rooms, we'll be in trouble."

"But—"

Voices sounded below. I recognized one of them as Luca's. He managed to fill a house with it; no wonder considering how big he was.

"They are here!" Fabiano dashed away and I was close behind him as we stormed down the staircase.

I spotted Gianna immediately. Her hair was brown now and she looked utterly exhausted but apart from that she was the sister I remembered. Father had often made it sound like she would be a new person if she ever returned; a horrible worthless person.

Father sent Fabi and me a glare when he noticed us, but I didn't care. I rushed toward Gianna and wrapped my arms around her. I'd missed her so much. When I'd first heard that Matteo had caught her, I'd worried he'd kill her, so seeing her unharmed was a huge relief.

"Didn't I tell you to keep them upstairs?" Father hissed.

"I'm sorry. They were too quick," Mother said. I peered over my shoulder to see her apologetic face as she came down the staircase. Since Gianna's escape Father had been on edge constantly and often lashed out at her as well. His screams had woken me more than once at night. I wasn't sure when he'd become so violent. I didn't remember him being like that when I was younger, or maybe I'd only been less aware of those things.

"Lily, Fabi, back to your rooms," Father ordered. I let go of Gianna and was about to protest but Fabi beat me to it.

"But, Father, we haven't seen Gianna in forever," Fabi grumbled.

Father advanced on us and I tensed. He rarely hit me but he looked furious. He grabbed Fabi and me, and dragged us away from Gianna. Then he pushed us toward the staircase. "Upstairs now."

I stumbled from the force of his push, but when I'd regained my balance I stopped and didn't move. I couldn't believe he wouldn't let us talk to Gianna after we hadn't seen her in so long.

"It's okay," Gianna said but her face told a different story. She looked hurt and sad, and usually Gianna wasn't someone who showed that kind of emotion. "We can talk later."

My eyes were drawn to something behind her: Romero. He stood strong and tall, his eyes firmly focused on my father. I hadn't seen him in seven months and over time I'd thought I'd gotten over my crush, but seeing him now my stomach fluttered with butterflies again.

Father's outburst drew my attention back to him. "No, you can't. I won't have you around them. You are no longer my daughter, and I don't want your rottenness to rub off on Liliana," he thundered. He looked like he would have loved nothing more than to kill Gianna. It scared me. Shouldn't he love us, his children, no matter what? If I ever did something he disapproved of, would he hate me as well?

"That's bullshit," Matteo said.

"Matteo," Luca said. "This isn't our business." My eyes darted between the two, then again toward Romero whose hand was below his vest. A twisted part of me wanted to see him in action. He was probably amazing in fight situations, and an even worse part knew Mother, Fabi, and I would be better off if Father was gone.

Mother wrapped her fingers around my wrist and took Fabi's hand. "Come now," she said insistently, tugging us toward the staircase and upstairs.

"That's right. This is my family, and Gianna is still subject to my rule, don't you ever forget that," Father said.

"I thought I wasn't your daughter anymore, so why do I have to listen to a word you say?"

My head whirled around, stunned by the venom in Gianna's voice.

"Careful," Father hissed. "You are still part of the Outfit." He looked like he would have beaten Gianna if it weren't for Matteo who held her by the waist. Mother tried to pull me along but Romero glanced up at that moment and his eyes met mine. His rejection on my birthday was still fresh in my mind, and yet I knew I still wanted to kiss him. Why was it that we sometimes wanted something that was impossible? Something that only led to hurt?

chapter *four*

Two years later
Liliana

Sometimes it felt like I had to prove myself to Father every day. He waited for me to mess up like Gianna had, but I wasn't sure how that was even possible; he never let me out of sight. Unless I started something with one of my ancient bodyguards, there was no way I could sully my honor. But Father hadn't forgiven Gianna yet, which was why I hadn't seen her in almost two years. She was forbidden from coming to Chicago, and I wasn't allowed to visit New York. If it wasn't for Aria's sneakiness, I wouldn't even have been able to talk to Gianna on the phone.

Sometimes even I felt anger toward Gianna because her escape had turned my life into hell. Maybe Father would have been less strict if Gianna had played by the rules. And then there were moments when I admired her for her daring behavior. There wasn't a night when I didn't dream of freedom. I didn't really want to run but I wished I could carve myself out more freedom in my life. Freedom to date, freedom to fall in love and be with that person.

I didn't even remember how it felt to be in love. Just like Gianna, I hadn't seen Romero in almost two years. What I'd felt for him back then hadn't been love, not even close. It had been admiration and fascination, I knew that now. But there had been nobody else either. Of course, it was hard to meet someone to fall in love with if you went to an all-girls school and weren't allowed to go anywhere alone.

The sound of glass shattering downstairs tore me from my thoughts. I jumped off my bed and opened my door. "Mother?" I called. She'd been gone all morning. There was no answer but I could hear someone moving in the kitchen.

I crept out of my room and down the stairs. "Mother?" I tried again when I'd almost reached the door to the kitchen. Still no answer. I pushed the door open and stepped inside. A wine bottle lay broken on the floor, red wine spilled around it. Mother was kneeling beside it, her cream-colored skirt slowly soaking up the liquid, but she didn't seem to notice. She was staring down at a shard in her palm as if it held the answer to all her questions. I'd never seen her like that. I walked toward her. "Mom?" I almost never called her that, but it felt like the right choice at the moment.

She looked up, her blue eyes unfocused and teary. "Oh, you are home?"

"Where else would I be?" I wanted to ask, but instead I touched her shoulder and said, "What's the matter? Are you alright?"

She stared down at the broken piece of glass in her hand again, then dropped it to the floor. I helped her to her feet. She wasn't steady on her legs and I could smell alcohol on her breath. It was still early for her to start drinking, and she wasn't really much of a drinker at all.

"I was at the doctor's."

I froze. "Are you sick? What's wrong?"

"Lung cancer," she said with a small shrug. "Stage three."

My throat constricted. "But you never smoked! How is that even possible?"

"It can happen," she said. "I'll have to start chemotherapy soon."

I wrapped my arms around her, feeling helpless and small under the weight of that news. "Does Father know?"

"I couldn't reach him. He didn't answer his phone."

Of course not. Why should he answer a call from his wife? He was probably with one of his mistresses. "We need to tell Aria and Gianna. They need to know."

Mother gripped my arm. "No," she said firmly. "It'll ruin their Christmas. I don't want them to know yet. There's no reason to worry them. I haven't spoken to Gianna in a long time anyway, and Aria has enough on her plate as wife of the Capo."

"But, Mom, they'd want to know."

"Promise me you won't tell them," she demanded.

I nodded slowly. What else could I do?

Two hours later I heard Father come home and another thirty minutes later, Mother's light steps came upstairs and then the door to the master bedroom closed. She'd been alone. Was Father still downstairs? I left my room and went to his office on the first floor. After a moment of hesitation, I knocked. I needed to talk to him.

Our Christmas party would be in two weeks and now that Mother was sick, Gianna should be invited. She and Mother should get the chance to spend some time together and reconcile.

"Come in," Father said.

I opened the door and poked my head in, half expecting to see him devastated and crying, but he was bent over some papers, working. I walked in, confused. "Has Mother talked to you?" Maybe she hadn't told him about her cancer.

He looked up. "Yes, she did. She'll be starting treatment with the best doctor in Chicago next week."

"Oh, okay." I paused, hoping for something else from Father but he watched me without a hint of emotion on his face. "I was thinking that Mother needs the support of her family now more than ever. Of her whole family."

Father raised his eyebrows. "And?"

"I think we should invite Gianna to our Christmas party. She and Mother haven't seen each other in a long time. I'm sure Mother would be very happy to see Gianna again."

Father's face darkened. "I won't have that whore in my house. Maybe Matteo has forgiven her and even married her despite her transgressions but I'm not that kind."

No, kind definitely wasn't a word I'd use for my father. "But Mother needs every bit of support she can get."

"No, and that's my last word," he growled. "And your mother doesn't want people to know about her sickness. They'd only start to get suspicious if we invited Gianna. We'll act as if nothing is wrong. You won't even tell your sisters or anyone else, do you understand?"

I nodded. But how could I keep that kind of secret from everyone?

The house was decorated beautifully for our Christmas party. Everything was perfect. The scent of roast beef and truffled mashed potatoes carried through the rooms, but I couldn't enjoy it. Mother had spent yesterday and the majority of this morning throwing up because of her treatment. With several layers of makeup, you couldn't tell how pale she was but I knew. Only Father and I knew. Even Fabi didn't have a clue.

Aria and Luca arrived only minutes before the other guests. They stayed in a hotel anyway so it wasn't too hard to keep Mother's state from them. Aria smiled brightly when she saw me and hugged me. "God, Lily. You look so beautiful."

I smiled tightly. I'd been so excited when I'd found the silver dress a few weeks ago because it made me feel grown up and accentuated my curves in just the right way, but today my excitement over something like a piece of clothing felt ridiculous.

Aria pulled away and searched my face. "Is everything okay?"

I nodded quickly and turned my attention to Luca who'd waited patiently behind my sister for his turn. He gave me a quick hug. It still felt strange to have him greet me that way. "Father is still in his office and Mother is in the kitchen," I explained. At least I hoped Mother wasn't in the bathroom, throwing up again.

Luca walked past me and my gaze landed on Romero who'd been hidden behind Luca's massive frame. My eyes widened at the sight of him. I hadn't expected him to come. Last year Luca had come alone with Aria. After all, he was more than capable to protect her.

"Hello," I said casually, sounding way more composed than I felt. I hadn't quite gotten over my crush on Romero but I realized with relief that I wasn't a quivering mess around him anymore. The last few months and weeks had changed me.

Romero

Luca had business to conduct with Scuderi and Dante Cavallaro; that was the only reason why I'd come to Chicago with them at all. And now as I stood in the doorway to the Scuderi mansion, staring at Liliana, I wondered if I shouldn't have come up with an excuse. The last time I'd seen Lily she'd been a girl, and while she still wasn't a woman, she'd grown a lot. She was fucking stunning. It was difficult not to look at her. It was easy to forget that there were still a few months until she'd be of age, easy to forget that she was way out of my league.

She tilted her head in greeting and stepped back. Where had the blushing, flirting girl gone? I had to admit I was sad that she wasn't giving me her flirty smile, though it had always bothered me in the past.

I followed Luca and Aria into the house. I could hear Lily's steps close behind me, could smell her flowery perfume and even see her slender frame from the corner of my eye. It took a lot of restraint not to glimpse over my shoulder to get another good look at her.

I spent the next couple of hours watching her discreetly as I pretended to be busy guarding Aria, not that I had much to do anyway. But the more I watched Lily, the more I realized that something was wrong. Whenever she thought nobody was paying attention to her, she seemed to deflate, her smile falling, her shoulders slumping. She was a good actress when she gave it her full attention but her few moments of inattentiveness were enough for me. Over the years as a bodyguard, I'd learned to be aware of even the smallest signs.

When she left the living room and didn't come back, worry overcame me, but she wasn't my responsibility. Aria was. I glanced at Luca's wife. She was deep in conversation with her mother and Valentina Cavallaro. I excused myself. She'd be safe here. Luca was just across the room in what looked like an argument with Dante and Scuderi.

Once I found myself in the foyer, I hesitated. I wasn't sure where Liliana had gone and I could hardly search the entire house for her. If someone found me, they might think I was spying for Luca. A sound from the corridor to my right attracted my attention and upon making sure that I was alone, I followed it until I caught sight of Liliana. She leaned against the wall, her head was thrown back, her eyes closed. I could tell she was trying to keep it together, and yet even like that, she was a sight to behold. Fucking gorgeous with long blond hair, immaculate skin, high cheekbones and slender figure. One day a man would be very lucky to be married to her.

The idea didn't sit well with me but I didn't linger on my inappropriate reaction. I walked toward her, making sure to make my steps audible so she knew she wasn't alone anymore. She tensed, her eyes fluttering open but when she spotted me, she relaxed again and turned away. I wasn't sure what to make of her reaction to my presence. I stopped a couple of steps from her, a proper distance. My gaze traveled over her long, lean legs, her narrow waist before I quickly moved on to her face. "Liliana, are you okay? You've been gone for a long time."

"Why do you insist on calling me Liliana when everyone always calls me Lily?" She opened her eyes again, blue eyes surrounded by thick dark lashes that kept you mesmerized, and smiled bitterly. She had fucking amazing eyes, and amazing pink lips. Damn it. "Did my sister tell you to watch me?" she asked with a hint of accusation in her soft voice.

As if I needed someone to tell me. It had been almost impossible to keep my eyes off Liliana tonight. "No, she didn't," I said simply. She didn't need to know why I had come to look for her. She was young and regardless of her immature attempts at flirting in the past, she was innocent.

Her blue eyes held confusion, then she turned her face to the side, leaving me to stare at her profile. Her chin wobbled but she swallowed and her expression evened out. "Don't you need to watch Aria?"

"Luca is there," I said. I moved a bit closer, too close. Lily's perfume wafted into my nose, made me want to bury my face in her hair. God, I was losing my fucking mind. "I can tell that something is wrong. Why don't you tell me?"

Lily straightened with narrowed her eyes. "Why? I'm not your responsibility. And last time we saw each other you didn't seem to like me very much."

Was she still mad at me for stopping her from kissing me at her birthday party more than two years ago? What kind of man would have returned that kiss? "Maybe I can help you," I said instead.

She sighed, her shoulders slumping. With that weary expression, she looked older somehow, like a grown woman, and I had to remind myself of my promise and oath again. Her eyes brimmed with tears when she peered up at me but they didn't fall.

"Hey," I said softly. I wanted to touch her, brush her hair away from her. Fuck. I wanted much more than that, but I stayed where I was. I couldn't go around touching a daughter of the Outfit's Consigliere. I shouldn't even have been alone with her.

"You can't tell anyone," she said.

I hesitated. Luca was my Capo. There were certain things I couldn't keep from him. "You know I can't promise you that without knowing what you're going to tell me." And then I wondered if maybe she was pregnant, if maybe someone had broken her heart, and the idea made me furious. I wasn't supposed to want her, I shouldn't want her, and yet…

"I know, but it's not about the Outfit or the Famiglia. It's…" She lowered her gaze and swallowed. "God, I'm not supposed to tell anyone. And I hate it. I hate that we're keeping up the charade when things are falling apart."

I waited patiently, giving her the time she obviously needed.

Her shoulders began to shake but she still didn't cry. I wasn't sure how she did it. "My mother has cancer."

That wasn't what I'd expected. Although now that I thought about it, her mother had looked pale despite the thick layer of makeup on her face.

I touched Lily's bare shoulder and tried to ignore how good it felt, how *smooth* her skin was. "I'm sorry. Why don't you talk to Aria about it? I thought you and her talk about everything."

"Gianna and Aria talk about everything. I'm the little sister, the fifth wheel." She sounded bitter. "Sorry." She released a long breath, obviously trying to get a grip on her emotions. "Father forbade me from telling anyone, even Aria, and here I am telling you."

"I won't tell anyone," I promised before I could really think it through. What was I doing promising that kind of thing to Lily? Luca and the Famiglia were my priority. I had to consider the consequences if the wife of the Consigliere was sick. Would that weaken him and the Outfit? Luca might think so. And not just that, I was supposed to protect Aria. Wasn't it my job to tell her that her mother was sick? That was the problem if you started to think with your dick. Then things always got messed up.

Lily tilted her head to the side with a curious expression. "You won't?"

I leaned against the wall beside her, wondering how I was going to get out of that corner. "But don't you think you should tell your sister? It's her mother. She deserves to know the truth."

"I know, don't you think I don't know that?" she whispered desperately. "I want to tell her. I feel so guilty for keeping it a secret. Why do you think I'm hiding in the hallway?"

"Then tell her."

"Father would be furious if he found out. He's been on edge for a long time. Sometimes I think it takes only the smallest incident and he'll put a bullet through my head."

She sounded fucking scared of her own father, and the bastard was scary. I took her hand. "Has he done anything to you? I'm sure Luca could figure out a way to keep you safe." What the fuck was I talking about? Scuderi would convince Dante to start a war if Luca took his youngest daughter away from him. You never got involved in other people's family problems. That was one of the most important rules in our world.

"Father wouldn't allow it," she said without hesitation. She really wasn't the kid I'd first met. This world took away your innocence far too soon. "And he didn't do anything, but he'd be furious if I went against his direct orders."

"You know your sister, she'd never tell anyone."

"Then she'd have to keep it a secret and she wouldn't even be able to talk to Mother about it. Why is everything such a mess? Why can't I have a normal family?"

She looked to me for answers I couldn't give. We both had been born into this world and were bound by its rules. "We can't choose our family."

"And in my case, not even my future husband," she said, surprising me. Something in her expression raised my walls. There were lines I couldn't cross.

She shook her head. "I don't know why I said it. This isn't what I should be worried about now." She looked down at my hand, which was still holding hers. I released her. If Scuderi or one of his men walked in on us, Scuderi would have a new reason to lose his shit.

"You know what? I will tell her," Lily said suddenly. She straightened and gave me a grateful smile. "You are right. Aria deserves to know the truth." Now that she didn't lean against the wall anymore, we were even closer. I should have taken a step back and kept my distance, but instead my eyes were drawn to her lips.

Lily surprised me by walking away. "Thank you for your help." I watched her turn the corner and then she was gone.

Liliana

My heart hammered in my chest, not only because I'd been alone with Romero and had barely managed to leave without kissing him, but because I was determined to go against Father's orders. Maybe Romero had told the truth and he wouldn't tell my sister and Luca about my mother, but really why should he keep a secret for me? We weren't a couple, we weren't even friends. We were nothing to each other. The thought buried itself like a heavy weight in my stomach.

It was better if I told Aria now. She'd find out eventually, and I wanted it to be from me. I headed back into the living room, where I found her deep in conversation with Valentina and a plate with prosciutto in her hand. Valentina smiled at me, but there was a flicker of pity in her green eyes. Did she know?

Of course, she did. Father probably had told his boss, Dante, right away, and Dante had told his wife. Had Father told other people as well? People he thought more deserving of the truth than his own family? "Hi, Val," I said with a smile. "Can I steal Aria from you for a moment? I have to talk to her."

Aria gave me a questioning look but Valentina nodded as if she knew why I needed to be alone with my sister. I linked arms with Aria and casually strolled through the room with her. Aria was tense. She knew something was up. I didn't want Father or Mother to get suspicious so I tried to keep a relaxed expression. I caught Romero's gaze across the room as he slunk back inside. He made his way over to where Luca and Dante stood beside the fireplace, but not without a last encouraging nod. Somehow that small gesture made me feel better. In the last two years I'd convinced myself that the thing with Romero was nothing but a silly crush but now I wasn't so sure anymore. I liked his calm protectiveness. It gave me a sense of safety I longed for.

"Lily, what's going on? You've been acting very odd all evening," Aria whispered as we headed toward the lobby.

"I'm going to tell you in a moment. I want us to be alone."

Aria's face clouded with worry. "Has anything happened? Do you need help?"

I led her upstairs and into my room. When the door had closed behind us, I released Aria and sank down on my bed. Aria sat down beside me.

"It's Mother," I said in a whisper, not bothering to hide my pain any longer. "She's got lung cancer." Maybe I should have broken it to her in a less direct manner, but it wouldn't have made the news less horrible.

Aria stared at me with wide eyes, then she slumped against the wall, releasing a harsh breath. "Oh God. I thought she looked exhausted but I blamed it on another fight with Father."

"They're still fighting and it's making everything worse."

Aria wrapped her arm around me and for a moment we held each other in silence. Mother hadn't always been as caring and loving as a mother should be, but we loved her despite her flaws. "Why hasn't she told me?"

"Father doesn't want anyone to know. He actually forbade me from telling you."

Aria pulled back, blond brows drawing together. "He forbade you?"

"He wants to keep up appearances. I think he's embarrassed by Mother's sickness." I hesitated. "That's why I didn't tell you right away. I didn't know what to do, but I talked to Romero and he convinced me to tell you."

Aria searched my face. "Romero, hm?"

I shrugged. "Will you tell Gianna when you're back in New York?"

"Of course," Aria said. "I hate that she can't be here." She sighed. "I want to talk to Mother about it. She needs our support but how can we give it to her if we're not supposed to know?"

I didn't know. "I hate how Father's acting. He's so cold toward her. You're so lucky, Aria, that you have a husband who cares about you."

Her face transformed at once. It always did if I mentioned Luca. Love—she'd found it. "I know. One day you'll have that too."

I really hoped she was right. Life with someone like my father would be a hell I couldn't survive.

With every passing day, Mother faded a bit more. Sometimes it felt like all I had to do was look away for a moment and her skin had already become a scarier shade of gray and she'd lost even more weight. Even her beautiful hair was gone completely. It was impossible to keep her sickness a secret anymore. Everyone knew. When other people were around, Father played the doting and worried husband but when we were alone, he could barely stand Mother's presence as if he worried that she was infectious. It fell on me to support her while I tried to get through my last year in school. Aria, Gianna, and I talked on the phone almost every day. Without them I couldn't have survived. And at night when I lay in the dark and couldn't sleep from worry and fear, I remembered the way Romero had looked at me at our Christmas party as if he saw me for the very first time, really saw me as a woman and not just a stupid child. The look in his brown eyes made me feel warmer even if it was only a memory.

A soft knock made me sit up. "Yes?" I asked quietly. *"Please don't let Mother be throwing up again."* I wanted one night without the acid smell in my nose. I felt bad for the thought. How could I think something like that?

The door opened and Fabi poked his blond head through the gap before he slipped in. His hair was disheveled and he was in his pajamas. I hadn't drawn the curtains so I could tell that he'd cried but I didn't mention it. Fabi had turned twelve several months ago and was too proud to admit his feelings to anyone, even me.

"Are you asleep?"

"Do I look like I've been sleeping?" I asked teasingly.

He shook his head before he put his hands in the pockets of his pajama pants. He was too old to come into bed with me because he was scared of something. Father would have ripped Fabi's head off if he'd found him with tears on his face in my room. Weakness wasn't something Father tolerated in his son, or anyone really.

"Do you want to watch a movie?" I scooted to the side. "I can't sleep anyway."

"You've got only girl movies," he said as if I was asking a huge favor of him but he headed toward my DVD shelf and picked out something he could tolerate. Then he sat down beside me with his back against my headboard. The movie started and we watched in silence for a long time.

"Do you think Mom is going to die?" Fabi asked suddenly, his gaze fixed on the screen. He had become better at masking his emotions in the last few months. It wasn't long before he'd be like all the other men in our world.

"No," I said with all the conviction I didn't feel.

My eighteenth birthday was today but there would be no party, no birthday cake, no sung Happy Birthday. Mother was too sick. There was no room in our house for celebrations or happiness. There hadn't been in a long time. Father was hardly home anymore, always gone on business, and recently Fabi had started to accompany him. And so I was left alone with Mother. Of course there was a nurse and our maid, but they weren't family. Mother didn't want them around and so I was the one sitting at her bed after school, reading to her, trying to pretend that her room didn't smell of death and hopelessness. Aria and Gianna had called in the morning to wish me a happy birthday. I knew they'd wanted to visit, but Father had forbidden it. Not even for my birthday he could be nice.

I put the book down that I'd read to Mother, A Wrinkle in Time, her favorite. She was asleep. The noise of her respiratory aid, a click and rattling, filled the room. I stood, needing to walk around a bit. My legs and back were stiff from sitting all day.

I walked toward the window and peered out. Life was happening everywhere around me, but I was left to stand at the sideline. My phone buzzed in my pocket, startling me from my thoughts. I took it out and found an unknown number on my screen. I pressed it against my ear. "Hello?" I whispered as I walked out into the corridor as not to disturb my mother, even though noises hardly woke her anymore.

"Hello, Liliana."

I froze. "Romero?" I couldn't believe he'd called me, and then a horrible idea struck me, and the only explanation for his call. "God, did something happen to my sisters?"

"No, no. I'm sorry, I didn't mean to scare you. I wanted to wish you a happy birthday." His voice was smooth and warm and deep, and it soothed me like honey did with a sore throat.

"Oh," I said. I braced myself against the wall as my pulse slowed again. I wasn't sure what to make of his call. I didn't want to see it as more than it was, didn't want to have my hopes crushed again. "Thank you. Did my sister tell you it was my birthday?" I smiled lightly. I could imagine Aria doing that, hoping to cheer me up. Aria couldn't help it. She needed to see us happy. She hadn't talked to me about Romero in a while but I was fairly sure she knew that I still liked him.

"She didn't have to. I know your birthday."

I didn't say anything, didn't know what to say. He remembered my birthday?

"Do you have birthday plans?"

"No. I'll stay at home and take care of my mother," I said tiredly. I couldn't remember the last time I'd slept through the night. If Mother didn't wake me because she threw up or was in pain, then I lay awake staring into nothingness.

Romero was silent on the other end before he continued in an even gentler voice, "Things will get better. I know things look hopeless right now but it won't always be like this."

"You've seen a lot of death in your life. How can you stand it?"

"It's different if it's someone you care for who's dying or if it's business-related." He had to be careful what he said on the phone, so I regretted having brought it up, but hearing his voice felt too good. "My father died when I was fourteen. We weren't as close as I'd wanted us to be but his death was the only one that really got me so far."

"Mother and I aren't as close as many of my friends are with their mothers, and now that she's dying I regret it."

"There's still time. Maybe more than you think."

I wanted him to be right but deep down I knew it was only a matter of weeks before Mother would lose her battle. "Thanks, Romero," I said softly. I wanted to see his face, wanted to smell his comforting scent.

"Do something that'll make you happy today, even if it's only something small."

"This makes me happy," I admitted.

"That's good," he said, but I caught a hint of hesitation in his tone. Silence followed.

"I need to go now." Suddenly my admittance embarrassed me. When would I stop putting myself out there? I wasn't someone who was good at hiding her emotions and I hated it.

"Goodbye," Romero said.

I ended the call without another word, then stared at my phone for a long time. Was I reading too much into Romero's call? Maybe he wanted to be polite and call the sister of his boss's wife on her eighteenth birthday to gain some bonus points. But Romero didn't seem to be the type for that. Then why had he called? Had it something to do with the way he'd looked at me at our Christmas party? Was he starting to like me as much as I liked him?

Two weeks after my birthday, Mother's health deteriorated even further. Her skin was papery and cold, her eyes glazed from the painkillers. My grip on her was loose, scared of hurting her. She looked so breakable. Deep down I knew it wouldn't be much longer. I wanted to believe a miracle would happen, but I wasn't a small kid anymore. I knew better. Sometimes I wished I were still that naïve girl I used to be.

"Aria?" Mother said in a wispy voice.

I jerked up in my chair and leaned closer. "No, it's me, Liliana."

Mother's eyes focused on me and she smiled softly. It looked horribly sad on her worn-out face. She'd been so beautiful and proud once, and now she was only a shell of that woman.

"My sweet Lily," she said.

I pressed my lips together. Mother had never been the overly affectionate type. She'd hugged us and read bedtime stories to us and generally tried to be the best mother she knew how to be, but she'd almost never called us nicknames. "Yes, I'm here." At least until Father would try to send me away again. If it were up to him Mother would be locked away from everyone she loved, only cared for by the nurses he'd hired until she finally passed away. I tried to tell myself it was because he wanted to protect her, to let a proud woman be remembered as she used to be and not only for her sickness, but I had a feeling that wasn't his main incentive. Sometimes I wondered if he was embarrassed of her.

"Where are your sisters? And Fabi?" She peered over my head as if she expected to see them there.

I lowered my gaze to her chin, not able to look into her eyes. "Fabi is busy with school." That was a blatant lie. Father made sure Fabi was busy with God only knew what, so he didn't spend too much time with our mother. As if Father worried her sickness would rub off on Fabi if he got too close. "Aria and Gianna will be here soon. They can't wait to see you again."

"Did your father call them?" Mother asked.

I didn't want to lie to her again. But how could I tell her that Father didn't want them to come visit our dying mother, that they wouldn't even have known she was close to dying if I hadn't called them. I filled her glass with water and held it up to her lips. "You need to drink."

Mother took a small sip but then she turned her head away. "I'm not thirsty."

My heart broke as I set the glass back down on her nightstand. I searched for something to talk to my mother about, but the thing I really wanted to tell her about, my crush on Romero, was something I couldn't trust her with. "Do you need anything? I could get you some soup."

She gave a small shake of her head. She was watching me with a strange expression and I was starting to feel uncomfortable. I wasn't even sure why. There was such a look of forlornness and longing in her gaze that it spoke to a dark place deep inside of me. "God, I don't even remember how it is to be young and carefree anymore."

Carefree? I hadn't felt carefree for a very long time.

"There's so much I wanted to do, so many dreams I had. Everything seemed possible." Her voice got stronger as if the memory drew energy from somewhere deep inside of her body.

"You have a beautiful house and many friends and children who love you," I said but even as I did I knew it was the wrong thing to say, and I hated this feeling of always doing the wrong thing, of not being able to help.

"I do," she said with a sad little smile. Slowly it faded. "Friends who don't visit."

I couldn't deny it and I wasn't even sure if Father was why they stayed away or if they'd really never cared about my mother in the first place. I opened my mouth to say something, another lie I'd feel guilty for later, but Mother kept talking. "A house that was paid for with blood money."

Mother had never admitted that Father was doing horrible things for our money and I'd never gotten the impression that she cared much either. Money and luxury were the only things Father had always given freely to her and us. I held my breath, half curious and half terrified of what she would say next. Did she regret having had kids? Were we a disappointment for her?

She patted my hand. "And you kids…I should have protected you better. I was always too weak to stand up for you."

"You did everything you could. Father would have never listened to you anyway."

"No, he wouldn't have," she whispered. "But I could have tried harder. There are so many things I regret."

I couldn't deny it. I'd often wished that she had stood up for us, especially for Gianna, when Father had lost it again. But there was no use in making her feel bad for something that couldn't be changed.

"You only have this one life, Lily. Make the best of it. I wish I had done it and now it's too late. I don't want you to end like me, to look back at a life full of missed opportunities and lost dreams. Don't let life pass you by. You are braver than me, brave enough to fight for your happiness."

I swallowed, stunned by her passionate speech. "What do you mean?"

"Before I married your father, I was in love with a young man who worked in my father's restaurant. He was sweet and charming. He wasn't part of our world."

I glanced toward the door, worried Father would overhear us. As if that could happen. *As if he would actually set foot into this room.* "Did you love him?"

"Maybe. But love is something that develops with time and we never got the chance. I could have loved him very much, I'm sure of it. We kissed behind the dumpsters once. It was cold outside and it smelled of garbage, but it was the most romantic moment of my life." A sweet smile was on her face, an expression I'd never seen on my mother before.

Pity squeezed my heart tightly. Had Father never done anything romantic for her? "What about Father?"

"Your father..." She trailed off. She took a few shuddering breaths. Even with the help of the oxygen tank, she was struggling to breathe. "He doesn't have time for romance. He never had."

But he had time for whores behind my mother's back. Even I knew about them, and I was usually the last person who got wind of these kinds of things. I'd never heard him say a kind word to Mother. I'd always assumed he could only show affection behind closed doors but now I realized he probably never did. The only nice thing he ever did was to buy her expensive jewelry.

"Don't get me wrong, I respect your father."

"But you don't love him," I finished. I'd always been sure Mother loved Father, even when he didn't return the feeling, but finding out that there was nothing between them somehow felt like a punch in the stomach. Aria and Gianna had made the best of their arranged marriages but now I realized that many weren't as lucky and never loved or even tolerated their husbands. Most women in our world were trapped in a loveless marriage with a cheating and sometimes even violent man.

She sighed, her eyes sliding shut, her skin becoming even paler than before. "I always told myself there was still time to do the things I love, to be happy, and now? Now it's too late."

Would those words always feel like a punch every time she voiced them? "No," I said shakily. "It's not. Don't give up."

She looked at me with a sad smile. "It won't be much longer. For me there's nothing but regret. But you have your whole life ahead of you, Liliana. Promise me you'll live it to the fullest. Try to be happy."

I swallowed hard. All my life my mother had told me to accept my fate, to be a good girl, to be dutiful. "I want to marry for love."

"You should," she whispered.

"Father won't allow it. He'll find someone for me, won't he?"

"Aria and Gianna made good matches. You don't have to marry for tactical reasons. You should be free to fall in love and marry that special boy."

An image of Romero popped into my head, and a swarm of butterflies filled my stomach.

"I remember that look," Mother said softly. "There is someone, hm?"

I blushed. "It's silly. He isn't even interested in me."

"How could he not be? You are beautiful and intelligent and come from a good family. He'd be crazy not to fall for you."

I'd never talked to Mother like this, and I felt incredibly sad that it had taken cancer for us to be this close. I wished she'd been that kind of mother before, and then I felt guilty for thinking something like that. "He's not someone Father would approve of," I said eventually. And that was a huge understatement. "He's just a soldier."

"Oh," Mother whispered. She had trouble keeping her eyes open. "Don't let anyone stop you from achieving happiness." The last few words were barely audible as Mother slowly drifted off to sleep. I slipped my hand out from beneath hers and stood. Her breathing was labored, raspy, and flat. I could almost imagine how it would stop any second. I backed out of the room but didn't close the door. I wanted to make sure I would hear it if Mother called for help.

I headed toward the staircase where I almost bumped into Father. "Mother will be happy to see you," I said. "But she's just fallen asleep, so you will have to wait a bit."

He loosened his tie. "I wasn't going to your mother. I have a few more meetings scheduled."

"Oh, right." That's why he smelled like a perfume shop and why his suit was wrinkled. He'd spent the morning with one of his whores and was probably on his way to the next. "But she'd love to see you later."

Father narrowed his eyes. "Did you call your sister? Luca called me this morning to tell me he and Aria were on their way to Chicago to visit your mother."

"They have a right to say goodbye."

"Do you really think they want to see your mother like this? Your mother was once a proud woman, if she were still in her right mind, she wouldn't want anyone to see her in this pitiful state."

Anger bubbled up. "You're embarrassed by her, that's all!"

He raised a finger in warning. "Careful. Don't take that tone with me. I know you are under a lot of pressure but my patience is running thin at the moment."

I pressed my lips together. "Are Aria and Luca still coming, or did you forbid them from visiting?" I didn't mention that Gianna would be visiting as well. He'd find out soon enough and then Luca would hopefully be there to calm him down.

"They'll be here in the afternoon. That'll give Luca and Dante the chance to discuss business."

That's what he worried about? Business? His wife was dying and he didn't give a shit. I nodded and left without another word. Half an hour later I watched my father leave the house again. There had been a time when I'd looked up to him. When I'd seen him in his black suit and thought he was the most important person in the world, but that hadn't lasted long. The first time he raised his hand against Mother, I knew he wasn't the man I thought he was.

Aria, Gianna, and Luca arrived two hours later. Matteo had stayed in New York. Not only because Luca needed someone he trusted there, but because Gianna's encounter with Father would be explosive anyway. If Matteo were there as well, someone would die.

Aria and Gianna hugged me tightly in greeting. "How are you?" Aria asked.

I shrugged. "I don't know. It's hard to see Mother so weak."

"And Father acting like a jerk isn't helping," Gianna muttered.

Luca gave me a small nod. "I'll wait in the kitchen. I still have a few phone calls to make."

I had a feeling he only wanted to give us time alone with our mother and I was grateful for that. I almost asked him about Romero but then I stopped myself.

I led my sisters upstairs. When we stepped into Mother's bedroom, shock flashed across their faces. Even I, who kept her company every day, was shocked every morning when I saw how broken she looked, and the smell was horrible as well. The nurses cleaned the floor and furniture with disinfectant twice a day but the stench of decay and urine still covered everything. It even seemed to cling to my clothes and skin, and clogged my nose when I couldn't sleep at night.

Mother was awake, but it took a moment before recognition shone in her eyes. Then she smiled, and for a moment, despite the tubes disappearing in her nose, she didn't look like death had already marked her as his. Aria immediately walked toward the bed and hugged Mother carefully. Gianna was tense beside me. She and Mother hadn't seen each other in a while, and they hadn't exactly parted on good terms. When Aria stepped back, Mother's gaze settled on Gianna and she started crying. "Oh, Gianna," she whispered.

Gianna rushed toward our mother and embraced her as well. It almost broke my heart that this reunion had such a horrible reason. I wished we'd come together like this long before today. I pulled two more chairs toward the bed and put them next to the one I'd spent countless hours in. We all sat down and Mother looked at peace for the first time in a while. I let Aria and Gianna talk and listened. Gianna leaned over to me when Aria told Mother about a new exhibition in New York. "Where's Fabi? Shouldn't he be home?"

"Father always has someone pick him up from school and then I don't see Fabi until dinner."

"Is he inducting Fabi already? Fabi's way too young for that bullshit."

"I don't know. It's difficult to talk to Fabi about it. He doesn't tell me everything like he used to. He's changed a lot since Mother got sick. Sometimes I don't recognize him."

"The mob changes them all. It sucks the good out of them," Gianna murmured.

"Look at Matteo, Luca, and Romero, they aren't all bad."

Gianna sighed. "They aren't good either. Far from it. With Fabi, I know how he used to be before the rottenness wormed its way into him, but with Luca and Matteo I always only knew them as Made Men, so it's different." Gianna narrowed her eyes in contemplation. "Are you still crushing on Romero? Shouldn't you have moved on to a new target by now?"

I flushed, but didn't reply. Luckily, Aria involved Gianna in the conversation and I could relax again.

Gianna, Aria, and I fell asleep in our chairs. Two hours later we were woken by Father's sharp voice. "What is she doing here?"

I sat up, taking a few seconds to get my bearings. Father stood in the doorway and was glaring daggers at Gianna. He still hadn't forgiven her for what she'd done. He'd probably take his wrath into the grave with him.

"I'm not here to see you, believe me," Gianna muttered.

Aria rose from her chair and went over to Father to give him a quick hug. Usually his mood always brightened when she was around, because she was the only one who hadn't disappointed him yet, but he didn't even look at her.

"I don't want you in my house," he said to Gianna.

I spotted Fabi a couple of steps behind him, obviously unsure how to react. I knew he'd missed Gianna very much and had always been eager to talk to her on the phone, but Father's influence on him had grown in the last few months and it was clear that my little brother wasn't sure which side to choose.

I stood, chancing a worried look at Mother. She was still out from her meds. I didn't want her to witness this. "Please, let's discuss this outside," I whispered.

Father turned on his heel and stepped out into the corridor without a single glance at Mother. The rest of us followed. Gianna didn't give Fabi a chance to make up his mind, she hugged him and after a moment he hugged her back. He was taller than her now, taller than all of us.

Father glowered at my brother. I couldn't believe he wasn't able to let his stupid pride take a back seat for once. Mother needed us in her last days, but he didn't give a damn. He didn't even wait for me to close the door before he went off again.

"I forbade you from stepping foot into this house," he snarled.

I slid the door shut and leaned against it. My legs felt shaky. The last few months had been draining, and I couldn't take it anymore, but I needed to be strong for Mother, for Fabi and even for my sisters.

"It's also Mother's house and she asked to see me," Gianna said. It was true. I'd lost count of the many times Mother had asked about Gianna. Regardless of how badly their last encounter had gone, they loved each other.

Father drew up to his full height. "I paid for this house and my word is law."

"Don't you have any respect for the wishes of your dying wife?" Gianna hissed.

I was pretty sure Father would have hit Gianna, even though she was Matteo's wife, but Luca came upstairs in that moment. It didn't stop Father from saying more nasty things and Gianna from firing right back at him. I couldn't take it anymore. I rushed past them. Their fighting followed me down the corridor and even downstairs I could still hear their shouting. I stormed into the kitchen, threw the door shut and leaned against it before I buried my face in my hands. The tears I'd been fighting for so long pressed against my eyeballs. I couldn't hold them back.

A noise made me look up. Romero stood at the kitchen counter and was watching me over his coffee cup. I cringed in embarrassment and quickly tried to wipe my cheeks clean. "I'm sorry," I said. "I didn't know someone was in here." I didn't even know Romero was here at all, but I shouldn't have been surprised. Since Matteo had stayed in New York, Luca needed someone who could keep an eye on my sisters when he was busy.

"This is your home," he said simply. His eyes were kind and understanding. I had to look away or I'd really start bawling, snot and sobs and all, and that was the last thing I wanted.

"It used to be," I whispered. I knew I needed to keep my mouth shut but the words kept coming. "But now it feels like I'm trapped. There's nothing good. Anywhere I look there is just darkness, just sickness, and hate and fear." I fell silent, shocked by my outburst.

Romero set down his coffee. "When was the last time you left the house?"

I didn't even know. I shrugged.

"Let's take a walk. We can get a coffee. It's really warm outside."

Euphoria burst through the dark cloud that had been my emotions in the last few weeks. "Are you sure that's okay?"

"I'll check with Luca but I don't see why it should be a problem. Just a sec."

I stepped aside so he could walk by. His delicious aftershave entered my nose as he passed me and I wanted to press my nose into his shirt to find solace in his scent. My eyes followed him, traced his broad shoulders and narrow hips. Mother's words shot through my mind again. Maybe happiness wasn't as far away as I thought.

Romero

I shouldn't even consider being alone with Lily, not now, not ever. Not when I couldn't stop noticing how grown up she looked. She wasn't the little girl I'd first met. She was a woman in marriageable age now, but she was out of my league, at least by her father's standards. I was one of the best fighters in New York, only Luca and Matteo were as good with the knife or the gun, and I wasn't exactly penniless, but I definitely wasn't mob royalty and couldn't afford a penthouse like Luca's. I wasn't even sure why the fuck I was thinking about those kinds of things now. I wasn't going to ask for Lily's hand, not now, not ever, and at this time there were more important things to take care of.

I climbed the stairs, following the sound of arguing. Gianna and her father were at it again and Luca seemed to try to keep them from ripping their heads off. Only problem was that he looked like he was close to losing his own shit. I walked toward them and Luca gave me an exasperated look. Scuderi was a pain in the ass, and Luca wasn't the most patient person on this planet. A bad combination. He came toward me. "I'm going to lose my fucking mind if Gianna and her old man don't stop fighting."

"Lily is taking it badly. She's had to witness her mother's deterioration for months now. I want to take her out for a walk and a coffee to take her mind off things."

Luca scanned my face with an expression I didn't like one bit. "Sure, but I really don't need any more problems. Things between New York and Chicago are already shaky."

"I won't do anything that'll hurt our relationship to Chicago."

Luca nodded but he didn't look convinced. He glanced back to Scuderi and his two daughters. "I better get back. Be back before dinner, then Scuderi doesn't have to know Liliana ever left the house. The bastard hardly pays attention to anything, least of all that girl."

I turned on my heel, leaving Luca to his shitty task of mediating between

Scuderi and Gianna. Lily sat at the kitchen table when I entered the room but quickly rose, a hopeful expression on her gorgeous face. Gorgeous. I had to stop thinking like that when I was around her. Lines easily got blurry, and Luca was right. We didn't need any more shit on our plate.

"So? Can we go out?" Lily asked with that same hopeful smile on her face.

I stopped more than an arm's length away. "Yes, but we need to get back before dinner."

That left a little more than two hours.

A hint of disappointment flickered in her eyes but it was gone quickly. "Then let's go."

We stepped out of the house and Lily stopped on the sidewalk and tilted her head up with a blissful expression. Sunrays cast her face in a soft glow. "This feels so good," she said softly.

I know so many things that feel even better.

How would her face look in the throes of passion? It was something I'd probably never find out. I didn't say anything, only watched her as she soaked in the sun.

She blinked up at me with an embarrassed smile. "Sorry. I'm wasting time. We were supposed to have coffee and not stand on the sidewalk all day."

"This is about you. If you'd rather stay here and enjoy the sun, we can do that too. I don't mind." Not one fucking bit. Watching Lily was something I could do all day.

She shook her head. Her blond hair settled in soft waves on her shoulders and I had to stop myself from reaching out and letting a strand of it glide through my fingers. For some reason I didn't know, I held out my arm for her. She hooked her arm through mine without hesitation, a grin twisting her lips as she peered up at me. Damn it. I led her down the street. "Do you know a nice café? I've been in Chicago plenty of times in the last few years but I'm not that familiar with the culinary scene."

"Just a ten-minute walk away is a small café with fantastic coffee and delicious cupcakes. We could go there. I usually only order everything to-go but we could sit down, if you want?" There were many things I wanted, and now that I'd seen her in those tight jeans and shirt, most of them involved Lily naked in my bed.

"That sounds good. Lead the way."

"You know what I like about you? You are so easygoing and relaxed. You seem like the guy next door. Nice and kind."

"Lily, I'm a Made Man. Don't make me into a hero that I'm not. I'm not kind or nice."

"You are to me," she said lightly. Her blue eyes were far too trusting. She didn't know the things I'd been thinking about her, most of them hadn't been nice. I wanted to do so many dirty things to her, she wouldn't even understand half of them, and that was why I needed to keep my distance. Maybe she looked grown up, but she was still too young, too innocent.

I only smiled. "I'm trying."

"You're doing good," she said teasingly. The sadness and hopelessness were gone from her face for the moment, and that was all the encouragement I needed.

Liliana

Romero smirked. "Thanks." I could have kissed him then. He looked so handsome and sexy.

"You're very welcome," I said. We strolled down the street toward the small café that looked like it belonged on a cobblestone street in Paris and not in Chicago. It was strange walking with a man who wasn't twice my age like my father's bodyguards. Only when we stopped at the counter did Romero release my arm, but until then we'd walked close like lovers. How would it feel if it were the truth? If he weren't just trying to distract me from my sick mother, if we were really a couple?

"Everything okay?" Romero asked in a low voice.

I had been staring. I quickly turned my attention to the girl behind the counter who was waiting for our order. "A cappuccino and a red velvet cupcake," I said distractedly. It was my standard order and my mind was too frazzled to check the blackboard for the daily specials.

"The same for me," Romero said and took his wallet out to pay for us both.

"You didn't have to pay for me," I whispered when we walked toward a free table near the window.

Romero raised one dark eyebrow. "A woman never pays when she's with me."

"Oh?" I said curiously. Romero looked like he already regretted his comment but it was too late. He'd piqued my curiosity. "How many girlfriends have you had?"

It was a very personal question.

Romero chuckled. "That's not something I'm going to tell you."

"That means many," I said with a laugh. The server brought our order, giving Romero time to compose himself. The moment she was out of earshot I said, "I know how things are with our men. You have a lot of women."

"So you know all of us?" Romero asked. He leaned back in his chair like he didn't have a care in the world. His white shirt clung to his muscled chest and arms, a very distracting view.

I took a sip from my cappuccino. "Women talk and from what I hear most Made Men don't say no to the whorehouses of the Outfit. For most of them it's some kind of hobby to have as many women as possible. I doubt it's different in New York."

"Many men do, but not all of them."

"So you are the exception?" I asked doubtfully. I wanted it to be true, but I was being realistic.

Romero took a bite from his cupcake, obviously considering what to tell me. "I've had wild days when I was younger, eighteen or nineteen maybe."

"And now? Do you have a girlfriend? A fiancée?" I'd always put the thought out of my mind but the way Romero had talked it was a valid option. I sipped at my coffee, glad for the feel of the cup in my hands. It gave me something to focus on.

Romero shook his head with an unreadable look on his face. "No, I've had girlfriends in the last few years but it's difficult to have a steady relationship if work always comes first. I'm a soldier. The Famiglia will always be my top priority. Most women can't bear it."

"Most women don't get asked if they want this life or not. What about an arranged marriage?"

"I don't like the idea of someone telling me who I should marry."

"So your family never tried to set you up with someone?"

Romero grinned. I could have jumped over the table and crawled onto his lap. "Of course they have. We're Italian, it's in our bloodstream to meddle with our children's lives."

"But you never liked any of the girls they suggested?"

"I liked some of them well enough but either they weren't interested in me or I couldn't see myself spending the rest of my life with them."

"And nobody ever tried to force you into marriage?"

Romero's expression darkened, turned more predatory. "How would they force me?"

I nodded. Yes, how? He was a Made Man, not a stupid girl. "You're right. You can make your own decisions."

Romero set down his cup and leaned forward, elbows on the table. "Luca could ask me to marry for political reasons. I probably wouldn't refuse him."

"But he wouldn't do that," I said.

Romero nodded. "Maybe you'll get to choose for yourself as well. You might meet the perfect guy soon and he might be worthy in your father's eyes."

The perfect guy sat in front of me. It stung that Romero suggested I'd find someone else. Didn't he realize I had feelings for him? I didn't want to find some guy my father would approve of. I wanted the man in front of me.

Perhaps he saw something in my expression because after that, we talked about random things, nothing of importance, and far too soon we had to make our way back to my home. This time we didn't link arms. I tried not to be disappointed, but it was hard. When we stepped into the entrance hall of the house, I could feel the weight of the lingering sadness return to my shoulders.

Romero lightly touched my arm. My eyes traced his strong jaw with the hint of dark stubble, his worried brown eyes, his prominent cheekbones. And then I did what I'd promised myself not to do again but right in this moment, in this cold, hopeless house he was the light and I was the moth. I pushed to my toes and kissed him. The touch was the briefest contact, hardly there but it made me long for more. Romero grasped my arms and pushed me away. "Liliana, don't."

I untangled myself from his hold and left without another word. Mother had said I should take risks for my happiness, and I was doing just that.

Romero

I stormed into the kitchen. I needed another coffee. The door smashed shut behind me with too much force. I wanted to tear something into tiny pieces. My lips still tingled from that ridiculous kiss. You couldn't even really call it that. It had been over too quickly, because I'd acted like the dutiful soldier I was supposed to be. Fuck it.

I made myself a coffee and emptied it in two gulps, then put the cup down with a loud clang.

The door to the kitchen swung open and Luca leaned in the doorway with a questioning look on his face. "You realize this isn't your home, right? I don't think Scuderi appreciates you destroying his expensive marble counter." The corners of his mouth twitched in an almost smile.

I relaxed against the kitchen island. "I don't think Scuderi even knows where his kitchen is. Where is he anyway? It's suspiciously quiet in the house. I thought he and Gianna would never stop fighting."

Luca's expression darkened. "They would still be at it, but Scuderi left for a meeting, which I'll have to do soon as well. Dante and I are going to discuss the Russians tonight at some Italian restaurant he loves."

"I assume I'll stay here to keep an eye on the women," I said tightly. The idea of being around Lily all evening worried me.

Luca came up to me. "Do I have to worry about what went on between you and Liliana while you were gone for coffee? Do I even want to know?"

I glared. "Nothing happened, Luca. You know me, I'm a good soldier."

"You are also a guy with a dick and Liliana is a gorgeous girl who's been flirting with you for years. Sometimes that can lead to unfortunate accidents."

I released a long breath.

"Fuck," Luca muttered. "I was joking. Don't tell me there's really been something going on."

"Liliana kissed me but you could hardly call it that. Our lips barely touched and I pushed her away so you have nothing to worry about."

"Oh, but I have to worry considering the look of regret on your face when you said that your lips barely touched. You want her."

"Yes, I want her," I muttered, starting to get annoyed by his interrogation. Luca used to be the guy who couldn't keep it in his pants and now he was acting all high and mighty. "But I'm not going to act on it. I can control myself. I'd never do anything to hurt the Famiglia."

Luca clapped my shoulder. "I know that. And if you're ever at risk of following your dick instead of your brain, just remember that Liliana is going through a lot. She's probably only looking for a distraction. She's vulnerable and young. I know you won't allow her to ruin her life."

That was a guilt trip if I'd ever heard one. I nodded, because the words waiting on the tip of my tongue were too harsh for my Capo.

Aria walked into the kitchen in that moment, but she stopped when she saw us. "Am I interrupting anything?" She glanced between Luca and me. "I thought we should start dinner. Father gave our maid the day off because he doesn't want anyone in the house right now. That means we have to cook."

"Let's order pizza," Luca said. He walked toward his wife and pulled her against him before kissing the top of her head. In the first few years of working for Luca, I'd have bet everything that he wasn't capable of that kind of affection.

"Did your conversation have something to do with Lily?" Aria asked casually as she rifled through several flyers from pizza delivery services.

I didn't say anything, and Luca shrugged. "Why do you ask?" he said.

Aria shook her head. "I'm not blind. Lily has been acting odd ever since she returned from her walk with Romero." She fixed me with a warning stare. "I don't want her alone with you."

Luca's eyebrows shot up. I knew I had to look pretty shocked too.

"Don't give me that look. You know I like you, Romero, but Lily has been going through so much recently and when it comes to you her brain stops working. I don't want to have to worry about her."

"So now you're protecting her virtue?" I asked sarcastically.

"Hey," Luca said sharply. "Don't take that tone with her."

Aria shook her head. "No, it's okay. I'm not protecting her virtue. I just don't want her to get hurt. You have younger sisters, don't you want to keep them safe?"

"I do," I said. "And I would never do anything that'll hurt Lily. But I respect your wish. I won't be alone with Lily from now on." With a curt nod in Luca's direction, I headed out of the kitchen. Aria's words didn't sit well with me. Luca had trusted me with her, though he was a possessive bastard, but Aria didn't trust me with her sister. Of course, truth was I'd never been remotely interested in Aria. I wasn't blind. She was beautiful, and definitely sexy, but I'd never fantasized about her, and not just because I knew Luca would cut my dick off if I made a move. Lily was a different matter. I'd imagined her naked body beneath me more than once and when I was close to her I wanted to press her against the wall and have my fucking way with her. That was a major problem. Maybe it was for the best that Aria's orders were now another barrier between Lily and me.

chapter *five*

Liliana

SOMEONE WAS SHAKING ME. I OPENED MY EYES BUT AT FIRST everything was blurry.

"Lily, get up. I think Mom's going to die," Aria said in a panicky voice. I jerked upright, my head spinning.

Aria was already on her way out of my room, probably to wake the others. One of us had always sat at Mother's bed to make sure she was never alone. Tonight it had been Aria's turn. I untangled myself from my blankets, slipped out of bed and hurried toward the bedroom at the end of the corridor. The smell of antiseptic and disinfectant greeted me even before I entered but my nose had grown used to the biting stench by now. Gianna was already inside, perched on the edge of the bed. Mother's eyes were closed and for a moment I was sure I was too late and she'd already died. Then I saw the slow rise and fall of her chest. I approached the bed hesitantly. Gianna barely glanced my way. She was glowering at her lap. I wrapped my arms around her shoulders from behind and pressed our cheeks together.

"I hate this," Gianna whispered.

"Where's the nurse?"

"She left so we could say goodbye in peace. She gave Mother another dose of morphine so she could go without pain."

Aria and Fabi came into the room. Fabi was wearing his brave face, and damn it, he looked so grown up. He was tall and strong for his age. Luca stood in the corridor but didn't come in, instead he closed the door, giving us privacy.

Mother's breathing was low, barely noticeable. Her eyes flickered back and forth under her lids as if she was watching a movie in her head. It wouldn't be much longer. Fabi grabbed the foot of the bed, his knuckles turning white. There were tears in his eyes but his face was like stone. I knew that look, *that posture*.

I turned away from him. Aria walked up to us. "How is she?"

I wasn't sure how to answer that question.

Gianna glared. "Where's Father? He should be here!" She'd spoken quietly but Aria and I still chanced a worried glance toward Mother. She didn't need to get upset in the last moments of her life. My stomach constricted painfully and for a second I was sure I'd have to rush to the bathroom to throw up. Death was part of our life, especially when you grew up in our world. I'd attended countless funerals in the last few years but almost all of them had been for people I'd barely known.

"I don't know," Aria admitted. "I knocked at his door and even walked in but it didn't look like he'd slept in his bed at all."

Gianna and I exchanged a look. Was he really with one of his whores tonight? Mother had been feeling very weak yesterday so it didn't come as a surprise that tonight was the night. He should have stayed home to be there for her.

"Do you know where he is? You've been acting like his best buddy the last few days," Gianna muttered with a scowl in Fabi's direction.

He stiffened. "He doesn't tell me where he goes. And I'm not his best buddy, but as his only son I have responsibilities."

Gianna stood, and I had no choice but to let her go. "Oh my God, what kind of bullshit is that. I can't believe it," she hissed.

"Gianna," Aria said in warning. "It's enough. Not here, not right now."

"It doesn't matter that Father's not here," I said firmly. "We are here for her. We are the most important people in her life, not him."

That was the last time we mentioned Father that night. Hours passed with Mother's state staying the same, and occasionally my eyes fell shut, but then her breathing changed.

I sat up in my chair and took her hand. "Mom?" I asked.

Aria was holding her other hand. Gianna didn't move from her spot in the armchair in the corner. Her legs were pressed up against her chest, her chin resting on her knees. Fabi had fallen asleep with his cheek on the wooden foot of the bed. I reached out and nudged him. He jerked up in his chair.

Mother's eyelids fluttered like she was going to open them. I held my breath, hoping she'd look at us once more, maybe even say something but then her breathing slowed even more.

I wasn't sure how much longer it took. I lost any sense of time as I monitored Mother's chest, the way it barely moved, until it stopped altogether. Fabi ran out to get the nurse, but I didn't need her to tell me what I already knew; our mother was gone. The nurse moved around us, and then with a sad nod, she disappeared again.

I let go of Mother's hand, stood from my chair and stepped back. Aria didn't move, still clutching Mother's hand. One moment Mother was there and the next she was gone. Just like that a life ended, and with it the dreams and hopes of that person. Life was so short, any moment could be your last. Mother had told me to be happy, but in our world happiness wasn't something that came easily.

Aria rested her head on the edge of the bed, sobbing without a sound. Just like me, Fabi stood back. He looked like he couldn't comprehend what had happened. Gianna walked up to Aria, for the first time in hours moving closer to the bed and put her hand on Aria's shoulder. She didn't even glance Mother's way, and I got it. Gianna's relationship with our mother had always been difficult and only gotten worse when Mother had accepted how horrible Father had treated Gianna after she'd run away. In the days since her arrival here, Gianna's feelings had often changed from one second to the other.

After a moment, Aria stood and pressed a kiss to Mother's forehead. To my surprise, Gianna did the same, though she quickly stepped back from the bed again. I could only stare. I knew I should kiss Mother's forehead as well as a last goodbye, but I couldn't bring myself to touch this lifeless corpse. That wasn't her anymore. That was something empty and lifeless.

I staggered out of the room. My throat was cording up and my eyes were burning. I wanted to run and never stop but in the corridor I bumped into Romero. If he hadn't grabbed my shoulders, I would have toppled over. I gasped for breath. Panic was slowly tightening around my body like a vise.

"Take her away," Luca ordered. I hadn't even noticed him.

"What about Aria's order?"

"I don't give a damn."

Romero wrapped an arm around my waist and steered me down the hallway. I was still trying to suck air into my lungs but it was futile. My legs buckled.

"Hey," Romero said in a soothing voice. "Sit down." He guided me to the floor and helped me put my head between my legs while he drew calming circles on my back. The feel of his warm hand steadied me.

"Just breathe," he murmured. "It's okay."

His voice pulled me out of the black hole that wanted to consume me and eventually my breathing returned to normal. "She's dead," I whispered when I was sure I could speak.

Romero halted in his stroking of my back. "I'm sorry."

I nodded, fighting back new tears. "Father wasn't there. I don't know where he is. He should have been there for her in her last moments!" The anger felt good, better than the sadness.

"Yes, he should have. Maybe Dante called him away."

I glowered up at Romero. "Dante wouldn't have done it, not in the middle of the night, not when he knows that our mother is so sick. No, Father didn't want to be here when Mother died. He barely visited her since she got worse. He's a selfish bastard and is probably screwing one of his whores right this moment."

Romero smiled darkly. "I sometimes forget that you're an adult now and know the ugly sides of our world."

"You better not forget," I said. "I know more than all of you think."

"I don't doubt it," he said. For an instant we only stared at each other. I felt calmer now.

"Thanks," I said simply. Romero pulled his hand away from my back. I wished he hadn't. His touch had felt good. He straightened and held out his hand. I took it so he could pull me to my feet. The door to Mother's room opened and Aria stepped out, her eyes zooming in on Romero and me. He let go of my hand, gave me an encouraging smile before he went to Aria to tell her how sorry he was about Mother's death. Aria nodded but then her eyes darted to me again. Her cheeks were wet with tears. I walked toward her and wrapped my arms around her. Romero took that as his cue to leave but before he turned the corner he glanced over his shoulder and our gazes met. The cold and empty feeling in my chest eased and something warm and more hopeful took its place. Then he disappeared from my view. I almost went after him, but my sisters needed me now. Steps sounded behind us and then Luca was heading our way, lowering his phone from his ear.

"He doesn't answer his phone? Did you try to send him a message?" Aria asked as she pulled back from me and hurried toward her husband.

Luca grimaced. "Yes, I sent him two messages, but he hasn't replied yet, and he doesn't answer my calls. I doubt he'll be back any time soon."

I returned into Mother's bedroom even though my body bristled at the mere idea, but Aria needed some time with her husband. I'd only be the fifth wheel. Before I closed the door, I saw Luca cradling my sister's face and kissing her eyelids. That was love and devotion. He wouldn't have left her side if she'd been dying. He wasn't a good man, but he was a good husband. I prayed that I'd be as lucky one day. I couldn't live the life my mother had, with a cold husband who didn't care about me. I knew Romero wouldn't be like that. But it wasn't like Father would choose him for my husband.

Gianna was back in her armchair but she was talking on the phone in a low voice, probably with Matteo. She, too, had found someone regardless of how hard she'd fought her marriage in the beginning.

Fabi was gone. I didn't want to interrupt Gianna so I went in search of my little brother. I found him in his room, sitting at his desk and polishing one of his many combat knives. They were shiny already.

"Do you want to talk?" I asked.

He didn't even look up, only pressed his lips together.

I waited before I finally nodded. "Okay. But if you change your mind, I'm in my room." He didn't react, only reached for the next knife and began polishing that too.

Romero waited outside. He nodded toward my brother. "Do you want me to talk to him? Maybe he needs someone who isn't family."

"You mean who isn't female," I said bitterly, but then I swallowed my emotions. "You're probably right. He'd rather talk to you than me."

Romero looked like he wanted to say more but then he walked past me and toward my brother. "Do you need help polishing your collection?"

Fabi's head shot up. Admiration flickered across his pale face. He didn't say anything but he handed Romero a cloth. Romero perched on the edge of the desk and unsheathed his own knife from its holster. A long, curved blade that looked absolutely deadly. Fabi's eyes lit up and he rose from his chair to take a closer look. "Wow," he breathed.

"I should probably polish it first. Your knives are in a much better condition."

"That's because they are only for show," Fabi said. "But yours is a weapon, it's real. How many have you killed with it?"

I closed the door quickly. I'd had enough death for one night. I didn't want to know how many Romero had caused in his lifetime. I glanced down toward the bedroom where Mother's corpse waited to be taken away, then I turned around and headed toward my room. Aria had Luca, Gianna had Matteo, and for the moment even Fabi had Romero, but I'd deal with this alone. I'd been doing it for weeks and months now.

Romero

I wanted to be there for Lily, wanted to console her, but I respected Aria's wishes. She too had gone through enough shit and didn't need the additional grief of worrying about her sister.

Instead I showed Fabiano how to handle my knife, how to unsheathe a long blade as quickly as a short one. It was easy to distract him from his sadness. But damn it, he wasn't the one who needed me most.

Needed you? Goddammit, if I started thinking like that now, I'd get myself in huge trouble. Lily wasn't my responsibility, and she definitely didn't need me.

Fabi drew his knife from the holster I'd lent to him and grinned at how fast he'd done it. I'd been like that once, eager to learn everything there was about fighting, about winning. Eager to prove my worth. My father had been a low debt collector, someone who never got to talk to the Capo directly. I'd wanted to be better, to prove my worth to him and myself. Fabiano had huge expectations resting on his shoulders, he had plenty of ways to fail, but very few options to excel.

"I need to go to Luca now," I said eventually. Fabi nodded, and settled back on his chair. He picked up a cloth and polished the same knife again. I guessed he would spend all night like that and maybe even the next few days.

I walked out and headed for the stairs but stopped in front of Liliana's door, listening for a sound. Maybe I wanted to hear crying so I could storm in and console her, be her knight in fucking armor.

I moved on.

chapter
six

Liliana

I looked deathly pale in mourning. Aria, Gianna, and I wore the same modest black dress and ballet flats, our hair pinned up in a bun. I didn't wear makeup, even though the shadows beneath my eyes were scary. Father had organized a huge funeral; expensive oak coffin, a sea of beautiful flowers, only the best food for the feast afterwards. He acted like the devastated widower everyone expected to see. It was a marvelous show. He should have been there for Mother when she really needed him. This was only to impress people and maybe to make him feel better. Even a man like him had to feel guilty for abandoning his dying wife.

The funeral was a big affair in our world. Father was an important man, and so Mother's death was a social event. Everyone wanted to attend, and everyone was crying crocodile tears as they said their condolences. My eyes were dry as sand. I could see people glancing my way, waiting for me to cry over my mother, to show the reaction they all expected from me. But I couldn't cry. I didn't want to cry, not surrounded by so many people with their fake tears. They pretended they'd cared for my mother, that they'd known her but none of these people had visited her when she was bound to the house. She'd been dead to them long before her death. The moment she hadn't been the glitzy society lady they'd ditched her like a dirty rag. They made me sick, all of them.

Father put his arms around Fabi's and my shoulders as he led us toward the coffin. I shuddered under his touch. I didn't think he realized it was revulsion for his closeness that had caused my reaction because he actually squeezed my shoulder. It took incredible self-control for me to stay where I was and not rip away from him.

The priest started his prayer as the coffin was slowly lowered into the hole. I peered up through my lashes and caught Romero's eyes over the grave. Unlike Luca and Matteo, who'd flown in for the funeral, Romero wasn't allowed to stand on this side with our family. His expression was solemn as we watched each other but then he lowered his gaze back to the coffin. He'd been avoiding me in the last few days. When I entered the room he was in, he usually left with a stupid excuse. It was obvious he couldn't stand my presence and didn't know how to tell me. Everyone was walking on eggshells around my siblings and me now. I wished he'd tell me the truth. I could handle it.

Father led us back toward the other mourners, away from Mother's grave and finally let go of me. I released a quiet breath, glad to be out of the spotlight and away from my father.

The moment people started to head for the coffin to say their last goodbye, I backed away. Nobody stopped me. Nobody even seemed to notice. They were busy putting on their show. I turned and didn't look back. I rushed down the path, away from the grave, sending pebbles flying as my feet pounded the ground. I wasn't even sure where I was going. The graveyard was huge, there were plenty of places to find peace and silence. I reached a part that was even more opulent than where Mother had been buried. Rows over rows of old family vaults surrounded me. Most of them were locked but one of the iron gates was ajar. I headed that way, and after having made sure nobody was watching me, I opened it and slipped inside. It was cool in the vault and the smell of mildew drifted into my nose. Everything was made from gray marble. I sank down slowly and sat with my back against the cold wall.

In moments like this I understood why Gianna had run away. I'd never had the urge to leave this life behind forever, but sometimes I wanted to escape at least for a little while.

I knew eventually someone would notice I was missing and come looking for me, but I didn't even care that Father would lose his shit on me.

It took less than an hour before I heard someone call my name in the distance. I opened my lips to reply but not a sound came out. I rested my head against the marble, and peered out through the bars of the iron gate. So often in my life I'd felt as if I was surrounded by invisible bars, and now I sought shelter behind them. A bitter smile twisted my lips. Steps crunched outside of the vault. I held my breath as someone came into view outside the gate.

A tall form with a familiar frame loomed in front of it. Romero. He hadn't seen me yet but his eyes scanned their surroundings. They passed right over the spot where I was hiding and he was about to turn away. I could have stayed hidden, alone with my anger and misery and sadness, but suddenly I didn't want this. For some reason, I wanted Romero to find me. He hadn't faked tears and he wasn't family; he was safe. I cleared my throat quietly but of course a man like Romero didn't miss it. He turned and his eyes zoomed in on me. He headed for me, opened the gate and stepped in with a bent head because he was too tall to stand. He held out his hand for me. I searched his eyes for the pity I hated so much, but he looked merely concerned and maybe even like he cared. I wasn't sure what to make of his concern when not too long ago he'd done his utmost to stay away from me.

I slipped my hand into his and his fingers closed around me before he pulled me to my feet. The momentum of the movement catapulted me straight into Romero's arms. I should have pulled back. He should have pushed me back. We didn't.

It felt good to be so close to someone, to feel his warmth, something my life had seemed so devoid of recently. He slowly backed out of the vault, taking me with him, still holding me close.

"We've been looking for you for almost an hour," Romero said quietly, worriedly, but all I could focus on was how close his lips were and how good he smelled. "Your father will be glad to know you're safe."

My father. Anger surged up in me at how he'd acted in the last few months. I was so tired of being angry, of not knowing where to go with my anger. I stepped onto my toes, closed my eyes and pressed my lips against Romero's. This was the third time I did this. It seemed I never learned, but I wasn't even scared of being rejected anymore. I was so numb inside, there was no way anything could hurt me again.

Romero's hands came up to my shoulders as if he was going to shove me away, but then he merely rested them there, warm and strong. He didn't try to deepen the kiss but our lips moved against each other. There was only the barest touch and even that was over too quickly. Something trailed down my cheeks and caught on my lips. I'd never imagined my first real kiss would taste of tears. I sank back down onto my heels and my eyes fluttered open. I was too drained, too sad, too angry, to be embarrassed about my actions.

Romero searched my face, his dark brows drawn together. "Lily," he began, but then I started crying for real, fat tears rolling down my cheeks. I buried my face against Romero's chest. He cupped the back of my head and let me sob. In the safety of Romero's arms I dared to give my sadness room, didn't fear it would swallow me whole. I knew Romero wouldn't let it. Maybe it was a ridiculous notion but I believed Romero would keep me safe from everything. I'd tried to forget him, had tried to move on, find someone new to focus my crush on but they all fell short.

"We should return. Your father will be worried sick by now."

"He isn't worried about me. He's only worried about how I make him look bad," I said quietly, pulling back. I wiped my cheeks. Romero brushed a strand away that stuck to my wet skin. We still stood close but now that I had a better grip on my emotions I stepped back, ashamed by the way I'd thrown myself at Romero. *Again.* I was glad I couldn't read his mind. I didn't want to know what he thought of me now.

Romero's phone rang and after an apologetic smile at me, he picked up. "Yes, I have her. We'll be there in a moment."

I stared off toward an elderly man who stood before a grave. His lips were moving and he was leaning heavily on a walking stick. I had a feeling he was talking to his deceased wife, telling her how his days had been, how much he wanted to be reunited with her again. That would never be my father. He seemed to have gotten over Mother's death already.

Romero touched my shoulder lightly and I almost flew back into his arms, but this time I was strong. "Are you ready to head back?"

Ready? No. I didn't want to see Father or the fake mourning. I didn't want to hear one more word of pity. "Yes."

Neither of us mentioned the kiss as we walked back toward my mother's grave. Romero had kissed me, or let me kiss him out of pity, that was the harsh truth of the situation. Luca and Aria were the only people waiting for us.

Aria rushed toward me and wrapped me into a tight hug. "Are you okay?"

I felt bad instantly. She too had lost our mother. She too was sad, and now she'd had to worry about me on top of everything. "Yes, I just needed a moment alone."

Aria nodded with understanding. "Father and the other guests have moved on to the house for the funeral feast. We should head there too, or Father will get even angrier."

I nodded. Aria shot Romero a look I had trouble deciphering. Then she led me toward the car, her arms tightly wrapped around my shoulders. Luca and Romero trailed behind. I didn't look back at Mother's grave again, knew it would have been too much for me.

"What was that look you gave Romero?" I asked quietly as we settled on the back seat.

Aria made an innocent face but I didn't buy it. I knew her too well even if we weren't as close as we used to be, due to the distance between us. She sighed. "I told him to stay away from you."

"You did what?" I hissed. Luca glanced over his shoulder at us, and I lowered my voice even further. I hoped he hadn't heard what I'd said. Romero seemed busy finding a good radio station.

"Why did you do that?" I asked in a bare whisper.

"Lily, I don't want you to get hurt. You think Romero will make you feel happier and help with the sadness, but it'll only make things worse. Maybe you think you've fallen for him but you shouldn't mistake loneliness for something else."

I stared at my sister incredulously. "I'm not an idiot. I know my own feelings."

Aria took my hand. "Please don't be mad, Lily. I only want to protect you."

Everyone always said they wanted to protect me. I wondered from what. Life?

Two days later, Aria, Gianna, Matteo, Romero, and Luca left for New York. I wasn't sure when I'd see them again. Aria had asked Father if I could visit them for a couple of weeks in the summer but he'd refused with a not so veiled look in Gianna's direction. I'd put on a brave face, told them I'd be busy spending time with my friends and taking care of Fabi. Romero hadn't even hugged me goodbye, and he and I never got the chance for a private talk. Maybe it was for the best that I couldn't ask him about the kiss.

Aria called the same evening, trying to make sure I was really okay. I wasn't but I didn't tell her.

Instead I learned to go through the motions, trying to pretend things were going well. But my friends were either on vacation or busy with family matters, and I spent my days alone in our house with only the maid and my ancient bodyguard for company. Father and Fabi were gone almost all the time, and when they returned they shared new secrets they couldn't talk to me about, and even in their presence I felt alone. The loneliness you felt when you were surrounded by people was the worst kind.

I often spent hours sitting in the chair next to the bed where mother died, thinking about her last words and wondering how I was supposed to keep my promise. Father didn't allow me to go to college, didn't allow me to visit New York, didn't want me to party with my friends. All I could do was wait for something to happen, for life to happen. Maybe if Mother hadn't died Father would have spent the summer introducing me to potential husbands and I would have a wedding to plan in the near future. Even that seemed preferable to the way my life unfolded now, without anything to look forward to.

Romero

Luca, Matteo, and I played cards when Aria's cellphone rang. She sat on the sofa with Gianna, drinking wine and laughing.

The moment Aria started talking I knew something was wrong. Luca put his cards down as well.

"Why didn't you call before? You should have sent her with us right away!"

Luca got up and went over to his wife.

"You can talk to me, too," Aria said before she raised her eyes to Luca. "My father wants to talk to you." She held out the phone for him and Luca took it with a worried glance at her.

Gianna crossed the room toward her sister. "What's going on?"

I had a bad feeling.

"Lily passed out today. Apparently she hasn't been eating much since the funeral."

I rose from my chair. "Is she alright?"

Aria nodded. "Physically, yes. Father called a doctor and he said she needs to eat and drink more. But it's more than that. From what Father said Lily's been alone almost the entire time since we left. Nobody took care of her. I can't believe I let Father talk me into leaving her there. I should have taken her to New York with me right away."

"By my honor, no harm will come to Liliana when she's here. She'll be well protected. I will make sure of that," Luca said. Then he listened to whatever Scuderi had to say on the other end. "I'm aware of that. Believe me, Liliana will be just as safe as she's in Chicago." He listened again and then he hung up.

Aria rushed toward him. "And? Will he allow her to come here?"

Luca smiled tightly. "He agreed to let her spend the entire summer here, maybe even beyond that. He seemed really worried about her."

"Really? That's great!" Aria said, beaming.

"I doubt he's doing it because he's worried but who cares as long as he allows her to stay with us," Gianna said.

"When will she arrive?" I asked, trying to sound casual, as if I was merely a concerned soldier making sure he could fulfill his bodyguard duties.

Luca's expression made it clear he didn't buy it for one second but Aria was too wrapped up in her euphoria to pay attention. "Tomorrow afternoon."

"She'll be staying in our apartment, right?" Aria asked.

Luca nodded. "I told your father I'd personally make sure that she'd be safe."

"You mean that she doesn't go around having fun or God forbid sully her purity," Gianna muttered.

"Yes, that," Luca said matter-of-factly. "And since war with the Outfit might be the outcome if I don't keep my promise, I'll do everything in my power to make sure she has only very limited fun." Again his eyes found me and I had to suppress a curse. He didn't even know about the kiss Lily and I had shared in the graveyard. I wondered how much worse it would be if he actually knew.

"We could spend the summer in the Hamptons. It's too hot and stuffy in the city and we're using the mansion not often enough anyway." Aria touched Luca's forearm and fixed him with one of her looks that always got him. "Please, Luca? I don't want Lily to be stuck in the apartment. In the Hamptons we can lie at the pool and swim in the ocean and take trips with our boat."

"Okay, okay," Luca said with a resigned look. "But Matteo and I can't stay with you the entire time. We have a lot to deal with at the moment. Romero and Sandro will have to keep you safe while we're gone."

Aria chanced a glance in my direction. She probably wondered if it was a good idea to have me around her sister, and to be honest I wondered the same thing.

chapter *seven*

Liliana

I HADN'T EVEN REALIZED HOW MUCH I'D NEGLECTED MYSELF IN THE last two weeks since Mother's funeral. I hadn't been hungry and rarely thirsty, so I hadn't eaten much.

Of course, I was happy that my fainting had changed Father's mind. Sending me to New York was the greatest gift he could have given me. In the last two weeks I'd wanted nothing more than to be finally out of this house.

When I landed in New York, Aria and Luca were waiting for me. After a brief moment of disappointment that Romero wasn't there, I allowed myself to be happy that I was here at all. Aria hugged me tightly. When she pulled back, her eyes wandered over my body. "How could Father not have noticed something before. God, you've lost so much weight, Lily."

"It's only a few pounds and I'll gain it back in no time," I said with a smile.

"You better," Luca said, giving me a one-arm hug. "I will have you force-fed if necessary. I promised your father to take good care of you."

I rolled my eyes. "I don't even understand why Father cares. He hardly paid attention to me and now he's suddenly worried sick over me? What is that all about?"

A look of worry passed Aria's face and I was about to ask her about it, when Luca nudged me and her toward the exit. "Let's get going. I hate this place."

"So what are we going to do today?" I asked as we headed toward the car. After weeks of doing nothing, of feeling nothing, I needed to get out, needed to *feel alive* again.

"Nothing," Aria said apologetically.

My face fell and Aria hurried to add, "But only because we're leaving for the Hamptons early in the morning. We'll be spending the summer at the beach."

"Really?" I asked.

Aria smiled brightly, and suddenly the dark cloud over my head burst open.

Romero

I was good at keeping a straight face even in difficult situations, but when I first saw Lily as she walked into the penthouse, I wasn't sure I could hide my fury. Fury toward her father for letting his own daughter drown in her sadness while he was busy improving his position in the Outfit by inducting his too young son.

Lily had lost weight, enough that her collarbones and shoulder blades stood out. She looked breakable, but still so goddamn beautiful. I wanted to protect her from everything.

Her eyes met mine, and the longing in them almost compelled me to cross the room, to wrap her in my arms, but I stayed where I was, not only because of the look Aria sent me. Luca had given his promise to Scuderi. We, the Famiglia, would keep Liliana safe, and that included her honor. Considering that most of my dreams included Lily in some state of undress I definitely needed to keep my distance, and I would.

In the last few weeks, I'd fucked several girls in the hopes that they'd dispel Lily from my mind, but seeing her now, I realized that it had been completely in vain. Of course, it hadn't really helped that I'd imagined it was Lily every time I'd been with a woman.

I was completely screwed.

Luca came up to me as I leaned against the kitchen counter and watched the reunion of the three sisters. "Is this going to be a problem, you being in a mansion with Liliana?"

"No," I said firmly.

"You sure, because that look on your face a moment ago told me a different story."

"I'm sure. Liliana is a pretty girl like you said, but I've been with pretty girls. I've been with prettier girls even. I won't risk Scuderi's wrath."

It was a fucking lie. None of the girls I'd been with could compete with Lily's beauty, but thankfully Luca couldn't read minds even though he tried to make the stupider soldiers believe he had some sort of sixth sense like that just to keep them in line.

"Not just Scuderi's wrath," Luca said. "This is fucking serious. I mean it, Romero."

Was that a warning?

I had to bite back a comment and nodded. Luca was a good Capo and I'd never had a problem following his rules but for some reason this didn't sit well with me. Lily tried to catch my eye during dinner but I made sure to keep my attention on Matteo and Luca. I didn't want Lily to get her hopes up.

And what was more important, I needed to get my own fucking urges in check.

Liliana

Romero was still ignoring me. Though ignoring wasn't quite the right word. He treated me with polite detachment, always friendly, but never too warm. If I hadn't known what Aria had told him, I'd have taken it harder but, as it was, I was fairly sure that he was interested in me.

The first day at the mansion, the sun was shining brightly and we decided to have dinner outside on the beach. I decided to wear my pink beach dress. It was low-cut, backless and hugged my curves. Well, at least it usually did, now it was slightly loose in certain places but it looked still very nice. When my sisters and I headed for the table that the men had set up, Romero looked up from the barbecue that he was manning and the look in his eyes when he spotted me was all the encouragement I needed. That was far from the polite detachment of the last twenty-four hours.

He tore his gaze away from me and returned to his task of turning the steaks. He looked amazing too, the way the sinking sun caught on his brown hair, the way his forearms flexed when he moved. I loved the way he'd rolled up the white sleeves and had opened the upper two buttons of his shirt, revealing a sliver of tanned chest.

"You're drooling," Gianna whispered in my ear.

I flushed and jerked my gaze away from Romero, then glared at my sister who sank down at the table with a sneaky grin on her face.

I took the chair beside her. "Did you tell Romero to stay away from me as well?"

Gianna took the bottle of white wine out of the cooler and filled our glasses. "Me? No. You know me. I'm all for the naughty and forbidden. If you want to have a piece of Romero, then do it. Life is too short."

I paused with the wine glass against my lips. Mother's words crashed into my mind, almost the same words. "Aria disagrees," I said, then I downed half of the wine.

"Aria's trying to act like a mother hen, but you have to decide what you want."

"Are you trying to get me in trouble?" I asked, feeling my stomach warm from the wine. I finished my glass in another long gulp.

"I don't think you need me for that, to be honest," Gianna said with raised red eyebrows. "But do me a favor and slow down with the wine."

"I thought you wanted me to have fun."

"Yeah, but I want you to be sober enough to realize what you want. And I don't think Romero will take you seriously if you're shitfaced."

"You're right. He's too much of a gentleman to take advantage of a drunk girl."

Gianna snorted. "Wow, now I know why Aria's worried." She watched Romero for a while. He was laughing about something Matteo had said. "I wouldn't put too much trust in his gentlemanliness, if I were you. Stay in control when you're with him. He's still a Made Man. Don't make me have to kill him, okay?"

"I thought you weren't a mother hen?"

"I'm not. I'm the angry mother bear who's going to tear his dick off if he hurts you."

I burst into laughter. Aria joined us at the table in that moment and regarded us with suspicion. "I don't know if I like you two alone together. It smells like trouble if you ask me."

"You don't want me alone with anyone it seems," I said, only half teasing.

Aria groaned and took a glass of wine for herself. "Are you still mad at me?"

"I'm not mad at you." I was only going to ignore Aria's orders, and I'd do my best to convince Romero to ignore them as well.

Aria glanced at Gianna who made an innocent face, then at me. "I don't like this. Promise me you two aren't getting into trouble."

"I've had enough trouble, thank you very much," Gianna said with a grin.

Aria fixed me with her older sister look.

"I'll behave, I promise," I said eventually. Then I poured myself more wine, trying to come up with a plan to get some alone time with Romero. I knew Aria would do her best to be my constant shadow.

During the day it was pretty much impossible to shake Aria off. She watched me, and particularly Romero like a hawk. When had she turned into such a killjoy? The nights and the early mornings were the only options I had. Since

I barely slept anyway, that wouldn't prove too much of a problem. For some reason the darkness made me afraid of falling asleep, so I spent the nights fantasizing about Romero and making plans on how to seduce him while I caught the occasional hour of sleep when my sisters and I were sunbathing in the afternoon.

It had taken me a few days to gather my courage for my next move. I knew how to put on a brave face but this wasn't something I'd ever done before. I had no experience with men, except for the harmless flirting I'd done with Father's soldiers over the years.

I wasn't as worried about Romero's rejection as I used to be. I'd caught him watching me too often in the last few days when he thought nobody was paying attention. When the sun came up, the first hesitant rays brushing my face, I slipped out of bed and crept toward my window facing the beach. Like every other morning in the last few days, I spotted a lonely figure jogging along the beach in shorts and without a shirt. This was the highlight of my day. I wasn't sure where Romero took the discipline to get up before sunrise every morning to work out, and I really hoped he wouldn't show that much self-control when it came to me. I watched him jog uphill toward the mansion and pressed myself closer to the wall so he wouldn't find me spying on him. After he'd disappeared from view, I waited another five minutes before I headed out of my room. It was deadly silent at this hour, barely six o'clock. My sisters were still asleep; they never got up this early, and Matteo and Luca had left for New York yesterday and wouldn't be back until tonight, so the only person who could have crossed my path was the other guard Sandro. When I passed Sandro's door I made sure to be extra quiet, but there was no sound coming from his room. I picked up my pace the closer I got to Romero's room.

I knew it was wrong. If someone found out, if *my father* found out, he'd keep my locked up in Chicago. He wouldn't even let me leave the house anymore. What I was doing was vastly inappropriate and unladylike. People were still bad-mouthing Gianna after all that time. They'd jump at the chance to find a new victim, and what could be better than another Scuderi sister getting caught in the act and with a mere soldier no less?

And deep down I knew I was exactly like Gianna when it came to resisting temptation. I simply couldn't. Romero's door wasn't locked. I slipped into his bedroom on tiptoes, holding my breath. He wasn't there but I could hear water running in the adjoining bathroom. I crept in that direction. The door was ajar and I peered through the gap.

Romero was a creature of habit, so I found him under the shower as expected. But from my vantage point I couldn't see much. I edged the door open and slipped in.

My breath caught at the sight of him. He had his back turned to me and it was a glorious view. The muscles in his shoulders and back flexed as he washed his brown hair. There was a cross, which was wrapped in barb-wire, inked into the skin over his spine. Naturally, my eyes dipped lower to his perfectly shaped backside. I'd never seen a man like this, but I couldn't imagine that anyone could compare to Romero. Even the fantasy-Romero from my dreams couldn't compare.

He began to turn. I should have left then. But I stared in wonder at his body. Was he aroused? He tensed when he spotted me. There was another tattoo over his heart, the motto of the Famiglia.

His eyes captured my gaze before they slid over my nightgown and naked legs. And then I found an answer to my question. He hadn't really been aroused before. *Oh hell.*

My cheeks heated as I watched him grow harder under my unwavering attention. It was all I could do not to cross the distance between us and touch him. I'd never understood the concept of wanting something so badly, it hurt; I did now.

Romero slid the shower open with unhurried movements and wrapped a towel around his waist. Then he stepped out. The scent of his spicy shower gel, peppermint and sandalwood, wafted into my nose. Slowly he advanced on me. "You know," he said in a strangely rough voice. "If someone found us like this, they might get the wrong idea. An idea that could cost me my life, and you your reputation."

I still couldn't move. I was stone, but my insides seemed to burn, to liquefy into red-hot lava. I couldn't look away. I'd spent hours going over the things I wanted to say once I had him cornered, but now I was speechless.

My eyes lingered on the edge of the towel, on the fine line of dark hairs disappearing beneath it, on the delicious V of his hips. My hand moved, reaching for Romero's chest, needing to feel his skin beneath my fingertips. I had no impulse control when it came to him. Maybe it should have terrified me. Girls weren't supposed to be like that.

Romero caught my wrist before I could touch him, his grip almost painful. My gaze shot up, half embarrassed and half surprised. What I saw on Romero's face made me shiver.

He leaned forward, coming closer and closer. My eyes fluttered shut, but the kiss I wanted never came. Upon hearing the creak of the door, I peered up at Romero. He'd opened the bathroom door wide. That's why he'd moved closer, not to kiss me. Embarrassment washed over me. How could I have thought he was interested in me?

"You need to leave," he murmured as he straightened. His fingers were still curled around my wrist.

"Then let me go."

He released me instantly and took a step back. I stayed where I was. I wanted to touch him, wanted him to touch me in turn. He cursed and then he was upon me, one hand cradling the back of my head, the other on my hip, the touch hot, warning and promise. I could almost taste his lips they were so close. His touch made me feel more alive than anything ever had, and I wanted more of this feeling, wanted to drown in it.

"Leave," he rasped. "Leave before I break my oath." It was half plea, half order.

I wanted him to break his oath, wanted nothing more, but something in his gaze made me back away a few steps. I was brave but I wasn't stupid. Letting my gaze travel the length of him one last time, I quickly rushed outside and crossed the bedroom, only stopping to check the corridor before I left. There was nobody around so I stepped out and hurried toward my room. I'd almost reached my door when Gianna showed up, still dressed in pajamas and a cup of hot chocolate in her hands. She halted, eyes narrowing in suspicion. "What are you doing sneaking around the corridor in your nightgown?"

Why did she have to choose today to get up early?

"Nothing," I said a bit too fast. I could feel heat creep up into my cheeks. When would my body ever stop betraying me in situations like this?

"Nothing," Gianna repeated, crossing her arms in front of her chest and taking a casual sip from her cup. "Right. Isn't Romero's room in that direction?"

I shrugged. "Maybe. It's not like he's ever invited me over."

"Doesn't mean you haven't been there."

"Are you done with your interrogation? I don't know why you suddenly try to sound like Father. It's not like you've always been playing by the rules."

"Easy, tiger. I was just curious. For all I care you can visit Romero and whoever else you want as often as you like, but you know how things are. If the servants catch you, rumors will spread like wildfire. You have to be clever about it and running around the house like a chicken without its head isn't going to help. If Aria had caught you like this, you'd have a lot of explaining to do."

"I did nothing wrong," I said stubbornly.

Gianna smiled bitterly. "I know, but that doesn't mean they won't punish you for it. Just be careful." She handed me her cup of hot chocolate. "I think you need it more than me."

I'd thought I was being careful, but at least my sisters seemed to see right through me. I could only hope they would keep my secret from their husbands. Both Romero and I would get in huge trouble if people started to believe something was going on between us, even if there wasn't. Nobody cared about the truth. I wished there was something to talk about, wished Romero had kissed me like I'd wanted him to, wished he hadn't stopped at kissing.

Romero

I almost chased after Liliana to drag her back into my room and have my way with her. Damn it. She'd wanted me. It had been written all over her face plain as day. The first moment I'd turned around and seen her standing there with huge blue eyes, I'd thought I was imagining it. After all, I'd been thinking about her during my shower. She was on my mind way too often. If Luca knew how hard it was for me to concentrate at the moment, he'd have someone else protect Aria, and he'd definitely have me sent back to New York, far away from Lily. If I was a good soldier, I'd ask him to do it, but I didn't want to go anywhere. I wanted to stay near Lily.

I ran a hand through my wet hair as I glared at the bathroom door. Why had I sent her away? She'd wanted me to kiss her. She'd wanted more than that. Why did I have to listen to my fucking conscience then?

But it wasn't even morals that kept me from kissing Lily. It went against my oath, my duty, but that wasn't the main reason. Even though she wasn't really mine to protect, I still *wanted* to protect Lily, even from herself. She couldn't possibly realize the consequences of flirting with me like that. In our world a girl's entire worth was based on her reputation, her pureness, that was true in particular for girls from high-ranking Made Men. But even among soldiers only very few women were allowed to date someone they chose. We still followed the same rules from more than a century ago and I doubted that would change any time soon. If I let Lily close, if I let this thing between us unfold, if I took her the way I wanted her, then she'd be ruined in our society's eyes.

Of course, there were plenty of things we could do that wouldn't destroy her virginity. So many things, damn it.

That was a very dangerous thing to consider because if I really started to think of all the ways I could have Lily without ruining her, the likelier it got that I actually acted on those ideas, and I wasn't sure if I was strong enough to stop at a certain point. At least, not if Lily didn't ask me to, and I had a feeling she wouldn't.

During breakfast, I acted as if nothing had happened. Aria was already too attentive. And Gianna seemed to know more than she should as well.

Lily met my gaze when her sisters weren't looking and the look in her eyes made my cock twitch. Today I'd given her an opening. She knew now that I wanted her.

I'd spent my life for others, always putting my own needs second. Would it really be so bad if I took what I wanted for once? Never in my life had I wanted anything more than the girl across from me.

Why should I deny myself this?

chapter *eight*

Liliana

I STARED UP AT THE CEILING, OR RATHER WHERE I KNEW IT WAS. THE darkness was impenetrable, I couldn't even make out my own hand. Sometimes it felt like darkness was all there was in my life. A long tunnel without an end. Especially at night Mother's words haunted me. I'd promised her I'd be happy, but I wasn't even sure how to do it. A deep loneliness filled me, had taken hold of me ever since Mother had died. We'd never been as close as some daughters were with their mothers, but she'd been there, a constant presence. And now it seemed like I was all alone. Of course there was Fabi, but he was young and would soon be involved in mob business, and Father…Right now, being here in the Hamptons made me happy but it was a temporary thing.

My sisters, they were always there for me, but they had their own lives, they had husbands, and one day they'd have their own families. They'd still love me, and still take care of me, but I wanted my own happiness, separate from them. I wanted what they had. And I knew the only person I wanted that kind of happiness with was Romero.

He had been watching me differently this summer. In the past years, his expression had made it clear that I was nothing but a girl to him, someone to protect. But recently something had changed. I wasn't an expert when it came to men, of course, but his gaze had held a hint of something I often saw on Luca's face when he watched my sister Aria.

At least, I was quite certain. I pushed my blanket off my body and sat up. I didn't bother turning on the lights from fear of attracting attention and instead felt my way toward the door. I inched the handle down and slipped into the corridor. It was silent and dark, but at least here I could make out schemes. Not that I needed to see something to find Romero's room. I knew exactly where it was. I had lost count of the times I'd imagined going there again. But so far reason had stopped me. Tonight I was tired of listening to reason, of playing it safe. I didn't want to be alone, didn't want to spend all night staring into the darkness, being lonely and sad. I crept down the corridor, careful not to make a sound, hardly daring to breathe. When I reached the door to Romero's room, I stood there for a long time. It was silent inside. Of course; it was already way past midnight and he always got up early for his run.

My fingers shook with nerves when I gripped the door handle and pushed it down. The door opened without a sound. I snuck in and closed it again, then I didn't move for a long time, only stared toward the bed and the contours of Romero's body. His curtains weren't drawn, so the moonlight provided some light. His back was turned toward me and the blanket only reached his waist. My eyes traced his muscled shoulders and arms. I moved closer, one hesitant step after the other. This was so wrong. Romero had caught me in his room before, and worse, he'd caught me spying on him in the shower, but this felt more intimate. He was in bed, and if things went my way, I'd soon join him. What if he sent me away? Or worse, what if he got angry and told Luca? What if they sent me back to Chicago into that dark and hopeless house with my father who didn't miss my mother at all?

I froze a couple of steps from the bed. My breathing had quickened as if I'd exerted myself and my hands were clammy. Maybe I was losing my mind. I was trying to tell myself that I was doing this because Mother had wanted me to be happy, but maybe I was only using that as an excuse for my insanity. I'd wanted Romero long before Mother had ever said anything, and had even tried to kiss him long before her death.

I shook my head, getting mad at myself for overthinking everything. There had been a time when I'd done whatever I wanted as long as I felt like it. I took another step toward the bed but I must have made a sound without noticing it because Romero's breathing changed and his body tensed. Oh no. There was no going back now.

He rolled onto his back in one fluid move, then his eyes settled on me. He relaxed but quickly tensed again. "Liliana?"

I didn't reply. My tongue seemed to be stuck to the roof of my mouth. What had I been thinking?

Romero swung his legs out of bed and he sat on the edge for a moment, silently watching me. Could he see my face? I probably looked like a mouse trapped by a cat, but I wasn't afraid. Not one bit. If anything, I was embarrassed, and strangely excited. I was a twisted and sick mouse, that much was sure. He stood, and of course my eyes did a quick scan of his body. He was only wearing boxer shorts. He looked too good to be true. Like he'd stepped right out of my dreams. It was embarrassing to think how often I'd dreamed of Romero and all the things I wanted to do with him.

"Lily, what are you doing here? Is everything okay?" There was worry in his voice, but there was also something else. Something I'd heard when he'd caught me spying on him in the shower. It was something darker and almost eager.

My stomach fluttered with butterflies and I took a step in his direction. I wanted to fly into his arms, wanted to kiss him, and so much more.

"Can I sleep with you?" The words shot out, just like that, and once they were out I couldn't believe I'd said them. Especially since they could easily be taken the wrong way.

Romero froze. Silence stretched out between us. I was sure it would crush me any second. I took another step in his direction. I was almost in arm's reach now.

The sound of Romero's breathing was incredibly loud. I could see his chest heaving. Was he angry?

"This isn't something you should joke about," he said quietly. "It's not funny." He was angry. Maybe I should have taken the hint and turned on my heel to leave his room, but like Gianna I had never been very clever in situations like this.

"I wasn't joking, and I didn't mean it like that," I whispered. "I want to sleep in your bed, just sleep." For now. I wanted more than that, eventually.

"Liliana," Romero murmured. "Have you lost your mind? Do you even realize what you're saying?"

Fury rose up. Everyone always thought I was too young, too naïve, too female to make decisions. "I know exactly what I'm saying."

"I doubt it."

I bridged the distance between us until our chests were almost pressed against each other. Romero didn't back away but he braced himself. "Every night I feel like darkness is swallowing me whole, like my life is spiraling out of control, like there's nothing good in my life. But when I think of you those feelings disappear. I feel safe when I'm with you."

"You shouldn't. I'm not a good man, not by any standards."

"I don't care about good. I grew up in this world. I know how things are, and I'm fine with it."

"You don't even know half of it. And if you really know how things are, then you should realize what could happen if someone found you in my room at night."

"I'm tired of hearing what I can't do. Can't I decide for myself? It's my life, so why can't I make decisions?"

Romero was quiet for a moment before he said, "Of course, it's your life, but your father has certain expectations of you. And not only that, Luca gave him and Dante Cavallaro his word that he'd take good care of you and keep you safe. That includes your reputation. If someone told them you were in my room right now, that could mean war between the Outfit and New York. This isn't a game. This is too serious for you to play around."

"I'm not playing around. I'm so lonely, Romero," I whispered. "And I like you. I really like you." That was an understatement. "I only want to be close to you. You kissed me back and I know how you've been looking at me. I know you are interested in me."

He didn't say anything.

Doubt wormed its way into my brain. Had I been imagining the looks he'd given me? "If you don't like me, then tell me. It's okay." It wasn't. I'd be crushed, but maybe it would be for the best. I'd move on with my life somehow.

"Fuck," he murmured, turning away from me and leaving me to stare at his back. "If I was a good guy, I'd tell you exactly that. I'd fucking lie to you for your own good. But I'm not good, Lily."

Relief flooded me. He hadn't said he didn't like me. I'd read the signs right. God, I could have screamed with joy. I rested my palms against his bare shoulder blades. His skin was soft except for a few small scars, but they made him only more desirable to me. They flexed under my touch but he didn't step away. "So you are interested in me? And you like me?"

Romero let out a harsh laugh. "This is crazy."

"Just tell me. Do you find me attractive?"

He turned around. I wasn't quick enough to pull my hands away so they now rested against his chest. That felt even better. I had to stop myself from running my hands up and down his body. Even in the half-dark I could see the fire in his eyes. He scanned me from head to toe. I was only wearing pajama shorts and a tank top, but I wasn't even embarrassed. I wanted Romero to see me like that, wanted to get a reaction from him.

"Lily, you are stunning. Of course I find you attractive. Look at you, you are too fucking beautiful for words."

My lips parted. That was more than I'd dared to hope for. I moved even closer and peered up at him. "Then why do you keep pushing me away?"

"Because it's the right thing to do, and because I know the risks."

"Isn't it worth the risk?"

Romero stared down at me with such intensity that I couldn't help but shiver. He didn't reply. He gripped my hips and pulled me against him before his lips came down on mine. I opened up without hesitation, eager for that kiss, eager for his closeness. His tongue plunged into my mouth. There was no flicker of hesitation or doubt in his kiss. I moaned. This was so different from our first kiss, more intense. He cupped the back of my head, guiding me the way he wanted it. I could hardly keep up. I stepped on my tiptoes and leaned against him as I gripped onto his shoulders for balance. The kiss consumed me, stirred a fire in my belly and made me long for much more.

Romero jerked away and I tried to follow him but he kept me at arm's length. His breathing was harsh and there was a wild look in his eyes. "Give me a second," he rasped.

He squeezed his eyes shut as if he was in pain. All I could think about was to kiss him again, to have his hands on my body. I wanted nothing more. But I did as he asked and gave him a few seconds to get control over himself. Eventually he opened his eyes again. The wild look was gone and was replaced by something more controlled. His grip on my shoulders relaxed and his thumbs lightly stroked my skin. I wasn't even sure he noticed. The light touch raised goose bumps of delight all over my skin. I waited for him to say something, but also feared what he would say. One of his hands traveled up to my cheek. "You should leave now," he said quietly.

I froze. "You're sending me away?"

Hesitation flickered across his face. "It's for the best, Lily, believe me."

I took a step back. I wasn't going to beg him. If he didn't want me to spend the night, then I'd have to accept it. "Okay. Good night." I turned around and hurried out of the room. I hardly paid attention as I crossed the corridor toward my room. I'd put myself out there today, had risked everything to get what I wanted. I wouldn't do that again. I had a huge crush on Romero but I also still had my pride. If he didn't want to risk this, then I'd accept it.

I closed the door and crept back into my bed. Like before, the darkness closed in on me. It was too silent in my room, too lonely and empty. Even the memory of the kiss Romero and I had shared couldn't cheer me up. Not when it was probably the last time I'd kissed Romero. It took a long time for me to fall asleep and then Mother's pale unhappy face haunted my dreams.

Romero and I barely looked at each other the next morning. I didn't seek his closeness like usual. I tried to avoid his eyes as much as possible but a few times I caught him stealing glances my way. I wasn't sure what they meant, but I was glad that he and I didn't get to spend time alone together. Of course he was almost always around. It was difficult to avoid your bodyguard, but I did my best to focus entirely on my sisters, to enjoy my time with them.

Romero

It was way past midnight when I headed for my room. Luca, Matteo, and I had played cards until an hour ago, a distraction I fucking needed, and afterward when they had joined their wives in bed, I'd sat on the terrace, and wondered why I couldn't have the same.

A noise made me pause. My hand went to my gun as I followed the sound toward Lily's door. She sounded like she was in distress, mumbling in her sleep and crying. I checked the corridor, but I was alone. Everyone was long asleep or at least busy behind closed bedroom doors. I pushed the door open and slipped in. It took my eyes a moment to get used to the darkness, which was worse than in the rest of the house. The curtains didn't let any light in. I kept the door ajar and moved further into the room. I knew what I should do, and it definitely wasn't being alone in Lily's bedroom with her at night. On my list of things to avoid that was really at the top.

She was in obvious distress and I'd vowed to protect her but a nightmare wouldn't harm her. There was no reason for me to be here. I could have called Aria or Gianna, or just let Lily sleep through her nightmare, but I was a stupid fucker.

When she'd come to my room two days ago, it had taken every fucking ounce of self-control to send her away. I'd wanted her in my bed, and not just for sleep. When I'd first heard her question if she could sleep with me, I'd almost gotten a hard-on. I knew she didn't mean it that way, but I'd never wanted to misunderstand someone more than in that night.

This was messed up. I'd always put my job and the Famiglia first. All the women in my life so far had been a nice distraction, but they'd never even come close to interfering with my duty. Lily was different. I wasn't sure how she'd done it, but I couldn't get her out of my freaking head. I glanced between the open door and Lily's bed, then I walked toward her. I left the door ajar, even though part of me wanted to close it and have total privacy, but if

I wanted any chance at keeping my promise I needed the risk of someone walking by and looking into the room.

As I stood over Lily, I watched her for a moment. She lay on her back, her blond hair spread out on her pillow, and her brows drawn together. Even in the throes of a nightmare she was fucking beautiful. Damn it. What had I gotten myself into? I touched her shoulder. She was dressed in only a tank top and my fingers brushed the naked skin of her shoulders, and the touch sent a freaking shiver all the way to my cock. Her fucking shoulder, not her boob or her butt or her pussy. I almost got a fucking hard-on from touching a shoulder for God's sake. This was pathetic on a whole new level. "Liliana?" Somehow it felt safer to use her normal name instead of her nickname.

Her eyes moved under her eyelids and she stirred under my hand but still didn't wake. I gently touched the side of her neck, feeling her pulse flutter under my fingertips. "Lily," I said a bit louder.

She jerked and her eyes flew open, staring straight at me. "Romero?" she whispered in a voice still heavy with sleep. I wanted to kiss her so badly.

Liliana

Someone touched my throat, tearing me from sleep. I opened my eyes but it took a few seconds before my brain registered what was before me: Romero.

"Romero?" Maybe I was still dreaming. It was definitely an improvement over my previous dream about my mother who had talked to me with lifeless eyes about happiness.

"It's okay," Romero said in his deep voice.

I looked around. "You are in my room." I sounded like a moron. But I was stunned. After all, he'd as good as thrown me out of his room two days ago and now he stood in my own. A bit of a twist I hadn't expected. Not that I minded.

Romero's lips twitched as if he wanted to smile but then he became serious again. Sometimes I thought he tried to keep in his smiles because he worried that if he allowed that kind of emotion, all of them would come up. "You had a nightmare. I decided to wake you."

I nodded. He stood beside my bed, half bent over me. If I'd reached out I could have grabbed his neck and pulled him down. My fingers itched to do just that, but I hadn't forgotten his rejection not too long ago. He needed to make the next step and I wasn't sure if coming into my room to wake me from a nightmare counted as one. I wanted it to. I sat up and my blankets fell down to my hips. I wore only a flimsy camisole. Romero's eyes followed the movement, and lingered on my chest.

"Thanks for waking me. I had a dream about my mother." I wasn't sure why I said it. My nightmare was the last thing I wanted to think about, much less talk to Romero about. His eyes returned to my face. Sometimes I thought I could drown in them. When he was around I felt so happy and light. Somehow I knew he was the one, the person I was meant to be with. I'd known it pretty much from the beginning. If there was something like fate, then this was it.

Romero brushed a strand of hair from my forehead and I leaned into the touch. Somehow he was closer now. "You miss her."

I nodded. I did, but her last words haunted me more than her death. Her sadness over the things she'd missed, the longing in her—I didn't think I could ever forget that. Romero and I locked gazes and just stared at each other. In the dim light spilling from the corridor I could see the conflict in Romero's eyes. I wanted to lean forward but I stopped myself. I had to be strong, had to have some self-respect.

I was about to say something, anything, to stop the mounting tension but then Romero leaned down and kissed me. I hadn't expected him to and gasped against his lips, but my surprise lasted only a couple of seconds before I wrapped my arms around his neck and kissed him back with everything I had. He put one knee down on my bed beside me and cradled my head. His kiss banished the last of my tiredness and the lingering sadness from my dream. I wasn't sure how long we kissed, Romero kneeling on the bed and I half-sitting, but I came more alive with every second. Eventually I pulled back, my breathing harsh. There was an insistent pounding between my legs but I knew it would have been wrong to take things further tonight.

Romero stroked my cheek and was about to straighten but I caught his arm. "I don't want to be alone tonight."

I waited for protest but it didn't come. My heart dropped when he walked toward the door. Would he leave without a word? Instead he closed the door silently before he returned to the bed. With every step that he took in my direction, my heart seemed to swell with emotion. Romero removed his gun holster and put it down on the nightstand, then slipped out of his shoes. I scooted to the other side of my bed to make room for him, excitement fluttering in my chest. He didn't slip under the covers with me as I'd hoped, instead he stretched out on top of it. I peered over my shoulder at him. He looked tired, even more tired than I felt. He smiled. It looked almost resigned, with a hint of regret. He snuck his arm around my waist and hugged me to his body, my back pressed against his chest, with the blankets between us. I wanted that barrier gone but decided to let him have his way for tonight. I'd won a small battle, the war could wait. Despite the material bunched between us I was fairly sure I could feel how much our kiss had affected Romero. Smiling to myself, I closed my eyes. "Thanks for staying with me."

Romero kissed the back of my head. "Get some sleep. I'll keep the nightmares away."

"I know you will," I whispered.

When my alarm woke me the next morning, I was alone in bed. I sat up and pressed the button that let the curtains glide open. Blinding light greeted me and I quickly squeezed my eyes shut. When I'd finally grown used to the brightness I looked around in my room for a sign of Romero's sleepover but there was nothing. It might as well have been a dream. For a heart-stopping moment I considered just that but when I pressed my nose into the pillow, I caught his scent. Not a dream. I slipped out of bed. Of course he didn't stay until the morning. Romero was cautious, one of us had to be. If one of my sisters walked in without knocking, which had happened before, then we could have been in huge trouble. Still it felt like a small rejection that he had left me alone without a word.

Get a grip, Lily.

We had to be careful or I'd be sent home and then we wouldn't get to spend any time at all together. This was a good beginning.

A beginning for what? I wasn't so naïve to believe that my father would accept Romero as a potential candidate for marriage. I wasn't even sure if Romero considered me as someone he'd want to marry. But I was getting ahead of myself. I wanted to take risks, enjoy life and be happy. This night with Romero was a step in the right direction.

I rushed through my shower but took extra care with my makeup and hair. Then I headed downstairs. I could hear my sisters already laughing in the kitchen and followed the sound. They stood at the kitchen counter, coffee cups in their hands. Nobody else was there but the big wooden table was set for six people, so the men would hopefully join us later. Trying to hide my disappointment that Romero wasn't there yet, I walked toward them. Aria poured me a cup of coffee and handed it to me with a worried look. "Didn't you sleep again last night?"

I paused with the cup against my lips, my pulse quickening. Had they seen Romero walking into my room? Or maybe even leaving it in the morning? "Why?" I asked hesitantly.

Gianna snorted. "Because you look fucking tired. There are dark shadows under your eyes."

I thought I'd put enough concealer on it. Damn it. "I'm fine. I dreamed of Mother, but it wasn't bad."

Aria wrapped her arm around my shoulders. "Is it still about what she said to you?"

"Yeah," I said evasively. "I can't get her words out of my head."

"Don't take everything she said too much to heart. She was sick. It's not your job to undo her mistakes. She was unhappy at the end but it was her own fault," Gianna said.

"Gianna," Aria said in warning.

"It's not like Mother tried to guilt me into anything. She only wanted me to be happy."

"And you're going to be happy. We'll make sure of it," Aria said, squeezing my shoulder lightly before stepping back. "Let's start to eat. Who knows when the men will show up. They had something to discuss."

"Oh?" I asked nervously as we went over to the table and sat down. "Business?" If I was already a nervous wreck when Romero and I hadn't even really done anything yet, how much worse would it be once there really was something going on?

Aria gave me an odd look. "I suppose. It's all they ever talk about."

"You're acting kind of odd," Gianna said as she grabbed a Danish from the bread basket. She scanned my face. "Did anything happen?"

"No," I said too quickly. I grabbed a bowl and some cereal and milk. Gianna's eyes seemed to bore holes into my skull and I could tell that she was going to push it, but male voices began to drift over to us from the entrance hall. I almost sighed in relief when they entered the dining area because Gianna's attention moved on to Matteo who gave her a grin. I froze as my eyes settled on Romero. His brown hair was in slight disarray and the white dress shirt hugged his chest in the most distracting way but his gaze barely brushed over me as he, Luca, and Matteo headed for the table. Despite knowing that we had to act normal and not draw any suspicions toward us, his blatant refusal to look my way sent a stab of worry through me. Things didn't improve when first Luca leaned down to kiss Aria and then Matteo did the same with Gianna before they settled on chairs across from them. Romero gave me a small nod and tight smile as he sank down on his chair. I grabbed my spoon and started eating my cereal. I could feel my sisters' eyes on me. They knew me too well but I wouldn't give them a chance to suspect anything. I didn't want them to have to keep a secret from their husbands, especially not that kind of secret. The rest of breakfast I made sure to keep my eyes away from Romero regardless of him sitting opposite me, and instead talked to my sisters. Romero didn't seem to have much trouble ignoring me, that was for sure. He and the other men were deep into an argument about the best way to handle a drug dealer who attracted too much attention from the police.

After breakfast, Aria and Gianna decided to head to the pool again. The weather was nice, barely a breeze and only a few white clouds adorning the blue sky. I went to my bedroom to change into a bikini, a cute pink thing with white dots with a halter top that accentuated my breasts. When I stepped out of my room, I bumped into a hard chest. Strong hands on my arms steadied but released me the moment I stopped swaying. I pressed a hand over my heart, not having expected someone to be in front of my door. "God, you startled me," I said with a small laugh but it died when I raised my head to Romero's face.

He didn't say anything and his jaw was locked tight as his eyes roamed my body. His lack of reaction made me feel self-conscious. I had never been around Romero half naked like this, or any man really. Romero had seen many women naked and I wondered if he compared me to them.

I took a step back, my cheeks heating under his steadfast attention, and I self-consciously crossed my arms in front of my body.

He checked the corridor before he moved closer, and said in a low voice, "You look breathtaking."

Dropping my arms, I couldn't hold back a jibe. "You didn't seem to notice at breakfast." Despite my attempt to sound flippant, my voice revealed my hurt, and it annoyed me.

Romero met my gaze, expression softening. "I did notice, believe me. It's impossible not to, Lily," he said quietly. We were alone in the corridor and standing close enough that I could smell his aftershave. "I didn't want to ignore you, but we don't have a choice. This has to stay a secret."

"This?" I asked. "What exactly is this?" We had hardly done anything yet. We'd kissed three times but that was it.

His shoulders tensed as if he didn't want to put a label on us. "I don't know. Maybe nothing. But I want you, Lily. I can't get you out of my head. No matter what I do there's always you."

I exhaled. It felt as if a huge rock had dropped off my shoulders. So it wasn't just me. "You want me?" I echoed, tilting my head up to peer at him through my lashes.

Romero's eyes travelled the length of my body again and it made me tingle all over. How would it feel if he touched every spot his eyes had wandered? He let out a small, dark laugh. "Oh yes."

"I want you too. So what are we going to do now?" I took a step closer until there was barely room between us and I dipped my head back to stare up into his face. He didn't touch me, even though I wanted him to but his eyes lingered on my breasts, and now that he wasn't masking his emotions I saw the hunger in his expression. "What I want to do is take you into your bedroom and rip off your bikini, then taste every inch of your skin. I know you'll taste absolutely perfect."

I hadn't expected him to be so direct and my face exploded with heat. "Why don't you find out?" My attempt at a seductive whisper came out breathless, almost shy.

Romero touched his fingertips to my heated cheeks. "So innocent." He shook his head and I could tell he was about to pull back physically and emotionally. I leaned against him, my breasts flush against his strong chest. "I don't want to stay innocent, Romero."

"Damn," Romero muttered. He cupped the back of my head and tilted it to the side, then he bent down and pressed an open-mouthed kiss over my pulse point before he traced my jugular with his tongue. I let out an embarrassing moan as my core tightened with arousal. I tipped my head further to the side, giving him better access, but he had moved on from my throat and kissed my lips. I pressed myself against him even harder. His shirt felt cool against my naked skin. A noise from somewhere in the house made us jump apart. There was no one in the corridor but it was a good reminder that we needed to be careful. After another glance down the corridor, Romero cupped my cheek again. "You do taste as perfect as I thought."

I smiled. "You haven't even tasted all of me." My cheeks flamed when I realized what I'd said and how Romero would understand it.

Romero's eyes darkened with what I suspected was desire. "I intend to, trust me."

I shivered. "You do?"

"God yes." He sighed, then took a step back. "But we need to be careful. This is a dangerous path we're on."

"I know but I don't care. I want this."

Romero kissed me again. He shook his head. "I don't know how you did it but I can't get you out of my fucking mind. And now this." He gestured at my bikini. "You're lucky you can't read my mind, you'd be shocked."

"Not as shocked as you, if you could read my mind," I said with what I hoped was a seductive smile. I turned around and walked away, making sure I swung my hips.

Romero

As I watched Lily prance away, I almost groaned. Her tiny bikini barely covered her perfect butt cheeks and her long legs drove me just as wild. I wanted to read her mind, wanted to find out what she desired and give it to her.

Her earlier comment about tasting her had filled my head with images of my mouth on her pussy. I couldn't wait to find out if it was as pink and perfect as I imagined it. I wanted to lick her until she begged for mercy.

My pants became uncomfortable and I had to shift to give my cock a bit more room. How would I be able to restrain myself if I kept thinking about tasting her? It had already been difficult enough to lie in her bed at night without those images in my head, torturing me. I knew Lily would visit me again at night. Now that she knew how much I wanted her, she would use her chance.

But I also knew that I needed to establish certain boundaries. Flirting and kissing was still tolerable, though I was fairly sure that Luca and Aria, and most definitely Scuderi, would disagree. Taking things further was something I couldn't risk. I'd given Luca a promise and I should at least try to keep it.

chapter *nine*

Liliana

THAT NIGHT I CREPT INTO ROMERO'S BEDROOM AGAIN. THE lights were out but he was sitting with his back against his headboard. He didn't say anything as I approached the bed and suddenly I was nervous.

"Hey," I whispered, then yawned because it had been a long day and as usual sleep evaded me. "Can I come into your bed?"

Romero lifted his blankets. I quickly slipped under them but didn't snuggle against him, suddenly shy. Romero peered down at me, then he reached out and brushed a few strands from my forehead. I braced myself on my elbows to kiss him, but he shook his head. I froze.

"I don't think we should be kissing when we're in bed together."

"You don't want to kiss me anymore?" Was I that horrible?

"No, I still want to kiss you and I'm going to kiss you but not when we're in bed. There are certain boundaries we shouldn't cross, Lily."

"Okay," I said slowly. Maybe he was right. Kissing in bed was only a small step away from doing much more, and some things simply couldn't be undone. "But can we snuggle?"

Romero chuckled. "I should probably say no," he murmured. "But I'm screwed anyway."

He lay down and opened his arms. I inched toward him and put my head down on his upper arm. I wasn't sure why I felt so comfortable in his presence. I wasn't someone who liked physical contact with people I didn't know, but with Romero I'd always wanted closeness.

I closed my eyes but I didn't fall asleep immediately. "Have you ever regretted working for Luca? As the son of a soldier, you would have had the option not to become part of the Famiglia. You could have lived a normal life."

"No. This was all I ever wanted," Romero said. His fingers ran up and down my forearm in a very distracting way but I wasn't sure if he even realized what he was doing. "I've known Luca and Matteo long before I was inducted. I always looked up to Luca because he was older and strong as a bear, and Matteo and I always got in trouble together."

"I bet Matteo got in trouble and you had to save his ass."

Romero let out a laugh. "Yeah, that's more like it. When Luca became a Made Man and when I heard the story of how he killed his first man at eleven, I wanted nothing more than to be like him."

"You were only eight then. Shouldn't you have been playing with matchbox cars instead?"

"I always knew I wanted to become a member of the Famiglia. I wanted to be their best fighter. I often practiced with Matteo and in the beginning even with Luca. They wiped the ground with me. But I was a quick learner, and when I was inducted a few years later, only a handful could see eye to eye with me in a knife fight, and I got only better with time. I worked hard."

I could tell he was proud of what he'd achieved. "What did your family want? Did they try to keep you away from the mob?"

"My father didn't want his life for me. As a debt collector he had to do many horrible things. But he and my mother trusted me to decide for myself."

How would it be to have people trust you to make your own decisions?

"This life, does it make you happy?" I asked softly. Sometimes I wished there was an easy definition for what made me happy.

"At times, but nobody can always be happy." He was silent for a moment. "What makes you happy?"

"I don't know. This, but I know it's fleeting."

Romero's chest rose and fell under my cheek until I was sure he'd fallen asleep but then he spoke again. "Happiness often is. That doesn't mean you can't enjoy it while it lasts."

Deep down I knew I needed to stop this madness. If someone caught us, both our lives would be ruined. But I couldn't. Whenever I was near Romero the sorrow that had rested so heavily on me in the last few weeks seemed bearable. Everything seemed lighter and more hopeful.

I eased the door open. As usual the lights were out but the curtains weren't drawn so the moonlight illuminated the contours of the furniture and showed me my path toward the bed. I closed the door without a sound and tiptoed across the room. Romero wasn't asleep. I could feel his eyes following me as I slipped under the covers. He lay on his back, his arms propped up behind his head. I couldn't make out his expression. He waited for me to put my head on his chest so he could wrap his arm around me. He'd never made the first move but tonight I didn't just want to fall asleep beside him. I wasn't exactly sure what I wanted, but definitely more. I was glad for the dark when I got up on my knees and straddled his hips.

Romero tensed beneath me and sat up, his palms flat against my shoulder blades. "What are you doing?" he murmured, a quality to his voice I'd never heard before.

"I don't know," I whispered before I lightly brushed my lips over his. I wasn't sure what kind of reaction I'd expected, definitely not the one I got. He flipped us over so my back was pressed into the mattress and he was hovering over me. He wasn't holding me down but his body caged me in, his knees between my legs, his arms beside my head, his upper body over me. Romero everywhere. God, and it felt good. Maybe there should have been anxiety and trepidation. We were alone in his bedroom, and if I called for help I'd get in more trouble than when I let him do whatever he wanted. But I wasn't scared of Romero. Maybe I was stupid not to be. I knew what he was capable of. He was a killer. And he was a grown man, who'd had many women before me who delivered when they offered their body to him. Everyone always told me that playing games would get me in trouble one day. Maybe tonight they'd be proven right.

Despite this, my body reacted to Romero's closeness. My center tightened in anticipation, of what I wasn't even entirely sure, and heat pooled in my belly. For a long time the only sound in the dark was our rapid breathing. "Lily," he said quietly, imploringly. "I pride myself on my self-control, but I'm a man and not a good one either. So far I've tried to be a gentleman. I know you're sad and lonely, and I didn't want to take advantage of you. But if you go the next step and offer more, then you can't expect me not to take you up on that offer."

"Maybe I want you to." My heart pounded in my chest as the words left my mouth.

Romero brushed his lips over my temple, the barest touch that made me tingle. "Do you even know what you're offering, Lily?"

I hesitated.

Romero released a long breath, kissed my forehead and began to pull back.

I gripped his shoulders, even through his t-shirt his heat seemed to scorch me. "Sometimes when I'm alone I try to imagine how it would feel if you touched me."

"Fuck," he breathed. And then he kissed me gently before pulling back again. Even my hands couldn't stop him this time.

"Why are you pulling away?"

"Lights."

"Lights?" I said nervously.

"I need to see your face." The lights came on and I blinked against the sudden brightness. He lay down beside me but he kept one arm around my waist. His hair was disheveled and dark stubble dusted his cheeks and chin. "When you imagine my touch, do you ever caress yourself?" he asked in a low voice.

My eyes widened a fraction and heat crept into my face. Romero cupped my cheek and traced the blush there. "Tell me," he said.

I lowered my gaze to his chin. "Yes," I admitted in barely a whisper. What would he think of me now?

Romero pressed his nose into my hair. "Fuck."

"You said that already."

He didn't laugh like I'd expected him to. He was very quiet. His hand on my waist tightened when he raised his head and fixed me with a hungry gaze. He brought his mouth down on mine and I parted my lips for him. His tongue slipped in and everything around me seemed to fade to nothing as I tasted him. It wasn't our first kiss but it felt like something else entirely, with me in bed with him, with nothing to stop us. His kiss was fiercer. There was no hesitation or surprise this time. He sucked my lower lip into his mouth, then my tongue, and I wasn't sure how it was possible that I felt the motion all the way between my legs.

"Is this okay?" he murmured against my throat and all I could do was nod. Aria and Gianna always called me a chatterbox but with Romero words so often failed me. His lips lightly traced the skin over my collarbone, then his tongue slid out to taste me. His mouth moved even lower to the edge of my camisole. His fingers traced the fabric and his lips followed the same path. I arched my back, wanting him to move even lower, to do more.

"You told me I should find out how you taste everywhere. I'm very tempted to do it," he murmured. He peered up. His eyes had a predatory look in them. The only expression that had ever come close was when he'd been down in the basement with the Russians. There was something dark and unhinged in his brown eyes, but this time I wasn't afraid. "What do you want?" he asked roughly.

If only I knew. "More," I said softly.

Romero lowered his gaze to my chest. My nipples strained against the thin material of my camisole, hard and aching for attention. Romero lightly traced his thumb over one nub and I gasped.

"Like this?" he asked.

I nodded furiously. "More."

Romero chuckled, and the sound made me ache even more for his touch. He took both of my nipples between his thumbs and forefingers, and lightly twisted them back and forth through the silk. I squeezed my eyes shut at the sensation between my legs. I pressed my thighs together, desperate for some kind of relief. Romero cupped my nipple with his lips, sucking it gently into his mouth. For some reason the fabric seemed to heighten the sensations even more. I was close to exploding. His hand brushed my hipbone before it moved under the hem of my camisole and softly traced my stomach. Goose bumps covered my skin at the light touch. He released my nipple but the wet fabric of my camisole stuck to it. I couldn't believe this was finally happening.

Romero moved onto my other nipple and repeated the same procedure. I rubbed my thighs together. The tension between them was almost unbearable. Romero's eyes followed the movement before they darted up to my face. "Do you want me to touch you there?"

I nodded quickly. Romero smiled. He trailed his hand down my side until he reached my thigh. He stroked the outer side lightly, his eyes never leaving my face, making sure I was okay. His strokes moved closer to my inner thigh until I wanted nothing more than to grasp his hand and push it into my panties. As if he could feel my impatience, Romero tugged lightly at my shorts. I opened my legs without even thinking about it, a silent invitation. Was I being too forward? I didn't care.

He slid his hand into the leg of my shorts and then his fingers traced the sensitive skin at the edge of my panties. He watched my face closely when he inched his index finger under the fabric and brushed my folds. I gasped and he groaned. I was already so wet that his finger slid over me easily. His lips claimed mine with less restraint than before, and I didn't mind. "Is this okay?" he rasped between kisses as his finger kept lightly tracing my folds. Sparks seemed to soar through my core. It felt so much more intense than when I touched myself.

"Yes," I whispered.

His finger moved up between my folds, spreading my wetness up to my nub. He started to rub back and forth, the barest touch that felt incredible. My hips jerked up from the intense sensation. I moaned into his mouth, my legs opening wider to give him better access. He kissed my neck, then he sucked my nipple into his mouth again, soaking my camisole even more. His fingers between my legs drove me higher and higher.

"You feel so good, Lily. So soft and wet and warm," he murmured.

I whimpered in response. Hearing him say those words made me relax further under his touch. He was gentle and unhurried. I ran my hands over his back and hair, wanting to feel as much of him as possible, wanting to have him closer in every way possible. I'd always wanted him and my sisters had often told me that feeling would cease with time, but my want had only grown. I didn't think it would ever stop, not that I wanted it to.

Romero's other hand moved to the edge of my pajama top and inched it down, freeing my breast. I had to fight the urge to cover myself up. For some reason it was more difficult to bare myself to his eyes than to have him touch me in my most private place. Embarrassment flew out the window when Romero lowered his head and captured my nipple between his lips. At the same time his finger on my clit started moving faster. I shivered. His tongue licked my nipple lightly and it felt even better without the fabric as a barrier. My embarrassing moans and breathless sighs became dangerously loud so I pressed my lips together, trying to hold the sounds in, but everything Romero did felt so good.

Romero released my nipple. "I wish I could hear your moans. I love the sound."

I lifted my head. "Really?"

Romero smiled a smile I'd never seen before. It was darker, more dangerous, and indescribably sexy. "Really. Can't you feel how much I love this?"

He pressed a bit tighter against me and something hard and hot dug into my leg. I couldn't believe I'd done this to him. Romero kissed my mouth, then the spot beneath my chin, my throat until he'd worked his way back down to my nipple. He trailed his tongue around it, then moved on to my other breast. "I've been wanting to do this for so long. Fuck, I don't care that it's wrong, that it goes against my promise, I can't resist you."

Hearing him say that felt like the ultimate triumph and when he sucked my nipple back into his mouth I fell apart, arching up, not caring when Romero pulled back to watch me. I stifled my cries in the pillow, knowing we had to be careful and I was being embarrassingly loud as waves of pleasures filled me.

I lifted my head when I'd calmed down and smiled at Romero. "Wow."

Romero kissed my throat. "Yes, wow. Watching you was fucking amazing."

I raised myself on my elbows, my eyes moving down to the bulge in his boxer shorts. I'd been wanting to see him naked again ever since I watched him shower. After a moment of hesitation, I reached out and rested my palm against his erection. Even through his boxers he felt incredibly hot.

Romero held his breath, his muscles becoming taut with tension. "I'm not sure that's a good idea," he said in warning, but he grew even harder beneath my touch.

I searched his eyes, wondering what had made him say it. Was he worried he'd lose control?

"I trust you," I admitted. He closed his brown eyes and when he opened them again they were even warmer and gentler than before, but I caught the hint of something darker in them as well. "I want to do it," I added.

Romero didn't protest, instead he sat back against the headboard before he lifted his hips and pulled down his boxers. His erection sprang free.

Last time I hadn't been this close and nerves and excitement curled in my stomach as I took in the sight. His girth was impressive. My first time with Romero would be painful, no doubt, but that was something I wouldn't have to worry about.

"You don't have to do anything, Lily," Romero said as he began to reach for his boxers, mistaking my hesitation for reluctance to touch him.

Pushing my thoughts aside, I curled my fingers around the base, surprised at how wide he really was. Romero sucked in a deep breath and dropped back against the headboard, his hands flat on the mattress. I stroked lightly up and down, ran my fingers over his tip and back down to his balls. I couldn't stop exploring him, curious and excited at the same time.

Romero cupped my cheek and I turned to look at him but didn't stop my explorations. "Damn it, Lily, you're driving me crazy."

"How do you want me to touch you?" I asked quietly. I wanted to make him feel as good as he'd made me feel. I'd overheard Gianna say something about blowjobs to Aria once, and that those brought any man to his knees, but I wasn't sure I could pull it off in a satisfactory way. Maybe I should have asked Gianna for instructions...

"You're doing good."

I didn't want to do good. I wanted to be amazing, wanted to show Romero that I was a woman and not the girl he still occasionally took me for. Pushing my worries aside, I bent over him and took him into my mouth.

Romero jerked under me in surprise and gripped the back of my head. "You don't have to do that."

It wasn't said with conviction. I licked from his base up to the top. He didn't taste of anything, except for the tip where a few droplets had gathered. I licked them away without thinking.

Romero cursed, raking his hand through my hair.

"Am I doing this right?" I asked after a couple of minutes.

"Fuck yes. You don't even know how hard it is not to thrust into your mouth."

"If that's what you want, you can do it."

"No, not today. Take your time and do what you like. I'll enjoy it all, trust me," he said in a low voice. And so I did. I licked around his tip and took him into my mouth, trailed my tongue along his length over and over again. Romero didn't make a lot of sounds but his hand in my hair tightened and he sucked in his breath every now and then.

"I'm going to come," he warned. I sucked harder, gripping his thighs to find better leverage, and then Romero came with a low groan. I kept him in my mouth, waiting for him to go soft, but he didn't. He wasn't as hard as he'd been but he definitely wasn't soft. I released him and swallowed, still unsure if I liked the taste or not.

My cheeks were hot as I met Romero's gaze and I shivered under the force of his expression, dark and hungry, but then it softened as his thumb stroked my mouth. "I meant that as a warning. You didn't have to swallow, Lily," Romero said. He gripped my waist and pulled me against him before he kissed me softly. "Are you okay? Or was it terrible for you? I shouldn't have allowed you to go this far," he said, voice thick with guilt.

My brows puckered. "Terrible? No, why? I wanted to make you feel good. I don't mind it when you come in my mouth."

Romero let out a breathless laugh. "Don't say those things to me. I won't be able to focus anymore."

I grinned, then my gaze flitted down to Romero's erection again. "Why isn't it going soft?"

I could see Romero's confusion, then realization set in and his mouth twisted in a grin that bordered on proud. "Only because I've come doesn't mean I'm not still turned on. It takes more than one orgasm to *make me go soft.*"

"Really?" I asked wickedly.

Romero shook his head, his fingers capturing my wrist and pressing my palm against his muscled chest to stop it from wandering. "Not tonight. It's late. You can't stay that long."

Disappointment banished my excitement. "I know."

Romero stroked my cheek. "We have to be careful. Believe me I'd love to spend all night with you."

I nodded and put my head back down on his chest. I wanted to catch a couple of hours of sleep before I had to sneak back to my room. *Enjoy the moment,* I told myself before I fell asleep.

chapter *ten*

Romero

After Lily had given me that blowjob, I spent the next day thinking about nothing but returning the favor with my tongue. It was a good thing that the mansion wasn't the most dangerous place, because my focus was gone. I didn't think I'd have done a good job protecting anyone if there had been an attack.

My cock was so hard it almost hurt as I waited in my bed that night for Lily to come over. When midnight rolled around and she wasn't there yet, I almost went in search for her. I couldn't remember the last time I'd been that horny.

When my door finally opened and Lily walked in, dressing in a flimsy nightgown, I had to stop myself from shoving her up against the wall and burying myself in her. That was the one thing I couldn't do. Many borders had already been crossed but that was where I had to draw the line.

Lily hopped into bed and kissed me eagerly. It seemed I wasn't the only one who'd waited for this. "Gianna and Matteo were in the corridor, so I had to wait," she said, her fingers already traveling over my chest and down my stomach toward my dick.

I loved her touch, but it was my turn. I grabbed her and flipped her on her back. She gasped in surprise. I hooked my hands in her waistband and slid her panties down her legs, then I paused. This was still new for Lily. I couldn't treat her like the women I'd been with before. "Is this okay?"

She lifted her legs to help me pull her panties over her feet. She nodded quickly. There was only need in her eyes. I smiled as I stroked her soft calf before I shifted it to the side so I could position myself between her legs and a hint of embarrassment showed on her beautiful face, but I didn't give her time to think about it. She had nothing to be embarrassed about. I lowered myself to my stomach, pushed her legs farther apart and after a moment to appreciate the sight of her arousal, I took a long lick. Lily let out a gasp, her hand flying to the back of my head.

"Romero," she said in wonder, and my fucking heart swelled at hearing my name from her lips.

I moved my tongue slowly up and down, and damn it, she tasted even better than I'd imagined. She was coming quickly undone, trembling and gasping so I pulled back and planted a few kisses on her inner thighs and trimmed curls. I didn't want her to come too soon. She was supposed to enjoy this for a while but her inexperienced body was so very responsive. I dipped my tongue back in and my cock twitched when she let out a long moan, legs falling open to give me better access. She raised her hips, fingers fisting the covers, and I closed my mouth over her clit. She exploded, arching up, legs shaking. She bit her lower lip, face contorted beautifully with passion and the effort to hold her moans in, and I watched her as I slowed my ministrations.

She was beautiful, and I didn't ever want to have to share her beauty.

Liliana

I'd heard girls talk about boys going down on them in school but I'd never been able to imagine how it would feel to have someone's mouth on me like that. Would it be strange? Wet? Disgusting? Awkward?

It was none of those things. It was mind-blowingly wonderful. Or maybe that was only because Romero knew exactly what to do, how to nibble and suck and lick until my fingers dug into the mattress because I couldn't take the pleasure anymore. And it seemed to get better every time we did it. Weeks passed and every night Romero pleasured me with his mouth. He seemed to enjoy it as much as I enjoyed going down on him.

Tonight, he was taking his time and I had no mind to rush him. It felt too good. Romero's stubble scratched me lightly at times and that intensified the sensations even more. He lifted his head and I huffed in protest.

He chuckled, but didn't lower his mouth. "Tell me when you're coming, okay? I want to know."

"Okay," I said uncertainly, wondering why he wanted to know, then moaned when Romero closed his lips over my clit and continued where he'd left off.

I could feel myself getting closer. My thighs began to quiver. "I'm coming," I gasped, too caught up in my pleasure to be embarrassed about it.

Romero's finger brushed my opening and then he slid it in. I arched off the mattress. There was a flicker of pain but for some reason it made me come even harder.

Eventually I lay motionless on the bed, trying to catch my breath.

Romero blew out a harsh breath. "Goddammit. You're so tight."

I couldn't say anything in response, too overwhelmed by the feeling of him in me. He moved his finger slowly, stroking the inside of my walls, tripling the sensations in my body. Romero's head rested on my inner thigh as he watched his finger slide in and out of me. I would have been mortified if he hadn't looked like it was the most amazing sight he'd ever seen. He curled his finger and my hips bucked off the mattress as I gasped in surprise and another orgasm rocked through me.

His eyes on me, he pulled his finger out and actually put it in his mouth. I could only stare, strangely turned on by the sight.

Romero crawled back up to me.

A question burned in my mind. What if the brief pain had meant Romero had broken my hymen? It was ridiculous that I even had to worry about something like that, but I knew the rules and I was still too terrified to break them.

Romero smoothed my brows. "Hey, did I hurt you?"

"No, I...I only wondered if..." I felt embarrassed to voice my worries.

Romero seemed to piece it together by himself, though, and regret crossed his face. "You're scared that you aren't a virgin anymore because I put my finger in you." I couldn't decipher the emotion in his voice. Was he angry? Annoyed?

He cupped the back of my head. "I wouldn't do that to you, Lily. I wouldn't just take your virginity without permission, and even then..." He shook his head. "I shouldn't even think about taking your virginity. But you don't have to worry. My finger isn't wide enough and I didn't go deep enough to do any damage. You're safe."

"I wasn't scared, I just..." Yes, what? I had been worried. There was no denying it. It wasn't that I didn't want Romero. I did. But that was a huge step, one I couldn't take back.

"It's okay. You should be scared about that. Your life would be ruined if you lost your virginity before your wedding night," he said in a strange tone. He wrapped his arms around me, so I couldn't look at his face anymore. "I want you to be the one, you know?" I whispered into the dark.

"But I cannot do it," Romero said, his fingers tightening on my arm.

"Why not?"

"Lily," Romero said almost angrily. "You know why not. So far we've been lucky that we didn't get caught. Your sisters and Luca are already suspicious as it is. Right now we could still deny everything and nobody would be able to prove the opposite, but if we slept with each other, then there would be evidence."

"Evidence?" I huffed. "We aren't planning to commit a crime."

"In our world it is. We don't play by the rules of the outside world and you know it."

"We only want to be together because we love each other. Is that so bad?" I snapped my mouth shut when I realized what I'd said. I'd practically put the words "I love you" into Romero's mouth when he'd never said them, nothing close to it. I hadn't either but I knew I loved him. Did he love me as well?

He'd become motionless and for a moment even stopped breathing altogether. "Fuck," Romero whispered harshly. He pressed a kiss against my temple. "This is spinning out of control."

"I meant it, Romero," I said in a small voice. "I love you."

He was quiet, and I realized he couldn't, he wouldn't say it back. "You shouldn't. We don't have a future, Lily."

My heart ached from his words. I didn't want to believe them to be true. "You don't know that."

"You're right," Romero said eventually but it was to appease me. He kissed my temple again and then neither of us said anything.

Romero acted a bit more hesitant around me the next couple of days but it only deepened my resolve. Mother had died with longing in her eyes and regret on her lips. This wasn't how I wanted to end. I didn't want to have a pile of "what-ifs" and "how could it have been" in my head during the last hours of my existence. I wanted to look back and not wonder how wonderful life could have been. I wanted Romero. I wanted Romero to be my first, wanted to share everything with him. Right in this moment, I wanted nothing more, and I knew that even if I'd come to regret it, that regret could never be as torturous as the one I'd feel if I didn't do it, the one where I'd always be left wondering how it would be to become one with the person I loved. Sometimes you had to risk something to live, and Romero was a risk I was willing to take. That was all I could think about as I relished the last few moments of my orgasm.

Romero climbed up my body and brushed a kiss across my lips. He was about to lie down beside me, as he always did after he'd taken care of me, but I held onto his shoulders. "I don't want to stop tonight."

He became very still. His dark eyes traced every contour of my face as if he was hoping for a hint of regret somewhere, but I knew he wouldn't find any. I'd spent too many nights longing and wondering and wishing, and tonight I'd finally get what I wanted. Of course, I needed Romero's cooperation but I had a feeling he wouldn't refuse me. He was dutiful and responsible, but he was also a man, and he wanted me. I could see it in his eyes, and his erection pressed up against my hip bone was a pretty good indicator as well. "Lily," Romero rasped, then cleared his throat. I had to stifle a smile. "That's something that can't be undone. Everything we've done so far is easy to hide, but beyond this point, there are ways to prove our…transgressions."

I laughed softly. "Transgressions?" I lifted my head and kissed him. "How can this be wrong?" Of course, I knew that Father and many other people in our world could have written a novel on all the ways it was wrong, but I didn't care. There was no part in me that thought what we were doing was wrong, and that was all that mattered.

"We discussed this already. I shouldn't do this. For God's sake, I made a promise to Luca to protect you. How is ruining your life protecting you?"

"You aren't ruining my life. I want this, doesn't that count for anything?"

"Of course it does."

I pressed myself against him and grasped his cock through his boxers. "I want you. Only you. I want you to be my first." I wanted him to be my only one. "Don't you want to be my first?" I said in a small voice, regarding him through my lashes.

Romero exhaled a tortured laugh and kissed the corner of my mouth, then my cheek before his eyes burned into mine again. "You know how much I want you. I can hardly think of anything else but I should resist temptation. I'm bound to the Famiglia, to my oath."

"Sleeping with me won't break your oath."

Romero cupped my cheeks. "Luca ordered me to stay away from you, and I haven't done it. Luca will see it as disobedience, and that's breaking my oath."

"I am the one who should decide if I want you to stay away or not. It's my body, my life."

"You know it's not that easy," he murmured, eyes so full of emotion my chest constricted with need and love.

I curled my fingers tighter around his erection. "I know but I don't care. And I know that you want me despite it all."

He released a harsh breath, then let out a quiet laugh. "You've got me in your hands in every possible way. That's not how it's supposed to be."

I smiled. It felt good to know that I had that kind of power over someone like Romero. But he held just as much power over me, and my heart. It was a scary thing, knowing that someone else had the power to crush your heart with a few words. Love was scary. "I want you to be the one, Romero. I don't want anyone else. Please."

He kissed me again, fiercer this time, and lightly thrust into my hand. He felt hot and hard, and I couldn't wait to feel him in me. "Are you sure?" he asked, but there was hardly any vehemence behind the words.

"Yes. I want you. Please."

Romero nodded. Excitement and nerves burst in my body. I'd half expected him to fight me again, but I was glad he hadn't tried to talk me out of it. Today I'd finally become his.

Romero

I was supposed to be the voice of reason, the one to protect Lily from herself and from me, but I wasn't as strong as everyone thought I was. Luca believed in me, trusted in my dutifulness and restraint. He didn't know me well enough. Trust and longing filled Lily's beautiful blue eyes as she peered up at me. She wanted me, and damn it, I wanted her more than anything. Every fucking time I'd fucked her with my finger, I'd imagined how it would be to have my cock in her, to feel her hot walls around me. I couldn't deny her, couldn't deny myself this gift she was offering. Maybe if there had been a flicker of doubt on her face but there was none. I tasted her mouth once more. She was sweet and soft and irresistible. Her fingers around my cock tightened and she bucked her hips lightly—an invitation I understood only too well, and longed to accept. I pulled away from her lips. "Not yet."

"But," she started. I slipped my hand between her legs and entered her with my middle finger. She let out a low breath and opened a bit wider for me. I loved how fucking responsive she was. Always so wet for me. There had been plenty of moments in my life when I had felt powerful but giving Lily pleasure beat them all. She didn't say anything else, only closed her eyes and relaxed, trusting me to make her feel good. I kissed her breast, then nibbled on her nipple as I slowly slipped my finger in and out. Her breathing quickened but I kept a steady rhythm. I moved lower and positioned myself between her thighs. I let myself enjoy the sight of my finger as it entered her perfect pink pussy. Everything about her was beautiful. I leaned forward, not able to resist a moment longer. I closed my mouth over her bundle of nerves and teased her with my lips and tongue while my finger kept thrusting into her, deeper and harder now. I could feel her hymen every time I pushed in. I pressed my tongue against her clit, and slipped another finger into her. I'd never tried it before and her walls clamped around me tightly. My cock was pretty thick so I would have to widen her as much as possible. Her breathing hitched in surprise and she tensed under me. I circled her lightly with my tongue the way she loved it, then took her between my lips and suckled. The tension left her body and a new wave of wetness followed, making it easier for my fingers to enter her. I found a slow rhythm as I listened to the sweet moans and sighs coming from her lips. I could have listened to her forever. I never got tired of giving her pleasure. There was no better feeling in the world than making Lily explode with pleasure, and the knowledge that I was the only one doing it to her. A darker emotion filled me. She wasn't really mine, might never be. One day she might have to marry someone her father chose for her and then that man would see her like this. Unreasonable fury surged through me, but I pushed the feeling aside. This wasn't the moment to think about those kinds of things. I didn't want to lose control only because I let my thoughts stray to dangerous places. Lily needed me to be careful and gentle with her, and I wanted to enjoy every fucking second of this, especially because I didn't know how many more chances we would get together.

I focused on Lily's sweetness, until she finally came apart, stifling her moans in my pillow. I wished I could hear her cry out without restraint, without the fear of getting caught. One day. One day, I'd really make her mine. I'd figure out a way.

I pulled my fingers out and sat back, relishing the sight of her heaving chest as she enjoyed the aftermath of her orgasm. Slowly her eyes opened and she smiled. Damn it. That smile got me every time. I bent over her and kissed her, then I reached for the drawer in my nightstand and grabbed a condom.

Lily watched me, and the briefest flicker of nervousness crossed her face.

I paused. "Are you sure you want to do this?" I wanted to shoot myself for asking. I wanted nothing more than to be in her, to make her mine, to feel her walls around my cock. Why did I have to act all noble? Who was I kidding?

She licked her lips in the most torturous way possible and whispered, "Yes, I want you."

Thank God. I kissed her lips again. I slid off the bed and got out of my underwear. My cock strained to attention. I quickly rolled the condom over it before I climbed back on the back. This wasn't the first time Lily had seen me naked, but today there was a flicker of anxiety on her face when she watched my cock. I moved between her legs, letting my fingers trace the soft skin of her thighs.

There was only trust in her eyes. I didn't deserve that much trust from her, and yet I fucking loved seeing it on her face. I supported my weight on my elbows and started kissing her gently. The tip of my cock rested lightly against her wet heat. I wanted to bury myself in her and it took every ounce of self-control to stay still and wait for her to relax under me. I hooked my hand under her thigh and pulled her legs wider apart. I looked deeply into her eyes, then I shifted my hips and started to push into her. I didn't take my eyes off of her as I inched into her tight heat, working the tip in. She felt so fucking amazing. Tight and warm and wet, and I just wanted to push into her to the hilt. Instead I focused on Lily's eyes, on the way she trusted me to make this good for her, to take care of her and be careful. Her face flashed with more than discomfort when I wasn't even halfway in. I paused but her fingers on my shoulders tightened. "Don't stop," she said quickly.

"I won't," I promised. Stopping was the last thing I wanted to do but if I didn't go slowly she might tear. I traced my lips over her temple, then I pushed further into her until I reached her barrier. I didn't tell her it would hurt. She'd only tense. I pushed the rest of the way into her and her walls squeezed my cock tightly as she gasped against my mouth. I didn't move.

Lily's face was contorted in pain. It took me a moment to realize what was happening, what I'd done. I'd taken what wasn't mine to take. It was unforgivable in our world, regardless of the fact that Lily had given it to me without reservation.

"It's okay," I murmured. "This was the worst part." At least, I hoped it had been. She felt so tight around me, I was worried if I started moving, I'd make things only worse for her, but I couldn't stay in her like that forever. And I really wanted to move, wanted to lose myself in her. "Lily?"

She gave me a shaky smile. "I'm okay. It's not as bad as it was."

That wasn't really something a guy wanted to hear from the girl he was with. I wanted to make her feel good but I knew it would be difficult during her first time. Even though I wanted nothing more than to move, I decided to stay as I was and kiss her for a while. My cock screamed in protest.

"You can really move," she whispered. And that was everything it took. I withdrew almost all the way before I slowly slid back into her.

She exhaled, fingers digging into my back. I slowed even further and tried to go not quite as deep and soon Lily's body loosened under me. I made love to her like that for a long time, and when she responded with the first hesitant moan, I wanted to fucking scream in triumph. But I couldn't last forever, not with the way her walls clamped around me and I had a feeling she wasn't going to come. Next time she would. And there would be a next time, I knew that now. When it came to Lily, I couldn't resist temptation.

I sped up even more until I felt my balls tighten, then my cock before I released into her. I held Lily tightly as I rocked my hips desperately, filling the condom with my cum as I stifled groans. Then I stilled.

She closed her eyes and rested her forehead against my chest.

"Are you okay?" I murmured.

She nodded, but didn't say anything. I pulled back slightly and tilted her face up, worried she was crying, but she merely looked exhausted and happy.

Relief washed over me. I pulled out of her slowly and removed the condom. Before I thrust it into the trash bin, I caught sight of the blood on it.

For some reason it took that image for reality to sink in. Fuck. What had I done?

"Romero?" Lily whispered. I lay down beside her and pulled her into my arms. She didn't need to know my thoughts. I didn't want her to worry.

It didn't take long for her to fall asleep but I lay awake for hours. Eventually I slipped out of bed and walked toward the window. I stared out toward the ocean for a long time. Regret wasn't a useful emotion. You couldn't undo the past. I turned back to the bed.

Lily lay curled up under the blanket, only her beautiful hair and peaceful face peeking out. She was deep asleep. I needed to wake her soon, so she could return to her own room. The sky outside the window was already starting to turn gray. Soon Luca and Matteo would get up and it would be too risky if Lily were still in my room then. I should have sent her away immediately afterward for her own safety, but I didn't have the heart to do it, and I didn't want to see her go so soon after what we'd done.

"Fuck," I muttered. So far everything Lily and I had done had been risky but untraceable, but this, this could destroy Lily's reputation and even start a war. Taking Lily's virginity had been a selfish thing to do. I knew better. I knew the rules. I'd learned to make reasonable decisions over the years, to make decisions that were good for the Famiglia, but today I'd ignored my duty and my promise to Luca. He and I were as close to friends as he could allow with him being my Capo but I knew he'd have to act if he found out what I'd done.

Lily sighed in her sleep and turned around. The blankets moved with her and the pink spot on the sheets became visible. I closed my eyes. *Fuck.* This was supposed to happen on her wedding night. But I knew that Rocco Scuderi would never give Lily's hand to me in marriage. I was only a fucking soldier. Respected and honorable, but a soldier nevertheless. Despite my guilt over having taken Lily's virginity, I knew I would do it again. I'd wanted to make her mine for so long, and this was the only way I could. At least now a part of her belonged to me, at least she'd never forget our night together, but I also knew it wasn't enough. I didn't want Lily to have only the memory of our shared night for the rest of her days, I wanted to remind her of the pleasure I could give her every night, I wanted to taste her, smell her, feel her every fucking night. I wanted to have her fall asleep in my arms and wake up next to me in the morning. I wanted to make her mine for everyone to know, but there was no way in hell I could do this without betraying Luca and the Famiglia even more.

Luca treated me like a brother but if I did this, if I went against the Outfit by claiming Lily officially, he'd have to put me down like a rabid dog for the good of the Famiglia.

With a sigh, I walked toward the bed and bent over Lily. I brushed her hair away from her face. "Lily, you need to wake up," I whispered.

Her eyelids fluttered and she turned on her back. The blankets slipped away, revealing her perfect breasts. Her nipples puckered at the cool air in the room and my cock stirred in response. I leaned over her. She even still smelled like me. Fuck. I was already getting hard again. She opened her eyes and gave me a sleepy smile. Happiness and trust shone on her face. Didn't she realize that I'd destroyed her life last night?

A light blush appeared on her cheeks under my scrutiny. I kissed her forehead. "You need to leave," I said.

She froze, eyes filling with insecurity. "Did I do something wrong last night?"

Good Lord. I wanted to stab myself with my fucking knife. I was such an asshole. I should have never let it come to this. Lily was a good girl and I'd ruined her. I kissed the spot below her ear, then her cheek. "No, you did nothing wrong, honey."

She relaxed and lifted her hand to the back of my head, looking hopeful. "Can we snuggle a bit?"

She sounded fucking vulnerable. Of course she wanted closeness after last night, and I wanted it too, but it was getting light outside, but the way she was looking at me I couldn't tell her "no." I slipped under the blankets and she pressed up against me. Her naked skin brushed mine, and all of my senses sprang to life. I pushed my lust down. This wasn't the time. I stroked her hair. "Are you okay?"

She nodded against my shoulder. "I'm a bit sore." She sounded embarrassed.

I pressed a kiss against her temple and I wasn't sure why I said it because it definitely didn't make things easier but it slipped out, "I love you."

And by God, it was the truth. I loved Lily, even though I knew our love was doomed.

She sucked in a breath before whispering, "I love you too."

I was digging my grave and hers too, only because I couldn't control my dick, my heart, and my mouth.

She let out a small happy breath. She didn't seem to realize in how much trouble we were. I couldn't stop feeling guilty. I wished I could say I would have acted differently if I got the chance, but I knew I'd sleep with her again. I'd wanted her, still wanted her. I would never stop wanting her.

chapter *eleven*

Liliana

I COULDN'T BELIEVE ROMERO AND I HAD ACTUALLY SLEPT TOGETHER. I didn't feel regret. Maybe it would come at some point but I couldn't imagine it.

It had been painful and yet it was the happiest moment in my life. And afterwards when Romero had admitted he loved me, I'd wanted to tell everyone about it. Let them get angry, let them call me names, what did I care? I was happy, and that was all that mattered. But I knew better. Romero and I needed to keep it a secret. Maybe one day we'd figure out a way to make it official without causing a war, but right now I only wanted to enjoy our time together. The summer was drawing to a close but Father didn't seem to want me back and I definitely didn't want to return to Chicago. Maybe he'd forget I existed and I could move to New York for good.

The first time I faced Aria and Gianna after losing my virginity, I'd worried they'd see something was different, but of course they hadn't. Nobody suspected anything.

Maybe that realization was why I got more daring.

It was almost noon and I could hardly keep my eyes open. Romero and I had made love until the early morning hours, and once I'd been back in my room I'd only managed two hours of sleep before I had to get up for breakfast again.

"Why don't you rest on the sofa for a while? You look tired," Aria said when I yawned again. We'd been rifling through a brochure that detailed events in the Hamptons for something to do in the next few days. Sunbathing and swimming were getting old.

Gianna wiggled her eyebrows behind Aria's back. "She does. She doesn't seem to get enough sleep at night."

Romero glanced over from where he stood with Luca and Matteo in the kitchen area, but he didn't seem worried. I decided to ignore Gianna's comment. I stood from the table. "You're probably right, Aria. I'll lie down for a bit."

Aria set the brochure aside and peered down at her watch before she looked over to Luca. "If we want to head out for lunch, we should leave soon."

Luca nodded.

I walked toward the sofa, stretched out and closed my eyes. I almost immediately drifted off into a light slumber, only interrupted by the sound of Aria and Luca leaving, followed a few minutes later by Gianna's and Matteo's laughter as they headed for the beach. In the following silence, I felt my mind drift off again.

"I'm wearing you out," Romero said from close by.

I opened my eyes to find him standing over me with a smirk. Slowly my own lips curled into a grin and my sleepiness began to disappear. I hooked my leg behind his knee in an attempt to make him fall forward and preferably land on top of me, but Romero was too strong. After a quick glance toward the terrace door he leaned down, though, and gave me a kiss. When he was about to pull back again, I wrapped my arms around his neck and my legs around his waist.

"Aria and Luca are out for lunch, and Gianna and Matteo will spend the day on the boat. That leaves the house to us."

Romero looked conflicted but when I pressed my core against his crotch, I knew I had him. He was already hard. With a growl, he lowered himself on top of me. Our lips eagerly found each other. After a few minutes of heated kissing and roaming hands, Romero drew back. "It's too risky to have sex out here."

"I know, but there are other things we can do," I said, before I pulled Romero's head back down for another kiss. He didn't protest again, which might have also had something to do with the fact that I was rubbing his erection through his pants.

For some reason making out with Romero in the middle of the living room made things seem more real between us, like we could maybe be an official couple, and not just something that needed to happen in the secrecy of darkness.

My lips were raw from Romero's kiss, but I loved it. Romero slipped his hand under my shirt and sneaked his fingers under my bra cup, finding my nipple. I gasped and arched off the sofa. Romero kissed me even harder. I swung my leg over his lower back, pulling him even tighter against me. I couldn't wait to feel him without the clothes between us. Maybe I could convince him to risk a quickie in the living room.

A door banged and steps rang out, but there was no time to react before Aria appeared in the living area. "Lily, I—" She snapped her lips shut and froze, so did Romero and I. Romero pulled his hand out from under my shirt and sat back quickly. He held his arms in a way that was supposed to hide his erection, but I doubted he was fooling Aria. My eyes searched the area behind her back but Luca wasn't there. That was the only good thing about our situation.

Nobody said anything for a long time. I tried to reposition my bra and straighten my hair but I wasn't doing a good job because my hands were shaking. "This isn't how it looks," I said, but stopped when I realized how stupid that sounded.

Aria raised her eyebrows as if she thought exactly the same thing. "That's why I didn't want you alone with her, Romero. I knew this would happen!"

"You make it sound like I had nothing to do with it. It wasn't only Romero's doing," I said, but Aria hardly paid me attention. She was glaring at Romero.

"Why are you back anyway? Shouldn't you be having lunch with your husband?" I asked.

"Are you blaming me for this?" Aria asked incredulously. "Luca got a call that there was trouble in one of the clubs. Something with one of the Russian underbosses, so he dropped me off in the driveway and headed straight to New York. You're lucky he didn't come in."

"If you tell Luca," Romero began but Aria interrupted him. "I won't tell him," she said angrily. "I know what he'll have to do if I do."

Romero helped me to my feet. "He's your husband. You owe him the truth."

What was he doing? He'd be in big trouble if Luca found out, and what if Luca told my father? I gave Romero a confused look but he didn't react. Then another thought struck me. Maybe he wanted people to find out. Maybe he hoped Luca would approve and would figure out a way for my father to agree on a union between Romero and me. Hope flared up in me.

"Lily, can I talk to you in private, please?" Aria asked, looking truly shaken. Her worry ignited my own.

I nodded, even though my stomach turned from anxiety. Aria was my sister. I loved her and trusted her, but Romero was right. She was also the wife of the Capo, and I wasn't sure where her loyalties lay. I followed her toward the dining room and then into the kitchen. She didn't say anything until we'd both settled on bar stools.

"How long has this been going on?" she asked. God, she even sounded like the wife of a Capo, so grown up and responsible.

"A while. Almost since I came to New York," I admitted. There was really no use in lying anymore and I actually wanted to talk to her about it. Romero and I had been keeping this a secret for close to three months.

Aria nodded slowly, her eyes full of worry. "I should have known. Sometimes I thought I saw you exchanging those secretive looks only lovers do, but I didn't want to believe it."

I wasn't sure what to say, if she even expected me to say anything. "We tried to hide it."

"Of course, you did!" Aria whispered harshly. "Oh, Lily. This is bad, you know that, right? If Father finds out all hell will break lose. You'll be in major trouble, and not only that. Father might very well start war over this. After all, Luca promised to keep you safe while you were in New York and having one of his men have an affair with you is definitely a breach of that promise."

"Affair?" I said offended. What Romero and I had was so much more than that. "You make it sound like it's just about sex."

Aria's eyes widened. "I didn't mean it like that, but…wait a second. Please tell me you haven't slept with him yet." Her expression was so pleading and anxious, I almost considered lying to her.

I bit my lip. "I really love him, Aria."

"So you did sleep with him," she said quietly. She made it sound like it was the end of the world.

I nodded. "And I don't regret it." I was so glad that I got to share that moment with Romero. I wanted to share so much more with him. Every time I'd slept with him in the last few weeks, I'd grown closer to him, though I didn't think that was possible.

Aria leaned back and released a long breath. "Father will kill you if he finds out. After the thing with Gianna, he'll completely lose it."

"Mother told me to be happy shortly before she died. And Romero makes me happy. I want to be with him."

"Lily, Father won't allow it. No matter what any of us says, he won't let you marry a mere soldier from New York. He can't gain anything from such a union, not when I'm already married to the Capo and Gianna to the Consigliere."

"I know," I said in a whisper. "But…I…" I trailed off. I knew Aria was right. I'd known it pretty much from the beginning. I hated that I had to apologize for loving someone, for wanting to be with that someone. It shouldn't be like that.

Aria took my hand and linked our fingers. "Some women manage to fake their virginity on their wedding night. Maybe you can do that too. And it's not like Father has already set up a wedding for you, so we can figure something out until then."

"Aria, I don't want to marry anyone else. I only want Romero. I mean it, I love him."

Aria looked into my eyes for a very long time. I wasn't sure what she was hoping to find there but I gave her time. "You do, don't you?" she said, resigned. "What about him? Does he love you?"

"He said it after we made love for the first time." I'd hoped he would say it again after our first night together but so far he hadn't. Maybe he wasn't the type to say it out loud very often.

"Are you sure he's serious about you?"

"Of course, didn't you hear what I told you?" I said, but even I could hear the flicker of uncertainty in my voice and I wasn't sure where it was coming from.

"Some men say things they don't mean after sex because they feel guilty."

My eyes widened. How would she even know? She had warmed the heart of one of the most feared men in the country. "He wouldn't do that. And if you're saying he only tried to get in my pants, that's ridiculous. You know Romero, he wouldn't use me like that."

Her blue eyes softened with guilt. "No, you're right. Romero isn't the type and he wouldn't risk so much for sex. He must care about you if he goes against Luca's orders."

"You won't tell him, right?"

"I told you, I won't. Luca's got enough on his plate already, I don't want him to worry about this as well. We'll figure something out. But until then, please be more careful. I'm not going to tell you to stay away from Romero because I suspect you'd just go behind my back, but if someone else finds out, things could really get out of hand."

"I know," I said. "Romero and I will be careful."

Aria pressed her lips together. "And there's really no way that you'd consider breaking things off with Romero?"

"No," I said without hesitation.

She smiled sadly and hopped off the bar stool. "I want to talk to Romero now."

I pushed to my feet and grabbed her arm. "Why? Will you try to talk him into leaving me?"

"Do you really think I'd do that to you?" Aria asked in a hurt tone.

I felt bad instantly but Aria had changed over the years. Maybe it was because she'd taken more responsibilities as Luca's wife, but sometimes I thought she acted too much like a meddling mother when it came to me. I didn't doubt she always wanted what she thought was the best for me, only problem was I wasn't sure if we both agreed on what that was. "No. But why do you want to talk to Romero?"

"I just do," she said stubbornly. "Please stay here while I talk to him. Do me that favor."

"Aria, please don't make a bigger deal out of this than it is."

"Oh, Lily, this is a much bigger deal than you think," she said before she walked off.

Romero

I wanted to tear my hair out in frustration. We should have been more careful. I usually never let my guard down. I always anticipated possible risks. Today I'd failed on so many levels, it was pitiful, and not just that, I'd risked both our lives.

Aria advanced on me. She looked royally pissed. And I couldn't blame her. She stopped right in front of me, her blue eyes blazing with anger. "How could you do that? What were you thinking?" she hissed, jabbing her pointer finger against my chest. "But you probably weren't thinking, at least not with your head." She made a gesture in the general direction of my crotch, then jabbed my chest again with more force.

My eyebrows shot up. This was so unlike Aria. She never touched me, because she knew how possessive Luca got over the smallest things. "This isn't only about sex."

"Lily said the same thing, but what is it then? You know the rules, for God's sake. It's ironic that I have to remind you."

"I know the rules," I said tersely, getting angry. But Aria was the last person I should be mad at. She was right.

"Lily said you slept with her." Aria shook her head, tears gathering in her eyes, and all my anger evaporated. "God, Romero, if someone finds out, Lily will be ruined. Or do you intend to marry her?"

"I can't. You know that. Your father would never allow it, and if we went against his wishes that would mean war."

"I *know it. You know it.* So why did you do it?"

"I didn't push Lily if that's what you think," I said. Did she think I'd forced her sister somehow? "Lily wanted it too."

"I don't doubt it. I see how she's looking at you. She loves you. Of course she wants to sleep with you, but you should have known better!"

Fuck, why did she have to be right? "I know. What do you want me to say? That I'm sorry?"

"You'd be lying," Aria muttered.

Indignation shot through me but she was right. I wasn't sorry that I'd slept with Lily, at least not enough that I wouldn't do it again. "Are you going to tell me to stay away from her now?"

"You'd be going behind my back. And Lily would hate me if I tried to get between you and her. You've slept with her already, so it's not like it matters if you do it again as long as you are careful not to get caught and not to get my sister pregnant."

"Are you going to give me the talk?" I said in amusement.

"I'm serious. If Lily gets pregnant, then things will get really bad."

"We're being careful."

"As careful as you were when I caught you on the sofa?"

"I mean it. Lily won't get pregnant."

Aria covered her face with her hands. "God, I can't believe we're having this discussion. I wanted Lily in New York so she'd have some fun, but not that kind of fun."

I wasn't sure what to say. Guilt weighed heavily on my shoulders, but like Aria had said it was too late now.

"Would you stay away from her if I threatened to tell Luca?" Aria asked as she lowered her hands.

"No," I said without hesitation.

"Good," she said, throwing me off track. "At least that means you're serious about her. Maybe we can find a solution for you and my sister. Let me think about it."

"I've been thinking about it for a long time. Unless we want war, we'd have to convince your father to agree on a union between Lily and me."

"Gianna and I married for political reasons. Why should Lily not be allowed to marry someone she wants?"

"If I was more than a soldier, then maybe your father would consider it."

Aria's eyes lit up. "You could become a Captain with your own group of soldiers. You've been working for Luca for so long and he always says you're his best soldier. The only reason why he hasn't already promoted you is because he trusts you with me and doesn't want anyone else as my guard."

I stared at her. Usually the position of Captain was handed down from father to son. Soldiers rarely received the honor of becoming Captain.

"Father still hasn't found a husband for Lily. That's a good sign. Gianna and I were long engaged when we were Lily's age, so maybe he's open for suggestions and it would be a good move to improve relations between New York and Chicago again."

"You'd make a good Capo too," I said with a smile.

"I'm married to a good Capo, that's all."

"You are," I said. "But I don't want to become Captain only because you talk Luca into it. I haven't worked this hard for a pity promotion."

"I won't have to talk him into it, and Luca never does anything because of pity. You should know that."

I nodded. She had a point. "Once you tell him, there's no going back. He might not take it so well. I went against his direct orders after all. That's still a crime."

"Yeah, you did," Aria said. "But he loves you like a brother. He'll forgive you. I'll just have to figure out a way to break it to him."

"I could talk to him. I have to own up to my actions."

Aria shook her head. "No, I can be more convincing than you, and he can't stay mad at me for long."

I laughed. "You Scuderi women have a way with men."

Aria smiled for the first time since she'd found Lily and me on the sofa. I took that as a good sign, even though I wasn't so naïve to think that I'd become Captain tomorrow and then Scuderi would gladly accept me as his future son-in-law. This would be a difficult battle.

chapter *twelve*

Liliana

I NERVOUSLY PACED THE KITCHEN. WHAT TOOK ARIA SO LONG? I didn't even want to know what she was saying to Romero. What if she convinced him to break things off with me? She'd promised not to do something like that but I wasn't sure. If she thought she had to protect me from harm, she'd play dirty if she had to.

The door opened and Romero stepped in. He looked almost relaxed. I hurried toward him. "What did she say?"

"That we should be careful."

"That's all? She's not going to tell Luca about it?"

"No, not right now."

"What does that mean?"

A slow smile curled his lips. "There might be a way for us to be together."

"You mean officially?" I asked excitedly.

"Yes, but first Aria needs to figure out a way to talk to Luca, and then we'll go from there."

I tried to hold back my joy, but it was difficult. I wanted nothing more than a real future with Romero.

I stood on my tiptoes and kissed him, but after only a few seconds Romero pulled back with a pained look. "We need to be more careful. Aria will rip my head off if she catches us kissing out in the open like that again."

"Probably not only your head," I said with a wicked grin, cupping him through his pants.

Romero groaned, gripped my wrist and pulled my hand away. "Lily, stop torturing me."

"I thought you like it when I torture you."

Romero leaned down, his lips brushing my ear. "I do, when we are *alone*."

"Then how about we head to my room?"

"There's nothing I'd rather do, but we shouldn't risk it during the day," Romero said regretfully. "And I really need to call Luca and ask about the problem with the Russian underboss."

I pouted playfully. "I hate it when you're being reasonable. Tonight is too far away. I want you now."

"Fuck," Romero muttered. Then he gave me a dangerous grin. "Go ahead. I'll come after you in a few minutes."

I dashed off toward my room, already feeling my core tighten with anticipation.

The next day, Luca returned from New York. He was on edge, so our confession would have to wait. During dinner that evening, Aria, Romero, and I acted as if nothing had ever happened. I really hoped Aria would figure out a way to talk to Luca soon so we could all find a way to make a future for Romero and me possible.

Gianna kept chancing looks at Aria and me as if she could smell that something was going on. Gianna had always been drawn to trouble so it was really no surprise.

Halfway through the main course, Luca's phone started buzzing. "What now?" he growled as he dropped his fork. Today definitely wasn't the day to tell him about Romero and me. I hadn't seen him in such a bad mood in a while. He got up, pulled the phone out of his pants pocket and answered it.

"Rocco, I didn't expect your call," he said.

We all turned toward the conversation.

Luca glanced in my direction. "Liliana is doing well."

My father had only called once the entire summer to ask how I was. For some reason I worried about the true reasons for his check-in.

"Tomorrow? That's short notice. Has something happened?"

I put my fork down, my stomach tightening with anxiety.

"Of course. She'll be there," Luca said with a frown. He hung up and returned to the table, lowering his large frame into the chair.

"What's going on?" Aria asked before I could even utter a word. She looked as worried as I felt. Did she think Father had found out something about Romero and me? If that were the case, the call wouldn't have gone over so peacefully, that much was sure. And who should have told them? Nobody in this house would.

"Your father wants Liliana to come home tomorrow," Luca said, lips tight with concern.

"What?" I said, shocked. Romero didn't quite manage to hide his surprise either. I had to force myself to tear my gaze away from him quickly before Luca got suspicious. "So soon?"

Matteo laughed. "You've been here for three months."

Gianna rammed her elbow into his side and he rubbed the spot with a smirk.

"I was joking, damn it. Why do you have to be so violent?" he asked.

I wasn't in the mood for jokes. I felt like the rug had been pulled out from under my feet. I'd always known I'd have to return eventually but now that I was being faced with my father's order, I felt heartbroken.

"He wants you on the earliest flight. He booked the ticket already," Luca continued as if his brother and Gianna weren't still bickering.

"Did he say why?" I asked.

"He said something about social responsibilities. Apparently there are a few parties he wants you to attend, but he wasn't very forthcoming with information."

My eyes darted to Romero again, but then I focused on Luca. "Did he say how long I had to stay in Chicago?"

Luca narrowed his eyes. "No. Chicago is your home, so I had no right to ask."

"Lily is of age, she could simply refuse to return," Gianna said snidely. Matteo had his arm wrapped around her shoulder. As usual their fighting hadn't lasted very long. They'd probably soon go to their room to make up.

Luca glowered. "Then I'd drag her onto that plane if necessary. If her father wants her to come home, she'll go. I won't risk a conflict over something as ridiculous as this."

I bit my lip. "It's okay. I'll go. I'll survive a few parties, and I'm excited about seeing Fabi again. I missed him. I'll plead Father to let me return to New York as soon as possible."

I didn't talk for the rest of dinner and was glad when I could finally get up. It was ridiculous of me to be so nervous about going home; because despite everything Chicago was still supposed to be *my home*. I headed out toward the terrace and wrapped my arms around myself, feeling inexplicably cold even though it was still warm.

The door slid open behind me again and Aria walked up beside me, giving me an understanding smile. "I'll call Father and ask him to send you back for another visit soon. It's not like he needs you in Chicago. You'll be back before you know it."

"You're probably glad I'll be gone because that means I can't see Romero for a while," I snapped. I felt instantly bad for lashing out at my sister. Closing my eyes, I said, "Sorry."

Aria touched my shoulder lightly. "Don't worry. And I really don't want you to leave, please believe me."

I nodded. "I've gotten used to life here. I've been happy. I don't even remember the last time I was happy in Chicago."

"This is only a temporary thing. You'll be back here in no time, and while you're in Chicago I'll talk to Luca about Romero. Maybe when you're back we'll have made a plan on how to convince Father to accept Romero as your husband."

Hope flared up in me. I looked at my sister. "You're right. I should see it as a short vacation. Maybe soon I'll be able to call New York my home for good."

We didn't say anything after that, only stood beside each other and watched the boisterous ocean. What I really wanted to do was talk to Romero, be in his arms and convince myself that this thing between us was meant to last, but it was way too early to retire to bed and we couldn't risk anything with everyone still awake.

When the breeze picked up, Aria and I returned into the living room. Romero caught my eyes from across the room. I couldn't wait to be alone with him tonight, to feel his body sliding against mine. I'd never needed him more.

Earlier than usual I crept out of my room and headed for Romero's. I wanted to spend as much time with him as possible. He didn't look surprised when I slipped in.

He was sitting on the edge of his bed, arms braced on his knees. He pushed to his feet when I closed the door. For a while we only stared at each other until the pressure in my chest threatened to crush my rib cage. Why was I being so emotional about this? Romero crossed the room and gripped me by the hips, then he turned us around and led me backwards toward the bed until my calves bumped against it and we both fell back on the mattress.

Our hands roamed each other's bodies almost frantically, undressing and caressing. Who knew when we'd get the chance to feel each other again? It could be weeks. *Too long.* We needed to make the best of our last night together.

Tonight I wanted to be in control. I pushed Romero onto his back and he didn't resist. I straddled his hips and lowered myself onto his erection, feeling it slide into me all the way. I closed my eyes for a moment, releasing a low breath at the familiar feeling of fullness. Romero gripped my hips and started pushing upwards, driving himself deeply into me. I leaned forward onto my forearms so my face was above his and my hair surrounded us like a curtain, our own personal sanctuary from the outside world. "I'm going to miss you," I whispered as I rocked back and forth. "I'm going to miss this, *everything*."

"You won't be gone long," he growled.

He sounded absolutely sure. I kissed him, moving even faster until we both came at the same time, but we weren't sated yet. We made love two more times that night as if we could stamp the sensations of our togetherness into our minds that way.

"I don't want to leave," I murmured afterwards as I lay in Romero's arms. "I want to fall asleep in your arms."

Romero reached for his alarm clock. "Then don't. We'll get up early so you can sneak back to your room without anyone noticing."

I smiled, and rested my cheek against his chest. It didn't take long for me to fall asleep with the sound of Romero's heartbeat like music in my ear.

The alarm woke us before sunrise and I quickly gathered my clothes in the dark room. Before I left, Romero pulled me against his chest and kissed me fiercely, then I slipped out and rushed back to my room. I caught a couple of hours of sleep before I really got up and prepared everything for my drive to the airport.

The hardest part about leaving was that I couldn't hug or kiss Romero when we said goodbye in the airport waiting hall. With a last glance, I walked away, trying to ignore the insistent worry that I wouldn't return.

When I landed in Chicago, my old bodyguard Mario was waiting for me. He wasn't the most talkative person so we didn't speak during the drive to my family home.

As I stepped up to the entrance door, my heart pounded in my chest like a drum. The last time I'd been here, the house had brimmed with sadness and death.

Mario opened the door for me and I stepped in. It wasn't as bad as it used to be but I definitely didn't feel at home here anymore. Was it my imagination or did the stench of disinfectant still linger in the corners?

"Where's my father?" I asked quickly before my mind conjured up more craziness.

"In his office. He wants to see you right away."

I doubted the reason for that was that he'd missed me. Mario headed off to take my luggage up to my room. I walked down the long corridor and knocked at Father's door, trying to ignore the way my stomach twisted with nerves.

"Come in," Father called.

I took a deep breath and slipped in. Fabi stood near the window. He had grown in the three months that I'd been gone and something about the way he held himself told me that wasn't the only change in him. The last few months seemed to have taken a toll on him. It would have been better if Fabi had been allowed to go to Chicago with me for the summer, but naturally that had been out of the question.

Father sat behind his desk as usual. He didn't bother getting up to hug me. But Fabi walked up to me and I wrapped my arms around him before he could decide he was too cool for affection. He was taller than me. I leaned back to take a look at his face.

I knew something was wrong the moment I saw Fabi's expression. Recently Father had involved him more and more in the mob business, even though Fabi wouldn't turn 13 for several more weeks. Had something happened? He couldn't have been forced to kill someone already, right? The idea that my little brother might already be a killer turned my stomach into an icy pit.

"Sit," Father said with a nod toward the armchair in front of his desk. Fabi immediately freed himself of my embrace, but what worried me more was that he made sure to keep his eyes on my chin.

"It's good to see you back in Chicago. I trust Luca and Aria took good care of you?" Father asked.

No mention of Gianna, which wasn't a huge surprise.

I sank down on the chair across from him. "Yes, they did. It was lovely."

I tried to catch Fabi's gaze; he'd returned to his spot at the window where he was busy avoiding my eyes, his hands balled to fists at his side and his lips a thin white line in his angry face. My stomach tied itself into a knot.

Father tapped his fingers against the smooth wood of the desk. If I didn't know better, I'd say he looked almost ashamed. Fear gripped me. Again I darted a look at Fabi but he was glaring at the floor.

The silence stretched between us until I was sure I'd suffocate. "You said to Luca that you wanted me here for a few parties?"

"That's part of the reason. You need to become part of our social circles again." Father paused, then he cleared his throat. He looked almost guilty. "Life must go on. Death is part of our existence but we must make sure that our family line stays strong."

Where was he going with this?

"I'm going to marry again."

I was torn between relief and shock. At least I wasn't in trouble but I couldn't believe, much less understand how he could be considering another marriage when Mother had been dead for less than six months. "But—" I stopped myself. Nothing I could say would change a thing. It would only get me in trouble. "Who is she? Do I know her?"

There were a few widows in Father's age I knew but I wasn't sure if any of them were his type. Even thinking that made me feel guilty and I wasn't even the one considering replacing Mother. Maybe Father was lonelier than he'd let on. I'd always thought he and Mother hadn't cared much for each other but maybe I'd been wrong. Maybe he had loved her in some twisted way. Maybe he hadn't been able to show it. Some people were like that.

Fabi let out a low sound, drawing my eyes toward him, but he was still glowering at his feet. Which was probably for the best because Father gave him a look that sent a shiver down my back. I noticed a fading bruise on Fabi's left temple, and I couldn't help but wonder if there were more hidden beneath his clothing and if Father was responsible for all of them.

Father's fingers took up their tapping again. "Maria Brasci."

I almost fell forward in my chair. "What?" I blurted. He had to be kidding. Maria was only one year older than me. She could have been Father's daughter. She'd gone to school with me, for God's sake!

I peered at Fabi again, needing him to tell me this was a joke, but his grimace was all the answer I needed. This was disgusting. Was this some kind of midlife crisis thing on Father's part? I couldn't even begin to understand how he could choose someone who could be his daughter.

"In turn," Father continued evenly. "You are going to marry her father, Benito Brasci."

And that's when my whole world shattered. I could see it right before my eyes. All the images of a future with Romero, of happiness and smiles, of sweet kisses and endless nights of lovemaking splintering into tiny pieces, and they were replaced by something horrendous and dark. Something people whispered about in hushed voices because they were worried the horrors might become reality if they spoke about them too loudly. Not in my darkest nightmares had I imagined that Father would marry me off to an old man like Benito Brasci. I didn't remember much about him, but I didn't have to. Everything about this was wrong.

I tried to speak but I was mute. I wondered when the first tears would fall. Right now, I still felt too numb.

"You're condemning Lily to a life of misery." Fabi said the words I could only think. He sounded so…old. Like he'd become a man some time when I hadn't been looking. I wanted to give him a grateful smile but my face was frozen, all of me was. Was this really happening?

This morning I'd still kissed Romero and now I was supposed to marry Brasci.

"I'm making reasonable decisions. You don't understand it yet, but you will."

"No. I would never do something like that."

"You will do worse, believe me, Son." He sighed. "We all have to make sacrifices. That's life."

What kind of sacrifice was it to marry a young woman who could be his daughter? I was supposed to do the sacrificing.

I couldn't stop wondering when the tears would come but there wasn't even the trademark prickling yet. There was nothing. I was nothing. Again I tried to call up an image of Benito Brasci, but I came up empty. It didn't matter. He wasn't Romero.

"You'll meet him tomorrow. He and Maria are coming over for dinner."

Maybe it could have been funny if it wasn't so terrible.

"Okay," I said simply. I sounded collected. Fabi frowned at me, but Father looked immensely pleased. I rose from my chair and crossed the room toward the door. "I'm going to bed. I had a long day."

"Aren't you going to join us for dinner?" Father asked, but he didn't sound like he cared.

"I'm not hungry," I said calmly.

"Then sleep well. Tomorrow is an exciting day for both of us."

My hand on the door handle stilled for an instant. A flicker of something, maybe anger, seized my body but then it was gone and I was numb again.

One foot in front of the other. One foot in front of the other. The mantra filled my head as I ascended the staircase. Steps thundered after me and then

Fabi was beside me. He grabbed my arm. He was stronger than I thought. He was so grown. These thoughts repeated themselves in my mind. Maybe my brain had been broken by shock, or shut down because the reality of the situation was too much to bear.

"What the fuck is wrong with you, Lily?" he growled. His voice wasn't man yet, but not boy either.

"Wrong?" I asked.

"Yes, wrong," Fabi muttered. He released me and I rubbed my arm from the force of his grip.

Was something wrong with me? Maybe that was the problem. I'd done many wrong things in the past. I'd slept with Romero, even though we weren't married. Maybe this was punishment for my sins. The pastor in our church would probably have said so.

"Why aren't you freaking out? Why did you just say okay? Do you even realize what you agreed to?"

I wasn't aware I'd agreed to anything. How could I have when nobody had ever asked me about my opinion? "Because there is nothing I can do."

"Bullshit," Fabi said, stomping his foot. Maybe not as grown up as I thought.

I almost smiled, if my face had been capable of movement. "When did you start swearing so much?"

"All the Made Men do."

"But you aren't one of them yet."

"But soon."

I nodded. That's what I'd feared. Father seemed keen on ruining both of our lives.

"And that doesn't even matter right now. You can't just accept this marriage. You have to do something."

"What? What can I do?" I asked with a hint of anger. That brief burst of emotion scared me because I preferred the numbness.

"Something," Fabi said quietly, blue eyes pleading with me. "Anything. Don't just accept it."

"Then tell me what I can do. You are the future Made Man. Tell me."

Fabiano averted his gaze, guilt on his face.

I touched his shoulder. "There's nothing either of us can do."

"You could run like Gianna," Fabi burst out.

"She got caught."

"But you wouldn't."

"I would." I was nothing like Gianna. I wouldn't even last one month, probably not even a week. I wasn't a rebel. I didn't even want to leave this life behind. There was no way I would survive on my own for long.

But maybe I wouldn't have to be alone. Romero could come with me. He knew how to evade pursuers. Together we could make it.

"You're thinking about it, aren't you?" Fabi asked with a boyish grin.

"Remember where your loyalties are," I whispered. "This is betrayal. If Father finds out, you're going to be punished harshly."

"I'm not a Made Man yet."

"But as good as, you said it yourself. They will judge you as they would a Made Man, and that would mean death."

"Father needs an heir," Fabi said.

"Father will soon have a young bride who can give him plenty of children. Maybe he won't need you after all."

Fabi made a gagging sound. "It's like he's marrying you. It's sick."

I couldn't deny it. "Benito Brasci is older than Father, isn't he?"

"I don't know. He looks ancient."

"I should go up to my room," I said absentmindedly. I needed to talk to Romero. Fabi didn't stop me as I walked up the remaining steps and headed for my room.

When the door closed after me, I feared for a moment that I'd actually burst into tears, but the stopper keeping my emotions in held fast.

I fumbled my phone out of the bottom of my travel bag and dialed Romero's number. My hands shook and when Romero didn't pick up after the first two rings like he usually did, I could feel panic slip through the cracks in my numbness. He didn't know I'd call, but I couldn't help but worry that something had happened to him. Or that he'd found out about my engagement to Brasci and didn't want anything to do with me. What if Luca had known all along? It was possible that Father had told him on the phone and Luca hadn't mentioned it because he knew Aria and Gianna would make a scene.

I was sent to voicemail and quickly hung up. I hadn't even put the phone away when the screen flashed with Romero's name. Taking a deep breath, I answered.

"Lily, are you okay? I was in a meeting and had the phone on mute."

I slumped against the wall at the sound of Romero's voice. It calmed me but at the same time it made me realize what I could lose if I had to marry Brasci. "Father has chosen a husband for me," I said eventually. I sounded like I was talking about the weather, completely detached.

Silence followed on the other end. I couldn't even hear breathing. I didn't dare say anything, although I was bursting with fear and anxiety.

"Who is it?" Romero asked in a low voice. I wished I could see his face to get a hint about his emotions. He sounded as emotionless as I had.

"Benito Brasci. You probably don't know him, but—"

Romero interrupted me. "I know him. I met him during a gathering last year."

"Oh," I said, then waited but again Romero was silent. Why was he so calm? Didn't he care that I was going to marry another man? Maybe this had always been a distraction for him. Maybe he'd never intended for us to have more than…what? An affair? I felt dirty just thinking about it. "He's much older than me."

"I know."

Of course Romero knew but I wasn't sure what else to say.

"I thought," I said hesitantly. "I thought we could…"

I didn't dare utter the words.

"You thought we could what?"

I closed my eyes. "I thought we could run away together." I cringed when the words had left my mouth. Could I sound any more pathetic and naïve?

"That would mean war between the Outfit and New York."

He said it matter-of-factly, like it had absolutely nothing to do with him. I hadn't thought of that but of course that would be the first thing that crossed Romero's mind. The Famiglia always came first.

I'd been stupid. Mother had always warned me that men promised you the world if they wanted something from you. Romero had been kind and loving, and I'd given him everything in turn. My body, my heart, every little thing I could give. I'd given it gladly and I didn't want to feel regret over a single thing, but it was hard.

I bit my lip, suddenly on the verge of crying. I could feel the floodgates open. It wouldn't be long now. "You're right," I croaked. "I—" I choked and quickly hung up. Then I hid the phone in my travel bag again and curled up on my bed, letting sobs wrack my body until my muscles hurt, until my throat hurt, until everything hurt, but nothing as much as my heart. Was this it? The end of every dream I had?

chapter *thirteen*

Romero

I STARED AT MY PHONE. WHAT THE FUCK WAS SCUDERI THINKING? I'D wanted to kill him so often in the past, now I wished I'd done it.

Nino came out of the meeting room and put a cigarette into his mouth. That guy grated on my fucking nerves. "Why the long face? Get yourself a nice long blowjob from one of the girls. That always puts a smile on my face."

I stormed toward him, gripped him by the collar and flung him against the wall. His head smashed against it and he dropped his stupid cigarette. "What the fuck, you asshole! Let me go!" he screamed like a fucking pussy.

I punched him in the stomach twice and he dropped to his knees. God, I wanted to fucking kill someone. I didn't even care whom. I hit him over and over again.

"Hey! What's going on here?" Luca growled. He gripped my arms and pulled them behind my back. "Romero, what the hell are you doing? Calm the fuck down."

I relaxed in his hold and took a deep breath.

Matteo knelt beside Nino who was bleeding from a wound on his head and from his nose. I hadn't even realized I'd hit him in the face too. Aria joined us after a moment. Since she'd started working the books of the clubs, she was here quite often. She gave me a questioning look, then worry twisted her face.

"I'm going to kill you, you bastard," Nino snarled. I'd love to see him try.

Matteo helped him to his feet. "You won't do anything. Go inside and have someone stitch up your head."

Nino staggered off, but not without sending me a death glare. As if I gave a fuck. Let him try to kill me. I'd wipe the fucking floor with his weak ass.

"Did something happen with Lily?" Aria asked fearfully, walking up to me.

"You can let me go now," I told Luca. He did and stepped back, his narrowed eyes flitting between his wife and me.

"Why would Romero know if something was wrong with Lily?" he asked carefully.

Aria didn't say anything, only looked at me, her eyes reflecting the fear that had settled in the pit of my stomach. Maybe I should have been worried that Luca might find out, but I didn't give a shit about that either.

"Your father has arranged a marriage with Benito Brasci for her," I said in a low voice.

Aria gasped. "What? He never mentioned that he was looking for a husband for her!" She glanced at Luca. "Or did he mention anything to you?"

Luca's expression was stone. "No, he hasn't. But right now I'm more concerned about the fact that Romero knows about this before anyone else does and that he almost killed one of my men because of it."

I leaned against the wall. I might as well tell him the truth. "Lily and I have been seeing each other during the summer."

Matteo let out a low whistle. For some reason it annoyed the crap out of me. I glared at him and almost lost my shit again when I saw his grin. What the fuck was so funny?

Luca got into my face. "Didn't you tell me not too long ago that you weren't interested in her? That there wouldn't be a fucking problem when she was around? I remember that conversation pretty damn well, and now you're fucking telling me that you were *seeing* Liliana behind my fucking back all summer?"

Aria touched Luca's arm and positioned herself halfway between us. "Luca, please don't get mad at Romero. He and Lily didn't mean any harm. They fell in love. It just happened."

"And you knew all along?" Luca muttered. "You knew and didn't tell me? Didn't we have a discussion about loyalty and trust when you helped Gianna run away?"

Aria blanched. "They are my sisters."

"And I'm your fucking husband."

"Luca, she didn't mean—" I began.

Luca jabbed his fingers against my chest. "You stay the fuck out of this. You're lucky I don't put a bullet into your head right this second for going against my orders."

"Hey, calm down, Luca. Maybe it's not as bad as it sounds," Matteo said, trying to be the voice of reason, which was a joke in itself.

"Oh, I suspect it's exactly as bad as I think it is," Luca murmured. His eyes fixed on me. "Just tell me this, will we be in trouble on Liliana's wedding night?"

I knew what he was asking.

"Lily won't marry that guy. Isn't he over fifty? It's ridiculous," Aria butted in.

"Over fifty and a nasty piece of shit," Matteo added.

Luca ignored them. His eyes bore into mine. "*Will* there be a fucking problem on her wedding night?"

"I slept with Lily," I said calmly.

Matteo let out another of his annoying whistles.

Luca cursed. He looked like he wanted to smash my head in with a sledgehammer. "Why couldn't you leave your dick in your pants? Couldn't you at least have drawn the line at actually fucking her?"

"I don't regret it," I said. "Now less than ever."

Luca took a step back from me as if he didn't trust himself this close to me. "This is a fucking mess. Do you realize what happens if Benito Brasci finds out his wife isn't a virgin? Scuderi will figure out it happened in New York and we'll be screwed."

"I don't think there will be a problem. I stood beside Brasci at the urinal once. That guy's cock is tiny. He can't possibly expect there to be any blood on the sheets with that small sausage. Liliana probably won't even notice his cock in her," Matteo joked.

I saw red. I lunged at him, my fist colliding with his jaw. But Matteo wasn't Nino. After my first hit, he blocked my second and pulled his knife. Mine was out too. We faced off, knives pointed at each other.

"Enough!" Luca roared, stepping between us and shoving us away from each other. "I'm going to put you down like rabid dogs if you don't get a grip on yourselves right this second."

"He started it," Matteo said, never taking his eyes off me. We'd never fought against each other, and I wasn't sure I could beat him in a knife fight, but I wouldn't mind to find out.

"You provoked him," Aria said. "What you said was horrible."

Matteo rolled his eyes. "My God, I was trying to lighten the mood."

"You failed," Luca said coldly. "Now put your knives away. Both of you."

I sheathed my knife and Matteo did the same. I exhaled. "I shouldn't have punched you," I said eventually.

Matteo nodded. "I should keep my mouth shut now and then."

We shook hands and I leaned against the wall again. My legs felt heavy. I peered down at my phone. I needed to call Lily, to tell her I wouldn't give her up.

"But she's not pregnant, is she?" Luca asked after a moment.

I shook my head. We'd always been careful.

"Then maybe we'll get out of this unscathed. Brasci might not notice, and there are ways to fake blood stains on the sheets."

"She won't marry that man," I said.

Luca raised his eyebrows. "Oh, isn't she? Are you thinking about stopping Scuderi? Maybe kidnap Lily and marry her?"

I didn't say anything. I wanted to punch Luca too, but that would definitely have been the nail in my coffin.

"Luca, please. Can't you talk to my father?"

"Talk to him and tell him what?" Luca growled. "That my best soldier screwed his daughter and wants her for himself? That I broke my oath to protect Liliana and now she's lost her fucking honor? That will go over *fucking well*."

"No, but you could tell him that Gianna and I want our sister in New York with us and if he wouldn't maybe consider marrying her to someone from the Famiglia. You wouldn't have to tell him who right away. It would give us time to figure something out."

"I can't get involved. It's none of my business. And if your father has already promised Liliana to Brasci, he won't change his mind. It would make him look bad and offend Brasci."

"But we have to do something!" Aria exclaimed.

"I won't go into war over this!" Luca hissed.

I understood him. He had to consider only the Famiglia. But I didn't have to.

Liliana

I was woken by the ringing of a phone. Slowly my conversation with my father and then Romero replayed in my mind. My eyes darted toward my travel bag in the walk-in closet, thinking and hoping it was Romero again before I remembered that it was on mute. Disappointment crashed down on me once more. I sat up, disoriented and exhausted from crying. The clock on the nightstand told me it was only 10 p.m. I walked toward my desk where the landline phone was and picked it up. It was Aria. She must have heard already. Had Father called her to tell her the good news?

I picked up. "Hi, Aria," I rasped. There was no hiding that I'd been crying. Aria knew that voice.

"Oh, Lily. I just heard. I'm so sorry. I can't believe it."

"We're not going to let Father get away with it. We'll figure something out," Gianna shouted in the background. They were together, they had husbands they loved, and I'd be stuck here with an old man I would never be able to love. How could things have gone so horribly wrong?

"Did Father call you?" I asked, my voice regaining some of the emotionlessness I preferred.

"No, he didn't. We found out through Romero."

"He told you."

"Yes, he did," Aria said slowly. "He attacked one of the other soldiers who said something to him, so Luca had a word with him, and figured it out."

"Why did he attack that man?"

"What do you think? Because he doesn't want you to marry Brasci," Aria said softly. "He's been trying to call you for the last hour but you didn't pick up. He almost went crazy over here. He wants to talk to you."

"He's there with you?"

"Yes. I'll hand him the phone now, okay?"

Fear corded up my throat. "Okay."

"Lily," Romero murmured into the phone. His voice was anything but detached now. I released a harsh breath and felt tears run down my face.

"Lily?"

I swallowed hard. "I thought you didn't want anything to do with me now that I'm promised to someone else."

"No, never. I know I didn't react the way I should have. I…I was so angry when you told me your fucking father wants to sell you off to that old bastard. I wanted to fly over there and kill him. I didn't want to let out my anger on you so I tried to push it back."

"Okay," I whispered.

"Do you still want to run away?"

Yes, more than anything else. "It would mean war. You said it yourself."

"I don't care. I would risk war for you."

"Is Luca there to hear you say that?"

"No, he isn't."

"He would kill you if he could hear you."

"Your sisters would risk war over you as well."

I didn't doubt it. Gianna, in particular, but even Aria who was the more reasonable would do anything to protect me, and that was what scared me so much. Fabi would soon be in the midst of mob business. The war with the Russians had gotten worse in recent years, and I probably didn't even know half of it. If New York and Chicago started fighting each other again, this could cost the lives of many people I cared about.

"I have to meet him tomorrow."

"I don't want you alone with him, Lily."

"But what if he asks me and Father says 'yes'? You know I can't refuse him."

"You can refuse him. You are an honorable Italian girl, play that card. If I have to worry that you'll be alone with him I'll book the next flight and be there tomorrow. Fuck. I want to do just that and kill him."

I smiled slightly, wishing he could. I wanted nothing more than to have him with me, to feel his arms around me. "I'm not an honorable girl anymore. Maybe if I tell my father I can get out of this marriage."

"He might kill you. Your father has been very volatile since that thing with Gianna."

"Maybe that would be better than marrying that guy."

"Don't say something like that. We'll figure something out."

I nodded, even if he couldn't see it. I wanted to believe him. "I know," I said quietly.

"Aria is going to call your father tomorrow morning to get a feel for his resolve."

"I don't think she'll be able to talk him out of it. Does Luca know everything about us?"

"Yes, at least everything he needs to know to assess the situation."

My cheeks flamed, but Romero was right. We needed to tell Luca the truth if we wanted him to be able to do something. "Was he very angry?"

Romero was silent for a moment. "He wasn't happy. I punched Matteo, that didn't really help matters."

"You hit Matteo? Why? I thought Aria said you'd attacked another soldier."

"I did both," Romero admitted. "I just really lost it."

"Please don't get in trouble because of me. I don't want you to get hurt, promise me." There was another moment of silence, before he said, "I promise."

But I had a feeling it was a promise he wasn't sure he could keep. If he'd already attacked Matteo, the Famiglia's Consigliere, that wasn't a good sign.

"Call me after your meeting with Brasci tomorrow. I'll go crazy if I don't hear from you. And don't let him try anything. He's got absolutely no right. I'll fucking kill him if he puts a toe out of line, if he even looks at you the wrong way."

"Didn't you promise to stay out of trouble?" I joked half-heartedly.

"I'll try, but I'll be on edge tomorrow, that much is sure."

We talked about a few unimportant things before we said good-bye and hung up. I clutched the phone against my chest. Slowly I lay back on the bed. I was relieved that Romero still wanted me but I was also scared that he'd do something that would get him killed. Luca liked Romero a lot, but he was also Capo and needed to keep his men in line. If Romero did something that publicly hurt the Famiglia, Luca might not have a choice but to punish him severely. I wouldn't let that happen.

I barely slept more than two hours. I'd known that my first night in Chicago wouldn't be easy but I hadn't expected it to be this horrible.

There were dark shadows under my eyes and I didn't bother covering them up. Maybe Benito would decide not to marry me if I looked like a corpse. I put on jeans and a shirt before I made my way downstairs. Fabi and Father were already sitting at the table, eating breakfast. I wondered if they'd done the same when I was gone. "Since when are you awake this early on a Saturday?" I asked Fabi as I took the chair across from him.

"Only because he doesn't have school doesn't mean he should laze around," Father answered in Fabi's stead. Fabi stabbed at his fruit with his fork, looking like he wished it was Father.

"Is he getting inducted soon?"

Father set his coffee down. "You know very well that that's none of your business."

I curled my hands into fists under the table. My throat tightened at my next words. "When are Benito Brasci and his daughter going to arrive?"

"Around six. I already told you we'd have dinner with them." His eyes narrowed. "I hope you don't intend to wear that tonight. Take out one of your cocktail dresses and let your hair down. That's how Benito prefers it."

I blinked a few times, too stunned for words. Fabi dropped his fork with a clang.

"And you should eat. I don't want you to faint again. Tonight is important," Father continued unimpressed.

I reached for a Danish and stuffed a few pieces into my mouth but I wasn't sure I could keep them down.

"Stop picking at your food, Liliana, for God's sake."

"Leave her alone!" Fabi shouted.

Father and I both froze.

"What did you just say?" Father asked in a dangerous voice.

Fabi glared back but then he lowered his eyes. "Why can't you leave her alone? I don't like how you treat her."

"I won't have you criticizing me, Fabiano. You better learn to keep your mouth shut or you'll be in major trouble once you're part of the Outfit. Understood?"

Fabi nodded, but his lips were a thin white line.

I forced the rest of my Danish down even though it tasted like nothing. Father picked up his newspaper and disappeared behind it.

Fabi and I didn't try to talk. And really what was there left to say?

chapter *fourteen*

Liliana

I CHOSE THE DRESS I'D WORN AT LAST YEAR'S CHRISTMAS PARTY. IT was more modest than my other dresses with a high-cut collar and a hem that reached my knees. It was more fitted than I would have liked for the evening though. Like Father had said, I let my hair fall down to my shoulders, even though the idea of being attractive for Benito terrified me to no end. I decided to wear ballet flats since Father had said nothing about high heels.

"Liliana, what's taking you so long? Our guests will arrive any moment. Get down here!"

I took a deep breath and walked out of my room. Everything would be alright. If I got through today, Romero would figure out a way to get me out of this marriage. Everything would be alright. I repeated the words over and over again as I walked down the stairs, but my throat tightened anyway. Fabi was dressed in a proper dark blue suit and a tie, but his expression was that of a sulking teenager.

Father, too, wore a business suit but he almost always did. He scanned my outfit critically. "You should have chosen a different dress, but it'll have to do now. We don't have time for you to change again."

I paused on the stairs. Anger surged through me again, fiercer than before. The doorbell rang, preventing me from saying something that would have probably earned me a slap across the face. Father gave Fabi and me a warning look before he went to the door and opened it.

My fingers on the handrail tightened painfully.

"Benito, good to see you. Come in, come in. Dinner is ready for us. I've let our cook prepare a wonderful roast," Father said in an overly friendly manner that he only ever used with people of importance, definitely not with his family.

I had to stop myself from running up the stairs and hiding in my room. I wasn't a child anymore. I'd handle this situation with grace, and then I'd do my best to stop this marriage. There had to be a way.

But what if there wasn't?

I walked down the last few steps and stopped beside Fabi.

Father opened the door wider to let Brasci and his daughter in. I held my breath. And when my intended husband entered the entrance hall, revulsion overcame me.

He was tall and thin, with graying brown hair that was combed back the same way as Father's, but where Father's was full, Benito's had thinned and his scalp peeked through. His skin was tanned from too many hours on the tanning bed, and looked almost like leather. He looked old. His dark eyes settled on me and a grin twisted his lips.

Benito's gaze felt like slugs crawling over my skin, the way they traveled over every inch of my body, already marking me as his. I wanted to wipe it off like slime. My eyes slid over to the girl beside him, barely older than me and with a look of desperate resignation on her face. She wasn't better off than me. She'd marry my father. Our eyes met. Was there accusation in hers? Maybe she thought I was the reason for the deal between my father and her own. I couldn't even blame her. Everything about this felt so unfair.

Father motioned for me to come over to them. Even though every fiber of my being was against it, I crept toward them. Fabi was a couple of steps behind me. When I reached Father's side, he put a hand on my lower back and said with a proud smile, "This is my daughter Liliana."

Benito inclined his head but his eyes never ceased their staring. He wasn't doing anything obviously inappropriate but for some reason his gaze felt like it was invading my personal space. "It's a pleasure to meet you," he said, then he stepped up to me and kissed my cheeks. I froze but didn't push him away. Father would probably have killed me if I'd done that.

"And Fabiano," Benito said, facing my brother, who looked like he tasted something bitter.

Benito waved his daughter forward. "This is Maria."

Father greeted her with a kiss on the cheek too, and I almost threw up. Maria glanced my way again. She looked so…resigned. But when she faced my father again, she gave him a smile. It looked fake to me but Father seemed satisfied with her reaction. I could practically see his chest swelling with pride.

Father nodded toward the dining room. "Let's have dinner. It'll give us the chance to talk."

Father held out his hand for Maria to take and she did so without hesitation. I knew what was coming, but instead of taking my hand, Benito put his palm on my lower back. I almost flinched away from him but I forced myself to remain still. I couldn't muster up a smile though.

We walked into the dining room and when I finally sank down on my chair I almost cried from relief of being rid of Benito's touch. He sat beside me though. Father and Benito were soon immersed in conversation, which left Maria and me to sit in awkward silence. I could hardly ask her anything of importance with our fathers sitting right beside us. I escaped into my mind, but every so often my eyes drifted to the man beside me who smelled of cigar smoke.

All I could think about was that I wanted to be back in New York with Romero.

"Why don't you girls go sit on the sofa, so we can discuss business?" Father asked, tearing me out of my thoughts.

I rose from my chair and led Maria toward the living area. We sat down beside each other and another awkward silence began. I cleared my throat. "It's strange, isn't it, that we're sitting here with our fathers who are planning our marriages?"

Maria watched me cautiously. "They want what's best for us."

I almost snorted. She sounded like a parrot. Had her father put those words into her mouth? "Do you really believe that? You're going to marry a man who could be your father. How is that the best for you?"

Again her gaze darted toward our fathers. She was very well behaved, that much was sure. What worried me was how she'd gotten that careful. Was her father that strict? Violent maybe?

"I'm going to be the wife of the Consigliere. That's a good thing."

I gave up. She obviously wouldn't talk honestly with me, or she'd been brainwashed so well that she actually meant what she said. "Yes, that's certainly a great achievement." I didn't mean to snap at her but my nerves were too frayed to be considerate. But she didn't catch my sarcasm. She was too busy chancing looks toward our fathers.

Father stood from his chair. "Why don't you take a moment to talk to Benito, Liliana? And I'll talk to Maria."

That was the last thing I wanted. Benito strode toward me and panic started to set in. Where would we go? I didn't want to be alone with him. Romero's words flashed through my mind. I was a reputable Italian girl, at least as far as they knew. Father and Maria sat at the dining table together and Benito took a seat beside me on the sofa. At least I wouldn't be alone with him.

He even left a space between us but he was still too close for my taste. I could smell the cigars on his clothes and breath, and his knee was only about three inches from my own. I could feel my vision tunneling. God, I wasn't getting a panic attack because he was sitting beside me, right? What would happen when he really married me? Then he'd do more than only sit beside me. I stared straight ahead, not sure what to do or say. I could feel him watching me.

"You are a very attractive girl," he said. He took my hand and lifted it to his lips. I couldn't even react, I was too shocked. When his lips brushed my skin, I wanted to sink into myself. I'd had many men kiss my hand at parties but for some reason, this was worse.

"Thank you," I choked out.

"Has your father told you the date of our wedding yet?"

There was a date? I'd found out about this only yesterday. How could there be a date already? I shook my head mutely.

"Four weeks from now. October twentieth. Your father didn't want to wait and I agree. He'll marry Maria the week before our wedding."

I stared at him, then toward my father who was leering at Maria like she was a piece of candy he wanted to devour. I was going to be sick. Any moment now, my dinner would come up again.

"Liliana, are you listening?" There was a hint of impatience in Benito's tone and something less kind shone in his eyes.

I shivered. "I'm sorry. I was only surprised." Surprised? Surprised? God, surprise didn't even begin to describe my feelings. If there was already a date, how could Romero possibly convince my father to choose him as my husband instead? He couldn't. I wasn't naïve. Father would never agree to it. He wanted Maria, and for him to get her, he needed to sell me off to Benito in turn.

Benito smiled but somehow that made him look even scarier. Maybe it was my imagination. "It's short notice of course, but people won't want to miss our weddings so I'm confident that we'll pull off a grand feast."

I nodded. I clasped my wrist, feeling my pulse and surprised to find it at all. I felt so numb, I might as well have been dead.

Benito talked about guests we needed to invite and food we needed to serve but I couldn't focus. I needed to talk to Romero. Benito touched my knee and I jerked out of my thoughts.

"You're jumpy," he said accusingly. He didn't take his hand off my knee.

"I'm glad you're getting along so well," said Father as he came up to us from behind, Maria trailing a few steps after him like a good dog. I'd never been so glad to see my father. Benito removed his hand from my knee and I quickly got up. I needed to get away before I lost it.

Thankfully, Benito and his daughter left shortly after that.

Father looked incredibly satisfied when he closed the door after them. When he turned to me, his smile dropped. "Don't give me that look. Benito is an important man. He's one of our most influential Captains with a big number of loyal soldiers. To have him on our side is important."

"Can I fly back to New York so I can go wedding dress shopping with Aria?" I didn't mention Gianna, even though I felt bad about it, but I couldn't risk Father getting angry again, and I definitely didn't want to remind him of Gianna's flight.

Father laughed. "You can go shopping here. I won't let you leave Chicago again. There's too much to do, and I don't trust you not to do something stupid if I let you out of my sight. I know you and Gianna aren't too different. I won't let you ruin this. You will marry Benito."

Once I was back in my room, I dialed Romero's number with shaky fingers. He picked up after the first ring. "Are you okay?" he asked immediately.

"The wedding is in four weeks."

"Fuck," Romero growled. I could hear him hitting something and then the sound of something shattering. Romero had always seemed so in control. "Your father has lost his fucking mind. I won't allow it. I don't give a damn that he's Consigliere."

"Please calm down." Part of me relished in his fury because it showed how much he cared for me but the other part was terrified of the consequences he might face if he acted on his emotions.

"How can you be this calm, Lily? Do you realize what that means?"

"Of course," I whispered. "What about Aria and Luca? Can they do something?"

"I don't know. Aria's talking with your father right now."

"Good," I said half-heartedly, but I knew it was no use. Father had looked determined.

"Will you be allowed to return to New York?"

"No, Father doesn't want me to leave Chicago. He wants to keep an eye on me until the wedding."

"Damn it. I'm going to talk to Luca. We'll find a way."

"Okay," I whispered.

"I won't lose you, Lily. I won't allow anyone to hurt you. I swear it."

"I know."

"I'll call you once I've talked to Luca."

"Okay." I sounded like a broken record. I hung up and sat cross-legged on my bed. I wasn't sure how much time passed until Romero called again. I picked up at once. I was oddly calm.

"And?" I said.

Romero released a harsh breath, and I knew everything was over. A bone-deep sadness overcame me. "Your father will go through with this wedding. Aria tried to talk him out of it but he got really mad and accused her of trying to weaken the Outfit. He warned her not to get involved or he'd see that as an attack on the Outfit and advise Dante to cease relationships with us."

"So there's nothing to stop this wedding."

"I can fly over to Chicago tomorrow and get you. I doubt your father's men could stop me."

"And then?"

"Then we'd figure something out."

"Could we return to New York? Would Luca protect us?"

Romero was silent for a long time. "Luca won't risk war over this. We'd be on our own."

"Would that mean Luca would hunt us too?"

Romero sighed. "Lily, we could make it. I could keep us both safe."

I didn't doubt it, but what kind of life would that be? I'd never see Aria and Gianna again, never see Fabi again, never be able to return to New York or Chicago, and we'd always have to live in fear.

"Can I talk to Aria?"

"Of course. What's the matter, Lily? I thought you wanted us to run away together."

"I did. I do. But you love the Famiglia, and you and Luca are like brothers. You'd lose all that if you ran away."

"You are worth it."

I wasn't sure that was true. "Can I talk to Aria now?"

"Sure. We'll talk later again, okay?"

"Okay," I said.

Aria's voice sounded on the other end. "Oh, Lily, this is such a mess. How are you?"

"I feel like I'm falling and there's nothing to stop my fall," I admitted.

"We won't let you fall, Lily. I'll convince Luca to change his mind. You are my sister. I won't let you be miserable for the rest of your life. If Luca loves me, he'll help you."

"He says he doesn't want to risk war. Does he think Dante will really start a war if I don't marry Benito?"

"If you run off to be with Romero, then Father will take that as an attack from the Famiglia and will convince Dante to retaliate. There will be war. Both Luca and Dante have to show strength. Their men expect it from them. Despite years of cooperation, New York and Chicago still don't like each other."

"If Romero decides to act on his own and take me away from Chicago, what would Luca do?"

"I don't know. He's really determined to avoid war with Chicago. To do that he would have to call Romero a traitor who acted without the permission of his Capo and in order to keep the Outfit happy, he'd have to hunt Romero and..." She trailed off.

"And kill him," I finished for her. "Could he do it? Could he really kill Romero?"

"I don't think he would do it," Aria said. "But he might hand him over to the Outfit."

"That would also mean Romero's death."

"I'll talk to Luca. If he loves me, he won't do it. Gianna will talk to Matteo as well. We will help you, Lily, no matter what it takes. I don't care if it means war."

"Fabi will soon be part of the Outfit. He might have to fight against Romero, Luca, and Matteo. Many will die, and the Russians might use their chance and kill even more of us."

"I don't care if the Russians take over parts of the city. This is all about money. I want us all to be happy."

"But could we be happy? What if Dante and the Outfit try to assassinate Luca? It's happened before when New York and Chicago were at war."

Aria was silent. She loved Luca. "It won't come to that."

"You don't know that." We were silent.

"Do you want me to give Romero the phone again?" Aria asked after a while.

"Yes." I could hear her move and then Romero was back on the other end.

"So have you and Aria talked everything through?"

"We did. Aria is going to talk to Luca again."

"He won't change his mind. And he's right to remain firm. He needs to think of the Famiglia," he said.

"I don't care about the Famiglia, but I care about you."

"Don't worry about me. I'll gladly die if it means saving you from Benito Brasci."

That was exactly what I feared. "Don't say that. My life isn't worth more than yours. Marrying him isn't a death sentence."

"Do you want to marry him now?" Romero asked tersely. He was so on edge. I wished I could touch him and calm him down.

"Of course not, but I don't want you to risk your life."

"There's no other way, Lily. But don't worry. I've done it before."

I knew he had, but this was different. We talked a couple more minutes before I promised to call him the next day for detailed plans about my escape.

When I'd hung up, I stared at the white wall across from my bed for a very long time as if it could give me the answers I needed.

The people I loved the most would risk everything to keep me safe, to save me from a loveless marriage, but at what cost?

Romero had sounded as if he didn't care at all that he might lose everything. I knew he loved the Famiglia, was proud to be a part of it. He loved this life, but he'd have to leave it behind if he helped me escape this marriage. Luca wouldn't risk war. His people would mutiny. He'd have no choice but to give up Romero and hand him over to the Outfit. Aria might destroy her marriage if she tried to blackmail Luca into helping me. He'd forgiven her once for betraying him, but would he do it again?

Could I risk everyone's happiness for my own?

Someone hammered against my door and then Father stepped in without warning. I stood immediately. His expression was thunderous. "What did you tell your sister? Why are she and Luca trying to get involved in our family? Did you really think they could make me change my mind about your wedding?"

"They want to help because they're worried about me."

"I don't care!" he roared. "You are going to marry Benito, end of story."

"I can't," I said desperately.

"You can and you will."

"I'm not a virgin anymore. If you don't want people to find out you can't let me marry Benito!" I blurted.

Father stormed toward me, gripped my arms and pushed me against the wall. The back of my head rang from the impact.

"What did you say?" he snarled.

I gaped up into his menacing face.

He shook me hard until my vision turned blurry. Suddenly Fabi raced into the room. He tore at Father's arm, trying to free me, but Father lashed out. Fabi landed on the floor, his face flashing with pain.

"Go back to your room, boy. *Now*, or I swear I'll make you regret it."

My arms hurt from Father's grip, but I gave Fabi a small nod. I wanted him to leave. He didn't need to get into trouble because of me. Fabi struggled to his feet and after a moment of hesitation, he limped out of my room. When he was out of view, Father turned back around to me.

I quivered.

"Tell me the truth."

I couldn't talk. I regretted ever having mentioned anything. Father really looked as if he wanted to kill me.

He slapped me hard across the face but didn't release me. "Who was it? Who turned you into a little whore? Someone from the Famiglia, wasn't it?"

Tears burned in my eyes but I didn't cry. I couldn't tell Father the truth. "No," I said quickly. "I met him in a club, it's no one you know."

"I don't believe a fucking word you say, you disgusting slut. And it doesn't matter. You will marry Benito and you'll scream like a little scared virgin on your wedding night so he doesn't doubt your innocence. I swear, if you ruin this for me, I'll break every bone in your body." He let me go and stepped back, eyes hateful. "And if you try to get out of this wedding, and maybe even ask your sisters for help, believe me, war between the Outfit and the Famiglia is only the beginning. I'll personally hunt you and your sisters down, and then I'll figure out who fucked you and skin that asshole alive. Do you understand?"

I gave a jerky nod. Father looked like he wanted to spit on me. Instead he turned on his heel and walked out.

I slumped to the ground. Everything was really over now. I couldn't allow Father to hurt everyone I loved only because I wanted to get out of my wedding with Benito. The image of Father's hateful eyes seemed burned into my brain.

If I married Benito, the Outfit and Famiglia would keep working together. Fabi would be safer, everyone would be safer. I'd be able to see my sisters and Fabi at least occasionally and Romero could keep working for Luca. He'd get over me and find someone else.

And I? Maybe things wouldn't be so bad. I didn't even know Benito. Maybe he wasn't a horrible guy. And it wasn't like I hadn't gotten a taste of happiness. Being with Romero had been amazing. It was something I'd never regret and would always cherish. It was time to do the right thing. Maria had accepted her fate. So many girls had before me. I should too, if only to keep my loved ones safe.

Once I'd made up my mind, I felt relief, then deep sadness. I lay down but sleep wouldn't come. I remembered the longing in Mother's eyes before her death and couldn't help but wonder if the same look would be in my eyes one day.

Romero

I'd have never thought I'd ever consider going against the Famiglia, but I could *not* watch Lily getting married to that man. She was mine and I didn't care what I'd have to do to keep it that way. Luca had been eying me almost all day yesterday. He'd never looked at me with true suspicion in his eyes before. I had to admit it hurt to know he didn't trust me anymore, and worse that he had every right to be wary of me. I'd gone against his direct orders, broken my oath, and betrayed the people who'd been as close, maybe even closer than my own family. When I came to Luca and Aria's penthouse that morning, I saw it in Luca's gaze that he knew he'd lost me. Another Capo might have eliminated me right then to prevent worse. Aria gave me an encouraging smile but I didn't miss that Luca left without kissing her. That never happened and was a fucking bad sign.

As soon as I could I called Lily. The phone rang almost two dozen times before I gave up. Aria shot me a worried look. "Maybe she's still having breakfast with Fabi and Father."

I waited a couple of minutes before I tried again. If she didn't answer this time, I'd book a fucking flight to Chicago today and get her. To my relief, Lily picked up after the third ring.

"Where were you? I tried to call you before. Are you okay?"

"I'm fine." The detachment in her tone made me pause. It felt like there was a barrier between us that had nothing to do with our physical separation.

"I've been thinking about the best way to go about it and I think I should fly over to you as soon as possible. Luca is getting more and more suspicious, so we need to act quickly."

"I don't think we should do it."

"Do what?" I asked carefully.

"Run away."

"I know you don't want to leave your sisters, but maybe Luca will take us in later. Aria might change his mind."

"No," she said firmly. "I mean I don't want you to come here and take me away. I'm going to stay."

I couldn't believe what I'd heard. "What are you saying? That you want to marry Benito? I don't believe that for one second. He could be your father."

"But he's an important man. He has many soldiers who follow him."

"Since when do you care about something like that?"

"I've always cared about it. I enjoyed our time together, Romero, but we have to be reasonable. It could never work out between us. You are a soldier and I have a duty to fulfill as the daughter of a Consigliere. We all have to do things we don't want to do."

"What the fuck did your father do? This doesn't sound like you, Lily."

"Romero, please. Don't make this harder than it is. You have your responsibilities to Luca. I don't want you to break your oath."

"I don't care about my oath."

"But you should!" she said angrily. "I don't want you to come here. It's over between us, Romero. I'm going to do the right thing and marry Benito. And you should do the right thing and follow Luca's orders."

Suddenly I was angry. "So what was this between us? An adventure for the summer? Curiosity about how it would be to fuck a common soldier?"

Lily sucked in a deep breath and I regretted my harsh words, but I was too proud to take them back or apologize. "We can't talk again," she said quietly. Was she crying? "We should forget what happened."

"Don't worry, I will," I said, then I hung up. I flung my phone away. "Fuck!"

Aria rushed toward me, alarmed. "What's wrong? Is it Lily?"

"She wants to go through with marrying Brasci."

Aria froze. "She said that?"

I nodded. I headed for the kitchen. I needed a cup of coffee. Aria hurried after me. "What else did she say?"

"Not much. Only that Benito is a good catch and that we should both do our duty. Fuck that."

"She doesn't mean it, Romero. She loves you. She probably only wants to protect us."

I wasn't sure anymore. And even if Aria was right, maybe Lily had a point. I'd devoted my life to the Famiglia. I shouldn't abandon my oath only because of a woman. I was a Made Man and my priority should always be my job.

chapter *fifteen*

Liliana

Aria called me thirty minutes after my call with Romero, trying to talk me out of my plan to marry Benito. But she was already fighting with Luca because of me. I wouldn't allow her to really put her marriage on the line for my own selfish reasons. I would marry Benito and try to make the best of it.

The next few weeks passed in a blur of wedding dress shopping with Valentina, choosing flowers and the menu, calling important guests to invite them personally. I only saw Benito on two occasions and there wasn't time for more than a few exchanged words and a kiss on the cheek. That and the fact that I was too busy to be worried, I almost managed to forget that I was actually preparing my wedding to a man I could hardly stand. But reality set in on the day of Father's wedding to Maria. He hadn't talked to me since I'd told him I wasn't a virgin, except on the few occasions when we had to pretend for Benito or other people.

While Gianna and Matteo would arrive later to attend my wedding only, Aria and Luca were also invited to Father's feast of course, and that meant Romero was with them. I'd hoped he'd decided to stay in New York, not because I didn't want to see him but because I was scared of facing him, of being confronted with what I was losing.

Luckily, they were all coming directly to church because their plane arrived so late; that meant there was a chance of me being able to avoid an encounter with Romero.

I sat in the front row, Benito beside me. He didn't touch me in any way, thank God, because it would have been improper before our marriage, but every time Aria looked my way I felt like I was doing something indecent by sitting next to a man I didn't even want to marry.

I wasn't sure where Romero was sitting. Since he wasn't family, probably somewhere in the back of the church. After the service we headed toward the hotel where the wedding celebration would take place. I managed to get through dinner without seeing Romero, but later into the evening when I was dancing with Benito I spotted him at the other end of the room. He was watching me. Suddenly the other dancers around me faded into the background. Shame washed over me. I wanted to push Benito away. I wanted to cross the room and fling myself at Romero, wanted to tell him that I needed him. I had to look away. When the song ended, I excused myself and quickly left the dance floor. I hurried toward the exit. I needed to get away from this for a moment before I lost it.

Once the door closed after me and I found myself in the hallway of the hotel, I could breathe easier. I didn't stop though. I didn't want to come across guests returning from the bathroom or heading in that direction. I wanted to be alone.

I turned two corners before I stopped and leaned against the wall, my chest heaving. In a few days we'd be celebrating my wedding. Panic flooded me. I squeezed my eyes shut.

Soft footfalls made me turn and my gaze fell on Romero. He stood a few feet from me, watching me with an expression that felt like a stab to the heart. Despite everything I'd gone through and despite my best intention to mute my feelings for him, they seemed louder than ever. Romero looked irresistible in his dark suit.

"What are you doing here?" I whispered.

"I hated seeing you with him. It's wrong and you know it."

I did. Every fiber of my being fought Benito's closeness, but I couldn't tell Romero that.

He took a step closer to me, his dark eyes burning into my own.

"We shouldn't be here alone," I said feebly, but I wasn't trying to leave. I didn't want to.

He took another step closer, every move so lithe and graceful, and yet dangerous. I wanted to fly into his arms. I wanted to do more than that. I stayed where I was. Romero bridged the remaining distance between us and braced one arm above my head, his gaze hungry and possessive.

"Do you want me to leave?"

Say "yes." If Father found us here, he'd kill Romero on the spot, and as distracted as Romero was at the moment, my father might actually succeed.

I released a shuddering breath. Romero bent down and kissed me, and then I was lost. I raked my hands through his hair and down his back. He kissed me harder. His hands cupped my butt and then he lifted me up. I wrapped my legs around his waist, so the skirt of my cocktail dress rode up but I didn't care. Romero's erection was hot against my opening despite the fabric of my panties and of his pants between us. I ground myself against him desperately. I was already so aroused. I'd missed this. I'd missed *him*.

I knew someone might come down this corridor and find us, but I couldn't stop. Romero pressed me against the wall and held me with only one arm. His other hand cupped my breast through my dress, making me moan into his mouth and my nipples harden. Romero groaned. He thrust against me, rubbing his erection against my panty-clad heat.

"I need you," I gasped against his mouth. Romero stroked his palm down my side, then slipped it between my legs and pushed a finger under the fabric of my panties. He found me wet and aching. I shivered at the feel of his touch.

"Fuck. You are so wet, Lily." He pushed a finger into me and I arched off the wall with a gasp. Only he had that effect on me.

He removed his finger again and opened his zipper. My core tightened with anticipation and need. I heard the rip of a condom package and then his tip pressed against my opening and he started to slide into me. My walls yielded to his hot length until he'd sheathed himself completely in me. We peered into each other's eyes. This felt so right. Why did it have to feel so right?

"You feel so fucking good, Lily. And so fucking tight, good God."

Our lips found each other again. It had been too long. Romero thrust into me, driving me higher up against the wall. I moaned when he hit a spot deep inside of me. "We have to be quiet," he murmured in a low voice, then his mouth swallowed my next sound. I wrapped my arms even tighter around his neck. It felt like we were one, inseparable.

I dug my heels into his butt, driving him deeper into me as I stared into his brown eyes. Eyes so full of emotions they threatened to unravel me. I loved him. How could I live without him, without this?

Romero didn't take his eyes off mine as he plunged into me harder. Pleasure surged through me and I came apart. Romero kept pounding into me until his own orgasm hit him. We clung to each other, still united. I kissed the side of his neck. His familiar scent flooded my nose and I closed my eyes. I wanted to stay like this forever.

Distant sound of laughter dragged me back into the realm of reality. Romero pulled out of me. I loosened my hold on him and let my legs slide down until my feet hit the ground. I couldn't even look up at him as I straightened my skirt. Romero threw the condom into a nearby bin before he returned to me. Neither of us said anything. From the corner of my eye, I saw him reaching for my cheek. I backed away. Bracing myself, I lifted my gaze. "This was a mistake," I whispered.

Shock crossed Romero's face, then it became emotionless. "A mistake."

"I'm going to marry Benito soon. We can't do this again."

Romero gave a terse nod, then he turned on his heel and walked off. I had to resist the urge to run after him. I waited a couple more minutes before I headed toward the restroom. I needed to clean up before I returned to the party or people would realize something had happened. To my relief, there was no one in the restroom when I stepped in. I checked my reflection. My hair was all over the place and my makeup needed touching up. Sweat trickled down my back. But worse than that was the telltale prickling in my eyes. I couldn't cry now. That would ruin everything. I took a few deep breaths through my nose before I started to redo my makeup. When I left the restroom twenty minutes later, I looked like nothing had happened, but my insides were twisting. I'd thought I'd made peace with my marriage to Benito, had hoped my feelings for Romero had lessened, but now I realized that was far from being true.

The moment I stepped onto the dance floor, Luca was there and asked me for a dance. I knew he wanted more than that. He steered us toward a part of the dance floor where there weren't as many dancers before he started to talk quietly. "You are still going through with this marriage? You and Romero were gone for a while."

"Yes. I will marry Benito, don't worry," I said tiredly. I couldn't even blame Luca for being so insensitive. He'd invited me into his home and taken care of me, and I'd paid him back by making one of soldiers break his oath.

"You don't have to stay married to him forever," Luca said casually.

"Father would never agree to a divorce." Father would kill me before that ever happened.

"There are other ways out of a marriage than divorce. Sometimes people die."

"He's not that old."

Luca cocked an eyebrow. "Sometimes people die anyway."

Was he really suggesting that I should kill Benito? "Why can't he die before my wedding?"

"That would look suspicious. Wait a few months. The time will pass quickly, trust me."

I wanted to believe him but months sharing a bed with Benito, of having him inside of me, like Romero had just been, sounded like hell.

"Romero won't want me anymore then."

Luca remained silent. He knew it to be true. Why would Romero still want me after I'd spent months sleeping with another guy? I was already disgusted by the thought, how much worse would it be for him? "There are good men in the Outfit too. You'll find new happiness. You're doing the right thing by marrying Benito. You're preventing war and you're protecting Romero from himself. That's a brave thing to do."

I nodded, but I wanted to cry. Luca and I returned to our table. Aria tried to talk to me again but she gave up when I barely said anything. I needed to survive this day somehow and then my wedding, and the months thereafter, and then maybe I'd get another chance at happiness. I searched the room until my eyes settled on Romero. He was pointedly not looking at me. I loved him, loved him so much it hurt. I knew there would be no happiness for me without him.

Aria and Gianna helped me with my dress. It was white of course, with a veil that trailed after me. I wore my hair down because Benito had wanted me to.

"You look beautiful," Aria said from behind me.

I checked my reflection but I could only see the look of utter despair in my eyes. I'd need the veil to hide it from the world. Gianna and Aria didn't know about my last conversation with Father, and it was better that way. If they knew how much he'd scared me, they'd take me away despite the risk for their own lives.

"This is crap," Gianna muttered. She touched my shoulder. "Lily, get the hell away from here. Let us help you. What's the use of being married to the Capo and the Consigliere of the Famiglia if we can't force them to start a war for our little sister? You're going to be miserable."

"Luca said I could get rid of Benito in a few months when it won't look suspicious anymore."

Gianna snorted. "Oh sure, and what until then? My God, could Luca be any more of a jerk?"

Aria didn't say anything, which was a sign in itself. She usually always tried to defend Luca.

"Are you and Luca still fighting?" I asked.

She shrugged. "I wouldn't call it fighting. We're basically ignoring each other. He's angry at me for keeping you and Romero a secret from him, and I'm mad at him for making you marry Brasci."

"He isn't making me, Aria. Father is. Luca's acting like a Capo should. I'm not his responsibility but the Famiglia is."

"Good God, Romero has really rubbed off on you. Please tell me you don't really believe what you just said," Gianna said.

"I won't have you all risk everything for me."

Gianna touched her forehead in exasperation. "We want to risk it for you. But you have to let us."

Even if I said "yes" now, what could they do? Both Luca and Matteo wouldn't help us, not when they were surrounded by Outfit soldiers. This would be suicide. And Romero? He would do it without hesitation and get himself killed. Father's words flashed in my mind again. No, I had to go through with this. It was the only option.

Someone knocked and a moment later Maria poked her head in. She was one of my bridesmaids, even though we still weren't talking much. "You need to come out now."

She disappeared before I had time to say something.

"I can't believe Father is married to her," Gianna said. "I don't like her but I still feel sorry for her. Father is a bastard."

I barely listened. My vision was turning black. Fear filled my bloodstream, made me want to bolt. But I held my head high and lowered my veil over my face. "We should go now."

"Lily," Aria began but I didn't give her the time to finish whatever she wanted to say. I hurried toward the door and opened it, startled to find Father right in front of it. I hadn't expected him to wait for me here. I knew he'd lead me to the altar but fathers usually waited in the ante-room. Maybe he'd worried I'd run off in the last minute.

"There you are. Hurry," he said. He slanted a hard look at Gianna when she and Aria walked by but didn't say anything. He held out his arm for me. An image of him with Maria popped into my head and I wanted to throw up. I put my hand on his forearm and let him lead me toward the main part of the church, even though every fiber of my being wanted to get away from him. Inside the church music was already playing. Before we entered, Father leaned down to me. "You better convince Benito you're a virgin or he'll beat you to death, and if he doesn't, I will." He didn't wait for my reply. We went through the double doors and every pair of eyes turned toward us.

My feet felt like lead as I walked toward the altar. Benito waited for me at the end of it, a proud grin on his face, as if he could finally present his catch to everyone. Despite the risk, my eyes searched the crowd until they settled on Romero. He leaned against the wall on the right, an unreadable expression on his face. I tried to catch his gaze, even though it would have made this walk even harder but Romero didn't even glance my way. He was completely focused on Aria, playing the part as her bodyguard.

I returned my attention to the front, hoping no one had noticed the detour my gaze had taken.

In the spot where my mother should have been was Maria, hunched shoulders, pale skin, sad eyes; maybe she thought nobody was looking because this was the first time she hadn't put on a brave face. This was a taste of what I would look like soon enough. I peered up at Father. He on the other hand seemed rejuvenated, as if the marriage to a barely twenty-year-old had allowed him to drop a few of his own years. Didn't he miss Mother at all? She should have been at his side for my wedding. My eyes sought Romero again. I couldn't seem to stop. And Romero should have been the one waiting at the altar for me. We reached the end of the aisle and Father handed me over to Benito. Old-man fingers curled around my hand, sweaty and too firm. Father lifted my veil and for a moment I was worried my disgust and unhappiness were plain as day but from the look on Benito's face, he didn't seem to notice or care. I didn't listen to the priest as he started his sermon. It took everything I had to stop myself from peering over my shoulder, seeking out Romero one more time.

While the priest and the gathered guests waited for my "I do," I considered saying "no" for a brief moment. This was my last chance, the last exit before I was forever stuck on a highway to unhappiness, or at least until I figured out a way to get rid of my husband. Was I even capable of something like that? I couldn't even smash a fly when it bothered me.

Just say "no." I wondered how people would react if I refused to marry Benito?

Benito would be furious, and so would Father. But my sisters and Romero, they would understand, would probably fight everyone else to protect me. Benito cleared his throat beside me and I realized how long I'd been saying nothing. I quickly said what everyone expected even when the words tasted like acid. "Yes, I do."

"You may kiss the bride."

Benito grasped my waist. I stiffened but I didn't push him away. His rough lips pressed against mine. I could taste cigars. I pulled my head away and turned to our guests with a forced smile. Benito shot me a disapproving look but I ignored him. If he knew how much restraint it had taken not to shove him away, he wouldn't be mad at me for ending our kiss a bit too soon.

Taking my hand, he steered me down the aisle. My eyes darted toward Romero but he was gone. I searched the entire church, not finding him. He probably hated me now that he'd seen me kiss Benito and didn't want anything to do with me. Would I ever see him again?

Romero

I should have never come to Chicago. Watching Lily stride down the aisle toward Benito, I felt like someone was squashing my heart under a boot. I wanted nothing more than to stick my knife into Benito's eye very slowly, see the light leave him, hear his last labored breath. I wanted to skin him alive, wanted to give him more pain than any man had ever endured.

I forced my eyes away from Lily and focused on Aria as I was supposed to do. She looked back at me and gave me an understanding smile. I didn't react. I shut off my emotions like I'd learned to do in the first few years after my initiation when seeing people get killed or tortured still bothered me.

"You may kiss the bride."

My eyes shot toward the front of the church where Benito *fucking* Brasci had put his hands on Lily's waist and was practically dragging her toward his body. I saw red. I wanted to kill him. I pushed away from the wall, turned around and walked out of the church. I didn't run like I wanted. I moved slowly, as if nothing was wrong. Fuck, what a fucking lie. Everything was wrong. The woman that was supposed to be mine had just married some old bastard.

I headed straight toward our rental car. I'd wait there until it was time to drive to Brasci's mansion for the feast.

Luca hardly left my fucking side at the wedding party. He probably worried I was going to lose my shit on everyone. He wasn't wrong. Every time I glanced toward Lily and Benito, something snapped in my brain. I couldn't stop imagining pulling my gun and putting a bullet in Benito's head, and then one in Scuderi's head for good measure. If I was lucky, they wouldn't stop me quick enough.

Aria came toward me after dinner. I wasn't sure if I could take her pity, but I wasn't going to send her away. She was only trying to be kind. "You don't have to stay, you know? Luca is here for my protection. This must be hard for you. Why don't you go ahead and find yourself a hotel? I'm sure you don't want to spend the night under the same roof with Benito."

Tonight. So far I'd managed not to think about the wedding night too much. "No. I'm fine. I can handle this."

Aria hesitated as if she wanted to say more but then she headed back to Luca.

When the party drew to an end, I could feel myself getting more and more agitated. And then what I'd been dreading happened. Benito and Lily rose from their chairs to head to the master bedroom for their first night together. A crowd followed them, cheering and making suggestions of what should happen tonight. My pulse quickened and my fingers longed to reach beneath my vest.

I trailed after them, though I knew it was the last thing I should do. I had always prided myself on my control but I could feel it trickling through my fingers.

I knew I'd said to Lily that I would accept her marriage. She had told me she didn't want me. As a soldier of the New York Famiglia it was my duty to put them first. Wanting Lily could mean war. No, it would lead to fucking war. Dante Cavallaro was a calculating man but his soldiers had been waiting for a chance to tear into us again. I'd seen it in many of their eyes today. Things between us had gone steeply downhill in the past few years. The honeymoon phase of our union had waned off quickly after Luca and Aria's wedding, and now this was a marriage of convenience, a marriage both the Famiglia and the Outfit wanted out of. The smallest infraction would be enough to blow up everything.

Without realizing it I'd followed the other guests into the lobby. I spotted Lily's dark blond locks at the top of the steps, next to Benito's ugly head, and a crowd of other men around them. And then my feet started moving, my hand going for my gun, my temples pounding with anger. I had to push through the crowd, and ignored the mumbles of protest. I couldn't let that fucker Benito have her. Lily was mine, and would always be mine. If that meant a fucking war, then so be it. I'd spend until the end of my days hunting Russians and Outfit bastards if that meant I could keep her.

I sped up and then Luca was suddenly in front of me. I ground to a halt, breathing hard. I had half a mind to punch him, but I fought the urge. If I made a scene surrounded by so many people, I could screw up everything. Luca grabbed me by the shoulder and steered me into an empty corridor. He pushed me against the wall, making my ears ring, then he released me.

"Goddammit!" He snarled and gripped my shoulder again. "She's not yours. She's a married woman now."

"She never wanted any of this," I said harshly and shook Luca's hand off. "It should have been me next to her at the altar."

"But you weren't. It's too late, Romero. This is Chicago. We won't start a fucking war because you can't keep it in your pants."

I got straight into his face. "This is much more than that and you know it."

"I don't care, Romero. You watched Liliana walk down that aisle and now you have to accept the consequences. She did her duty and so should you. Go to your room and get some sleep. Don't do anything stupid."

Luca was Capo. It was his job to look out for the best of the Famiglia, but right then I wanted to kill him. I'd never wanted to kill my Capo. "Yes, boss."

Luca grabbed my arm. "I mean it. This is a direct order. I won't have war over this. I've warned you about how this would end a long time ago, but you didn't listen."

"I won't do anything," I gritted out. Even I wasn't sure if it was the truth or if I was lying. I hadn't made up my mind yet.

chapter *sixteen*

Liliana

When people started to call for Benito and me to retire to his room, I felt the blood leave my face. Benito didn't waste any time though. He took my hand and pulled me to my feet, and before I knew what was going on we were heading toward our room.

His palm stuck to the thin material of my wedding dress. It was sweaty and heavy and too warm. Slowly it traveled lower until it rested on my butt. I suppressed a shudder. I wanted to push his hand away, push him away but he was my husband and soon enough he'd touch me there without the protection of fabric, he would touch me everywhere, would see every inch of skin that was supposed to be Romero's only.

Sickness washed over me, and I almost threw up. Sheer power of will kept my wedding dinner in my stomach. I glimpsed over my shoulder, even though I'd promised myself I wouldn't do it. My eyes searched the crowd for Romero but he wasn't there. Part of me was glad that he didn't have to witness Benito pawing me, but the other, the bigger part, was disappointed. That silly part had hoped that he'd somehow stop this. Of course that would have only gotten him killed. They would have shot him on the spot and then war would have broken out. Many people would have died, maybe even Fabi, Aria, and Gianna. It was a good thing that he'd kept his oath, that he hadn't interfered and let me do what was expected of me.

I turned back around and realized that we'd already arrived in front of our room for the night, a guest bedroom because the Brascis believed it was bad luck if a married couple spent their first night in the master bedroom. Benito opened the door and half shoved me into the bedroom. I froze in the middle of the room, listening to the sound of the door closing and Benito's steps. "You're a real beauty," he said, his voice already thick with desire. "I wanted to be alone with you all evening. If it hadn't looked rude, I'd have taken you to our room hours ago."

Bile clogged my throat. I didn't dare move from fear of vomiting onto my shoes. He gripped my arms and turned me around to him, then before I could even gather my bearings his mouth pressed against mine. I gasped, and he used the chance to thrust his tongue past my lips. He tasted of the cigars he'd smoked with the other men, and it made me feel even sicker. His tongue was everywhere. He didn't give me the chance to do anything. God, this was horrible. My hands grasped his shoulders, fingers digging into his suit, and I shoved as hard as I could, but his arms wrapped around my waist, pulling me even tighter, giving me no chance to escape. His breathing was quick and excited. He was so eager.

I didn't want this. I squeezed my eyes shut, fighting back tears and desperately trying to imagine it was Romero kissing me, but everything about this felt wrong. The clumsy hands on my waist, the taste of him, the way he moved his tongue like a dying slug.

Ripping away from him, I drew in a few desperate breaths. His taste lingered on my tongue. I wanted to rinse my mouth to get rid of it.

Benito stepped in front of me again and leaned close. "Don't worry, sweetheart. I'm going to take good care of you. I'm going to make you a woman. You'll never forget this night."

I knew I'd never forget it. I'd probably have nightmares about it for the rest of my life. Mother's last words, the look in her eyes filled my mind. How could I have let it come this far?

"No, I can't." I took a step back. I needed to get away, out of this room, needed to find Romero and tell him that I couldn't survive this marriage, that I wanted only him, that he'd always been the one I wanted and would keep wanting him till the day I died. I was being selfish, I knew. But I didn't care about causing a war anymore if the alternative meant having to spend my life being touched by Benito. Maybe Luca could handle the situation. He was a good Capo. He could prevent war. Right?

Benito's expression tightened, that sugary sweet smile being replaced by something more leery and hungry.

Fear settled like a weight in my stomach. He grabbed my arms too tightly, making me wince. "You are my wife and you will do what's expected of you."

"No, please. I'm not ready. I need more time." Time to figure out a way out of this without getting everyone killed. There had to be a way where nobody got hurt.

Benito chuckled. "Oh, don't try this bullshit with me, sweetie. I've been jerking off to the image of your perfect perky ass for weeks now. Tonight I want to bury my cock in it. Nothing in this world will stop me, not even your big puppy dog eyes."

I opened my mouth for another attempt at begging but Benito pushed me backward. I cried out in surprise.

My heel caught in the hem of my wedding dress and then I was falling. I braced myself for the impact, instead I landed on something soft and bouncy: the bed. How could I have been this close to it?

I tried to scramble off immediately but didn't get the chance. Benito leaned over me, his knees between my legs, pinning my dress beneath him. I was stuck. I struggled, but my legs were tied down by the fabric. And I panicked. Panicked like I'd never had before, not even when I saw the torture scene in the basement.

Benito lowered his face down to mine and then he kissed me again. I turned my head to the side so he slobbered all over my cheek. His fingers clutched my chin, forcing me to face him. His cigar breath washed over me and his chapped lips were too close. His eyes narrowed to slits. "Listen, sweetheart. We can do this the easy or the hard way. For your sake, I hope you work with me. I don't give a shit either way. I like it rough."

He meant it. He'd force himself on me if I kept up the struggling, I could see it in his eyes. I couldn't expect any kindness from my husband tonight. Tears and pleading wouldn't change his mind.

I willed myself to relax beneath him. He smiled in a condescending way and shifted his body, finally letting my dress free. He pressed up against me, his mouth wet on my throat. He licked his way down to my collarbone. I tried to imagine it was Romero and when that didn't work, I tried to stop thinking about him altogether. Tried to be empty and numb, tried to cast my mind to another place and time, away from my husband who would have his way with me, no matter what I wanted. Benito shoved my skirt up and slipped his hand up my calf. He grunted appreciatively and pressed his body even closer against mine. I could feel how much this excited him. Whenever I'd felt Romero's erection, I'd been excited, but this? Oh God. I couldn't do this. But he was my husband and I was his wife. I'd chosen this way to protect everyone who wanted to help me. This was my duty, not only to him but to my family, to the Outfit. It was the fate of many women. They had survived and so could I.

I hated the sounds my husband made, the smell that wasn't Romero's, the way his clumsy fingers tugged at my dress. He was my husband. His hand traveled up to my knee.

My husband.

Then up to my thigh.

My husband. My husband. My husband.

His hand reached the edge of my panties and I couldn't take it anymore. I lay my palms against his chest and pushed him off me. I wasn't sure where I found the strength. Benito had at least seventy pounds on me, but he lost his balance and fell to his side. I leaped off the bed but my dress was slowing me down. I staggered toward the door, arms extended. My fingers were mere inches from the doorknob when Benito caught up with me. His fingers bruised my forearm with their grip, and he flung me back toward the center of the room. I couldn't gain my footing quick enough and fell forward, hip bones colliding with the desk in the corner. I screamed out from pain. Tears burned in my eyes.

Benito pressed up behind me as I was bent forward and his erection dug into my butt. "Tonight, doll, you are mine."

And there it was, right in front of me. I barely noticed Benito's hands squeezing my breasts through the fabric. My eyes were fixed on the gleaming silver letter opener. Benito squeezed again, harder, probably angry because of my lack of reaction. I gripped the letter opener. It felt good in my hand, cold and hard. My husband tore at the edge of my corset. I tightened my grip on the opener and jabbed my arm backward as hard as I could. Benito stumbled away with a gurgling gasp, letting me free. I whirled around. The letter opener stuck out of his right side of his stomach. Blood soaked the white fabric of his shirt. I must have hit him really hard, maybe even injured him seriously. I'd never done something like that.

My lips parted in shock. I'd really plunged a knife into my husband's stomach. His wide eyes stared. "You bitch, I—" He gasped and dropped to his knees. His ugly beetle eyes grew even wider as he rasped in pain.

I stumbled away from him. What if he called for help? What if someone saw what I'd done? I'd stabbed *my own* husband. They would kill me for that, and even if they didn't, Benito surely would beat me to death if he survived the wound.

There was only one thing I could do, only one person who could help me and I wasn't even sure if he still would after everything I'd put him through. After what I'd said and what he had to witness today. Maybe he wasn't even in Chicago anymore. Maybe he'd already taken the next flight back to New York to get as far away from me as possible.

I rushed toward my bag, ripped it open and fumbled for my phone. With shaking fingers I keyed in the number I knew by heart. Benito seemed still dazed but he had gotten up on his elbows. He was gasping for breath, obviously trying to find his voice to scream for help. What if he came toward me? Could I finish what I'd started?

A new wave of panic hit me hard.

After the first ring, Romero's familiar voice rang out. "Lily?"

I'd never felt more relieved in my life. He hadn't ignored my call. Maybe, just maybe, he didn't hate me.

"Please help me," I whispered, voice hoarse with tears. They were streaming down my face. It wasn't because I'd just stabbed someone with a letter opener, I felt no regret over that.

"I'm coming. Where are you?"

"Bedroom."

"Don't hang up," he ordered. I wouldn't have. I could hear him moving, could hear his calm breathing, and it calmed me in turn. Romero would be here soon and then everything would be all right.

After everything that had happened, he still rushed to help me.

Less than two minutes later, there was a knock. He must have been close or it would have taken him much longer to reach the bedroom. For a couple of seconds, I wasn't sure if I could even move. My legs felt numb.

"Lily, you have to open the door. It's locked. If I break it down, people will be up here in no time."

That was all it took. I crossed the room in a few steps and opened the door. My heart was beating in my throat, and only when I saw Romero's worried face did I dare to lower the phone from my ear and hang up. I felt safe now, even though I knew I was far from it. We both were in grave danger if anyone found us like that. By calling Romero, I'd put him in harm's way. How could I do that to someone I loved? Hadn't I gone through with this marriage exactly to protect Romero?

Romero's eyes wandered over my half-open corset, my disheveled hair and ripped skirt, and his face flashed with fury. He stepped into the room, closed the door and cupped my face. "Are you okay? Did he hurt you?"

I shook my head, which I realized a moment later, could be taken as an answer to either question. "I stabbed him. I couldn't bear his touch. I didn't want his hands on me. I..." Romero pulled me against him, my cheek pressed against his strong chest. I listened to the sound of his pounding heart. Outside he looked calm but his heart betrayed him. "I didn't sleep with him. I couldn't."

"He's still alive," he murmured after a moment before he pulled back. Deprived of his warmth, I wrapped my arms around myself. Romero advanced on my husband whose eyes were darting between Romero and me like he was watching a tennis match. His breathing rattled in his chest, but he'd dragged himself closer to the desk and was reaching for his phone. Romero stood over him, then calmly pushed his arm back down to the ground, his expression predator-like.

Benito fell onto his side with a pained gasp. He reminded me of a beetle who was trapped on his back, its legs helplessly pedaling above its body. I didn't feel any pity though.

"You," Benito snarled, then started coughing. Blood speckled his lips. "Did your Capo set this up? Chicago will make him pay tenfold. Dante won't let you make a fool out of me and everyone else."

"You aren't important enough for Luca to give a shit about you," Romero said coldly. He had the same expression I'd seen when he'd watched the Russians getting tortured in the basement.

I shivered.

Realization settled on Benito's face as his eyes swiveled from Romero to me. "You and her." His mouth pulled into a nasty grimace, spittle clinging to his lips. "You nasty whore let him fuck you. You—"

He never got the chance to finish his sentence. Romero stepped up to Benito, jerked him up by his collar and then in one practiced motion he pulled his knife and plunged it in an upward angle between my husband's ribs, silencing his rattling breath. Without even blinking, Romero let go of Benito, who fell to his side, lifeless.

chapter *seventeen*

Liliana

ROMERO HAD JUST KILLED A MEMBER OF THE OUTFIT FOR ME. OUR eyes met, and cold fear spread in my chest like fog. Romero wiped his knife clean on my husband's pant leg before he sheathed it in its holster.

My throat constricted as I walked toward him. "This means war."

"We can come up with a story. I'll pretend I've lost my mind. I've been lusting for you forever but you were never interested in me and today I snapped, and barged into your bedroom and attacked your husband, who tried to defend himself with the letter opener, which I then used to stab him. We can make it look like I tried to rape you so nobody suspects you were involved. Nobody would doubt it the way you look." He stroked my cheek. "The bastard died too quickly for how he treated you."

I couldn't believe he was suggesting something like that. It was bad enough that I'd dragged him into this at all. I wouldn't make him look like a disgusting rapist to save my own hide. "I won't pretend you tried to rape me. You are the only man I want to be with."

Romero wrapped me in a tight embrace. His smell, his warmth, the way my body perfectly fit against his; this felt right. My eyes found Benito on the ground. I'd tried to be his wife and failed, but I couldn't be sad about it. I'd never wanted this, and he'd known it from the start. He would have forced himself on me, maybe that didn't deserve a death sentence but he lived in a world where death was almost always the punishment. His eyes were still open and it seemed they were staring straight through me. The longer I stared at him, the worse their look seemed to get. I shivered violently.

Romero pushed me gently away. "Don't look at him." He walked toward the body and turned Benito so he was facing the ground, and no longer me. And just like that I felt better. He was still dead, but at least he wasn't looking at me with that reproachful expression anymore.

I stumbled toward the bed and sank down. My legs were too shaky to hold me. Romero stood for a moment before he joined me. He brushed his thumb over my cheek, catching a few stray tears. I hadn't even noticed I'd started crying again. "He's dead now. He can't hurt you ever again," he said roughly. "Nobody will ever hurt you again. I won't allow it."

"If you confess to murdering Benito, you'll be killed and then you won't be around to protect me from anything." Maybe it was a low move to play the guilt card but I couldn't let Romero take the blame.

Romero's gaze settled on Benito and the puddle of blood slowly spreading around him, turning the beige carpet into a sea of red. "We can't cover this up. Even if we got him out of the house without anyone noticing, we could never get the blood out of the carpet. People would suspect something. Someone will have to take the blame for this."

I buried my face in my hands, desperation clawing through my insides. "I should have let him have me. I should have endured it like so many other women before me. But I had to act like a selfish bitch."

"No," Romero said sharply, wedging a finger below my chin and tilting my face up. "I'm glad you stabbed him. I'm glad he's dead. I'm glad he didn't get what he doesn't deserve. You are way too good and beautiful for this bastard."

I pulled him down to me and kissed Romero. I would have deepened the kiss, despite everything, would have lost myself in Romero as I always did, but he was more reasonable than I and pulled away. "I have to call Luca. As his soldier, I need to confess to him at least, and then it's up to him to decide what happens next."

"And what if he decides to kill you so he can keep the peace with Chicago?" I asked quietly. "You know how angry he was when he found out about us. Even Aria couldn't convince him to risk war for me."

For a long time Romero merely looked at me, then he picked up his phone and lifted it to his ear. "Then I'll accept his judgment."

"No," I said suddenly. I shoved his phone away. "Let me call Aria. She can reason with Luca. He listens to her."

Romero smiled sadly. "This is something even Aria can't do anything about. Luca is Capo and if he needs to make decisions that protect the Famiglia, he won't let Aria mess with his mind. You said it yourself. He refused to listen to Aria."

"Please."

"I need to do this. I can't hide behind you or Aria like a coward." He raised the phone again and this time I didn't stop him. He was right. Luca would probably be pissed if I tried to use Aria to manipulate him.

I held my breath as I waited for Luca to pick up.

"Luca, I need you to come to Benito's room." I heard Luca's raised voice on the other end but couldn't make out what he said. It didn't sound nice. "Yes, I'm there. You should hurry."

"Damn it!" Luca growled loud enough for me to hear, then he hung up. Romero lowered his phone slowly and put it back into his pocket.

I took his hand, needing to convince myself that he was really there.

Romero glared at Benito's body but he didn't try to tell me things would be okay. I was glad he didn't try to lie to me. I rested my cheek against Romero's shoulder.

There was a soft knock. I straightened, but my grip on Romero's hand tightened. I didn't want to let him go. Once Luca saw what had happened, I might never get the chance to touch Romero's hand again, at least not while it was still warm. I shuddered when I remembered Mother's lifeless corpse. I wouldn't allow that to happen to Romero.

Romero kissed my forehead, then he untangled himself from my grip and got up. I rose too, my eyes darting to Benito. Anger for him welled up in me. If he'd never stepped into my life, then I could have been happy. But Father would probably have found another horrible husband for me. Fear corded up my throat as I watched Romero push down the handle and open the door. What if Luca really decided to kill Romero as punishment?

Romero didn't open the door all the way, so Aria had to slip in. She sucked in a harsh breath at the sight of my dead husband, then she rushed over to me and clutched my shoulders, but my eyes were frozen on Luca who had walked in after her. His gaze settled on Benito, on the letter opener still stuck in his side and on the hole in the shirt where Romero's knife had gone in. Romero closed the door noiselessly but didn't move away. I wished he'd bring some distance between himself and Luca. It was a ridiculous notion. It wouldn't protect him.

"My God, Lily," Aria said shrilly. I couldn't remember the last time she'd sounded so scared. I met her gaze.

"What happened? Are you okay?" she asked. She ran her hands over my arms, her eyes lingering on my ripped skirt.

I didn't reply. Luca had started moving toward the body and knelt beside it, scanning the scene without saying a single word. His face was stone. This was it. Suddenly I was sure that Romero and I wouldn't find Luca's mercy today. Maybe Aria would manage to convince Luca to protect me, but Romero wouldn't be so lucky. I knew I wouldn't be able to watch him die.

Luca raised his head very slowly and fixed me with a look that turned my blood to ice. "What happened here?"

I glanced at Romero. Did he want me to tell the truth? Or should I lie? There had to be a story that wouldn't make Luca angry enough to want to kill us.

Luca straightened. "I want the fucking truth!"

"Luca," Aria scolded. "Lily is obviously in shock. Give her a moment."

"We don't have a fucking moment. We have a dead Outfit member in a room with us. Things will get ugly very soon."

Aria squeezed my shoulder lightly. "Lily, are you okay?"

"I'm fine," I said. "He didn't have time to hurt me."

She pursed her lips but didn't argue.

"Enough," Luca said harshly. He turned to Romero. "I want answers. Remember your oath."

Romero looked like a man resigned to his fate. It scared me senseless. "I always do."

Luca jabbed a finger toward the dead body. "That doesn't look like it. Or are you saying that Liliana did this alone?"

"Liliana is innocent," Romero said firmly. He never called me Liliana. What was he trying to do? "Benito was still alive when I arrived. She'd stabbed him with the letter opener because he attacked her. It was self-defense on her part."

"Self-defense?" Luca muttered. His gray eyes fixed on me. "What did he do?"

"He tried to force himself on her," Romero said for me.

"I didn't ask you!" Luca growled. Aria let go of me and walked toward him and put a hand on his arm. He ignored her completely as he said, "And if he tried to consummate the marriage, nobody in this fucking house will see it as self-defense. Benito had a fucking right to her body. He was her husband for God's sake!"

Romero took a step forward but stopped himself.

"You can't be serious," Aria said, eyes imploring.

"You know the rules, Aria. I'm stating the facts," Luca said in a much calmer voice.

Aria always had that effect on him. "I don't care. A husband doesn't have the right to rape his wife. Everyone in this house should agree on that!"

I shivered. The events of the evening were catching up with me. I just wanted to lie down in Romero's arms and forget everything. Romero came over to me and wrapped an arm around my shoulders.

Luca narrowed his eyes. "I told you this would end in disaster. So let me guess, Liliana stabbed her husband, called you and you finished the fucking job to have her for yourself."

"Yes," Romero said. "And to protect her. If he'd survived he would have blamed Liliana and she would have been punished harshly by the Outfit."

Luca let out a dark chuckle. "And now she won't? They will put her on trial and they will not only punish her harshly. They will also accuse us of having set this up and then there will be a fucking bloodbath. Dante is a cold fish but he needs to show strength. He will proclaim war in no time. All because you can't control your dick and your heart."

"As if you could do it. You'd take down anyone who'd try to take Aria away from you," Romero said.

"But Aria is my wife. That's a huge difference."

"If it was up to me, Lily would have been my wife for months."

I stared at him in surprise. He'd never mentioned marrying me. My heart swelled with happiness, only to turn to stone at the sight of Luca's expression. "Someone is going to pay for this," he said darkly. He paused. "As Capo of the New York Famiglia I need to put the blame on Liliana and hope Dante buys it and doesn't start a war."

That would mean my certain death. Maybe Dante wouldn't give the orders himself but he would have to submit me to my father's judgment and I didn't expect any mercy from him. He hated Gianna for what she'd done and that wasn't nearly as horrendous as my crime.

"You can't do that," Aria whispered. Her knuckles were turning white from her tight grip on his forearm.

Romero let go of me and walked a few steps toward the center of the room where he got down on his knees and held out his arms wide. "I'm going to take the full blame for this. Tell them I lost my mind and ran after Liliana because I've wanted her for months. I killed Benito when he tried to defend Lily and himself, but before I could rape her, you noticed I was missing and went in search of me. Then there won't be war between the Outfit and New York, and Lily will get the chance at a new life."

"If that's the story we want them to believe, there's something missing," Luca said.

Romero nodded. He met Luca's gaze straight on. "I will put my life down for this. Shoot me."

I staggered forward. "No!" Aria, too, screamed the same word.

Luca and Romero ignored us, locked in a silent staring contest. I stepped between them. I didn't care if that went against some secret mafia rule. I walked toward Luca. From the corner of my eye I saw Romero getting up. He looked like he was worried about me getting close to Luca but I wasn't worried for me. If Luca killed Romero because of me, that would be the end of me. I'd never be able to live with myself.

"Please," I whispered, peering up into Luca's emotionless face. "Please don't kill him. I'll do anything, just please don't. I can't live without him." Tears started streaming down my face.

Romero put his hands on my shoulders and pulled me back against him. "Lily, don't. I'm a soldier of the Famiglia. I broke my oath to always put the Famiglia first, and I have to accept the due punishment."

"I don't care about any oaths. I don't want to lose you," I said as I turned in his grip.

Aria rested her palms flat against Luca's chest. "Please, Luca, don't punish Romero for protecting someone he loves. He and Lily belong together. I beg you." She said the last in the barest whisper. I wanted to hug her, but I was scared to move. She and Luca were gazing at each other and I didn't want to break their silent understanding, especially if it saved Romero's life. I glanced up at Romero. He looked so calm, not like someone whose life could end any moment.

Luca finally tore his eyes away from my sister and gently removed her hands from his chest. "I can't base my decisions on feelings. I'm Capo and have to make decisions that benefit my Famiglia."

Romero nodded, then he walked past me and stood across from Luca. I began shaking, completely terrified. Aria's wide eyes settled on me.

"You are my best soldier. The Famiglia needs you, and I don't trust anyone with Aria as I do with you," Luca said. He put a hand on Romero's shoulder. "War has been inevitable for a while. I won't end your life to postpone it for a few fucking months. We'll stand together."

I almost sagged with relief. Aria rushed over to me and hugged me tightly. My moment of euphoria was short-lived however.

"Of course, we might not get out of this house with our lives," Luca added. "We're surrounded by the enemy now."

"Most guests are either drunk or asleep. We could try to sneak out. They won't notice Benito's death until morning; by then we'll be back in New York," Romero said. A flicker of relief showed on his face. I wanted to be in his arms but he and Luca needed to deal with our dilemma, a dilemma I'd started. What if we really didn't get out alive? The Outfit outnumbered us greatly. This was their territory and we were thousands of miles away from reinforcement.

"I'll have to call Matteo and Gianna. They need to come here so we can figure out the best way to get out of this house," Luca said, already raising his phone to his ear.

Romero strode over to me and smoothed the crease between my brows. I pressed up against him. Aria headed for Luca, giving us space.

"I was so scared," I whispered.

Romero buried his face in my hair. "I know."

"Weren't you? It was your life on the line."

"My life has been on the line since I've become a Made Man. I've grown used to it. The one thing that fucking scared me today was when I had to watch you walk toward your wedding night with that asshole Benito. I wanted to kill him then. I've wanted to kill him every day since I found out you were forced to marry him. I'm glad that I finally did."

"Me too," I said, then rose to my tiptoes and kissed his lips.

"Damn it. Matteo isn't picking up his fucking phone."

"Do you think something happened to them?" Aria asked.

Romero let out a small laugh, and exchanged a look with Luca.

"The only thing happening is that he's probably fucking your sister's brains out right now and ignoring his fucking phone," Luca said.

I wrinkled my nose. Of course I knew my sisters had sex, I just didn't want to be reminded of it, or worse: imagine it. "Can't we go over to their room?"

Luca shook his head. "It's farther away from the back entrance." He dialed again. "Damn it!"

"We should carry Benito into the bathroom and cover the blood stain in the carpet with something. That way if someone walks in tomorrow morning, it might buy us a bit more time."

Luca shoved his phone into his pocket, then gripped Benito by the feet while Romero took the arms. I shuddered as I watched them carry the corpse into the adjoining bathroom. My husband was like a sack of flour in their hold.

"You should get out of your wedding dress and wear something more sensible," Aria suggested softly. She touched my arm lightly, drawing my eyes away from the dead body. After a moment, I nodded. Luca and Romero came back out of the bathroom and discussed how best to go about our flight.

I grabbed jeans and a pullover from my bag in the corner, before heading toward the bathroom to change in peace, but froze in the doorway. Benito was sprawled out in the bathtub. I didn't want to be alone with a dead man. Bile traveled up my throat.

"Hey," Romero said gently, coming up behind me. "Do you want me to come with you?"

I nodded merely and finally stepped into the bathroom. Romero entered after me. I quickly got out of my dress with his help. "Somehow I always imagined it would be different when I'd help you out of your wedding dress," he murmured.

I laughed breathlessly. I dropped the dress unceremoniously on the ground. For me it was only a symbol for the worst day of my life. I wasn't sad to be rid of it. Maybe one day I'd get the chance to have another wedding, one I wanted, with a husband I loved. I changed into my other clothes.

Romero picked the dress up, and for a crazy moment I thought he wanted to keep it for our own future wedding. "What are you doing?"

"I want to cover the blood stain in the bedroom with it. Nobody will get suspicious if your wedding dress lies on the floor after your wedding night." He headed out of the room and set the dress down on the ground.

Luca nodded. "Good. Now let's get going. I don't want to risk staying here a moment longer than absolutely necessary." He held out his hand for Aria, who took it. I suspected the tension between them would be over after tonight. The way they looked at each other gave me hope that Luca would forgive her for her secrecy. After pulling his gun, he opened the door and peered out into the corridor.

"Stay close to me," Romero told me, drawing his own gun and grasping my hand with his free one.

Luca gave a curt nod, then pushed the door open wider and stepped out, Aria a step behind him. Romero led me after them. Nobody said anything. The long corridor was empty but from below you could hear scattered laughter and music from the party. The smell of smoke travelled up. Immediately I was reminded of Benito's breath and the taste of his tongue in my mouth. I shoved the thought out of my mind.

I needed to focus. I really hoped none of the guests would decide to head our way. Luca or Romero would have to shoot them. What if it was someone I knew? I didn't even want to think about it. Aria glanced over her shoulder at me as Luca pulled her along. The same worry I felt was reflected on her face.

chapter *eighteen*

Liliana

Romero and Luca showed only determination and vigilance as they led us through the house. Eventually we arrived in front of Gianna and Matteo's door. Luca knocked lightly, but I could tell from the thunderous look in his eyes that he'd have loved to take the door down if it weren't for the risk of getting overheard. Again nobody reacted and I was starting to freak out, when after another louder knock the door finally opened. Matteo appeared in the gap, hair ruffled and only dressed in boxer shorts; they looked like he might have put them on the wrong way in his hurry and there was a bulge hidden beneath them. I drew my eyes away.

"Didn't you get the hint that I didn't want to be interrupted when I didn't answer your fucking call," Matteo muttered, then his eyes settled on Romero and me, and he grimaced. "I have a fucking bad feeling."

Luca shoved Matteo's shoulder. "For fuck's sake, Matteo, pick up when I call you. You need to get dressed. We have to leave now."

"What's wrong?" Gianna asked, coming up behind Matteo in a satin bathrobe. Her lips were red and swollen. There was really no doubt what they'd been doing before we arrived. Her gaze darted from Aria to me. "Shit, something bad happened, right? Did the asshole hurt you?" She slipped past Matteo despite his and Luca's protests and hugged me.

"He's dead," I whispered.

"Good," she said without hesitation. She patted Romero's shoulder. "You did it, didn't you?"

Romero smiled tightly. "Yeah, which brings us to the reason why we need to hurry."

"Romero is right. We need to get out of this house before someone realizes that the groom is dead," Luca said impatiently.

"I always thought that I'd be the one to start a war between the Outfit and the Famiglia. Kudos to you, Romero, for proving me wrong for once," Matteo said grinning.

"I thought that too," Romero said.

Luca sighed. "I hate to interrupt your chitchat but we need to get the fuck going."

Matteo nodded and motioned for Gianna to get into their room. The rest of us followed and waited while Matteo and Gianna got dressed. Every time I heard voices, I jumped, half expecting Father or Dante to rip open the door and shoot us all on the spot. Romero brushed a few strands that had fallen over my eyes away from my face. The look in his eyes made me realize that it was worth it. Love was worth risking it all. I just wished I hadn't dragged others into danger with me. Five minutes later, the six of us left the room and continued our journey through the house. The sounds of the party had dwindled further, which meant more people could be walking back to their rooms and potentially cross our paths, but so far we'd been lucky.

We took the second staircase in the back of the house down to the first floor and headed for the door that led to the underground garage. Most houses in this area had them because outside space was limited. There was the sound of steps from the corridor to the left of the door. Romero pulled me to a stop and pointed his gun ahead. Both Matteo and Luca did the same. My pulse pounded in my temples. They had silencers on their barrels but a shooting always made some noise, and I really didn't want to have more blood on my hands.

Someone turned the corner into our hallway and I clutched at Romero's arm to stop him from shooting. It was Fabiano. He jerked to a stop with his own gun pointed at us. I didn't even know he wore a gun, especially to my wedding. He was too young for this. His eyes scanned our small group, his brows drawing together in suspicion. He was still in his festive vest and trousers. What was going on here?

Aria put her hand on Luca's arm with the gun but he didn't lower it, neither did Matteo despite Gianna's urgent whispering.

"Don't hurt him," I pleaded. Romero didn't take his eyes off my brother but he lightly squeezed my hand in response.

"What's going on here?" Fabiano asked firmly, standing even taller than usual and trying to look like a man. With the gun and that serious expression he almost managed to look like more than a teenage boy.

"Put that gun down," Luca ordered.

Fabiano laughed but it sounded nervous. "No way. I want to know what's going on." His eyes moved from Aria to Gianna then to me, and finally settled on Romero's hand, which was clutching mine.

"Why are you even running around with a gun? Shouldn't you be in bed?" Aria asked and was about to take a step toward our brother but Luca pulled her back.

"I have guard duties," Fabiano said with a hint of pride.

"But you aren't inducted yet," I said, confused. I would have noticed if he'd started the process, right? Fabi had always told me everything. It had been us against the rest after Gianna and Aria had moved to New York.

"I started the induction process a few weeks ago. This is my first task," Fabi said. The hand with his gun was shaking slightly. If I noticed it, Romero, Luca, and Matteo definitely had. I wasn't sure it was a good thing because his nervousness made them realize he was still a kid, or a bad thing because it made him an easy target in their eyes.

"Father gave it to you because he thought it would be an easy first job, right? Nothing bad ever happens at weddings," I tried to joke.

Fabi didn't even crack a smile, neither did anyone else. I exchanged a look with Aria and Gianna. We had to escape, that much was clear, but we couldn't risk Fabi getting hurt.

"He gave me the job because he knew I was responsible and capable," Fabi said, sounding like Father's personal parrot. My chest tightened. What if Fabi really didn't let us go? The way he pointed his gun at us, he appeared absolutely determined. Had he changed so much?

"You don't really think you can kill all three of us, do you?" Matteo asked with a twisted grin.

Gianna shot him a glower. "Shut up, Matteo."

Fabi shifted on his feet but his face remained hard. When had he learned to wear a poker face like that? "I can try," Fabi said.

"Fabiano," Luca said calmly. "They are your sisters. Do you really want to risk them getting hurt?"

"Why is Lily here? Why isn't she with her husband? I want to know what's going on. Why are you trying to take her with you? She's part of the Outfit, not of New York."

"I can't stay here, Fabi. Do you remember how you told me I shouldn't marry Benito? That it wasn't right?"

"That's been a long time ago, and you said yes to him today. Where is he anyway?"

I glanced at Romero. Something in my expression must have given it away.

"You killed him, didn't you?" Fabi accused, his narrowed eyes switching between Matteo, Romero, and Luca. "Was this some kind of trick to weaken the Outfit? Father always said you'd stab us in the back one day." He raised his gun a bit higher.

Aria tried to move toward him again, but Luca practically shoved her behind him.

"He's my brother!" she hissed.

"He's a soldier of the Outfit."

"Fabi," I said. "The Famiglia didn't try to weaken the Outfit. This isn't about power. It's all my fault. Benito tried to hurt me and I stabbed him. That's why I need to leave. Father would punish me, maybe even kill me."

Fabi's eyes widened, making him look younger at once. "You killed your husband?"

Romero's hand around mine tightened, but the hand with his gun was steady. He hadn't moved it at all. It was still pointed straight at Fabi's head. If he killed my brother...I couldn't even finish the thought.

"I didn't know what else to do," I said. I decided not to mention that Benito had still been very much alive when Romero plunged his knife into his heart. That would have complicated things even further.

"What about you and him?" Fabi nodded toward Romero. "I'm not stupid. There's something going on between you."

There was no denying it, and I had a feeling that Fabi would get angry if I tried to lie to him. Matteo had inched closer to Fabi while we'd been talking. I wasn't sure what he planned to do but knowing Matteo it wouldn't end well.

"We've been together for a while. You know I never wanted to marry Benito but Father didn't give me a choice."

"So you want to leave Chicago and the Outfit for New York like Gianna and Aria," Fabi said.

"I have to," I said.

"You could come with us," Aria suggested. Realizing her mistake, she peered up at Luca, who would have to accept Fabi into the Famiglia.

"You could become part of the Famiglia," he said immediately.

Fabi shook his head. "Father needs me. I'm part of the Outfit. I made an oath."

"If you're not fully inducted yet, it's not as binding," Matteo said, which was not quite a lie, but really, he'd be treated like a traitor if he ran off anyway and the punishment would be the same.

Fabi glared. "I won't betray the Outfit."

"Then you'll have to stop us from leaving," Luca said simply. "And we won't let you. There will be blood, and you will die."

I stiffened and was about to say something but Romero gave a small shake of his head.

"I'm a good shot," Fabi said indignantly.

"I believe you. But are you better than all three of us? Do you really want your sister Lily to be punished? If you force her to stay, you sign her death warrant."

Conflict showed on Fabi's face. "If I let you leave, and someone finds out, they will kill me too. I could die an honest death if I tried to stop you."

Luca nodded. "You could, and they would sing your praises, but you'd be dead all the same. Do you want to die today?"

Fabi didn't say anything but he'd lowered his gun a few inches.

"Nobody has to find out that you let us leave. You could have tried to stop us but we were too many," Romero said suddenly.

"They will think I was scared and ran away, and that's why you escaped."

Luca gave Romero a small nod. "Not if you got wounded. We could shoot you in the arm. This was meant as an easy first job, nobody expects you to be capable of stopping the best fighters of New York. They won't hold it against you if you got shot."

"You want to shoot my brother?" Aria asked incredulously.

"What if you injure him seriously?" I added.

"I could hit the zit on his chin if I wanted to, I think I can manage to hit an unproblematic spot on his arm," Matteo said with his shark-grin. "And we're taking a risk by not just killing him, so an arm wound is really nothing."

"So what do you say, Fabiano?" Luca asked quickly before Matteo could say more. None of the men had lowered their guns yet.

Fabi nodded slowly and aimed his weapon at the ground. "Okay. But I will have to call for help. I can't wait more than a few minutes or they'll get suspicious."

"A few minutes should be enough for us to drive away," Luca said. "They will follow us once they figure out what's going on but five minutes will bring enough distance between us and them. Dante isn't someone who likes fighting in the open, so I doubt he'll send his men on a wild car chase. He'll attack us later, once he's figured out the best way to hurt us."

My stomach tightened. All because of me. How selfish could a person be to let others risk so much for her?

Romero gave me an encouraging smile, but for once it didn't manage to cheer me up. "War with the Outfit was inevitable. Things have gotten worse by the day."

Luca looked over to us. "That's true. If it weren't for Aria and Gianna, Matteo and I wouldn't even have come to Chicago for the wedding."

That might have been the case, but Benito's death would put fuel into the fire. Things would get very ugly now.

"Let's do this now," Matteo urged. "We're wasting time."

"I think we should move our shooting to the garage. Maybe that will buy us additional time. People won't hear your scream as easily," Romero suggested.

Together we headed for the door and down a flight of stairs into the underground garage. It wasn't as big as the one I'd seen in New York. Despite our decision to work together, none of the men had put their guns back into their holsters yet. When we stopped close to our two rental cars, I slipped out of Romero's grasp and walked up to Fabi. I didn't miss the way Romero tensed and raised his gun, but I trusted Fabi. Maybe he was on his way to becoming a soldier of the Outfit, but he was also my little brother. That wouldn't change. I hugged him and after a moment he wrapped his arms around me. In the last year, he'd avoided public displays of affection because he'd tried to act cool, but it felt good to have him close, especially since I didn't know when I'd get another chance to see him.

"I'm sorry for getting you into trouble," I whispered. "I wished things were different."

"I never liked Benito," Fabi said. "Father shouldn't have married you off to that guy."

Suddenly Gianna and Aria were there too, and took their turns embracing him.

"We have to go now," Luca reminded us.

I pulled away from Fabi and returned to Romero. He motioned for me to get into the car, while Aria and Gianna got into the other. I watched as they tried to figure out the best way to fake a shooting. Eventually Fabi fired two muffled shots, and then it was Romero's and Matteo's turn. When Matteo's bullet, sliced through Fabi's upper arm, I winced. My brother dropped his gun and fell to his knees, his face scrunched up in pain. Nothing about that was fake. Romero rushed toward our car and slid behind the steering wheel before flooring the gas. Luca pressed the button that made the garage doors slide open. Most guests had parked in the driveway so I worried that the sound would draw attention to our flight even before Fabi started screaming. I doubted anyone had heard the silenced shots through the thick ceiling of the underground garage. Romero steered our car up the slope and down the driveway. Matteo was behind the steering wheel of the other car and close behind us. We raced down the driveway, past a couple of drunk guests who sat on one of the marble benches on the side. My heart stuttered in my chest, but there was no time for worry. I clutched the seat as we drove off the premises at a dizzying speed. I glanced through the rearview mirror, but the only car behind us was the one with my sisters and their husbands. "Nobody is following us," I said.

"Give it a moment. Most of them are drunk and it'll take a while for them to figure out what's going on, but someone will be sober enough to chase us," Romero said.

He looked calm about it. This wasn't something new to him, even if the circumstances that had led to us here were, but Romero had been a Made Man for a long time. This wasn't his first chase and it wouldn't be his last.

I squeezed my eyes shut, trying to come to terms with everything that had happened in the last twenty-four hours. I'd walked down the aisle toward a husband I hated, a husband who had been killed by the man I loved. Romero linked our fingers and my eyes shot open. Despite our speed, he was driving with only one hand. He'd stashed his gun in the compartment between our seats. I gave him a grateful smile. "When we're back in New York, what happens then?"

"You move in with me." He paused. "Unless you'd rather stay with one of your sisters."

I shook my head. "I don't want to be away from you again."

Romero brought my hand to his lips and kissed it gently, but then his eyes darted to the side mirror and he tensed. He let go of me and grabbed his gun.

I peered over my shoulder. Three cars were chasing us. I sank deeper into my seat and folded my hands, sending a quick prayer above. I wasn't particularly religious but it seemed like the only thing I could do. So far not a single shot had been fired from either side and it made me wonder if the Outfit had set a trap somewhere. "Why aren't they shooting?"

"This is a residential area and Dante doesn't like to draw attention to the Outfit. I assume he gave orders to wait until we're out of the city limits, which will be any minute now. We're crossing over to an industrial area."

He was right. Once the family homes were replaced by storage facilities, the Outfit cars closed in and started firing. Since Matteo was close behind us with the other rental car, Romero didn't get a clear shot at our pursuers, but I could see Luca shooting bullet after bullet through the open passenger window. I couldn't see Aria and Gianna; they were probably crouched on the back seat so they didn't get hit by bullets.

What if we didn't get away? What if all of our lives ended here?

One of the bullets tore through the tire of one of our pursuers. The car spun around and stopped. But the other two cars closed in. I couldn't even see their license tag anymore.

I wasn't sure how long they chased us but I knew at one point either Matteo or Romero would make a mistake and lose control of their car.

Suddenly both cars slowed and then they did a U-turn.

"Why have they stopped following us?"

"Dante's orders, I assume. I told you, he is a very cautious man. He'll wait for a better opportunity to make us pay. This is too risky for his taste," Romero said.

I exhaled. I knew it was far from over. From what I knew of Dante, Romero was right, but I was simply glad that we'd all get away unscathed tonight. We'd figure out the rest tomorrow. I glanced at Romero again. I couldn't believe I'd finally be allowed to be with him.

Except for two toilet breaks, we didn't stop on our drive to New York and then we barely spoke. When the skyline of New York finally rose up outside of the car, relief flooded me. For some reason the city already felt like home and I knew we'd be safer here. This was Luca's city. It wouldn't be easy for Dante to attack us here.

chapter *nineteen*

Romero

After more than fourteen hours on the road, we arrived at Luca's penthouse. Lily had fallen asleep a couple of times during our drive but she'd startled awake almost instantly. She was probably having nightmares about Benito. I was so fucking glad that I'd killed him. When I'd walked into the bedroom and seen Benito with a letter opener in his body, I'd wanted to scream with joy. I knew the next few weeks and months, maybe even years, would be hard on the Famiglia, and for each of us. Dante would retaliate with everything he had.

I parked the car in the underground garage and got out. Lily could hardly stand on her own feet from exhaustion but she put on a brave face. I wanted nothing more than to take her home with me, but first, Luca, Matteo, and I needed to have a talk without the risk of an Outfit attack.

When we stepped into the penthouse, Aria and Gianna led Lily toward the sofa. A protest lay on the tip of my tongue. I still felt very protective of her after almost losing her and wanted her at my side at all times, but it would have been ridiculous to say something. She was still in the same room as me. Her longing gaze in my direction when she sat down between her sisters told me that Lily felt the same way.

"We have to call everyone in for a meeting. They need to know that the truce between the Outfit and us is no longer in effect. I don't want anyone to walk into a trap because they thought they could trust an Outfit bastard," Luca said. I could tell that he was still pissed at me, and he had every right to be. That he hadn't killed me was a bigger sign of his friendship than I'd ever hoped for.

"Some people might not be happy with Liliana and you," Matteo said. "They probably won't act on their anger but I'd be careful if I were you."

"Don't worry. And if someone lays a finger on Lily, I'll rip their throat out."

"I think you have done enough damage for a while," Luca said tightly. "And nobody will try to hurt Liliana. She's now part of the Famiglia and under my protection. I assume you're going to marry her?"

I had never asked her but I wanted her to be my wife. "If she says yes, then I'll marry her."

"After all the drama of today, she better marry you," Matteo muttered. He leaned against the dining table and yawned widely.

"I'll ask her soon enough."

Luca raised his hand. "This isn't our main concern right now. We have to double security measures. We didn't only kidnap Scuderi's daughter, we killed a Captain with a loyal following of soldiers. There will be blood to pay."

I chanced another look at Lily. The Outfit might try to kill her. Knowing her father, he'd probably do it himself. He'd have to go through me if he tried to hurt her.

Liliana

After two hours in Luca's apartment, we were finally at Romero's place. I'd never been there and I was curious despite my exhaustion. I could tell that Romero was tense but I wasn't sure why. Maybe he regretted everything that had happened? Or maybe he was only worried about what was to come.

Romero unlocked his door and opened it wide for me. I walked past him into a long hallway. Family photos in pretty silver frames decorated the walls. I promised myself to take a closer look at them later. Several doors branched off of the hallway. Romero led me toward the last one on the right. A master bedroom waited behind it but we didn't stop there. We had been on the road for hours and I'd been awake for more than twenty-four hours. It was already past noon but I wanted to sleep.

I could still smell Benito on me though; his blood, his sweat, his body odor. It made me sick. Romero opened the door to the adjoining bathroom. I quickly shimmied out of my clothes and stepped into the glass shower. Romero watched me silently, an unreadable look on his face. He looked exhausted. When the warm water streamed down my body, I felt some of the tension leave my limbs.

"Do you want to be alone?" Romero asked after a moment. He sounded…uncertain. That wasn't something I was used to from him. Maybe I needed to take into consideration that he needed some time to work through everything.

I shook my head. "I want you to join me."

Romero got out of his clothes. I didn't try to hide my admiration as I watched him. I loved Romero's body. I loved everything about him. I moved to the side so he could step into the shower with me. I slipped my arms around his waist and pressed my cheek against his chest as the water poured down on us. I'd missed the feel of his skin against mine. I squeezed my eyes shut. So much had happened and so much was still to come.

"Things will get really bad for Luca and the Famiglia now, won't they?"

Romero stroked my back. "The union between the Famiglia and the Outfit was bound to break at some point. I'd rather have it over something as important as you than over money or politics. You are worth a war."

"I'm not sure Luca agrees. He's probably already regretting taking me to New York."

"I know Luca. He doesn't regret his decision. Once he's made up his mind, he stands by his decision. And this wasn't only for you. It was also for Aria and Gianna. They want you to be happy."

I tilted my head up and smiled up at him. His body shielded me from the water. Romero lowered his head and kissed my forehead, then my lips. We didn't deepen the kiss, though. His closeness was enough for now.

We finished showering quickly. Romero stepped out first and took a towel. He wrapped it around me and gently started drying my body. I relaxed under his gentle ministrations. The last bit of tension slid out of me. After he was done with me, I took a towel out of the shelf and dried Romero in turn. He closed his eyes when I massaged his shoulders. "How do you feel?" I asked softly. I knew men, and Made Men in particular, didn't like to talk about their feelings, especially sadness or fear.

He looked at me. "Tired."

"No, I mean because you had to kill Benito for me. Are you okay?"

Romero let out a humorless laugh. He took my hand and led me back into the bedroom. He sank down on the bed and pulled me between his legs, then made me sit down on one of them. "He hasn't been my first and he won't be my last, but I enjoyed his death more than the others, and I don't regret it. I'd do it again and enjoy it just as much."

Romero

It was the truth and now that Lily and I would start living together, she needed to know it, needed to know every dark part of me. I searched her eyes for a sign of revulsion but there was none. She kissed my cheek before resting her head on my shoulder. Her fingers traced my chest lightly. That and the feel of her firm butt on my thigh stirred my cock, but now wasn't the time to follow that urge. Not too long ago Lily had to fight off her new husband, had to stab him and watch him die. She needed time to recover. I stood and lifted Lily into my arms before I lay her down. She kept her hands wrapped around my neck and didn't let go even as I tried to straighten. "Lily," I said quietly. "You need to rest."

She shook her head and pulled me down on top of her. I braced myself on my elbows so I didn't crush her under my weight. Lily wrapped her legs around my hips and dug her heels into my lower back, pressing me down.

I didn't resist. Slowly I lowered myself until our bodies were flush against each other and my cock pressed against her pussy. She raised her head to claim my mouth for a kiss. I stared into her eyes; they were soft and filled with longing. I wasn't sure how I could have ever believed that Lily didn't want me. Her eyes showed her love for me as plain as day.

"I need you," she murmured, lifting her hips a few inches and making my tip glide over her lower lips. I let out a small hiss at the sensation. She was wet and warm. She always felt so fucking inviting. I didn't need to be asked twice. I always wanted her. I quickly put on a condom, cupped her head and eased into her slowly, and as I did I realized just how much I needed it too. She was tighter than usual, maybe from tension and exhaustion, and I made sure to be careful.

I made love to her slowly. This wasn't about getting off, about being consumed by desire and lust, this was something to show us everything was okay. A few days ago I'd thought I would lose her forever and now she was mine.

Between soft moans she told me she loved me. I kissed her lips. I'd never been the overly emotional type but I never got tired of her saying those words. "I love you too," I said quietly. It still felt strange to admit it to someone.

When we lay in each other's arms afterward, I felt a deep, all-encompassing peace I'd never felt before.

I woke at sunrise but Lily wasn't there. I jerked upright, reaching for my gun on the nightstand, as usual expecting the worst, but Lily was there at the window, looking out. I didn't have floor-to-ceiling windows like Luca's penthouse, but they weren't exactly small. But Lily had grown up as the daughter of a Consigliere. She'd had the best of everything all her life.

I swung my legs out of bed and walked toward her.

"It's not as grand as you're used to. Your family's townhouse and Aria's penthouse are much bigger than my apartment. You're going to be the wife of a mere soldier."

Lily jumped slightly, then she peered over her shoulder at me.

"Do you really think I care about things like that? When I lived in a huge house and had more money than I could possibly spend I was never happy, but when I'm with you, I am."

"Still, this will be a big change for you," I said. I wasn't exactly poor but she wouldn't be able to afford as much as she had done before.

Lily turned to me fully and touched my cheeks. "I want only you, Romero. I don't care about money." She motioned around. "And this is a gorgeous place. Most people would be happy to live here. I love it."

That was why I knew Lily was the one.

The sun finally peeked over the surrounding skyscrapers. "Look," I said, pointing out toward the city.

Lily turned around in my arms, her back pressed against my chest, as we watched the sunrise. I wanted to enjoy this moment of peace and quiet, because I knew there wouldn't be many more moments like that today. The Famiglia was at war with the Outfit now.

"I'm worried about Fabi. I wished there was a way to find out if he's alright. What if Dante and Father don't believe his story? I could never forgive myself if something happened to him because of me."

"I'll figure out a way to get information, but I'm sure he's fine. He's your father's only son. Even if your father is unhappy with him, Fabi won't be punished too hard."

"He's married to a young woman now. He could produce a new heir," she said bitterly.

"Let me call Luca and see if he knows anything," I told her and untangled myself from her. Luca would probably be awake already, if he'd gone to bed at all.

Luca picked up after the second call. "Did you kill another Outfit member?" It was mostly said in a joking way, but I could hear the strain in his voice.

"No. Have you heard anything? Did Dante try to contact you?"

"He didn't. He only sent me an email through one of his men that our alliance is terminated."

"He didn't even contact you himself, or at least through his Consigliere?"

I asked. That was a blatant show of disrespect and showed how bad the situation really was.

"I don't think Scuderi is very keen on talking to me right now," Luca said wryly.

Lily came up to me, an anxious look on her face.

"I suppose not," I said. "Listen, Luca, Lily is really worried about her brother. Do you have any way of finding out if he's okay?"

"Aria has been trying to get in contact with Valentina but so far she hasn't had any luck. She'll try again later. You and Lily should come over anyway. We have a lot to discuss and the women can spend time together."

"Alright. We'll be there soon." I hung up.

"And?" Lily asked hopefully. I hated having to crush her hopes.

Liliana

Romero's expression caused a lump to rise in my throat.

"Luca doesn't have any information about your brother yet, but he and Aria are trying to contact Valentina."

"Do you really think Val will respond to Aria's calls? She's Dante's wife and now that there's war between New York and Chicago, she'd risk a lot by getting into contact with Aria."

Romero touched my cheek. "We'll find out about your brother, Lily, I promise."

We showered quickly before we headed for Aria's apartment. When we stepped into the penthouse, Gianna and Matteo were already there despite it being only seven in the morning. The scent of freshly made coffee greeted me and Danishes waited on the kitchen counter. My sisters were standing and talking and I steered toward them while Romero walked up to Luca and Matteo who sat on the stools at the kitchen island.

Aria put her arm around me. "How are you, Lily?"

"Okay. I didn't sleep much but I'm just happy to be here with you and Romero."

"Of course, you are," Gianna said. "I'm so glad Romero got rid of that sick bastard Benito."

An image of Benito's blood-covered body popped into my head but I pushed it aside. I didn't want to think of him anymore. He wasn't part of my life anymore.

Aria handed me a cup of coffee. "Here, you look like you need it. And you should eat something."

"Mother hen mode active," Gianna teased but then she too fixed me with a worried look. "And? How was your first night with Romero?"

"Gianna," Aria warned. "Lily has gone through a lot."

"It's okay. I loved spending the night in Romero's arms without being afraid of getting caught. For the first time we could watch the sunrise together."

"I'm so glad you are happy," Aria said.

I nodded. "But I can't stop worrying about Fabi. I want to know if he's okay."

"I've left two voicemails on Val's phone. I really hope she'll call me back."

"Even if she does," Matteo said. "We don't know her motives. She might be doing it on Dante's orders and be looking for information."

"Val wouldn't do that," Aria said uncertainly.

"She's the wife of the Capo and the Outfit is where her loyalties lie. You are part of the Famiglia and that makes you the enemy," Luca said.

I glanced at Romero. All this because I loved a man I wasn't supposed to love, and because I wanted to be with him. Was I a selfish bitch? Romero met my gaze. I wished I could say I wouldn't do it again but looking at him now, I knew I'd stab Benito again to save myself from a horrible marriage and be with the guy I was supposed to spend my life with.

"Hey," Aria said gently. "Don't look so sad."

I turned back to her. "You and Val got along so well. I know you talked on the phone often and now you can't because of the mess I caused."

"You are my sister, Lily, and seeing you happy and having you in New York with us is more important than my friendship with Val. And maybe Luca can negotiate another truce with Dante. Dante is a pragmatic man."

"Not as long as your father is Consigliere. It would be like a slap in the face for your father if Dante didn't seek revenge," Romero said.

"I hate this revenge crap," Gianna muttered. Matteo stood from his stool, went over to her and pulled her against him with a grin. "I know you do, but it's how things are."

Gianna rolled her eyes but let Matteo kiss her. In the past that would have sent a stab of envy through me, but now I walked over to Romero and leaned against him. His arm came around my shoulders and he kissed my temple. "We've been at war with the Outfit before. We'll handle this."

"I don't want people to die because of me."

"Romero is right. We will get through this. And I don't think Dante will kill one of ours. The Russian threat is still too strong. He can't risk his soldiers' lives in a war with us."

"Nor can we," added Matteo.

A phone rang, making us all jump. Aria snatched her phone off the counter and peered down at the screen, then she raised her head with wide eyes. "It's Val."

Luca got up. "Don't let anything slip that Fabi helped us and be careful."

Aria nodded, then she lifted her phone to her ear. "Hello?" She paused. "I'm so glad you called. Can you talk?" Aria listened for a few seconds, her expression dropping. "I know. I only wanted to ask about Fabi. He got shot when he tried to stop us and I'm just so worried about him. He's so young. He shouldn't have been involved in this. Can you tell me how he's doing?"

Aria released a breath. "So he's okay? He'll be able to use his arm like he used to?"

I slumped against Romero in relief, but at Aria's next words I tensed again. "Is he in huge trouble because he wasn't able to stop us?" Aria nodded, then gave us a thumbs-up. She was silent for a long time after that, listening to Val.

"Okay, I will tell him. Thank you so much, Val. I won't forget it. I hope our men figure something out soon. I'll miss talking to you. Bye."

"So?" I asked, the moment she had hung up.

"Father and Dante seem to believe Fabi's story. Nobody blames him for letting us get away. He didn't have enough experience for the job. Only because of Father's insistence did he get it in the first place."

Luca looked like a bloodhound on a trail. "Did she say anything else? About Dante's plans and his mood?"

"He's furious," Aria said with a shrug. "But he wanted Val to give you a message," she told Luca, her eyes flitting to me.

Romero became still beside me. I had a feeling I knew what kind of message.

"If we send Lily back today, they might consider not retaliating."

Romero pushed himself off the stool. "She won't go back."

Luca narrowed his eyes but then he took a deep breath. "Of course not. Dante knows we won't agree to that offer. That's why he made it."

Romero rubbed my arm lightly and brought his mouth down to my ear. "Nobody will take you away from me. I'll fight a million wars if it means I can keep you."

Two days had passed but they might as well have been a lifetime. Romero had been busy and I'd spent most of my time with my sisters. But tonight Romero wanted us to have dinner together alone in his, no, *our* apartment. He'd ordered food at his favorite Italian place and spread it all out on the dining table in his huge kitchen.

A few minutes into the dinner, Romero set down his fork. "Luca made me Captain."

"Really? That's wonderful!" I could see how much this meant to him. I'd never gotten the feeling that he was unhappy as Aria's bodyguard but of course it was a big deal if you got promoted, especially because the mob was a place where people usually took over their father's position. "What business are you going to get?"

"I'll be taking over a few clubs in Harlem. The old Captain has cancer and needs to retire, but he's got only daughters so Luca decided to give me his businesses. I'll be making more money for us."

I smiled. "You know I don't care about that. I'm just happy for you because you deserve it."

Romero grimaced. "Some people don't think so after I caused war with the Outfit."

"I thought the majority was eager to stop cooperating with Chicago?"

"Those think I deserve to be Captain," he said in amusement.

"So who will be guarding Aria?"

"That's a bit of a problem. Sandro will guard Aria and Gianna for now. But that won't be enough especially when you're with them often. He can't protect all three of you, but we'll figure something out."

When we were done with dessert, Romero got up and walked around the table toward me. I watched him in confusion. Did he look nervous?

Without warning, Romero dropped to his knees right in front of me and pulled a small satin box from his pants pocket. I froze as he held it out to me and opened it, revealing a beautiful diamond ring. Of course I'd hoped we'd marry soon. It was expected in our world but I didn't think Romero had bought a ring already. He hadn't wasted any time, that was for sure!

"I know you've been through a lot and your last wedding experience was horrible, but I hope you give it another chance. I want to be the husband you deserve. I want to make you happy and love you, if you let me. Will you marry me?"

I flung myself into his arms, my knees colliding with the hard floor but I hardly felt it. "God yes." I kissed him fiercely.

Romero grinned when he pulled back. We didn't get up from the floor. As long as I was in Romero's arms I didn't care where I was. "I understand if you want to wait a bit before you marry me. You're probably not in the mood to plan another wedding."

I shook my head quickly. "This is a wedding I want to plan. This time I will enjoy it. I can take Aria and Gianna wedding dress shopping with me and actually be excited about it."

He chuckled. "But I want you to meet my family first. That way we can tell them the good news."

"Oh, sure," I said slowly. I was excited to meet Romero's family but I was also worried that they wouldn't like me, or worse despise me. I could only imagine what was being said about me and what had happened in Chicago.

The next day Romero took me to his family. His mother lived with her new husband and Romero's three sisters in a modest apartment not too far from us. I shouldn't have worried that they wouldn't like me. They were kind, humble people. I knew his two oldest sisters already from my birthday party many years ago but we'd grown and his oldest sister, Tamara, had already started college. Something I'd never considered because I knew Father wouldn't approve of it.

Dinner in my family had always been a formal affair, with my father sitting at the end of the table and with everyone on their best behavior, well, except for Gianna perhaps. But this was easygoing and fun. We talked and laughed all evening, and when Romero told them that we were going to marry, they hugged me and were actually happy. Nobody looked at me strangely because I'd married Benito less than a week ago.

I knew right then that I would be happy in this new life, not just because of Romero's love, but because of my sisters and my new family. That wouldn't stop me from missing Fabi but I had to trust that he would find his own happiness one day even if we'd never see each other again.

epilogue

Liliana

I'D WAITED FOR THIS MOMENT FOR A LONG TIME, HAD IMAGINED IT SO often that it felt almost like a deja vu. A few weeks ago at my wedding to Benito, there had been only anxiety, sadness, and fear. But today I felt like I could fly. Happiness and euphoria buzzed in my body. I couldn't wait for the party to be over so Romero could undress me and make love to me over and over again. The only thing missing for a perfect day was Fabi. I hadn't seen him since my wedding night and I wasn't sure if I ever would. I didn't even know if he was alright. If he'd gotten in trouble for getting shot and letting us get away.

When the priest declared Romero and me husband and wife, Romero lifted me into his arms under the excited cheers of our guests. I couldn't help but laugh. I'd never felt lighter, as if any moment I would soar up into the sky. I risked a glance up, wondering if Mother was watching. I'd done what she'd wanted. I'd risked happiness, and it was worth it. Romero kissed my cheek, drawing my attention back to him. Our eyes met and my heart swelled with love. I wanted to spend my life with him, and now I could.

Later at night, after the festivities, when Romero carried me toward our room in Luca's mansion, my stomach fluttered with butterflies. This time I couldn't wait to arrive, to be alone with my husband, to have him to myself for the night. This was how it was supposed to be. Every woman should be happy on her wedding day, should feel safe in the arms of her husband, should have the right to marry for love and not because someone decided her match for her.

I pressed my face into the crook of his neck, smiling to myself. From the corner of my eyes, I caught sight of my sisters and their husbands. Aria beamed at me, and Gianna wiggled her eyebrows. I stifled a laugh. Romero brushed his lips across my ear. "I can't wait to undress you and kiss every inch of your silky skin."

Desire rushed through me. "Hurry," I whispered.

Romero chuckled but he did actually speed up. He opened the door to our bedroom with his elbow, then kicked the door shut before crossing the room toward the bed and setting me down.

"God, you're so damn beautiful. I can't believe you're finally mine."

"I've always been yours."

Romero cupped my cheek and kissed me fiercely before his hands started their work on my dress, slowly uncovering inch by inch of my body. He kissed every new spot, but not the places I wanted him to. When I lay before him in my corset and panties, his eyes traced my body with hunger and reverence. I loved that look. It made me feel like the most beautiful girl in the world. He let his fingers glide over my ankles then up my calves and thighs until he reached my panties. I lifted my hips. Romero let out a low laugh and kissed my hip bone, then licked the spot. "Romero, please." He hooked his fingers under my panties and slid them down. When he came back up, he parted my legs and closed his mouth over my folds. I exhaled. With slow strokes of his tongue Romero drove me higher and when he slipped a finger into me, pleasure rolled over me. My toes curled and my butt lifted off the bed but Romero kept up his pleasuring until I couldn't take it anymore and pushed his head away, laughing and gasping.

"Your first orgasm as my wife," Romero said with a self-satisfied grin as he crawled up until he hovered over me.

"I hope not the last," I teased.

"Are you saying you're not done yet?" He slipped a finger into me again and moved it slowly.

I shook my head.

Romero pulled his finger out and unlaced my corset, laying my breasts bare. He sucked one of my nipples into his mouth as he eased his finger into me again.

It felt so good, and I could feel myself getting close, but I needed to feel Romero inside of me. "I need you," I begged.

Romero didn't waste any time. He climbed out of bed and quickly undressed. His cock was already hard and glistening. He moved between my legs. I closed my hand around his shaft, enjoying its firmness and heat. I stroked a few times before I guided it toward my entrance. When the tip brushed my opening, I relaxed against the pillows. Romero started moving into me slowly. I could feel every inch of him until he finally filled me completely. I wrapped my fingers around Romero's neck and pulled him down to me for a kiss. I loved kissing him, the way his stubble lightly scratched my lip, his taste, everything. I never got enough.

Romero moved in a slow rhythm, sliding almost all the way out, only to drive his cock all the way into me again. "Caress yourself," he ordered in a low murmur.

I didn't hesitated. I sneaked my arm between our bodies and my fingers found my clit. I started to draw small circles. My fingertips brushed Romero's cock occasionally and it drove me even higher.

"Yes, baby, come for me," Romero rasped. He kissed my neck and one of his hands grasped my leg and hooked it over his hip. I caressed myself even faster and when Romero pushed into me again, I shattered. My body arched off the bed as Romero groaned, his pushes coming harder and faster and then I felt him release into me.

I trembled from the aftershocks of my orgasm. Romero buried his face against my neck and I ran my hands through his hair and down his back. After a moment, he rolled off me and onto his back, pulling me with him so I half lay on his chest. I raked my fingers through his chest hair and listened to his fast heartbeat.

"I can't believe you're finally mine. Nobody can take you away from me now." Romero pressed a kiss to the top of my head. I smiled, sated and happy. Briefly, my thoughts drifted to Fabi, wondering what he was doing now. Without him and my sisters, I wouldn't be lying beside Romero right now. They'd risked so much for my happiness, so had Romero. I would always be grateful for what they'd done. I'd try to make their sacrifices worth it. I'd try to live life to the fullest.

I turned around and Romero wrapped his arms around me from behind. It was late and I was exhausted. Eventually Romero drifted off to sleep. I loved listening to him sleep beside me. It always set me at ease.

Romero's even breathing fanned over my naked shoulder. I couldn't fall asleep even though I was sated and exhausted. I slipped out under Romero's arm and slipped out of bed. I grabbed a bathrobe and put it on before I made my way toward the balcony door and walked out onto the balcony, which had a beautiful view over the premises and the ocean. Tomorrow we'd return to New York and then our lives as a married couple would really start. I watched the night sky. The stars were always brighter out of the city, and yet there were always a couple of stars that shone the brightest. As a small kid I used to think they represented people who had died and who were watching over us as stars. I'd stopped believing in that a long time ago. Still I couldn't help but wonder if somewhere somehow Mother was watching me. Would she be happy for me? Maybe even proud? I would never find out, but I'd kept my promise to her. I'd risked everything for love and happiness. I glanced over my shoulder at Romero's sleeping form, then with a last glimpse at the stars, I returned into bed and snuggled up against him. He wrapped his arm around me. "You were gone," he mumbled.

"I needed fresh air," I said softly.

"I'm glad you're back."

"I love you," I whispered.

Romero's arms tightened around me and he kissed my temple. "And I love you." Maybe things wouldn't always be easy in the future, but I knew I'd never regret taking this risk. Love was worth every risk.

THE END

more books by
Cora Reilly

Born in Blood Mafia Chronicles:

Bound by Honor
(Aria & Luca)

Bound by Duty
(Valentina & Dante)

Bound by Hatred
(Gianna & Matteo)

Bound By Temptation
(Liliana & Romero)

Bound By Vengeance
(Growl & Cara)

Bound By Love
(Luca & Aria)

Bound By The Past
(Valentina & Dante)

Bound By Blood
(anthology)

The Camorra Chronicles:

Twisted Loyalties
(Fabiano & Leona)

Twisted Emotions
(Nino & Kiara)

Twisted Pride
(Remo & Serafina)

Twisted Bonds
(Nino & Kiara)

Twisted Hearts
(Savio & Gemma)

Twisted Cravings
(Adamo & Dinara)

Mafia Standalone Books

Sweet Temptation

Fragile Longing

about the author

Cora Reilly is the *USA Today* bestselling author of the Born in Blood Mafia Series, The Camorra Chronicles and many other books, most of them featuring dangerously sexy bad boys.

Cora lives in Germany with a cute but crazy Bearded Collie, as well as the cute but crazy man at her side. When she doesn't spend her days dreaming up sexy books, she plans her next travel adventure or cooks too spicy dishes from all over the world.

Made in the USA
Middletown, DE
07 October 2023

40422198R00440